THE CELLULOID CLOSET SERIES:

NOTHING VENTURED, NOTHING GAINED

Brennen Tammons

© 2019 Grassroot Station
All Rights Reserved

Special consideration to Right-Think for brand design marketing.
https://right-think.com

Do not duplicate, copy, scan, reproduce, transmit, transcribe, translate, any part of
this book, without permission or consent from the author/publisher.

If you pirated this book, please still support the author/publisher in other ways, by
leaving a review on this title, and recommending this title to others as well.

Do you like the cover design? So do I. It was illustrated by Andrew Gaia
https://andrewgaia.com
https://www.deviantart.com/gurugaia

TITLE: NOTHING VENTURED, NOTHING GAINED (THE CELLULOID CLOSET SERIES #1)
AUTHOR: TAMMONS, BRENNEN
1st EDITION
ISBN: 978-1733776202 (Paperback)

This story is a work of fiction. Any correlation between people, names, places, events,
or politics, are simply coincidental. Although, in this and in practically every other
story, there are elements of inspiration based on actual events. However, any exact
correlations are simply coincidental.

This story is graphic. There is strong vulgar language, criminal activity, drug use, and
strong violent content. Due to the extreme subject matter, reader should be advised.

The opinions expressed by characters in this story, may reflect the opinions of the
author, or may not. The author wishes to have a neutral stance.

CHAPTERS

To my twin brother, Berton.
To my mother, Brenda.
To my grandmother, Sharon.

To everyone else close to me, I appreciate you as well.

To God Be The Glory

CHAPTER 1:

NOTHING STARTED, NOTHING FINISHED

Los Angeles, a vibrant and loud city. A very populated city with an array of activity, and never that many dull moments apart of it. A city that has a lot of action and entertainment to offer, and for those to participate and take part in such agendas. A city that has many opportunities available. In this city, there are many who hold onto dreams of success in their life. Very driven on compassion and desire, with a very competitive edge for those to reign supreme above others in many aspects. This is a city which has many characters and personalities apart of it, all of which are finding their piece of the puzzle in the success and business ladder. It is also a city where crime and masterminding also come into play. In these difficult times to where those who have desires to achieve what they want, will do just about anything to obtain them, it becomes a very complex and complicated industry to understand. Everyone tries their best to fit into a loop or place to which they feel the most comfortable by, and willing to accept and understand their full potentials and abilities toward.

In the heart of the downtown Los Angeles area on Sunset Boulevard, contains a small shopping center called the "Oakwood Shopping Center", which for the most part generally isn't that busy. Business has come and go as the years have gone. The shopping center itself has been around for over forty years. Many patrons use their businesses but all in all, it's a very low profile strip. Nothing out of the ordinary usually happens. This "L" shaped shopping center which has three outlets facing north, and one single outlet facing east, in total containing four outlets. The northern facing outlets consist of a health and organic type grocery store called "Healthy and Fresh." The grocery store is open from 9 a.m. to 8 p.m. West of the grocery store contains two more businesses. One which is a family owned Korean dry cleaning business called "Happy Dry Cleaning." Which is open from 8 a.m. to 4 p.m. Monday through Saturday, and closed on Sunday. Directly to the left of the dry cleaners is an Armenian Deli which serves donuts, sandwiches and coffee called "Sunset Deli." They are primarily open during breakfast and lunch hours every day, as they close typically early at 3 p.m.

The single eastern facing outlet which is connected to to the end of the Deli, is a bank called the "Sunset Credit Union." This is a privately owned bank, which very seldom has incidents occur. The bank which has gone over numerous name and management changes of the years, has been called the "Sunset Credit Union", for the past twenty years. The bank is open Monday through Friday, from 9 a.m. and closes at 6 p.m. The bank by far is the most populated business apart of this shopping center by far. It does cater to the most patrons and clientele. The bank not only is in charge of personal and private accounts, but also takes care of credit payment transactions that customers may need to take care of. The bank is also the oldest business apart of this complex, and has a long history of serving those who live in this particular part of the metropolis. Unlike the other stores apart of this plaza, it contains little to no natural light apart of the building. The most light which protrudes into the building, comes from the entrance door. The bank does not have much security measures. Having very few surveillance cameras, and there isn't any safety glass behind the tellers. It has an open infrastructure into the whole layout of the bank. In addition, the bank does not have a security guards or security officers present. It is a privately owned quaint bank which very seldom runs into any issues or problems, so the need for that must not be necessary.

It is 5:45 p.m., which is around closing time for the bank. It is the first Friday of the month, which incidentally is payday for many companies. So the bank is usually quite active on days such as today. With many customers wanting to deal with transactions and business related to their paychecks. Being that it is on the verge of closing, many of the patrons have mostly been helped and tended to already. Patrons generally try to do their business at the bank as early as possible, as the bank is very cordial on closing time. The bank is also closed on the weekends, so it is usually a day that the bank wraps all of its ties and transactions together. So patrons also realize Friday is a very important and detrimental day to get their business taken care of. Just in case patrons are not able to be make it into the bank before closing time, there are there is an automatic teller machine located to the left of the front door of the bank, which can also take care of some transactions that a patron may need to use.

Today seemed like any other typical Friday at the bank, with everything going according to plan and operating as it usually regularly does. This was until closing time was approaching, to which the attitude and aura suddenly changed for some reason. Today seemed totally different and peculiar. Everyone inside of the bank which included five employees, and three customers currently, for some reason had a very strange unexplainable emotion running through their bodies. As if something unsuspecting was about to happen and occur. Just a very dark and negative energy was just roaming about, and not a single soul could put the pieces together to figure out what the issue and problem exactly was. But nevertheless, it is business as usual and everything is usually going according to plan as it usually does, and these dark feelings and emotions at this particular point and time have to wait and be put on hold. Things must continue to go on, despite feelings everyone has lurking in their minds.

The five employees in the bank consist of two bank tellers, one financial advisor, one bank manager, and one operations manager. The employees have all been with the bank at separate durations; some longer than other. Even though for the most part, they are all familiar with the protocol and procedures of the bank. The last incident the bank has had was over four years ago shockingly enough. There was only one person currently working in the bank who experienced that particular event, whom is the operations manager. However, each employee has been thoroughly trained on how to handle robberies if they were to occur. Despite the very lax security this bank has, the employees seem confident on their code of conduct on how to act and approach a situation such as that if it were to happen. It still doesn't take away any ill feelings that generally everyone in this building has at the moment. The bank in total has eight employees. Four bank tellers, two financial advisors, an assistant operations manager or bank manager, and an operations manager. Of those eight, only five are currently working on this particular day. The other three employees consist of two bank tellers whom are not currently working, and a financial advisor not scheduled to work today. The bank tellers and financial advisors alternate days when they work. The operating manager, and the bank manager are the only employees who work Monday through Friday, without alternating their shifts. There aren't any other personnel associated with the bank aside from the Senior Branch Security Manager, who is not an employee of the bank, but an employee of the federal security branch the bank is involved in. He is present from time to time at the bank for security purposes.

All five employees currently inside of the bank, are anticipating closing time. Performing their usual rounds, awaiting time for the business to close. The bank tellers are currently assisting patrons with their business, a financial advisor is currently helping a patron with their issue. The operations manager who also fulfills the duties of a financial advisor is helping a customer at his desk. The bank manager is standing behind the bank tellers terminals, with a very stern and strict look on his face. Watching the bank tellers to make sure they are doing everything in order and correctly. If they were to encounter any problems, the bank tellers are easy able to call upon the bank manager to help with any assistance.

This newly appointed twenty-nine-year-old bank manager is Russell McCoy. A slightly chubby man who is robust. He is an auburn haired, tall man with a goatee, with sharp light blue eyes. As far as his face, he has very pudgy cheeks, and a spherical face. He has a short tapered wavy hairstyle, and very bushy sideburns on the side of his face, which neatly connect to his goatee. He has in a way a very grizzly, yet professional look about him. He has on a navy blue tailored patterned suit, which he goes to the dry cleaners located in the same shopping center to get altered quite often. He has on brown leather shoes, that are well polished. He usually has a stoic look on his face most of the time. He is a very introverted man, who keeps many of his feelings and emotions to himself usually. Having a very neutralized relationship with the other employees of the bank. A reason for Russell's strange demeanor, would have to be his very damaging upbringing and background. Russell is not originally from Los Angeles. He was born and raised in Milwaukee, Wisconsin under a middle and working class family. He is of second generation Russian and Jewish descent, although he wasn't very committed to his religion that much at all.

While the day is winding down to closing time on this Friday evening, Russell begins to drift and daydream and reminisce on his past and current life a bit. Russell lives by himself in his luxury condo that he bought in downtown Los Angeles. It is located in a short driving distance from the bank. He is a man of solitude generally and keeps to himself. Although he is friendly and cordial to others, he is realistically a man of much mystery. Russell who self-diagnosed himself as having antisocial personality disorder, and narcissistic personality disorder, has kept this fact about himself very secret. He is particular with his daily life and he has certain routines that he's happy with, and he's very strict into going against them. He has many hobbies; he likes to play football, and he is really into watching NFL football games. His favorite teams are the "Oakland Raiders" and the "Green Bay Packers."

Russell holds both liberal and conservative opinions about himself. He is involved with anarchy and politics; to which he can be obsessed at times with it. Russell is also a gun enthusiast. He currently owns two guns. A "Smith & Wesson" handgun, and a "Smith and Wesson M&P" rifle. Which he is legally licensed to own both. In his spare time, he goes to the shooting range. Russell virtually struggles with friendships, as his introverted personality doesn't allow him to connect with others. He has not had any romantic endeavors in his life. That part of his life is kept ambiguous. He doesn't consider himself the fatherly type, and doesn't plan on getting married, having children and starting a family. He considers himself a very strict person when it comes to romantic affection. Russell in a way considers himself a bisexual man, with homosexual tendencies. Being both romantically attracted to men, women, and people in general. He is very private about his sex life, and it's very unknown and obscure at times.

Russell looked back at how his childhood is one of much trauma and disappointment. An only child, he did not have any siblings. He led a very sheltered young life with his parents, Vladimir and Karla. Due to the fact his parents were sadly killed when he was only five years old in an automobile collision, under intense winter snow weather conditions. His father whom was driving, lost control of the vehicle. While Russell was the sole survivor in the accident riding as a passenger in the back seat. An event which Russell very rarely mentions or discusses due to the extreme amount of depression it causes him. His paternal grandparents were already deceased by this time, so he lived under the care of his maternal Grandmother and Grandfather, to which he had a distant and difficult relationship with, yet still appreciated their support. Russell turned to athletics in his teenage years to suppress these feelings he had. Excelling in football, and becoming very proficient in that. However, despite all of that Russell did not decide to pursue athletics in college, as it just didn't interest him really.

He decided to take a different outlook and lease on his life, with his major being business accounting. A dream of his was to be a stock broker in Wall Street, making a career and living out of that. He was accepted into the "University of Southern California", to which Russell has now lived in and relocated to Los Angeles for over ten years now. He later received his master's degree in Business Finance. Since he has moved to California, both his paternal grandparents have passed away, and he doesn't keep in contact with his remaining extended family members in Wisconsin. Devoting all of his time to his new life in California.

Since earning his degree, Russell decided to turn his passion into working for banks and financial institutions for the time being, with his dream of working in Wall Street still on his mind. He has worked for two bank branches. The first bank being a major branch chain called "First National Bank of Los Angeles", as a bank teller. During his time as a teller, Russell only witnessed only one incident of a bank robbery. A female teller working two terminals to the left was given a note by a man wearing sunglasses, a brown trench coat and a top hat, to empty all of the money inside of her terminal. She complied with the note, and the man dashed out of the bank. Russell who was busy assisting a patron of the bank, noticed the man's strange behavior, but did not pay him much attention. With that aside, Russell has not had any issues or problems while working in this bank. Very rarely calling out sick or missing work, due to the enjoyment he had working and helping his customers. He was very devoted to his job, and it was very vital for him to do his absolute best at all times. His main goal was to eventually become a manager at this bank.

As much as it hurt for Russell to realize, he did feel at times management of this bank did not have his, or many of the customer's best interest at all. He began to question his importance at this company, and whether or not he wanted to continue his services here. Career growth seemed to be an issue, and he also had doubts about different rules the company had, which he felt wasn't fair to some of the patrons of the bank. Russell then strived to find a way to assess and fix this problem. Although he cared for the company and was thankful for his position at the bank, he felt he deserved better. He decided to go for a change of pace and direction. After a few years of working at this bank as teller and gaining experience and knowledge from this position, Russell wanted to advance himself in a smaller bank, working as a manager in charge of all operations. He noticed an opening in a bank across town called the "Sunset Credit Union", that was hiring for a management position. Russell inquired for this position, and decided to take a risk with it. He put in a two weeks' notice with the "First National Bank of Los Angeles", and decided to no longer to work at that branch. He decided to move forward in hopes that this new opportunity was one that was well worth it.

On the morning of his interview at the "Sunset Credit Union", Russell arrived an hour before opening to meet with the operations manager of this bank named Peter Jones. Peter Jones is a forty-five-year-old slender, clean cut, skinny and short heighted man of Irish descent, who has a very severe receding hairline, with his salt and pepper hair thinning on a low buzzed level, and spherical metal frame glasses. He looks as if he's a college professor. He always wears a bow tie and suspenders with every outfit he wears to work. He is gentle and kind hearted man who has a big sense of humor about him. He lives with his wife Linda, and his 10-year-old daughter Louise in Los Angeles. Originally from New York, Peter is a man who has many experience working in banks and the financial world. He has various opinions on an array of topics, mainly because of his age. He holds a lot of virtues along with that. He is an open minded guy for the most part, willing to accept and understand things that most people generally don't. Peter's family consist of many immigrants, who came to the United States to seek a better life for themselves, so Peter uses that to fuel his hard working attitude to better himself.

Peter is the Operations manager of the "Sunset Credit Union". He is basically in charge of the bank, and acts as an administrator to all the daily duties of the bank. He also is the one that hires, and hired all of the employees that are currently working in the bank. He has been working in the bank the longest, and has the most experience and knowledge of the bank. Peter's main tasks are to make sure the bank is running as smoothly as it can, although he does hold other tasks and job duties that he performs as well. Peter is looking to hire another bank manager/assistant operations manager. This is because the past manager who held this position, moved onto another bank, and he has to replace him. Peter has interviewed a handful of prospects, but he hasn't been satisfied at all with the potential candidates for some reason. Russell would be the sixth man that he would be interviewing to hire onto this position.

Russell who is feeling very nervous and anxious from meeting Peter, is although enjoying Peter's company and liking his attitude upon greeting him. Russell took a seat behind Peter's desk. Peter began to interview Russell for the position. Asking him several questions.

"Russell, it's great to finally meet you. I know I spoke to you over the phone a couple days ago, and thanks for coming by. This resume is very nice...., so I must ask, how was it at First National?". Russell replied, still feeling anxious.

"I loved it, I learned a lot about the banking and financial business, there wasn't a single day that I didn't like. Dealing with computers and technology and records and bookkeeping, and dealing with other objectives I had to complete. Working in a bank is very high profile, and I took what I knew about that particular branch, learned specifics and tricks to make things more efficient. Dealing with customer payments and solving issues they had. I enjoyed my time at that bank, I really did."

Peter who seemed satisfied with that response asked Russell another question.

"So, why aren't you at First National anymore?".

Russell began to feel even more anxious, as he had several different answers in his head. He was debating as to whether or not to make himself look good and fib, and say in some shape or form that the company was laying off employee's hours and wages, or to just tell the truth and say that he wasn't happy with how he was being treated at the company, and how the bank was treating other customers. Russell very anxiously replied,

"Well, I just decided that logistically I felt I was being overshadowed, and I wasn't as important as I once was. It was becoming an issue as we were understaffed at times, and it was getting very hectic. Many people were coming and going, and...," Russell stopped himself, looked towards the ground and hesitated for a few seconds. He then continued.

"I'm sorry, I'm not going to lie. I had some issues with management, and I felt they were, please excuse my language, doing some very shady shit, and I wanted nothing to do with that. I noticed a pattern that everyone was getting the hell out of there rather quickly. So I decided to follow suit. No disrespect to them at all. Again, I loved working there, and I learned so much. Above all of that, I was hard working and gave my all to that company. But to be honest, I felt that wasn't where I was supposed to be at all, and I decided to take my talents elsewhere."

Russell felt very uneasy after that response, but was glad that he was truthful, hoping the benefit of that would reap success. Peter responded to Russell.

"You know what, I really appreciate your honesty man. You seem to not give a damn, and that's a good quality for a man who wants to manage a bank to have. Really between you and me, I have like four other guys I'm considering, but to hell with that. I doubt they have what you have. You're such a well put together young man. I'm really feeling you, and I would love to have you join us. I want you to start right now. That is if that's alright with you, please say yes."

Peter with a big smile on his face, put out his hand for Russell to shake and acknowledge.

Russell not expecting at all for Peter to be gratified for his rather blunt way of putting things, was shocked to see Peter's acceptance towards his personality. Russell very briskly shakes Peter's hand, and accepts his offer smiling,

"Well I don't mean to brag, but I am the best. Come on now. Thank you so much sir, I appreciate it.".

Peter under his breath calmly responds to Russell, while still shaking his hand.

"Don't call me Sir, call me Pete, were partners now. It's alright. Welcome to the team."

Russell who has now been working for the bank for only three months, was then hired onto become an assistant operations manager, ergo just simply a bank manager. His duties included managing bank teller activities, solving customer complaints and issues, making sure security protocols are met, and to be an acting bank teller if customer flow is very active, be an acting financial advisor if need be, and to most importantly in relation to that, be an acting operations manager if the operations manager is not working.

Russell out of all the other employees became very close with Peter, and develops a close bond with him. Peter has been with the "Sunset Credit Union", for many years. Originally transferring as a manager from another nearby bank before then. Russell's relationship with Peter reaches out even further, as they mingle outside of work numerous times. Despite their wide age difference, with Russell being in his late twenties, and Peter being in his forties, they still seemed to orchestrate a very close and supportive friendship. Also minding the fact that Russell has only been an employee of this company for a few months, that doesn't seem to matter. Peter has invited Russell to his house a couple times, and has introduced him to his family in addition to that. Russell who was sort of an introverted man himself, did not have any friends. He had close associates when he was in university that he later lost contact with. He began to confide in Peter quite closely. Peter was a very talented golfer, and Russell not quite being as skilled as him, still enjoyed to golf with Peter.

Russell temporarily snaps out of his daydreaming, and leaves from behind the bank counter, when he goes to assist an elderly African American woman departing the bank who drops her pocketbook from her purse onto the ground.

"Sweetheart, I believe you dropped this."

The woman thanks him for alerting her on this, and she walks out of the bank. Immediately following that, a young woman with curly hair, wearing a T-shirt and blue jeans and sunglasses, who works at a restaurant around the corner, walks into the bank, and asks Russell if they are still open. He responds to her politely.

"Yes, you're just in time, we are about to close, but you're okay."

Russell proceeds to go back to his work location, overlooking the bank. Aside from Peter the operations manager who is working, the other employees consist of two tellers. One of which is a twenty-five-year-old, attractive blonde haired Caucasian girl, named Jennifer Reynolds. Jennifer is a very beautiful woman, who is still trendy yet professional with her image. She has been hired as a bank teller at the "Sunset Credit Union", for almost two years now. Before then, she took up various jobs as being a waitress. Being born and raised in Los Angeles, growing up in a typical nuclear upper middle class background. She has many siblings, three brothers and two sisters. Jennifer is the youngest. She lives with her parents not that far from the bank, and she is in school at, "California State University, Los

Angeles" to become a school teacher. She recently decided to change her study to that, after she originally wanted to study fashion design. Jennifer is a very outgoing and bubbly woman, and she has a friendly spirit about her. Her relationship with the other coworkers is generally well liked. Due to her conflicting school and work schedule, she very rarely has much of a social life despite her exuberant personality, but she manages to still take control of her life in a positive way.

Jennifer is single and she does not have any children. She at this point is concerned about her career and her work, and is not concerned about love or relationships. Jennifer enjoys exercising and going to the gym frequently. She has many friends who also work at the bank, and some that do not, that she usually associates with. Despite their wide age gap, Jennifer keeps a very professional relationship with Peter, as she is always respectable with him. She isn't close friends with him outside of the bank, but she is very professional towards him.

Russell has a very conflicting relationship with Jennifer. They are cordial to each other, however they aren't really that close. Russell thinks of her as a nice woman, but he isn't that devoted or concerned to her that much at all. Jennifer also seems to not really show that much attention to Russell at all. Despite the fact Jennifer has associated with every other employee of the bank in some shape or form, she has never really developed any type of relationship with Russell outside of work. It seems to be a mutual feeling between them both, that they aren't really interested in each other for whichever reason. Russell does respect Jennifer though, and really is happy to see her apart of the company. Jennifer seems to be safe around Russell, although they aren't close on any personal levels.

The other bank teller is a twenty-eight-year-old African American man named Jesse Watkins. Jesse is a very slender, childish, flamboyant and eccentric, brown skinned man, with natural afro textured hair and full lips. He as a very loud and high pitched voice. He is wearing a blue vest, with a white shirt and black tie. He is also wearing black shorts, to which he likes to wear shorts quite often, along with black loafer shoes. Jesse is an openly homosexual man, that has an artistic personality about him. Jesse was hired as a bank teller only a couple weeks before Russell was hired as manager. He along with Russell, are both recently hired to company. Jesse has had a very damaging upbringing, with many obstacles he had to overcome. Not only being a black man, but also a homosexual man as well. Adapting to the issues of society with that. He was born and raised in Atlanta, Georgia living in the inner city of the southern United States. He was in a terrible family situation in a working class background. He was born an only child. His mother Claudette who passed away when he was only three years old, was a drug addict and succumbed to her drug addiction, and he never met his father at all. Jesse who had no other family, lived his entire life in a foster care system, with many other black children. Due to how proficient he was in High School, Jesse was offered a Scholarship at the "University of Southern California." The same school Russell attended, however he and Russell have never met each other before working at the "Sunset Credit Union", nor do they both know that they went to the same school.

Jesse decided to move from Atlanta, to Los Angeles. He decided to go onto study communication studies. Jesse had a desire to become a journalist and a news anchor. Jesse holds a very neutral political opinion, and feels maybe due to the fact of his own personality and profile, that his opinion doesn't matter, and he doesn't know where he fits in. Jesse does not have any friends, and like Russell seems to have social issues befriending others. Unlike Russell, Jesse is more outgoing than he is, and Jesse sometimes uses that as a defense mechanism to hold his feelings. Jesse lives by himself also in the south Los Angeles area. He was going to continue school and graduate however, it wasn't until a couple years ago that Jesse decided that he no longer wanted to pursue that, and decided to drop of school with an undeclared major.

Jesse who suffers from Bipolar Disorder, which he was diagnosed with in his teenage years. He began to work an array of odd jobs. Such as working at working at a fast food restaurant, a retail clothing store, and at a hotel, which was his previous job. He then decided with no prior experience working in a bank, to apply for a bank teller position at the "Sunset Credit Union", to which he was hired on by Peter, who seemed to be enthralled by Jesse's strange personality.

He along with Russell, is very secretive about his mental disorder and this fact about himself, and doesn't disclose it. Likewise, with Jennifer and all of his other coworkers aside from Peter, Russell has a very distant and complicated relationship with Jesse. Being that they are both relatively new to the company and only working there for a few months, they still do not have much good rapport with each other. Jesse respects Russell as his manager, and he leaves it alone at that. Although, Russell and Jesse are very professional with each other as far as work is concerned. Even though Russell is aware that Jesse is homosexual, he has not come out with his sexuality to him at all, nor does Jesse know about Russell's sexuality, or anything about his personal life outside of work. Russell feels Jesse doesn't need to know that information about him, and so he keeps it to himself.

Jennifer and Jesse do not associate much outside of work. They are at a friendly professional level when working, but they are not closer than that when they are outside the bank. Jesse has a friendly and respecting relationship with Peter, though when Jesse is not working, he doesn't keep in touch with Peter that much at all. Jesse tries to keep a professional relationship with him. Jesse all around is a well-liked employee apart of the bank.

The final employee currently working in the bank is Yvette Martinez. She is a thirty-eight-year-old curvy Hispanic woman, who has long brunette hair, and long dangling earrings. Yvette has been working at the bank longer than Russell, Jesse, and Jennifer, but she hasn't been working in the bank as long as Peter. She has been working in the bank for over twelve years. Yvette is a financial advisor. Unlike the bank tellers, she has a separate desk that's adjacent to the lobby. Similar to that of Peter. Her job is to assist customers with opening up new checking or savings accounts, dealing with loans and payment plans, and dealing with any other customer issues regarding their account. Yvette originally started out as a bank teller, then she was moved onto becoming a financial advisor. Yvette is a woman in which not much of her personal life is known. She is a mother of two young children, a seven-year-old son Ricky, and a nine-year-old daughter Laura. She was once married, but is now divorced. She is currently dating a forty-year-old bearded Caucasian man named Matt Meyers. Not much else is known aside from that. She was born and raised in Los Angeles, and comes from a very big family. She is Catholic and is very devoted to her faith. Yvette keeps a conservative and professional attitude towards her work. Yvette coincidentally used to previously work at the grocery store which is now called, "Healthy and Fresh". She used to work at the store when it was under different management and called "SaveCo Foods", as a checkout lady. Yvette was laid off when the store changed management directions, and she was left without a job. She decided to apply at the bank belonging to the same shopping center as a bank teller, to which she was hired.

Although Yvette keeps a very direct and professional attitude when at work, she is still a very welcoming person and gets along with everyone else at the bank. Her relationship with Peter seems to be the strongest. Yvette like with Russell, has also met Peter's family, and Peter is also very close to Yvette's family. Yvette and Jennifer despite being both female, aren't as close as they should be. Yvette is much older than Jennifer, and she also feels Jennifer's personality is too loud for her, so that is a reason for the fact they are distant. Yvette isn't that close with Russell or Jesse, but she has a very safe and comfortable working relationship with the both of them. Yvette does at times feels close with Russell, yet she doesn't always trust him. She feels he is hiding much about himself, and therefore her relationship with him is damaged because of that.

The other three employees who are currently not working at the bank, consist of two bank tellers. One of the bank tellers is a twenty-six-year-old, slender professional looking Chinese American woman that wears glasses named Tiffany Wong. Tiffany's parents immigrated to the United States, so she is first generation Chinese. Tiffany has not been working in the bank for that long. She was hired as a bank teller a month before Jesse was. Due to that, her relationship with virtually everyone else at the bank isn't as strong. She is a very kind and friendly young woman at the bank, and is accepted by everyone else generally. She is currently studying psychology at "Pepperdine University." When she is not at school, she is working at the bank. Tiffany keeps private at work, and doesn't explain much about her personal life that much at all. Because they work alternating shifts, Jesse, Jennifer and Yvette rarely get much contact with her. Peter seems to have a friendly and nice relationship with Tiffany. Russell who is also new like Tiffany, seems to not mind her company, and they have a good bond together usually.

The next absent employee is another bank teller. She is a forty-four-year-old Caucasian woman with short hair named Sally Richardson. She has been working at the bank for a long time, longer than Yvette. She has been working at the bank for fifteen years as a teller. Sally unlike the other employees, is a very difficult woman to be around, including Peter who doesn't really seem to care for her truth be told. All the other employees of the bank, along with Tiffany whom she works shifts alongside with, also doesn't give any special treatment to. She has an equal relationship with her, in which it isn't really a positive or happy one at all. Russell tends to leave her alone, and keeps his distance with her to avoid any conflict. Her work performance is satisfactory and she shows good contributions to the bank, so even though her personality with the other workers isn't that well, she still is a good employee to the company. She has a very scornful and passive personality about herself. As far as her history goes, she was born and raised in California, and she used to work as a librarian. She has a son who is in University on the eastern part of the United States. She lives with her husband in Los Angeles.

Tiffany and Sally work alternating shifts every other day each week, with Jesse and Jennifer. With whoever didn't work on Friday, works on Monday, and the pattern continues. There are times to where bank tellers would fill in for each other and they would work conflicting shifts, but for the most part generally there are two bank tellers who work each day. With Russell sometimes filling in if the bank becomes too overpowered with patrons. The bank is generally low profile, so this system works well with the employees, and is managed and operated quite well with little issues involved.

The other employee currently not working, is the other financial advisor. He is a thirty-four-year-old Caucasian man named Abel

Albertson. He is the son of one of Peter's close friends, which is how he got hired. Abel has been working in the bank for five years, so he's one of the more veteran employees. He is a very attractive and handsome athletic built man. He is bald, and has tan skin. Abel is married to his wife, and has two very young daughters. When Abel is not working as a financial advisor, he spends most of his time exercising in the gym and working out, occasionally he also likes to go surfing. Unlike Russell, and like Peter and Jesse, he is way more engaging with his personality. Abel grew up in California, and he had a typical family life growing up. Abel went to "Berkeley University", and graduated studying finance. Most of Abel's personal life other than the fact his father is really close with Peter, is not really known. The financial advisors, likewise with the bank tellers also work alternative shifts. So therefore his relationships with Yvette, Jennifer and Jesse aren't as strong, as he usually and typically doesn't work when they are scheduled, but he's still a gentleman to everyone he comes across. Russell although not extremely close with him, enjoys being around him and has no issues with him.

The only other employee who sparingly comes into the bank, is the Senior Branch Security Manager, who is not a direct employee of the bank, but is in charge of the federal operations that the bank belongs to, and is part of the main operations of the bank. His name is John Marshall. He is a thirty-six-year-old half Dutch, half Mexican American man who has black hair in a flat top, and he has bushy mustache. John is a single man with no children. He is bisexual, and antisocial. He is seen in the bank a few times a month, usually for safety and security reasons. He has been the Senior Branch Security Manager of this bank for only a few years. He is not sociable to the other employees of the bank, and he doesn't have to be. His job is simply to go over company records, and safety regulations and records, and to review camera surveillance video records. His relationship with Peter isn't very strong, as Peter seems to only have a strict relationship with him. John is only in the bank for a couple of hours a few times a week, so his interactions with the other employees actually isn't that existent. Russell seems to be scared of him usually, and seems to not really trust him, and trembles in fear every time he sees him. If an incident were to happen such as a robbery, the Senior Branch Security Manager would have to come to the branch and assess the issue and follow procedures and rules according to that.

The very dark and fearful wave of energy surrounding the bank is still very much present. It's a very peculiar and unknown sense of fear, that although not a single soul inside the building wants to mention or bring up vocally, they know that it exists and is lingering in the air. As the bank is soon to close in minutes, usual behaviors and actions continue to go on.

Russell once again decides to snap out of daydreaming and reflecting. As closing time is very rapidly approaching, Russell decides to keep himself occupied to refrain from daydreaming and flashbacking once again. He decides to step from behind the teller's counter, to unplug the coffee machine, and put away the complementary coffee cups, coffee creamer, and other coffee supplies that were set out in the lobby. Meanwhile, two more customers, who are young females dressed very clad, dash into the bank in an effort to take care of their business before the bank is closing. Russell jokingly acknowledging their presence.

"Ladies, you look stunning, However, we do close in a few minutes just to remind you. I understand you guys want to cash your paycheck before you head to the club. I understand. It's alright. But we are about to close."

The two women laugh at his remark. At the same moment, Russell then begins to take his phone out of his pocket. Russell and Peter planned earlier this week that after this shift, they were going to a sports bar to enjoy themselves. Russell decided to arrange reservations, so that right after their shift ended, himself and Peter could go directly there. After making and confirming the reservations, Russell notices Peter is wrapping things up and is tidying up his desk for the branch to close. He decides to walk over and stand next to Peter's desk. Although it is still technically business hours, he finds a sly way to in an unprofessional manner, converse with Peter.

"So, I just got done putting in the reservations, and everything is all set. I can't wait, only...,"

Russell looks at his Rolex watch.

"Eight minutes left until we are out of here. It will only take us three minutes to close all the terminals, shut the lights off, and lock the cash drawers up. Shit, I just want to call it a day. Ugh."

Peter while looking at his computer terminal smiles at him. Russell begins to look down at the ground to daydream once again. One thing Russell liked about the "Sunset Credit Union", is that it was a very small bank branch, which unlike major federal banks didn't have to follow the same safety and security measures. When Russell was working at the bank he was previously, during closing time more steps needed to be done before the building was closed and employees were allowed to depart from the business.

Peter begins to shut his terminal off, and starts his usual routines and customs when it is closing time. He looks up to Russell who is standing, and in a sly method talks to Russell.

"Doesn't it always seem like when it's the final minutes of the day, they seem to tread on for what seems like forever?".

Russell in a response to Peter's statement, sucks in his lips and shakes his head and scoffs to himself. He then whilst still standing next to Peter's desk, glances around the bank. He notices about four customers standing in line in front of the tellers, and he also sees Yvette gathering her bearings, and getting ready for the business to close.

Russell then decides to walk over to Yvette's desk and engage in small talk with her, with his arms crossed.

"How you doing girl? Can't wait to get out of here huh?".

Yvette shaking her head, looking slightly drained and agitated, looks up at Russell and sassily responds,

"You have no idea, my daughter has an appointment at the salon in an hour, and I have to get on the 110 and drive clear across town, as her hairdresser has other clients. If I'm late, she's going to skip over me. We have a function on Sunday, so, it's always something."

Russell in response to her comment, laughs and grins heavily showing his clenched teeth, also shaking his head. To which Yvette while still sitting at her desk, then slaps Russell on his behind in a friendly manner. Russell then decides to walk away from her desk, heading towards the back area of teller's counter. Directing his comments both to Jesse and Jennifer.

"You guys alright? Are you guys all ready and set to close?"

Both Jesse and Jennifer respond by telling him yes, and continue to work. Russell while still behind the counter makes sure everything is in proper order to close. He then decides to leave from behind the teller's counter, and head out into the lobby. Russell then goes into a separate room located to the left of the entrance, which is a multi-purpose room. Which contains printers and photo copiers, that employees use to make copies for customers and to print out other important documents. In a separate hallway in the back of this room, contains another room which has a refrigerator, a microwave, and cupboards with each employee's name on it. This connected adjoining room is for employees to eat lunch in, and to also put their belongings in. Russell opens his personal cupboard and grabs his car keys and puts him in his pocket, and also grabs his briefcase.

Russell then with his briefcase in his hand, walks over to Peter's desk one more time. Peter is still sitting at his desk. He sets his briefcase down on Peter's desk, and Russell takes a seat in front of the desk. He then makes himself comfortable and puts his hand under his chin, assessing the entire bank at the same time. Peter who has finally wrapped everything up, opens and goes through one of the lower drawers of his desk, and pulls out a piece of paper that was a very odd drawing on it. He hands it to Russell. The drawing is of a man and a young girl with hearts drawn across it.

Russell looks at the picture and smiles. He then knowingly responds to Peter.

"Your daughter made this? This is very cute and sweet."

Russell then hands the drawing back to Peter. To which Peter takes his glasses off and is looking down at the drawing, while still talking to Russell.

"Yeah she did. She made that for me when she was in Kindergarten. I don't know why, but I get so emotional with this picture. I just love how detailed she drew me, and how her teacher asked her to draw the one thing she's loves the most in the world. She decided to choose me. I kept this drawing all these years. She's ten now. Time just flies doesn't it?"

Russell then looks away from Peter, temporarily freezing his emotions and keeps a stoic and cold stare for a few seconds, then continuing to keep this same expression, nods his head slowly. Peter then opens the lower drawer of his desk, and puts the drawing back inside, and shuts the door. Peter then pulls his chair back and leans back and puts his hands behind his head looking up. Russell is looking down at the floor, smiling and shaking his head, he then however brings his head up and notices Peter staring into space. Russell then speaks to him.

"What are you thinking about?".

Peter while he is still leaned back into chair, looks at Russell and tells him,

"I'm just thinking about how blessed I am to have a guy like you working for me. Russell, you are a remarkable man, you are.".

Peter then seals his mouth and grins at Russell.

Russell once again looks away from Peter, erupts a stoic and cold look on his face for a few seconds, then looks down towards the floor and shakes his head, this time scoffing while he's doing it.

CHAPTER 2:

NOTHING GIVEN, NOTHING TAKEN

As the "Sunset Credit Union" is in preparation to close, emotions are winding down to suspend the business day. All the employees in the bank are anticipating about their agenda once they exit work, in addition to any plans for the weekend they may have. Putting all professional related thoughts aside, and positing themselves for the end of the shift. Having in mind that this typical Friday at the bank, is coming to an end. With everyone comfortable with the idea and notion that once work is finished, they can wind themselves down and can be satisfied to proceed with their own personal matters.

However, the mood is soon to change. There is a dark and unpleasant energy floating about. One that is sure to bring much danger and negative signals. The "Oakwood Shopping Center", is about to be the epicenter of extreme disaster. Disaster, that not a single soul is ready and prepared to deal with. This disaster and peril is not unexpected though, as everyone in this area can sense the fear, although it is difficult for anyone to quite put their finger onto what the fear actually is. It is just very devastating and upsetting that this feeling is just overpowering the building. What is for certain is that something negative is creeping up, and it's not something that anyone is looking forward to. This was supposed to be an ordinary typical Friday, but according to the shift and mood that lingers in the air, this might not all be the case. It is very unfortunate that anxiety has to be on high rise, and comfortable and relaxed vibes instead aren't present. Actions do in fact speak louder than words, but due to the high anxiety which everyone inside the bank has, the actions cannot be committed. Thoughts and emotions are only available, and these thoughts and emotions people generally keep to themselves. Even though there is a disgusting surge of negative harsh energy at this point, people have to accept and deal with it. It is a harsh truth to understand but basically, it is the only thing that anyone can do. Simply conform to normality and carry on with regular routines and customs. As generally there shouldn't be any reason to think otherwise, or to assume anything otherwise. What people feel and what emotions they have shouldn't have any merit or any reason or rhyme, so all of that just simply has to be ignored so there isn't any cause for concern. If only it were as simple and as smooth as that.

Rushing down the street is a white 1994 Chevy Astro van with tinted windows, including the rear window, and a tinted windscreen. The tires on the van are quite large and look brand new. There is no license plate at all on the vehicle. This van is driving very erratically and recklessly, and driving in an unsafe and unnatural fashion. Although the van is following the traffic signals for the most part, that seems to be dismissive. The driver is weaving through the road and speeding at an exorbitant rate. Other cars that are on the road are very fearful of this vehicle. They realize the person behind the wheel is either intoxicated, or they are under some type of adrenaline rush to where the safety of others isn't their priority at all. The van continues to travel down the street making an unsafe right turn, barely sideswiping a car. It is very clear the driver of the van has his own agenda, and that particular agenda is a dangerous and disastrous one. Presenting an extreme wave of mystery, due to the ambiguity this vehicle has. The unknown is a reasonable thing to be in fear of, and this van is the unknown. The van has tinted pitch black windows; so it is impossible to see inside the van from the outside. Taking note perhaps all of that is done for good reason; as most likely the occupants of the van do not wish for any other parties to see who is inside the vehicle. Keeping in mind as well, the lack of plates on the van, as realistically there is no way to identify or place a name as to who exactly the vehicle belongs to. This is not at all a good sign to those who are in some type of unsettling feeling about this van. All of this only adds more suspicion and fear to an already boiled over pot.

The driver at this point seems to be getting impatient, almost as if they are running late for an appointment they need to attend. The van which was previously obeying traffic laws, is now running red lights, and speeding past intersections. If the driver of the van could avoid stopping at light, he would. The driver has lost all control, and it's too much to bear.

There are two men that are inside of this van. Both of these men know each other well, and they are very close to each other. These men exterior wise seem innocent and normal enough, however that contradicts their actual true details and profile. The men inside the vehicle are dressed in rain ponchos and both wearing dark black pants. Both of their faces are concealed, with a stocking cap covering their face and mouth. There are holes in the eyes of the stocking cap, yet their eyes are also covered and hidden as they are wearing sunglasses. Over their hands, both of the men sport thick leather gloves. The men are also wearing very thick combat boots. Their attire clearly seems intimidating and serves a purpose. The purpose is so their identity is not accessible to be known to others. No other details of the men can be known, although the men are virtually similar in age and body type. The men of course are dressed to commit some type of crime, which now explains the wild behavior and antics they are exhibiting. We are dealing with two very sinister men with cruel intentions, and violent demeanors to themselves.

These men are very prolific bank robbers, and they are very skilled with their actions. Both of the men lock their heads straight ahead, and they do not stray or look away from the windscreen. During this intense moment, these two men honestly have two completely different emotions. The driver of the van is tamer, calm and determined with his actions. His hands stick to the steering wheel as if they were glued or sewn on top of it. He knows exactly what he's doing, and how he's going to do it. The well-being of others isn't running past this man, and he wants to focus only on what benefits him. The passenger however, is not showing an identical attitude. He seems to be timid and nervous, yet he doesn't want the driver of the van to recognize or notice this. His legs and knees start to shake, and he starts to feel anxious on his current position. The passenger then takes his head away from facing in front of the windscreen, and turns to the face the driver, looking concerned and doubtful. The driver who is continually to drive in an outrageously manner, then directs his head and eyes away from the road, and makes eye contact with the man sitting in the co-pilot seat for a split second. The passenger awkwardly and quickly turns and faces front again, locking his view to the windscreen, not expecting the driver to notice and look at him.

A few seconds later however, the passenger feeling even more nervous and uncomfortable, glances at the driver once again. This time, expressing himself.

"Hey man, just take it easy alright? You are going way to fucking fast man, and I know we gotta do what we gotta do, but just chill it and take it down a notch."

The driver ignores the passenger and continues his unsafe driving performance. After saying what he had to say, the passenger shakes his head and turns away from the driver and locks his view forward. Seconds after this, the van makes another sudden illegal right turn, only this time the van does in fact swipe another vehicle. The impact is not that severe, however there is significant damage to the other vehicle. The car that was hit pulls over to the side of the road, the van continues to speed past the accident scene. The passenger then turns his head to the driver once more.

"We just fucking hit a car! I knew I should have drove; I just knew it. I just got done telling you to watch yourself. Damn."

The driver then quickly scans behind himself to take a look at the car he hit, and then returns his view to the road. The driver while continuing to look forward, responds to his passenger.

"Quit acting like a bitch. That car is fine; all I saw was a scratch. We're about to do an armed robbery. You think I give a fuck about a hit a run? Just sit tight, we're almost there. I know you jacked this car, but I'm driving and that's final. All I need for you to do is shut your trap, and sit down and be quiet."

The passenger puts his hand over his forehead, and is in complete shock over what the driver said, and is in complete disbelief of himself. He stares at the driver for a few seconds, and responds to him.

"Yeah, but you know, can we like, not draw attention to ourselves? It's shit like that which is going to ruin us. It's bad enough you're driving like Batman, people are already probably calling the cops on us for that shit alone, but here you go and hit a fucking car. Jesus. Just please, I'm begging you to just ease yourself will you?"

The driver then grunts at the passenger, and proceeds to slightly lower his speed, whilst still driving in uncustomary reckless way. He then replies to the passenger, in a determined and triumphant way. Even though his face was covered, you could tell he was smiling and grinning.

"This is going to be our third and final hit. How many people can say they took three banks, all in the same state on the same day? We hit Sacramento, then we hit San Jose, now were gonna hit LA. This is our home turf too as we both cased this bank before, so this is gonna be a piece of cake. After this, we count what we got and we're leaving California for good. We're off to New York."

The passenger even though his face is concealed, has a nervous like grin while looking at the driver. He then looks behind him to the cargo area of the van. The van only has two seats, the driver and the passenger seat. Behind these seats is an open cargo area. This area has contents that are neglectfully arranged and aligned. It contains an array of weapons and items these men have used in their robberies. These include six giant burlap sacks, in which four of the sacks are filled with dollar bills, with the remaining two which are empty. It also contains two semi-automatic machine assault rifles, and ammunition. In addition, there is rope, tape, three small handguns, a bottle of whisky, a can of gasoline, a laptop computer, two steel hammers, a ladder, a chainsaw, grenades, and smoke bombs.

The passenger although he already knew everything was already properly accounted for, checks to see if all the items are in order and ready for use. He once again looks at the driver, and converses with him.

"Yeah, everything is all set man, we should be in and out no problem. As soon as we get to the bank, we're gonna roll out and roll back in, and we're done."

However honestly, the passenger inside did not feel as enthusiastic as he was claiming to be. He was feeling apprehensive and unsafe. The driver looks at the clock on the dashboard, and starts to worry and panic. He then begins to divert himself into speeding the vehicle again.

"Look man, if I don't go any faster the place is gonna close. I lost track of time, and didn't expect us to get here this late, we gotta get there fast, so sit down and shut the fuck up. Why don't you make yourself fucking useful and reload the magazines?"

The passenger then starts to gets out of his seat to comply with the driver's demand to reload the guns in the back of the van, however he briskly returns to sitting down.

"Are you sure man? We're not gonna shoot anybody, those are just a scare tactic. I mean we never have, that's not our style. Don't worry about it."

That was not the response and reply which the driver was hoping to expect from his partner. Out of frustration and anger, the driver then purposefully swerves the steering wheel of the van left and right causing the van to jerk in a fast motion, whilst looking at the passenger when doing so. He then ferociously and beastly snaps back at the passenger.

"I said reload the fucking magazines, and do it now. I don't want to hear another word out of your damn mouth, or I swear to god, I'm gonna throw you out of this fucking car. We're almost there. I don't want to hear another word from you."

The very shocked and stunned passenger then out of instinct shakes his head, and immediately obeys the driver's instructions, and directs himself to the back of the van. The passenger very quickly assembles the guns and brings both weapons up to the front of the vehicle and sets them in the space between the driver and passenger seat. He as well then goes to get the two empty burlap sacks and sets them on top of them guns. The passenger then returns to his seat and sits down. He puts his head down toward his lap, with his hand covering his forehead. The passenger hesitates to himself as to whether or not to say what's on his mind, despite the fact the driver told him to stay quiet. However, he just couldn't keep in it and had to mention what his feelings actually were. While still in a dazed state looking down at his lap, he utters something to the driver.

"I don't know what has gotten into you man. I've known you for almost eight years and I know I have my moments too man, but I don't know what's gotten over you. This is our last hit and I think the thrill is making you act crazy."

The driver turns his head halfway to look at the passenger, who still has his lead lowered, then proceeds to direct his view back facing forward. The driver does not respond to the passenger. He continues to rush through traffic, and continues to speed through lights. The passenger however no longer can look at the road and keeps his head facing down. The driver then makes a sharp turn through an alley, cutting through many streets. He seems to know of a shortcut to get to their destination, and figures this route will be the fastest and most efficient. The passenger starts to calm himself down. Yet however after noticing their surroundings he seems to be puzzled at something. Due to the fact he had his head lowered down and wasn't paying attention to the streets, he realized that they had passed the bank they were supposed to arrive at. Although he was hesitant to speak after being threatened to stay silent by his partner, he was too concerned and confused to not speak up and alert the driver of the current situation.

"Man I think we passed it. "Washington Credit Union" is on Wilshire, and that's four blocks over. This is the wrong way I think. Man, you're going the wrong way."

The driver at this point is feeling very impatient and fed up with the passenger. He is not comfortable with his remarks and with his bickering. His patience which is already wearing thin, seems to overpower his emotions and actions. The driver, with one hand on the steering wheel, then reaches for one of the assault rifles laying in the center of the floor of the dashboard divided between the both of them, and aims it at the passenger. While still aiming the gun at this head, he gives some remarks to the passenger.

"This is your final warning. If you say one more word I'm pulling the trigger and doing the job myself without you. Shut the fuck up, I know what I'm doing. I'm going to go to a different better bank on Sunset, which I've cased before. This is going to be our last hit, and there is no better place to target than this one."

The driver then puts the gun on his lap with the barrel of it pointed at the passenger. The passenger then instinctively lowers his head once again. Filled with fear and intimidation, the passenger this time promises himself to stay tight lipped and to not speak to his partner again. He feels the proceedings will perhaps will run more smoothly if he just complied and kept to himself during this whole ordeal. Although the passenger has thousands of thoughts running into his head that he wishes to present to the driver, he simply cannot make them known public and he has to keep them to himself. The driver then returns the gun back to the ground, and puts both of his bands back on the wheel. The van continues to make rapid turns, and swerves through the road. The passenger brings his head up with his eyes closed, and leans his head back towards the headrest of the seat. He then looks at the driver again, and deep breathes. He starts to question why his partner is acting so erratically, and unusual towards him. In any other case, the relationship between these two men is generally a more positive one, and they both exhibit good rapport. This would in fact be the third bank heist they would commit today, as earlier in the day they successfully were able to do two. Perhaps the driver is feeling some type of superior confidence boost, and doesn't want the stress to overpower his emotions, and in turn is acting in a more violent way. The passenger however wants to keep a calmer profile to himself, and try and attempt to keep things more mellow and peaceful. The fact they are now switching plans and deciding to heist a bank they weren't originally planning to visit, worries the passenger. He has no idea what tricks the driver has up his sleeve, and it makes him uncomfortable. However, the driver proclaims to have quite extensive knowledge on this bank, and thus decided to change plans and direct themselves to this bank instead, saying the benefit would reap the reward better at this bank.

These men are headed straight for the "Sunset Credit Union." The driver who is finally stopped at an intersection, looks towards his right and points his finger in that same direction. Following that, he proceeds to brief himself with the passenger who is also looking in that same direction out the window.

"That's the Sunset Strip right there. Where that grocery store is, you can't see it, but the bank is almost kinda hidden behind it. But that's our spot right there. That shopping center is a bitch to get inside of, especially in this traffic. I got a solution and a plan though, don't worry. There's an alley creeping up right beside it, and like cats we're just gonna sliver our way up in there. We're gonna draw the least amount of attention to ourselves."

The passenger while still looking out the window, nods his head quietly in agreement. He is still anxious about what's about to occur, and is feeling doubtful on himself. The driver is still in control and showing authority. His submissive attitude towards the passenger is definitely showing and coming into light. The van is still stopped at the light, and the driver decided to take advantage of this instance, and continues to relay more information to the passenger.

"You do exactly as I say. I'm the one that picked this spot out, so whatever I say, is whatever goes. If I tell you to do something, I want you to do it, and I want you to do it without any fussing. Do I make myself clear?"

The passenger then nods, but very quickly then shakes his head in astonishment. The signal turns green and the van speeds up. The driver then grabs one of the guns that were laying on the floor, and sets it on the passenger's lap. The passenger then turns his head to the driver, in which the driver who still has his eyes on the road, continues to give the plan of attack to the passenger, and directions for him to obey.

"We're gonna be in there in like a minute in a half, so you're gonna need this. Again, just do as I say, and we'll be in and out. You don't know this bank, I do. So just do as I say, and everything will be okay. If you don't do as I say, then things will get ugly. Very simple."

The passenger who continues to obey the driver in a polite respectful way, then picks the gun up from his lap and positions the gun in his hands. He looks down towards the ground holding the gun, shaking his head. The passenger is aware his only option is to follow orders and to go with the flow. He doesn't have any other choice to make for himself at this point. The driver then takes one hand off the wheel, and proceeds to grab the other gun which was laying on the floor, putting it on his lap. Both of the men prepare themselves for the heist, and are very close to approaching the bank. They seem to have mapped and planned everything out, and they seem very confident in themselves. The van makes one final turn creeping up towards the "Oakwood Shopping Center.". The van pulls up into the parking lot of the shopping center, and parks in an obstructed corner in front of the "Happy Dry Cleaners" and "Sunset Deli" storefronts. The driver then turns the ignition off, and puts the keys into his pocket. While looking at the bank, the driver notices the bank is still open, and people are still patronizing inside. He then looks at the passenger, briefing him some more on how they are going to operate their heist.

"Okay, we need to hustle right now. This bank is a couple minutes from closing and we need to act fast now. This is the plan, and I want you to follow it, that way we'll both be satisfied and walk out happy. This bank has a vault attached to it, and there is a lot of cash in it. This is most likely going to be our jackpot and worth all of this bullshit and trouble."

The passenger again respects everything the driver asks and confirms to his actions. He doesn't dare wish to go against his plan of attack or protocol, he has to just listen to everything he says without complaint or defiance. The driver then makes sure his mask is snug around his face, and his gloves are properly fit around his hands. The passenger then in an identical custom way also makes sure his mask is concealed over his face, and his gloves are set tight as well. The driver reaches behind his seat towards the cargo area, and grabs the tape and the rope that was included in the miscellany items and weapons. He hands them to the passenger.

"What I want for you to do, and to only do, is make sure nobody runs outside. You shouldn't have to use these, but just in case; this is only to make sure people stay quiet, and stay put. Shoot a few rounds in the floor to scare them too. I can't promise you that nobody is going to get hurt, I just can't, but if you listen to me, everything will be smooth and fine. I don't know why I'm telling you all this shit, you should already know this."

Even though the passenger felt disrespected and hurt by his remarks, he in accordance nods his head, and without any trouble puts the tape and rope the driver gave him into his poncho pocket. He has an intense unsure feeling for some reason. Even though they both seem prepared and ready, the passenger isn't as comfortable and at ease with the plan as the driver is. Knowing he has to put all of those thoughts aside and just get ready for the plan. The driver is very sure of himself, and now understands there is no time like the present. They need to act now. The driver looks down at the floor of the van, and reaches for the burlap sacks, and puts both of them into his pocket. The driver would be the only one who would be taking control the money. The passenger would merely and simply be the backup, and act as an aide for the driver. Having everything in order, the driver then picks up his machine gun and makes sure it is loaded and set accordingly. Before both men exit the vehicle, he turns to the passenger, and gives him final words of advice to follow and to understand.

"Here we go, it's Showtime. I'll do all of the action and grab all the money, so don't worry about any of that. I'm just gonna fill both sacks, and we're home free. We are out of here. I'll get the cash from the carts at the teller, and clear the vault and were done, and we are out. This is it, let's roll."

The bandits then dart out of the van guns drawn, and rush straight towards the bank. The patrons inside the bank have no idea a robbery is about to commence. Even though both men seem focused to get their job done, one of the men is clearly not as sure as optimistic and positive as the other is, and is starting to feel scared and is worried. Mind you, these men have robbed two banks earlier without any issue. This shouldn't be any different to them at all. From the way their van was parked in front of the other shopping outlets, and the way the bank is positioned, the two of them went virtually unnoticed walking to the entrance of the bank. The driver reaches towards the entrance of the bank and opens the door. Immediately upon entering the bank, the passenger of the van reluctantly inside his mind, but in a very menacingly way, makes his presence known, and yells the following while waving his gun.

"Everyone get the fuck on the floor, you know the drill. I want all of you on the floor right now. Get your asses on the floor, and I want all of you with your faces down. I'm a nice guy, but I can turn into a mean guy too!"

Russell who was sitting in front of Peter's desk, immediately falls to the floor with his hands behind his head. Peter also does the same. Yvette, who has been a part of a robbery in the past, although was scared and terrified, knew she had to act accordingly and act in a dignified way, and she as well does what the robber tells her to do. A few other customers in the bank also were on the floor, trembling in fear. Everyone in the building shocked that a bank robbery is currently taking place. Russell at this moment, began to fear for the safety of the people in the bank. Russell did witness a bank robbery from when he previously worked at "First National", but all of that really didn't matter now. He was terrified and felt frozen. This was the first time that he witnessed a robbery working at the "Sunset Credit Union." Even though himself and Peter have gone over robbery routines and procedures many times, unfortunately being that the moment is live and is happening now, Russell out of shock and fear could only lay down on the floor like a dog at this moment. He knows being the assistant operations manager, that situations like this fall under him. As tellers such as Jesse and Jennifer, and financial advisors such as Yvette, do not hold responsibility towards robberies, and aren't instructed to act in reliance towards them.

According to network regulations, Russell was to immediately listen to the robber's commands, and deescalating the situation so it ends in a peaceful manner. Making sure the silent security alarms located in the bank were pushed, which were located in Russell's terminal positioned behind the bank tellers. Peter as well was not doing the proper procedure either. Being the bank manager, he's essentially in an identical manner as Russell, is supposed to mediate the situation and deal with the robbers so that other employees and patrons are not hurt. Making sure the silent alarms located behind the tellers are also pressed and set and that the incident is well established and safely done in a correct way. The men supposedly could have realized that in this particular situation, it was best for them to not cause any immediate action towards themselves, and to just let robbers do their duty. Peter assumed the robbers simply wanted money from the tellers, and they would go on about their business. However, Russell felt extreme guilt that instead of being in his position behind the tellers where the silent alarms were, he was at Peter's desk mingling with him due to the bank reaching closing time.

The passenger who was in the van aimed his gun sporadically to the other patrons in the bank, continuing to exclaim threats to them.

"I want everyone on the floor, and I also want you all to stay still. I don't want to see anybody talking, moving, or doing anything. Keep your heads on the ground, and stay still!"

The driver in the van then walks up to Jesse's terminal, pointing his gun at his head, alerting him to empty the contents of his terminal till, and cash cart into his bag.

"Put all the fucking money into the bag. Go faster, or I'm gonna fucking shoot. I want everything in the bag. Everything in the cart I want in the bag too, now!"

This was the first robbery Jesse was involved in with this bank. He however was trained on dealing with robberies, and as a teller he is to do whatever they ask him to do. Jesse emptied all of his contents of his terminal drawer into the bag. Jesse was aware that he could use a dye pack, which is a stack of fake money which detonates a bomb of hard to wash paint onto the robber and cash bag to thwart the robbers, but he decided not to do so. After emptying his cash drawer, he unlocked his cash cart located behind his drawer, and emptied the money into the bag. Jesse did not to give the robbers any emotions or eye contact. He also did not show any fear as he was trained and instructed not to do so in such occasions. The robber continued to aim the gun towards Jesse's head as he was emptying the substantial amount of cash from the cash cart into the burlap sack, going as fast as he humanly possibly could. The robber was getting very impatient over this.

"You need to move faster, and put the money in the fucking bag. I will kill you if you don't go faster. Hurry up. Get the money in there now!"

Jesse then emptied all of the money from his cash cart. As soon as he was finished with that, the robber with his gun aimed at Jesse the entire time, instructed him to step behind his terminal and into the lobby with the rest of the accosted patrons of the bank.

"I want you to lay the fuck down, don't get up or I will shoot you. Lay down!"

The passenger of the van then took over his position, and aimed the gun at Jesse and the other hostages in the bank. Everyone in the building was under intense mental anguish and panic, as this stressful and unprecedented event takes place. Russell again was just overthrown with guilt that he's not managing the robbery accordingly. Thinking to himself he's being a terrible and irresponsible bank manager, and not stepping up to his duties. He could only think that he's letting Peter down, and not living up to the expectations set onto him. Russell's only defense at this point is to just continue to stay down and to not get involved, under the pretenses that hopefully all of this would be over and be done with relatively soon. He could only lay motionless on the floor for right now.

Peter however was on the brink of losing control. Bank robberies are the one thing Peter was always scared and afraid of in the banking and finance industry, as according to him, they either end well, or they end bad. It always scared Peter to be in situations such as this, and for that reason Peter likewise with Russell was going against company protocol, and decided to distance himself from the action.

The robber who as driving the van, then proceeded to walk himself over to Jennifer's terminal. While pointing his gun at her, in a very forceful and demeaning loud tone, instructed her to empty her cash drawer.

"I want all the money, all of it. Empty everything out of that drawer, and put it in the bag. Empty the whole drawer, and empty it now. I want to see that drawer empty now. Empty everything, and do it quick!"

Jennifer was also trained to deal with bank robberies, however this was the first time she had ever been involved with one. She was extremely terrified with panic and fear due to being in this situation. Like Jesse, she did not give the robbers any eye contact, and simply responded to whatever demands they asked for. Although Jennifer wanted to try to see if she could control the situation, putting an end to it. Out of fear, Jennifer decided to do something that Jesse opted out of doing which was to use a dye pack in other to halt the heist. In an inconspicuous way, Jennifer lifted the bottom of her cash drawer, and attempted to place a dye pack into the burlap sack. However, the robber quickly noticed her charade and fired shots onto a wall inches away from Jennifer, in order to scare her to a deeper extent.

Due to the fact there was a silencer enabled on the gun, the gunshots did not make any impactful or forceful noticeable sounds, or cause any attention. The bullets from the gun, did however startle and make Jennifer feel uncomfortable than she already was. The robber who is very furious from that, aimed the gun at her head again.

"Do not fuck with me, I saw that shit. Put the money into the bag. I'm not going to warn you again, the next time, I will kill you. Put the money into the fucking bag, and do it now!"

Jennifer then began to go into an extreme panic mode, and rapidly emptied her cash drawer. After she finished emptying her cash drawer, she went over to unlock her cash cart. The robber was starting to become more and more impatient.

"Open that up now, very quickly. We should have already been done at this point. Open that drawer up and put everything into the bag, and do it fast!"

Jennifer finally got her cash cart open, and she quickly put the stacks of money into the sack. Trembling with anxiety, Jennifer tried her best to overcome this fear, making sure that she managed to empty the cart as fast as she could. Knowing that the robber was losing his patience and cool with her, she tried her best not to damage his emotions with her. After Jennifer finally emptied her cash cart, the robber unlike with Jesse did not instruct her to go into the lobby. He instead grabbed her very forcefully by the back, aiming the gun towards her head.

"Because you pulled that stunt earlier, I'm not done with you. You clearly want to play hero and savior to everyone. You listen to everything I tell you to do, or else the results might be unfortunate. I will not hesitate to shoot you. Don't scream, don't say shit!"

Even though his head was down to the ground, Russell knew that one of the tellers were being held hostage by the robber. Russell was very close to reaching his boiling point towards this situation. He began to really feel upset and scared; even more scared and nervous than he already was, now that the robber was taking one of the teller's hostage. He was in a predicament to where he was unsure of what to do, and what was the safest and sensible action for him to make. With that, he decided to continue to stay down the ground despite that. Peter as well noticed a teller was being held hostage. Like Russell, he didn't want to act on any impulses quite yet, and continued to stay silent on the floor. Peter was under stress seeing one of the bank tellers in that condition, and worried for their safety. He just wanted everything to be over with, and for the event to end in a positive way. Peter just wanted the robbery to end as soon as possible.

The robber who still had Jennifer hostage, escorted her over to the entrance of the vault, and the safe deposit lockers. He wanted to complete the second portion of his job, which was to get whatever he wanted out of the vault and the safe deposit lockers. The robber was aghast to find out the vault was security locked. In order to go inside, he needs an employee of the bank to give him access to it. The robber was unaware that by Jennifer being a bank teller, she would be able to assist him with this at all. She had no access to any of this, and that only Russell and Peter being bank managers could open the vault and safe deposit lockers. They were the only ones who had security access to the vault. The robber still had no knowledge of this, and aimed the gun towards Jennifer's head, instructing for her to give him access to that section of the bank.

"I want you to open all of this up. Once you do all of that, I'm gonna take what I want, and we're gone. You'll never see us again. So just open all of that up now!"

Jennifer stood in shock, as she is not able to comply to what the robber wants. She cannot open anything in this part of the bank. She began to panic and was scared as to what she could do. She thought the only right thing to do, is to honestly tell the robber that she cannot allow him to go in to that room of the bank. Jennifer very nervously responds to the robber.

"I can't let you in there, I don't have access to the vault and the safe deposit boxes. I'm sorry I don't. I can't get you inside of there."

The robber who was the passenger in the van, began to feel very remorseful of himself, and didn't expect for the robbery to drag on this long, and for it to go onto this harsh of a level and degree. He wasn't as rough as the other robber was, and he felt a lot of hurt from taking a part in all of this. The previous two robberies they committed earlier in the day, weren't this savage or this drawn out. He began to wonder what a mistake they possibly made, by deciding to choose this bank to rob. All the sorrow building up inside of him was starting to become too much, and he just had a feeling of something not being quite right.

The other robber snapped once again, and began to produce great anger from the current situation. He was planning on already being done with the heist at this point, and knowing the possibly that someone in the shopping center perhaps called the police already by this point. They have been in the bank at the present moment for about three minutes. Which was longer than what they originally anticipated and structured for. The robber is at his wits end, and wants to get out of the bank as fast as he can. He starts to act more on impulse and on anger. Still pointing the gun at Jennifer, he gives her more threatening demands.

"Well I'm not leaving until I get inside that vault. So somebody in this bank has to have the key to let me in. There has to be someone in here that can do it. Come on!"

The remaining inhabitants in the bank stay silent, and do not respond to the remarks of the robber at all. Basically ignoring his remarks and claim most definitely out of fear and shock, to not cause any escalation to an already damaging and frightening stance. The robber likewise is not at all content with this behavior or response that he was given, and in desperate need to get what he wants. He fires several rounds onto the floor, giving an ultimatum.

"If I don't get inside this vault in ten seconds, everyone in this bank is going to die. Every single one of you. Let me in this fucking vault, right now!"

Directly after hearing of all that, Russell without much thought about it all, began to get the vault keys from his pocket, and positions himself up off the floor. Before he could raise his whole body up, Peter immediately starts to spring up from the floor before Russell was able to. While Peter is kneeling on the floor with his hands raised, he notices the robber holding Jennifer hostage.

"I'm the bank manager, and I have the vault keys right here. Don't harm the woman. It's okay, just let her go, and I'll let you inside of the vault, just let her go please."

The robber refused to take his hands off Jennifer, in fear that she would press a silent alarm, or do something else that would foil the robbers wishes. Peter while standing up whispered something to Russell.

"Russ, stay down and be quiet."

Everyone else in the bank, aside from Peter and Jennifer, remained on the floor with their heads down. With the fact that Peter was currently taking care of the situation, Russell felt temporarily more safe with himself, and wasn't as tense as he was earlier in the robbery. The other robber who was in the lobby watching over the rest of the patrons in the bank, still in a more scared and compliant mood over the more overbearing and threatening robber. The other robber who still had the gun pointed to Jennifer's head, and still restraining her, was refusing to let her go.

"That's not gonna happen. She's not leaving my sight, I don't trust her at all, so no I'm not letting her go. I'll let her go once I get what I want from the vault, and that will be it."

Peter at this point had no other choice but to reluctantly decide to open the vault. He did have a plan which he wasn't completely sure would work and would be the safest, but one which he thought would definitely calm the situation down. Peter's plan would work as follows; as soon as the robber entered the vault and demanded money to be into the sack, Peter would engage the emergency lock of the vault, in which the door would very quickly close behind the robber. Peter would run outside of the vault and press this button in a hidden location on the outside of the vault door that would within a split second lock the robber inside of the vault. It would also cause the building to trigger an emergency silent alarm in which the authorities will quickly arrive at the bank. Peter knew that this was possibly the only plan that could possibly work, due to the unpredictable behavior that the robber was exhibiting towards everyone, he needed to rectify and deal with this problem. Peter grabbed the vault keys from his pocket, and walked towards the vault, with the robber still pointing the gun at Jennifer.

"Yes, I'm going to open the vault right now, calm down. It's fine. I'm opening it."

Peter then unlocked and opened the vault door. With the vault door now open, the robber walks inside the vault with Jennifer still as his hostage. He set down his full sack of cash inside the vault, and went inside his pocket to grab the other empty burlap sack. While continuing to hold the gun towards Jennifer's head, he ordered for Peter to open the vault boxes which contained the most amount of money, and to quickly put the contents into the sack. Peter began to unlock the safe deposit lockers however; he was struggling to get them open. The robber being impatient demands Peter to get the lockers open.

"Put in the money in the bag, right now. Then I'm gone, and nobody gets hurt. I need you to put the money in the bag from the boxes right now!"

Peter was struggling to open the lockers, and the robber was mistaking this as Peter disobeying him. The robber in an out of control psychopathic rage, does the unfortunate. While Peter's back is turned opening the locks, the robber aims his gun towards Jennifer's chest.

"Maybe I need to send a clearer message to you, because you aren't understanding me."

The robber then shoots Jennifer, several times. She falls onto the floor, due to the impact of the shot. Her body lays motionless and unconscious. Due to the fact the rest of the patrons are held hostage on the floor, and unable to see what sadly just occurred, and also due to the fact the robber's gun had a silencer, they unfortunately do not understand the severity as to what just happened. Peter turned his head behind and stood in frozen shock seeing Jennifer.

Upon seeing Jennifer shot, the robber who was sitting in the passenger seat, decides to run outside of the bank and rapidly leave the scene throwing his gun away in a trash can located in the lobby of the bank. The other robber who was inside the vault, didn't see his partner run out of the building. The robber then threatens Peter.

"I'm not playing. Open the fucking boxes, Do it now. Just open it and I'm gone!"

Peter now in immense panic and shock, is finally able to get the boxes open. He quickly empties the contents of the vault inside the burlap sack. After emptying the money into the sack, the robber ordered for Peter to carry his other money sack outside of the vault to the lobby of the bank, while still holding the gun at his head. Instantaneously, Peter decides that now is the right time act out on his plan that he originally had in mind, to lock the robber inside the vault until the police arrived in the bank. Peter knew this would be his only chance he would have to trap the robber inside the vault.

Peter dropped the sack and started to go outside of the vault, right after pressing the emergency lock button. Unfortunately, the robber saw him press the button and was able to get outside right in the nick of time, yet the robber left behind his gun and money sack while trying to leave the room. The robber is extremely agitated. Out of sheer anger and frustration that the robber locked his money and his gun inside of the vault, the robber acting despicable rapidly reaches inside his sock and pulls out a long handgun. He shoots Peter in the back of the head as he's running out of the vault entrance. Everyone else in the bank did not hear this gunshot, as the handgun the robber used also had a silencer and the shot went unheard. They have no idea that Peter was just shot, so they remain outside in the lobby on the floor. As his unconscious body lays on the floor, the robber then reaches into Peter's pocket to get the vault key to retrieve his gun and his money bags. He successfully opens the vault door, grabs the items and starts to run outside of the vault. However not even within a couple seconds later, the police finally arrive. Several police officers storm into the bank guns drawn on the robber.

"Down on the floor now! LAPD! Get down on the floor now!"

The robber realizes he's in tough spot, and doesn't know what to do. In a last ditch effort, he decides to sprint out of the bank entrance, darting through the police.

"Fuck, you'll have to kill me before I leave this fucking bank. Fuck you all!"

The robber is fatally shot in the chest, by the police instantaneously. He drops to the ground, with his money bags he had in his hand also dropping to the floor. The police then confirm the robber is dead, and search the bank for suspects, before clearing the bank.

It was finally over. This hell hole was now finished. The police instruct for all hostages and the rest of the patrons in the bank that it is now safe for them to get up. Russell who was laying down the entire time finally gets up. He can't believe this madness is now over. That entire time full of unpleasantness has come to an end. He notices Jesse and Yvette, but he doesn't see Jennifer or Peter. Russell then proceeds to walk away from Peter's desk area towards the vault area. A police officer restrains Russell from entering the area, and asks Russell who he is. Russell then responds to the officer.

"I'm one of the Bank Managers. I'm authorized to be in this area."

The police officers ignore Russell and allow him to proceed. Russell notices Jennifer's body, and he starts to buckle under shock and pressure. He begins to immediately sob over the sight of this, and is overwhelmed with depression and sorrow. He kneels down and starts to caress her.

Russell moments after that gets up sees Peter's body as well. Upon noticing Peter's body, Russell has a panic attack, and begins to have a temper tantrum. He starts to scream and express his depressive emotions.

"NO, NO, FUCK, WHAT THE FUCK, NO. THIS CAN'T BE RIGHT. FUCK!"

The police and other patrons in the bank notice Russell's fit, and the officers at the scene try to console and calm Russell down. The pain he is currently going through is just too much to handle and he is not in any control of how he feels. Russell then begins to throw papers and chairs located in the bank. He is restrained by a couple police officers. His outrage and impulse depressed actions show a clear sign that Russell feels totally at fault to this instance. Feeling that Jennifer and Peter's death could have been avoided. He doesn't understand why Jennifer had to be shot, and why Peter was the one who volunteered himself to go into the vault. Russell felt himself to blame, and that even though Peter told him to stay down, he over estimated how brave Peter was. He had so many rushed emotions that he couldn't control.

The police inform the other patrons in the bank that the bank is currently on lockdown for a pending investigation, and that two of the bank employees have been killed. Jesse and Yvette immediately go into shock and horror, and understand the severity of the event. Russell then walks over by Peter's desk. He takes his suit jacket off, hanging it on the back of a chair in front of Peter's desk. Russell sits down in that same chair, with his head lowered and his hands covering his face, crying heavily.

CHAPTER 3:

NOTHING LOST, NOTHING FOUND

The investigation of the robbery starts, with everyone who witnessed this terrible event still in shock. This bank is now considered a crime scene, with a robbery ending with three deaths. Even though the robbery is over, it is almost as if it's still active. How could such a heinous act happen in just a few moments? So many unanswered questions and thoughts running though everyone's mind in the building. Russell who above everyone else is the most shook over the ordeal. He is still feeling extremely guilty over what happened. Blaming himself for a myriad of reasons, saying to himself what he could have done to prevent what happened from occurring. Telling himself that if he didn't listen to Peter and got up anyways, would Peter and Jennifer would have survived? Having to accept the fact that the disgusting scenario that happened a while ago, actually happened and now having to deal with the feelings that follow. Trying to come to terms that two of his fellow employees of the bank, were killed as a result.

Officers quickly cover Peter and Jennifer's body and barricade the vault foyer from allowing anyone into that area. The robber's deceased body who was also near the vault foyer area, is also covered up. Russell who watches them do so, is unable to keep his emotions controlled at this time, and it is taking a major toll on his mental health. The two surviving employees Jesse and Yvette, are also overwhelmed with multiple mixed emotions. A police officer dismisses the customers that were in the bank after getting witness statements. However, for investigation purposes at this time, all employees must stay in the bank. He relays a few statements to the employees.

"Everyone, we are going to try to make this investigation move as quickly as possible, we are here to help you and we want all of you to hang on for just a bit with us. After our investigation, all of you can be released."

This same police officer walks over to Russell who is now sitting in front of Peter's desk with his hands over his face and his head lowered, to confer a few things with him.

"So you mentioned that you were the manager of the bank correct? Okay, one of our chief detectives is going to be arriving very momentarily as a part of our investigation. He is specifically going to ask you questions and ask to see surveillance videos and such. After he gets his information, all of you can go home then. The branch operations manager should also be arriving as well I believe due to federal regulations and rules."

Russell who had his hands covering his face the entire time the officer was speaking to him, looks at the officer and responds to him in an angry condescending manner.

"Well, I'm actually the assistant manager. Being that the manager of the bank was just killed half an hour ago, I guess you can say I'm now the acting manager of the bank. The Branch Operations Manager is John Marshall, and whenever there is a robbery or incident at the bank, he must gather information and send it to the financial corporate office for records."

Russell after speaking with the officer, lowers his head into his hands again still feeling defeated and upset from the situation, and feeling confused as to what to do. He then starts to look at the pictures on the desk of Peter with his wife and daughter, which in turn makes him more upset than he already was. He glances around the bank and sees Jesse speaking to a police officer, and Yvette crying while she is on the phone on her desk. Yvette then hangs up the phone, while right soon after an officer comes over to speak with her. Russell then eavesdrops on what she says.

"I was talking to my sister, and to the school my kids go to. She's going to pick them up. I don't know how long we are going to be locked in here I can't believe any of this, I can't."

Yvette then responds to the officer by explaining her witness accounts of what happened.

"We were all told to just lay face down on the floor, and all I remember is that he asked for someone to open the vault. Only Peter and Russell can open the vault, and I don't know why Russell allowed for Peter to get up, I don't. I don't want to blame Russell, but I don't know."

Russell then starts to get agitated over what Yvette said, and tries his best to restrain himself from talking it over with her. He does ultimately decide to get up from Peter's desk, and walk over to Yvette's desk to go over and assess this issue with her. Shockingly, Yvette is not at all in the mood to speak to Russell and refuses to give him eye contact. By the way she is behaving and the way she's exhibiting her body language, she wants nothing to do with him. Yvette feels extremely angered towards him, and would rather not deal with Russell right now.

"Don't talk to me, get away from me Russell. I'm sorry, I do not want to talk to you right now, or perhaps ever. You should have had Peter's back. The amount of things that man has done for you, you should have taken that bullet for him, and you didn't."

Russell then looks down to the floor and reflects over what Yvette has said. In his mind, he does feel she is correct, and that as the assistant manager of the bank he should have done more to to prevent the actions that happened. He also feels that at the time, he made the choices that he felt were necessary. Peter himself told Russell not to get up, so he didn't. Russell felt if that he knew the robber had intentions to murder two people, he most definitely would have acted in a more active way. Hindsight doesn't mean anything once the situation is over, so Russell doesn't blame himself in that regard. He does blame himself that he should have ignored what Peter said and gone over to the vault area regardless.

Yvette continues to lament herself over the situation, giving her accounts and opinion towards the robbery, and says exactly what is on her mind.

"I don't know if I can work in this bank anymore. All of the memories, they were shot and I wasn't. I wasn't that close with Jennifer, but she was a young pretty girl that had so much for herself. Peter, oh my god, was the nicest guy you would ever know. The man I believe was Christ reborn, he was a saint. Very nice man he was."

Russell who continues to eavesdrop on Yvette, goes back to Peter's desk to get his suit jacket, putting it on. He then reaches in the front pocket of the jacket, taking out his handkerchief. He wipes his forehead with it, folds it up and puts it in his pants pocket. Russell then gets up and goes over to the water cooler to get himself a drink of water. While he's drinking his water, he sees Jesse standing near the lobby area talking to the officers. Unlike Yvette, Jesse seems to be taking a different approach to the situation, and because of the shock he is feeling wants to display everything in a more cordial and relaxed manner. Russell listens closely to Jesse conversing with the officers.

"This has to be a dream. I refuse to believe this is real life. This is like the Twilight Zone. I cannot believe what happened at all. I'm just surprised that I'm still here and alive. Peter and Jennifer didn't deserve any of that."

Jesse then begins to take deep breaths and scoff, while shaking his head. He also has a very confused and depressed look on his face. He makes eye contact with Russell, and stares at him for a handful of seconds. Russell returns this by giving him a disgusted look, which causes Jesse to look away from him. Jesse then takes a seat in the lobby area staring at the ground. Russell then walks over to Jesse is seated and stands over him, leaning his face near Jesse's and speaks to him, in a very hushed and intimate tone.

"If you don't want to talk about it, it's fine. I won't pester you at all. Let me know, and I'll walk away and you don't have to worry about it. It's cool, don't worry about it at all."

Russell after noticing after a few moments that Jesse isn't going to reply to him, pats Jesse on the back of his shoulder and walks away from him. Jesse then glances at Russell while he's walking away to the other side of the building. Jesse decides to ask the officers a question.

"May Yvette and I get our belongings from the employee break room?"

The officer allows the both of them to get their items. While Jesse and Yvette go and attend towards that, Russell receives a text alert on his phone, reminding him that he is late for the reservations he made from himself and Peter. This causes Russell to start to cry, and he begins to again have depressed waves of emotions. Russell while still crying, walks to a supply closet located near the entrance of the bank, and takes out two medium sized cardboard boxes. Russell beings to pull all of Peter's personal belongings that were on his desk, inside the boxes. These include pictures of his family, his name plate, his certifications and awards, and the drawing that his daughter drew for him. Russell then set the boxes on a counter in the lobby. He then notices that Jesse and Yvette have left the break room, and goes inside after that. He opens up Peter and Jennifer's lockers, to grab more of their things. He takes Jennifer's purse out of the locker as well. Returning to the lobby, he puts all of the items together. Russell then taps an officer on the shoulder, speaking to him.

"These belonged to Peter, and this purse belonged to Jennifer. Their family members can have all of these, I just wanted to make sure they were all properly accounted for."

Russell then once again walks over to Yvette who's sitting at her desk crying still, in a second attempt to open up towards her. Russell calmly speaks to Yvette.

"I know your upset, okay. I need you to listen to me for a minute though, I..."

Yvette stops Russell by snapping back at him rather quickly. She still feels unsafe around his attitude, and holds some type of resentment that the consequences over Peter and Jennifer's death, the fault in some shapes and form revolve around Russell.

"Don't fucking talk to me Russell. I wish you the best of luck in your future life endeavors, but I never ever want to see you or your face again. It's a miracle myself, you and Jesse weren't killed, and I feel you should owe it to yourself over that. Russell, you're a lovely man, you are, but don't talk to me, don't look at me, I need you to leave me alone."

Immediately, Yvette then goes to the same supply closet Russell went to moments earlier, and gets an identical looking cardboard box similar the ones Russell used earlier. She while talking to herself, begins to clear things off her desk and put them in the box.

"I'm not working for this damn bank anymore, I'm not. Too many bad memories, and it's like a horror movie. I refuse, I can't work at this bank anymore. After today, I'm never, ever coming back to this bank. I never thought by working in a bank I'd ever see something as scary happen that happened today. I have proven myself wrong, and I'm done. I've had it up to here."

Russell shakes head and walks away from Yvette's desk. He notices Jesse is still seated in the lobby. He goes over to sit in another adjacent chair by him. Jesse and Russell accidentally for a few split seconds make eye contact. This in turn causes Jesse to smile at him in an irritating way. Russell then in an agitated manner laughs at loud to himself over that. He then takes more gulps of his water emptying the cup. He gets up, while asking Jesse a question.

"Hey, would you like a drink of water?"

Jesse then nods in acceptance to his question. Russell then walks over to Yvette's desk.

"Can I get you some water at least? Will that calm you down?"

Yvette then finally gives Russell eye contact, and responds to him.

"Russell, yes you can give me some water, that will be the last thing I'll ever ask from you in this world, then I won't bother you for a single thing ever."

Russell shakes his head and walks over to the water cooler. He gives Yvette and Jesse a cup of water, and refills his own water cup. He returns to the chair he was sitting at in the lobby near Jesse. Russell while sitting down, looks outside of the bank entrance and notices a sea of police cars and crime scene tape. He has never seen the "Oakwood Shopping Center", this bombarded with policy activity. Russell gets up to throw his cup away in the trash can. While looking in the trash, he notices a massive rifle. He immediately alerts the officers inside the bank, that there is a gun inside of the trash can, and he of course recalls it for belonging to one of the robbers. The officers quickly confiscate the gun and put it apart of their evidence. Russell then in that moment started to realize that he himself owns a handgun, and that if he brought his gun to work today, most of what happened possibly could have been prevented. Russell never carried his gun while he was working, but it was a mere thought that he had. An officer comes over to ask Russell something.

"So you're the guy in charge of the bank right? The detective will be here probably in a couple minutes, but in the meantime, I'm going to ask you to do me a favor if you don't mind, just for the investigation procedure. I need to know if you can identify the deceased suspect for me. All I need for you to do, is tell me if you recognize him, that's all."

Russell agrees to comply with the officer. He goes over to the area where the robber was shot, and the officer pulls back the cover of the corpse. The officer also removes his mask. Russell sees the robber was a Caucasian man with a shaved head, and he looked to be in his late twenties or early thirties. Russell did not know who this man was.

"No, I don't recognize him at all. I've never seen this man in my life. I don't know him."

The county coroner's soon come into the bank right after the officers asked Russell if he could identify the corpse of the suspect. Jennifer, Peter and the robber's bodies are each taken away out of the crime scene. Russell watches as they are all strolled outside of the bank in an eerie sense of sorrow and depression. He immediately begins to feel upset and comfortable, being triggered by that. Russell goes over by the water cooler, and gives himself another cup of water to calm himself down. He takes out his handkerchief and wipes his face once more. While he is wiping his face, Russell noticed that he hasn't yet checked the security feed of the ordeal. He thought to himself, he wasn't even sure if it worked or if it was in proper order. As such, he proceeds to go back near the front of the bank, into a room next to the break room. This room contains the surveillance feed of the bank on three small monitors. Russell has always hated the fact the bank used inferior technology when it came to their security systems. The bank did not have a security guard, and it had obsolete security cameras and feed hardware and software. Russell then using the surveillance DVR machine, takes it back to the time when the robbery started, which was approximately forty-five minutes ago. The picture quality sadly is very poor, and the cameras also do not pick up certain angles, especially near the vault area. However clear shots of the robbers entering the bank were taken. Russell then shakes his head in disappointment and astonishment over the lackluster security camera system. Because the door to the surveillance room was open, an officer leers into the room and asks to see the video feed. Russell allows him to, and also converses with him.

"It sucks we have a shitty security setup. This crap is possibly from the nineties, it's so bad. But you can see when they came in, there are two robbers and the other one ran away."

The officer and Russell flashback the entire robbery, as it was shown through the security cameras located in the bank. The picture quality is in black and white, and at times due to the aging of the hardware, ghost grained images also appear making it difficult to assess and see what exactly is happening in the camera at times. All by witnessing on camera, albeit in very poor quality Jennifer and Peter being shot by one of the robbers. Russell notices that one robber virtually stayed in the lobby the entire time, while the other was behind near the vault. Russell continues to chat with the officer while looking at the security tape.

"You see this guy, we all assumed he was the more dangerous one, which is why we didn't get up and stayed on the ground. We didn't know this guy wasn't as dangerous as the other was one. This was the one that most likely ran out."

They also see on the surveillance cameras when the other robber ran outside of the bank before the police arrived. The robber that shot both Peter and Jennifer, was the one that the police were able to accost. After viewing the whole situation, Russell rewinds it back to the beginning, reaffirming this with the officer.

"I'm gonna set it back and when the detective comes, he can just look at it again. I can only output it towards VHS though, as again this is a very crappy security console. This is the best that I can do, and I really wish that we had a more updated system with the latest and greatest, but we don't. I am happy that there are still some good shots that were captured."

The officer seems to understand, and isn't at all bothered by the weak surveillance cameras. He along with Russell walk of the security camera room. Russell walks back into the lobby who notices a very obese man with spiked hair wearing a suit. The man quickly scans his head around the bank, then makes eye contact with Russell.

"Is this guy the manager, if he is then I need to speak with him. I have a lot to discuss and talk with him, and there are some things I have to go over with him."

Russell extends his hand out for the detective to shake, however the detective simply looks at him in a rude manner, and does not acknowledge or reciprocate the handshake. Russell puts his hand back, and then introduces himself to the man.

"Yes, I am the bank manager. I'm Russell McCoy sir. If there is anything that you want for me to do, or need for me to do for you let me know. This is a very upsetting time, and me and my employees are very shaken over it, and it is extremely terrible sir."

The detective gives Russell a dismissive look and walks past him. The detective for a minute looks around the bank, with Russell following behind him. The detective seems to be puzzled and confused, and has a lot of concerns which are plaguing his mind. The detective is going around many corners over the bank, and having peculiar looks on his face while he is doing it. He is not at all satisfied to the current state of the investigation and senses something is wrong. The detective then starts to angrily shout out his feelings out loud to everyone.

"First of all, I can already tell by looking this bank shouldn't even be operating. With all due respect, I'm not surprised a robbery happened today."

Russell immediately scrunches his face at the detective and harbors a lot of negative thoughts towards the detective's comments. Russell knows that the "Sunset Credit Union", wasn't the best when it came to security and aesthetic, but it was still a bank that Russell was proud to be the manager of. Listening to the detective say that, almost gave Russell a frenzy of frustration and anger of having to deal with that. Russell continues to walk behind the detective as he is surveying the bank, from the results of the robbery. The detective continues ranting.

"Where is that branch manager at, because I have a bone to pick with him. These security cameras just by looking at them aren't regulated, in addition to that, they aren't positioned right at all. There should be a camera in front of every teller, there is not."

Russell folds his arms together while listening to the detective's qualms and gripes. He keeps his feelings to himself and doesn't wish to respond or give into what he says. The detective continually finds more things to nitpick about the bank. He feels there are so many incorrect policy and regulation penalties that the bank is committing. The detective continues venting.

"Banks apart of the Los Angeles Federal Credit Union branches do not have to have safety glass over the tellers, but if there were safety partitions, it could prevent a lot of things from happening. Being that this bank is located in a metropolitan downtown area, there should be safety glass in front of the tellers. I can understand why there isn't any, but just a thought."

Although Russell was taking much of the gripes the detective was giving as being dismissive at this point, he did agree that because the tellers weren't protected by glass, he at times did feel apprehensive on that. But according to Peter's wishes, he felt customers felt more safe and homely at banks which didn't have protective glass covering the tellers. In Peter's mind, he felt that it would make the bank feel like a jail, and seem unattractive to patrons. The detective continued to add his opinions and commentary towards things in the bank he felt weren't correct, while Russell was steadily listening in chagrin.

"The way this vault area is set up is also a big violation. It shouldn't be constructed this way. There should be more security barriers around this vault foyer. This is beyond unacceptable and not even almost close to following current safety regulations."

Russell kept quiet and continued to not reply to the detective, as he didn't see the need to offer his own sentiments or responses. Russell was in agreement that there were certain things here and there with the bank that weren't up to par, and needed to be improved and upgraded. For the most part however, Russell was very content with the way the bank ran and was comfortable to attend work. The behavior the detective is exhibiting is attacking Russell very much, but he is allowing him to have his opinions and concerns nevertheless. The detective shows more concern and worry on the state of affairs of the bank, and the ongoing investigation. He goes over to an officer and in a very loud tone, shows tense impatience and exclaims his feelings.

"Why isn't the branch manager here yet? There is no official incident report yet filled, and the branch manager along with the bank manager here needs to notarize that a robbery did take place, so that it goes on record. It's the law, and everything has to be done properly."

The detective then shakes his head at the officer, and glances over at Russell for a few seconds, looking very agitated and displeased by his company. He then walks over by where Russell is standing, and asks a question strictly directed towards him.

"How long have you been working at this bank as a manager for? I need you to tell me that, because I want to know how experienced you are with this."

Russell responds to him in a proper, polite, and formal manner.

"Sir, I'll be honest, I've only been manager of this bank for a few months. I am quite new to this bank yes, but I do have experience. Having said that, my knowledge in banks is quite well. I used to work for "First National" across town before I came here."

The detective is not pleased with Russell, and continues to show much disdain and an assumed disrespectful attitude towards him. The fact Russell admitted he's new to being manager at this bank, didn't sit well with the detective. After Russell mentioned that, the detective with a smug look on his face, walks away from him and inspects the bank more. Russell then decides to once again return to his seat in the lobby by Jesse, and sits down. While he is seated, he notices Yvette continuing to pack her things away. Russell begins to recollect the day, and get his thoughts situated. He feels very punished by the way the detective is treating him, and feels guilt and embarrassment over his position as assistant manager. Russell then looks outside the entrance of the bank again, and sees the barricades outside of the doors of the bank. He is very much enthralled over the storm of activity centered around the bank. While he is still sitting in the lobby leering outside into the area outside of the bank, his thoughts are interrupted when the detective walks over to where Russell is seated to talk to him. Russell stands up to listen to the words the detective wishes to tell him.

"I never introduced myself to you, for that I apologize. I am Detective Mike Henderson. I've been with the LAPD as a detective for many years, and I'm very knowledgeable on armed robbery investigations, and I've basically seen and witnessed it all."

This time, the detective however does reach out his hand for a shake, and Russell returns the favor by shaking his hand. Russell reintroduces himself, and the both of them attempt to turn a new leaf into their relationship and their social actions. The detective explains to Russell that due to the hectic activity and poor investigation protocols, is the cause of the way he's behaving. Detective Henderson is a thirty-five-year-old, police detective who's a very chubby man. Like Russell, he is always wearing a tailored suit to work. The detective has spiked black hair, which he uses hair gel to make his hair styled in that from. Overall he's a good detective with good intentions towards his work. However, generally he is serious and strict with his job. He continues to talk to Russell.

"I'm sorry if I'm prodding and making you uncomfortable, I am very frustrated right now that people aren't doing things according to the law. The branch manager should have been here at this point, and I can't believe how people are acting. Can you please show me the surveillance tapes? I don't believe I had the chance to look at those yet."

Russell agrees to let the detective into the surveillance room, but this time, he also allows Jesse and Yvette to view the whole ordeal on tape as well. He felt that they deserved to see the whole situation and how it evolved, being that they are all victims in the robbery. He directs each of them to the security room. Everyone watches the monitors and reviews the entire robbery, from every camera angle. Jesse and Yvette, being that this was their first time reviewing everything, are in shock and in much disbelief of how everything panned out. The detective is not happy or thrilled on the way the security tapes are managed, and considers it unprofessional in a sense. However, he feels it is acceptable enough to be taken into evidence, as most of the action is able to be seen by the cameras. The detective then offers his own take on how the events ran down, based on the security monitors.

"So it appears there were two robbers, and they had an interesting approach. One of the robbers stayed in the lobby to scare those on that side of the building. The other robber was the one who looted the money, went inside the vault, and killed two employees. The robber located in the lobby of the building ran, and is at large."

Russell is then able to take the feed from the robbery into a VHS tape, and hands it over to Detective Henderson for evidence. Everyone in the room walk out after this. Jesse returns to the lobby, and Yvette returns to her desk. Russell walks behind Detective Henderson, who proceeds towards the entrance of the bank. He looks up and notices a strange peculiar looking van situated near the dry cleaners and deli of the strip mall. He wonders if that was the vehicle the robbers had used to get themselves to the bank. The detective then instructs the officers that are inside the bank, to go outside and check it out.

"I need you guys to investigate that van right now. I believe that's their van; I have a good feeling that it is. There were keys recovered on the suspects corpse right? So go out there and diagnose the van, and see if it belongs to them."

The officers sprint outside into the parking lot towards the van to investigate it. The detective's assumptions were correct, and the van did indeed belong to the robbers. However, the van did not contain any identifying factors. The license plates and VIN plates were removed from the vehicle, and no registration information was inside the van. The only contents that were contained inside, were simply miscellany items. The detective later deduced the van was most likely scrapped and stolen, explaining why it was hard to identify who the vehicle belonged to. Detective Henderson then asked Russell to unlock the vault as a part of their investigation, and to explain the emergency vault system which Peter attempted to use. Russell opened the vault and inside contained the deceased robbers assault rifle, and both sacks of money which the robber had looted. The detective was able to match the gun which Russell found in the trash can, with the gun located in the vault. Both of the weapons matched, and belonged to each of the suspects. Russell also demonstrated how the vault uses an emergency shut in lock, which automatically alerts the police.

The detective then reveals that the police were actually notified from an anonymous 911 call from someone who was witnessing the robbery right as it happened in the parking lot, and that the vault alarm had no impact or any purpose in this particular case. The detective also redirects information on who the robber that was accosted by the police was, hoping to get information as to who his partner that ran was, based off that. He also confirmed that the robbery took place for a little over three minutes. Although according to Russell, it felt extremely longer than that, and he couldn't understand how all of what happened did in just three minutes. The detective at this point continues to wait for the branch manager to arrive to officially close and wrap up the investigation at this time. The detective then makes a statement.

"I want to thank you all for your cooperation, I am truly sorry for the events that sadly took place. I'm waiting for the branch manager to attend, so we can continue with the proceedings. Again, I apologize for my initial attitude, and please disregard that and forgive me."

Russell accepts and acknowledges his apology, and shakes the detective's hand again. Russell then walks away from him, and meanders and roams himself inside of the lobby with his hands in his pants pockets. Observing an array of different things in the lobby, he notices Yvette retouching her makeup at her desk. Jesse is simply sitting in the lobby with his arms crossed. Russell then decides to yet again return to the lobby area and sit down near Jesse. Russell sits back in the chair with his head back, and closes his yes. A couple minutes later, Detective Henderson approaches Russell and Jesse. He gives each of them both a form and a pen.

"I almost forgot, I'm going to need you guys to fill out an incident statement. I gave the woman sitting over there one as well. Be honest and truthful, and explain as much as you know. I understand the robbers acted fast, and it's possibly all a blur now, but try to record it all again."

Russell and Jesse then start to write their events as to what happened. Russell peeks over at Jesse writing his form out of curiosity, yet quickly returns to minding his own business and continues to fill out his incident form. Russell was having difficulty refreshing his memory of the events. He really just wanted to leave all of that behind him, and not think about it again. He was struggling to write the graphic and gruesome details that happened. Russell is able to power through writing his incident form, and explains everything he is able to. The detective then reminds both he and Jesse to sign their names at the bottom of the incident form. The both of them give their forms to Detective Henderson, and he thanks them both and walks away.

Feeling tired and overworked, Russell returns to putting his head back in the seat, and closes his eyes, as if he were taking a nap. However, he is wide awake and simply resting his eyes. Jesse stares at Russell for a bit, but then gets up from the lobby and goes over to Yvette's desk. Jesse then tries to talk to Yvette who is still putting her makeup on.

"Sweetheart, you okay? I wanted to check up on you girl. What's up with you?"

Yvette puts her compact down and gives eye contact at Jesse in a disappointed, defeated and agitated manner. She is giving the same treatment that she gave to Russell, over to Jesse. By her tone and actions, she is making it very clear that she doesn't wish to be bothered at this time, and she is under high stress at the moment. Russell being nosy, watches Jesse and Yvette talk and listens in on their conversation.

Yvette snaps at Jesse, and exhibits some very harsh truths on the matter towards him, yet still being somewhat polite.

"Honey, leave me alone. I don't hate you as much as I hate Russell, because unlike him, I can see you're a free spirited person, and a more open minded person. Russell he's very two faced and stuck up, and he's an asshole. I believe most of this mess is his fault indirectly. But please leave me alone. I don't want to talk right now Jesse. Okay hun?"

Jesse shows concern towards her, and wishes to speak more with her, yet decides to let it lie, and walks away from Yvette's desk. He returns to his seat at the lobby by Russell, who laughs at him once he is seated. Jesse ignores Russell and doesn't respond to his laugh. Jesse then pulls out a men's fashion magazine out of his tote bag, and begins to skim through the pages. Russell peeks over at Jesse reading the magazine for a bit, but returns to resting his eyes.

About ten minutes later, Detective Henderson alerts for Russell. He has a big stack of papers in his hand, waving them in the air.

"Excuse me, can I talk to you once more for a few moments? We have some new interesting developments, that I just wanted to let you in on. It will only take a few moments"

Russell gets up and walks over to the detective in a private area of the bank so the both of them can talk. The detective informs him that he was just faxed some information by the state on some interesting details over the robbers. Detective Henderson explains this to Russell.

"I decided to send pictures of the van that belonged to the suspects in, I also sent the grainy surveillance video of the suspects to the state. It turns out, these guys have actually hit two banks upstate earlier today. Go figure, wow. Can you believe your bank was the third?"

After taking in this news, Russell was amazed that the police were able to gather all of that rather quickly, and put the puzzle pieces together. The detective also had some more papers that he was faxed, which had information on the identity of the deceased robber. He proceeds to show this to Russell.

"I also was able to find out the robber that was shot is named Scott Anderson. He's thirty-three years old, and this guy has robbed at least ten banks that we have on account. He is serious business and a very dangerous man. Unfortunately, we don't know who the other robber that ran away is, and we couldn't find any ties as to connect them both."

Russell thanks the detective for also explaining this information. Detective Henderson gives Russell the stack of papers that had the developing news on the robbery. Russell standing in the middle of the lobby, then calls Jesse and Yvette to come over where he is. He then allows the both of them to look at the papers Detective Henderson gave him minutes ago. Russell relays this to them.

"I was just given all of this, and I wanted to share it with the both of you. These guys robbed two other banks today. That is so crazy, and we were the third. This is also the robber that killed Peter and Jennifer. They don't know who the other robber is, but this is one of the guys."

Jesse and Yvette accept what he tells them, and are amazed at this information just as Russell was. The both of them after analyzing what Russell presented to them, however go back to what they were doing before. Yvette returns to her desk, and Jesse goes back to his seat in the lobby to read his magazine. Russell also directs himself back to his seat. He notices more and more officers leave the bank, and assuming the investigation is leading to a close.

Russell then starts to look at Yvette and is in disbelief at her constant disdain for him. Before the robbery, they were both reasonably close, now she has extreme hatred over him. He as well seems to notice all of her things are taken off her desk, and are packaged and put away. Russell then gets reminded of the fact Yvette told him that she does not wish to return to bank ever again. This causes Russell to think about his own position at the "Sunset Credit Union", and if he himself will assume his position as manager of the bank. After the events which panned out today, Russell truly feels he can never look at the bank the same away again, and will always have this memory etched and engrained very closely. He will never forget the man who hired him to be manager of the bank, was murdered while doing his job. All of these thoughts are hard to ignore, and the traumatic experiences are a lot to deal with and to handle. This is something that didn't really cross his mind until this point. Most likely due to the shock and trauma of the robbery, Russell never once considered what he plans to do now moving forward. Is he going to stay at the bank, and continue working? Russell then looks over again at Jesse reading a magazine. He then also realizes that his relationship with Jesse is nonexistent, and doesn't know that much about him except very little minor details, despite the fact they have been working at the bank as coworkers. Russell also wonders how Jesse is handling the situation, but finds it odd that unlike Yvette who is showing malice towards Russell, Jesse is simply ignoring him. Russell continues to leer at Jesse for a bit, but then looks away from him. He sits back into his seat looking up at the ceiling. After a few moments, he looks outside of the bank and noticing it is getting dark outside, and dusk is approaching. He turns his head away from the entrance, and scans around the building again. Russell then gets up and roams around the bank looking down at the floor, with his hands in his pants pockets.

A minute later the branch manager, John Marshall finally arrives to the bank. Russell and John have a convoluted relationship, and for the most part Russell is not very fond of him. He has only met him a few times, as despite him being an official employee of the "Sunset Credit Union", he is not present inside the bank that much; he visits very intermittently. Russell simply doesn't care that much for him. His position as the branch manager is to simply take note of records of logistics of the bank. John after all is a very strict man, with an even more rigid and difficult personality. He is a very tall and skinny lanky man with a bushy mustache. His profile is not to be messed with, and he has a stern agenda. Russell notices him walking into the bank entrance, and moves over to his direction to greet him. However, the branch manager ignores Russell and goes straight towards the detective. Russell is not surprised at his behavior, and watches the both of them converse to each other.

"Detective Henderson, I'm the branch manager for this bank unit. I'm John Marshall. I want to apologize for my late arrival. I was attending a very important council meeting as a part of the "Los

Angeles Federal Credit Union" for security measures ironically and incidentally, and I had no idea that the "Sunset Credit Union" was robbed until about twenty minutes ago. "

John shakes hands with the detective, and Detective Henderson updates on the proceedings of the robbery. John after being informed on all the details of the robbery, gives his opinion towards the ordeal, and is outraged and angered in the process.

"This is preposterous. Peter was killed in the robbery? Oh my, this is just unbelievable. That man was something else, he was pleasant to be around. This is terrible, as he was a very good friend to me, and he was a big support system as manager of the bank."

Russell knew that John was fibbing. As of a matter of fact, he actually hated Peter, and Peter hated him. They fought like cats and dogs usually over petty things, and he would constantly try to get Peter to retire or transfer to another bank, so that he could take his position away from him. This was all a façade that John was trying to promote to Detective Henderson, to make him out to be a model person. Russell decides to try again to greet himself to John. He walks over to him and extends his hand out for him to shake it. John and Russell are able to shake hands, and acknowledge each other.

"Ah yes, hello Russell. I'm so sorry on the death of Peter, I really have no words. This is such an unfathomable experience for everyone involved. So unfortunate. Well I'm just going to go over some routine things, and take care of a few matters and then we will be done."

Russell had a feeling that John was being totally insincere with the way he was acting. He did decide to push that to the side and move on from that, due to this very devastating situation at hand. Even though his relationship with John isn't a pleasant one, he must allow for John to do his job. John also greets himself to Jesse and Yvette. Russell, John and Detective Henderson for one final time go inside of the surveillance room. Russell allows John to view the surveillance video of the robbery, to which he responds in a shocking manner, looking at Russell the entire time with a disappointed expression.

"This is very bad; I don't understand; this is very tough to watch. But I feel that Russell should have stepped in over Peter. I don't understand why Peter opened the vault and Russell didn't. That really shows his character as a bank manager and how he's unfit for the position and should have never gotten it in the first place."

All three men return to the lobby of the bank, but Russell unable to control his emotions, responds to John over his comments.

"That's it John, I can't take any more of your shit. You weren't fucking here when the robbery took place, you weren't. You have no fucking idea what went down. Two guys came in here with guns and told us to get to the ground. Peter told me to stay down, and he went to the vault. I had no idea Jennifer and Peter were shot until after the cops came."

John gives an angry look of disagreement to Russell. He then goes into his briefcase and pulls out a sheet of per and starts to write on it. Then responds to Russell.

"Russell, on Monday I want you to head to the Federal Union building here downtown. I want you go to this room, and speak with myself and a Union head Superior. We'll talk about this issue more. I'm not saying you're a bad manager, you're not. You're a very intelligent man Russell, but we need to dissect his issue further."

John gives the paper to him, but Russell rips and shreds the paper throwing it on the ground. Russell then in a fit of rage fires back at John.

"I'm not going. How dare you come in here with that bullshit. This shows how much of a psychopath you fucking are. You always were one. You're never ever fucking here, we had a robbery today, it takes you almost two hours after it happened to get here."

John then grins at Russell, and sets his briefcase down on a counter and replies to him.

"You have some fucking nerve. If anybody is a psychopath, it's you Russell McCoy. You are the creepiest, and scariest man I've ever fucking met in my life. What Peter ever saw in you I don't know. Peter himself was a crazy quack anyways. I always told him this fucking bank was unsafe and because he never listened to me, I guess he now learned his lesson."

Russell then starts to chuckle, and smile at John. He then looks away towards the ground giggling to himself some more and shaking his head. John responds again to him grinning.

"There you go again, always doing that creepy head shake. I don't know why you ever got that manager's job. You are clearly not fit for the position, and I'm definitely letting the Federal Board know about this on Monday rest assured."

Russell stays silent for a few seconds, but then raises his head giving eye contact to John. Russell lifts his eyebrows and nods to John. Jesse stops reading his magazine and watches both men quarrel. Yvette who was also watching the fight, cannot take it anymore. She grabs her box of things and asks Detective Henderson a question.

"Can we all leave now? I gave my statement, the branch manager is aware of the incident and took note of it, are we free to leave now?"

Detective Henderson says that the investigation at this point is temporarily suspended and that all the employees are free to leave the building. Over the next few minutes, all of the officers that were inside of the bank leave except for Detective Henderson, and the crime scene tape is removed from the outside entrance of the bank. Yvette makes another statement, before she decides to leave the building.

"Well Russell, John, Jesse, today was my last day working in this bank. I'm not returning, I can't. I'm way too stressed out and dealing with all the damn mess from that to come back. I'm done, and I'm taking my services elsewhere. Goodbye."

Yvette then grabs her things, and proceeds to walk out of the bank towards the parking lot. Russell, Jesse, John and Detective Henderson watch her leave, but all three men quickly divert their attention back to where it was before. Jesse continues to sit in the lobby. John continues to strike Russell in a humorous tone.

"See what you fucking did Mr. Bank Manager, you lost not one, but three employees today. How does that feel? I'm not surprised, because that's the work of Satan and The Devil. You look like the fucking devil by the way."

Russell once again does not respond to John, he just raises his eyes at him, and smiles and nods. Detective Henderson is not amused by this behavior and tells them both to stop.

"Alright gentlemen, that's quite enough of that. Knock it off. I don't want to see any of this continue. I want you both to stop all of that."

John continues to undermine Russell's character in an indirect fashion.

"I'll lock the bank up tonight, and I'm most likely going to take the place as bank manager on Monday, as Mr. McCoy clearly based on his actions today needs to be reassigned. This man has no business managing a bank. So pitiful. What an ugly man."

Russell refuses to hold back and finally unleashes his fury. He launches at John at tackles him to the ground due to his football skills, pushing his chest and neck towards the floor. Jesse stands up from his seat and watches in shock and in amusement. Detective Henderson then is able to break the two of them together, so that they can stop fighting. While restraining Russell who is much larger and overpowering John. John manages to get up, and Detective Henderson starts to massage Russell on the back calming him down. He then berates the both of them for their actions.

"I told the both of you to knock that shit off. Now knock it off. It has gone tough enough, and you need to quit. That is quite enough. You need to quit."

John straightens his tie after Russell tussled him on the floor, and starts laughing. John then responds.

"Yeah I agree; you need to quit."

Russell then angrily looks at John, then smiles and laughs to himself. Russell picks up his briefcase and then laughs once again at John's face.

"You know what John; I agree with you. You are absolutely right, you are. I need to quit. So therefore, I fucking quit. You can take this job, and you can shove it. I'm done, I'm gone. You want to be bank manager so bad, be my fucking guest. I'm outta here."

Russell then takes his car keys out of his pocket, and heads out of the entrance of the bank. John stands in shock not at all expecting for Russell to act and to respond in that way. John in a very disrespectful way quickly responds to Russell walking out.

"See what I tell you, he was just not fit for this job, there is something really off about that man, and he's so troubled and disturbed. So pitiful."

Jesse depressingly looks at Russell walk out the building. He then gets up walks over to John and Detective Henderson, and tells the both of them something.

"Um, I quit as well. If Russell leaves, I leave. I don't want to work in this bank anymore either. So goodbye."

Jesse grabs his tote bag, and walks out of the bank.

CHAPTER 4:

NOTHING RIGHT, NOTHING WRONG

After his fight with John, Russell decided to terminate his position at the "Sunset Credit Union". He already was contemplating suspending himself at the bank originally, but his argument with John solidified it. The future being unclear and unknown for him, he advances forward with his life. Understanding that the traumatic event which happened this evening, will forever haunt his memory. Russell left with his dignity intact and his virtues kept together and in order. Even though he has been through many hardships and troubles in his life, comparing them to what happened today. Along with the death of his parents, this event is also difficult. He moves on, and doesn't intend to look back during the times that he had at the "Sunset Credit Union." It is almost as if he is vowing to himself as a defense mechanism, to just erase the whole situation from existing. However, he sadly cannot magically remove the memories. The event did indeed happen in all it's unfortunate glory. Russell must come to terms that he must find a way to proceed in a manner, which causes him to be comfortable and safe with himself.

Had Russell not had the quarrel with John, would that have mattered at all? Would that have leveled his choice to stay or leave his position at the bank? These are thoughts Russell himself possibly deep down cannot be certain to answer. Many signs are leading that this was a choice he was going to make regardless, due to the outcome of the event. He is of course very concerned and anxious about his future ahead. He is now without a job, and now has many horrific traumatic thoughts inside of his mind. Russell now has to take charge of this, and get all of this prioritized. Leaving the bank possibly was a good decision to make for his mental health capacity, to remove himself from the negativity. Choices that people make sometimes don't always make sense to an outside party, but to the person themselves it is the logical and most sensible one to choose. In the case of Russell, he had to frankly do what was right for his own personal agenda.

He is still trying to also cope with losing both Peter and Jennifer, two of his fellow employees. An extremely hard pill to swallow, accepting the truth of witnessing and going through all of that. Peter was Russell's close friend, losing someone that you shared a close connection with is unbearable to imagine and understand. Trying not to recollect all the harsh and depressing moments, Russell tries to stay strong minded from it. After all, he has had one of the most excruciating days in his life, and he's not having an easy time dealing with all of the results which have reacted from that.

Russell no longer wanted to associate himself with that bank, and simply wanted to move on. All the turmoil he was feeling, toppled any hope of wanting to stay and stick around in that arena. The guilt he was being accused of by John, also played a major toll. Being humiliated and attacked by him, Russell felt buried under all of that, and the stress wasn't enough to hold onto. Understanding that there is an even bigger problem of proceeding into the unknown and undetermined future that he has for himself. Those issues and problems he would rather not ponder about at this time. Russell is well aware that a moment ago, he made an extreme rash life choice concerning his career. Yet again, it was a choice that he felt he had no choice to make. It was something he simply had to do, and there isn't any way around it. Mental anguish is very difficult to heal. Russell feels finding a way to mask or hide what he is going through, is a good solution. He will attempt to erase the multiple hardships that he went through earlier, and strive to find some type of explanation or improvement to deal with it all. It will seem difficult and complex at first, but Russell tries not to feel much worry about it. With the right routine and mental stability, he can overcome it. With so much to think about and so many thoughts he is confused about, it's a lot to carry. He is willing to advance from it, and be optimistic with whatever comes next.

As the sun is setting and nighttime is beginning to start, it is still a humid night in Los Angeles. Russell is in the parking lot of the "Oakwood Shopping Center", still fuming and tense from his fight with John. He holds his car keys clenched in his fist, walking to his car. When finally reaching his vehicle, he starts unlocking his car. He drives a black Chevrolet Suburban, which Russell himself always treasures his car. He gets into his car and sets his briefcase in the back seat. Then he starts to lock the doors, and turning the air conditioning on with the windows rolled up. Russell turns his car stereo on, and listens to one of his favorite songs. "Scar Tissue", by the Red Hot Chili Peppers. He opens the sunroof of his car, puts his head back on his seat, turns the volume of the stereo up, and closes his eyes for a bit.

He begins to feel very comfortable and relaxed, if only for a moment in this condition. Feeling weightless and light, and wanting to escape to some non-existent parallel world inside his mind. Escaping to some make believe heaven which he daydreams in his head. Intermittently, he is distracted by being reminded of foul events which happened in the day, although quickly trying to cover up those thoughts with happy ones. He realistically is in his own bubble and paradox, and doesn't want to think of anything that would ruin or soil this scene he's currently brewing in his mind. Russell opens his eyes, and looks up in the sunroof, and sees the dusk sky. The humid air also is orchestrating a gentle and smooth breeze. He takes his phone out of his pocket and notices the battery is quite low. In order to remedy that, he plugs his phone into the electrical port under the car stereo. Immediately following that, he leans his head back into his seat, and closes his eyes.

A few moments after this, he hears a soft knock on his passenger side door. This noise at first scared and startled Russell, who was in his comfortable mood. He looks out the passenger door window, and notices the person who is knocking is Jesse. He realizes that Jesse is looking rather depressed and puzzled, and possibly is in some type of trouble mentally. He turns the volume on his stereo down, and rolls the windows down. Russell then softly speaks to him.

"What's going on, you okay? Talk to me."

Jesse looks away from Russell right after he said that, and glances all over the parking lot. He then looks down on the floor, and beings to cry. He then asks Russell for a favor.

"I know the both of us aren't on good terms, but I don't have a car. I always take the bus to work. I been saving up to buy one...look that doesn't matter. Russell I'm feeling really upset and I don't feel like waiting for the bus tonight. Can you give me a ride home, please?"

Russell puts his hand on his forehead and laughs to himself. He looks around the parking lot for a bit, then starts to unlock the car door and reaches over and opens the door.

"Okay, only because you said please, I'll give you a ride home, get in."

Jesse takes a seat in the car, and puts his tote bag on the ground. He looks straight ahead and doesn't look at Russell. After turning the stereo back up, Russell and Jesse both put their seatbelts on, and he starts the car. Russell then backs out of the "Oakwood Shopping Center", and drives down Sunset Boulevard. For a moment, Russell looks at Jesse who seems very timid. Jesse is keeping to himself and seems nervous and shy. Russell then turns his head towards the road. He continues to drive, until he reaches a stoplight. He lowers the volume on the stereo, and begins to ask Jesse a concern he has on his mind, while looking straight ahead.

"You never told me where you lived, so, yeah. Where do you live at?"

Jesse then peeks out the passenger side window, and hesitates to answer Russell. He looks down at the ground for a couple seconds. It didn't occur to him that he would have to give Russell his personal information, such as that. However, he did submit to Russell.

"Well, I live in a studio in Inglewood by myself. It's okay, I like it. I know Inglewood is kinda far from here, and I would have to take several busses but ugh. I really liked working at the bank so I would deal with the commute. You do you know where Inglewood is right?"

Russell glances at Jesse who is looking straight, and turns his head back forward. Russell nods his head in agreement to his question. When the signal changes, Russell continues to drive. When he reaches another stoplight, he turns the music on his stereo to some loud Hip-Hop music. Russell then begins to perfectly mouth the lyrics to the music. Jesse then looks at him in amazement and in confusion, before letting his intentions show to him.

"Oh, I never knew you were that type of guy Russell. You always seemed stuck up to me."

Jesse then looks out the window in a bitter pushy mood. Russell then turns up the volume of the music, and continues to mime the words. As the men are riding the road, Russell realizes that he hasn't had anything to eat the entire day. He was saving his appetite, as himself and Peter were supposed to go out to eat. Russell who is a man who enjoys food, lowers the volume on the stereo, and proceeds to proposition Jesse something.

"Hey, I'm hungry as hell. I need to get a bite to eat. I can't go on much longer without eating something. So, it's not up for discussion. I'm going to get something to eat, and you can decide not to eat if you want, but I'm hungry, so if that bothers you, I can let you out right now."

Jesse then scoffs at Russell for saying that, and crosses his arms in his seat, looking out of the passenger window. Jesse then playfully responds to Russell.

"Okay, yeah I can eat something. But you're paying right? It's on you?"

Russell turns his head over at Jesse, then laughs out loud, he then turns his head back forward and nods. Immediately following that, he turns the music on the radio back up. A few minutes later, Russell makes a turn onto the highway heading towards Hollywood. He lets Jesse know where the both of them are going.

"I don't know if you've ever been, but there is this really nice Italian restaurant on Santa Monica Boulevard, called "Rome" that me and Peter have visited a couple times. It's kinda a fancy place, good vibe too. Their food is really good. They might... no fuck that, they are gonna be packed because it's Friday night, and we don't have a reservation, but we can wait for a table. You aren't in a rush to get home are you?"

Jesse for the first time in this moment, starts to become more comfortable with Russell and turns his head and smiles at him. He jubilantly replies to him in agreement.

"No, I'm not in a rush to get home Russell. I don't care, even if we go to KFC, I don't care. I trust your intuition and, I trust you."

Russell laughs at Jesse, and continues to drive down the highway. Eventually, he gets off of the highway and drives down Hollywood boulevard. Russell displays minor agitation.

"This LA traffic is really getting on my damn nerves. The restaurant is around the corner, but because of this traffic, it's gonna be a while before we get there."

Jesse shakes his head to conform what Russell said as being sincere to the situation. He then looks out onto the Hollywood Strip, seeing many performers and people walking down the sidewalk. It is a very entertaining and busy scene, with a lot of different characters and events happening. The stars on Hollywood Walk of Fame, and looking at buskers and people in costume as well. It's a very interesting and eclectic site to say the very least. Traffic finally starts to expand itself, and move at a smoother rate. Russell continues to drive, and then turns into a private parking lot building located a reasonable walking distance from the restaurant, and parks his car.

"We're gonna walk over there from here, it's not far. They have valet at the restaurant, but I'm more comfortable with this. Come on, let's go."

Russell then unplugs his phone from the charger and puts it in his pocket. He unlocks the car doors, with Jesse taking a few items out of his tote bag, then setting it on the floor, leaving it inside. He and Jesse both get out of the car, and walk down Hollywood Boulevard. Russell is walking with his hands in his pockets grinning, and Jesse is walking with his arms crossed. Russell is beginning to relax himself and be more calm. Jesse seems to be anxious, yet safe walking with Russell. Perhaps he is wanting to give off a false impression towards him. While they are strolling down the sidewalk, they temporarily stop walking and are mesmerized by something.

They see a Michael Jackson impersonator dancing, and Russell gives him some money. After that, they continue walking heading towards the restaurant. Upon reaching the restaurant, Russell informs the host that he and Jesse wish to have a table. They are told that they are going to have to wait possibly twenty minutes for one. Both of the men agree to wait for a table, and Russell is given a buzzer which would light up when their table is available. They both go to an outside courtyard area adjacent in the back area of the restaurant, in the meantime. They are both sitting on a bench near a marble fountain. For a few awkward seconds, they both wander their eyes around in the air, before Russell takes his phone out his pocket. In this same moment, he reaches in his pants pocket and takes out a pack of Marlboro cigarettes and sets them in the middle of himself and Jesse. He puts a cigarette in his mouth, then starts to go through all of his pockets, including his suit jacket pocket. In frustration, Russell grunts and seems to be upset over something. Talking with the cigarette still in his mouth, he looks over at Jesse.

"Aww Damn, I left my lighter in my car. You wouldn't have a light?"

With the cigarette still in Russell's mouth, Jesse picks up Russell's pack of cigarettes and takes one for himself, concurrently reaching in his pocket and letting Russell use his lighter.

"You're lucky. Something told me to bring my lighter. I left my pack of cigarettes in my bag in your car, because I know you smoke because I saw you put a pack in your pockets."

Russell then smiles at Jesse, and Russell lights the cigarette in his mouth before returning the lighter back to him. Jesse then lights a cigarette for himself. Russell with the cigarette in one hand, picks up his phone in the other, and is reading the sports scores. Jesse while taking puffs of his cigarette, is feeling curious about something, and he heavily gazes and scans at Russell, asking him a question while doing so.

"Russ, can I ask you a question?"

Russell still looking down on his phone, shakes his head and grunts at Jesse.

"You can ask me anything, but I have one rule okay. We don't talk about anything that happened today. I just want to go inside, have dinner, and eat. All that shit is gonna ruin my appetite. So don't bring it up, and remind me. Anything in that realm I'm not gonna talk about, and don't want you mentioning. Is that a Deal?"

Jesse then feeling attacked by Russell's comments, takes a puff from his cigarette, and gives an ugly look at Russell, and very angrily replies to him in a harsh manner.

"You know what, forget it. I didn't want to listen or believe it at first, but everyone was right about you, you are an asshole. There are so many rumors about you that me and the rest of the gang at the bank would always make, and I totally see it now."

Russell who is continuing to look down on his phone, takes a puff of his cigarette and shakes his head and laughs. The men continue to smoke their cigarettes. Russell finishes his first, and throws the butt away in the trash can. Jesse soon finishes his cigarette and disposes of it. In awkward silence, the both of them sit and wait. Jesse looks at Russell again, and speaks to him.

"Russ, I just wanted to let you know, that I quit working at the bank. Possibly the for the same reasons you and Yvette did. I can't be in that building anymore. I'm going to go mad."

Russell with his phone still in his hand, looks up at Jesse for a couple seconds, raises his eyebrows and shakes his head at him, then goes back to looking down on his phone. Jesse then proceeds to ask Russell another question.

"Everyone else at the bank, I knew about their family and their personal life, and I'm just the token black and gay guy. Yet I don't know a single damn thing about you. You're such a man of mystery. Are you married, do you have any kids Russell? I'm just curious."

Russell while still looking on his phone, makes an angry face, and for almost a minute it seems as though he's avoiding and refusing to answer the question. Remarkably, Russell opens up more about himself to Jesse.

"Well, no I'm not married. I'm single. I'm also not the fatherly type, so I don't have any children either. And no, I've never dated any of the women that ever came into the bank."

Jesse continues to express himself more towards Russell on personal matters.

"Well, when you're not acting like an asshole, you're a beautiful man. I'm not saying that because I'm gay, I'm saying that because I feel inside you're an alright guy I suppose."

Russell continuing to read his phone, smirks at what Jesse said, and laughs to himself. Jesse continues to stare at Russell, profiling him. He is wondering as to whether or not he should continue to throw more questions at him, or to just leave him alone. A few more minutes of awkward silence passes, when Russell who is still going through his phone, raises his head at Jesse who is purposefully staring at him in confusion and in amusement. Russell following that lowers his head to his phone again, and starts to grin and laugh to himself. A few seconds later, he then becomes curious towards Jesse, and doesn't hesitate to be frank with him by forcefully explaining something.

"You know, if I was such an asshole, I would not have given you a lift, and left you in that parking lot, I wouldn't have taken you out to dinner for free, and I sure as hell wouldn't have let you bum one of my cigarettes, and don't act like I didn't catch you do that. I also wouldn't be telling you private information about myself. But I'm such an asshole right?"

Jesse starts to unintentionally laugh over what Russell said, and folds his arms together. He then looks up at the night sky, and looks at all the tall buildings in the surrounding area. Russell puts his head up from his phone, and notices Jesse looking up at the sky. He as well interestingly looks up with him. Jesse while still looking at the sky talks to Russell.

"Despite today being what it was, this is strangely such a beautiful night. The air is so lovely, it's kinda humid but still lovely. The sky is kinda a mix between orange and blue, and it's so lovely. This is why I like Los Angeles a lot, because you see a lot of this."

Russell while still looking up at the sky nods over Jesse's comment. He then proceeds to look down to his phone again. This time, Russell is reading political and finance news on the CNN app. Russell likes to be very involved with these sorts of things, and has always been a conspiracy theorist in a sense. He is always trying to get involved with issues that others very seldom talk about, dealing with money, politics, crime, and social studies. In addition to that, Russell always has a more out of the box perspective on how things happen the way they do, and seems to think that there might be outside sources which control the unknown. Jesse continues to gaze at Russell, second guessing to himself to bring up a thought in his mind, or not to. Russell is finished going through his phone, and sets it down on the bench. He puts his hands in his pants pocket, and looks over at the fountain situated next to the bench himself and Jesse are sitting on. He notices how peaceful the water is coming out of the faucet, and how beautiful the marble on the outside of the fountain shines. There are LED lights on the bottom of the exterior of the fountain which are in blue, green, and white. They complement the artistry of the way the fountain is designed, and displays a beautiful and colorful arrangement. Jesse who is still glancing at Russell, notices him paying close attention to the fountain, and starts to offer his own personal feelings and remarks towards the beauty of it.

"That is a nice fountain huh Russ? If I were filthy rich, I would have one of these in my backyard. It's so nice, and breathtaking. Ugh, I really like this fountain, and it's very rare you see beautiful and artistic things like this anymore."

Russell continues to look up and down at the fountain, being fascinated by it. He then begins to agree with Jesse on his opinions of the fountain.

"It's eye catching yes. It reminds me of Italy kind of, I'm getting that sort of theme from it. It also looks very regal and royal. The only thing I don't like is the way it's kinda positioned. It would have made more sense if they put it in the middle of these benches, instead of having it behind all that shrubbery. To me that looks beyond ignorant, but alas."

Jesse turns his head away from the fountain towards Russell, giving him an innocent submissive look. He stays silent, and doesn't respond verbally or indirectly to Russell's comments over the fountain. Russell then looks away from the fountain and puts his head down, with his hands still in his pockets. He notices Jesse yet again staring at him, which this time he grunts at him as if he were bothered. Jesse begins to refrain from staring at Russell, and looks away from him. He is starting to become aware that perhaps Russell is starting to find him doing that unpleasant. Jesse still had a million things on his mind that he wanted to explain to Russell, and is very captivated by his presence at the moment. However, he simply kept his responses to himself, and didn't wish to reveal them.

A couple minutes later, the buzzer the restaurant host gave Russell started to go off. Their table was finally available, and they could both now go inside. Russell and Jesse proceed to walk through the restaurant. It was a magnificent setting, with the theme being Rome, Italy, hence the name of the restaurant entitled "Rome". From the way the restaurant was designed, it was almost as if it were outside, but it wasn't. The whole restaurant was orchestrated to follow that particular pattern and design. There are no windows inside, possibly done in an illusion so that he patrons inside of the restaurant, feel engulfed in the scenery and ambiance. There were many paintings hung up on the walls, and a lot of plants and other botanic motifs. Upon looking at the ceiling, you can see many chandelier's and other sparkling attractive compliments. The restaurant was lit in an intimate and passionate way, to give a very comfortable and compassionate feeling. Inside, it is crowded with many people, with virtually every single table being occupied. This is clearly a popular and well liked restaurant due to that happening.

Russell and Jesse were seated into a booth located in the center of the restaurant, very close to the bar area of the restaurant. There were big screen TV's showing sports games. They each took a seat on the opposing sides of a booth, sitting across from each other. Russell starts to remove his suit jacket, folds it up and puts it down next to him.

The waitress then presented them both with menu's, not before asking what type of libation they would like.

"Alright gentlemen, what can I get you both to drink?"

Russell looked at Jesse for a couple seconds before responding to the waitress.

"Uh, I know you guys have beer. Hmm.... uh. I'll just have two bottles of Blue Moon please. That's just for myself. Two bottles of Blue Moon. Yeah."

Jesse, while looking at Russell gives his drink order as well.

"Yeah, I'll just take a glass of Chardonnay. Thank you."

Right before she is about to leave the table, Russell grabs the waitress arms.

"Just bring the whole bottle. Get me two bottles of Blue Moon and a bottle of Chardonnay. We had a long day, I appreciate it. Thanks."

Russell then grins at Jesse. Jesse began to talk about the interior of the restaurant.

"Oh my, this place is just fantastic. I never seen a restaurant like this before ever, this was a very good recommendation Russell, thank you very much."

Russell smiled at Jesse, and began to read over the menu. Russell was very fond of this restaurant and has been a couple times before with Peter. He not only likes the environment and the experience, but also the food. He really enjoyed eating Italian food. Despite him being Russian and Jewish, he still had an affinity for Italian cuisine, and would prefer it above all. Russell continued to scan the menu, trying to make his mind up over what he wanted to eat. The choices at this restaurant were plenty, and thus it makes it very difficult to decide what to actually order. Jesse has never been in this restaurant before, mainly because he very seldom eats Italian food. So unlike Russell, he wasn't as experienced with the menu and what to order. Russell had a feeling this might be the case when he glances over at Jesse reading the menu looking puzzled.

"Do you know what you want? Do you want me to make a recommendation for you?"

Jesse seemed to be in control, and could manage just fine. He replied to Russell very sharply, letting him know that he didn't need his help, and that he could pick out what he wanted from the menu without any issue.

"Actually Russell, I'm trying to make my mind up on a few things, but thank you for your concern. I'm just fine, thank you. You've helped me enough tonight."

Russell then smiles at Jesse, and looks back at his menu, glancing it over to decide what he wanted to eat. He would occasionally take a peek over a Jesse, who was reading the menu as well. When Russell figured out what he wanted to order, he set his menu down on the table. Jesse however was still looking over the menu, still in an indecisive mood. Russell then watched the sports games featured on the big screen televisions sitting over the bar area. Jesse was then able to decide what he wanted to eat, and set the menu aside on the table. He makes eye contact with Russell. Russell then whispers to Jesse.

"So. Have you made your mind up as to what you wanted to eat?"

Jesse nodded his head. The waitress came to their table seconds after this.

"Here are your two bottles of Blue Moon, and here is a bottle of Chardonnay, and I have two glasses for you. Now have you gentlemen decided as to what you wanted?"

Russell begins to place his order.

"I'll have the stuffed crab mushrooms, lobster diavolo, a side salad and I would like some garlic bread as well."

Jesse then immediately gave his order to the waitress.

"Well, I'll just have the shrimp scampi, and could I please have some scallops with that. Thank you."

Russell started to drink one his beers, while watching a basketball game on the big screen televisions in the restaurant. Jesse started to grab the wine bottle to pour himself a drink, but he is stopped by Russell.

"No no, let me. I'm treating you out, so I'll pour it for you."

Russell then poured Jesse a glass of wine. Jesse starts to take sips of his wine, while staring at Russell watching the sports game. Russell finishes his first beer, and pours himself a glass of wine. Russell then proceeds to take a couple swallows of it. Immediately following, he then takes the opportunity to talk to Jesse.

"How is the wine? To me it's kinda sharp, but I like it like that."

Jesse takes another drink of the wine before responding to Russell.

"Oh it's just fine, it's very good. Thank you for asking."

Russell returns to watching the game on the television, while Jesse continually stares at him. Both of them are continuing to wait for their food to arrive. Jesse peering at Russell, asks him a personal question which he has on his mind.

"Russell, I was trying to avoid asking you this question, and I feel I'm possibly going to regret asking it, but I can't help myself. That's just the way I'm programmed I suppose. But here it goes. Would you be bothered if I said that in some cosmic way, I'm attracted to you?"

After taking another glass of wine, Russell opens his second beer, and looks at Jesse looking very puzzled. He then responds to him.

"Why would you think I would be bothered?"

Jesse rests his arms on the table and puts his hands over his cheeks and under his chin, and waits a minute before replying to Russell.

"Well because you know, I'm a gay guy, and you're straight. So I am just assuming that you might get bothered by it. I'm also black and loud, and you're a quiet white guy, but I guess that's kinda dismissive, but still. So many things I'm curious about, and that's my fault. You don't have to answer that. Forget it. Pretend I never said that, okay?"

Russell starts to laugh to himself shaking his head, and takes a gulp of his beer. With the beer still in his hand, he reveals shocking information to Jesse.

"I have a feeling this might be the liquor and alcohol making me act this way. But you should know that I'm actually Bi. So I don't give a fuck that you're gay, and I really don't give a fuck that you're black. I'm not in the KKK, so. You're also not my type, so it's all good."

Jesse then scoffs at Russell and gives him a disgusted and appalled look.

"Well, excuse me. How the fuck was I supposed to know you were Bi? You don't give a bi/gay vibe to me at all. You seem like a regular straight guy. Also, there were rumors at the bank that you were racist and kinda closed minded and conservative. So I'm sorry, I just had to ask. I still find you attractive, and you're an alright guy to me."

Russell takes another swallow of his beer, and laughs at Jesse, shaking his head. Jesse then starts to share his gripes about a habit Russell is doing.

"Why the fuck are you always doing that? It's getting annoying and I want you to stop. You're like the damn Heat Miser, shaking your head and laughing like that all the damn time."

Russell sits back in his seat, folds his arms and responds to Jesse.

"Why do you have to act so gay? It's bad enough you're black, so why make things more difficult for yourself, and act all faggoty like that. Be a man."

Jesse realizes that Russell is joking with him, and doesn't fire back at that comment. He is slightly offended and bothered by his remarks, but quickly ignores it and moves on. The both of them continue to wait for their meals. Russell drinks his beer again, asking Jesse a question.

"What about me do you like? You like ginger guys? You like Jewish guys? I'm also Russian, you like Russian guys as well? I mean you called me the Heat Miser, so that shows you are observant on my outside looks. Just curious I suppose."

Jesse takes a couple swigs of his wine, before answering Russell's question.

"I don't know; I had no idea you were Jewish and Russian so it's not that. You are ginger haired yes, I don't mind that. I just feel safe with you. I just find it odd that before tonight, I've worked at that bank with you for a while, yet this is the most we've ever really connected. I do like how weird and crazy and mysterious you are."

Jesse then feels guilty for saying that, and looks down on the table feeling discouraged to continue talking. Russell looks at Jesse with a cold stare, and finishes his second beer. Russell begins to open his mouth to say something, but then is interrupted. During this time the waitress comes to the table as their food order is now ready.

"Okay, I have some stuffed crab mushrooms, lobster diavolo, and a side salad. I also have shrimp scampi with scallops, and some garlic bread for the table. Alright, is there anything else that I could get for you gentlemen."

Russell responds to the waitress.

"Yes just two glasses of water, and the check. That's all, thanks."

They both then begin to eat their meal. Russell while eating his meal then proceeds to talk about what he was going to mention, before the waitress came with their food. He starts to talk about Jesse in a playful and cruel, yet sincere way.

"Jesse, you have an attitude problem, and you need to fix that. You're not going to succeed in life unless you do. You also shouldn't let other people dictate how you should act, and how you should be. You think if Peter was like that, you would have gotten hired at the bank? I don't think so. He saw the good in you, and gave you a chance. Think about it."

Jesse also eating his meal thinks to himself as to whether or not he should reply to Russell. However, a few moments later in the same exact fashion as Russell, he doesn't hold back and does let his true opinions and thoughts out for him to know.

"Well I also want to add that Russell, you are an asshole and I might have an attitude problem, but you have a narcissist problem. You are such an inconsiderate man, and you are also scary and weird as well. But I just find you so damn attractive for some reason. Oh well."

Russell raises his eyebrows at Jesse while eating his food, reiterating a question he asked before, that he still did not get an adequate answer on.

"Okay Jesse, I'm going to ask you again. What about me do you like? Because that's now the second time you said you were attracted to me, but again you failed to really say what you liked about me. Actually, you started to say very unappealing things about me. You called me an asshole, which I am, and a narcissist, which yes I am, but I'm still confused. Help me out."

Jesse continues to eat his meal and doesn't respond to Russell. Russell who is also eating adds on to what Jesse said previously, wanting to clarify that.

"You also said that I was scary and weird. Okay. Yeah so what, I'm a scary and weird guy. That still doesn't answer what you find attractive about me. Just let it out, I'm not gonna get mad. In fact, it's healthier that way. If you continue to sulk, it's going to make it worse."

Russell pours himself and Jesse more wine, and Jesse responds to Russell.

"Um, I don't know, you're just the type of guy I dream about I guess. It might sound funny to you, but I just can't explain it Russell. I'm sorry. I just like what I like."

Jesse looks down from Russell after saying that, very ashamed to look up and give him eye contact. He continues to eat his meal, without paying attention to Russell. A few minutes later, Russell taking a sip of his wine, does decide to follow up what Jesse said to him.

"You've never had a boyfriend Jesse, have you?"

While still avoiding to look at Russell, Jesse tells Russell the truth.

"No, I've never had a boyfriend. How did you know?"

Russell takes another swallow of his wine, shakes his head and laughs at Jesse.

"Because I'm the Heat Miser and I'm just magic. I just know."

Jesse then looks up at Russell and laughs at him. They both continue to eat their meal in silence. Russell watches more of the basketball game on the television at the bar. Jesse watches him staying quiet. The both of them finish all of their food, and occasionally stare at each other. The waitress soon then returns to the table with the check. Russell puts his credit card in the checkbook, and puts it on the side of the table. Russell then speaks to Jesse.

"Would you like to go and get some dessert? Like some ice cream or something? I know this really awesome place that you're gonna love. My treat of course. Would that make you feel better, because you seem kinda depressed now."

Jesse responds to Russell's question.

"I would yes, that sounds nice. Thank you for offering Russell. I appreciate it."

Russell pours the remaining amount of wine left in the bottle and evenly distributes it to himself and Jesse's glass. They both then finish the wine. Jesse asks Russell a question.

"Russell, you've never had a boyfriend either have you?"

Russell while looking at the basketball game on the television and not giving Jesse eye contact, responds to the question that he asked very abruptly.

"No Jesse, I've never had a boyfriend. I've never really had a girlfriend either if I think about it. I just focused on school really. I always wanted to be an accountant and work on the stock exchange, and be a fucking billionaire. The next Trump and shit I guess. So the answer is no."

Jesse with his elbows on the table and his hands on his cheeks, looking down replies.

"That's a shame, because whoever would have you would be the luckiest person in the world, I swear to god. They would be the luckiest person in the world."

Russell smiles and continues to look at the basketball game on the television, complaining about the gameplay.

"The Kings are just getting whooped by the Golden State Warriors tonight. Usually they play better than this, I don't know what's going on. I can't believe this game at all."

Jesse then looks at the basketball game on the television, and nods his head. The waitress returns with the checkbook and Russell's credit card. After signing the receipt, he gives the waitress a cash tip inside of the checkbook. He then proceeds to put his suit jacket back on while staring at Jesse, asking him if he's ready to leave.

"You all set, we were good to go now?"

Jesse then stares at Russell for almost a minute, then immediately laughs at him. A few moments later, he responds to him.

"Yeah, I'm ready. We can leave now."

They both then leave out of the restaurant, and walk down the Hollywood strip. Walking through the night they see an entertaining setting, full of action and many diverse happenings going on all at once. After all it is Hollywood, and it's only customary to notice things like that. Russell and Jesse see more performers and buskers on the street, and window shop at the many different storefronts located on the strip. During this time, Jesse ever so often would take peeks and glances at Russell, being very thankful and blessed to be a part of his company. He was filled with so much excitement and anxiety, being close to him. This was turning into one of the most amazing nights he has had. Compensating to the traumatic events which have happened to both of them earlier. It was their time to be happy with themselves, and to escape. They eventually make their way to an ice cream shop that has an extremely long line out the door. The shop is called "Freeze Play", and looks very 1930's candy shop themed and old fashioned. It has a very vintage and sophisticated look towards it. While they are both standing in line outside of the shop, Russell explains to Jesse that this is a very well-liked ice cream shop with a lot of flavors and options, so that's why it's crowded.

"I come here all the time, I like it. They can pretty much put whatever you want with your ice cream. You want fruit, you want candy bits, you want peanuts, it doesn't matter. You can basically get what you want, however you want it."

Jesse listens to Russell talk, becoming more and more infatuated with him. This was very struggling for him to accept, as he feels that Russell doesn't at all feel the same way he does. The line in the ice cream shop dissipates little by little. When they both reach the counter, they begin to order the type of ice cream they would like; with Russell going first.

"I'll have chocolate ice cream, with marshmallows and brownie bits."

He then looks down at Jesse, alerting him it is now his turn to make his order.

"Oh, I'll take vanilla with chocolate chips and cookie dough."

They both then take their cups of ice cream and sit on a table located on the other side of the building. While eating his ice cream, Jesse starts to converse with Russell.

"This is really good, I've never been to this place before, but I definitely want to come back. This is some damn good ice cream. Thank you very much for taking me here."

Russell eats some of his ice cream and smiles at Jesse, playfully teasing him.

"You don't have to thank me, I wanted to come here. Even if you said no to wanting ice cream, I still would have gone. I came here for myself, I didn't come here for you. I don't care about you at all. I only came here and suggested this place, because I like it here."

Jesse while eating more his ice cream, decides to tease Russell in return.

"Bullshit, that is not the truth at all, and I don't believe it one bit. But you can lie all you want. I find it cute. It's okay. I don't care."

Russell while eating more of his ice cream grins at Jesse. They both are enjoying themselves and feeling free in the moment. Jesse while eating his ice cream, continues to talk to Russell, and gives him an honest confession. It was something that he was scared to confess, but knew Russell had to know the truth about.

"This is an amazing night, and I wasn't expecting this. I'm going to be honest, I was just gonna catch an Uber home, and not get in your car. But because of what happened today, I said fuck it, and decided to take a risk and see what happened. I see it paid off."

Russell looks up at and smiles at him for a few seconds, and replies.

"I understand, and I don't blame you. If I were you, I would have done the same exact thing, so don't let yourself down over that. I completely understand."

Jesse then begins to look around the ice cream shop, noticing the decorations and how everything is presented. Taking note at conversation pieces on the wall.

"It's funny how they have pictures of Coney Island up, when we're in LA, but I don't know. It seems like a silly thing for me to gripe at, but just something I've noticed."

After taking in what Jesse said, Russell does notice as well the New York homage in the pictures and portraits hung up on the wall, and the lack of Los Angeles related material.

"Yeah everything is New York come to mention it. There's the Statue of Liberty, and that's the George Washington Bridge. Why do they not have anything California related? That doesn't make any sense to me at all. But oh well, I agree it's kinda trivial to argue at."

Jesse then begins to uncontrollably laugh at loud due to what Russell said, which the infectious laugh also causing Russell to slightly giggle. The two continue to enjoy their ice cream, also continuing to look at more pictures on the wall. Jesse then is curious as to what Russell's ice cream flavor tastes like, and allows Jesse to sample some of his ice cream. He likes the taste of it, and Jesse does allow Russell to do the same and taste his flavor of ice cream. Russell after trying it, shows approval that he likes it.

They finish their ice cream and walk out of the building heading out towards the Hollywood strip. Russell walking with his hands in his pockets, and Jesse walking by his side in a comfortable and confident way. Even though they stay silent, they both show positive body language from being near each other. Jesse in particular being comfortable with Russell, as he continues to take peeks as Russell when they are walking down the sidewalk, with Russell unaware that Jesse is staring at him. They continue to look at the different nightlife and entertainment in the street.

Minutes later, they arrive at the parking structure where Russell has his car parked. He unlocks the car, and they both get in. Before starting the ignition, Russell turns his head and talks to Jesse.

"Alright, it's been lovely and I've had a wonderful night, but look how late it is. I'm really tired, and I need to get to bed. So let me take you home."

Jesse looking very depressed, looks down on towards the ground, and is silent for almost a minute. He then looks up ahead and for a short while looking out the windscreen. Jesse looks at Russell for a few seconds and lays his head on his shoulder, and puts his hand on Russell's lap. Jesse then sadly exclaims to him.

"I don't want to go home."

Russell with an uncomfortable look on his face, shakes his head and laughs. Then starts the car engine.

CHAPTER 5:

NOTHING REMEMBERED, NOTHING FORGOTTEN

Russell was not expecting for Jesse to do that, and is in shock. He doesn't know how to react to the current situation, and doesn't know the correct response to give. He is not a very touching or romance orientated person himself, and doesn't do well at all to affection. These types of things are Russell's main weakness, and it's something he'd rather not partake in. Love, romance, personal relationships and such. All of this is a new experience for him, and it's only understandable for him to feel estranged from anything related to love. That is of course a quality of his personality, to give off that agenda and trait to himself. His mysteriousness and ambiguity as far as his personal life is concerned, makes sense. Any close bonds that Russell tries to attach himself to, cause an issue and bring much difficulty. Honestly, they both have problems surrounding this particular category. Jesse as well is quite innocent and inexperienced in this department as well, taking advantage of Russell's kindness that he's portraying. Attraction, both physical and mental is just something that you cannot control. So whereas Russell is finding it hard to express himself towards compassion, Jesse seems to be the exact opposite, and letting his feelings and colors show. There has to be some kind of equalizer in this conundrum somehow, in which both parties are satisfied in their virtues. There has to be a way for everyone in this situation to be at peace, and to not be insecure with their feelings.

Russell gets on the highway, which has moderate traffic. The night sky is turning a light tan color, and the city lights surrounding Los Angeles are an interesting sight to see. It's a very cool, yet humid night. Thus it being a Friday night, a lot of action is still presenting itself. Keeping his mind towards the road, Russell still has a heavy case of emotions on his mind. While driving the car, he thinks about how he should resolve this with Jesse, so that wrong ideas aren't being harvested. He is also wondering if he should leave it alone, and pretend Jesse's advances never happened. Part of him wishes to ignore what Jesse did, and blame it on the fact that he acted on emotional impulse and didn't mean to do it. Especially if you factor in everything which did pan out today, you can't really blame anyone. Russell believes that he'll excuse that act just this one time. The other part of him does want to confront Jesse, and inform him that he's not comfortable with his gestures. Jesse however in some ways doesn't feel guilty or wrong, he did what he wanted to it and that settles it. He feels that it isn't his fault that he can't keep his patience and feelings to himself anymore, and acted accordingly to the way he did. Trying his best to respect Russell's boundaries, he was just able to contain how he really felt. Jesse is very much attracted to Russell, and doesn't want to part from him right now. Wanting to hold onto this setting with him.

Russell continues to drive the car, and the both of them stay silent with Russell concentrating on the road. Jesse is keeping to himself with an innocent look on his face, staring straight out of the windshield of Russell's car, in a mute state. The car stereo is on, playing music very loudly, and they both remain quiet towards each other. Russell occasionally would direct his eyes towards Jesse, but only for a second. As he continues down the highway in silence, Russell finally snaps, and he isn't in a flirtatious or affectionate mood. He tries to make it clear to Jesse. He turns the stereo down to talk to him.

"Don't ever do that again okay. That really made me feel uncomfortable, and you need to keep your fucking hands to yourself; you don't touch people like that. Especially men, and you being another guy. Don't do stuff like that, it's not right."

Jesse is sitting with his back in the seat with his arms crossed, and rudely responds to Russell.

"I'm going to do what I want, I gave you so many hints that I was into you, and if you can't get them that's not my fault at all. If I want to touch you, I'm gonna touch you, sorry."

Russell stays silent for a couple minutes, and looks at Jesse very angrily. Jesse looks at Russell with an entitled look and turns the stereo up. Jesse feels he should say whatever is on his mind towards Russell, due to assumed rapport and connection that they both seem to have. Wanting to be comfortable and free spirited, and not having to filter or conform himself under Russell's wishes. Russell is still having issue with this situation, and how to correctly assess it. Frankly, he wasn't really offended and disgusted by what Jesse told him, but surprised and shocked that Jesse has much disregard to others personal space. His rudeness and the way goes about it brings much concern. But again, Russell reminds himself of the moment they are currently in, and perhaps he was being far too nice, which why why Jesse reacted that way. Under a lot of stress from recent events, exceptions should probably be made under certain conditions. That still shouldn't matter, as Jesse's approach to the situation in Russell's mind isn't the proper one. If Jesse feels he needs to get and do whatever he wants to feel happy on his own personal status, that's good for him. But Russell feels it is an incorrect method for him, and he does decide to take the situation into his own hands, displaying his side of the ordeal. He takes another look at Jesse, turns the stereo down again, and continues to converse with him.

"There's that attitude problem of yours yet again. It's interesting how it approaches itself like that. Like a wave in the ocean. It comes up, and springs itself. Jesse, you have a terrible attitude problem buddy, and it's something you really need to work on."

Jesse starts to laugh to himself, and turns the radio up on high volume. He then proceeds to put his hand on Russell's lap for a second, and then he removes his hand and laughs again. Jesse then looks straight forward, and doesn't say a single word. Russell turns and looks at Jesse with an irritated face, and he's not amused. He turns the stereo down again to talk to him.

"Stop touching me Jesse, I'm trying to drive. Which reminds me, I need to drop you off at home, so I need you to tell me where I can drop you off at. You don't have to give me your address I don't care, but I do need to drop you off, as I need to get home myself."

Jesse turns the radio up again, and sits back in the seat with his arms crossed, ignoring Russell and looking out of the window. Russell looks at him, and shakes his head. Jesse then starts to become angry and defiant. The fact Jesse is testing him this way, makes Russell impatient with him. He yet again turns the stereo down, and begins to attempt to get an answer out of Jesse.

"Well, I'm gonna drop you off now. I gotta get home because I'm tired, and we can hang out some other time I promise. Just tell me where to drop you off at."

Jesse gives Russell an agitated look, and doesn't respond to him. Immediately following that, Jesse once again increases the volume of the car stereo. He relaxes himself in the seat more, sitting with his head back, and his arms crossed, looking out the window. Russell being extremely fed up, drives towards the exit ramp, and moves off the highway. Continuing off the highway, down a street. The music still blaring in the car, Jesse sits relaxed in the passenger seat. Russell is trying to keep calm towards this, and lowers the volume on the stereo again.

"If you don't tell me where you live, I'm going to drop you off at some random place, because I'm not your babysitter or your bodyguard. I have shit I need to do, and I need to go home and rest. So tell me where I can drop you off at please."

Jesse this time laughs at what he said, and continues to ignore him. He turns the radio up, and starts to dance and mime to the music. Russell being very irate and stressed at this present time, acting strictly on impulse, starts driving to an unknown location. After passing a few streets, he turns into an abandoned department store parking lot. This is a very desolate and terrifying location, and there are no other cars in the parking lot, and being in this location gives a very unsettling vibe.

Jesse looks around in fear and shock, and in total confusion. Russell then lowers the volume of the radio down, turns the ignition off, and unlocks the car doors. He then directly looks at Jesse in a very strict manner, and forces his seatbelt off him. Jesse looks at him in total shock not knowing how to act, but Russell doesn't hold back how he feels.

"Get the fuck out of my car right now. I was patient with you, and I let you get away with touching me inappropriately twice, and I was nice to you, but no more Mr. Nice guy. Jesse, it's been a lovely time, but I need you to get out my car. So please get out of my car."

Jesse continues to look at Russell with an appalled face, and refuses to get out of the vehicle. He is very shocked that Russell is acting this way towards him, and wasn't envisioning this type of behavior from him at all. Russell then loses more of his patience, and reaches over the passenger seat, and flings the door open. He then points out to the desolate parking lot.

"Yes, so I'm gonna need you to get out. So get out before I throw you out."

Jesse then looks around the parking lot for a few seconds, and then closes the door. He becomes comfortable and sits back in the chair, folding his arms together as if he had authority in this particular situation. He has no intentions of listening to Russell, and has his own agenda in mind. He turns up the volume of the stereo in Russell's car and sits tightly.

Russell puts his hands over his face, feeling very tired and frustrated. He is scared that he is going to turn violent, as Russell does have a sharp temper at times. It's during events like this which causes him to lose patience with others, and to discontinue his gratitude. Jesse continues to listen to the blaring music playing, and relaxes himself in the seat. Russell then loses control, and in a tirade cuts the car stereo off and runs out of the car, shutting the door behind him. Very angrily, he marches himself over to the passenger side door and tries to open it. This fails, as Jesse has quickly locked the doors from the inside. Jesse looks at him in amusement and laughs, while turning the car stereo up on high volume dancing and miming to the music. Russell takes his key fob out and attempts to unlock the door, however Jesse is quickly locking the door in the same process. Russell runs his hands through his hair, and crosses his arms, staring at Jesse in disappointment and in anger.

He allows Jesse to act childish, and continue this game for a couple minutes or so, before he returns to the passenger side door, to unlock it. Jesse steadily locks the door as soon as Russell tries to unlock it using his car remote. Russell then returns again to letting Jesse milk this moment, and just stands and watches him from outside his car. He is thinking to himself that he will get restless at some point, and eventually cave in. Jesse continues to act very immature and to Russell for another few minutes or so.

However, he starts to become bored soon, and figures to himself that enough is enough and he's not going to torture Russell anymore. He cuts the radio off and sits back in the seat, and finally decides to give in, and allow Russell to open the door. Russell one final time unlocks the car using the key fob, and this time he is able to open the door. Like he was a professional wrestler, Russell grabs Jesse up from the seat and flings him towards his back, carrying him. Because Russell is much larger and stronger than Jesse, he sadly cannot defend or protect himself from this. Russell while still carrying Jesse, carries him quite a distance from the car, towards a delivery truck dock station of the defunct department store, and sets him down on an elevated ramp. He then slightly out of breath looks at Jesse, and begins to talk to him in a very frightened and puzzled tone.

"What's wrong with you? Are you a psychopath? I'm not being funny, I'm really concerned and scared of you. Where did you come from? Who are you? It's like you're an entirely different person from earlier tonight. Who exactly are you?"

While still sitting down, Jesse looks down towards the ground for about thirty seconds, then directs his head up looking at Russell, and starts to cry. Russell looks at him feeling confused, and not knowing how to react or what to say either. Jesse then while sobbing and trying to gather himself, responds to Russell.

"Russell, you're such an asshole, I swear to god. You were really gonna leave me here out in the middle nowhere? I should be asking you those same questions. I might be a psycho, but you're like the epitome of that, and in a whole another ball park and level."

Russell then puts one hand over his mouth, and looks up at the sky. Jesse is still crying, and wiping his tears with his hands. Russell watches him for a few seconds, then reaches into his pocket and takes out his handkerchief and starts to wipe Jesse's face and nose.

"If I was a psycho, I wouldn't be doing this, now would I?"

Jesse then starts to laugh at Russell, while he's cleaning his face. Russell then decides to take a seat on the ramp next to Jesse. He sits with his hands in his pockets, and stares out into the desolate area. They both sit in silence for a minute or so, then Russell starts to converse with Jesse, displaying an act of kindness towards him.

"Okay, you can spend the night at my place tonight. But just for tonight; tomorrow, you don't have to go home, but you can't stay. I'm not your bodyguard. Okay?"

Jesse who is still wiping his face with Russell's handkerchief, then smiles at Russell and starts to laugh. He then asks him a question.

"Russell, you think I'm crazy don't you? Well I'm not crazy, I'm just different. You're different as well, so I figured you would understand. Clearly I was wrong."

Russell who is still looking away from Jesse, answers him.

"Yes I think you're crazy, but you know what, I'm crazy too, so it's okay. I'm just really tired and that's probably why I'm acting so berserk like this. But I did ask you multiple times where I could drop you off at, and you continued to bullshit with me."

Jesse who is continuing to wipe his face with Russell's handkerchief, looks up at Russell and in a depressing way, replies to him.

"Russell, I told you that I didn't want to go home, and you didn't listen. I kept giving you hints that I wasn't going to separate from you, at least not tonight. So I don't feel I did anything wrong, and it's your fault for not understanding, and wanting to leave me in this unsafe place."

Russell while still looking out in the distance away from Jesse, responds.

"Well, I also put my foot down towards you many times. I made it clear that I wanted to go home, and we could hang out some other time. Again, I'm not your bodyguard and I'm not your goon or some toy that you can play with whenever you want. I'm a human."

Jesse then intentionally puts Russell's handkerchief in his pocket, to which in his peripheral vision Russell saw him do it. Jesse then starts to lament himself to Russell.

"I've just had bad luck all my life. Being black and gay I feel like I'm living some type of curse. I've never had a family, and my mother died before I got to even get to know her. Seeing Jennifer and Peter killed today, was unbelievable. That could have easily been me Russell. The fact you, me and Yvette survived that, I just don't understand it at all."

Russell continues to look out into space, yet still carefully listening to Jesse, who continues to express his concerns and deep emotions he kept buried and concealed.

"I don't have any friends, I felt Peter possibly only hired me for affirmative action reasons, as I feel I was hired just strictly because I was different. I've never worked in a bank before, and I feel I'm not supposed to be here, and the two of us were never supposed to meet or come together. It's fucked up because I really like you, yet hate you Russell. I don't know."

The both of them continue to sit together while both analyzing the situation they are currently in. Jesse is clearly feeling depressed at the moment, and is using this time to seek empathy from Russell, or at least try to. He is aware that emotions are running high, and he's willing to share and risk deep personal traits of himself to Russell. Jesse continues to cry out.

"I moved out here to LA and to California for school and because this was supposed to be an open minded area, and I dropped out. I didn't know what to study, and I feel so lost. I don't know why I'm here, and what I'm supposed to do. I feel like an alien sometimes."

Jesse then incidentally rests his head on Russell's shoulder, and stares into the distance along with him. Looking at the night sky, and observing the barren and desolate shopping center. Russell then in this moment as well reveals more personal issues about himself, in an effort to make himself more comfortable with Jesse.

"My parents died when I was young, I never knew them. Growing up I've always been a chunky guy so I've dealt with shit for that. I was also the weird kid that they avoided and stayed away from. I was into science fiction stuff and paranormal stuff. I liked horror movies a lot."

Jesse while still having his head on his shoulder, continues to listen to Russell, and starts to close his eyes. Russell continues to describe his personal matters to Jesse, and finding common emotional ground for them both.

"I'm not originally from LA. I'm from Wisconsin actually. "The Cheese State" ... ha. Yeah California is pretty cool I guess. This place can get a little wild I suppose. But I like it. I also like politics and money, and that's why I went into banking..., not anymore. I'm probably at this point gonna consider going into stock exchange, I never want to work at a bank again."

Jesse opens his eyes and stares into the distance and responds to Russell.

"Me either, fuck that shit. After today, I'm permanently scarred for life. I don't ever want to be a bank teller again. So much pressure from what happened today. Ugh."

Russell who's continuing to look away from Jesse, laughs. Russell then starts to devilishly reveal a confession to Jesse.

"I know this is going to sound morbid, but I'd rob a bank before I work in a bank again. I'm being very serious. I would rob a fucking bank, and I'm sure I could do it well."

Jesse with his head still on Russell's shoulder, mutters to him.

"You can do whatever you want Russell. You're an intelligent man, you're a big strong man, you smell good, you look a little scary looking, in a handsome way though. But fuck it, if you want to rob a bank Russell, I don't care. I wouldn't blame you at all after the shit which happened today. I wouldn't blame you at all. I totally get it."

Russell continues to stare in the distance, nodding his head at Jesse. Russell continues.

"But I'm not gonna half ass it at all. I would be in the zone about it, and take it very seriously. I would need help of course. I can't do something like that alone."

Russell then looks down at Jesse for a while wanting his confirmation and reply. Then Jesse looks up at him, snapping back and feeling disturbed by what Russell said.

"I didn't say anything about helping you. I just said I feel for you, and I completely get why you would want to do something like that. Never did I once say I would help you out, and join your crusade on this. Russell, I don't want to talk about this shit okay?"

Jesse while gazing out of the horizon, then starts to develop an angry and bitter look on his face for a bit, still having his head on Russell's shoulder. Russell then sarcastically responds back to Jesse's request that the both of them suspend talking about this topic.

"Okay, I won't bring it up ever again in this lifetime Jesse. I didn't mean to offend or hurt you, and I won't talk about it anymore. I apologize, and I won't mention it."

Russell then takes his phone out to check the time. It is almost 11 P.M. He had not realized it was that late in the night. He looks down at Jesse who still has his eyes closed resting his head on his shoulder, looking very depressed. Russell looks out into the distance and smiles and chuckles to himself. The both of them continue to sit together at this location completely silent for a few minutes. Russell looks up at the night sky and starts to notice how unusually tan and orange the night sky is. There are some stars that are visible in the sky as well. This area that they are currently in is very quiet, and the environment makes it so that gazing and observing the night sky seems like a beautiful occurrence. Being in the city makes it extremely more difficult to appreciate natural earthly tones such as that. Whereas if you are situated in a more barren location, you can easily notice beautiful happenings like that.

The night air shows a gentle breeze, however there is still a humid vibe towards it as well. Russell feels safe and contempt with himself, and starts to feel guilty. He originally came here to this unknown location to dispose and get rid of Jesse, as he was starting to get irritated and annoyed by his company. Evidentially, the whole agenda backfired in a somewhat positive way, as he is in a calm and mellow mood. Jesse also seems to have gotten his wish, which was to spend more time with Russell. He was able to manipulate and control him into submission and control. Gradually showing great mental stress from not being in Russell's company. Ordinarily, Russell should have seen right through this, and understood the type of game Jesse was trying to play and convey. Due to the fact Russell himself also deals with mental issues, he is unable to deduce this and falls victim to unprecedented traps and digs himself into trouble.

Russell then started to investigate the outside area of this defunct department store himself and Jesse were at. It was indeed scary looking if you were there by yourself. But if you were with someone you trusted or loved or cared about, it would be an interesting spot to possibly make the sky the limit, and to look at it in a different perspective and shade. On the right of the store faces the highway that Russell got out off, surrounded by shady bushes, and tall evergreen trees. This area was located only about fifteen or so minutes away from the downtown Los Angeles area, but it seemed as though it was settled in a deep dark isolated forest area. Russell then saw how the windows and doors of the department store were covered and patched with wooden boards.

The delivery truck dock area himself and Jesse were sitting on, in which trucks can attach their trailers delivering goods to the store, were as well slammed with wooden boards and covered. There were however about twenty or so shopping carts that were pushed to the wall behind this area they were in. Russell stood himself off of the ramp, and continued to stare at the shopping carts with his hands in his pocket. Finally hatching an idea and thought inside his mind. He then started to offer Jesse a suggestion.

"There are some shopping carts over there. This lot is pretty large, and I just thought it would be fun if you sat in one of those carts and I pushed you around. I won't take no for an answer. Don't act like you don't want to do it. Come on."

Jesse then got off the ramp and stood up. He then started to look behind them, glancing towards the shopping carts with a puzzled look on his face.

"Well, alright. But if this is a trick for you to hurt or harm me… ugh. I'll play along, this sounds so ignorant, yet fun at the same time. Yeah, let's do it."

Russell while staring at Jesse, smiles and laughs at him.

"I don't know; it just might be a trick; I am psycho after all right? So you never know."

The both of them walk towards the shopping carts and Jesse arrives towards them first. He sits in one with his legs crossed, and his arms hanging holding onto the sides of the cart. Russell then removes his suit jacket and sets it down on the ramp area that they were sitting on. Immediately after that, he proceeds to push the cart that Jesse is sitting in all over the parking lot. While he's moving the cart, Jesse starts laughing. Russell is grinning heavily and enjoying the moment, pushing the cart with great speed and strength. It is almost as if he is using the shopping cart as a race car, and they are on a track.

Russell roughly and rapidly pushes the cart through the ground; swaying and turning the cart. Getting some sort of inspiration that it could also be an amusement ride as well. Jesse continues to laugh and giggle, and be amused by this activity they are doing. He trusts Russell completely, despite the fact this is perceived to be dangerous and hazardous stunt they are pulling, he seems to not care at all. Jesse wants to relish this moment and be completely engulfed in the magic of it. Russell decides to add humor to the situation, while obviously becoming lethargic and breathing his words out.

"…I'm gonna pretend this is "NASCAR" and I'm Jeff Gordon and you're the car. We're cruising through the circuit, we're gonna set a world record. Here comes the checkered flag, making another sharp turn. If we keep this speed up, we'll make it. We did it. World Record!"

Russell stops pushing the cart due to him being exhausted and puts his hands behind his back to rest and stretch himself. Jesse while sitting in the cart, starts to clap and whistle, and pretends to make crowd cheering noise like they were at a racetrack. Russell continues to catch his breath for a bit, with Jesse remaining in the cart. Jesse starts to get out of the cart, but Russell quickly lifts him out of it. They both then sit down at the ramp area they were at before. Russell then puts his suit jacket back on. While sitting in silence for a minute, Russell is still feeling winded from pushing the cart. Jesse turns to look at Russell who is looking around the lot, laughing at him with a smile on his face. Jesse was able to have fun and experience that random bout of happiness by riding in the cart. Russell although feeling tired, seemed very happy to be silly with Jesse. The both of them developed more connection over that, and it really shifted the mood that they were in. Jesse then starts to talk to Russell.

"I can't remember the last time I've done some wacky shit like that, it's been a while. Thank you so much for that, that was so much fun. I remember when I was like ten years old or so, me and some of the bay bay kids that lived in my block, we would take trash cans and use them as go karts and take them down hills."

Russell laughs at Jesse and they both stare out into the distance, and look at their surroundings. Russell then starts to explain similar antics he has done.

"Man, I was most likely in Junior High School I believe, but as I said I lived in Wisconsin, so it would snow like fuck over there. I remember the teachers at my school were really mean as hell, so we would build snow forts in the school parking lot, and take sleds and do ski jumping over the teacher's cars. Yeah, that was some pretty crazy stuff."

Jesse begins to wonder about how crazy Russell actually is, and how he comes up with these ideas he has. He wouldn't never think that Russell would suggest something as unusual as that, but he is happy that he did. Jesse asks Russell a question based on that.

"About the shopping cart thing, that was so random and I wasn't expecting that. I'm just kinda curious. I used to watch "Jackass" on

MTV a lot, and they would play around with shopping carts. You didn't have that in mind did you? I think you did?

Russell continues to look out from Jesse, and waits a while before he gives his response. He starts to laugh and smile for a bit, then responds to Jesse.

"I did watch Jackass yes, but no I didn't get the idea from that. I have a creative mind, and I am able to think of spontaneous things such as that. I like pranks, and I like foolishness sometimes. I think most people do as well, they are just too ashamed to admit I think."

Jesse laughs at Russell and they both look around the area. The fact they are both reminiscing about their youth, brings a lot of joy towards this originally deep situation. Unbeknownst to Jesse, Russell has a very untraditional, unconventional, and unpredictable imagination like that. It is not uncommon at all for Russell to come up with silly and inane ideas as he did, such as pushing Jesse in the shopping cart. Jesse as well seems to be his perfect candidate or partner for that, by being a willing participant. Not feeling scared or apprehensive from the mysterious actions that Russell exhibits towards him. Russell begins to profile the defunct department store, and wanting Jesse's opinion on his current thoughts.

"What do you think this store was? Possibly a "Kmart". A lot of "Kmart" stores went bankrupt and out of business here in California, and that's what this possibly is. Probably because this lot is out in a destitute area, is why another store hasn't resurfaced here. I just have a feeling that this used to be a "Kmart", and it makes sense to me."

Jesse also starts to gaze at the store, and examining it before responding to him.

"I can see why you would think that. I'm gonna agree with you. You seem like the kind of person that would know about that type of stuff. So I'll take your word Russell."

Russell then pulls out his phone again, and checks the time. Taking note as to how late it is, he puts his phone back in his pocket, and gets up from the ramp. He turns to look at Jesse, being very direct with him.

"Ah, it's getting really late, and I'm so tired. I think we've had more than enough fun tonight, so let's get going. Now if you want to stay, you can stay, I don't care. But I'm really gonna leave you this time. So if you want to come with me, I'm leaving now."

Jesse then looks at Russell and nods his head. He gets up from the ramp and walks with Russell back to his car. Jesse started to refresh all the shenanigans that they did in this abandoned lot. Understanding that Russell intended to actually reject him here at this location, they bonded more than they didn't really anticipate for. Jesse would never in a million years ever imagine that Russell would act the way he did. Being thankful for all the glory that was brought onto him. Still knowing that Russell being the mysterious person that he is, anything could happen.

As Jesse was walking back to Russell's car, he could only be in complete suspense over what is to come of their relationship next. Jesse isn't completely sure that this is leading to romance or not, or if Russell is alternatively simply being kind due to some other measures. Russell is not the type of man that is typically like that. He is a difficult person to study and to research on, especially when it comes to his emotions and personal relationships. Jesse for one last time gazes around this area they were in, and looks up at the night sky.

Russell as well for one final time takes note of this abandoned setting. He and Jesse both reach his car, and he unlocks the door. After getting into the car, they both sit in the vehicle for a couple minutes staring out of the windshield into the lot, in complete silence of each other. This silence isn't one of any negativity, but one of feeling safe and close towards each other's positions. Soon enough, Jesse peeks over at Russell and smiles at him. Russell also looks at Jesse and also grins at him. A few moments later, Russell starts the engine of his car, turns the car stereo on, and drives out of the deserted lot.

Russell continues to drive down the highway, headed towards his apartment in downtown Los Angeles. He did allow Jesse to sleepover, to which Jesse is very excited and anxious over that. Both of the men continue to stay quiet. Slowly but surely, it subconsciously feels like they are forgetting that the robbery that took place earlier, and that it didn't even exist. It's funny how the human mind can go into a temperamental escape zone such as that. Finding different coping methods to deal with trauma. Russell does that quite often when he is faced with events in his life that he isn't happy with. Attempting to find the bright side of a dull event, and being content with the results. Russell and Jesse continue to stay silent, but both of them are still thinking of plenty.

Russell in particular is most likely still doubting himself and unsure of the relationship that he's forming with Jesse. Wondering if he's being tricked by some type of voodoo or magic that Jesse is spraying onto him. Russell originally did not feel this type of way around him, now he seems to be captivated and attached to his energy. Jesse can also say the same, being somewhat attracted to the unpredictability that Russell continually puts out. Thinking to himself, he has Russell right where he wants him, in total control and showing some type of forced sympathy or empathy to him. Perhaps Russell feels sorry for Jesse which could explain his actions he's showing and displaying around him.

Russell continues to drive on the highway, continuing on their way towards his residence. Russell for curiosity reasons glances over at Jesse, who notices that he has started to close his eyes and lay his head back on the seat. He continues to drive before looking at Jesse again, and starts to feel concerned. Russell smiles and laughs to himself for a bit, and lowers the volume on the radio. He starts to talk to Jesse.

"Hey, are you alright? Are you tired? Are you sleepy? You seem kinda tired to me and I was just making sure that you are okay."

Jesse immediately opens his eyes and sits up in the seat. He looks directly at Russell and tilts his head at him. Right after he laughs at him, and turn his head forward. Jesse reaches for the stereo to turn the volume up, but before he does, turns his head and talks to Russell.

"No I'm not sleepy, I was just putting my head back in the seat. I'm fine."

Jesse then proceeds to turn the music on the radio up, and lays back in his seat again. Jesse then closes his eyes once more, relaxing. Looking at the way Jesse is behaving, it causes Russell to laugh. He for some reason finds it funny when Jesse shows an attitude towards him. He might not always like it, or be comfortable with it, but he does find it amusing. He continues to drive down the highway, having minor flashbacks of all the events that happened today. This day will be a very monumental one in his life, and one that he will always remember and play a major part from this point forward. Understanding all the twists and turns which happened, and all the problems he was faced with. The deaths of Jennifer and Peter are also flashing themselves in his memory. Harboring every single dramatic detail of the robbery that happened, just having to accept the emotional scars which come with the territory.

He and Jesse both are dealing with it the best way they can. He quickly is able to think about how the evening turned completely around. His new unprecedented bond with Jesse seems to mask most of it, and acts as a tool to make it easier to move on from the terrible memories. Becoming a changed man, and altering his mood and personality.

As Russell was approaching his residence, he began to glance at Jesse more and more, who looked as if he were asleep. In some ways, Russell was happy that Jesse was finally being obedient. Even though he had to basically pamper him in many ways this past evening in order for that to happen. It seems as though he has found some type of work around, to give into Jesse's behavior. He doesn't know how long he can keep this up for, as he doesn't wish or intend to be that nice to him and for Jesse to get too comfortable. That's all a part of the complexity of Russell's mind and how he operates. This will cause a butterfly effect for Jesse, as he will only try to manipulate Russell more into giving into him, and agreeing with his needs and wants.

Russell continues to drive down the highway, still thinking and contemplating over several things in his head. Jesse soon opens his eyes and sits up and looks out the window. Peeking at Russell, who has his eyes directed at the road. Jesse thinks about asking Russell a question, and turns his head towards him and is about to open his mouth, but then suddenly changes his mind. He leans his head back in the seat and shuts his eyes. Russell noticed Jesse attempt to talk to him as well, and is now curious as to what he wanted. The fact Jesse went back into his relaxed state makes Russell even more doubtful and curious as to what Jesse had on his mind. Russell continues to drive, until he reaches the highway exit, leading onto the surface streets. Russell continues to cruise the downtown Los Angeles area creeping up close to Midnight. Which it being the weekend, the streets are still booming with action. There are many nightclubs and bars still in operation, and still people walking around the sidewalk enjoying the nightlife. Los Angeles in many senses is a city that never sleeps, and it's always action packed. It's very customary to witness activity late in the night, and these types of occurrences happen.

Russell reaches a stoplight and takes a look at Jesse who is now again opening his eyes, and sitting himself up in the seat. Jesse scans the area and perceives that he's no longer on the highway, and getting closer to Russell's apartment. Jesse gazes at Russell for a couple seconds, then sits back in the seat with his arms crossed. While Russell is stopped at a red light, Jesse looks concerned over something. This time attempting to talk to Russell yet again. He lowers the volume of the stereo and turns his head to Russell's direction, and talks to him.

"Russell, I again want to say thanks for everything. I really mean it. This really does feel like the weirdest dream I ever had, but I'm happy I'm spending this time with you. Thank you for everything that you've done, and I'm so happy and blessed to be with you."

While he is still stopped at the light, Russell turns his head and smiles at Jesse. He then whispers to him in a soft tone, while running his fingers though Jesse's hair.

"You don't have to thank me. You don't have to do anything right now. All I want for you to do is be comfortable, and to feel safe. Everything is fine."

Jesse then smiles back at Russell, and turns the music on the radio up again. He then sits back in his seat shutting his eyes. Following this, the signal changes. Russell continues to drive down the road. Within a few minutes later, Russell approaches the parking lot of his apartment complex. Before entering the parking structure, he looks over and notices again Jesse has his eyes closed and is leaning back in the seat. Russell taps Jesse on the shoulder to get his attention. He then explains to him that they are going to be exiting the vehicle momentarily.

"My place is on the eighth floor of this building. You see that elevator there? We're gonna take that, and it's going to bring you up to my unit."

Jesse nods his head, and starts to pick up his tote bag from the ground and sets it on his lap. Russell then parks in his assigned parking lot, and proceeds to park and turn the engine off. He unlocks the car doors, and the both of them exit the vehicle. Russell after locking his car, forgot that he left his briefcase inside. After he retrieves he's briefcase, he locks his car again putting his keys in his pocket. Jesse then starts to follow Russell towards the elevator, standing directly behind him. After Russell hits the elevator button, he takes his phone out and checks some sports scores.

Jesse is both trembling with excitement, yet also feeling very anxious that he is going inside Russell's apartment. The elevators doors open, and Russell sticks his arm out, alerting Jesse that go in before him. While in the elevator, Russell keeps his head focused down towards the floor shaking his head, looking exhausted. Jesse continues to gaze and leer at him, being fascinated by him. The elevator then stops on the eighth floor, and once again Russell directs his arm out for Jesse to proceed. As they are walking through the hallways, Russell pulls out his phone yet again, and continues to browse through sports scores. While still looking at down at his phone, he speaks to Jesse.

"I'm in unit 822. It's further down. We're gonna make another turn to another hallway. It's quite a long way from the elevator which I hate, but I get used to it."

Jesse nods his head in agreement and continues to walk with Russell. Within a few moments, they finally reach Russell's apartment. Russell goes through his pocket and retrieves his keys again. He unlocks and opens his door and turns the lights in the living room on.

Upon walking into his apartment, Jesse starts to diagnose all the contents located inside. Looking inside his living room, Jesse notices that Russell has a pretty large fish aquarium, in which he is able to quickly figure out the type of fish inside.

"Those are clownfish right? They are so beautiful and pretty. Wow."

Russell after closing the door, nods towards Jesse, and takes his suit jacket off. He folds it up and places it on the back of the sofa. Jesse continues to observe many different things in Russell's apartment. Another thing that captivates him is the sports memorabilia that are hung on up on the walls. Russell has many framed sports jerseys, which captives Jesse very much. He seems to find them very fascinating, and begins to talk to Russell about it.

"I see some NFL stuff. I see a John Elway Bronco's jersey. I see Brett Favre Green Bay Packers jersey as well. I see some basketball stuff as well. I see a Magic Johnson and Kobe Bryant jersey too. I didn't know you were a Laker fan. You have a Michael Jordan Bulls jersey as well. You're a baseball fan too; That's a Babe Ruth jersey. I see an autographed hockey jersey as well. Russell, I'm not that familiar with hockey can you explain that one for me?"

Russell sets his briefcase down on the coffee table of his living room, and while looking at the jersey, answers Jesse's question concerning that particular one.

"Um, yes that's Gordie Howe. He passed away recently. I remember I had to probably been like six years old. My grandparents took me to go see him. That jersey I actually bought off eBay. I barely won the bid as a matter of fact. Yeah... that's the story behind that."

Russell then notices the frame is askew, and starts to straighten it out. Jesse continues to walk around his apartment, mentioning anything he deems noteworthy. He then notices an Andy Warhol Marilyn Monroe art piece.

"I really like this. I know that's Andy Warhol right? You like Marilyn Monroe too?"

Russell returns from the kitchen with two cans of Bud Light, handing Jesse one of them.

"I love Marilyn Monroe, yes. I like Andy Warhol's creativity. This I also barely snagged of eBay, and I'm so happy that I did. I really wanted it and had to have it."

Russell then walks towards his kitchen, as Jesse continues to look around Russell's apartment for a bit being very enthralled by what he picks up, then deciding to take a seat down on the sofa in the living room. Jesse then opens the beer Russell gave him, taking a few sips. As he's returning to the living room with bowl of potato chips, Russell sets them down on table in front of the sofa. Jesse eats a few of the chips. Russell stands next to the sofa, and starts to drink his beer. While still standing, he turns the big screen television set in his living room on. SportsCenter on ESPN is showing with Russell watching it, but the volume is on mute. Russell then takes his phone out of his pocket, and charges it in an electrical socket by the television. Jesse also notices that Russell has a PlayStation 4 console under the television set. After charging his phone, Russell then takes a seat on the sofa next to Jesse. He then proceeds to watch the television. Jesse is not at all interested in what Russell is watching, despite the fact Russell is enjoying looking at his program.

Minutes pass by, and they continue to stay silent as they both watch the muted television program. Russell continues to drink his beer, and Jesse does the same. At this point, Jesse is feeling nervous to ask Russell anything being that he is a guest. It seems as though Russell is going about his usual business and routine, as if Jesse weren't even in the room with him. Jesse eats some more of the potato chips, while looking at Russell. Jesse then can't take the silence anymore. Feeling bored, he tries to talks to Russell who has his eyes locked the television.

"So, you like watching this show huh? Why do you have it on mute like that, you can't hear what they are saying? I don't understand, that seems stupid to me."

Russell ignores Jesse's commentary, and continues to watch the television screen. Jesse who is now starting to feel like he's being ignored, is craving for attention. He lays his head on Russell's shoulder. Russell then in that moment shoves him off.

"I'm trying to watch my show, knock that shit off."

Jesse being ultimately upset at being ignored and being shunned by Russell, once again rests his head on Russell's shoulder, in addition he also starts to rub his hands across Russell's face. Russell this time doesn't brush him away, and continues to watch his program on the television and not paying Jesse any attention. Jesse takes even more risks in this current situation, and starts to rub his hand across Russell's chest. Russell however doesn't react at all to this and continues to ignore him. Jesse stops touching Russell, and finishes drinking his beer. Jesse sets his empty can down on the coffee table. He then eats a few more potato chips. After the television program goes to commercial break, Jesse gets up and walks behind the sofa where Russell is seated. He starts to massage Russell on the neck. This causes Russell to snap at Jesse again.

"I said to knock that off. I didn't tell you to do that. So knock it off."

Jesse walks back around the sofa, and sits down, staring at Russell very angrily. He then fires back at Russell.

"I'm sorry, If I want to touch you, I'm going to touch you. You're just going to have to understand that and get used to that. I always get what I want."

Jesse then takes the television remote that was on the table, and turns the television set off. Jesse then walks towards the other side of the living room, as Russell gets up after him.

"I don't find that funny. Give me the remote back now."

Jesse continues to tease Russell by running across the living room with the remote control. Russell feeling extremely agitated chases him until Jesse opens his bedroom door and runs in there. Jesse lays on top of Russell's large bed, still hanging onto the remote. Russell who's now starting to lose it, follows him in there, and turns on the light. While Russell is standing on the side of his bed, he tries to snag and grab the remote from Jesse who won't let it go. Jesse then starts to make a deal with Russell.

"I'll give you the remote, if you give me a kiss, and tuck me into bed. All you have to do is give me a kiss, that's all. I'll go straight to sleep and won't make any noise. You can go back to watching your television show, and I won't bother you at all. Is that a deal?"

Russell then starts to smile and laugh, and nods his head. Shortly after that, Jesse gives Russell the remote control, and Russell leans his head in and passionately kisses Jesse for almost ten seconds. Russell still smiling tucks Jesse into bed and covers him up, giving him another peck on his cheek. Jesse smiles back at Russell as he turns the lights in his bedroom off, and closes the door behind him going into the living room. Jesse falls asleep a couple minutes later.

CHAPTER 6:

NOTHING NEW, NOTHING USED

The morning sun gleaming through the curtains in Russell's bedroom, wakes Jesse. He struggles to open his eyes, yet finally accomplishes to. He looks around and peeks out the bedroom window. He notices that it is now daylight, and is curious as to what time it is. Jesse notices that Russell has a balcony connected to the bedroom window. He also takes note that Russell is not lying in the bed with him. Although Russell must have come back into the room at some point while he was resting, as Jesse is well aware than when he went to sleep, the curtains in the bedroom were shut. Still present in bed, Jesse turns his head and takes a peek at the alarm clock located on the nightstand. It is showing that it's 11 A.M. Jesse decides to remain in bed and closes his eyes again, with the blanket covering his head so the light from the sun doesn't disturb him. Jesse feeling still sluggish, starts to think about everything which happened the evening before and leading to Russell kissing him before he drifted off to sleep. Understanding that it was most likely not a dream, and having to be comfortable that he actually kissed Russell, although out of force and coercion to do so. Feeling very anxious and scared to get out of bed and face Russell now, wondering if he's upset or disappointed at him. Twenty minutes later the door to the bedroom opens. Even though Jesse heard he door open, he persistently remained motionless in bed. Russell comes into the room carrying a brown paper bag and two Styrofoam cups. He is wearing a red "USC" sweatshirt hoodie, and black Adidas sweatpants, he also has some sneakers on. He notices that Jesse is tucked away in the bed, and assumes he is asleep. He very delicately walks over to him without making much noise. He shakes him over the covers and and precedes to shout at him.

"Get the hell up, it's time to get up. This is isn't Motel 6, it's time to get up Jesse."

Jesse removes the covers and rises himself up from the bed, with his eyes still closed waking himself up. He is still wearing the same outfit he wore the day before. A few seconds later, he manages while still sitting on the side of the bed, to open his eyes completely and look at Russell who who's laughing at him. Russell then proceeds to walk out of the bedroom mentioning something to Jesse. While waving the paper bag and cups in the air.

"I went and got you something for breakfast, and some coffee. You drink coffee right? Well, anyways, it's time to get up, and if you want something to eat I got something for you."

Jesse who was looking out of Russell's bedroom window the entire time he was talking, turns his head towards Russell who is still standing in the doorway to ask him a request.

"Do you have something that I can change into? I've been in these clothes for two days now, and just ugh. I appreciate it if you do. I also noticed your USC jacket, you went there? I did too, but I dropped out. I didn't know what to study, so I dropped out."

Russell raises his eyebrows, then walks into the living room setting the coffee and bags of food hand on the living room table. As he reenters the bedroom, he slides open his closet doors, revealing his extensive collection of attire of all types and themes. Jesse decides to be nosy and take note of the articles of clothing in the closet. Russell has over fifteen different types of suits with different patterns. Across his closet door are also at least a hundred different neck ties. Russell starts to pick up different things in his closet with a serious look on his face.

"You attended USC too? Very interesting. Yeah that's the school I graduated from. Hmm, I think I might have something in here for you. You're being kinda prissy for whatever reason, but I'll never mind that. You're a lot smaller than me, so I don't want to give you something that isn't going to fit you."

Jesse then gets up from Russell's bed and crosses his arms standing behind Russell sifting through his closet. He responds to Russell feeling very angry.

"Russell, just give whatever you have that you can lend or borrow for me to wear. Is that too much to ask? If I knew it was going to be this difficult, I would have never asked you, and frankly just would have kept these clothes on really."

Russell ignoring Jesse, continues to goes through the items in his closet. When a couple minutes pass with Russell rummaging through clothes, Jesse sees something that catches his eye, and something he would be fine wearing. He walks over to Russell's closet, and grabs a white artistic graphic T shirt that has Abraham Lincoln with sunglasses on it.

"I'll just take this Russell. I'll keep my bottoms on, none of your pants will fit me."

When Jesse goes to the bathroom to undress and freshen himself up, Russell proceeds to close his closet doors, and walk into the living room. He immediately directs himself to his kitchen to grab to plates, and returns to the living room setting the plates down. Russell begins taking the contents of the brown paper bag out. Inside the bag are ham and cheese bagel sandwiches, which he had gotten at a donut shop he likes not far from his apartment. He then turns his television set on and turns to a college basketball game and sits on the sofa. Russell then starts to eat one of the bagel sandwiches. A couple minutes pass, and Jesse comes out of the bathroom. He folds his discarded clothes, and puts them next to this tote bag sitting under the coffee table. Right after that, he sits down next to Russell. Jesse takes a look at the food on the table and begins to take a few bites of it, seeming to enjoy it.

"This is nice, I haven't had a ham and cheese bagel in quite some time."

Russell while looking at the television screen also eating, smiles at him.

"Yeah, I figured you like it. I was just very hungry and I figured it would be rude as hell if while I was out, I didn't get you something either. Their coffee is good too."

Jesse scrunches his face at Russell, and picks the starts to drink the coffee.

"Russell I don't really drink coffee. I mean I do, but I don't. But this tastes good to me."

The both of them eat their breakfast, and Russell continues to chat with Jesse.

"Man, you are a strong sleeper. I slept here on the couch because I didn't want to bother you, and were not lovers. If I would have slept with you, that would have presented the wrong idea. I know we kissed last night, but I just did that because I was little buzzed from that beer I drunk, and you would have continued to be a whiny bitch if I didn't give in, so congratulations. But I woke up at 9 and saw you were still deep asleep, so I left you alone."

Russell takes another bite of the bagel sandwich, still paying attention to the basketball game on the television, and continues to talk to Jesse.

"I was just playing around and enabling you. So just pretend that never happened okay? We're just friends if you want to call it that."

Jesse then starts to feel anxious again and scared, and wants to reply to Russell about the kiss they had. He takes a couple swallows of the coffee and turns to Russell, yet decides to bring up an unrelated issue instead, before talking about it.

"You're watching basketball, that's cool I guess."

Russell while still keeping his head towards the screen responds to Jesse.

"Of course I'm watching College Basketball. It's Saturday and that's all I really watch is sports on Saturday. It better be cool, it's my house and I can watch what I want, thank you."

They both continue to eat, when Jesse this time talks about something on his mind.

"Russell, you're so full of shit. You don't play around like that. You kissed me because whether you want to admit it or not, you possibly feel sorry for me, or...forget it. Ugh."

Russell finishes his sandwich and starts to drink the rest of his coffee. When the basketball game takes an advertising break, he turns the channel to CNN. He then while having his vision directed at the television, replies to Jesse very harshly.

"Right, that's exactly what I said. I only kissed you because you were being a whiny bitch. If I said no, you would have had a fit and cried. You're like a damn woman, Jesus Christ. I was also a little drunk, I was tipsy all last night to be honest, and so you were you. So enough."

Jesse finishes his food, and turns to look at Russell watching television. While still watching the screen, Russell proceeds to attack Jesse.

"I want my handkerchief back too. I saw you snag it last night. Yeah. I never said you could keep it, and that's one of my favorite ones too, so I need it back, right now please."

While drinking his coffee, Jesse then goes through his tote bag. As he is going through it, Russell takes his eyes off the television, and watches him. Jesse then pulls Russell's handkerchief out the bag, but instead of handing it to him, he swings it in the air teasing him with it. Russell then looks puzzled and tries to grab it form Jesse who swings it back from him.

"Oh you mean this handkerchief? With my tears, spit and snot on it? No, I'm going to keep it. Since you want to play around, I'm going to play around. Now we're Even Steven."

Jesse then puts the handkerchief in his pocket. Following that, Russell storms into his bedroom and comes out with a leather belt and with force, swats it at the back of the couch which causes Jesse to quickly get up and run to the other side of the living room in fear.

"I said give me my fucking handkerchief back Jesse."

Jesse then stops running around the room for a minute, and laughs at Russell. He then notices Russell looking unapprovingly about this situation, and stops laughing. He walks over where Russell is, pretending to hand him the handkerchief, but quickly swings it away.

"I don't care if you whip me with that belt, Russell you used to scare me, but you don't anymore. You're not getting the handkerchief back, so forget it."

Russell then scoffs to himself, and shakes his head.

"Yeah because you're sadistic. I'm sadistic at times as well, but you're completely different. I don't know what's the deal with you sometimes."

Jesse looks him straight in the eyes and begins to mock him.

"Go ahead Russell, hit me with the belt, I'm not scared of you."

Russell hesitates for a few seconds, but then in a swift manner playfully beats him on the behind softly with the belt. Jesse then laughs at Russell.

"That hurt so much. NOT! I knew it. Russell. I make you so weak, ha-ha."

They both continue to stare at each other in silence for a few seconds, before Russell raises the belt up in the air, and responds to Jesse.

"You should know that was only a test, the next one won't be like that at all."

Jesse is not at all convinced and doesn't believe him, and starts to laugh at him. Russell then throws the belt on the ground, and crosses his arms together, grinning.

"You can have my handkerchief, but don't lose it okay. That's the handkerchief that I had in my pocket during everything that went down yesterday, so it's a piece of history if you think about it. I trust you with it, so don't lose it, alright?"

After Jesse nods his head, Russell goes to the bedroom to put the belt away. Jesse then takes a seat on the couch and watches the television set, although not being interested as to the particular program that is being shown. Russell returns to the living room and sits beside Jesse. Upon returning, he changes the channel back to the basketball game. Both of men sit in silence on the couch with Jesse being extra obedient watching the basketball game as well. Jesse then remaining on the couch goes through his tote bag, and decides to check his phone. Russell continues to watch the television ignoring Jesse. Jesse gets himself up from the couch and walks to the other side of Russell's living room with a concerned look after looking at his phone. He starts to listen to his voicemails, having a worried and shocked expression on his face as listens on the phone. He covers his mouth and starts to pace back and forth around the room. Jesse is beginning to panic to a dangerous extent, feeling depressed and roaming around the room feeling anxious. After Jesse hangs up his phone and puts it in his pocket, Russell looks up at him and starts to feel concerned.

"What's wrong? Something happened, so just go on ahead and tell me."

Jesse remains silent towards Russell and storms back to the sofa area to grab his tote bag located under the coffee table. Jesse then roughly walks towards Russell's front door. He stops himself at the door, and out of anger, Jesse throws his tote bag on the floor, and begins to cry. Russell who's watching him the entire time gets up from the sofa and rubs him on the shoulder. Jesse cries out to Russell.

"You need to take me home now; I'm might be getting evicted, I don't know. My landlord doesn't listen, and she's a lunatic. It's a complex situation I'm in."

Jesse then leans his head inside Russell's chest, as Russell comforts him by running his hands through his hair. Jesse continues to cry.

"I'm usually good with finances, I always pay my rent; but I did refuse to pay this month's rent which was due yes, for good reason. The landlord like I said, this woman is just an evil witch. The building I'm in isn't fit for people to rent out of, and she refuses to fix the issues. So I refused to pay the rent until she did. I was looking for a new place to stay, and was gonna move out anyways. With what happened yesterday, I totally forgot I was dealing with this."

Russell continues to embrace and comfort Jesse, as Jesse explains more of his troubles.

"She just left me a voice mail this morning, and she basically said all of my stuff is going to be in the hallways, and if I want my security deposit back, to come and see her. All of what she is going is technically legal as well, so. This is not fair at all, nothing is going right."

Jesse continues to hold onto Russell for a minute, and then separates from him. He proceeds to grab his bag off the floor, but Russell grabs it, and hands it to him. Russell then immediately grabs his keys from his pocket, and shuts the television off. He walks back towards the doorway and notices that Jesse is still crying. He stops to talk to him.

"I can take you there right now. Don't worry, everything will be fine."

They both hug again for a minute, before walking out of Russell's apartment. They both head towards the parking lot of Russell's complex. While walking, Jesse looks down towards the ground ashamed of himself feeling much sorrow. Under so much anxiety to even give Russell eye contact, thinking as though he's a burden towards him. Jesse is under a great deal of stress, and trying to keep himself together. Although he has much on his mind he isn't talking to Russell at all. Russell is walking beside him, also staying silent. They eventually reach Russell's car, and they both get in. Jesse continues to pan down at the floor, and continues to stay silent and cry. Russell shows empathy and tries to comfort him.

"Hey, it's going to be fine alright. Don't cry. I don't like to see you sad okay? So don't cry, it's gonna be fine. Whatever happens, I'm here for you. Okay?"

Jesse continues to cry and look down towards the floor. Russell takes his phone out of his jacket pocket, and charges his phone in the socket located under the car stereo. He glances at Jesse feeling very concerned over him, and shakes his head. Russell directly following that, goes through a pocket located above next to his sun visors and pulls out his aviator sunglasses. He then starts the engine. He backs out of the parking structure and heads towards the road. Jesse looks up from the floor to stare at Russell who's driving. Jesse tries to toughen himself up, and reaches in his tote bag to pull out a pair of sunglasses. He then turns the car stereo on, laying back in the seat. Jesse while looking out of the window, notices how much of a clear and perfect sunny day it is. In any normal circumstances, it's a lovely Saturday afternoon. The California weather in this particular day is really working overtime. It is quite warm, but it's not that humid either, as there is wind that intermittently shifts the air. The temperature is clearly perfect and this day strictly has immaculate weather. Jesse continues to peek out the window as Russell focused on driving. He looks at all the palm trees, which stand unbelievably tall. These types of trees are plenty in Los Angeles, and are a wonderful sight to look at. Jesse thinks to himself, how this would be lovely beach weather. On a warm day such as this, being able to go to the beach being trapped in a view such as that. To be captivated by the beauty of the ocean waves and the scent of the sea. Feeling comfortable and looking at the beauty of that scene. Jesse continued to get lost in his thoughts, before he is interrupted by Russell.

"I don't mean to fire you up, but you never told me where you live."

Jesse looks at Russell feeling very puzzled. He turns forward before responding to him.

"I thought I did. I'm pretty sure I told you were I lived didn't I?"

Russell takes one hand off the steering wheel and rubs the back of his head, and then laughs to himself. He then glances over at Jesse still smiling.

"No you didn't. You just said you lived in Inglewood. You never told me an exact address or street you lived on. You simply said you lived in Inglewood."

Jesse then covers his mouth with his hands and looks ashamed. He then without asking him grabs Russell's phone and opens up a map application. He starts to enter in information through the phone, and sets Russell's phone back under the car stereo. Jesse then turns his head towards Russell who is focused on the road, and talks to him.

"I hope you don't mind, I went through the GPS on your phone and put in the exact location. It's extremely hard to get into, it's off Crenshaw and there are a lot of one way and dead end streets in South LA, so you have to be careful and know what you're doing."

Russell looks at Jesse and grins at him. Then turns his head back forward.

"Well yes I do mind, that's my phone and that's my property. I have personal things on my phone. But I trust you and it's okay. I'm gonna let that slide this time."

Jesse smiles at him and returns to looking out the window. Russell continues to drive towards their destination, listening to the GPS system shout out directions. It instructs him to get on the highway. When exiting the highway as instructed by the GPS system, he returns to the surface streets. As they both are soon approaching where Jesse lives, Jesse starts to be alarmed over something he didn't consider up until this moment. He starts to become scared, and nervous and afraid to bring it up. There are many controversial social stigmas going through his mind as he is not sure how to bring them up. Most importantly, he is not sure if Russell is aware of the area that he lives in. Being that Russell lives in a more simplistic part of Los Angeles, and Jesse does not. Jesse stays silent about it, and tries to brainstorm how he can relay these thoughts to Russell, in the most proper way. When Russell reaches a stoplight, Jesse uses that time to mention it. He turns his head towards Russell, to mention something to him.

"Russ, I need to be honest with you. The part of town where we are going is kinda rough. I've been robbed and had guns pointed at me and all types of shit. There are gangs, and you will most likely see gang members walking about. I might be okay, but because you're a white guy, I don't know. If someone says something or if you see something don't take it personal."

The light changes and Russell proceeds down the road, and responds to Jesse.

"I wish someone would try something. I do play football and I'm a pretty big guy, so to me that's foolish for me to be insecure like that. I appreciate the concern though."

After hearing Russell say that, Jesse has an unsure look on his face. Still concerned over Russell's profile and if he was truly understood, Jesse goes more in depth to the point he was trying to make, giving somewhat dismissive truths about Russell.

"Russell, that's not quite what I meant. You might think that, but you're never lived in the hood. You're just a white guy from Wisconsin who lives in downtown LA. Yeah you listen to rap music, but you still have no idea, you don't. All my life I've been accustomed to this lifestyle, and you haven't. I'm just telling you to watch out. That's all."

Russell reaches another stoplight and fires back at Jesse disagreeing with him.

"Hey, stop all that bullshit. All of that is going in one ear, and out the other for me. I don't think like that, you shouldn't either. Again, I appreciate you looking out for me, but now you're starting to mix things up. You have a very negative liberal mindset to think like that. What you just said is also kinda racist too. Making all of those assumptions. Wow."

Russell shakes his head and turns to give Jesse an aggravated look. He is confused and doesn't know what Jesse is really trying to convey. He doesn't truly understand, and doesn't wish to analyze or compartmentalize any of it. Russell continues down the road, with Jesse looking guilty with this head looking down towards the floor. Jesse was afraid that the conversation would turn into something like that, and still feels that Russell doesn't understand the nature of the topic. Sometimes the truth does hurt, and certain agendas need to be explained in a certain form in order to get their correct meanings and value across. It becomes difficult to explain it in a way, so the other party isn't offended or feels damaged because of it. Jesse continues to peek out the window as Russell continues to drive. He takes peeks at Russell every few seconds, fermenting his own personal thoughts and feelings. Perhaps Jesse is making snap dismissive judgments and stereotypes, that don't merit anything. Jesse wonders why Russell feels so confident in himself towards the matter, yet he himself doesn't. Ultimately feeling that maybe he clearly just didn't get his point across in a clear and concise manner as much as he wanted to. Jesse then sits back with his arms folded, feeling silenced and censored. Russell turns his head towards Jesse, and notices his body language. He returns this by scoffing to himself and shaking his head. Standing by his own personal stance, that Jesse is possibly generalizing and undermining

Russell as well. Not at all understanding why Jesse would quickly turn to opinions and thoughts like that. Russell once more turns to look at Jesse, who still has head down, and pats his shoulder. Jesse looks up at him and smiles.

A couple minutes after that, Russell arrives down the neighborhood where Jesse lives. As he's driving down this neighborhood, he is experiencing a culture shock to himself. He immediately becomes struck in his mental thoughts, and starts to almost feel that possibly Jesse was right. He notices the unusual display of graffiti on practically every building. He notices a high amount of vagabonds sleeping in the street. Russell then observes the amount of defunct and closed storefronts, and is completely stunned and shocked. He looks at all the condemned houses and residential buildings that are in terrible condition. He starts to think to himself how could this stretch of town get to this type of level and state? It didn't make any sense to him at all, and a rush of confusion goes through Russell's head. Alternatively, Russell then starts to feel glad about himself thinking of the positives towards this; that he was immersed and introduced to this type of experience. He gains a bigger picture and idea towards something that before witnessing, he had very minor prior knowledge on. Russell went back to the conversation he had minutes ago with Jesse. Thinking to himself that although he was not completely agreeing with what everything Jesse mentioned, starts to understand and discover a different point of view, and listening to another person's observations on a particular issue is still beneficial. Russell steadily drives through the neighborhood, and investigates more of the area.

Jesse grew up attached to life like this, so none of this is a surprise to him. Jesse just knew that he had to look at it through Russell's eyes as well, and offer sentiment's based on that. As they are proceeding through the street, Russell becomes more and more amazed and surprised at his findings and new discoveries. Jesse turns his head towards Russell; could tell by the look on Russell's face that he seems frozen by this.

"Yeah, this is the hood Russell. Welcome. I tried my best to explain it to you, but you needed to see this. You can think what you want to think, but I tried to tell you."

Russell continues to scan around the area taking in everything that he is witnessing. They finally reach their destination; outside of Jesse's building. Russell parks his car on the side of the building, and they both exit the car. As they are approaching the building, Jesse and Russell remove their sunglasses. Jesse then takes a look at the landlord's window, and notices that she is peeking at the both of them through her curtain. She quickly closes the curtains when she is spotted. Jesse continues to the entrance of his building unlocking the front door. Russell looks around the apartment building which has many tenants playing loud music in their units, and a bunch of children running up and down the staircases. He also sees a homeless man sleeping on the far end of the hallway. Jesse takes a look at Russell observing the building, and taking note of his puzzled face.

They both continue to proceed down the hall, with Russell being in shock. A short while later, they finally reach Jesse's apartment. When they arrive at his door, Jesse reaches into his bag, and pulls his keys out. Unfortunately, he starts to struggle to unlock the door. He puts the key into the door, but it will not turn or open. Russell watches him have trouble with this, but he stays silent not knowing what to say. Jesse continues to try to unlock the door with no success. Starting to panic, Jesse then realizes that the landlord has possibly changed the locks on the door, so that he wouldn't be able to get in. He explains this to Russell.

"She changed the locks. I can't believe she changed the fucking locks. That's why I can't get in. Ugh, I can't stand that woman. This is some bullshit. Come with me."

Jesse is well aware that the landlord is in her apartment, as when they were entering the building, he saw her looking out her window. With Russell following him, he proceeds to walk towards her door. Jesse knocks on the landlord's door. A couple minutes pass, and no one comes to the door. Jesse knocks once more, but this time the door opens. The landlord steps out of the door, and quickly shuts it behind her. She is named Lisa Corrigan. She is forty-nine-year-old Caucasian woman, who has short brunette hair. She wears thick circular glasses, and wears very off color makeup. She has a very creepy stature. Her body is extremely thin and shaped like a spider, and the woman is always smoking a cigarette. She wears a nightgown with blue fuzzy house slippers consistently, even during the daytime. She then turns to look at Jesse and talks to him smoking a cigarette. In a very rude tone, she

"What do you want? I'm very busy right now, so what is this about?"

Jesse shouts out to her in emotional rage.

"You know damn well what this is about. I just went to my door, you changed the locks. It's one thing if you want me out of here, that I can understand and deal with. It's another thing if you keep me from getting my things and lock me out. This isn't kosher at all and you know it."

Russell after hearing that, starts to unintentionally snicker at Jesse, but tries to quickly contain himself. Lisa who's smoking her cigarette looking away from his face into the hallway, then in a very harsh and strict tone responds to Jesse.

"I gave you plenty of time to get your shit and move. You haven't paid rent in almost three weeks, so to me that's grounds for an eviction. So I can't help you. Sorry."

Jesse looks at Lisa in disgust and tilts his head at her, firing back.

"Sweetheart, the reason I didn't pay you rent, is because the plumbing sucks here. We don't get any gas or hot water. Everyone here on the first floor myself included, our ceilings are always leaking from upstairs units. Electricity is always cutting off. Do you want me to continue? You refuse to fix these problems. I also told you I was moving as well."

Lisa takes more puffs of her cigarette looking away from Jesse.

"Look, I don't have time for that bullshit, I don't. The fact is, you don't live here anymore, and I have to rent your unit out to make money, so hit the road."

Feeling aggravated Jesse continues to talk to her.

"I'm not asking for my security deposit back, you can have it, I don't care. I do want for you to unlock my unit so I can get my belongings and I can go. That's all I'm asking for."

Lisa continues to scan her head across the hallway of the building, taking puffs of her cigarette. She then persistently continues to yell at Jesse.

"Well I wasn't going to give you back the security deposit back anyways. I only mentioned that if you want it back to come and see me, in which I was going to tell you that you can't have it anyways. Ha-ha. I never said I was going to give it to you. Now beat it!"

Jesse continues to look at her sideways and spout out his anger. Russell decides to try and talk to Lisa who is still looking away from them, hoping to coax her attitude.

"Hey lady, this guy has been through a lot okay. I'm his friend and he's going through issues. Just give him a break this time please. Have some heart lady."

For a few moments, Lisa stays silent, then turns her head towards Jesse shouting at him.

"I said no, and my answer is no, and I need you to leave right now. I'm not going to change my mind, so leave and get out of my face!"

Russell puts his hands over his face in rage, and begs towards Lisa.

"Lady please, just let him get his stuff. We'll leave."

Lisa then ignores the both of them, and continues to smoke her cigarette looking bothered. Jesse spouts at her, reaching his breaking point.

"Bitch can you at least let me get my things? I need to get my things and I'll be gone. You'll never see me again. I want to get my stuff. That's all I want."

Lisa stays silent for almost a minute, taking puffs of her cigarette. She turns his head towards Jesse looking at him in a disgusting manner feeling defeated and stuck. She then reaches in the pockets of her nightgown, and pulls out a set of keys and hands them to Jesse.

"You have one hour to get your shit and get the fuck out of my building. I don't ever want to see you again after that. Consider yourself lucky you caught me on good day."

Lisa then immediately goes into her residence, and slams the door shut behind her. Jesse then walks towards the door of his apartment, then stops himself and is about to tell Russell something. However, Russell has an idea of what he has on his mind and cuts him off.

"You don't have to say anything. You can stay with me for as long as you want. Don't mention it. I can help you move whatever you need."

Jesse then gives Russell a hug, and opens the door to his apartment. As the both of them enter, Jesse asks Russell a request.

"Russ, I need you to go and get me some cardboard boxes and tape. I'm pretty much only gonna take a few things. My clothes, and other important stuff. Everything else I'm gonna leave behind. I don't want any of it. Thanks again."

Russell nods his head and directs himself to pick up the items that Jesse requested. Jesse puts everything that he's wanting to keep in separate piles of the room, so it's easy for him to know that to take. When Russell arrives back at Jesse's apartment with the boxes and tape, he doesn't hesitate to help him pack his things. Jesse notices his kindness.

"Russell you don't have to do that, but I appreciate it. Thanks."

Russell smiles at Jesse and takes his phone out of his pocket to turn on an internet radio station playing pop music. He then continues to put his things into the cardboard boxes. Jesse while putting his things away is sidetracked when he picks up a picture. He diagnoses the picture for quite some time, with Russell looking curious. Jesse then explains the picture to him.

"This is my mother and I in this picture. I was three years old in this picture, and she passed away of a drug overdose soon after this sadly. This is the only picture I have of her."

Jesse then starts to cry and feel depressed over the picture. Russell noticing how upset Jesse looks, then walks over to him, and starts to rub the back of his shoulder. He then offers his empathy and compassion, and whispers to him.

"I'm so sorry, Jesse."

Jesse begins to calm himself down after that, and puts the picture in a cardboard box. Russell then goes back to helping Jesse store his things in the boxes. Russell starts to understand Jesse even more, considering his tough background. Russell himself hasn't had it easy, but looking at it from the perspective that Jesse has gone through puts it into another light. Knowing that this time yesterday, he was only his boss, now becoming a very strong intricate person in his life. Russell prides himself on having that type of perception on how events manifest. Jesse seems very blessed to have developed this bond with Russell, and appreciates all of his actions. Going through a lot stress, he perseveres with it from his contact with Russell. The both of them continue to pack things away, until they finally conclude. Jesse then turns to Russell.

"Okay Russell, that's it. That's all I'm taking. Everything else I don't care about and it can stay, I don't want it. From what I do have, all of this will fit in your truck right?"

Russell after scanning the room and examining the moderate amount of boxes Jesse has, he nods his head in approval and responds to him.

"Yeah it will no problem. This will all fit okay. I'll start carrying these right now."

Russell very easily lifts a couple of the boxes and walks them out the building. He then puts them in the back of his vehicle. Jesse right behind him also brings a couple boxes. Within the next few minutes, they manage to transport all of the boxes into Russell's car. Russell takes a seat in the car, puts his sunglasses back on and turns the stereo on. Jesse then walks over to Lisa's door, and returns the keys to her. Following that, he gets into Russell's car putting his sunglasses on, and they both drive off. During the drive back to Russell's residence on the highway, Jesse turns the stereo up his car and starts dancing to the music. The song he is listening to is Spice Girls "Love Thing". Jesse is miming to the music almost perfectively, and completely in his own zone. Russell while keeping his eyes focused on the road, would occasionally look at him in amusement laughing and grinning. He is happy to see that Jesse enjoying himself and in experiencing a happy and satisfied mood. Russell starts to become relaxed himself, understanding the good deed he did, allowing Jesse to stay with him. As Jesse carries on listening to the music, Russell simply watches him have fun. Being more laid back with his personality; being more of an introvert to Jesse's extroverted personality. Russell believes that as long as he can make others happy, he's fine with that. He's more than contempt that Jesse is feeling safe. He is also well aware that Jesse is performing for him and craving attention. At this point, he has gotten used to how his behavior operates and constructs itself. Russell approaches the parking lot of his residence and parks his car. He and Jesse take their sunglasses off, and Russell turns the ignition off and opens the back hatch of his vehicle. After grabbing a couple boxes, Russell talks to Jesse.

"Go and hit the elevator button and wait for it to come. When the door opens, hit the switch to keep the doors open, we can put all your boxes in the elevator lift easily that way."

Jesse nods his head in agreement and obeys what Russell told him to do. With the doors of the elevator held open, they load all of the boxes onto the elevator without any issue. As the elevator reaches Russell's floor, Jesse holds the elevator doors open again. Russell reaches his door and sets the boxes down. After unlocking the door, he puts the boxes in the living room, instructing for Jesse to do the same.

"You can put them all right there, that's fine."

About ten minutes later, himself and Jesse are able to transport all of the boxes. Russell goes into the kitchen and grabs two bottles of water, giving Jesse one. He takes a seat on the sofa, and turns the television set on, watching a baseball game. Jesse proceeds to walk over to the sofa and lounge on it next to him with his legs extending on the sofa, laying his head down on Russell's lap like a pillow, also looking at the ball game. Russell continues to watch the baseball game going into later innings; it seems to be evenly matched. When the game reaches a commercial break, he apparently begins to experience a bout of mental depression from the events which happened the day before. He tries to escape himself from that and advance from it, but it still haunts his mind. The trauma is still presenting itself, and it's impossible to forget at times. Being completely understandable that a situation such as that would forever cause horrific feelings. Russell tries to squash his depression and find a solution to cover it up. The fact he is now with Jesse watching baseball which he loves, is a good start. Slowly but surely erasing the negativity from his mind and drifting into a state of pleasure. Wanting to feel safe in this current time. He continues to lay back on the sofa with Jesse laying down on the couch. Jesse then asks Russell a question while still resting his head on Russell's lap.

"You said you weren't going to go bank to banking, and that you wanted to do stock exchange. So you really want to do that for work?"

Russell while looking at the baseball game responds to Jesse.

"It was kinda just me suggesting things. You're damn right I no longer want to work in a bank. I'll repeat what I said last night as well. I'd rob a bank before I work in one again."

Jesse laughs at Russell, but wants to reaffirm he's being sincere with his comments.

"Russ, do you really mean that or are you joking. I think last night you were joking, and I think you might be joking again today, but I want to make sure if you are, or aren't."

Russell ignores him, and watches the baseball game and stays silent. In actuality, Russell was not joking and he was contemplating these thoughts. The issue and problem was if he wanted to let Jesse be aware of these thoughts. The baseball game takes another break, and Russell decides to be honest, expressing all of his feelings.

"I'm being serious, and I was being serious last night as well. I would totally rob a bank, and do it well. I mean, I don't see why I couldn't be able to. I know everything about banks, corner to corner. It would be the perfect way to avenge Peter's death if you think about it too. How much I fucking hate working for banks. Never again will I work in one."

Jesse then oddly starts to completely understand where Russell is coming from.

"You know what Russell; I don't blame you. If you were you I'd rob a damn bank too. I don't know, I mean, the free money would be nice, but it's more of being a rebel. Society is so shit nowadays and it's so easy to just not give a fuck anymore you know?"

They both continue to lounge on the couch thinking about this drastic subject. Russell continues to press about the subject of robbing a bank.

"I wouldn't be able to do it alone, I would need a team, I would need a system. I would be the inside guy, or the mastermind behind the operations. Like I said, I know everything you need to know about banks, I could totally do it."

Jesse then shockingly while still resting his head on Russell's lap, looks up towards Russell and agrees and encourages Russell's insane thoughts.

"Russell you know what, if you need my help, you can count me in. If you want to rob a bank, and you can promise that we won't get caught, I'm there every step of the way. I think you're crazy for wanting to do it, but I'd be lying if I said I wasn't excited over this."

Russell smiles and laughs at Jesse's reply. Russell can have a dangerous imagination at times. Even though he is an intelligent, he on occasion can be a dangerous and unpredictable type of man. He is well aware of his harmful agendas, yet he strives on the enjoyment on fulfilling them. He continues to grin, while keeping his head facing the baseball game on the television, as he runs his fingers through Jesse's hair very softly. Russell then speaks to Jesse.

"Yeah, I'm gonna rob a fucking bank. Do I feel bad about doing it? Hell no. Just one bank though. Well, maybe two depending on how well we do for the first one. People rob banks all the damn time. They robbed ours yesterday and we nearly got fucking killed. I agree with you Jesse; how do they expect us not to react this way?"

Russell continues to rub his fingers through Jesse's head on his lap. When the baseball game takes another break, he turns the television to CNN. Russell then after watching the stories on the news network, begins to feel emotional, and continues ranting in a devastating manner.

"Peter and Jennifer died, just like fucking that. They didn't deserve any of that. Jennifer, beautiful girl. Peter, he was like fucking Christ himself. The man was amazing. They are now gone, and I just don't fucking understand it. Me, you, Yvette, everybody is fucking scarred for life. I just don't understand. I was a good bank manager Jesse wasn't I?"

Jesse nods his head as Russell continues to cry and vent out his emotions.

"This world is sick and sad Jesse. This is a sick sad world. It's rare that there are people like you and me, and we just don't give a fuck. From this point on, fuck it. I'm going to do what I want, and follow what I want. If I want to work for the stock exchange, I'll work for the stock exchange. If I want to rob a bank, I'm gonna rob a damn bank. That's the damn truth."

Russell starts to grin heavily, and Jesse proceeds to nod his head to agree with Russell. With the both of them continuing to stay on the sofa, Jesse responds to Russell.

"This is a dog eat dog society Russell. That's how it works, and that's how it's always gonna work and operate. What happened yesterday happens all the time. The government does it just more sneakily and in a more secret way. But when they do it, it's extremely worse."

Russell takes a swallow of his water, and turns the television back to the baseball game. Still caressing Jesse's hair, he returns to exclaiming his thoughts.

"Government does a lot shit. They are spreading chemtrails to brainwash all of us Jesse to think and act certain ways. Probably why I'm attracted to other men because of that shit. No offense to you, I mean, I love you Jesse, but you know I wouldn't be myself if I weren't honest. So I know you won't take offense to that. But yeah, fuck the government."

Jesse laughs while looking at the television screen, and responds to Russell.

"It's okay Russell, I'm used to the way you talk by now. But you know that's bullshit. Sexuality has nothing to do with that. Well at least not for me, I don't know about you Russ. I've always been gay, ever since I was little, so I can't agree with you on that one."

Russell while grinning continues talking about what's on his mind.

"People are being replaced by robots too. I don't understand that shit either. Money is being replaced by virtual funds and crypto currency and shit. Wow. It's unbelievable how society works and how the government can piece together all of that. I can't wrap my mind on it."

Jesse stays silent as Russell continues to ramble and rant. Russell gets highly involved with conspiracy theories, and once he has started with these thoughts, he's usually on a roll and continues to fire out his opinions. Jesse seems to be somewhat entertained and amused by Russell, and listens well when he speaks of such things. This is more than likely some type of tool Russell is using to deal with the mental stress he experienced the day before, and using the discussion on delicate topics and on phenomena, to make sense of trauma that is on his mind. Wanting to escape into his own thoughts, with Jesse being his metaphorical lap dog, listening and agreeing to anything that Russell says. For nearly a half hour more, Russell continues, sometimes being unaware that he's ranting, with Jesse laying on his lap. Eventually, he is interrupted when someone begins to knock on his door. Jesse gets up to answer it.

"Russell, I'll go get it."

Jesse approaches Russell's door and opens it. Standing on the other side of the door was a pudgy and geeky Caucasian man wearing glasses. Jesse beings to speak with him.

"Yes, what can I do for you?"

The man responds in a very energetic and hyper manner.

"What's going on man, I'm Kevin Peterson. Does Russell McCoy live here? Last time to my knowledge he did, but I just want to make sure. It's really important, I speak to him. I'm an old friend of his. I don't have his number anymore I lost it, and part of me forgot where he lived as well, but if Russell is here, may I speak to him please?"

Jesse seems to be amused at the way the man talks, and freezes in his thoughts for a second. He eventually gets himself together and responds to Kevin and shakes his hand.

"Hey Kevin, I'm Jesse Watkins, I'm one of Russell's friends too. Yes, thankfully he does still live here. I'll go get him right now. Hold on."

Kevin replies back to Jesse.

"Alrighty, thanks so much."

Jesse returns to the living room and updates Russell.

"Russ, there is a guy at the door wanting to see you named Kevin."

Russell has a confused look on his face and gets up. While walking to the door without Russell making eye contact to him, Kevin starts to scream out for Russell in absolute joy.

"RUSS, OH MAN! IT'S BEEN AGES SINCE I LAST SAW YOU MAN, FUCK! HOW YOU BEEN MAN?!"

After recognizing Kevin at the door, Russell becomes hysteric and starts to panic and responds to Kevin, feeling very aggravated and annoyed by his presence.

"Aww shit, not you. Damn."

Kevin then shouts back at Russell.

"YES RUSS, IT'S ME MAN. YOU KNOW IT! YEAH BABY! HOW YOU BEEN?!"

Russell shakes his head and laughs.

CHAPTER 7:

NOTHING WEAK, NOTHING STRONG

Kevin prances himself inside with much glee and feeling jubilant, with his arms flared out. Russell then closes the door, then starts to reluctantly hug Kevin. As he's hugging him, Kevin has a wide relaxed grin on his face. They both hug for what seems like thirty seconds or so. Kevin is the same age as Russell; he is twenty-nine. He has light brown/dirty blonde wavy hair. He is wearing a dark grey T-Shirt with video game characters on it, and he has blue jeans on as well. He is a reasonably short heighted man, being only five foot five. With his weight, he along with Russell are slightly husky and pudgy with their stature. Unlike Russell, Kevin does not have any facial hair, and has a smooth face. Kevin is nearsighted, so he wears eyeglasses. His hobbies include video games, comic books, science fiction stories, and above all working on computer hardware and software.

Kevin in addition to Russell and Jesse, also suffers from anti-social behavior disorders. He likewise with Russell at times can have a split personality towards his emotions. Kevin also speaks and acts as if he's a cartoon; speaking extremely fast and vibrant, and is always coming up with comical comebacks towards people. He isn't afraid to say what's on his mind. Most of the everything he says is very active and hyper. Because of all this, he has gone through many issues and problems in his life. He considers himself a hermit towards society, and finds it difficult to make friends. Kevin is also Bisexual, but prefers relationships with women as opposed to men. His family life is also full of disaster. Being an only child similar to Russell, Kevin grew up in total isolation by himself. When Kevin was ten years old, his parents tragically died in a plane crash, which ever since that moment Kevin has lived with different family members in Chicago, before moving to California for University. He now lives by himself in a studio apartment very close by Russell's residence. He was a close acquaintance of Russell, but they both haven't seen each other in over four years. Just by sheer chance and luck, he has resurfaced himself in Russell's life again.

Russell first met Kevin when he was attending the "University of Southern California". Russell at the time was taking computer finance courses, which is where he bumped himself into Kevin. Even though they were studying different things, and had separate majors. Russell wanted to go into banking and finance, as Kevin had an unrelated study. His specialty was computer programming and electronics. Kevin unfortunately due to complicated circumstances was expelled from the school. He was caught trying to hack transcripts, grades, and finals test scores, to benefit himself and his fellow classmates in order to make money. Kevin successfully was able to find a trick in order to do this without being traced back, and originally it worked. He was quite skilled from his computer knowledge, but sadly Kevin made an amateur mistake of not trusting the right people.

He didn't realize that doing this could backfire, and cause him to get in trouble by running his mouth. Kevin was eventually ratted out by a decoy staff member at the school, posing as a student. This was done after students whom Kevin helped out, became bitter and angry after they still failed their tests, and got suspended from their classes using his services. Out of revenge, they later teamed up to get the staff board of the university to investigate this issue. Kevin was later not only expelled, but blacklisted from many other schools and Universities as well. Kevin now runs his own freelance computer, electronic device repair, and data recovery programming business. He is generally successful with that; thought at times he does struggle with his business, which causes him great stress.

The reason that Kevin and Russell distanced themselves from each other, is that Russell doesn't trust Kevin at times, and he cannot take his outrageous behavior. Similar to his position with Jesse, Russell can be wishy washy as far as his friendships and personal relationships are concerned. He usually only gives people one chance, and if they do not prove themselves after that chance, Russell usually avoids that person. As of late, Russell is trying to be more open minded and let situations slide. This is possibly because of the robbery that happened the day before, as to why Russell now has a change of heart. Russell last saw Kevin over four years ago, before he was even working in a bank, while they were still enrolled in university.

Kevin tried to convince Russell to participate in his test score scheme, but Russell refused, wanting nothing to do with it. Russell usually has always been a man that wanted to win and gain things fair and in the correct way. Cheating, in Russell's view wasn't the right way to go about it. After Russell rejected Kevin's offer, the both of them got into a heated argument surrounding that. They both clashed and distanced themselves from each other. Russell and Kevin would congregate outside of class very often, and due to similar opinions they both had, befriended each other relatively quick. Russell and Kevin are both Jewish, which was a main similarity in which both of them shared. Kevin has always regretted destroying his friendship with Russell, and has tried to find ways to recover from that and patch up their differences. After all, Russell was one of Kevin's closest contacts he has ever been around, and it meant very much for him to have Russell there. Russell to be frank, had totally forgotten about Kevin, and had moved on with his life. He did enjoy being around him when it lasted, but considered him to a be hurdle as far as his own personal goals. Russell's big plan was to work in a bank, and thankfully he was able to accomplish that. Being around Kevin's energy would have served as a distraction and a complication for Russell. He tried as much as he could to erase anything related to Kevin, so his professional agenda did not have to be wrecked because of that.

As Russell continues to bear hug Kevin, he has a rush of flashbacks in his mind. This person whom he would never think he'd see again, is now reuniting with him. Russell under much panic due to his past dealings with Kevin, can only be optimistic that perhaps this is a new leaf. Things can possibly change for the better between the both of them. The past shouldn't matter in the present, and Russell generally begins to allow most of that to diminish. Kevin of course never had any resentment towards Russell, or at least not at the same value. He merely was upset that Russell didn't join him for his escapades, and that caused most of the friction between them both. Kevin always thought that if Russell was a true friend, he would stand by him no matter what. Although he didn't realize that what he was doing was wrong, he felt Russell should have had his back regardless. It was far too late at that point, and Kevin soon understood the mistake he made. Deep down he knew that Russell had every right to turn his back on him, and to move on with his life. Kevin still always doubted himself and began to feel depressed that his friendship with Russell, retracted the way it did.

Russell and Kevin finally stop hugging, and stare at each other for a couple seconds. They stand in the living room, with Jesse watching them. Kevin then actively starts to chat with Russell in a jovial fast tone.

"Russ, I can't believe it's really you. Damn. It's been a long time hasn't it? Wow man, I just don't know what else to say, I'm just surprised to see you buddy."

Russell then awkwardly grins at Kevin and responds to him brashly and sarcastically.

"Kev, yeah...I uh...it's good to see you too. What a surprise, it has been a while Kev."

Kevin then scurries around Russell's apartment inspecting it. He then in a very authoritative manner while he's walking around, shouts out to Russell.

"From when I was last here, you really spruced this place up. I'm really liking all the stuff you have on the wall, that's really awesome. Hey, wait a minute, what the hell are these boxes here for? You moving Russ?"

Russell and Jesse look at each other, and Jesse quickly responds to Kevin in a polite way.

"I'm staying with Russell for the time being, he's helping me out."

Kevin then with a confused look on his face, walks over to Jesse and starts to be fascinated by his afro textured hair. He then starts to rub Jesse's head. Jesse allows him, not being bothered or disturbed by it. Kevin then talks to Jesse.

"Wow man, I love your fro. Cool. Nice hair. Yeah, me and Russ go way back."

Jesse then smiles and laughs at Kevin. For another few minutes, Kevin continues to look around Russell's living room as if it were a museum. Russell who was being patient, then can longer hide his true feelings, and snaps at Kevin in a harsh way.

"Kev, what the hell are you doing here? I thought I'd never have to see your goofy butt again, and here you are. What mess have you gotten yourself into this time?"

Kevin ignores Russell and continues to walk around his living room for a short while. He then looks at Russell, and answers his question.

"Russ, I'm not in any trouble. You know I live around the corner from you, I haven't moved. I was scared you might have possibly moved back east. I don't know Russ, I woke up today, and a bird told me to check on you, so I did. Turns out you still live here. Go figure."

Russell then walks over to Kevin who is continuing to be distracted by the things hung on up in the living room. Kevin picks up an autographed Mark McGwire foul baseball next to the television set, and fondles with it. Russell then quickly snatches the ball from him, placing it back. Kevin then continues to wander his eyes at different things in the room. Russell then takes out his phone, and while going through his phone, he responds to Kevin.

"Kev, now is not a good time. Some other time okay Kev? I have a new number; you can call me whenever you want. Just... now is not good."

Kevin then takes out his phone, and he saves Russell's telephone number, after Russell gives it to him. After doing so, Kevin proceeds to return gazing around Russell's apartment. Russell then becomes furious.

"Kev, you need to go. I wasn't expecting you, and again it's not a good time right now."

Russell proceeds to push Kevin out of his apartment, before Kevin begs and screams for him not to eject him. Kevin reaches in his pocket and pulls out a small plastic bag that has marijuana in it. Kevin hides the bag inside his hand, without Russell noticing.

"No wait Russ, I came all this way and you're kicking me out? Wait!"

Russell takes his hands off Kevin and gives him a skeptical look. In that moment, Kevin then waves the plastic bag in his hand towards Russell's face teasing him with it.

"Russ, I got that good good. Don't act like you and Michael Jackson don't want it. I know you smoke weed Russ. Don't act like you don't."

Jesse then runs over to Kevin, and snatches the bag from him. Kevin then smiles and laughs at Jesse. Jesse then walks over to Russell, begging for Kevin to stay.

"Russell please, he's your friend. Don't treat him that way. Come on, he has weed. How can you say no to that? Russell come on. Please?"

Russell looks down, and thinks to himself. He then looked up at Kevin, and replied back to him very sternly, in order to give him a false sense of security.

"Kev you brought pot? You're lucky I'm in that mood. Come on let's blaze."

All three men then proceed outside towards Russell's balcony which is connected from his kitchen to his bedroom. Russell's balcony facing the kitchen is very quaint and safe, as it overlooks a back courtyard covered with trees that give a more private feeling. Over the other side of his balcony facing his bedroom, you can see a panoramic view of downtown Los Angeles. Russell also has various plants on his balcony. They all sit on deck chairs on the balcony. The sun is shining bright this afternoon, and the weather is still very moderate and fair. It is simply a very clear beautiful day. Russell takes his phone out of his pocket and puts on some Reggae music. Kevin proceeds to take some tobacco paper out of his pocket, and starts to roll a marijuana joint. Kevin is focused, rolling it very accurately.

"I'm going to make this one really fat, because I can tell you guys have a lot to talk about. Something is up, and I'm going to get to the bottom of it. I don't judge, so it's okay."

Kevin finishes rolling the marijuana joint. Immediately after, Russell then reaches in his pocket and gives Kevin a lighter. Kevin puts the joint in his mouth, and before Kevin lights it, Russell snatches the joint from him.

"I take the first hit. It's my house and my rules."

Russell takes a couple puffs from the joint, then hands it to Kevin. After handing it to him, Russell while looking out towards the distance of his balcony patio, starts to explain everything which happened the previous day to Kevin, who is taking hits from the joint.

"You know Kev, how I explained I wanted to be a banker. Well, my dream kinda came true. I got a job at this bank, then I got a job at another bank as a manager."

Kevin while looking at Russell, hands the joint to Jesse who takes hits from it.

"Damn Russ, manager? Look at you. I'm proud of you of man. I'm still doing all the computer stuff. Here's my business card, I designed it myself."

Kevin hands both Russell and Jesse his business cards. Russell quickly puts it in his pocket without examining it, while Jesse compliments how it looks to Kevin.

"You're really talented man, I like the way this is designed."

Jesse then puts the card in his pocket, and hands the marijuana joint to Russell who takes more hits from it. Kevin while looking at Russell continues.

"Yeah I got fired from Best Buy; remember I was working there Russ? I kept giving guys I know discounts and shit, and they canned me. Oh well. I now have my own business, and I help out people who break their phones, or download shit they shouldn't. You know, stuff like that."

Russell hands the marijuana joint to Kevin, while looking away from him, and while still looking out into the city from his balcony, Russell continues to update Kevin.

"Yeah Kev, I lived my dream I guess. That was until yesterday. The bank I was a manager at; I never seen you walk in a customer Kev I don't think. That bank on Sunset near Santa Monica Boulevard, in that shopping center with the deli and cleaners? The "Sunset Credit Union.""

Kevin after taking more hits of the joint, passes it to Jesse. He then responds to Russell.

"What happened yesterday Russ? You didn't get fired did you? What happened?"

Russell then looks directly at Kevin and continues to explain everything.

"No Kev, not exactly. The bank was robbed yesterday. These two guys just came into the bank, and robbed us like that. One of the guys was way more brutal than the other one was. He killed two of my coworkers, but the police came and shot him, he's dead. The other one didn't kill anybody, but he still ran away, they weren't able to catch him. "

Kevin then looks at Russell in complete shock. He widens his eyes and shouts at him.

"Wait, WHAT?! Russ hold on, you're being serious right? What?!"

Jesse hands the joint to Russell. Jesse then replies to Kevin.

"It's sadly true. It happened. I was there, I was a teller and Russell was one of the bank managers. Me, Russell and another woman we worked with, thankfully survived it all."

Russell after taking hits of the joint, passes it to Kevin. Russell continues to talk.

"I decided to quit because of that. Jesse also decided to quit. Yvette, the other woman who we worked with, she decided to quit as well. I don't think any of us ever want to work in a bank again after all of that. I am still shaken over all of that. In fact, Kev only because you used to be my best friend until you fucked up, and you know you did; I'll let you in on a secret. Me and Jesse are thinking of robbing a bank ourselves."

Kevin takes couple hits from the joint and passes it to Jesse. Kevin then turns his head towards Russell, and responds to Russell in an energetic rant.

"Man, I can't believe any of this. Russ, you are crazy. I woke up today and had the strangest feeling, and this feeling is so hard to explain. This feeling told me that you were in some type of mess, and it turns out it's true. Wow. There is no doubting that at all, you are a crazy guy, messing with my mojo and my inner feelings like that, causing me to predict stuff and that's why I love you man, and you're my main bro."

Jesse takes more hits from the marijuana joint and passes it to Russell. Kevin then while looking at Russell, continues on with his rambling.

"Well, if you guys are serious about this, you can count me in. You're gonna need a guy that knows how to make diversions and shit. I can hack into bank alarms. It's not 100 percent fool proof no, but I'll be a good asset. I know I'm just spouting shit but, I'm here if you guys need me. I'll be a good member to the team."

Russell after taking hits of the joint, hands the joint back to Kevin. Russell starts to put his head towards the ground, and responds to Kevin nonchalantly.

"Sure Kev, if you want to help out you can. We're only gonna rob one bank though, and that's it. If we get caught, we get caught. But after yesterday, we've given up on society"

All three men continue to sit on the balcony, feeling relaxed and chatting to each other. Kevin takes more hits of the joint and passes it to Jesse, asking Russell a question.

"So Russ, this pot is making me hungry. Let's get something to eat yeah? We can talk about this bank robbing crap later. I want to get something to eat right now."

Russell continues to look down towards the floor, and Jesse then hands the marijuana joint towards Russell who starts to smoke it once more. Jesse then converses with Kevin.

"Russell is such a nice guy, and it's sad it took what happened yesterday for me to really get to know him. I used to always be scared of him, and now I love his personality. He's not like anybody else, and I can see why the both of you are so close."

With Russell still smoking the marijuana joint, Kevin raises his eyebrows at Jesse and curiously asks him a question that is on his mind.

"I'm not really a politically correct guy, I'm kinda a jerk. I say what's on my mind. But are you and Russell dating? I just have a feeling that you guys are. I don't care, I don't judge. I'm Bisexual, but I don't really date guys. I would never date a guy like Russ, he'll always be a friend to me, but again I'm just a jerk and inquiring minds like myself want to know."

Jesse starts to respond to Kevin, but Russell interrupts him, and hands Kevin the joint.

"It's complicated Kev, I don't know about him. I think he has me on some voodoo or magic curse or spell or something. He's head over heels about me. Really though, he's crazy like us so that's the only reason why he's here. He's like a damn woman sometimes though. Attitude problem too."

Jesse turns and looks at Russell in disgust. He quickly attacks him.

"What the hell? Wait a minute. Because I'm black, I do voodoo? Wow, really? Fuck you Russell."

Russell while looking at the floor, under his breath talks to Kevin.

"You see Kev, what I tell you?"

Kevin smiles and laughs and turns his head towards Jesse. He speaks to him softly.

"You're lucky to have a guy like Russ, he's an amazing man. I've known him for years, and sadly we've been estranged for that same amount of time, but he's a good guy."

Kevin while smoking the marijuana joint in one hand, runs his other hand through Jesse's hair laughing at him. He then hands Jesse the marijuana joint. Russell who's continuing to look down, then continues to express himself towards Kevin.

"Kev, nothing is making sense man. First, the shit that happened yesterday happened. Now, my best friend who I've haven't seen in I don't know how long pops up. If that isn't trippy or weird, I don't know what is. None of this is making any sense to me man."

Jesse hands Russell the joint, and Russell takes a hit from it. Kevin then responds to Russell.

"That's life man, none of it makes sense sometimes. You should be thankful that I'm here, because I could have easily said, 'Fuck Russell, I don't care about him. He can fuck off'. But I didn't, I came to see you anyways. You're still here, Jesse is still here. We're all here to serve some type of purpose man, what that is I don't know, ha-ha, but think about it."

Russell gives Kevin the marijuana joint once more, and Russell raises his head up, looking out of the balcony in a very relaxed and comfortable way. Kevin takes a couple more hits of the joint, and starts to hand it to Jesse, who shakes his head and refuses it.

"Oh no thank you, I've had enough. That was some good shit, thanks Kevin."

Kevin smiles and laughs at Jesse, taking more hits of the joint.

"Pleasure is all mine, it's okay. A friend of Russ' is a friend of mine, you know it."

Kevin then gives the joint to Russell who takes more hits of the marijuana joint. He then puts his head down, and starts to whisper to Kevin.

"Thank you Kev, I really needed this. I did. Thanks."

Russell gives the joint back to Kevin who takes a couple hits from it. The joint becomes too small to smoke at this point, and Kevin puts it in the plastic bag with the rest of the raw marijuana. All three men sit on the balcony in silence for about ten minutes, keeping their thoughts and feelings quiet. They continue to listen to the reggae music playing from Russell's phone, with Jesse moving his head to music. The sun continues to shine on all of them sitting on the balcony, as the afternoon continues to pass. The climate is ideal, with the weather being very immaculate and perfect today. Russell has many thoughts on his mind, and being reunited with Kevin wants him to bring them all out, however he can't. He's relaxing himself on the patio, as the music is playing with two of his friends. Kevin however is starting to feel hungry, and is craving something to eat. Jesse feels very happy listening to the music on the balcony, and unwinding himself, being involved with Russell and Kevin's circuit. Another ten minutes pass in total silence, then Russell looks up at Kevin and asks him a question.

"Kev, you said you were hungry bro, what did you want to eat man?"

Kevin then rubs his hand under his chin, and begins to ponder on what to eat. He has many choices that he is currently thinking of, and can't decide as to which one he wants. Kevin enjoys all different types of food and isn't a picky eater. After a couple minutes pass, Kevin looks towards Russell, and finally is able to make his choice.

"How about "In-N-Out" Burger? I'm really craving some of that right now. Yeah Russ, that's what I want. I want to get some of that. Yeah."

Russell turns his head towards Kevin and shakes his head and laughs. Immediately after that, Russell stands up from his chair and sticks his hand out towards Kevin.

"Give me the bag of pot Kev. You're not taking all of that out with us."

Kevin grunts and grumbles at Russell as he's going through his pocket to get the bag.

"Damn, why Russ? I'm not going to smoke it. Man, come on."

Russell continues to stick his hand out towards Kevin, while staring at him with a sharp and strict look on his face. Jesse looks at the both of them in silence.

"Kev, you're not taking that shit in my car, so give it to me. I'm gonna put it on top of my refrigerator and you can get it when we come back. But you're not taking all of that in my car."

Kevin shakes his head and mumbles under his breath, before reluctantly giving Russell the bag of marijuana. All three men then proceed off the balcony into Russell's kitchen. Once in the kitchen, Russell takes the bag of marijuana and sets it on the surface of the refrigerator. Kevin watches him do this, and shakes his head.

"Russ, you just want to take my shit and smoke it later, that's all."

Russell then walks over to Kevin, and proceeds to frisk his pants.

"I just want to make sure you don't have anything on you, because you're sneaky and sly like that. I can't trust you as far as I through you Kev, so I have to do this."

Kevin laughs and shakes his head at Russell. He then responds to him angrily.

"Russ, I don't have shit on me, I don't have anything, you took my stash. I'm hungry, I just want to eat. Can we eat? God, this is unnecessary Russ, let's go."

Russell stares at Kevin with a doubtful look on his face, and responds.

"Okay Kev, we can go now. I'll just have to take your word for it."

All three of them head out the apartment towards Russell's car, and they each take a seat. Kevin sits in the passenger seat, with Jesse sitting in the rear seat. Kevin begins to talk to Russell.

"Russ I parked my car at my place, and walked over here. So you don't have to worry, I'm not gonna get towed or anything, so don't even worry about that."

Russell scrunches his face at Kevin and snaps back at him.

"Kev, I don't care where you parked your car, I wasn't even thinking about that."

Russell, Jesse, and Kevin all put on their sunglasses. Kevin then begins to look around Russell's car offering his opinions on it.

"This is a nice ride Russ, I really like the upgrade. I remember the last time I was with you, you had a plain old Honda Civic. Really digging the Suburban man, gotta love it."

Russell laughs at Kevin, and starts the car ignition. As Russell proceeds down the street, Kevin reaches for the car stereo and turns it on. Kevin then starts to recollect on their conversation on the balcony. He turns his head and talks to Russell.

"Russ, are you absolutely serious about the bank robbing thing? Because I'm going to be honest with you Russ, if you need my help I'm here. I mean that man."

While he's driving, Russell has a wide grin on his face, and thinks of a clever response to give to Kevin. A few moments later he then responds to him.

"Well, yes...Kev. I'm very serious. At this point, it's just a matter of when and how. You know what I mean Kev? But yes I'm serious, and I could use all the help I could get."

Kevin shakes his head at Russell and looks out the window. He then begins to finally perceive that Russell is persistent towards his agendas and thoughts. He softly responds to him.

"Russ, you are so crazy. I understand you're going through a lot of shit right now, but you are one crazy guy. You're so lucky I'm the same level of crazy you are to accept all of this mess. You tell that crap to anybody other than me, you would have been shit out of luck Russ."

Russell stays silent, although taking in what Kevin said. Jesse remains in the back seat eavesdropping on their conversation, but remaining silent. As Russell proceeds down the street, Kevin starts to feel more comfortable with Russell, and refreshes their past unrequited friendship. He instantly remembers all of the positive and happy times they both witnessed and been through. Kevin only came to Russell's residence, as he had a gut feeling that something wasn't right. A part of him didn't want to act on it, and Kevin at first did ignore it. Kevin also felt that he had nothing to lose. The worst scenarios that could possibly perhaps happen, is that Russell would either not live where Kevin thought he lived anymore, or Russell would simply reject and not forgive Kevin for their past quarrel that caused them to distance themselves from each other. It seemed as though everything did pan out accordingly towards Kevin. Russell continues to drive, also finding it odd that during this specific time, he was able to meet with Kevin at long last. Having such a wide gap and time from when they last saw each other, only coming together during these intense bouts of turmoil Russell is experiencing. How could this merely be fate, it can't be at all. Russell in addition starts to see this as a sign, towards his agenda of actually wanting to rob a bank. The fact Kevin now sprung back into his life, he can now use him as a tool in order to support his rebellion. Knowing full well that Kevin just like himself is a major outcast towards society, and struggles through daily life. He's glad he now rehashed their friendship, and is now able to start over with Kevin. Russell would need to have a good system of support in order to move forward with whatever plans that hatch into his mind.

The men sit quietly in the car, as Russell proceeds to the hamburger stand. Jesse remains quiet as a mouse in the backseat. Kevin however still has much to say to Russell, yet is far too anxious to speak to him. To remedy this, he starts to bite his nails. Russell notices him do this and quickly peeks at Kevin, but ignores and shuns it off. Kevin continues to be tense, wanting to talk to Russell. Kevin starts acting very anxious and proceeds to remove his sunglasses, cleaning them with his shirt, even though the lenses weren't dirty. While he's doing this, he starts to ask Russell a question he was thinking about.

"Russ, you should know...ah...fuck it. Russ...forget it."

Russell reaches a stoplight and turns to look at Kevin with much concern. He realizes that Kevin is feeling very scared and terrified with himself.

"Kev it's okay, if there's something on your mind say it. Use your words man."

Kevin lifts his hand up to his mouth and continues to bite his nails, trying to overcome his nervousness and anxiety. Moments later he is able to calm himself, and talks to Russell.

"Russ, I was just going to say that doing something like that is kinda dangerous. We could get hurt and stuff you know. I'm all for the rebelling part of robbing a bank, and sticking it to the man and fucking over the government and stuff. But I don't know about the other stuff. Russ I'm scared, I don't know if I'm down for something like this."

With the car still stopped at the light, Russell rubs Kevin's shoulder.

"Kev, it's going to be fine alright. If we act clever enough, nobody is going to get hurt. I'm your friend Kev, and I'll always be here man."

Kevin taking Russell's kind words into heart, is more comfortable with himself.

"Thanks Russ. You're absolutely right man. We can totally do this. This is a crazy idea, but sometimes crazy ideas might work out, and it's okay to do crazy things."

Russell smiles back at Kevin, and he continues down the road towards their destination. A few minutes later, Russell arrives at another stoplight. While the car is stopped, Kevin sees a promiscuously dressed woman walking down the sidewalk and starts to profile her very accurately and precisely. Kevin then starts to gossip about her to Russell.

"Russ, you think she's a prostitute or hooker? Why else would she be dressed like that and walking like that. Something doesn't seem right. She looks hot, but I don't know."

Russell while looking at the woman also very closely, starts to rub his chin. He starts to analyze her carefully, before giving his opinion about it to Kevin.

"I mean; she could also be a cop as well. You have to think about that too. But I agree with you Kev, something about that picture just doesn't look right at all."

Kevin turns his head to the back seat to look at Jesse.

"What do you think man?"

Jesse who was also watching the woman offers his opinion.

"Yeah, I agree with Russell. I think she's a cop, and that's some type of trick or game they are playing. They do that a lot and I don't get it. But yeah, I'm sure she's a cop."

The signal then turns green, and Russell continues down the road. Another few minutes pass and they eventually make it to "In-N-Out Burger". Being that this is a Saturday, it is extremely crowded. There is a long line of cars queuing outside of the drive thru. This frustrates Russell somewhat, as he at times can be an impatient man. He turns the stereo in the car up and rests his hand on his forehead. The drive thru line very slowly dissipates. Russell turns his head towards Kevin who is playing a game on his phone. He then talks to him.

"Kev, what game you playing man?

Kevin with his head down towards his phone answers Russell's question.

"Oh, this game is called 'See You Later Alligator.' Basically it's a memory and strategy game where you take this alligator and he can only eat similar objects. For example, in this particular level, the alligator can only eat things that are round. It's a fun game. I like it."

Russell with his hand still over his forehead, acknowledges Kevin and faces forward. Jesse continues to sit in the back seat, staying very quiet. The line is moving so slow that Russell turns the ignition in his car off. He sits back in the seat very frustrated. Russell becoming more tense waiting in this drive thru line which is moving terribly slow, starts to ask Kevin something.

"Kev, what do you want to order? Tell me now, so when it's finally our turn I can just give it to the people. I feel like we've been in this line for fucking ever man."

Kevin while still looking down on the phone playing his game, responds to Russell.

"Oh, uh, Russ, I'll take two double double cheeseburgers, animal style man."

Russell shakes his head at Kevin, and turns his head towards the back seat.

"Jesse, what did you want to order?"

Jesse immediately responds to Russell.

"Oh Russell, I'll take two double double's but with pickles please. Thanks."

Russell then starts to think about what he wants to order. Unlike Kevin and Jesse, he's not sure what to get, and has not yet made his mind up. He continues to wait in the drive thru line watching Kevin play a game on his phone. Russell turns the car stereo up to listen to music. He turns his head over to Kevin, who is still focused on his game and vents his frustration.

"You just had to come here Kev, we could have just gone to McDonalds and been done with it. We've been in this line for a least forty-five minutes. This burger better fucking taste like gold as long as we've been waiting in this line. Damn it Kev."

Kevin looks up from his phone and notices the extremely long line sticking out of the drive thru. He turns his head to Russell who's looking very aggravated.

"Russ, calm down man, it's okay. Take it easy man. The food here is good. You've been to 'In-N-Out' before man. The line is always long like this. I don't know why, it just is."

Russell rolls his eyes at Kevin, and changes the music on the car stereo. The line finally starts to proceed to move forward. When they reach the drive thru menu speaker, Russell then figures out what he wants, and gives the order through the speaker.

"Yeah, can I have six double double burgers. Two I want animal style, another two with pickles, and another two with extra onions. I also want three fries and three cokes. That's it."

After placing the order, Russell continues to wait in the line, to get the food from the service window. He turns the volume on the stereo louder, and Kevin recognizes the song. While still playing the game on his phone, Kevin begins to hum the melody of music. Russell looks across at Kevin, and his humming causes Russell to laugh at him. He finds it hilarious and cannot contain himself. The line slowly and steadily moves ahead and Russell pulls up. As he is approaching the service window, he reaches in his pants and pulls out his wallet. Kevin while still having his head down, focused on the game on his phone, ask Russell a question.

"Russ you still play Grand Theft Auto and Call of Duty? I remember you used to."

Russell continues to have his hand on his head feeling stressed out and ignores Kevin. Jesse who heard Kevin mention that to Russell, taps Kevin on the shoulder and responds.

"Kevin, I play Grand Theft Auto sometimes. I like Street Fighter, I like Tekken, I like Final Fantasy sometimes, I also like Pokémon. I like to play Dance Dance Revolution. I like Mario and Donkey Kong too. I don't play World of Warcraft, but I like RuneScape though."

Kevin then turns his head towards the back laughs at him and gives him a high five.

"Nice Jesse, I used to work at GameStop like when I was in High School and going into college. Russ likes video games too, he's just being a dick right now. We use to play together."

Jesse nods his head at Kevin, and Russell beings to laugh out loud. Ten minutes later, Russell reaches the service window. He turns down the volume on the car stereo, and hands the employee his credit card, and they hand him a receipt. They still continue to wait, as there is an additional window in the drive thru line that hands them their food. Russell becomes impatient again and raises the volume on the stereo, tapping his fingers on the steering wheel according to the music. Jesse reaches from behind the rear seat, and begins to stroke Russell's hair. Russell is not receptive towards that and hints for Jesse to stop, by swatting his hands away from his head. When another few minutes pass, they inch up closer to the window to pick up their food.

The employee asks if they are going to be eating in the car, to which Russell agrees. He is given two brown boxes which contains all of their food. Russell also asks for ketchup; in which they give him some. He then drives away from the drive thru line, towards the parking lot. When examining the area, he quickly notices there is a nice bluff area which shows a remarkable view of Los Angeles in the lot, to which Russell feels would be nice spot for them to eat. Russell pulls up to the parking spot and turns of the engine. He then gives Kevin and Jesse their food. The guys then start to eat their, food; Kevin looks out of the windshield to acknowledge the landscape.

"This is so spectating, you can see all of the buildings in the city from this hill."

Jesse pulls up a YouTube video on his phone, and sits in the back not paying attention to Russell or Kevin. Russell while eating his hamburger chats with Kevin.

"You were right Kev; this burger is delicious. I don't know if it was worth the wait, because we've been in that line for over a damn hour, but I'm not gonna lie, this burger is good."

Kevin takes another bite of his hamburger and laughs at Russell.

"Told you Russ, you just didn't want to listen. You've always been a hot head. It must be because you're a ginger and you don't have a fucking soul."

Russell while staring out the windshield takes another bite of his hamburger and laughs at Kevin. Russell then hands Kevin his French fries.

"Kev you can have the rest of these, I don't know if I can finish them. I probably could, but I'm gonna be nice and give them to you, I know you'll scarf them down no problem."

Following that, Kevin immediately snatched the fries from Russell, eating them.

"Thanks Russ, and yeah you're right. I'm gonna kill these fries right now. See?"

Kevin raises the empty box of fries smiling, which causes Russell to laugh hysterically.

"Aww, Kev. You're such a ray of sunshine aren't you?"

Kevin takes a bite of his hamburger and continues to chat with Russell.

"Russ, I'm glad I was able to meet you again man. It's been so long, and I thought I've lost you as a friend forever. I didn't, and you're still here. You're such a good friend Russ."

Russell balls up his fist, and playfully punches Kevin across the chin. He then starts to value Kevin's friendship at maximum capacity. Russell feels so overjoyed with Kevin, and their friendship which despite the lack of contact for so many years, is now being repaired and cherished. Russell continues to eat his food with Kevin and Jesse in the car, settling himself with the happiness of being surrounded by his close friends which for only a short time, he developed strong emotional experiences with them both. The three of them eventually finish their meal, and Russell takes all of the trash to a garbage can nearby. He then gets back into the car, starts the ignition and drives off. Russell arrives outside of Kevin's apartment complex and pulls up to the curb to procced to drop him off. He turns off the ignition and turns his head towards Kevin.

"Okay Kev, you have my number, we're definitely gonna keep in touch this time alright? You take care Kev, okay man?"

Kevin disembarks himself out of Russell's car and shuts the door behind him. Once he is outside his car, Jesse climbs from behind the rear seat, and sits in the passenger seat. Kevin then immediately talks to Russell through the open passenger side window.

"Yeah yeah Russ, thanks man. It was so good to catch up with you again man, after all these damn years. It was nice meeting you Jesse. See you later Russ. Bye."

Russell and Kevin fist bump, and Kevin shakes Jesse's hand. Kevin then walks inside of his apartment building. Russell drives away from outside Kevin's residence. Jesse lays back on the passenger seat, staring out the window feeling exhausted. He was glad to have met one of Russell's estranged friends. Jesse was comfortable with Kevin's personality, and felt happy that he now has him apart of his life. Friends and connections hold much value in a person's life, and it's very important to hold onto these special relationships you get presented with. Russell continues to pay attention to the road, reflecting on the day's events. He proceeds to drive towards his apartment. Upon reaching the parking lot of his complex and parking his car, Russell then remembers that Kevin left his marijuana bag on top of the refrigerator. Russell while preparing to exit the car, turns to Jesse, and lets him know about what he remembered.

"Oh shit. I totally forgot that Kevin left his weed. I didn't want him to bring it, because I was scared that he was going to smoke it while we were out. He gets like that sometimes, and he's very careless. I worry about him, so I look out for him. I'll give it to him tomorrow I guess."

Jesse laughs at Russell, and they both exit out his car. After getting off the elevator, they walk into Russell's apartment. Jesse still has his boxes in the living room, from when he moved into Russell's apartment earlier on in the day. Jesse then starts to unpack his things.

Russell notices that Jesse is starting to unpack his clothes, so he directs himself to his bedroom closet to clear some space for him to use. Jesse follows him, carrying a box of his clothes. As Russell is clearing out his closet, Jesse once again takes note of the amount of professional tailored suits Russell has.

"Russ, I'm looking at all those suits and going back to your bank manager days. Ha-ha. You're so dapper with your clothes, and you always look fresh."

Russell heard Jesse but doesn't reply to him, and continues to clear out space in his closet. While he's doing that, he violently throws bundles of clothes, forming a pile on the floor.

"I'm gonna give most of this shit to Goodwill, I don't even wear have this crap anymore. Let the homeless wear it or whatever. Because I don't wear any of this."

A few minutes later Russell manages to free a moderate amount of space up in his closet for Jesse to hang his things up in. When he's done he turns to Jesse.

"Is this enough space for you? If it isn't I can clear more things out."

Jesse nods his head and starts to hang his clothes in this closet.

"Yes Russell it's perfect, thank you so much."

Russell smiles and sits on the edge of the bed watching Jesse pack his things into the closet. He looks out the curtains of his bedroom, and notices the sun is slowly setting. He turns the television set in his bedroom on, and an NFL football game is playing. He takes his sweat jacket off, to which he's wearing a white undershirt over, and takes shoes and socks off as well. He then proceeds to lay down on the bed. Jesse then slips off his loafer shoes and sets them outside of the closet door. As Jesse continues to hang his clothes in the closet, Russell remains laying on the bed staring at him. He then softly speaks to him.

"Jesse, I want to show you something. Do you want to see my guns? I don't think I've ever shown them to you yet. Do you want to see them?"

Jesse who's still hanging his clothes in the closet, responds back to Russell.

"I'm trying to put my clothes up; I'll see them later alright?"

Russell then sits up on the corner of the bed and while still staring at Jesse put his clothes in the closet, tries to coax him in a soft way.

"Yeah, but, you can go back to that later, I want to show you my guns. You don't want to see them or something? Come on, let me show them to you."

Jesse then very quickly walks over to where Russell is and stands by him. Russell begins to kneel down under his bed, and pulls out a titanium steel chest and lays it down on the floor. He unlocks and opens it, and inside of the chest are two guns. One handgun, and one assault rifle. Jesse remains standing still watching him, as Russell pulls the assault rifle and starts to position it in his hand, waving it around every corner of the room. He notices that Jesse looks slightly anxious and scared, and starts to whisper to him.

"It's okay, it's not loaded. Ha. Don't be scared."

Russell then puts the rifle back in the titanium case and locks it.

"Yeah, I go practice shooting sometimes. I love my guns, and it's my hobby. I wanted to show you my guns. That's all".

Jesse nods his head, and returns back to the closet to continue the task. Russell then begins to feel tired, and lays himself in the bed and then slowly drifts off to sleep. Jesse finishes hanging up his clothes, and doesn't realize Russell has fallen asleep. He looks over at Russell who is fast asleep, and climbs on the top of bed lying next to him. Russell has now awoken due to Jesse's motions on the bed. He then opens his eyes and at smiles at him. Jesse lays his head on top of Russell's chest, and Russell wraps his arm behind Jesse's head, rubbing his hair. Russell closes his eyes again, and begins to talk to Jesse, in a very raspy and lethargic voice.

"Jess, I'm so tired of this shit. Yesterday was a long scary day. Today was a long scary day. Please God, let tomorrow which is Sunday be just a regular relaxing day."

Jesse then starts to feel sleepy himself and slowly closes his eyes laying on Russell's chest staying quiet, while continuing to listen to Russell speak.

"If only life can be peaceful and lovely like this all the time. If only life could always be this easy. Damn."

He then with his eyes still closed, kisses Jesse on the forehead.

They both a minute later fall asleep.

CHAPTER 8:

NOTHING HAPPY, NOTHING SAD

The following morning, Russell awakens. He looks at the curtains in his bedroom, and takes note of the sun peering through the curtains. Russell had a good and strong deep sleep, and feels very energized. He takes a quick flash glance over at the clock; it is 8 A.M. Russell turns his head to the other side of the bed, and realizes that Jesse is still sleeping. He rearranges the covers on the bed so that Jesse is more comfortable. Without trying to disturb or wake him, Russell carefully treads himself off the bed. He then proceeds to towards his closet to grab an outfit to wear; picking out a blue polo shirt, and a pair of black sweatpants. After setting the articles of clothing down on a separate section of his closet, Russell then heads straight towards the bathroom to take a shower. Russell while bathing himself, begins to reflect on the past couple of days yet again. He has been introduced to so many outrageous situations, tallying up each and every one of them in their full glory detail. Each day passes by, still having memories which he does not want to think about still reaming on his mind. These terrible photographs and mental pictures gathering a pit of sorrow for him. Russell starts to wonder if this day will possibly be more level pegged to how his life was before what happened on Friday. He can only imagine this will be a more mellow and somber day for him to grow and lean on.

Russell finishes taking his shower, and wraps a towel around his nude body. He walks towards his bedroom where Jesse is still resting. Without making much noise to disturb him, Russell takes the clothes he set aside in closet and begins to dress himself. He also puts some sneakers on as well, as he plans to go out jogging. Once he finishes putting on his clothes, he looks at the pile of clothes he discarded the evening before. As he has free time, he decides to donate the clothes to a nearby thrift store. Russell proceeds towards his kitchen to get a black plastic bag. Returning to the bedroom, he puts the pile of clothes in the bag and begins to grab his car keys from the side of his bed. Russell then walks out his apartment towards his car.

He gets into his car and directs himself to the Goodwill donation center, which is approximately a fifteen-minute drive from his residence. Looking out his car window, today like the day before has very clear weather. The sun is shining bright this morning, and the weather feels moderate and fair. Russell reaches the Goodwill center, and drops the clothes off. Immediately after that, he wishes to surprise Jesse by cooking him a nice breakfast, and stops at a convenience store to pick up some eggs, milk, bacon and fruit. He pays for the items and leaves the store. He arrives back at his apartment and opens the front door. Russell saw that the bathroom door was shut, and could hear that water was running. Inside his mind, he was well aware that Jesse was currently taking a shower. Just to be sure, Russell walks into his bedroom and Jesse is not present in the bed. He then starts to make his bed, and walks out the bedroom. Russell walks into the living room, and turns on the television playing "Law and Order", which is on mute with subtitles on. Russell after that quickly marches towards the kitchen, and pulls out a waffle iron next to his sink. He starts to mix the eggs, milk and flour to make the waffles. Once he's finished making the waffle batter, he puts many strips of raw bacon in a pan on the stove.

Jesse right at this time, walks out of the bathroom, and walks into the bedroom. He starts to dress himself; he picks out a very colorful tank top, and some denim shorts. He decides to go barefoot. As soon as he's dressed, Jesse walks straight into the kitchen, smelling the food Russell is preparing. Russell smiles at him as he walks into the kitchen.

"I wanted to do something special for you, so I have some waffles, some bacon, and I have some pineapple as well. You like pineapple right?"

Jesse nods his head and sits down on a stool in the kitchen. Jesse takes a piece of pineapple that Russell cut, and while eating it asks Russell a question.

"So, what is your plan for today?"

Russell while pouring the waffle batter into the waffle iron responds to Jesse.

"Well, I have a couple bills to pay. My cable and utility bill, I can do that online. Then I have to gather all the shit that belongs to the bank. My ID card, the keys to the bank, all that shit, and send them to the federal office tomorrow. Other than that, I might go out and jog today."

Jesse runs his hands through his hair looking tired and takes another piece of pineapple and eats it. He looks in the direction towards the television set in the living room and watches it. Russell takes the bacon from the pan, and puts it on a plate that has napkins on it. Russell then takes a strip of bacon and eats it. A few minutes later, he removes a waffle from the waffle iron, and puts it on another plate. He takes the bacon from the separate plate and puts it on the plate with the waffle. He then gives the plate to Jesse. Russell makes another waffle and talks to Jesse.

"There's butter in the refrigerator and here is some syrup. Enjoy."

After thanking Russell, Jesse takes his plate into the living room and sits down on the sofa to eat watching "Law and Order", putting his plate on the coffee table. Russell still in the kitchen, puts more strips of raw bacon on the pan. Jesse then grabs the remote and turns the volume up, screaming at Russell while he's doing it.

"Russell why do you have it on mute? That's so ignorant. Ugh."

Russell ignores him, and continues what he's doing in the kitchen. Jesse then walks into the kitchen very briefly to make himself a cup of hot tea. A couple minutes later his tea is finished, and he proceeds back into the living room. Russell takes the waffle out of the waffle iron, and takes the strips of bacon out of the pan; putting them both on the same plate. Russell then pours himself a cup of coffee. He then walks over to where Jesse is and sits next to him on the sofa. They both proceed to eat their breakfast in silence. Jesse would at times look over at Russell eating his breakfast, in a very rapid manner and would display a skeptical smile. This seemed to be a very calm Sunday, and the both of them wished to eat in peace and without bringing up whatever thoughts on their mind, if any. Eventually, they both finish eating and Jesse takes his and Russell's plate into the kitchen. With Russell watching television, Jesse then without hesitation begins to wash the dishes they ate off. Jesse as well washes all the pots and cookware that Russell used when he was preparing breakfast. During a commercial break, Russell reaches under the television set, and grabs his laptop computer. While Jesse is continuing to wash the dishes, Russell starts to pay his cable/internet/phone and electricity and utility bills online. Once Russell is finished paying his bills, he puts his laptop back under the television set.

Russell then walks into the kitchen to grab a plastic Ziploc bag. He walks into his bedroom and begins to put things which belonged to the bank, inside of the bag. Once he's completed that, he returns to the sofa in the living room. Jesse at this time has concluded washing the dishes, and returns to sit next to Russell. A couple minutes later, Russell takes out his phone, and his car keys. He turns his head towards Jesse to speak to him.

"I'm gonna go out for a run for a while You want to come with me? You don't have to."

Jesse while shakes his head while keeping his head towards watching the television set.

Russell smirks at him, and starts to head towards the door. He briefly stops himself before opening it to talk to Jesse, remembering something he forgot as he is leaving.

"Oh damn, right. Jess, If Kev pops up and wants his pot, just give it to him. Thanks."

Jesse turns his head towards Russell, nodding at him in agreement. Russell then walks out of his apartment, and gets into his car putting his sunglasses on. He then starts to drive to towards Venice Beach, to do his customary jog. Russell enjoys jogging, as it gives him time to relax himself and exercise. When he reaches the jogging path at the beach, Russell takes out some ear buds, and plugs them into his phone. He then starts some music as he's jogging on the beach path. This would be the perfect day to jog. The weather is simply exquisite. The breeze coming from the beach is also splendid. Russell continues his jog, and escapes into his own fantasy land for this particular time.

Back at Russell's apartment, Jesse who is lounging on the sofa, and now watching "SpongeBob Squarepants", hears a knock at the door. He goes to open the door and Kevin is standing in front of it. Kevin like Jesse is wearing a graphic tank top, he has on cargo shorts and is wearing flip flop sandals. Kevin also has a "7-Eleven" Slurpee in his hand.

"Hey man, what's up? Don't mean to bother you, but I left my you know what in the kitchen yesterday. Do you mind if you can go get it for me? Thanks."

Jesse quickly goes to the kitchen and grabs Kevin's property. He returns to the door and while smiling, hands the bag over to him. Kevin then waves the bag in the air.

"Since I'm here, do you want to smoke for a bit?"

With an unsure look on his face, Jesse shakes his head and refuses.

"Okay, well tell Russ I stopped by. See you Jesse."

Kevin and Jesse immediately hug after this, and Kevin proceeds on about his business. Jesse returns to the sofa, and this time starts to relax. He extends his whole body on the couch, and makes himself very comfortable. Russell meanwhile is wrapping up his jog, and starts to head back towards his car. He gets into his vehicle, and drives straight back to his apartment. When reaching home as he's walking inside, he removes his sunglasses and sees that Jesse is laying on the couch. Russell sets his keys down on the kitchen, with his back towards Jesse. With Jesse still focusing on the television, Russell begins to speak to him.

"Did Kev come and get his shit?"

Jesse silently nods his head, but Russell is not facing Jesse and was unable to see his nonverbal emote. Russell checks the top of the refrigerator anyways. After that, Russell joins Jesse on the sofa. He then talks to Jesse.

"Today is just going to be a slow day. I'm not going to do anything else."

Jesse still focused on the television, nods his head to Russell.

Russell was indeed correct, the remainder of the day seemed uneventful really. As the afternoon continued they both remained in the living room, with the both of them taking a cigarette break on the balcony later in the afternoon. When evening approached, Russell directed himself towards the kitchen to make fettucine alfredo pasta for himself and Jesse for dinner. Jesse soon follows him into the kitchen, and watches in amusement as Russell prepares their dinner. He boils a pot of noodles and cuts up pieces of chicken, simmering them in another pan. Eventually Russell is finished cooking, and he and Jesse go in the living room to eat. As soon as they finish eating, Jesse goes into the kitchen to wash their dishes, and Russell starts to play "Call of Duty" on his PlayStation. After Jesse finishes the dishes, he goes through one of his boxes that contains his belongings, located in the corner of the living room, and takes out two fashion magazines. He then brings himself back over to the sofa, where Russell is continuing to play his video game. A few hours later, they both begin to feel sleepy. They decide to retire themselves to the bedroom. Russell changes into an undershirt and pajama pants. Jesse decides to wear a t shirt, and a pair of underwear briefs. They both get in bed, and quickly fall asleep.

The next morning, Russell wakes up and carefully gets out of bed to not wake Jesse. He immediately takes himself to the shower. After bathing, he returns to the bedroom and takes out one of his tailored suits. The one he picked out was a dark gray color. He picks out a red tie to complement the suit, and has on black polished shoes. Jesse continues to sleep as Russell quickly puts his outfit on. As he's leaving his bedroom, he goes to kiss Jesse who's still sleeping on the forehead. Russell then gets his briefcase and puts the Ziploc bag full of items which belong to bank, inside of his briefcase. Russell heads towards his car, and drives to the "Los Angeles Federal Credit Union", business office. He looks outside and notices that today is a clear sunny day. He approaches the front desk, and talks to the receptionist.

"Good Morning, I'm Russell McCoy. I suspended myself from one of your banks, and I was one of the superiors at that bank. I'm returning all my classified items."

The receptionist directs him towards the personnel office. Russell securely drops the items off, and signs certified papers, which prove that he returned the items. As he's leaving the building, waiting outside the elevator he sees Yvette. In this moment, she begins to run toward his direction shouting his name.

"Russell! Not that I'm glad I caught you, but I guess I'm glad that I did catch you. This is really important. On Thursday, Peter and Jennifer's funeral will take place. Peter's family all chipped in to help bury Jennifer as well, and they are going to have the same memorial service."

Russell puts his hand over his mouth, and he continues to listen to Yvette.

"They originally wanted to have the funerals private, but then they changed their mind, and the funerals are now open to the public. They are still being hush hush about it. I wrote down all the information here. Please tell Jesse about this. I have to go now."

Yvette quickly hands Russell a piece of paper that has the address of the memorial, and the time it will take place at. She then vanishes from the current scene. Russell scans over the paper very quickly, then directs himself inside the elevator. He then heads over to his car heading home. When he reaches his residence, Jesse is in the kitchen preparing himself a bowl of cereal. Jesse has on a T-Shirt, and a pair of denim shorts. Russell sets his briefcase down on the kitchen counter and starts talking to him.

"While I was out, by chance I ran into Yvette. She told me that they are having a funeral service for Peter and Jennifer on Thursday. Peter's family is paying for the service for Jennifer as well, so that's nice. Here is where it will take place at."

Russell hands Jesse the paper with the information on it. While Jesse is reading the paper, Russell starts to loosen his tie and takes his suit jacket off, and folds it on the back of the sofa in the living room. He then sits down on the sofa, turning the television on. Jesse quickly follows sitting beside him. Jesse gives the paper back to Russell, as he puts it in his pocket. Russell then puts his arm around the back of Jesse's neck, and starts to softly speak to him.

"I don't like funerals. I just don't. I don't like sad stuff like that. I never have."

Russell starts to run his hand through Jesse's hair, and pulls out his phone.

"I gotta call Kev, because I want him to come with me for moral support. I just don't like funerals, and I want to go and honor Peter and Jennifer the right way."

Russell calls up Kevin who's at his apartment fixing computer hardware for his clients. When he notices that Russell is calling his phone, he answers it.

"What's up Russ? Is there something you need man?"

As he's looking down toward the ground, Russell converses with Kevin on the phone.

"Uh no Kev, I'm alright. On Thursday I have to go to a funeral and you're coming with me whether you want to or not. It's going to be on Thursday morning. So yeah."

Kevin who's continuing his work, responds to Russell.

"Yeah Russ, I'll be there, no problem. Hey, you don't have to pick me up. I'll be over there on Thursday. I'll see you then. Alright, Ok man."

Russell and Kevin disconnect the call. Following that, Russell gets himself up from the sofa, and starts to prance around the living room rubbing one hand behind his head.

"I'm trying to see where I put my Tanakh at. I want to give a eulogy to Peter and Jennifer in Hebrew, and I want to practice. You've never heard me speak Hebrew either, so you're in for a treat. I know where my yarmulke is. It's right here."

Russell walks over to under the television set, pulling out a box. He then shows Jesse his yarmulke. It is a small black cap, with a blue and white cross stitched design. Jesse begins to feel the texture of the yarmulke. This is very important for him to wear, as it is custom as Russell is Jewish, that they wear one during a funeral service. Russell puts the box back under the television set, and starts to head in the bedroom towards the closet.

"If it's not in here, I'm gonna be really mad. Because I think...ah here it is. Yes."

Coming back into the living room, Russell presents Jesse a black book with Hebrew written on the outside of it. The book looks very old.

"This is my Tanakh, or my bible. This is my grandfathers, and I've had this since, wow, I want to say I've had this since I was five. It's been that long. Damn."

Jesse continues to be captivated by Russell's culture, and Russell continues to talk.

"This is the verse I'm gonna use. Here I go, it's been a while since I spoke Hebrew, but I'm going to try my best;"

אֶחְסָר לֹא ,רֹעִי יְהוָה :לְדָוִד מִזְמוֹר.

יְנַהֲלֵנִי מְנֻחוֹת מֵי-עַל ;יַרְבִּיצֵנִי ,דֶּשֶׁא תִּבְנָאוֹ.

שְׁמוֹ לְמַעַן ,צֶדֶק-בְמַעְגְּלֵי יַנְחֵנִי ;יְשׁוֹבֵב נַפְשִׁי.

עִמָּדִי אַתָּה-כִּי --רָע אִירָא-לֹא ,צַלְמָוֶת בְּגֵיא אֵלֵךְ-כִּי גַּם;

יְנַחֲמֻנִי הֵמָּה ,וּמִשְׁעַנְתֶּךָ שִׁבְטְךָ.

צֹרְרָי נֶגֶד --שֻׁלְחָן ,לְפָנַי תַּעֲרֹךְ;

רְוָיָה כּוֹסִי ,רֹאשִׁי בַשֶּׁמֶן דִּשַּׁנְתָּ.

חַיָּי יְמֵי-כָּל --יִרְדְּפוּנִי וָחֶסֶד טוֹב ,אַךְ;

יָמִים לְאֹרֶךְ ,יְהוָה-בְּבֵית וְשַׁבְתִּי.

Russell closes the book, and starts to cry. Jesse gets up from the sofa and hugs him.

"Russ, that was so beautiful, such a lovely language."

While he's still hugging Jesse, Russell responds to him.

"Yeah, that was the Psalm of Comfort. It's a pretty verse. In addition to speaking Hebrew I can also speak Russian as well Jesse. It's been a while since I spoke Russian as well too. I'm going see if I can say the same verse in Hebrew in Russian. Hold on."

а надеющиеся на Господа обновятся в силе: поднимут крылья, как орлы, потекут – и не устанут, пойдут – и не утомятся.

Russell and Jesse continue to hug, with Jesse complimenting his different lexicons.

"Russell, that is so lovely. I never knew you spoke both of those languages."

They separate from hugging each other, and Russell puts his Tanakh under the television set. He walks towards the kitchen to grab a beer from the refrigerator returning to the sofa after.

"Well, I only know some stuff. I guess I'm semi fluent. I kinda memorized all the religious shit. My Grandfather taught me how to speak Hebrew and Russian, and I just held onto the words I guess."

Jesse nods his head and sits down on the sofa. Russell starts to drink his beer, and also takes a seat. He cuts the television off, and they both sit in complete silence. Jesse then rests his head on Russell's shoulder and closes his eyes. While he's drinking his beer, Russell continues.

"I'm tired Jess. Both physically and mentally. I'm a fucking wreck. Life is becoming so tough to deal with, and I miss Peter and I miss Jennifer as well. This is not right. I don't understand, and I'm scared that I probably won't ever understand why life is like this."

Russell has been approached with the thought of death so many times. The deaths of his parents being most significant and prominent. Dealing with funerals was also one that caused him much grief and sorrow. Being remembered and reminded of the deceased, is depressing and seeing others congregate for such an upsetting occasion. Russell struggled to power himself into dealing with such events, and ultimately he would always feel drained in the process. Stuck into this mental trap of sadness, and trying to escape into peacefulness. Russell becomes too closed with himself, and from the emotional anguish he's seen. Honestly, he's far too scared to deal with these thoughts. As so, this is a weakness he must improve on.

Thursday, the day of the funeral approaches, and Russell and Jesse start to get ready. Russell picks out an all-black suit, with a black tie and black shoes. Russell also puts on his yarmulke. Jesse decides to wear a black vest, with long black slacks. As they are getting ready, someone knocks on the door. Russell proceeds towards the door, and its Kevin. Likewise, with Russell, Kevin is Jewish. He also wears a yarmulke. Also slightly identical to Russell's, his is black with a white stitched design on the outside borders of the cap. Very identical with Russell as well, Kevin is wearing a black suit with a black tie. He walks into the living room and hugs Jesse, and proceeds to chat with Russell.

"Russ, how do I look? I look fine right? You look sharp man."

Russell starts to investigate Kevin and looks all over his body.

"Kev, your collar is all crooked. Here, that's a lot better. Wait hold on. Let me fix your tie as well, that's looking off too. Alright, you look okay to me now. Oh hell, wait. Your fly is open. Let me fix that."

Kevin starts to feel uncomfortable over Russell's behavior.

"Russ, you didn't have to do that, I could have done that myself."

Kevin and Jesse then laugh at each other over the way Russell is behaving. Jesse decides takes a seat on the sofa and sits quietly. Immediately after this, Russell walks towards the television set to grab his Tanakh. While he's doing so, Kevin starts to get bored. He decides to grab the remote control on top of the table in the living room, and turns the television set on. Kevin then proceeds to takes a seat on the sofa, and make himself comfortable. Russell as soon as he heard the sound of the television being turned on, looks at Kevin with an angry disappointed look. Kevin laughs and smiles at him, and Russell quickly snatches the remote from him, and turns the television off. Right after that, Russell walks back under the television set to get his Tanakh. He then starts speaking to Kevin in a very strict tone, looking for his Tanakh.

"Kev, I don't want you acting up at this funeral okay? I'm going to get up to give a eulogy, and I don't want to hear you laugh or do any type of outbursts. I'm having second thoughts on inviting you to be honest, but just promise me that you'll behave. I don't want any monkey business from you Kev. I want you to behave at this funeral."

Kevin looks over at Jesse and begins to mock Russell while he's talking. When Russell turns his head over to Kevin, Kevin quickly knocks it off, and responds to him.

"Wow Russ, is that really what you take me for? Yeah I'm an ignoramus, but you really take me for all of that Russ? I can't believe you man. What kind of friend are you?"

Kevin then begins to laugh out loud hysterically, and Jesse mildly giggles with him. Russell finally gets his Tanakh, and walks over to the kitchen counter to grab his car keys.

"Kev, Jesse come on. We're leaving now."

The three men then proceed towards Russell's car, on their way to the funeral. Russell still very anxious and feeling uneasy about attending. As they are walking to the car, Kevin tries to grab Russell's Tanakh, and Russell swipes his hand away from him.

"Russ, I want to read your Tanakh man. I'm not completely orthodox like you. Wait a minute Russ, you're not orthodox either, so why do you even have that?"

Russell unlocks the car doors and leers over at Kevin. Jesse watches the both of them bicker and is quietly keeping to himself over the current situation. Jesse gets into the back seat, and Russell runs over to the passenger side to berate Kevin.

"Kev get in the damn car; I don't need you to act like a comedian right now. I don't have time for your bullshit man. Get in the car and behave yourself please."

Kevin smiles at Russell and takes a seat inside the car. Russell, Kevin and Jesse all put their sunglasses on, and Russell starts the car ignition. As he is pulling out of the parking structure of the apartment complex, Kevin turns on the car stereo, but Russell quickly mutes it. He's not in the mood to hear music right now, and would rather have a quiet car ride. Russell while driving notices that the weather is awfully ugly today. For Los Angeles, which is noted for their sunny warm weather, is not the case this time around. The sky is a very hazy and gray tone. The gloomy overcast clouds that surround the atmosphere, give off a very off vibe and theme, not one to bring joy. Russell continues to drive to the funeral, but for a second turns his head towards the passenger seat. He notices Kevin using his saliva and fingers to clean his tie, and without Kevin noticing, Russell winces to himself. Jesse remains in the rear seat quiet and obedient. Russell continues to approach the memorial service. It will be held outside, despite the terrible weather conditions for the day. They continue towards the funeral for several more minutes. Kevin starts to fidget to himself, and then takes out his phone, to pull up a funny YouTube video. He then reaches behind the rear seat, showing the video to Jesse. Jesse looks at Kevin's phone, but doesn't give a reaction, and remains quiet. Russell while he is driving, then snatches Kevin's phone from his hand and confiscates it by putting his phone in his pocket. Kevin then immediately snaps at Russell.

"Russ, give me my phone man. Why did you do that for?"

Russell keeps his eyes forward on the road, and ignores Kevin. He then starts to shake his head, and rest his hand across the bottom of his neck. When he reaches a stoplight, he digs into his pocket, and throws Kevin's phone back at him; landing on his lap. Kevin then quickly picks his phone up and continues to look at videos on it. While they are all still waiting at the stoplight, Jesse then pulls out a sympathy card that Russell gave him earlier, and a pen from his tote bag, and starts to sign it. He then hands the card to Kevin who signs it as well. Russell signs the card and hands it back to Jesse soon after. The signal changes, and Russell continues towards the funeral. About twenty minutes later, they finally arrive.

The procession which is being held outside, has many white chairs across the graveyard. Peter and Jennifer's coffins are positioned behind the pulpit. Many flower arrangements are around the coffins. Russell parks his car and, they all get out. Russell starts to profile all of the attendees at the funeral. He immediately sees Yvette and her children. Also present at the funeral, are all the other employees at the "Sunset Credit Union". Sally, Tiffany, Abel, and John. John in particular who is now the manager of the "Sunset Credit Union." Incidentally, which happened to be Russell's past position. Russell and

John last met on difficult terms. He started to get into a physical fight with him, which led him to resign himself from the bank. Russell on purpose tries not to give any eye contact towards John.

Russell continuing to scan the attendees, also notices not one, but two strange looking gentlemen looking out of place at the funeral seated at opposite sections. These two gentlemen don't know each other, but Russell seems to have a feeling that he knows the both of them. He has never met them before, but has a feeling as if he has. One of the men is a very handsome well-built man, with short styled hair. He like Russell is wearing a black suit with a black tie. The other man however is very odd and creepy looking. He has very pale skin, and has a very cold straggly face. The man is very unconventional looking. He is wearing a white shirt, with a black tie. Russell however ignoring this strange feeling he has, still feels anxious about it. He doesn't understand why he feels so uncomfortable over those two men. He, along with Kevin and Jesse all sit together.

The memorial service then begins. Russell starts to feel emotional upon witnessing the funeral proceedings. He starts to cry when Peter's wife starts to speak about him. Jennifer's mother and father also say a few words in her memory. Russell remains seated under much sorrow, well aware that the time to give his eulogy is approaching very soon. Things for Russell start to become tense, when he notices John walk up to offer his words. Russell tries his best to calm himself down, as John brings him much aggravation. He starts to remember all of the harsh things that he has said to Peter, and how much John envied him as well. When John finishes, it is now Russell's turn to offer his peace to both Peter and Jennifer. He walks up towards the pulpit, and gives his eulogy.

"My name is Russell McCoy. Peter and Jennifer worked with me. Peter was a beautiful man, and he was like a father to me. He was. Jennifer, lovely young woman. Going to miss them both very much. I'm going to say a passage for commemorate them both."

מִזְמוֹר לְדָוִד: יְהוָה רֹעִי, לֹא אֶחְסָר.

בִּנְאוֹת דֶּשֶׁא, יַרְבִּיצֵנִי; עַל-מֵי מְנֻחוֹת יְנַהֲלֵנִי.

נַפְשִׁי יְשׁוֹבֵב; יַנְחֵנִי בְמַעְגְּלֵי-צֶדֶק, לְמַעַן שְׁמוֹ.

גַּם כִּי-אֵלֵךְ בְּגֵיא צַלְמָוֶת, לֹא-אִירָא רָע-- כִּי-אַתָּה עִמָּדִי;

שִׁבְטְךָ וּמִשְׁעַנְתֶּךָ, הֵמָּה יְנַחֲמֻנִי.

תַּעֲרֹךְ לְפָנַי, שֻׁלְחָן-- נֶגֶד צֹרְרָי;

דִּשַּׁנְתָּ בַשֶּׁמֶן רֹאשִׁי, כּוֹסִי רְוָיָה.

Russell while giving the eulogy, becomes mentally frozen. He reads the passage incomplete. Physically, he is strong enough to deliver the words. However mentally, Russell is currently being reminded of all the events that he and Peter have gone through. He's being reminded of the beauty Jennifer had. The fact they are now gone and being put under that much depression. Russell continues to give the eulogy, trying his best to remain from crying. More and more flashbacks of Peter and Jennifer run rampant in his mind. He would have never envisioned that this would happen. Russell felt that he could be strong enough to deliver this eulogy, but he now begins to feel this force of depression. He cannot move, and he feels like a concrete statue. One of Russell's biggest fears he had, was that he would cry during the eulogy. Alongside that, not being powerful enough to deliver the words. Unfortunately, this fear came true.

Although he started the eulogy off well, Russell all of a sudden cannot control himself, and begins to sob during the last line of the scripture. He stops reading the eulogy and looks out into the audience, continuing to sob. He looks down at his Tanakh and tries to speak out the words, but he cannot. As he continues to cry, Yvette then notices how hurt he is. She puts her past differences of Russell aside, and walks up to the pulpit and hugs him tightly. She then kisses Russell on the cheek several times, as she continues to hug him. Kevin starts to shake his head, and also feels sad seeing Russell in this condition. Jesse begins to cry and feel upset as well. Yvette continues to comfort and calm Russell down, as Russell cries and is choked up on his words. A few moments later, Russell with the help from Yvette, has pulled himself together, and manages to finish the eulogy.

חַיַּי יְמֵי-כָל --יִרְדְּפוּנִי וָחֶסֶד טוֹב ,אַךְ;

יָמִים לְאֹרֶךְ ,יְהוָה-בְּבֵית וְשַׁבְתִּי.

Yvette then kisses Russell on the cheek again, and holds his hand as they walk away from the pulpit. Russell was disappointed with himself that he wasn't able to give the eulogy, without having a mental breakdown. He was thankful and glad that he was able to make amends with Yvette. When he returns to his seat, Kevin starts to rub Russell's shoulder. They both stare at each other, in which Russell has a stoic face. Kevin gives him a smile nevertheless. Jesse also does the same as Kevin, and rubs Russell shoulder, but Russell gives Jesse a cold stare as well. Russell then takes out his handkerchief and begins to wipe his face.

Shortly after Russell's eulogy, the funeral continues with a couple more speakers coming up to talk and offer their respects. The memorial service was soon over and finished after that. As the funeral was concluding, patrons began to hug, and then walk towards their car to leave. Jesse walks over to Yvette, and they both hug and kiss and say goodbye. Russell signals for Kevin and Jesse to follow him. Russell decides to walk over to one of the guys he had a strange feeling about, the handsome one. The man is sitting by himself looking very nervous and unsure of himself. Russell decides to approach him, and sticks his hand out for him to shake it.

"Excuse me, I have weird feeling that we've met before. I'm Russell McCoy. I was a very close coworker to the deceased. I don't know why I feel like I've met you before."

The man shakes Russell's hand and introduces himself, yet fibbing about his name.

"I'm Martin. Martin Caputo. I look familiar? Funny, you look familiar as well. I can't put my finger on to where I know you from though. But you look familiar as well."

Russell looks at the man very suspiciously, and presses him some more.

"If you don't mind me asking, how are you in relation to the deceased?"

The man then starts to rub the back of his head, and stops for a couple seconds. He then starts to laugh and grin. He then responds with another fib.

"Oh, well I'm an old golfing buddy of Peter's. Me and him go way, way, back. Yeah. He was such a nice friend to have. I'm gonna miss him."

The other man Russell seemed to have a feeling that he recognized, the unconventional creepy one, remains in his seat, listening to Russell speak to this man. Russell snaps back at the man exposing him.

"Peter never played golf. In fact, hated it very much. He always thought it was boring, and Peter was more of a hang-gliding and more extreme sport type of guy. So why don't you start to tell the truth now. Just stop lying, because you're clearly bad at it."

The man then looks around, and continues to rubs the back of his head. He waves his hand signaling for Russell to follow him to a more intimate area.

"Okay, Okay, you caught me. My name isn't Martin. Tell you what, why don't we go out for a drink? Does that sound good, and we can talk about this more?"

Russell stares at the man for a few minutes, and then responds.

"Alright, you seem innocent enough. I want to get to the bottom of this right now. Something fishy is going on. But yeah, we can talk about this over a drink."

The man smiles back at Russell and replies to him.

"I know this really good bar; it has a good vibe. The drinks are nice, it's really good. It's quite far from here though. Just follow me and I'll take you there. Okay?"

Russell, Kevin and Jesse then walk towards Russell's car. Russell notices that the man gets into a luxury Mercedes that has no license plates. He shrugs this off, and gets in his car and starts the engine. Russell starts to follow this strange character to the bar he recommended to them. He continues to caravan behind this man for almost a half an hour. Kevin starts to get suspicious and screams and hollers at Russell.

"Russ, this guy could be a psycho killer and you're just following him. I mean, at first I thought it was cute that he wanted us to go for a drink with him. But the longer we drive, the more I think this man is just plain creepy. I don't about this Russ."

Russell ignores Kevin, and continues to follow this strange man. Russell was on a mission to find out why this man seemed so familiar to him. As soon as he noticed him at the funeral, Russell began to have so many thoughts in his head. He somehow is connected towards this man, and the fact he is still in mystery over the circumstances around him, Russell feels determined to find out the ties that they both share. The more minutes that pass driving behind this man, is the more anxious Russell gets. He anticipates breaking this guy, and cracking the code towards his ambiguity. Russell looks at the passenger seat and notices Kevin acting scared.

"Russ, I think we should stop following him. Let's just leave him alone. The reason he looks familiar; is you probably saw him on Unsolved Mysteries or something Russ. He's a psycho and that's why his face sticks out. Russ, I'm your old college buddy listen to me. You're gonna follow and listen to this guy you don't even know, and ignore me Russ? I don't believe this at all. You're starting to scare me Russ."

Jesse remains in the back seat quiet and under anxiety as well. He doesn't question Russell at all, only trusting his intuition. Russell continues to follow the man. Kevin then continues to worry and try to convince Russell to stray away.

"Russ, listen to me man. This guy is bad news. You're gonna look back at this and say to yourself, 'I should have just listened to Kev'. Russ you're starting to scare me and Jesse."

Russell then gives Kevin a very terrifying grin and begins to laugh. Jesse starts to frown and worry, yet continues to stay silent and not speak at this time. Russell continues down the road following behind the mysterious man in the Mercedes. Kevin continues.

"Russ, pull over. I can't do this. I don't want anything to do with this man. I hate it when you get like this Russ. You're transforming into some evil devil, and I want nothing to do with this Russ, so just pull over and let me out because I don't want any part of this."

Russell turns his head towards Kevin and laughs at him.

"Kev, shut the fuck up. I know what I'm doing okay. I would never put you or Jesse in any harm alright. This guy isn't going to hurt us either. I do want to find out who he is though."

Kevin looks down towards the floor and takes his glasses off. He starts to cover his hands with his eyes, and continues to scream at Russell.

"Russ, I can't watch this. This is nothing but trouble. You're gonna get us all killed man."

Russell laughs at Kevin and continues to drive behind the man. Jesse remains silent in the back seat, also in fear of Russell's actions. Russell is fired up now, and nothing is going to stop him from pursuing who this strange man is. He doesn't sense any danger from him, or else Russell would have distanced himself. The mysterious feeling he had at the funeral however, had to have meant something and held some type of value. Russell also feels that he has travelled too far at this point, to turn back and leave this man alone. He has wasted too much time already to give up and leave the man alone. He has been following this man for over two hours, since they have met at the funeral, so Russell felt he deserved to resolve this particular issue. If he honestly felt that Kevin and Jesse were in immediate danger, he wouldn't proceed. Russell didn't feel that way. He knew that wasn't the case with this man, this was something more ethereal than that.

The man finally pulls up to a deserted saloon in an industrial area of San Pedro. An area located South West of Los Angeles. There are many factories and warehouses adjacent to the bar. Russell, Kevin and Jesse get out of the car, and the man gets out of his car. All four men then walk inside the bar. Upon entering the bar, Russell starts to notice the art style and how extravagant the interior looks. The bar has a Wild Wild West theme, and it shows as there many frontier and western influenced decorations and styles scattered all across. The bar stools look like they were made in the 1800s, and have a classical vibe towards them. There are many cowboy hats hung up on the wall. The dark brown wooden paneling the walls have, add to the ambiance of the building. There is an old style jukebox, and most of the popular playlists are of country western music. All of the booths and tables of the bar look like stagecoaches to pay more homage to the western vibe. There is also a pool table located in the bar.

Russell approaches the mystery man who's looking smug.

"Okay, now we can do this the easy way or the hard way. Tell me who you are. Now!"

The man looks at Russell and begins to smirk and chuckle to himself. He then walks over to the bar, and orders drinks for everyone.

"Let me get a double shot of scotch, and what I can get you?"

He turns to look at Russell, who gives him his drink order.

"I'll take three Jägerbombs."

The mysterious man then turns to look at Kevin and Jesse wanting their drink order. Kevin gives his drink order to the mysterious man first.

"I'll have a Long Island Iced Tea."

Jesse then gives his drink order to the man.

"I'll have a double shot of Jack and Coke."

The mysterious man then turns towards the bartender, and hands him dollar bills.

"You heard what they wanted, now fix us all up."

The bartender quickly serves their drinks. Russell takes one of his shots, and turns to look at the mysterious man grinning at him ferociously. He then screams at him.

"Okay, now you tell me who you are. No more playing around."

The mystery man laughs at Russell, and starts sipping on his cocktail. Kevin and Jesse sip their drinks and watch Russell and the strange man with fear and in confusion. The man then starts to walk towards the pool table. He takes a pool cue and begins to rub chalk on the end of it.

"Do you play pool?"

Russell beings to scrunch his face up at the man, and marches over to the pool table. He takes his suit jacket off, handing it to Jesse.

He then proceeds to take a pool cue and also begins to rub chalk on the cue stick, staring at the man while doing it.

"Unfortunately for you, I do. I can also play it quite well. What's the deal? You want to play a game? I'm down. I'm gonna beat you, but I'm down."

The man then gives a devilish laugh towards Russell and puts quarters inside of the pool table. He then begins to set up the pool balls. As he's doing it, he starts to make a bet with Russell.

"If you win, I'll tell you where you know me from, and believe me you're gonna flip once you find out. However, if I win, you and your friends not only have to buy the next round of drinks, but I won't tell you my name, and you'll never know who I am. You'll always be in suspense about me, and wouldn't that be a damn shame?"

Russell gives the mysterious man a very competitive look and starts to crack his knuckles. Kevin then starts to give Russell words of encouragement.

"You can do it Russ, kick his ass. I've seen you play pool a bunch of times before, you used to always whoop me in it. You got this Russ, you can beat him!"

Russell ignores Kevin, as he watches the man of mystery set the balls on the table. Russell is indeed very skilled in billiards. However, he does not know the skill level of this man, and he could be more advanced than Russell is. Russell is well aware that he must win this game if he wishes to know who the identify of this man actually is. The mystery man goes first, breaking the balls originally quite well. He is having great accuracy with his shots, and is giving Russell a run for his money. The man continues to sink his set, hitting every correct pattern accurately. He is down to only one ball left. However, the man suddenly misjudges the aim of his shot, and sinks the 8 ball into the hole. It is now Russell's turn to shoot. Russell begins to sink the first of his balls perfectly. Russell is completely focused, and has his eye on the prize. It all comes down to the moment where the mystery man made his mistake. Russell only has to make this shot, without the 8 ball or the cue ball being sunk. Feeling extremely confident that he can win, he prepares to take his final shot. Russell successfully manages to sink his last ball into the hole. Kevin immediately goes up to hug Russell, and Jesse as well applauds for him. Russell then gives the man a triumphant look, and talks to him.

"Alright now, you said If I won the game, you would tell me who you were, now spill the beans. You need to keep your end of the bargain now."

The mysterious man then begins to wade by the pool table. He is feeling scared, and starts to act very nervously. He then walks up to Russell and whispers at him.

"Okay, I'll tell you. But you have to come outside with me though."

Russell frowns at him, but nods his head. Jesse hands Russell back his suit jacket, and Russell proceeds to put it on. The mysterious man and Russell then walk out to the bar's parking lot. The man then covers his mouth with his hand, and in a shy way, speaks to Russell.

"Now look, you have to promise that you won't freak out once I tell you who I am. Because I'm not a bad guy, I just make bad choices sometimes. I'm scared, and part of me thinks once I tell you who I am, you are going to freak the fuck out. Please don't."

Russell continues to frown at the man and give him impatient looks. Russell then crosses his arms, and moves in closer to the man, and softly speaks to him.

"Man, just tell me who the fuck you are. I don't want to turn on my mean switch, but I will very quickly if you don't hurry up and tell me who you are."

The man becomes even more scared and nervous and puts his hands in his suit jacket. He starts to waddle himself around the parking lot. He walks back to Russell who is looking very angry and fed up with him. Russell has had enough and grabs him by the collar. He finally reveals who he is with a guilty look on his face.

"I'm the guy who ran in the robbery."

Russell while still grabbing him by the collar, starts shaking his head, and laughs.

CHAPTER 9:

NOTHING LOVED, NOTHING HATED

For almost a minute, Russell continued to grab the man by his collar, staring at his eyes with a confused grin. Russell had a strange feeling about this man, and it turns out the feeling was justified. He was now looking in the eyes of the man who got away in the robbery. The first thing that can only come to Russell's shocked mind, that this is the more cowardly man in the robbery. He wasn't that one that killed Peter and Jennifer, yet he was still involved in the robbery. Russell if he was programmed like a normal human being which he isn't, would be calling the authorities right now on this man and doing a citizen's arrest. However, he isn't going to. Russell is sociopathic, and doesn't think in that manner. He starts to over analyze everything on the table. Consider the fact this man was brave and stupid enough to admit that he was the other person in the robbery. Russell felt this guy wasn't as tough as he was leading himself out to be. This man was clearly just as confused as Russell was, and maybe misplaced in society, not knowing what category to put himself under. Russell finally let's go of his collar, and the mystery man starts to dust his jacket off looking at Russell while he's doing it. Russell then starts to give the man a threatening look, and starts to speak to him.

"You're not so tough. If you were a real tough guy, you wouldn't be stupid enough to just admit you're at large for an armed robbery. You robbed my fucking bank, your buddy killed two of my friends. I don't know how you have the balls to stand there. I should fucking kill you right now. There is something completely off about you. What is your name? Your real name."

The man looks around the lot for a few seconds, then turns his head to Russell.

"Look, I'm sorry, okay? I'm a car jacker and I'm a mechanic. That's my thing. I don't rob banks. I hang around the wrong crowd. The other guy, Scotty. I thought he was a cool guy, but he wasn't. He always tried to convince me to rob banks with him. The day of the robbery, was the first day I ever robbed a bank. We robbed two banks that day, and yours was the third."

Russell gives the man a disgusted look and walks closer to him.

"What's your fucking name. I didn't ask to hear any of that. I mean, I'm glad you told me, but I would like to know what your name is. What is your name?"

Another few seconds pass with the man looking around the parking lot with a scared look on his face, before he finally reveals who he is to Russell.

"My name is Brian. Brian Fratelli. I'm originally from New York. I'm not from LA. I only came out here because I was into street racing and cars like I said. I'm not a bank robber, I'm not a murderer or any of that. I just jack cars, and rich people cars. That's it."

Brian then begins to explain himself more to Russell.

"I was reading the newspaper, and on the obituaries, I remember the faces of the man and woman that Scott killed. I just had to go to the funeral to pay my respects."

Russell then reaches into his pocket and pulls out a pack of cigarettes and a lighter. He takes two cigarettes of the carton and hands one to Brian who quickly snags it from him. Russell lights the cigarette, and after giving him the lighter, Brian lights his cigarette up as well. Brian was a handsome, and medium built, shaped and heighted man. He had brown hair, in the form of a tapered crew cut. Brian spoke in a clear and smooth east coast accent. He is of Italian descent, and even though he was thirty-one-years old, he could easily pass for being in his twenties. Brian like Russell, suffers from narcissist personality disorder, and also deals with anti-social issues in addition to that. His personal life is very complex to explain. Brian never met his father, and his mother passed away he when was young. His family lives all across the country, but mainly on the east coast of the United States. He struggles with relationships, and considers himself a self-proclaimed "trisexual", and struggles finding bonds with both men and with women. So he lives a single life by himself. Ever since he was young, Brian was always a juvenile delinquent, and he had a bad habit of stealing cars. Which he has been cautioned by the police many times for. It was something he could never control himself over. The more luxurious the car was, the more he wanted to get his hands on it. But Brian claims he would only steal cars, from people that looked like they were high profile. Such as wealthy and prolific people.

Brian would use his carjacking skills to earn money for himself by taking the cars to chop shops, participating in illegal street racing actives, or taking the parts from these cars, and using them to help out less fortunate people who he would do car repairs for. Brian used to work for an auto repair shop in Los Angeles not long ago, but sadly was fired when he was caught trying to used unauthorized parts to fix cars. Many years ago, Brian formed and on and off relationship with a dangerous man named Scott. Brian would work for him by stealing cars and delivering them for profit. Brian began to feel guilty from stealing cars and didn't want to continue doing that. He wanted to change his life around, or at least find something else to earn a hustle off from.

A couple months ago, Scott who has robbed many banks in the past, approached Brian and asked if he wanted to help him rob three separate banks on the same day. Brian reluctantly agreed to help him out, despite not having any past experience as a bank robber. He was unaware of Scott's history, and that he was an extremely violent man. Brian managed to steal the van they used for the heist. Upon witnessing Brian shoot Jennifer, he became scared and ran out of the bank. Brian didn't receive any money from the robbery, as the other robber was killed by the police, leaving the stolen money in the bank. After Jennifer was shot, he quickly ran to his residence, without going into the van to retrieve the rest of the stolen money.

Kevin and Jesse who were secretly watching Russell and Brian the entire time, walk to the area of the parking lot which they are standing in, and join them. Kevin then talks to Brian.

"This is a small world huh? Every fucking thing is connected. Wow. We're not gonna snitch on you, don't worry. We're a bunch of psychos too. Welcome to the club."

Kevin then takes a pack of cigarettes from his pocket, and gives Jesse one as well. They both light their cigarettes. Kevin then turns his head to Russell, and continues to talk.

"Wow Russ, you have some sort of sixth sense or something. You knew this guy was hiding something, I just don't know how you were able to figure that out. Damn."

Russell starts to take puffs of his cigarette smiling at Kevin.

"Yeah Kev, I'm the devil remember. I'm just using my satanic powers. I'm not like anybody else, and I can tell when someone is hiding something. I'm magic."

Jesse then turns his head towards Brian and asks him a question.

"So, you were really the guy that ran? I can't believe any of this, how does all of this come full circle like that? I also find it funny that Russell had a feeling about you too."

Brian smiles at Jesse and takes a puff from his cigarette. Then replies to him.

"Yup, that was me. I'm not proud or anything. I mean, I'm sorry. All I can do is apologize, and I feel so stupid admitting this to all of you. I trust you guys, like you all trust me. I'm not an evil guy at all, I just make really bad choices and hang with the wrong people."

Kevin then puts hand on Brian's shoulder and speaks to him in a soft tone.

"We all make mistakes, it's fine. The important part is that you feel remorse, and that you are honest with all of us. That's a good start, that's all that really matters if you think about it."

Russell takes another puff of his cigarette and begins to trust Brian, and realize that he is a safe guy to be around. He sticks his hand to out Brian.

"I'm Russell. I was the manager…well ex manager of the bank. That's Jesse, you know he was another of the workers at the bank. This is Kevin, he's my best friend."

Brian begins to shake all of the guy's hands. There is an awkward silence for almost two minutes, until Brian turns his head towards Russell, and converses with him.

"Uh, do you want me to buy you guys some more drinks? Is there anything I can do for you guys? Just let me know, and I can do it. I really owe all of you anyways."

Russell takes another puff of his cigarette, and starts to look around the parking lot. He squints his eyes, and then notices a suspicious looking Volvo with tinted windows. Russell clearly deduces that he also saw this same car at the parking lot of the funeral. Whoever this person is, followed them to the bar. He starts to have an identical feeling that he had towards Brian, and that the person that car belongs to, is as well in some shape or form connected to the incident that happened at the "Sunset Credit Union". Russell then wonders if he should investigate about this more, or to leave this feeling alone. At this point, Russell feels he has absolutely nothing to lose, and throws his cautions to the wind. He immediately begins to walk over to the car. Kevin notices him doing this, and screams out to him.

"Russ, where are you going? Why are you going to the car man? Russ!"

Russell continues to walk towards the car, with a furious look on his face. He reaches the driver side window, which is tinted to such a deep level, you cannot see who's inside. Russell then knocks on the driver window, and doesn't get a response. He knocks again, yelling.

"Open the door. Who are you? I know you're in there. Open the damn door now."

Kevin, Jesse and Brian look at Russell in shock. Kevin runs over to Russell.

"Russ come on, there is nobody in that car. Calm down man. You're starting to scare me again. Just leave it alone Russ. There's nobody in the car man."

Russell ignores Kevin, and cups his hands over the car window, in order to see who is inside. The windows are so deeply tinted, it's impossible to tell. Russell knocks on the door again, and doesn't receive an answer. He then turns his head towards Kevin.

"Kev, this guy followed us from the funeral. It's the same car. There was a guy at the funeral I had a weird feeling about, similar to the feeling I had with Brian. This is just crazy."

Kevin takes a puff from his cigarette and also cups his hands towards the window.

"Russ, he's probably a cop or something. That's more than likely what this is. An unmarked cop car, and that's why you're acting like that. So if it is a cop, leave him alone Russ."

Russell turns his head towards Kevin, and snaps back at him.

"Kev, he's not a cop. Or at least I don't think he is. He's just from what I remember a kind of weird looking guy. Kev, this guy looked creepy, I mean you had to have seen him. He was at the funeral but was sitting in the back. I don't know why he was there either. Hmm."

Kevin looks down towards the floor and is speechless. In this same moment, Jesse and Brian walk over to the suspicious car, and start to cup their hands on the window. Brian starts to walk around the car and assess different things about it.

"This is a really nice classic Volvo. That's an unbelievable tint job. I can do something like that quite easy, I'm really good with auto detailing and stuff. Wow, beautiful ride."

Russell looks at Brian and shakes his head. He continues to knock on the door.

"Hey man, I know you're in there, so just open the door. I believe you know who I am, so stop fooling around. I'm not gonna hurt you or get mad. Just get out the car man."

A second after this, the window on the driver's side lowers a half an inch. The men outside of the car stand in shock and horror from this. A few seconds more later, a voice starts to speak from inside of the car, in a very hushed and eerie manner.

"I'll get out right now. Hold on, I'll be out in just a second."

The window then immediately rolls up, and Russell crosses his arms together. All of the men start to feel anxious and wait in anticipation as to who this actually is. The person eventually exits out of the vehicle; it was the same man Russell had a suspicious feeling about. The man reluctantly starts to position himself out of the car, locking it once he's out. The man is slender and very pale skinned. He has a grainy and bony childish face. He has short straight black split wavy hair. He walks towards the other four men. He then smiles at all of them and speaks.

"You guys wouldn't happen to have another smoke would you?"

Russell laughs at him, and Kevin immediately gives him a cigarette. The man then starts to take several heavy puffs of the cigarette. He then starts to introduce himself.

"My name is Victor Romero. You can call me Victor, Vic, Romero. I don't care."

Russell relights his cigarette, and starts to talk to Victor.

"Where do I know you from? Why do you look so damn familiar Victor?"

Victor while looking down at the ground smoking his cigarette, remains silent for nearly a minute. He finally looks up towards Russell giving him eye contact and finally responds to him in a very reluctant and nervous tone.

"Two weeks ago, I went inside the 'Sunset Credit Union'. I didn't go in there as a customer, I went in there to case the bank. I remember noticing how easy the bank looked to rob. I was planning on robbing it, the same exact day he and his friend came inside to rob it."

Victor then looks up and points to Brian. Brian looks at Victor with a shocked look. Russell then starts to laugh out loud due to shock, which then also causes Kevin to laugh finding the situation hilarious. Jesse then starts to profile Victor more, and speaks to him.

"I think you're now starting to look familiar. As a bank teller, I usually keep track of customers that come in. I saw you that day. No offense, but you looked creepy and like a Nazi. You had the same exact outfit you have on now, that day."

Victor looks up, and walks over towards where Jesse is and smiles. He then proceeds to put his hand on his shoulder, and softly whispers to him.

"Interesting observation. In a past life I may, or may not have been in the Nazi Party."

He then runs his fingers through Jesse's hair and smiles at him some more.

"I really love your afro man. I'm not a bad guy. I'm just creepy looking that's all.

Kevin then starts to laugh at Victor, and starts to tease him.

"Creepy looking? That is such an understatement. Russ, he looks like the fucking Scarecrow from Wizard of Oz. He's like a scary Nazi, scarecrow guy."

Victor then gives Kevin a terrifying cold stare, which causes Kevin to quickly silence himself. Russell then smacks Kevin on the back of the head. He turns and sticks his hand out.

"I'm Russell. That's Kevin, Brian and Jesse."

Victor then shakes the hands of all of the guys. Russell profiles Victor to a great degree, and stares at him deeply.

Victor out of all the five men currently together, is the most ambiguous to assess. Not only does Victor struggle with dissociative personality disorder; a mental illness which causes people to have split personalities and have unoptimistic views towards life and society, Victor also suffers from Obsessive Compulsive Disorder. He has social delusions, and dissociation from society. Similar toward Russell, Victor is not very trustworthy with people, and believes the government is out to murder and eliminate him from the world. He has basically given up towards conforming himself to society in many aspects. Victor is twenty-nine-years-old. He was born to a foreign Japanese mother, and a German American father in California. He has both facial traits of Asian and European features. Victor can speak conversational Japanese and German. His father was in the military, and died during infantry when he was only two years old. His mother died of an illness not long after that. Victor then grew up in foster care all of his life. He hated school, and would always be bullied by his other classmates from the way his face looked. He always struggled with friendships and tried to find a way to fit in. He considers himself a Bisexual/Asexual man, and ignores most romantic relationships. He finds people attractive regardless of gender or body identity. Victor always considered himself an alternative learner, and didn't take in education and information as others did. Victor dropped out of High School when he was sixteen years old. He then went into a deep depression, and escaped and ran away from his foster home. Victor then joined a Nazi Nationalist cult group in Los Angeles, and stayed in their residence for many years. They practiced a racist and homophobic agenda, promoting and producing hate. A few years ago, Victor developed a change of heart and left the cult. Although the result of that has left him homeless. Victor does have a handgun; which he claims he uses for protection as he lives in the street. When he was in the cult, they provided him with a car, which Victor now lives out of. He has worked a number of odd jobs, mainly being a maintenance handy man for office buildings. Money is still very tight for him, and Victor uses food stamps and dumpster dives to feed himself sometimes.

For the past few months, Victor has contemplated robbing a bank. He has cased many banks in the Los Angeles area. He tried to look for one which he felt had the most inferior security, and would be the easiest for him to do the job. He decided to pick the "Sunset Credit Union", and planned to rob the bank the same day Brian and Scott did. Victor arrived at the bank at four that afternoon, yet sat in his car feeling far too scared to actually go inside. A couple minutes before Brian and Scott arrived at the bank, Victor finally decided to commence with the robbery. He got out of his car and proceeded to wait beside the bank, with the handgun tucked behind his pants. He stood behind a column which was hidden in the corner of the "Happy Dry Cleaners", and waited for the right time to enter the bank. However, he was already beaten to the job. Victor watched the entire robbery pan out. He felt guilty that he didn't walk in the bank as he had a gun and could have potentially deescalated the situation, but he felt scared.

Victor began to tell the rest of the men information about himself.

"I was supposed to rob the bank, but I didn't because two other guys got there first. I saw everything go down, I was hiding in that bench in front of the dry cleaners on the side of the bank. I kept thinking to myself, should I walk in or not? I decided not to because I was too scared, and I just didn't want to get involved. I saw both the people get shot, and I saw this lady who was hiding near the deli call the cops, and I just ran back to my car and drove away."

Russell looks at Victor in complete shock and Victor continues and starts to cry.

"I mean, I'm just an ugly creepy homeless guy that scares people. I live out of my car, I don't want to harm anybody. I'm happy with that, and I don't ask for much. I just wanted some easy money, and I regret everything I did. I should have gone in and helped, but I didn't."

Victor takes another puff from his cigarette, and Kevin starts to laugh at Victor. Brian begins to feel sorry for him. Jesse walks over to Victor and starts to rub his shoulder. Russell continues to fold his arms, and locks his eyes at Victor. Gazing at him with an angry look. Seconds later, Russell responds and starts to snap at him.

"Sour grapes. I should have gone to the vault and not Peter. I feel just as guilty about that, as you do for not coming in. But you can't turn back time, so it is what it is I guess. We're all here now, and that's how it is I guess. I don't understand how things happen anymore."

Victor continues to take puffs of his cigarette, and continues to to talk.

"I read the paper all the time. I'm a millennial, but I'm weird and I read the paper. I saw the obituaries were of the people in the bank. So I decided to go to the funeral out of respect. I felt I should have done something and gotten involved. I didn't, so it was the right thing to do for me to come to the funeral to show my respect."

Russell then starts to feel more comfortable. He was able to piece together the two people he saw at the funeral, and have a more eased feeling about that. All of the men then stay quiet for a few minutes, taking in everything. With heavy emotions on everyone's mind, they remain silent. Brian then starts to find a way to equalize this current situation.

"Hey guys, my pad is just around the corner from here. I have a bunch of booze too. How about I order some pizza's, and we all just go and chill. I mean, that is if you trust me or not. It's the least I can do, and we can talk about everything there. Because this is some freaky shit how all of us came together like this, and we all need to go somewhere private."

Kevin immediately jumps and down and starts to hug Brian.

"Man, you said the magic words. Pizza, beer, oh my god yes. I wanna go. Can we Russ?"

Russell looks over at Kevin and smiles. He then nods his head. Victor then puts out his cigarette, and starts to walk towards his car.

"I'll follow you guys over there. I'll be right behind you guys."

All of the men get into their vehicles, and caravan from each other. Brian leads the way, with Russell carrying Kevin and Jesse; with Victor riding right behind them. While in Russell's car, Kevin turns the stereo on and beings to talk with Russell.

"Russ, who do you think is more relatable and more trustworthy? The handsome "GQ" model guy, or the Nazi Scarecrow guy. Because to me they each have their pros and cons."

Russell while he's driving, responds to Kevin in a very harsh way.

"Kev, that was fucked up the way you made of him. I look just as creepy as he does."

Kevin begins to laugh at Russell, and responds to him, speaking fast.

"Yeah but Russ, he looked like the damn Scarecrow, come on man. You have to agree with me on that one. That guy just looked so scary. I feel so sorry for him. Poor guy."

Jesse remains quiet in the back seat, listening to both Russell and Kevin talk to each other. Russell when he reaches a stop light, puts his hand over his head, and talks to Kevin.

"Kev, you need to shut your mouth and stop making fun of people, okay man?"

Kevin shakes his head and listens to the music on the car stereo. Russell continues following Brian until he reaches a commercial warehouse building, located in a harbor area of San Pedro, with the Pacific Ocean a few minutes away. They continue until they reach a unit with a big metal door. Brian parks his car outside of the building and waves his hand for the rest of the guys to come in. Russell, Kevin, Jesse and Victor then get out of the vehicles they were in, and stand outside of the building. While he's unlocking the door, Brian begins to chat with the other guys.

"Okay, so I figure I would give you guys a treat and reveal this to make up for my behavior. This is my safe house. This is where I live. I don't want you guys telling anybody about this place, okay. I bought this unit for myself a while ago. This is where I work on cars, and where I eat, sleep and shit, Ha-ha. Alright guys, just wait a second and you guys can come in."

Brian finally opens the door to his warehouse. After all the men walk in, he quickly shuts the metal door and turns on the lights. Inside this commercial loft building, is an area where Brian does his auto body work. He has his tools and car jacks located in this section. This side of the building also contains two classic cars. A 1960 Oldsmobile convertible, and a 1970s Chevy El Camino car. Behind the cars is another locked door which leads outside towards a driveway path. Brian likes classic cars, and he modifies them. Spread across the walls of the warehouse, are 1950s inspired art and neon signs. The other sides of the room contain a bathroom with a shower, a kitchen with a refrigerator and stove, and a large lounge area which features a bed, two sofas, and a big screen television. This warehouse has been converted by Brian as his own personal apartment. He was able to obtain this unit from an old acquaintance of his. Brian mostly takes cars that he carjacks and brings them to this unit temporarily to fix them, or to scrap them. Taking the automobiles to a chop shop after. This warehouse is also located in quaint and hidden area away from town. Once all the doors are shut, it is virtually soundproof. It offers the chance for more privacy.

The men continue to look around the unit, before Russell begins to speak with Brian.

"This is not bad. Nice place you got here. This is a nice setup you have."

Brian then walks towards his kitchen area, and brings beers for all of the guys. He then takes out his phone, and begins to order some pizzas. All of the guys start to open their beers and drink them. Kevin then sits down towards the sofa area, and turns the television on. Russell laughs at him, and continues to look around the warehouse. He notices that Jesse is looking at Brian's classic cars. Russell pats his hands over Jesse's shoulders, and talks to him.

"Those cars are nice huh? Isn't it crazy how he worked them up like that?"

Jesse nods his head towards Russell in agreement. Victor being nosy, watches them in amusement and smiles. He then walks around the warehouse for a bit, before deciding to sit down at the sofa area with Kevin who is watching the television. A couple minutes pass, and Kevin who kept peeking at Victor, hesitating whether he wanted to chat with him or not, finally decides to speak with Victor in a playful way, almost teasing him.

"Hey man, look. I apologize if I offended you. It's just that you look kinda creepy to me, and I mean that in the nicest of ways. I'm not trying to make fun of man, it's just you look scary, and I tell it like it is. But, you seem like a cool guy and I think you're misunderstood."

Victor takes a sip of his beer not giving eye contact to Kevin, as if he were offended by what he said. Kevin looks at Victor feeling guilty over what he said, and turns his head towards the television. Victor doesn't wish to deal with Kevin's behavior, and removes himself from his company. He decides to get up from the sofa, and walk over to where Russell and Jesse are. They continue to be captivated and fascinated by the classic cars. Brian gets done ordering the pizzas, and he screams out to let all of the other guys know.

"Okay, the pizza should be here shortly guys. Hang on for a bit. In the meantime, just make yourselves at home, get comfortable. Mi Casa is Su Casa. Okay?"

The other men nod their heads towards Brian, and go back towards their business. Brian then walks over to where Russell and

Jesse are standing and takes a rag and begins to dust off the classic cars in the warehouse. He then cleans and adjusts the mirrors on both of the cars as well. He then takes a sip of his beer and taps Russell on the chest.

"These are my prides and joy. That's an Oldsmobile, and that's an El Camino. No, I didn't steal them; I got them at a scrap auction. They didn't look like this when I first got them. No sir, I had to do a lot of work for all of this. But believe me, it paid off."

Russell takes a sip of his beer and compliments the cars some more.

"I wouldn't mind driving that convertible down PCH. Damn. That car is so fine, and I can see myself behind the wheel of that one, cruising down the road. Shit man."

Russell and Brian then fist bump each other. Brian continues

Victor then asks a question he is curious about to Brian.

"So, do you ever take these out on the road or not? Shit, I know I would always want to show these off. But I also know some car guys don't like to take their cars out, and they are scared people are gonna breath on them wrong, or scratch them or whatever."

Brian takes a swallow of his beer and snickers at Victor. He then responds to him.

"I took them out a couple times yes. But as you said yes, I am very temperamental when it comes to my cars. I don't want people stealing my parts, or stuff like that. I was thinking on taking them to car shows as well to show them off that way too. Yeah."

Victor nods his head and takes more sips of his beer. Kevin is still sitting at the sofa area, watching "Family Guy" on the television laughing hysterically. Russell turns his head over to where Kevin is sitting, and starts to laugh at him. Victor continues to inspect the cars.

"I see with the convertible, that's a brand new engine. Must have cost a fortune huh?"

Brian fires back at Victor, possibly misunderstanding his intentions.

"That's none of your fucking business. I don't appreciate you being all nosy and perceptive like that. I'm watching you okay? I'm gonna give you another chance."

Victor starts to give Brian a depressed look, and Russell snaps at Brian.

"You didn't have to talk to him like that, I don't think that's what he meant. He was just being curious that's all. I think you need to chill man. Alright?"

Brian puts his hand under his chin, and nods his head towards Russell. Victor then walks over to inspect the other car, and Brian leans into Russell's ear to whisper something to him.

"I don't trust him, I don't know what it is, I don't. It's not the way he looks... ha-ha well maybe it is. I don't get a good vibe from him, you and the other two guys are golden for me."

Russell while staring at Victor, takes another swallow of his beer and responds to Brian.

"He's okay to me. I think every guy in this damn room is psycho to some degree. So it's not fair at all to pin point him as the grand prize winner you know?"

Brian while staring at Victor, takes a swig of his beer and nods his head in agreement. Russell then starts to realize how eccentric all of the guys are in their own way. With Russell being a tough grizzly who stands by his own principles and opinions. Jesse who is a flamboyant and feminine clown, yet compassionate in his own right and has his own artistic qualities. Kevin who is a chatterbox and comedian, with an exorbitant sense of humor. Brian who attempts himself to be a Happy Day's reject, liking classic culture and classic cars. Finally, Victor who is a mysterious man with an even more mysterious personality towards himself. He embraces the thoughts of this newly found group of confidants that he has. For the first time in quite some time, Russell begins to have flashbacks of his original idea to rob a bank. In an attempt to rebel against the troubles he had from working at a bank. In another attempt to avenge Peter and Jennifer's death.

This seemed like the perfect time to bring all of this up into action and to discuss it. He begins to ponder if he should bring up this thought he has to the other guys or not. Russell at least for now, keeps that to himself. More than likely he will bring it up sooner or later, as when Russell has an idea or agenda he's determined to follow, he accomplishes it. He structured himself to not hold back, or resist his any mental temptations that he has anymore. It's not as if he's giving up, he simply doesn't care anymore.

A few minutes later, Brian gets a notification on his phone that the pizza's he's ordered are ready. He turns his head towards Russell and asks if he wants to go with him to pick them up. Russell agrees to ride with Brian, and they both immediately leave the warehouse. Leaving Kevin, Jesse, and Victor behind. Russell gets into Brian's car. On their way to pick up the pizza, while he's driving, Brian begins to converse with Russell at a deep level.

"Hey, I appreciate you not flipping out earlier. I was scared to admit any of that to you, but just like you had a feeling about me, I had a feeling that you were a nice guy. So I said, what the hell, and just flat out told you. Part of me still feels bad about it, and part of me also thinks you probably partly hate me, but I think it's okay now and I'm happy."

Russell looks out the passenger window, and doesn't respond to Brian. He feels that it's no use trying to put any blame on him, when he genuinely feels that Brian is a nice guy which like himself, is someone misunderstood in the world. Russell a few minutes later, does decide to turn his head towards Brian, and reply to him speaking in a low tone.

"Man, I've already forgotten about that shit. I just want to move on, and be happy with my new friends. Today was a crazy day, and I've been having a lot of crazy days anyways, so I get used to it at this point. I don't waste my time sulking over crap anymore. Not worth it."

Brian nods his head to agree with Russell. They both continue on the road to pick up the pizzas. After reaching the pizza place, they get their food and proceed to head back towards Brian's warehouse. When walking into the unit with the pizza, Kevin runs up from the sofa area, and starts to lose all control.

"I'm hungry! I'm hungry! I want some of that pizza now. I want to eat now."

Russell starts to laugh and sets the pizza boxes in the kitchen area. All of the men then grab pieces of pizza, and sit at the sofa area. They watch "Family Guy" on the television, with Kevin laughing extremely loud and reciting lines from it. As they are eating their pizza, Russell figures that there is no time such as the present, to bring up something that is on his mind.

"Okay men, what I'm about to say to some of you might not be a surprise. To some of you, it wouldn't be something that you're hearing for the first time. However, to some of you it may be shocking. To some of you, it might be surprising. But, I'm gonna tell it anyways."

Everyone then gives their eye contact to Russell.

"Alright, I think with the help of each and every guy that's sitting around here, we can a rob bank. Seeing how good that goes, we can rob two banks, and really stick it to the man. I don't see why we can't accomplish this at all. If everyone played their part."

Russell had already offered this idea up to Kevin and Jesse, however this comes as a complete surprise to Brian and Victor, who both have shocked and confused expressions on their faces. Brian then notices how Kevin and Jesse aren't phased by what Russell mentioned. He then understands that Russell is not joking, and offers his own opinions on this.

"My thing is this, what if we get hurt or we get caught? I really do think we are smart enough to get away with it, yes. I hate playing the what if game, but you saw how I robbed your bank, and look at what happened. Two of your friends were killed."

Russell takes a sip of beer, and a bite of pizza while watching the television. He then responds to Brian in a very passive way.

"That's because you and your partner did it the wrong way. I'm not gonna tell where the both of you messed up at, but due to my knowledge of banks, we can totally do this. If we are all smart and we do it the right way, nobody gets hurt and above all, we don't get caught."

Kevin starts to nod his head and laugh at Russell agreeing with him, while taking bites of his pizza. Russell then while still looking at the television, continues.

"It's the perfect crime, we just need the right team and the right setup. Once all of that is covered, the rest of it will be smooth like butter, and it will work out fine."

Kevin while facing the television, eats more of the pizza and takes more sips of beer. While shaking his head, he starts to egg Russell on over his ideas.

"Yeah Russ, you're such a beast man. You're a sick man, and that's why I love you man. How does he come up with this shit, I don't know? But that's Russ, and he's my friend. That's my friend right there. Nobody else is like him, he's original. Damn Russ."

Brian continues to scratch his head and continue to feel apprehensive about the idea. He looks at Russell with a puzzled look, and then replies to him.

"Do you really think we could pull it off? Yeah we have an inside guy on our team and I guess that's an advantage. I'm still not over the robbery I originally did at your bank?"

Russell while continuing to look at the television, takes a sip of beer and laughs at what Brian said. While still having his head positioned towards the television, he responds.

"You'll be fine. Based on your experience from that, you'll be a good member towards the team. You have to look at it from the outside man. Also, if you don't do it, I'll snitch on you to the police. So you can make you choice at this point."

Kevin then starts to burst out laughing from what Russell said. He immediately starts to get up from the sofa, and starts to run around Brian's warehouse, laughing like a hyena. Russell watching Kevin, shakes his head and laughs at him.

"Kev, sit the fuck down man. You are really something, and you are such a handful Kev. Never a dull moment with you, I swear. Ha-ha. Sit down man"

Seconds later Kevin returns to the sofa area, still giggling to himself. Jesse who's eating his pizza and watching the television, is quietly shaking his head at Kevin's behavior. Brian feels cornered. He gets up from the sofa and prances around his warehouse with his hands in his pockets. He is still doubting himself to whether or not he wants to join with Russell's idea. Victor who is being unusually quiet and not sharing his input, is eating a piece of his pizza while looking down towards the ground. He then looks up towards Russell and starts to speak to him.

"If you need my help, you can count me in. To make up for me not acting fast during your robbery. This is my way of helping out. Also, I need the cash, and fuck the law. I'm ready to be an outlaw so you can count me in."

Russell and Victor then smile at each other, and Victor returns to eating his pizza. When commercial break hits, Kevin takes a swallow of his beer, and turns his head to Russell.

"Okay Russ, so you have four guys that's ready. You have yourself, me, Jesse and Victor. All we need now is Brian to stop acting like a bitch, and to come on board with us. He has nothing to lose, so why doesn't he just do it and say yes? That's five guys. What a team."

Russell pats Kevin on the back and takes another sip of his beer. Following that Russell turns his head toward Brian, wanting to know his response as to whether or not he wants to join the rest of the guys. Brian continues to roam around, acting very jittery and nervous with his hands in his pocket. Russell begins to feel impatient with Brian. He doesn't understand why he just won't get on board with the program. Perhaps Brian is seeing right past Russell's manipulative behavior. He is able to tame Kevin, Jesse, and Victor, but Brian doesn't think that he can be controlled in the same way.

Brian also unlike the other four guys, has more doubt on his mind. He was the robber at the "Sunset Credit Union" robbery that got away, and was involved in a failed robbery. These thoughts run in his head, that the chance of a repeat occurrence might happen, and disastrous events could happen to them. The other side of Brian feels this is a chance from him to redeem any debts to Russell, by agreeing to do this. He was involved with the robbery that killed two of his friends, and this would be an interesting way to repay all of that. He is torn to make a choice. Russell starts to lose all patience with Brian and takes his phone out of his pocket.

"Alright Brian. I'll just call the cops and say 'the guy who robbed my bank is standing ten feet away from me, come get him now.' Is that what you really want Brian?"

Kevin starts to laugh out loud again towards Russell. He picks up his hand and pretends to have a fake telephone conversation.

"Call the cops Russ. '911? Yeah he's right here, come quick'. Ha-ha. Ha-ha."

Brian continues to walk around unsure of himself, and not responding to Russell. This goes on for another few minutes until Russell starts to dial numbers on his phone. When Brian notices him do so, he immediately charges at Russell and grabs his phone.

"Don't you fucking do that. Okay you win. I'll join you guys. But only on one condition. I'll tell you what the condition is in a second, but you have to agree to it first."

Brian swiftly hands back Russell his phone. Russell then responds to him.

"Okay, what's the condition? What do we have to do?"

Brian then smiles at Russell and roams around his warehouse with his hands in his pockets. The rest of the guys watch him in confusion, not knowing what to expect. A minute later Brian pulls out his phone, and begins to call someone, while looking at the rest of the men.

"Hello? Max? Are busy man? This is Brian, and I have a situation that I really need your assistance with. Do you mind if I come and get you right quick? Okay, be right there."

Brian then hangs up his phone, and directly leaves the unit without saying a word. The other guys in the building look at Brian, not knowing what to say or think. Finally, Kevin decides to turn to Russell, and whispers to him very softly.

"Hey Russ, where do you think he went? What did he mean by condition? He's probably gonna come back and kill us all. I didn't like how he said condition. What's going on?"

Russell rubs his hand under his chin for a few seconds, and then turns to look at Kevin, also replying to him in a very soft whispering tone.

"I don't know Kev, but as long as he's on our team, I don't care. I don't know what's going on, but I don't think it's anything too bad or something terrible like that."

The rest of the guys sit in the sofa area, waiting for Brian to return. Almost ten minutes pass and he still has not arrived back at the warehouse. Kevin then starts to worry.

"Russ, maybe we should leave. I don't know about this. Maybe we made him mad, and he's now calling all of his goons to take care of us or something like that. I just don't like the way he said condition, and that makes me uncomfortable. I don't know Russ."

Russell while looking down towards the ground, responds to Kevin.

"Kev, he's not going to do anything okay? He's not that type of guy. Sit back and relax and shut up man. Nothing is gonna happen, and we are all going to be okay. He went to go take care of the 'condition', and he'll be back in a minute and everything will be alright man."

Kevin shakes his head at Russell and starts to grumble under his breath at him.

"I don't know Russ, if you say so. I'll shut up now I guess."

Honestly, Russell was starting to worry somewhat at this current time. He wasn't sure at all what Brian meant by "condition", and starts to wonder what the "condition" actually is. For now, he just has to wait to see what exactly will come from this. He decided to ask Brian to join the team, and if it has to take a "condition" for Brian to comply with the rest of the guys, then so be it. That's a risk that Russell had no problem taking. All he wanted was for Brian to be on board with everyone else, and to stick with the program. Russell is slightly nervous because of this, but is confident that everything is satisfactory.

The rest of the guys sit and remain on the sofa area in silence, waiting for Brian to come back. They keep their thoughts to themselves, although many of them stare at each other intermittently to break the tension. A few minutes later, Victor gets up from the sofa area, and he heads over to where the classic cars are. Russell then immediately gets up and walks over to that area himself. While they are both staring at the cars, Russell in a very kind fashion, starts to talk to him.

"You really like these cars huh? Hey, I don't think you're a weird guy, I think you're awesome, and that's why I want you to be involved with our team. You're a winner in my eyes, and I don't think you're weird at all. I care about you. Hey, think of it this way, us scary and creepy guys have to stick together, okay?"

Russell then playfully punches Victor in the chin. Victor then smiles and laughs at Russell. Victor while still looking at the cars, responds to Russell in a muttered voice.

"Yeah, we are both kinda creepy looking huh? I'm not offended by it, and it's an interesting way to look at it. From one creepy guy to the other, I agree. We do have to stick together, and support each other. I really appreciate you coming over here to speak with me Russell. Thanks. It really means a lot to me, and I want to thank you."

Jesse observes Russell and Victor interact with each other, and he smiles as well. Kevin continues to sit on the sofa areas feeling very anxious. A couple minutes later, the door to the warehouse begins to open. Russell and Victor then walk away from the area the cars were at, and head back towards the lounge area. All of the men in the room stand up, and watch in suspense as the gate opens. Brian walks into the warehouse, pushing an elderly Caucasian man with long gray hair with glasses, in a wheelchair. This man has no legs at all. Brian continues to push him into the sofa area of the warehouse. He pushes the man closer to where Russell is standing and introduces him.

"Max, this is the sicko I was talking to you about. This is the psycho bastard that wants us to rob a bank. Russell I'd like you to meet Max. This guy is gonna help is out."

Russell looks at the man in the wheelchair. He sticks his hand out and he shakes Max's hand. Max smiles at Russell and replies to him in a friendly way.

"Nice to meet you Russell."

Russell shakes his head and laughs.

CHAPTER 10:

NOTHING SHORT, NOTHING TALL

All of the men in the room are in complete shock. Who is this strange man in the wheelchair? They all gaze at him in such surprise, and in total confusion. A few minutes pass, and all of the men in the room continue to remain quiet. Russell starts to stare at Max, being very curious about him. Max then while scanning his head at all the men, finally starts to speak.

"I was speaking with Brian, and he informed me on everything top to bottom. This is an interesting situation we have here, and I can't say I don't somewhat feel for each of you. I might not agree to do the same things that you all want to do, But I at least understand and feel for each and every one of you."

Max then looks to his right, focusing on Brian. He then immediately directs his comments towards him. While occasionally looking at the other guys.

"Brian was in that robbery last Friday. A robbery that virtually almost all of you in this room, are in some ways are directly involved with. I might not always agree with what Brian does, but he's a good guy and has done much for me. I'm going to forgive his awful mistakes, and help him out and help the rest of you out as well."

Brian then smiles at Max. He turns his head to the other guys, and starts to explain more.

"Okay everybody, this is Max. If we're actually serious on robbing a bank, we won't be able to do it without him. No he's not a bank robber. It's not because he's not physically able to rob a bank, but that's not his thing. He would be the perfect person to trust, and will always have our backs. He used to work for the police, and has connections, and can help us out."

Max then turns to look at Russell, smiling at him again, and talks to him.

"Brian has told me so much about you. He said you were the mastermind behind this whole idea. It's such a small world how everything is connected like that. Brian robbed your bank and got away, now you want to work with him in organized crime. He told me that earlier today at a memorial service for the deceased in the robbery, you two were able to meet and come together. That's so strange how that happened. You were the manager of the bank. Now you have this sudden change of heart and want to rob a bank now? Interesting."

Russell grins at Max, and nods his head to agree with him. He then responds.

"Matter of fact I was. I was always in suspense as to who the guy who ran off was. I still can't believe it's him, but I don't sense any type of evil spirit from him. Damn right I want to rob a bank now. Fuck the government, and society really as well. I'm tired of it all."

Max then looks around again and starts to point his finger at Jesse.

"You were also in the robbery too. You were one of the bank tellers involved. It's crazy how you and Russell survived that. Now you want to rob banks?"

Jesse looks down on the floor and then looks up at Max to reply to him.

"Yes it was a very traumatic experience for me. At this point, I got kind of suckered into involving myself with the group. I'm fine working these guys. All my life, people have always treated me badly and I think all of us have been treated bad, so it's tough."

Max then points his finger at Kevin, and starts to smile at him.

"He then said that you were the comedian and court jester of the group. You're Russell's best friend and have nothing to do with this robbery. You're just here because you live for excitement and amusement, and you want to ride along with them. I understand, I suppose."

Kevin nods his head very fast, and also responds to Max speaking rapidly.

"Russ is one of the most interesting guys I've ever met. Whatever he's down to do, I'm going to support him every step of the way. I don't blame Russ at all for feeling the way he does, and wanting to rebel all of a sudden. The man has been through a lot. I'm here for him."

Max then gives Victor a strange look and points his finger at him.

"Now you, you were the guy that was supposed to rob the bank, but was thwarted because Brian and his criminal partner got to the bank just slightly before you. You saw the whole thing happen, and didn't do anything. You feel guilty and that's why you're here."

Victor starts to laugh at Max, and responds to him.

"I had seconds thoughts of robbing the bank originally, and I didn't really want to do it. I stood back and watched yes, but I was too scared to do anything. That's why me and Brian went to the funeral today, we just felt guilty about everything that happened."

The rest of the guys continue to look at Max, and remain in shock and in surprise in this current time. Max is an older man in his sixties. He has long silver grey hair that goes to his shoulders, and wears big black eyeglasses. If you were to look at him, you would think he was a mad scientist. He cannot walk and is wheelchair bound, as he was born with a disorder that caused him to be born without legs. He has never married, and keeps a solitary life. He isn't a very social relationship type person, and prefers his own company. He considers himself an asexual man. Max is a licensed surgeon and criminal pathologist. He retired from the job after he noticed many corrupt police practices and procedures. Following that, through difficult and undisclosed circumstances, he gotten himself involved in black market cartels and crime syndicates. Offering weaponry and other services to help these organizations, and groups.

Max because he involves himself in illegal activity, keeps a neutral opinion towards choices he disagrees with by others. He was mainly used as a reference when crooks need weapons or other items. This is mainly because he has a hobby for shooting and gun collecting. The exact circumstances as to how Brian first met him are very unclear and complex. Although alternatively and simply, Brian met him through acquaintances during his past lifestyle of being a kingpin carjacking vehicles. In fact, it was actually Max that helped Brian buy the warehouse which he converted into his home.

Max lives in the adjacent unit next door to him. When Brian was approached to do the bank robbery with Scott, he suggested to him that they use the help of Max. However, Scott refused, and the services of Max were not used. When Brian told Max about what happened at the "Sunset Credit Union" robbery, he became devastated, and felt that the heist shouldn't have turned into something that brutal. If they had inquired with Max, he had drills that more than likely would have opened the safe, without the use of having to take someone hostage in order to open it. He also has other tools such as detonation and explosive devices, used to divert or distract themselves during the heist to take attention away from that. If they would have used the aide and help from him, the robbery might have not been orchestrated in the way it was. Max no longer works for these black market organizations, but due to his complicated relationship with Brian, he's making an exception this time to do things under regular circumstances, he probably most likely wouldn't.

Brian knew that being all the men were determined to succeed forward with the robbery, he had to gain the support from Max. This was Brian's condition. He will only take part, if they all agree to allow Max to help them as a guide. Brian looks at Russell and the rest of the men, then proceeds to discuss his condition.

"Guys, I'll only do this if you let Max help us. I don't see why you guys wouldn't agree to this. We have nothing to lose, and this guy knows his stuff. If we need guns or ammo or tools, he has them. If we need disguises and masks, he's got those. Let's say if one of us gets shot or injured god forbid, the man knows how to operate on people. We have nothing to lose. Come on guys."

Max then starts to stare at all of the guys in the room, and exclaims out to them.

"Brian told me you guys wanted to rob a bank, and I refuse to let you guys do something as crazy as that without allowing me to help you. I can give you guys guns and anything else you might need. I have a whole supply of items located in a unit, that you can walk to from here. All of it is free and no cost for you to use. This is however going to come with two requests that I ask from you all."

Russell looks at Max very deeply, taking in everything that he is saying and listening closely. He raises his eyebrows at him. Max then continues.

"The two things that I ask for, is number one is that you all get along and you don't betray each other. If you're gonna do bank heists, communication and teamwork is key. If one of you doesn't work well the others, then the whole plan is going to fail due to poor communication and interaction between you all. The results could possibly be dangerous."

All of the men continue to listen to Max, having focused expressions.

"Number two, is that you all have to work for my office cleaning business. This isn't up for discussion. You guys are just going to have to do that to earn my help. Also, it will help you guys learn to handle each other better. If you can't work together cleaning office buildings, taking out trash, cleaning bathrooms, mopping and vacuuming floors, then you can't work together and rob a bank. So I think this will work out perfect for each and every one of you."

The guys then start to look at each other with disgust. Max continues to talk to the guys.

"From Monday to Thursday, you guys will have to clean various buildings in downtown Los Angeles from noon, to nine at night. You guys get an hour break at four, and that's it. On Friday's you get the day off. So you guys can plan to do the heist on a Friday."

Russell grins at Max, and quickly responds to him.

"So, when are we going to be able to see what you have to offer to help? It sounds like we could definitely use some of what you have. Can we take a peek at it?"

Max turns to look at Brian, and while giving Russell a relaxed look, answers his question very quickly in a smooth way.

"You guys can come take a look at all of that tomorrow. It's a big unit full of all the things you all need. I have other goodies and toys as well. You'll have to wait and see all of that tomorrow."

Russell runs his hand under his chin and nods his head towards Max.

"Okay, tomorrow all of us will check out your supply and see what you have. Because I have a couple guns myself, but that's not going to be enough for all of us. So I appreciate your help. I'm not really looking forward to us having to work as janitors. But oh well."

Kevin walks over closer to Max, and starts to ask him a question.

"Um, I have a two concerns. For starters, I wanted to know if you have anything that could disable security alarms and security cameras. This is something I think which would help us greatly."

Max smiles at Kevin, and reassures the question that he asked.

"I believe I do. Whatever you need, I'm sure I have it, and it would be useful when you guys decide to do the bank heist. What was the other concern that you had?"

Kevin then nervously looks at Max, and continues to speak with him.

"Well, I have a side gig, I work from home working with computers and electronics. I work with both hardware and software and tech stuff like that. Do I still have to clean with the rest of the guys?

Max while giving Kevin an angry look, quickly responds to him.

"Yes you do, because I said so. All five you need to work, and all five of you need to work together with each other this way. You guys don't have to work until noon. You can still do that earlier in the day can   you   not?"

Kevin leans back his head and starts to moan and groan.

"I suppose I could, but I just don't think it's fair I have to do this. It's not, and I don't feel comfortable doing that crap. Ugh, to me this is bullshit, and I don't know why we have to do any of this. This is just complete bullshit."

Russell walks over to Kevin and smacks him hard behind his head. He then cordially turns his head towards Max and starts to reassure him.

"That's no problem at all. We will all show up to work without any fight or fussing or issues or problems. We can handle this just fine, and all of us will agree to do it."

Brian then looks toward Max and beings to speak to him.

"I want to thank you Max for everything. This is truly amazing, and I want to thank you for supporting us and wanting to work with us."

Max smiles at Brian and and pats him on the back.

"It's fine, the pleasure is all mine, and I'm happy to do this. I understand the situation, or I wouldn't have brought myself into it. I do have to depart now, but I wish all of you the best. I shall see all of you tomorrow. You gentleman have a good evening."

Max then starts to shake all of the guy's hands, and Brian starts to push Max out of the unit. Once Brian walks out of the building, Jesse and Victor creep their way back to the sofa, and watch television. Kevin who's still standing on the other side of the room with Russell, turns his head towards his direction, and immediately starts to snap at him.

"Russ, I'm not cleaning buildings with the rest of you, and I'm not changing my mind. I just don't want to do any of that. I have my own business, so let me do that."

Russell gives Kevin an agitated look, and responds to him very sharply.

"Well too bad Kev, you're going to have to suck it up and do it. If you were truly my friend, you would agree to do it, and not whine and bitch like you're doing right now Kev. Every other guy didn't whine, but you did. You need to get with the program Kev if you want to ride with us. It's not going to hurt you to mop floors and take out trash Kev. Stop playing yourself."

Kevin walks over to the sofa areas shaking his head, and responds to Russell.

"Okay Russ, I'll do it. But I can't promise you I'm not gonna continue to be mad about it. This isn't something I'm thrilled about. That's just me Russ. Come on, you know I'm fussy."

Russell then smiles and pats Kevin on the back. They both then join the rest of the guys on the sofa areas. The men continue to watch the television, waiting for Brian to come back. Russell and Kevin continue to look at "Family Guy", laughing at it. A few minutes later, Brian returns. He opens up the unit door and after shutting and locking it, quickly runs over to the sofa area with the other guys to ask them a question.

"It occurred to me just now, that we should probably call this 'Home Base'. I mean, if we're gonna be a heist team, we have to have a safe haven right? Why can't this be it? This is where we all would gather when we need to discuss business, or whenever something goes down. We all have our own lives yes, but this is our safe spot. This will be our hub I guess."

Brian looks over at the rest of the men, who are each taking in what he just said with very thoughtful looks on their faces. They remain quiet for a while, then Brian continues.

"So, is that cool with you guys? This will be our safe house. Our secret hangout where we all can be in private and deal with each other. Again, if something were to happen or whatever to where we are separated, we are to always meet up back here. I just want to make sure everyone understands this and we are all clear. This will be called 'Home Base.'"

The rest of the guys each agree, and they all shake each other's hand in agreement. Brian then gets up from the sofa area with his hands in his pockets, walking around the unit pacing. He then turns his head towards Russell who's watching the television and speaks out loud to him.

"So, if we have to work Monday through Thursday, that means we would have to do the heist, on a Friday. So that's already one major development out of the way. I know we have a long way to go with planning and everything. But we've covered that part already."

Kevin then while sitting at the sofa area, makes a disgusted face at Brian and attacks him.

"Wait, hold on. We only have to work on from noon to nine. Banks are open before noon, and we can strike then. Wouldn't that make sense? I think it does. I mean we have more time and all day to plan on Fridays, but I don't know, I think we can pull it off if we do it early."

Brian then leers at Kevin for a while, having an expression of disagreement. Brian then continues to walk around the room looking flustered before coming up with an idea.

"Alright, we'll just take a vote. Anybody who wants us to do the heist in the morning during Monday through Friday, raise your hand right now."

The only person who raises their hand is Kevin. Who then lowers his hand, while making a disappointed face immediately after. Kevin then grumbles under his breath something.

"Again, I'm always fenced in. Nobody ever listens to me or takes my ideas. It's like you guys don't even want me in the group anymore. What the fuck?"

Russell with his head directed at the television, responds to Kevin.

"Kev, knock it off. You know we need you in our group. Friday is the most logical option giving our circumstances. Working as janitors, it will give us a chance to talk and plan more and gain rapport with each other Kev. We'll use your ideas later buddy. Don't feel like that Kev."

Kevin looks at Russell and gives him a grin. He turns his head towards the television. They all remain silent for a while, but Kevin then decides to reply to Russell.

"You're right Russ, and thanks for cheering me up man. Everything is just happening so fast and so sudden man. That's probably what the problem is. We are storming up all of these ideas and plans and everyone is on board with stuff, and I don't know. I got caught up with all of that, and we need to discuss and compromise over these things more as a collective group."

Victor who's looking down on the ground, agrees with Kevin.

"Yeah this is happening way too fast, and I'm already starting to doubt everything. I only met you guys today, and already we're talking about this stuff. I mean, I live in my car, and I don't know who any of you fucking guys are. This doesn't seem right, and all of us are crazy as hell and lunatics. I need a smoke. Can we all go out for a smoke break please?"

Brian while looking at Victor, pulls a pack of cigarettes out from his pocket. He then hands the pack to Victor, and starts to walk towards the door, talking to him.

"Call I call you Vic? Is that alright? Vic, it's okay man. Most of us are strangers and getting to know each other. Sooner or later, everyone will be familiar with everyone. Don't worry man, don't feel that way. You can take as many cig breaks as you want man, and you can also sleep here during the nights. It's fine."

Victor gives Brian eye contact, slightly frowning. He then whispers out to him.

"Yeah, you can call me Vic, or you can call me Romero. But I prefer Victor. Also, thank you for letting me stay here, I appreciate it. I don't mind sleeping in my car, but this is very nice of you to do that, and I'm very thankful that you are allowing me to stay."

Brian walks over to Victor and pats him on his shoulder. He continues to talk to him.

"There is a shower here too man, if you want to take a shower you can. I don't mind you staying here at all. You're one of us and a part of our group. We all have to stick together."

Victor starts to give Brian a weak smile. Brian smiles back at Victor. Brian then directs his attention to all of the guys in the room, and shouts out to them.

"You all want to step outside for a smoke? Might as well."

All of the men agree, and they prepare to step outside to smoke a cigarette. Kevin shuts the television set off, and they all walk outside. The night sky is dark, and there are many stars above. The moon is shining bright, and the air is very warm with a slight breeze. All five men gather outside of the warehouse unit, and start to smoke a cigarette. Kevin takes a puff of his cigarette, and notices Russell is staring down at the ground. He taps his shoulder to get his attention, and starts to talk to him very softly.

"So Russ, you think by next Friday we'll be ready by then? I think so. I think the quicker we do it, the better. The longer we wait to plan; I think we might change our minds by then."

Russell continues to stare down towards the ground, firing back at Kevin.

"Kev, let's talk about all that later. Tomorrow maybe. We all came out here to take a smoke and just to relax and gather our minds. We can deal with that a little later."

Kevin looks away from Russell and takes another puff of his cigarette. He quickly takes another look at Russell, then whispers a reply towards him.

"Okay Russ, I won't mention anything related to that. My bad man."

Russell laughs at him and takes a puff of his cigarette. Jesse while smoking his cigarette, starts to profile Victor who's scratching his arms for whatever reason. He notices that the top of Victor's arms has healed self-harm scars on them. He can see them from under the sleeve of his shirt. Jesse upon realizing that, begins to feel sad for him, and frowns. Brian is looking down towards the ground, being silent walking with his hands in his pockets. Russell looks up and watches him. With his eyes still focused on Brian, Kevin taps on Russell again.

"Russ, can I spend the night at your place tonight?"

Russell to shut Kevin up, quickly responds to him, while he's still looking at Brian.

"Yeah Kev, whatever you want man. Yes. Whatever."

Brian then continues to look down towards the ground roaming and waddling around with his hands in his pockets. He looks up towards the other guys and speaks to them.

"You know what guys, let's call it a night? Alright. Regroup tomorrow?"

Russell then looks up at Brian and smiles at him. He quickly responds.

"Okay, yeah let's call it quits. Me, Kev and Jesse will meet you and Victor in the morning, and we'll take it from there. I'm getting very tired too. So, that's gonna be it."

Brian smiles at Russell. Brian then walks over to Russell, giving him a very strong hug. He then starts to softly whisper something into his ear.

"You're a good man. Thank you again for giving me another chance. I guess I'm lucky you're crazy like me, or else I probably wouldn't have gotten that chance, but thanks a lot man."

While he's still hugging Brian, Russell also whispers something into his ear.

"I don't want to put the blame entirely on you. I don't feel that the whole thing is fully your fault, so I don't think it's fair to only attack you. I have faith in you, and I trust you too."

Brian smiles at him and the both of them separate from each other. Brian then walks over to Kevin and starts to shake his hand. He begins to talk to him as well.

"It was nice meeting you Kevin. You're a hyper guy and you don't know when to quit. You have a nice sense of humor though, and I like that about you; that's a good thing."

Kevin laughs, rubs the back of his head and responds to Brian.

"Aww, thanks man. It was nice meeting you too Brian. I really like this pad and secret hideaway you have. I have to get me one of these someday I suppose. Nice meeting you."

Following that, Brian walks over to Jesse and shakes his hand. Jesse smiles at Brian for a few seconds and they remain quiet looking at each other, then Brian decides to talk to Jesse.

"It was nice to meet you Jesse. You're an interesting guy, and you seem much more level headed than the rest of us. I feel as though you have witnessed a lot harsh stuff, and you still stay strong. It was nice meeting you and I'll see you later man."

Jesse then responds to Brian while smiling at him.

"I'm trying to be more observant and take everything in. I'm a more sensitive type of guy and I guess you're right, I deal with it that way. Thank you for everything Brian."

Brian then smiles at Jesse, and he walks away. All of the guys then stand together outside in silence for a few minutes continuing to smoke their cigarettes. The silence is clearly interrupted when a strange occurrence happens. Victor remaining distant from the group with his head still down smoking his cigarette, begins to have an episode. Victor starts screaming out loud to himself. While he's screaming, he takes his hands, and rubs them on the back of his neck very vigorously. Russell, Brian and Jesse watch him in shock and are speechless. However, when Kevin notices this, he immediately unintendedly starts to laugh hysterically and loudly. He then turns his head towards Russell to whisper to him.

"Russ, this guy is nuts. Wow. What is wrong with him? Poor guy."

The rest of the men watch, as Victor begins to get himself together. Victor notices that everyone is watching him, and starts to laugh. He then starts to talk while laughing.

"I'm sorry guys, that was just a tension breaker. I usually do those like once a week. That was my weekly one, and I can't control them. Honestly you guys. I should have said something and warned you guys that it was coming, and I was gonna do that. I'm not used to being around this many people, so it never dawned on me. Sorry. I'll warn you guys next time. I'm so sorry. Now you guys know, and it's no big deal right?

The rest of the guys look at him in silence for a few seconds, then they all support him, and exclaim remarks that show that they agree and understand the situation. Victor then finishes his cigarette and while looking down, and walks into "Home Base". The rest of the guys continue to stay outside during this time. Russell starts to worry about Victor, and wonders how his mental capacity will play a role from this point forward. He still doesn't know much about him, and his history. Russell doesn't want to immediately rush to snap judgments about him either. He ignores that situation for now, and gives Victor the benefit of the doubt. Brian then proceeds to dismiss himself from the group, and tells everyone goodbye.

"Well, what just happened was very interesting. I don't know what that was about, but I'm gonna try to talk to him and find out. He's gonna be staying with me anyways, so might as well pick at him. Goodnight gentlemen, see you all in the morning."

Brian then walks into "Home Base", but stops himself and walks back towards the rest of the guys. He takes out his phone and starts talking to Russell.

"Russell, can I have your number man so we can all stay in touch? Thanks."

Russell then immediately pulls out his phone and exchanges numbers with Brian. Immediately following that, Brian walks into the unit shutting and locking the door behind him. Russell, Kevin and Jesse then all look at each other for a minute. Russell then starts to speak.

"Alright boys, I'm totally beat, and I'm tired. If I'm tired, I know you guys are tired as well. So let's head back."

Jesse and Kevin both nod their heads at Russell. Jesse then walks over to Russell who wraps his arm around Jesse's back and all three men walk towards Russell's car. They all get inside the car, and head towards Russell's apartment. While in the car, Kevin turns the stereo on and talks to Russell very fast and loudly, with Jesse remaining quiet in the rear seat listening.

"Russ, Brian is cool. He's like a younger George Clooney. He's kinda smooth and cool. I mean, yeah he did rob your bank but that's old shit right? Now the other guy, the one who looks like the Scarecrow from the Wizard of Oz, Victor his name was? He's just plain scary and weird, and I don't know about him. That conniption fit he did was also very strange...and"

Kevin is interrupted when Russell turns his head over his direction giving him a disappointed look. Russell mutes the stereo volume, and proceeds to scream at Kevin.

"Kev not another word okay? I'm too tired man. Please Kev."

Kevin then gives Russell a scared expression and turns his head forward.

"Okay Russ, I know your tired man. I'll shut up and leave it alone. I'm sorry Russ."

Russell turns his view towards Kevin, and shakes his head. He then turns his head back forward to the road. They continue to drive to Russell's apartment in silence. Back at "Home Base", Brian starts to clean up, with Victor sitting on the couch rocking back and forth. Brian becomes concerned and goes over to talk to him and pats him on his leg.

"Victor, Yo. You okay man? Do you want me to get you some water buddy?"

Victor looks up at Brian and nods his head. He then replies to him.

"I would like some water, thank you. I'm sorry, I get anxious like that a lot. I'm so tense and again, I'm not used to being in these types of situations. I'm so sorry about that."

Brian then proceeds to get Victor a glass of water. Victor continues to sit on the couch rocking back in forth. Brian gives Victor the glass. Victor starts to take gulps of the water.

"Thank you. Brian, you wouldn't have any Tylenol or aspirin or something? I have a really bad headache, and if you could give me something for that, I'd appreciate it."

Brian smiles at him and pats him on the leg again. He then replies to him.

"Tell you what, Victor why I don't I walk you to your car. I want you to pick out a change of clothes. I then want you take a shower after that okay? Once you get out of the shower, I'll give you some aspirin alright? Can you work with me on that?"

Victor takes more sips of the water and nods his head towards Brian, replying to him.

"Yeah, okay. I can do all of that. I think I'll feel better after too."

Brian and Victor then walk out of "Home Base", towards Victor's car. Victor picks out a clean pair of clothes. A black t shirt and some khaki pants, and they walk back inside. Immediately after that, they both walk back into the unit, and Victor then heads into the bathroom to take a shower. Brian continues to clean the building, while Victor is bathing. When Victor is finished cleaning up, he goes over to where his bed and located and opens up his wardrobe dresser. He then starts to undress himself. He takes off his shirt and tie, then he takes of his pants. Brian then puts on some pajama bottoms while still remaining shirtless. He proceeds to return to the sofa area, but walks back and grabs another pair of pajama bottoms. Following that, Brian goes over to the bathroom door and knocks on it, screaming out to Victor to get his attention.

"Hey Victor, I have some sleeping pants for you when you get out. Okay?"

Victor doesn't respond, but Brian walks away. He sits at the sofa area, and watches the news on the television.

At Russell's apartment, himself Kevin and Jesse are now walking in. Upon walking into the building, Kevin directly runs to the sofa area and flings off his suit jacket. Russell and Jesse remain over by the front door watching him. He turns the television set on, and coincidentally "Family Guy" is on. He then takes his shoes and socks off and shouts out to Russell.

"Russ, you wouldn't have any beers would you? I could really use a cold one right about now. That is, if you have any."

Russell puts his suit jacket on the kitchen counter and gives an angry look directed towards Kevin, who has his view towards the television screen. Russell then goes into the refrigerator and pulls out three cans of beer, which incidentally he only had three left. He walks over to where Kevin is lounging, and gives him one of the beers.

"Thanks Russ, you're a good friend man."

Russell then hands Jesse a beer, but Jesse sets it down on the counter. Jesse then walks towards the bedroom, talking to Russell while walking in that direction.

"I'm going to go change clothes."

Russell nods his head, and takes a sip of his beer. Russell then walks over to sit by Kevin on the sofa. While he's sitting down, he removes his tie and sets it on the coffee table. Russell unbuttons the top of shirt, and takes his shoes and socks off, setting his shoes under the table. He then takes another sip of beer and starts to watch the television. Kevin while he still is facing the television, starts to talk to Russell.

"Thanks again for letting me spend the night Russ."

Kevin takes a sip of his beer, and Russell does the same. He responds to Kevin after that.

"It's okay Kev, you can stay as long as you need to man. You know that."

Jesse walks out of the bedroom wearing a white graphic t shirt that's covering his boxer bottoms, with a celebrity tabloid magazine in his hand. He takes a seat on the other side of the sofa. Russell looks at him puzzled, and speaks to him.

"Jesse, is that what you really want to wear? Okay. It doesn't seem at all appropriate, you could have picked something else. In fact, I almost feel like telling you go to back into the room and change, but I don't know."

Jesse tilts his head and opens his mouth towards Russell, and is appalled.

"Fuck you Russell, I can wear what I want. This is what makes me comfortable, so I want to wear this. I'm going to bed soon anyways, so why does it matter?"

Jesse then takes a sip of beer. Russell while looking at the television screen, takes another sip of beer, and responds to Jesse in a soft manner.

"Well, I don't care what you wear, but Kev is here and he's company and..."

Kevin takes a sip of beer, and while watching the television, claps back.

"Russ, he's gay. I'm bi, you're bi. We're all men here. Fuck you Russ. Leave him alone."

Russell while still having his vision towards the television screen, laughs and shakes his head. He looks over at Jesse who is reading his magazine. Russell then gets up from the sofa and stands in front of Jesse softly slaps him on the back of the head. Jesse laughs, and Russell then starts to rub his hair, then kissing him on the forehead. Jesse smiles at him, and Russell smiles back. He returns to where he was seating at the sofa, takes another sip of beer and watches television. Kevin who was watching them both, smiles, and turns his head back facing forward. Kevin takes another swallow of his beer, and starts to talk to Russell.

"Russ, you're a good man, but sometimes you act so crazy. Let the boy wear what he wants, shit. But anyways, Russ, there is something I need to talk to you about."

Russell starts to scratch the back of his head and responds to Kevin while keeping his vision ahead watching the television program.

"What is it now Kev? I'm all ears, go on ahead and shout it out."

Kevin takes another sip of his beer, and turns his head towards Russell.

"Russ, I left my yarmulke in your car I think. I don't have it. I left it in your car."

Russell starts to laugh while having his view still at the television.

"Kev, you can get it tomorrow then. That was it? That was what you had to tell me? I know you Kev, that isn't what you wanted to tell me, so again, shout it out."

Kevin laughs and turns his head towards the television replying to Russell.

"Yeah you're right Russ, but seriously…, OH MY GOD RUSS, WHAT'S THAT!"

Kevin starts to scream and point towards the front door area. Russell and Jesse both look in that direction and don't see anything noteworthy. Kevin then starts to laugh.

"Made you look. Ha-ha. You guys are so stupid. Ha-ha. Suckers."

Russell then reaches over, and smacks Kevin in the back of the head hard. Kevin then starts to laugh, and turns his direction towards the television screen again. All three men sit in silence for about ten minutes, then Kevin calls out for Russell yet again.

"Okay Russ, scouts honor. This time I'm not fooling around and I have something important I need to tell you. I promise this isn't a joke this time."

Russell puts his hand over his forehead, and replies to Kevin.

"Kev, what the fuck do you want? This is now the third time you're trying to tell me this. I'm starting to think this is some type of game you're playing. I don't find it funny Kev, if there is something you need to say well then just say it, stop fooling and joking around like that."

Kevin then takes another sip of his beer. He stops laughing, and begins to act more serious and responds to Russell in a formal tone.

"Russ, I wanted to say that today has been very long and eventful, and just this morning I remember I was goofing off, and flashback to now, another game changing day Russ. Every day seems to be something else with us. I don't know how you handle it Russ."

Russell laughs and turns his head towards Kevin, and takes another swallow of his beer.

"Well Kev, I don't know how I do it. I don't know how I do anything. I'm just an insane, crazy, psychopathic, ginger, demon looking, evil, hot headed, asshole right?"

Jesse begins to giggle to himself, then continues to read his magazine. Kevin takes another swallow of his beer, and turns his head towards Russell.

"That's correct Russ, and that's why I love you man. Ugh, Russ this is the most unfunniest episode of "Family Guy" I've ever seen. This episode sucks so much man."

Russell takes another sip of his beer and laughs. He responds towards Kevin.

"Yeah this is really bad. "Family Guy", is hit or miss for me. This one is not funny at all."

Kevin laughs at Russell, and takes another swallow of his beer. He then responds to him.

"Russ, do you remember that episode of "Family Guy", where they did a crossover with "The Simpsons"? That one was so funny, I was laughing so much. The part where Peter and Homer began to fight like that was so damn hilarious. You remember that one Russ?"

Russell laughs at Kevin, and drinks more of his beer keeping his vision forward.

"Yeah I saw that one Kev. I agree, that was a good one."

Kevin continuing to watch the television, asks Russell more questions.

"Russ, do you like "Futurama"? Do you ever look at that show? I watch it sometimes, it's pretty funny. I think I've seen all the episodes of that I believe."

Russell looks up towards the ceiling and scratches his head, he then responds to Kevin.

"Hmm, "Futurama" is alright. I mean I don't like or hate it, it's alright. I'm not that well known about it like you are, so. But it's an okay show I guess Kev."

Kevin takes another swallow of his beer, and continues to ask Russell questions.

"Russ, do you like "Stargate"? Oh man, I love that show so much. I wonder if it's on."

Kevin takes the remote control and flips through the channels. Russell then starts to close his eyes and put his hands behind his head. He roughly responds to Kevin.

"Kev, I'm not a fan of "Stargate", but yeah I've seen it. You're more of a Sci-Fi guy, that's not really my thing."

Kevin while still going through channels on the television, replies to Russell.

"Well, you like "Star Wars", right Russ? I know you said you don't care for Sci-Fi, but you do at least like "Star Wars" don't you? How could you hate "Star Wars?"

Russell grumbles out to Kevin with his eyes closed feeling extremely tired.

"Uh, "Star Wars" is alright Kev. I like "Star Wars". I like Darth Vader, Kylo Ren, C3PO, R2D2, Yoda. You know I like "Star Wars" Kev, stop acting silly like that. Now Kev knock that off, I way too tired for all of that man."

Russell then begins to close his eyes and fall asleep. Kevin while he's flipping through the channels, starts to doze into sleep while responding to Russell, whom he doesn't know is asleep.

"Sorry Russ, I was just asking and making sure. Ugh. I'm so sleepy."

A few minutes later Jesse starts to feel tired and decides to close his magazine. He looks across the sofa and notices that both Russell and Kevin who are sitting on different ends of the sofa, are fast asleep. He laughs to himself, and turns the television off. Jesse then walks over to Kevin who's sleeping, and removes his glasses. He sets them on the table in front of the sofa. After cutting all the lights off, he walks into the bedroom and lays down on the bed. He then falls asleep.

Back at "Home Base", Victor begins to walk himself out of the shower. He has on a towel and starts to walk towards the sofa area not giving Brian eye contact. Brian who was paying attention the television, quickly takes a peek as Victor walking from the shower. He notices Victor's self-harm scars on his arm. He tries to keep his eyes on the television and away from Victor's body, but he cannot help himself and continues to watch him. Victor starts to put the pajama pants that Brian left for him on, and sits down on the couch. After he's dressed he looks down towards the ground. Brian looks at Victor's self-harm scars one more time and becomes more distraught over it. He talks to him.

"Hey Victor, were you bullied a lot in school man? Growing up did other kids pick on you or make fun of you? I'm curious about that, and you can tell me. Because I was bullied when I was young and I know it's tough being made fun of."

Victor continues to look down towards the ground and ignores Brian. Brian starts to frown and feel extremely sad for Victor. He then cuts the television off and talks to him again.

"Victor, what's wrong with you man? What's going on? How old are you?"

Victor looks up towards Brian, and whispers out his answer.

"I'm twenty-nine. I haven't done shit with my life. I'm nobody. I look like a fucking creature feature. People fucking hate me. I always have mood swings like this. I'm sorry."

Brian then smiles at him, and responds to him in a calm way.

"Well I'm only a little older than you. I'm thirty-one. I don't think you look like creature. If everyone looked the same, this would be a boring world right? I just think you're a misunderstood man, and I see a lot of myself in you. Me and you are quite similar really"

Brian starts to feel much empathy for Victor, and feels that he's a very damaged person. He tries to continue to make him feel comfortable and happy with himself. Brian continues to press Victor in an attempt to get him to feel more relaxed.

"Victor, you don't have any friends do you? You feel alone, don't you Victor? People make fun of the way you look, people bully you. You start to feel isolated and alone. You start to hate yourself. I don't have much friends either. But I'll be your friend."

Victor looks back towards the floor again, feeling ashamed of himself. Not realizing that Brian is using psychology tactics to mess and control with his emotions. Brian continues.

"We're a part of a special group now, and we all need to stick together and be there for each other. I don't want for you to feel alone or neglected Victor. I care about you, and I feel you're such a lost soul, and you never had anybody love you before have you Victor?"

Victor starts to become very enraged and upset. He still doesn't realize that Brian is offering him words of kindness. Victor views it as

Brian trying to make fun of him or harass him. Victor has been victimized in this situation many times before, so it becomes difficult for him to assess when people are being sincere with their thoughts, and when people are not. Victor starts to have pent up anger. He keeps his head down towards the ground. Brian then continues.

"Victor, you don't have to be afraid. You don't have to hate yourself. I'm your friend."

Brian then starts to rub Victor's self-harm scars on his arm and speaks to Victor very softly.

"Victor, I'm your friend and I'm here for you man."

Immediately following this, intensely, Victor grabs Brian's neck and tackles him to the ground. They begin to wrestle and fight each other on the ground. This continues for a couple minutes until Victor manages to grab Brian's neck, and brings Brian's face, to his. Victor then kisses Brian for almost a minute. Following that, he pushes Brian to the floor, stands up and laughs and screams very loudly.

"Ha-ha. Brian, DON'T YOU EVER TOUCH ME, AND DON'T YOU EVER TALK TO ME AGAIN LIKE THAT! Do you understand me Brian?"

Brian while still down on the ground with an angry look on his face, nods his head. Victor continues to laugh, then sits back down on the couch watching the television, laughing to himself. He looks down on the ground where Brian is and and talks to him.

"Brian, I'm happy to be your friend, just don't ever talk to me like that."

Brian while still on the floor responds to Victor.

"Okay, I won't. I promise."

Brian then gets himself up, laughing and shaking his head. He then walks over to his bed, and starts to go to sleep. A few minutes later, Victor turns off the television, and falls asleep on the couch.

CHAPTER 11:

NOTHING BIG, NOTHING SMALL

The following morning, Russell begins to wake up. As he's waking himself up, still feeling slightly tired, he slowly stands up from the sofa. He then turns his head and notices that Kevin is deep asleep on the sofa. Russell smiles to himself and starts to walk inside of the bedroom. He sees that Jesse is also sleeping, and smiles at him as well. Russell glances over at his alarm clock, and it says it is 10 A.M. He proceeds towards his closet to pick out an outfit to wear. He picks out a black polo shirt, and some blue jeans, with some black Adidas shoes. He then sets his clothes on the side of his bed, where Jesse is still resting, and takes a towel and heads into the shower to bathe himself. When Russell is finished bathing, he returns to the bedroom and puts his clothes on. Immediately after that, he walks into the living room, and sees that Kevin is still sleeping. He then starts to jolt Kevin back and forth on the sofa, and screams at him.

"Kev, get up man. We have to meet the other guys remember? Get up."

Kevin wraps his arms around his eyes and ignores Russell. When Russell notices that Kevin is still not getting up, he continues to bother him until he does.

"Kev, I said get up. You gotta get up now. You have to wake up man."

Kevin then composes himself and starts to wake up. With an angry and irritated look on his face, he reaches for his glasses on the table, and begins to snap at Russell.

"Russ, okay I'm up. Shit. You didn't have to go through all of that. Damn. I'll be back Russ, I'm going to go to my place to change, and I'll be right back."

Kevin then gets up from the sofa, and proceeds to walk towards the front door. Russell who is walking towards the bedroom, stops to yell out to Kevin.

"Kev, come straight back here once you're done. I'm not playing with you Kev."

Kevin before turning the doorknob, moves his head towards Russell and responds.

"Yeah Russ, I'll be right back, I'm only going to change clothes man. Be right back."

Russell shakes his head at Kevin, and Kevin leaves the apartment. Russell then immediately walks into the bedroom. He sees that Jesse is still asleep. Likewise, with Kevin, he also forcefully wakes him up. Russell grabs one of the pillows on the bed, and starts to bop Jesse with it very violently and roughly, screaming at him while doing it.

"Sleeping beauty, get up. It's time to get up now. Wake the hell up."

Jesse then immediately wakes himself up, and gives Russell an aggravated look. He starts to walk himself out of the bedroom, and while he's walking out screams at Russell.

"Was that really necessary Russell? Damn, I don't understand you sometimes."

Russell laughs at him. Jesse walks into the bathroom to freshen himself up. Russell at this time goes into the living room and picks up his phone. He starts to call Brian and lets him know he, Kevin and Jesse are on their way, and they will be there soon. Russell then takes a seat down on the sofa, and turns the television on. He begins to flip through channels, before finally settling to watch a tennis match. Jesse minutes later comes out of the bathroom and walks straight towards the bedroom to get dressed. Jesse picks out a light green button up shirt, and some black shorts with a pair of boat shoes. After getting dressed, he walks into the living room, and joins Russell on the sofa. The both of them look at the tennis match on the television. Ten minutes later, Kevin starts to knock on the door. Jesse lets him in.

Kevin then proceeds to the sofa, and sits with the rest of the men. Kevin is wearing a gray polo shirt, with denim jeans and sneakers. All three men sit in an awkward silence for a while, before Russell pulls up his phone to look at the time. He then puts his phone in his pocket, and walks towards the kitchen area to get his keys and his sunglasses. Kevin and Jesse watch him, and start to get the hint that it's time to leave. They precisely get themselves up from the sofa. Jesse turns the television set off, and grabs his tote bag from under the coffee table. Kevin and Jesse then put their sunglasses on, and all three men walk out of the apartment. They head towards the elevator. While inside, Kevin starts to complain.

"Russ, I'm hungry. Can we stop and get a bite to eat? I'm really starving man."

Kevin and Jesse turn to look at Russell who's shaking his head and looking down. Jesse looks back at Kevin who seems upset, then exclaims out to Russell as well.

"Russell, Kevin and I haven't had a damn thing to eat. If it isn't going to trouble you, would you mind if we could go and eat something?"

Russell continues to look down at the floor remaining silent. Kevin and Jesse turn their heads away from Russell, and stay silent as well. They get inside of the car, with Kevin sitting in the passenger seat and Jesse sitting in the rear seat. Russell starts the ignition of the car, and Kevin then turns his head towards Russell, screaming at him.

"Russ, I'm hungry. I need to eat something. Have some heart man, please?"

Russell ignores Kevin as he drives out of his complex, and heads down the road. He notices the weather is clear and looking very fantastic and moderate today with the sun out. Jesse cries out to Russell in defense of Kevin.

"Russell, can you stop somewhere to eat please? Kevin is hungry and so am I. Please?"

Russel reaches a stoplight and turns his head to look behind at Jesse, and gives him a defeated look. Russell then looks across towards Kevin who looks upset, and talks to him.

"Where do you want to go Kev?"

Kevin then begins to rub the back of his head with his hand, and starts to think. He then looks out of the window, still rubbing his head. He then responds to Russell.

"Russ, can you stop at "IHOP"? I really have a taste for that. That sounds really good."

Russell while he's still stopped at the light, quickly claps back at Kevin angrily.

"Kev, hell no. "IHOP" is going to take too damn long. I can take you somewhere else though. Not "IHOP", because we have an agenda and I don't want to go against it."

Kevin shakes his head at Russell and fires back at him.

"Russ, please. I'll pay for you and Jesse. It's on me. I really want "IHOP". I know we are supposed to meet Brian and Victor at "Home Base", but that's still miles away on the other edge of town. There's gotta be an "IHOP" in that area, I just know. I'll check right now."

The light changes and Russell continues to drive, while Kevin pulls out his phone and starts to find an "IHOP" location near their destination. He then is able to find one.

"Okay Russ, there's one only a few minutes away from where Brian and Victor are. So we can eat, and head right there after. Come on Russ, there's no reason to say no now."

Russell puts his hand under his chin, and turns his head towards Kevin.

"Alright Kev, you win. We'll go to "IHOP", but after we're done eating we leave. We don't have a bunch of time to kill or waste. We're gonna eat and leave. That's it."

Kevin smiles at Russell and beings to laugh. He turns up the stereo volume which is playing urban pop music, and then responds to Russell.

"Thanks Russ. Damn right I win. I always win against you Russ. You always lose. Ha."

Russell shakes his head at Kevin, and continues down the road. Back at "Home Base", Brian is at his work station, organizing his mechanic tools. Brian is wearing a blue polo shirt, and blue jeans and black shoes. He looks at the sofa area and sees that Victor is still asleep. Knowing that Russell, Kevin and Jesse are on their way there right now, Brian walks over to the sofa, and then begins to wake Victor up by pushing his body.

"Hey you, the guys will be here soon, so get dressed man. Alright?"

Victor then aggressively rises from the couch and pushes Brian to the ground.

"Don't fucking touch me. I'm a heavy sleeper, and I'll get up when I'm ready to get up. I don't need you touching me. I warned you about this shit last night, don't make me do it again."

Brian then looks at Victor in shock, and nods his head very reluctantly. Victor then gives Brian an evil smile, and remains sitting on the couch feeling anxious. Brian then starts to walk back to his work station, talking to Victor while doing it.

"I have some cereal here if you want some. I don't know if you're hungry or not, but just in case if you are. I want you to eat something. Don't be afraid, I'm a nice guy."

Victor looks around for a few seconds, then he gets himself up and starts to dress himself. He puts on the same clothes he picked out the night before. A black t-shirt, with khaki pants. After he's finished putting his clothes on, he walks over to the kitchen area and pours himself a bowl of cereal. He then sits down at the table and silently eats his cereal. As he's eating, Brian looks at him and starts to smile. He then talks to him.

"I wanted to say sorry if I'm making you uncomfortable Victor. I want to be your friend man, that's all. You have to chill though, I'm a cool guy. I don't know your history, and don't give a fuck. I want us to be friends, and I need for you to calm down a bit. Alright? Oh and another thing, I didn't like you kissing me like that. Respect me and I'll respect you. Okay?"

Victor continues to eat his cereal and looks over at Brian to reply to what he said.

"Well, I don't want you touching me first off. Next, I'm working on friendships and dealing with other people. It's very difficult for me, so I'm sorry if I come across as creepy to you, but as long as you don't touch and don't sweet talk me, I'll be cool with you Brian. I did kiss you, and you're a handsome man Brian, but I only want to be friends for now. Okay?"

Brian continues to organize his tools, and softly responds to Victor.

"That's just fine. If you're cool with me, I'll be with you. I won't touch you, but I don't want you kissing on me either man. So you can touch other people, but I can't touch you?"

Victor continues to laugh looking at Brian, while eating his cereal. Brian becomes annoyed at this and starts to frown at him in disappoint. Victor then responds.

"Yes, that's exactly right. What I get to do, you aren't able to do. If I want to touch you, it's okay. But If I don't want you touching me, then I don't want you touching me. If I want to kiss or touch you Brian, like this..."

Victor then runs up from the table towards Brian's work station, and grabs one of his wrenches. He intentionally aims and throws it at the wall startling him. He then forcefully starts to kiss Brian; the same way he did the night before. Brian pushes Victor off him and starts to smile at him. He then responds to him.

"Victor, go over there eat your cereal man. You've proved your point, I get it. If you want to touch me or do what you just did, it's fine. I'll also respect you, and not touch you. That makes zero fucking sense, but whatever I can do to calm you down. I'll take one for the team I guess."

Brian then returns to what he was doing, and Victor returns to his seat. Victor continues to eat his cereal while staring at Brian, laughing and smiling to himself. A few minutes later, Victor finishes his cereal, and walks over to the area Brian is. He speaks to him.

"I don't know much about repairing cars, but I do know that you're not lining these tools or socket wrenches right at all. They are supposed to be sized up like this. Here I'll show you."

Victor then proceeds to help Brian out with his task, and they both manage to develop a closer both with each other. Brian then softly speaks to Victor.

"Thanks man, see I told you that you weren't a bad guy. You're misunderstood."

Victor smiles back at Brian, and he continues to help him arrange his tools.

Meanwhile, Russell, Kevin and Jesse arrive at "IHOP" and walk inside. There are not that many people inside, and they are immediately seated at a booth with Russell and Jesse sitting adjacent from each other, and Kevin sitting across from them on the other side of the booth. The waitress arrives and gives them their menu. Russell then gives his drink order.

"Can I have a coffee please?"

Kevin while looking at the menu, then gives his drink order.

"Hmm...Yeah, I guess I will just take a Coke Cola, thanks."

Jesse then immediately gives his drink order after that.

"I'll go with an Iced Tea. Thank you."

The waitress then leaves the table. While he's still looking through the menu, Kevin then begins to speak to Russell in a whispery tone.

"I can't decide what I want, it all looks so good. Hmm. This is gonna be tough."

Russell keeping his eyes towards reading the menu, responds to Kevin harshly.

"Kev, make your mind up and pick something. We don't have all day to spend here."

Kevin continues to skim through the menu, and replies to Russell.

"Okay Russ, I'll will figure something out I suppose. I have to make a choice."

The waitress a couple minutes later returns to the table with their drinks, and then begins to take their order. Russell goes first and gives his order to the waitress.

"I'll take the hotcakes, scrambled eggs, bacon and hash browns. Thanks."

Kevin who's still indecisive about what he's wants, gives his order to the waitress.

"Ah, this is tough, but I'll go with the chocolate cream filled pancakes. I'll take sausage, scrambled eggs, hash browns, and I also would like some toast as well. Thanks."

Jesse then directly after that, gives his order.

"I will go with the strawberry and banana pancakes. I'll have hash browns, sausage and scrambled eggs. Thanks."

The waitress then leaves the table, and Russell begins to put cream and sugar in his coffee. Kevin while sipping his soda, decides to quietly talk to Russell.

"Hey Russ, so we're gonna meet up with the rest of the guys after this right? What for again? Is it for the 'you know what'? That's still going down? We're gonna so that still?"

Russell takes a sip of his coffee, and gives a cold stare towards Kevin ignoring him. Jesse listens to Russell and Kevin interact, but doesn't to respond them. When Kevin notices that Russell is not paying him any attention, he starts to throw sugar packets at him. Russell throws the sugar packets back at Kevin, and confiscates the sugar container. Russell becomes fed up.

"Kev knock that shit off, it's not funny man. Knock it off Kev."

Kevin laughs at Russell, then behaves and composes himself. All three men sit at the table in silence for a few minutes. The waitress then eventually returns with their food, and they begin to eat. While they are eating, Kevin takes a piece of Russell's bacon.

"I forgot to get bacon Russ, let me have some of yours man. Thanks, appreciate it."

Russell lets Kevin pick from his plate without any care. They continue to eat their food quietly. The waitress around this time comes and drops of the check, and sets it at the corner of the table. As they are all finishing their food, Russell grabs the check and gets his wallet out. Kevin then snatches the check out his hands, and pulls his wallet out.

"Russ, I'd said take care of it, and I will. Don't worry. This one is on me."

Russell laughs and shakes his head at Kevin and puts his wallet back in his pocket. All three of them get up from the table, and head to the lobby of the restaurant where Kevin pays for the check. They then walk out of the restaurant and get inside the car. Russell then drives directly to "Home Base". They get out of the car, and Russell takes out his phone to let Brian know that they are outside. Brian quickly unlocks and opens the front gate, and greets them.

"Hey guys, good to see you again. Come on in."

As Russell, Kevin and Jesse walk in, they notice Victor on the other side of the building walking around in a circle looking down at the ground, laughing to himself. Brian sees that Russell, Kevin and Jesse look puzzled over this, and he then explains.

"He's been doing that for the past ten minutes. I ignore it, because as long as he's comfortable that way, I'm not going to bother or disturb him. Anyways guys, I'm going to tell Max we are all here. Russell, can I speak to you outside for just a second."

Russell raises his eyebrows and nods his head. He and Brian then walk out of the unit. Brian closes and locks the door behind them, and he quietly speaks to Russell.

"Hey, I don't know if we should let Victor be involved. The guy is really damaged and out of control. I was talking to him last night, and also dealing with him this morning. I don't know. I mean, he can be a nice guy when he wants to be, I'm just worried that's all."

Russell looks at Brian, and puts his hand on his shoulder. He then responds.

"Well, it's not fair to single out Victor. All five of us are crazy in some shape or form. We are all in this together, and we have to all be included. Think of it that way."

Brian shakes his head and looks out to the distance. He then quickly replies to Russell.

"I suppose you're right. He deserves the same amount of equal treatment as the rest of us. He is still weird, and you can't doubt that. I'm not ideal and perfect either, but he's different. I mean, he kissed me twice though. He says that he can touch me all he wants, but I'm not allowed to touch him. I don't understand that at all. Ha-ha. Crazy guy."

Russell and Brian both laugh. Brian unlocks the unit door, and Russell goes inside the building. Brian then walks away to go and get Max. Minutes after this, Brian returns back to "Home Base" with Max. As Max walks into the warehouse, all of the men gather around him. They start to greet him and shake his hand. They then stand by him, as he begins to talk.

"It's very good to see all of you again. This only proves to me that you guys indeed are serious with this venture, and you all want to rebel against the world. I'm just a man with no legs, so who am I to judge? As I promised you all yesterday, I want to show you my collection."

They all then proceed to walk out of "Home Base", and follow Max around a short distance towards another warehouse unit. Once they arrive there, Max gives Brian a key. While Brian is unlocking the door to the unit, he then turns to the rest of the guys, and speaks to them.

"You guys are going to have to copy that key so that each of you will have one, and will be able to get in here whenever you want. I'm afraid I don't have any additional copies."

The rest of the guys nod their heads to agree, as Brian begins to unlock the unit. Upon entering, they all assess the contents inside. The unit which is considerably smaller than "Home Base", but still a reasonably big warehouse unit, contains a driveway space that has a black passenger van, many automatic machine rifles, handguns, smoke bombs, grenades, detonation devices, and other artillery ammunition. There are also industrial drills, sledgehammers, walkie talkies, wireless security alarm detectors, and many disguises and clothes used to conceal identity. Max then talks to the other men who are continuing to observe the unit.

"All of these items and tools are yours. I'm sure they will be of much help to you. This is as far as I can offer though. The rest of the choices will be up to all of you."

Russell turns his head towards Max, and responds to him.

"This is perfect, and yes this will help us a lot. Thank you very much."

Max smiles back at him, and Kevin then starts to talk to Max.

"I'm going to try to work on those alarm detectors. I can most likely connect them to my laptop, and they might be very useful to disable silent alarms in the banks. I can also use the same wireless software to plant the detonators as well, to act as a distraction or diversion."

Kevin was extremely skilled in this department, and felt this would possibly be his biggest contribution towards the group. Brian looks over at the black van, and starts to speak.

"I don't know how many getaway cars we would need, but I suggest we use more than one. Kevin can use that black van to do all the tech stuff in there. It's not a registered car, so it's okay. I can get more vehicles if need be, so you can leave that all to me."

Victor stars to walk around the unit, and notices the industrial drills. He begins to talk.

"These are interesting, and I don't know if we are going to use them, but these are very interesting tools. They might turn out be beneficial for us."

Jesse walks around the building, and starts to offer his opinion.

"It's unbelievable how we are actually going to go through with this, but we are all prepared at this point. We have all our tools, so this is good."

All of the men continue to walk around the building for a few minutes. Max then speaks.

"Okay gentlemen, I'm going to retire now and I've hope that you guys are satisfied with this. Remember, Monday, you guys start your first day of work in exchange for allowing me to help you. I know you guys don't work until noon, but because Monday will be your first day, I want all of you to show up here in front of this unit at 10 A.M. I have stuff to run by all of you. Wear something comfortable, and something you're not afraid to get dirty, and something to clean in. It's very important for you to not be late. I shall see all of you later."

Brian then looks at all the guys, and starts to shout out to them.

"Alright guys, I'm gonna go back to my pad. You guys can stick around if you want, but make sure you lock up when you're all done and all set. Okay. Here you go Russell."

Brian throws Russell the key to the unit, and also a spare key to "Home Base", and Russell catches them. Immediately after, Brian and Max leave the unit together. The other guys stay inside assessing it. Kevin starts to walk around the unit more, and then turns his head towards Russell, speaking at him with much excitement and happiness.

"This is so awesome Russ. We are really kicking it into overdrive now. Yeah."

Russell smiles at Kevin, and walks around the unit. Russell is becoming more confident towards his plans to commit the heist. They have instruments now in order to successfully help them through a task such as that. He is grateful that Max offered to put his profile on the line, for the rest of them. A little part of him starts to worry about the dangers of proceeding. The chance of himself or other members of his circuit getting hurt, or getting into trouble. He feels slightly more at ease that they have tools to make their crusade easier.

Russell believes he has gone too far at this point to give up. His adrenaline rush is at a high level for him to quit, and to change his mind now. He plans for this time next week, next Friday in fact, for all of them to commit the heist. Russell continues to walk around the building, gazing at the different materials. He is then interrupted when Kevin taps him on his shoulder to ask him a question.

"Russ, we have to copy those keys huh? Why don't we go to the hardware store right now and get copies? Because I know you Russ. You'll say we'll do it later, and we don't."

Russell then smiles and laughs at Kevin and pats the back of his shoulder.

"Alright Kev, you're right. Let's get this done now. Let's go get copies of the key."

The men all leave the building, locking the unit as they leave. Victor heads back to "Home Base", and Russell, Kevin and Jesse then travel to the nearest hardware store. They arrive, and make an additional copies of the key to the "Home Base" unit, and an additional copies of the key to the other unit. Russell hands Kevin and Jesse one each. Russell then returns back to "Home Base", and gives Brian and Victor copies of the keys. Russell then starts to talk to all the other four guys.

"With these keys, these are just in case we get separated and have to end back either here, or at the other unit. Only in case of emergencies and things like that."

The rest of the guys nod their heads and agree with him. Right after this Russell, Kevin and Jesse say goodbye to Brian and Victor, and they leave "Home Base". Russell drops Kevin off at his residence, and then proceeds to his home with Jesse. When he gets inside his apartment, Russell starts to feel extremely tired for some reason. Jesse goes over to the sofa area and turns the television on. He begins to watch "The People's Court". Russell starts to feel fatigued and lethargic. He struggles to walk. Feeling out of it, he begins to talk to Jesse.

"Jesse, I'm just feeling tired. I'm gonna go and take a nap."

Jesse looks away from the television, and is concerned about Russell's current condition.

"Russell, do you need me to get you something? Are you alright?"

Russell continues to struggle to walk and speak. He responds to Jesse.

"Yeah I'm fine, I'm going to go and get some rest, that's all. You can chill out here if you want, I don't care. I'm just don't feel okay right now. I don't know."

Jesse continues to worry about Russell, and goes over to feel his forehead. He notices it feels slightly warm. Jesse then asks Russell a question.

"You probably caught a cold or something Russell. You have any Dayquil or Tylenol?"

Russell nods his head, and tells Jesse to go in the medicine cabinet in the bathroom. Jesse gives Russell a glass of water and some of the medicine. Russell then goes into the bedroom and falls asleep. Jesse's assentation was correct; Russell did catch a cold somehow. For the next few days, he tried his best to fight it by remaining in bed. Knowing that he and the rest of the guys had to report to work for Max on Monday morning, he has to get himself together by then.

Monday morning arrives for all the men to start their first day of work. Russell slowly wakes feeling very nervous and not very optimistic on what the day will bring. His cold has finally subsided, but he still feels slightly woozy from the effects. He peeks out his bedroom curtains, and notices that today is a very cloudy and hazy overcast day. That already makes him feel more glum than he already is. He looks at his alarm clock on the side of the bed, and it's showing that it's 8 A.M. Jesse is still resting, but Russell goes into the bathroom to take a shower. After departing from the shower, he returns to the bedroom to put on a white graphic hoodie, and some black sweatpants and white New Balance tennis shoes. After dressing, he wakes Jesse up. Jesse also starts to get himself ready.

Russell walks into the kitchen and makes himself a cup of coffee to spark himself up. He puts the coffee in his travel mug and sets it on the counter. Jesse at this time is getting dressed. He decides to wear a red graphic t shirt, grey sweat pants with some Vans shoes. The both of them put their sunglasses on, Russell gets his coffee mug, and they then head over to Kevin's residence to pick him up. Kevin is wearing an old beat up blue T-Shirt, some black sweatpants and white sneakers. Kevin gets into Russell's car and greets them in a very cheerful and perky voice.

"Morning Russ, Morning Jess. I'm not happy about today, we have to clean buildings, but I guess it's not that bad. It's not like none of us having nothing to do."

Russell laughs at Kevin, and Russell takes a sip of from his coffee mug.

"Kev, that wasn't what you were saying before. You were the main one complaining and trying to hassle your way out of doing the work. Now you're all happy about it? Please Kev."

Kevin starts to bite his fingers, and looks out the window. He then responds to Russell.

"Well that was then, this is now Russ. I changed my mind. I'm gonna deal with it."

Russell laughs at Kevin. They proceed towards the unit near "Home Base". They arrive there at nine thirty, slightly before the time Max told them to be there which was at ten. Russell, Kevin and Jesse, notice Brian and Victor standing outside looking tired. Brian is wearing a white polo shirt with black denim jeans. Victor is wearing a white plain t shirt with khaki pants. All of the men start to greet each other, and Brian gives out a remark.

"I'm surprised that everyone is here. Well, I don't know if surprised is the right word, I guess I wasn't expecting for everyone to show up I guess. I don't know. But we're all here."

The rest of the guys ignore Brian, and they give him very agitated looks. The men continue to wait outside the unit, until 10 A.M. finally approaches. Max appears in his wheelchair. He starts to look at all the of the guys, and begins to laugh. He then speaks.

"You guys are all present, and on time. Great. That's the hard part over already. Everything else for today, is going to come easy and smooth. Alright. I'm going to give a set of keys; and no, you can't copy these; and two guide binders to both Russell and Brian. The rest of you will have to borrow these items if you need to use them, or ask Russell and Brian."

Max then hands the set of keys and binders to Russell and Brian.

"The keys are to unlock the office buildings you guys have to clean. The guide binders tell you what keys unlock which building, safety regulations, if one of you gets in contact with chemicals, and a to-do list. All items must be completed before you guys lock up for the night."

Russell and Brian then start to skim through the binders, as Max continues explaining.

"I decided to give Russell and Brian the keys and the binders, because I only have two sets of keys, and I only have two of the guide binders. I gave them to the two guys whom I felt were the most responsible to be in charge of them. But all five of you can read the guide and use the keys. It's really important that you guys do not lose them. I don't have replacements."

After skimming through the binders, Russell and Brian close them. Max continues to talk.

"Well, I guess that's about it. Now all of you get to work. The guide tells you which buildings you guys clean each day. So I wish you guys all the best. Catch all of you later."

Max then departs from the area. Brian skims the guide again, and starts to speak.

"Okay, so on Mondays and Tuesdays, we have to clean the "Wittberg Law Offices" on 7th St.; On Wednesdays and Thursdays, we have to clean the "Porter Professional Building" on Flower St; Alright. Victor you can ride with me; Russell I'll meet you there by twelve. Okay."

The men then follow each other on their way to the "Wittberg Law Offices". They reach the surrounding area an hour before they are scheduled, at eleven. They all take advantage of this extra time, by going to McDonalds drive thru for lunch. After leaving the McDonalds, the men reach the building. Russell and Brian park in the indoor parking structure of the building they are going to be cleaning. Russell, Kevin and Jesse eat in Russell's car. Brian eats with Victor in his car. While they are all eating, Kevin decides to ask Russell a question.

"So Russ, you still want to do the heist this Friday? Is that still okay for you?"

Russell who is eating, and doesn't really wish to be bothered by Kevin, responds roughly.

"Yeah, I guess Kev. We can do it this Friday. We have to plan fast, but I think it's possible if we all work together and stay focused. I already have a few locations to consider."

Kevin eats more of his food, and continues to talk with Russell.

"Okay Russ, that sounds good. I only wanted to make sure, and thanks for updating me."

Russell tilts his head down, puts his hand over his face, and shakes his head.

"No problem Kev. Don't worry about it anything man, everything is going to be fine."

The men start wrapping up eating their food, as they continue to wait until it is time for them to work. Russell looks at the clock on his dashboard and it's a quarter until noon. He gets out of his vehicle, and heads over to Brian's car. He knocks on his window and speaks to him.

"So, do we go in now? I think this is the right time, wanted to make sure with you first."

Brian looks around, and rubs his hand over his neck looking as if he were unsure. He and Victor then get out of the car. Brian then confirms with Russell.

"I think so. By the time we get on the elevator and check in, it shouldn't be too early. I don't think they would care if we started to clean a few minutes early."

Russell nods his head, and he directs himself to his car to alert Kevin and Jesse. They get out of Russell's car, and Russell then locks the doors. All five of them proceed towards the elevator in the parking lot, to get inside the building. Once they are inside, they officially start to work. Each of the guys must figure out which man will do which task, at which time. They have until noon until nine to finish all their tasks, and they get an hour break at four. Each building they have to clean, has ten floors. They must find a way to alternate, or find some type of system to get the tasks done. The tasks they have to do are as follows.

Each floor has two restrooms, meaning twenty toilets in total. They must be kept clean and tidy at all times. The bathrooms must also be stocked and maintained. Soap in the dispensers must also be filled. Trash must also be emptied regularly. Trash cans are in hallways, lobbies, offices, in conference rooms, the restrooms, copy rooms and breakrooms. They typically have to be checked every two hours, and the trash bag must also be replaced. Trash must be emptied in trash bins that each guy must wheel around. The trash bins can be emptied in the dumpers in the parking structure on the bottom level to get rid of. Lobbies, hallways, breakrooms and copy rooms must always be vacuumed and mopped. They can only vacuum and mop private offices from five until nine.

The first floor must be power mopped every night, and this should typically be the final task. Once all their tasks are finished for the day, they must turn off the lights, and lock the doors. The first, fifth, and tenth floor of the buildings contains a supply closet, with their tools and materials. Each building, although located on two different streets in walking distance of each other, are owned by the same company. Thus, the layouts and floor plans of the building are very identical and look exactly the same as far as design and structure. The buildings give a professional and new age modernized theme to them. Both of the buildings are for professional business law firms, and legal businesses.

The men quickly decide that each man will be in charge of cleaning two floors for both buildings. Brian will clean floors one and two, Russell will clean floors three and four. Jesse will clean floors five and six, Kevin will clean floors seven and eight, and Victor will clean floors nine and ten. They will also be in charge of the trash and other duties, including nighttime duties and cleaning private rooms. Once they are all done, Brian will lock down floors one through five, and Russell will lock floors six through ten. The men promptly get to work. Russell thinks to himself that just a couple weeks ago, he was a manager at a bank. Now he's cleaning office buildings. Although, he has had to do similar cleaning work like this in the past. Russell had a part time job as a busboy at a Greek restaurant when he was in High School. He doesn't complain due to that, and rather get the work done, than to complain and be angry about it. Jesse has had jobs to where he had to clean up after other people, so this wasn't new to him. Kevin used to have a job as a janitor before, and he didn't care for it. This explains why he wasn't thrilled to be doing this with the rest of the guys. However, Kevin quickly accepted himself into doing the tasks, and he is now comfortable. Brian has worked a cleaning job before, but it's not the type of work he prefers to do. He still stays positive about it. Victor has worked as a janitor, and as a maintenance man many times before. So all of this is second nature for him. Out of all the guys, he is the most experienced and most comfortable at cleaning. The men continue to do their tasks, even though many of them are starting to feel slightly exhausted. Being their first day, this is quite a lot to get accustomed to. Despite that, they are managing quite well. They strive through above all of that.

Jesse who has his headphones on listening to music on his phone, goes to the supply closet which contains all of their cleaning tools. He walks in to get a vacuum, to start vacuuming the hallways and the lobby. After turning the vacuum on, it cuts off after a few seconds. The vacuum is out of commission, and won't work. Jesse heads up to tenth floor supply closet, with intentions to grab a replacement vacuum located there. However, Victor stops Jesse, and asks him what he's doing. Jesse explains the situation. Victor somehow manages to fix the vacuum Jesse was using. Jesse returns to the fifth floor to continue his task, without any further issues.

Russell has his earphones in listening to music on his phone. He is very focused on the tasks which he must do. He starts to empty all the trash cans located on his floors, and replaces the trash bags as well. He notices that for such a large building, there aren't that many trash cans in the halls. He also notices that due to the amount of trash, he's surprised he doesn't see that many employees roaming about. This is very peculiar and puzzling to him, but he carries on with his work. He continues to empty all the trash, as he pushes his trash cart. It fills up father than Russell anticipated for. As his trash cart is full, he needs to empty it in the dumpster. He steadily hauls the full trash cart on the elevator, and heads down to the parking structure to empty it in the dumpster. He then takes the empty trash cart back in the building, storing it in the supply closet.

Kevin is starting to become agitated and irritated doing his work. He is listening to political podcasts on his phone, with his earphones on. He begins to clean the toilets on the floor he's assigned. He makes sure that the soap in the bathroom is full, and that the bathroom is structured nice and neat. Kevin then begins to mop the floor of the bathroom. Once he's done with that, he carries on to the other bathroom to do the same tasks as he did in the one before. Kevin already is feeling tired, and its only day number one. He's not happy cleaning bathrooms at all, but understands quite frankly the job must be done.

Victor is doing his tasks rather well, and doesn't seem to be irritated or bothered. He goes into the break rooms of the floors he has to clean, and makes sure they are all cared for. He empties the trash, sweeps and mops the floor. He mops the floor on the lobby, and mops all the floors in the foyers of the private rooms. The last two floors which Victor is in charge of, remarkably are the biggest, and contain the most vestibules and common rooms and lobbies. But the final two floors usually are the quietest. For someone like Victor who likes things peaceful and quiet, that is an advantage for him.

Brian is on the main floor, and doing his tasks and having a happy attitude to himself, keeping a smile on his face. The first floor is typically the busiest, but for Brian this is something that doesn't really phase him. He gets to see patrons in the building, talking to them and greeting them. Occasionally having small talk. Brian is always making sure all the tasks on the first floor are done accordingly, as the first floor has the most activity. It has to be kept in a proper clean pristine condition, due to that very reason. The trash can in the first floor seems to always be full, which kind of makes Brian annoyed. It's understandable as it's the first floor, and he doesn't mind it as much, once he puts it in that perspective.

As the men continue to work, their break time is slowly approaching. All of them are beginning to feel drained from all the work they are doing. This is in fact hard work, having to clean a large building such as this. While doing this however, it causes them to bond and work together to accomplish all of their tasks. Intermittently, they come into contact with each other while they are working. Usually to get items from the supply closet, or when they have to empty their trash on the lower level. The men endure and persevere through their tasks until break, which is slowly but surely coming. Kevin is really anticipating his break, as he really wants to relax for a while. Out of all the men, he's the one whom is the most tired. He pulls out his phone almost every ten minutes checking to see if it's break time, as he's that anxious about it. All of the men continue their work, despite the fatigue they are feeling.

Finally, break time soon approaches. The men are each able to have a one-hour break from four until five. They can leave the building and get something to eat, but they must be back working at five. Once five approaches, the men must now do evening tasks such as cleaning private office rooms, and the first floor must also be power mopped, which this is typically the final task of each day. Then they must lock all the doors. Kevin who's feeling very jubilant and excited for break, takes out his phone and starts to order samosas from a nearby restaurant. samosas are deep fried foods that have chili peppers, potatoes, onions, peas, and meat in them. After placing his order in his phone, Kevin tries to locate Russell, as he has something to tell him. He continues to walk through the building looking for Russell, feeling anxious. When Kevin finally sees Russell down a hallway, he runs towards him, talking to him very fast

"Russ, Russ! It's break time man come on. I've ordered us some samosas. You like those right Russ? Hey Russ, follow me right quick, I want to show you something. But you have to keep quiet man, don't go running your mouth and don't overreact either."

Russell gives Kevin a very skeptical look, and follows him to a secluded staircase. Kevin shuts the door to the staircase, and they stand in the stairwell, off the side. Kevin pulls out a bag of marijuana, waving in it Russell's face who looks shocked. Kevin then whispers to him.

"I got that good good, sticky icky, skeet skeet, cheeba cheeba, reefer, Mary Jane, Russ! This is enough for all five of us. Like I said I ordered some samosas they should be ready in about a few minutes. We have to find a place to smoke this."

Russell is extremely aghast, and snaps back at Kevin angrily, whispering to him.

"Kev, you are beyond repair man. Beyond repair. I should have known you had pot on you, I should have checked you. Fuck. We can't smoke that shit here; we have to find a park or something. Damn, Kev. You brought pot? Really? Ugh."

Kevin starts to laugh at Russell, and puts the bag of marijuana back in his pocket. He then hears someone about to open the staircase door, and its Brian. Kevin then waves the bag at him. Brian widens his eyes and looks at Kevin in shock, angrily clapping at him.

"Oh no you didn't. Tell me that isn't what I think it is. We can't smoke that here though. I can take a few hits, I could use some, but all of us are in deep trouble if we smoke that here."

Russell starts to shake his head, and Kevin who was staring at him begins to laugh. The three of them locate Jesse and Victor, and all five of them head down to the parking lot. Brian buys five bottles of water from the break room vending machine, and hands one to each of the guys. Once they are in the parking lot, Kevin then starts to wave the bag of marijuana at Jesse and Victor, who are shocked and surprised over this as well. Russell, Kevin and Jesse then get in Russell's car, and Victor rides in Brian's car, as they drive towards the restaurant to pick up the samosas. Leaving the restaurant, they then drive a short distance to a park that Russell recommends. While Russell is driving, Kevin reaches in his pocket, taking out the marijuana bag. He begins to roll two small marijuana joints. Russell watches this and laughs at him, shaking his head. Kevin while he's rolling the joints, then softly speaks to Russell.

"Russ we don't have much time, we gotta get back to this cleaning shit. So if I roll two joints, there wouldn't be so much waiting and repetition passing. I want all of us to get high."

Russell again shakes his head and laughs at Kevin. Both he and Brian a couple minutes later, reach this very quiet and quaint park with many trees, flowers and natural plants. From the park, you can see the downtown skyscrapers. Russell looks around this quiet and peaceful park, and notices a young hippie couple, a man and a woman kissing under a nice shaded tree, with their bikes located right next to them. This park is simply wonderful and magnificent. Not only is the scenic view breathtaking, but the scent of nature and the plants is also splendid. Brian takes his phone out his pocket, and begins to play some Hip-Hop music on an internet radio application on his phone. The five men walk through the park, until they see an intimate area on the back corner of the park that has a table with a bench attached. They all sit down on the bench. Russell sets the box of samosas down, and Victor quickly scarfs one. Kevin then hands one of the marijuana joints to Jesse who's lights it, and Kevin lights the other one for himself. While he's taking a hit from the joint, Kevin starts to whisper to Russell, with a very soft relaxed voice.

"Oh man Russ, this park beautiful man. Nice secret little spot. Very cozy and lovely."

Kevin passes the marijuana joint to Russell, who takes a puff of it. Jesse after taking a hit from the joint, gives it to Victor who takes a hit. Jesse then grabs a samosa, and while eating it speaks to Kevin in a very quiet tone.

"Thanks Kevin. You have balls for doing that, but thank you so much. That was good."

Kevin socks Russell on the shoulder to get his attention, passing him the joint. Kevin and Jesse then fist bump. Kevin also fist bumps Victor. Russell takes a couple hits from the joint, then passes it to Brian. Russell then reaches into the samosa box and starts to eat one. Brian fist bumps Kevin, and takes a hit from the joint. The guys then start to feel the effect of the marijuana, and become more relaxed with themselves. Victor takes another hit of the joint, and passes it Jesse. Brian then takes another hit, and hands the joint to Kevin, who takes another hit. Brian then grabs a samosa and eats it. Brian then starts to talk to Kevin.

"Thanks man, this is what I call a good break. Russell, you got a good friend man. Ha-ha."

Kevin fist bumps Brian again. Kevin then punches Russell on the shoulder passing him the joint. Kevin while smiling at Russell, takes a samosa and begins to eat it. He then talks to Russell in a very smooth manner.

"Hey Russ, you feeling good man? You feeling relaxed buddy? Shit, I know I am."

Russell takes another hit of the joint. While looking at the scenery, he responds to Kevin.

"Ha-ha, fuck you Kev. You're something else man. What will I do without you Kev?"

Russell shakes his head and hands the joint to Brian. Jesse takes another hit, and passes it to Victor, who's chomping down on the last samosa. After eating his samosa, Victor gets up and throws the empty box of away in the trash. Victor then takes another hit from the joint. Jesse begins to get up from the bench, and starts to dance and mime to the Hip-Hop music that Brian is playing on his phone. He is dancing in complete rhythm and timing towards the music. The track is a remix of "Runaway Love" by Justin Bieber. Featuring Raekwon from the Wu-Tang Clan, and Kanye West. Russell, Kevin, Brian and Victor watch Jesse's performance, laughing at him in a friendly and encouraging way. While Jesse is dancing, he walks over to where Russell is and stands in front of him. Jesse begins to rub Russell's shoulders, while he's continuing to dance to the music. The rest of the guys laugh at this as well. Russell then rubs Jesse on his back, and Jesse then returns to the area he was before, and resumes his dancing. Brian after taking hits from the joint, quickly passes it to Kevin. Kevin takes another hit from the joint. Kevin passes the joint to Russell.

"Hey Russ, we gotta start heading back man in a bit. All of us are so fucked up, but we gotta get back to work. But we are so relaxed now to finish off the day. Right man?"

Russell takes another hit of the joint, and doesn't respond to what Kevin said. He passes the joint to Brian, and Russell looks down towards the ground, shaking his head. Victor takes another hit of the joint. Victor then hands it to Kevin, who puts the joint in his marijuana bag. Brian hands the joint he has, back to Kevin. Kevin puts this joint in the bag as well. The men hang around the bench area for a while, relaxing themselves. They must report back to work very soon however. Jesse continues to dance to more music on the phone until the internet radio on the phone takes an advertising break. Brian then grabs his phone and shuts the application off. All of the guys except Russell, start heading out of the park.

Russell looks out towards the horizon of park, and takes a swallow of his water. He laughs and shakes his head. He then gets up from the bench, and joins the other guys as they head back to work.

CHAPTER 12:

NOTHING COLD, NOTHING HOT

The men returned to work after their break. They quickly got started on their evening activities, that they must complete before they are allowed to end their work day. After they return from break from five until nine, they have additional tasks they must do. Including the tasks they are in charge of doing before going on break, which they also have to finish. These additional tasks include cleaning private office rooms and conference rooms. The first floor must be power mopped, and all doors in the building, including the front door, must be locked before they leave. During this time, employees and patrons of the building have gone home, and are usually not present. It allows more freedom from the guys to work in peace and quiet. Each of them perform their tasks without any issues or problems. The evening tasks however, are more difficult and more stressful. There are more rooms and areas to cover, which equals to more work and effort that has to be done. But due to them already being established on how the cleaning procedures work, it makes the job slightly easier to deal with and handle.

Russell continues with his work, and he has his headphones on. He is now vacuuming the rooms located on his floors, and continues on with his cleaning duties. However, while he's cleaning, Russell notices there are many private vacant board rooms in this building. He starts to wonder if they all complete their tasks early enough, they could possibly hang out in these rooms and talk in private. Russell continues with his tasks, yet still having this thought on his mind.

Kevin who is vacuuming a room which has many computer terminals, gets distracted and bored for a minute. He wants to play a game on one of the computers, but he is feeling scared about the chances of getting caught. He looks around to see if there is anyone else in the area. Once he finds out no one is there, he sits down at one of the monitors. He starts to play an action space game. After twenty minutes, Kevin starts to feel guilty for slacking off, and shuts the computer terminal off. He grabs the vacuum and continues with his work.

Jesse is paying attention to his work, and has his headphones on listening to music as he continues to clean and accomplishes all of his tasks. He proceeds to empty all the trash located in the office rooms, and refills each of the trash cans. Now that they have to clean the office rooms, there is more trash to collect and to dispose of.

Victor is completing his tasks without any issue. He does realize that the top two floors have the most amount of rooms, and the biggest sized rooms. Because of this, he works extremely efficient, to get everything clean and done. Although he still deals with issues surrounding his anxiety, cleaning makes him comfortable.

Brian, who's in charge of the first two floors, is arguably working the hardest out of all the men. The first floor has much space to cover, and as it's the first part of the building people usually see, it must be always kept in a perfect condition. He is listening to music on his headphones. Brian cleans all the lobbies and rooms on the main floor. Once he's finished with most of his tasks, Brian goes into the supply closet to get the power mop. One of the final tasks, requires that the first floor must be power mopped before all of them can leave. He then starts to deep clean the floor, with much accuracy.

All the men begin to wrap up most of their tasks, and prepare to suspend their work day. Russell and Kevin end up making a trash run at the same time. They both run into each other in the elevator, heading down to the lower level. Kevin begins speaks to Russell.

"Hey Russ, you almost done man? After this I am. All my floors are clean as a whistle."

Russell looks over at Kevin and he responds to his question.

"Yeah Kev. I'm basically done myself, and I did everything I had to do."

Kevin nods his head at Russell. They both get out of the elevator and head to the lower level parking structure. After dumping the contents of the trash carts into the dumpsters, they immediately head back inside the building to return their trash carts to the supply closet. Once they return their carts, Kevin pulls out his phone and notices that they still have quite some time before their day is over. Russell also pulls out and checks his phone to check the time. He then goes back to the idea he had in his head earlier and reveals this to Kevin.

"Hey Kev, this building has a lot of empty rooms. This could be a perfect place for us all to talk about the 'you know what'. These rooms are very private and nobody will bother us. We are gonna have all this extra time before we have to go out anyways? Let's use that time."

Kevin rests his hands behind his neck, and nods his head towards Russell. He then responds.

"You're absolutely right Russ. Especially if you're planning on doing the 'you know what' this Friday. That only gives us a few more days to plan and prepare for it."

Russell nods his head, while looking down at the floor. Jesse, Victor, and Brian during this time, are in the process of finishing all of their duties. When they finally finish, all five men congregate with each other on the main floor. Russell then starts to speak to everyone.

"Guys, we have quite some time left before it's time to go. I figured we could go to one of the rooms on the top level, and have some private talk. I believe you are all aware as to what the talk is going to be about, but we have to go somewhere private, and that's the best place."

The rest of the men nod their heads to agree with him. All of them get on the elevator and proceed towards the tenth floor. Getting out of the elevator, everyone heads into a reasonably large board room with the lights turned off. The board room has giant windows; they overlook the entire downtown area of Los Angeles. The night sky glows through the room, that displays a beautiful view. Russell turns on a lamp on the corner of the room, which gives off some minor illumination in the room. However, most of the light is coming from the night sky outside. The men then sit on different ends of the table, scattered around on different sides and areas. Russell and Brian sitting on opposing ends of the table. Jesse and Kevin sit next to each other on one side, and Victor sits by himself on the other side.

Russell then looks down at the table, and they all sit in silence for nearly a minute. Russell starts to gather his thoughts, on how exactly he wishes to plan the heist. This was something he's been thinking about for several days now. He's feeling anxious, that it is now time to put all of his ideas to the test. His main objective was to get together a solid team; he was able to check that off the list. The next thing he must do in the order of business; plan out how exactly they wish to act. Careful planning is very necessary, as if they do not plan accordingly or correctly, their plans might not orchestrate the way they intended them to.

This is a very serious venture they are about to proceed in, so it's vital that things are done in a proper method. All of the men in the room are seeping with anxiety, feeling excited and scared to discuss these proceedings. Russell continues to silently look down at the table, preparing himself to explain how the events will flow to the other men. Kevin then takes out a bag of Cheetos he bought from the breakroom, and starts to eat them. Russell at last is able to compose himself, and then begins to speak to all of the men at the table very seriously.

"I don't want to waste any more time on this. I have to cut to the chase, and get right down to business. So I need all of you to listen well, and listen good to what I'm about to say."

The men all look at Russell with attentive expressions on their faces. Russell continues.

"Alright men, on Friday, we do our first heist. Depending on how things go, we may do a couple more before calling it quits. Because nobody just robs one bank, they don't. Right now, I want to get one thing out the of way first. Figuring out which one we are going to hit."

All of the guys look at each other with blank stares. Russell then carries on.

"The bank we are going to hit, is "United Farmers Savings." It's actually not that far from here. This would be the perfect spot for out first time. I been to this bank many times before, and it's an easy setup. Tomorrow morning before we have to work, just to be sure, we're gonna check it out. Kevin, you can also put all the wireless tech stuff to the test as well."

Kevin while he's continuing to eat his chips, nods his head towards Russell. Russell then gets up from his seat at the table, and while looking out the window, continues to speak.

"All five of us will play some sort of role with this job. Brian and I, are going to do the hard stuff. We're just gonna hold up the tellers, and their cash supply. We're not gonna deal with the vault this time around. Next time we will though. Jesse and Victor are going to be the look outs. Kevin, I want you to be the getaway driver, and to be in charge of all the security and computer stuff. That's how it will go down."

Brian then starts to ask Russell a question.

"So as far as the getaway vehicle. Do you want to use the black van that we have? So Kevin's going to drive the van the whole time, and we're all gonna escape in it? That can work well. That way nobody gets split up during this. But just so you know, if you need me to steal any extra cars, I can. Just wanted to offer and put that out there."

Russell while still staring outside the window, nods. He then explains more of the plan.

"Yeah so tomorrow morning, only to be safe, we'll case the bank and check things out. Brian will go in wearing some glasses that have a camera attached to them, and Kevin using his computer magic will then capture the video to us, so we get an inside look inside. Kevin will also use his hacking skills, to see how the security alarm system in the bank is set up."

Kevin continues to eat more of his chips. He responds to Russell while he's eating.

"Sounds good Russ, I can handle that no problem. I'm glad I can help towards that."

Victor then starts to look across the room feeling nervous. He asks Russell a question.

"I was wondering about guns and disguises and stuff. It seems like a stupid question, but we're all gonna keep our identities hidden and be armed right? We want to look legit I suppose."

Brian then looks at Victor very angrily, and responds to him.

"Of course man, we have all of that covered. You don't have to be concerned over that."

Jesse starts to put his hand over his mouth, and then starts to speak.

"When we go into the bank to do the job, me and Victor are going to be scouting the floor as backup. You and Brian are going to be collecting the money. We are not, I repeat, we are not going to even try to deal with the vault, right? Kevin will be our getaway driver and working out all the alarms, he's not going to be in the bank. Is this right?"

Russell continues to gaze out of the window of the board room, and nods his head. Jesse continues to have his hand over his mouth and then asks another question on his mind.

"We are going to all leave from "Home Base" to the bank. After the job is done, we are then going to head back to "Home Base". I think everything seems solid and understandable."

Jesse then nods his head and rubs his hand through his hair. Brian then starts to speak.

"I need to remind this to everyone. Timing and speed is very important. We don't want to be in that bank longer than a few minutes. The longer we are in the bank, the longer ugly results could happen, and we get caught. The chances of us getting caught are very slim and none if we plan smart which is what we are doing now, and act fast. I have to remind you all about this."

All of the men, including Russell who's continuing to look out the window, nod their heads. Brian then while looking down at the table, continues to speak to the of the guys.

"I'm not a professional bank robber, no. None of the guys in this room are. We have all given up on how the world operates, and every guy in here has been hurt by society. We can do this you guys. We have to believe in ourselves, and work as a team to accomplish this goal."

Kevin continues to eat his bag of chips and laughs. He responds out loud to the men.

"This is some psycho shit you guys. We are actually going to rob a bank? I can't believe any of this. This seems like one of those realistic dreams you sometimes have that you think is real life, but it's not. Seriously, I feel safe that I'm in the group with you guys though. We make a strong force."

Russell then starts to return to his seat with a grin on his face, and stares at Kevin.

"Kev, that's the spirit man. We are all in this together, everyone in the group matters."

Kevin nods his head and smiles at Russell. The men continue to explain more of their game plan moving forward with the robbery. Victor then asks a very interesting question.

"The money we get from the job, we all each get an equal share right? All five of us?"

Brian then immediately raises his eyebrows, and responds to Victor shouting at him.

"Well, that would be the proper thing to do. When I was with my past partner, I don't want to bring him up because he's an asshole, but he kept urging to me that I was only going to get twenty-five percent of the cut. I kept thinking about how unfair that was. Being involved with this group, I believe that everything should be fair, and everyone should be treated equal."

Russell rubs his hand under his neck. He then nods his head. The guys carry on with discussing tactics about the heist, and talk about other details. Russell feels extremely confident that he, along with the rest of the guys are ready. Knowing that there is a small chance that things could perhaps go wrong, that doesn't worry him that much at all. Russell believes that if all the guys are able to form an established unit together, there shouldn't be any issues to occur. Brian although he doesn't feel that experienced, has been in three bank jobs before, and feels confident that they have a solid chance to succeed towards this. They all want to reach the same exact goal. Being ostracized by others, and wanting to rebel against the normalcy of the regular routine that society lives by. Only having a few more days until they plan to commit the heist, they take advantage of this time to make sure that their setup is properly planned ahead of time, to avoid any mistakes from happening.

Russell decides to stand up again, to stare out the window of the board room. This time however, Brian walks up and looks out the window as well with him. They both observe and look at the night sky, and the other skyscrapers and buildings in the surrounding area. Many cars are driving down the downtown area, and you can see all the headlights from them, forming a very artistic view. Russell is quickly reminded of the heist which happened on his last day of working at the "Sunset Credit Union". A day that will have a permanent place in his mind, as it was one filled with much trauma and sadness. Everything in this moment basically came into formation, because of that day. It made Russell a completely different man now, from the one from which he used to be. How that one day quickly changed his entire mind on how he views the world and other people. His interactions have never been the same since that day. Russell is well aware that one of the robbers in that heist, is standing next to him right now. He then tells himself that he needs to look at this event from another shade. Brian is not an evil guy, and Russell trusts him enough to let him start over.

Brian then starts to feel how in this particular moment that being a member of this team, he is offering some type of compensation towards Russell. Feeling guilty on being there that day, he wants to do all he can to rectify himself from that. Brian reflects more and more on past events. He starts to flashback towards the day himself and Scott robbed the "Sunset Credit Union". A day that both Brian and Russell won't ever forget in their lives. How things which had no intentions of going the way they did, sadly ended in a terrible way. He is confident that this time around, things will be different. Brian has never been a violent person, but he was always caught up around the wrong people with different agendas. He turned to crime of opportunity and his intentions were never, and are never to hurt or harm anybody else. He's thankful that Russell understands his position, and has decided not to cause any type of vendetta or any other personal issues directed at him. Brian and Russell smile at each other, almost as if they could read each their mind, and are thinking about the same exact thing. Brian stands with Russell for a few minutes more, then he returns to his seat after that.

Kevin continues to eat his chips, as he watches Russell stand by the window. He is amazed at how brave Russell is, and can't believe his oppression is causing him to think about dangerous ventures and ideas. Kevin is proud to have Russell as a friend, and considers himself lucky that Russell is acting as a main support towards his personality. Even though he has no direct involvement with the "Sunset Credit Union" heist, he still feels connected to everyone somehow and someway. Kevin is also wanting to rebel against the world.

He has always been rejected by other people, and feels this is the time for him to fight back in a sense. Participating in the bank job with the other guys, gives him an ultimate rush. Kevin gets up from his seat and stands by the window where Russell is. He then looks out the window looking at the view of the city, and pats Russell on the back. Kevin then returns to his seat.

Jesse sits in anxiety, and watches the other guys. He then begins to think to himself how did he get involved with this? Being a gay black man, he tries his best to have an open minded neutral view to different aspects on how people operate in the world. Never would he think that he'd be sitting at a table, with four guys whom are polar opposite of himself; discussing organized crime activity with them.

He is glad of the relationship he has with Russell. Which before the bank robbery at the "Sunset Credit Union" happened, Jesse never paid him any attention at all. He always thought of him as someone he wasn't supposed to linger and mess around towards. Understanding Russell's pain and suffering, Jesse also being involved in the same heist that caused him to break. He offers his support to this team, and someone who has worked in a bank as well, he wants to disestablish himself from any type of professional agendas, and rebel with the rest of the men.

Victor was originally supposed to rob the bank, and not Brian and his partner. Dealing with his own social issues, and feeling neglected with the rest of the world, he contemplated robbing the bank to make his life better. He had no idea that someone else was thinking of hitting the same bank. Victor witnessed the entire robbery happen, and stood back watching in fear. Perhaps it was the bystander effect, but Victor was frozen at the events which took place.

He feels he's indirectly responsible for all the events which took place, as had Victor gone inside the bank and acted as a hero, would the events which conspired happened the way which they have? These are things which he doesn't and will not ever sadly know. Victor is now more concerned about what he can do to redeem himself. Agreeing to join the rest of the guys in the bank job, is a way for him to do that. Victor himself dealing with his own mental issues, he's thankful that he's being understood for once in his life. His silly quirks are being rewarded.

All of the men continue to sit in the board room, and it creeps up closer to the time in which their work shift is over. Russell begins to stare at the other four guys in the room. Examining them, and pinpointing how each of them are the key to a successful bank heist. Russell being the inside man with his past knowledge of banks. He looks at Brian, and sees how he's a very cool spirit, yet can get into that criminal edge when he has to. He has Jesse, who worked with him at the "Sunset Credit Union." Jesse has a vibrant personality, and is like a sponge, and takes anything he's presented with. Victor, who Russell sees many positive traits and aspects about him. His eccentric and weird personality, makes him very dependable when it comes to looking at scenarios outside of the box. He then finally gets to Kevin. An estranged acquaintance of his from when he was attending school, and how Russell quickly made amends with best friend in such a short time span. He is glad to be connected to him.

The guys remain in the room, but they suspend talking about the heist for now. They decide to change the subject, and start to offer small talk to pass the time. As they are all each comfortable among each other, they develop more personal discussions. They begin to laugh and joke with each other among miscellany subjects and topics.

This goes on for quite some time, and the mood in the room changes from an informal, to a more humorous one. Almost slightly forgetting that they are going to commit their first bank heist in a few days. This might be intentional, to sort of clean their attitudes and moods. Many of them feel ready to take on the heist, and are prepared to head into the next few days. The men then talk about their first day working, and how eventful and interesting it was. Russell takes out his phone to check the time. It is now 8:55, and almost about time for them to leave. All five of the guys then get up from the table, and look out the window of the board room one final time.

This is truly a lovely night, and how the buildings shine through the city lights; looking at the aesthetic of Los Angeles. They are high up above, and have the perfect view to look over the area. After they gaze out the window, the men then prepare to leave the building. They tidy the room up, as if they were never there. Russell turns the lamp off, and when all of the men walk out, he locks the door behind them. Following that, they each begin to lock up all the doors, and turn out the lights. With Russell shutting off the lights and locking the doors from floors six through ten. With Brian turning the lights off and locking the doors from floors one through five. When this task is done, all the men proceed towards the parking structure.

Brian and Victor say goodbye to Russell, Kevin and Jesse, and Brian gets in his car with Victor, heading towards "Home Base". The other three men then get into Russell's car, and Russell then drives out of the parking structure of the building. Russell turns the stereo in his car on, and listens to the music. He continues to drive down the road, noticing that there isn't that many other cars on the road, finding it strange.

As he's steadily driving, Russell sees flashing red and blue lights in his rear view mirror. A police car is following him. The police cruiser then sounds his siren. Russell starts to feel nervous, as he does not like being around the police. He immediately turns off the car radio. Russell begins to feel scared, and quickly figures out that Kevin has marijuana on him. As soon as this thought occurs to him, he turns his head towards Kevin. Incidentally Kevin as well quickly notices the policeman and he starts to panic too. He then cries out to Russell very nervously.

"Shit, Russ. That's a cop. There's pot in my back pocket man. Shit. Damn. That's a cop Russ. What am I gonna do man? Damn. What am I gonna do?"

Kevin then takes the bag of marijuana out of his pocket, and holds it in his hands, which are shaking very fast. He then looks around the car for a place to stash it. Russell turns his blinker on, signaling to the officer that he will pull over soon. Russell then opens his glove compartment, and snatches the bag of marijuana out of Kevin's hand. He then quickly stashes the bag deep inside the glove compartment, and slams it shut. Russell then while he's still driving and looking ahead, finding a spot to pull his car over, whispers to Kevin.

"Kev, I want you to do one thing, and one thing only. That thing I want you to do, is to shut your fucking mouth. Kev, don't say a motherfucking word. Please."

Kevin looks straight ahead out the windshield, and Russell finally is able to find a spot to pull his car over. He pulls over, and turns his ignition off. Kevin starts to shake his legs up and down repetitively, and Russell grabs his knees to get him to stop doing it. Jesse sits still in the back very quiet. Russell then locks his hands on his steering wheel. The police officer at this point starts to walk out of his car with a flashlight. The officer is a muscular bald Caucasian man. Russell rolls down his window, when the police officer walks closer to his car. The officer continues to tread towards Russell's car, shines a flashlight on him, and then speaks.

"Sir, can I have your license, car registration, and proof that you have insurance please."

With the officer still shining at flashlight at him, Russell while keeping one hand on his steering wheel, uses reaches over using his other hand to open the glove compartment which has many things inside of it. He is very careful to make sure the officer doesn't see the bag of marijuana which Russell carefully hid. Russell then takes out a small folder setting it on his lap. He opens the folder taking out his registration and insurance papers. He then immediately reaches in his pocket to get his wallet. He then takes out his driver license. Russell hands all the items to the police officer at that point. Russell then sticks his hands back on the steering wheel after that. The police officer continues to flash the light at Russell's face, and begins to scan his light on all of the items Russell gave him for a short while. Following that, the officer then proceeds to walk back towards his police car, with the items Russell gave him in his hands. Kevin while looking straight ahead, then starts to whisper to Russell.

"Ugh Russ, I feel so nervous man. I don't know what's going on. Russ..."

Russell while he's still facing his head forward, instantly takes one hand off the steering wheel, and reaches across to squeeze Kevin's knee. He then places both hands back on the steering wheel, and under his breath begins to whisper to Kevin.

"Kev, what part of shut the fuck up, didn't you understand? Shut your damn mouth man."

Russell continues to feel nervous as the police officer remains in his police car for a few minutes. He eventually returns to Russell's car and hands him back the items. The police officer begins to write a ticket. As he's writing it, he speaks to Russell.

"You were going a little fast. Speed limit here is forty, and the meter said you were doing fifty. Was there any particular reason why you were speeding for?"

Russell gives the officer a puzzled look for a few seconds, he then responds to him.

"I guess I was trying to get home. I'm really tired, and I want to get home. I had no idea I was going fifty, I usually mind the speed limit. I'm so sorry officer."

The police officer looks out in the distance for a short while, and continues to write the ticket. He receives a call on his radio, and directly after that, he rips up the ticket. After destroying the ticket, the police officer then talks to Russell once more.

"I'm going to let you off this time. I was going to give you a ticket, but I don't think you meant any harm in what you did. You were speeding past the limit though, so I want you to obey the speed limit in the future. Okay sir? Good night."

Russell smiles at the police officer, and he thanks him.

"Thank you officer, and I will. Thank you very much."

The police officer returns to his car, and quickly drives off. After that, Kevin then starts to laugh at Russell as he's starting the ignition to his car.

"Ha-ha, Russ. We had weed in the car and the cop let us off free. Wow, unbelievable."

Russell turns to look at Kevin, and shakes his head out of disapproval. Kevin quickly composes himself and remains quiet, as Russell proceeds back to driving. Russell takes Kevin to his residence, and drops him off. He says goodbye to him, and he continues driving towards his own home. Russell and Jesse get out of the car, and they head inside the apartment. Russell heads straight to the sofa area, and turns on a basketball game. Jesse walks into the kitchen and makes himself and Russell a tuna fish sandwich. Jesse returns to the sofa area, and they both eat their sandwiches. They watch television for a couple hours, then they both walk into the bedroom. Soon after this, they both fall asleep.

The next morning, both Russell and Jesse wake up early at 8 A.M. to get ready for the day. They have to be at "United Farmers Savings", early enough to do their heist planning, then having enough time to immediately get to work after. Russell is wearing a black polo shirt and some blue work pants with his black Adidas on. Jesse is wearing a blue sweat jacket and some cargo shorts, and has blue Nike sneakers on. Russell drives over to Kevin's residence to pick him up. Kevin is wearing a red polo shirt, and some black dickies pants and black converse all-star shoes on. He's eating an "Eggo" frozen waffle, wrapped in a paper towel. He is carrying his laptop in a large computer case. He gets in Russell's car, and they all head to "Home Base", to meet up with the rest of the guys.

Russell uses his key, and unlocks the door to the unit. As he Kevin and Jesse are walking in, they do not see Brian, as he stepped out. Victor is asleep on the couch shirtless, only wearing pants. When Victor hears them walk in, he wakes up. He looks at the three of them with an angry look. They wave at Victor and say hello to him, but he ignores them, and Victor heads towards the bathroom. They all wait in the sofa area waiting for Brian to arrive. Kevin then quickly turns the television on to a morning news program.

Today is the day that they case the "United Farmers Bank", to prepare themselves for their planned heist on Friday. Kevin has brought his materials in order for them to get a better look at how the bank operates as far as the layout plan is, and to also see how the security systems of the bank work, and how Kevin can use his software to set off nearby security diversions both inside and outside of the bank. They continue to wait for Brian to arrive. Victor walks out of the bathroom, and then puts a plain white T shirt on. Victor does not greet the rest of the guys. Russell, Kevin and Jesse are also not acknowledging Victor either. Victor walks over to the kitchen area to fix him a bowl of cereal. Russell gets up from the couch, and walks over to the kitchen area Victor is. Russell then softly speaks to Victor, who's eating his cereal.

"Hey Victor. Do you know where Brian went? We have to be at work by twelve, and today is the day we were going to go check out "United Farmers Savings", for our heist on Friday. Kevin bought all of his stuff, and we were gonna let Brian go in and be our lab rat to check the place out. But he's not here, I don't see him. Do you know where he went?"

Victor without giving Russell eye contact, continues to eat his cereal. Russell continues.

"Victor. I'm not trying to bother you man, I only want to know if you know where Brian is. Did he tell you he was leaving before he did? We have a time frame that's all."

Victor continues to eat his cereal, but turns to Russell and shakes his head. Russell smiles at him and returns to the sofa area with the rest of the guys. Russell then starts to worry about where Brian is. He assumed that everyone was fully aware of the program, and how things were supposed to go the evening before in the board room. He starts to wonder if there is anybody he can truly trust, or depend on for situations. Their planned heist is supposed to start on Friday, yet they can't even all meet up on time, to examine the bank they are supposed to hit later on in the week. Events such as this stress Russell out, and he becomes anxious as to whether this is a sign for what's yet to possibly come. Russell turns his head towards the news station on television, and watches a news story about a temporary art museum exhibit. Russell then puts his head down towards the ground, rubbing his hands over his face, shaking his head. He continues to try to calm himself down. Victor finishes his cereal, and walks over to the sofa area with the rest of the guys and takes a seat.

Russell a few minutes later, is slowly losing his patience. He takes out his phone and begins to text Brian. Ten minutes pass, and Russell starts to lose it. Russell then calls Brian. The telephone rings but he does not get an answer, only an automated voicemail alert. Russell is now angry, and quickly dials Brian's phone number once more. It continues to ring with no answer. Russell then contemplates as to whether or not he wants to leave a voicemail. He decides to leave one.

"Brian, this is Russell man. Call me please right now. It's important. Thank you."

Russell puts his phone in his pocket and looks down to the ground, shaking his head. He is extremely stressed that Brian is not with them, and he's already breaking the rules of them sticking together, especially during times where they all agreed to. With Russell still having his head to the ground, Jesse rubs the back of his shoulder. Kevin notices that Russell is feeling tense; he talks to him.

"It's gonna be alright Russ. We don't know what's keeping Brian, so hold on for now."

Russell lifts his head up, looks towards the door of the unit hoping it will magically open. He turns his head back towards the television, which is having a report on business, finance and electronics. Russell then looks back towards the front door, again hoping out of some miracle it will open up. They all continue to wait on the sofas, and it is now 9 A.M. Russell gets up from the sofa, and goes over to the kitchen area to get himself a glass of water. Kevin watches him, feeling concerned, however he quickly turns his head back to the television screen. Russell continues to stand in the kitchen area with his arms crossed, looking down on the floor feeling outraged.

The front door of the unit then suddenly opens. Russell unfolds his arms, and rushes straight to the door very fired up. Brian opens the door and steps into the unit. Brian has on gray polo shirt, and he has on khaki pants. He is immediately restrained by Russell, who pins him to the wall. Brian is also tussling with Russell as well. They begin to wrestle on the ground. Kevin, Jesse and Victor then try to break them up. Russell and Brian are separated, and Russell starts to stare down Brian harshly. Brian then starts to speak to Russell.

"Russell, I know why you're mad, and I'm sorry. My phone died. I wanted to go and surprise you guys with coffee and donuts, but my car hit a flat tire. Because I'm stupid, I didn't bring my car jack, and all my spare tires are here. I had to get a can of "Fix-A-Flat". Russell you need to control your temper man. Now are we all ready to fucking go?"

Russell puts his hand over his mouth and shakes his head at Brian. He then walks closer to him and gives him a tight hug, patting him on the back of the shoulder. He then responds.

"I'm sorry Brian, your right man. I overreacted and that was my bad. I need to work on that. Yeah we are all ready to go. Let's head on out boys."

Brian stares back at Russell shaking his head and giving him an ugly look. All five of them leave "Home Base", and Russell, Kevin and Jesse get in Russell's car, and Victor rides with Brian. They then start to head towards the "United Farmers Savings" bank. This bank is located not that far from the buildings the men have to clean. It is located on Grand Ave. The bank is moderately sized, and is slightly larger than the "Sunset Credit Union", but there are banks which are much larger located in the area.

The bank is located in a somewhat concealed area, attached to a back parking structure extending out towards the street which hides the entrance. The bank also receives a moderate patron base. It's not that crowded usually, but there are still many people that patronize the bank, and do their financial matters there. The bank like the "Sunset Credit Union", has very lax security. A security guard is not present on duty. The bank tellers are easily accessible, and so are the cash carts located right behind them. The guys are not going to get inside the vault for this heist, but the vault similar to the way it was positioned at the "Sunset Credit Union", is located in an area adjacent to the bank tellers.

Russell and Brian park a few blocks away outside the bank, to not draw attention to themselves. Kevin immediately begins to open his laptop case in the passenger seat of Russell's car. He removes his laptop, and then begins to open up the black market security software on his computer. The main objective is to analyze all the features of the bank, so they are prepared for their job on Friday. Kevin will place a pair of eyeglasses on Brian which look typical, but they are not. These eyeglasses are a camera, which also give a live feed to the other guys to what the inside of the bank looks like. This is so the other guys don't have to walk in, and draw suspicion to themselves.

Kevin is also pulling a pirated black market program on his laptop, which isn't guaranteed to work and can run into hiccups and issues, but can be useful and helpful. The program allows the user to disable silent alarms in the bank, and the program can also detonate diversions from a nearby area It can set off a smoke bomb, causing the police to check that area out, and not the bank. Kevin doesn't intend to test this feature, as they don't need it for this heist. It also has dangerous repercussions, if the detonators are not calibrated right towards the program. Kevin only wants to see how strong the security silent alarms are, and if they are hackable according to his software. Brian also has a tiny earpiece, so that Kevin and the other guys can talk to him while he's in the bank, and give him directions. The ear piece doesn't have a microphone, so Brian will not be able to speak back to them. After Kevin is just about all set, Russell inconspicuously waves his hand out the door, to signal for Brian and Victor to walk towards his vehicle. They reach Russell's car, and Victor opens Russell's back door, and sits in the rear seat with Jesse. Brian walks up to the passenger side door, standing outside on the sidewalk. Kevin sets the glasses on Brian's head. Kevin then warns Brian, before he goes in.

"Now Brian, these glasses may give off static electricity vibes or waves. That might sound scary because it is. Static electricity won't kill you, but it will give you kind of an oogy and uncomfortable feeling. I can't promise you that it won't happen once; it will probably zap you once, but if it happens multiple times, just take the glasses off, and come back to the car. I'll check it out. There is a program that I can run, that can adjust the frequency so it doesn't do that. The picture won't come in as clear, but your health means more to me that that man. Okay?"

Brian nods his head, and he proceeds to walk to the "United Farmers Savings" bank. In order to make Brian's presence at the bank more believable, the men all hatched a plan that Brian would go to the teller, and ask to get change for a twenty-dollar bill. That way they get a clear picture to the bank teller areas, as he's doing his money transaction in front of the teller. As Brian continues to walk to the bank, Kevin positions his laptop in front of Russell's center console.

Kevin's laptop contains a live video feed player, so they can see in real time Brian casing the bank. Brian walks into the bank, and Russell, Jesse and Victor begin to analyze where everything is located based on the video feed. While they are watching the video feed, Kevin slightly minimizes the video screen, and on the other side of the screen, pulls up a separate program on his laptop computer. The bank isn't currently crowded, but there are a handful of people doing business at the bank. All the bank tellers are busy helping patrons. Brian is currently standing in line. In the meantime, Kevin continues to work with another other program. The program that he pulls up, is checking to see if the silent alarms in the bank can be hacked and disarmed. It turns out in this particular bank due to the obsolete alarm system, with some slight effort which will take a short amount of time, the alarms can be disabled. Kevin looks at more diagnostics on his computer, before turning to Russell to speak to him on his findings.

"Okay Russ. I've got some good news, and some kinda good news. The good news is that the alarms can be disabled, so that's good. The kinda good news, it's going to take some time, especially if I don't want to seem suspicious. It gonna take like almost four minutes. My only suggestion is I can start disarming the alarms before you guys walk in. My only choice sadly."

Russell while looking at the video feed of Brian standing in line, nods his head. Kevin then closes that program, and pulls up a separate program, used for the detonation devices. Kevin doesn't intend to use them for this particular heist, but wants to show them off to the other guys anyways. Brian is still waiting in line, so they use this free time they have. The detonation software is quite dangerous, and if it's isn't used correctly, the results could lead to unsafe results. It is mainly used to distract law enforcement into creating an explosion, which will cause the police to investigate that, rather than the bank heist. It can also be used for defensive purposes as well.

The detonators can be placed outside outside the entrance of a bank, causing a big smokescreen distraction as well. This could possibly be used if law enforcement is right outside the doors of the bank, and this diversion could be used as an easy escape. However, if these detonators are not calibrated or computed correctly, it could cause catastrophic results. Kevin is not that experienced with both the detonator tools or the detonator software, but he is still eager and determined to educate himself more about their use. While Brian is still in line waiting to see the teller, Kevin continues to look at the software. He talks to Russell.

"Now Russ, this is the interesting stuff. Marvel in the technology of today Russ. Ha-ha. Don't ask me where I get my programs Russ. You know the rules, and that's how we originally fell out anyways. But this is awesome stuff. Look it here. The only downside is I'm still quite inexperienced with this, and I maybe want to do some test runs at "Home Base", just to be on the safe side. Because if you don't learn how to do this right, it's not going to be pretty at all."

Russell continues to look at the feed on the computer and nods his head at Kevin. Jesse and Victor are silently watching the video feed as well. Even though Brian has an earpiece and can hear all of the guys in the car, they aren't giving him any instructions. Brian however is not drawing attention to himself, scanning his head and giving hints to the guys, showing them different areas around the bank while he's standing in line. Kevin continues to speak.

"Maybe I can use this stuff in our future heists Russ. It's way too useful for me to not mess with it. We could really make the heists a lot easier if I did. But as I said, I don't want to risk or chance it at this point Russ. So maybe later. But boy, is this shit cool man."

Russell looks at the feed Brian is on, and notices that he's next in line to see the teller. While still having his vision towards the laptop, he softly responds to Kevin.

"Be careful Kev. If you're not ready to use those, then don't. I do agree, they seem cool, and that software is also interesting. However, we can use those later Kev. Don't worry about it man. I am trying to look out of you. I really appreciate your help Kev. I do. I mean it."

Kevin quits the detonation software, and leaves the video feed turned on. He turns his head to look at Russell, and pulls out a large bag of "Famous Amos" cookies from his computer case, and begins to eat some of them. He turns his head towards Russell again and laughs at him. Russell looks at the video feed, and he asks Brian to move his head slightly upright to the ceiling. Brian heard Russell through the earpiece, and he does. Russell notices that as he was examining the video feed, for whatever reason, this bank mostly has their security cameras positioned towards the vault. There is only one camera positioned at an interesting location by the tellers, and one camera by the entrance. Russell is then immediately reminded, that this terrible camera setup is similar to that at the "Sunset Credit Union." Kevin eats some more cookies, then taps Russell on the shoulder asking if he wants some. Russell laughs at him and eats some of the cookies. Kevin reaches behind the rear seat. He then sticks the bag of cookies out to Jesse and Victor, grunting to get their attention. They both eat some of the cookies and thank Kevin. Brian continues to wait in line to see the teller, and the men continue to watch the feed. Finally, Brian makes it to the teller, and they get a good view of this area. Russell quickly begins to scan through this area. Taking note of how the bank drawers are set up, and where the cash carts are. Jesse and Victor continue to watch the feed, also taking in their own personal observations. Russell is easily able to deduce from his past experience as a bank manager, the relatively easy difficulty it would be to commit this heist. He begins to laugh to himself, and he then turns to speak to Kevin.

"This is going to a be so easy Kev. We might not score that big no, but as far as this being our first hit together as a team, we got this man. This bank is just basically begging to be robbed, it's not funny. I thought my bank was bad. Wow. I'm happy to see this man."

Kevin eats a few more of the cookies, and turns his head to laugh at Russell.

"Yeah Russ, I trust your knowledge of this stuff man. I have a good feeling about this, and I don't see any reason why we won't do this heist with flying colors man. This is gonna be good. I can't wait until Friday Russ. We are going to do our first heist man. Yes."

Russell turns his head away from the video feed, and looks out the windshield, into the distance. He starts to smile to himself, feeling very confident and overthrown with excitement and success. Brian is finished doing his business at the teller, and is now walking back to the car. Kevin proceeds to close the camera feed software, and shuts down his computer. Brian approaches the car, and begins to the take the glasses off. Brian then looks at Kevin, and starts to laugh. This also causes Kevin to laugh as well, still unaware to what Brian is laughing at. Kevin then looks at Russell who's also laughing. The laugh seems to be very infectious, as Jesse and Victor laugh as well. Kevin then finally asks Brian what's funny.

"Man, why are you laughing? What do you know, that we don't know?"

Brian continues to laugh, but at this time the rest of the guys don't find the suspense funny anymore, and actually want to know why Brian is laughing. He then responds.

"Kevin, those glasses actually shocked me quite a few times, and it hurt like hell. I don't know how you knew they were gonna do that, probably because you used them before, and that's what happened. I was just a man about it, and suffered through with it. I found that funny that's all."

Kevin looks at Brian with a disgusted look and shakes his head at him. Brian hands Kevin the glasses, and Brian then talks to Russell.

"Alright Russell. You saw what you needed to see, right man? So we're all set. I think we'll do fine Friday. Now come on, we're almost running late for work."

Russell nods his head at Brian, and Brian walks towards his car. Victor stays in Russell's car. Both Russell and Brian drive off, heading towards the "Wittberg Law Offices", so they can start their work day.

CHAPTER 13:

NOTHING EASY, NOTHING HARD

After mapping out their plan of attack for the upcoming heist, all of the guys return to work. Casing the bank gave them a great confidence boost, and their findings were more than satisfactory for them. Obtaining that information, allowed them to be prepared for when the day actually comes. When it comes to this heist, they only have once change to do it, and only one opportunity to do it correctly. Should a mistake or mishap occur, that would of course be a disaster. The chance of them also getting caught or thwarted by the police is also a chance. Due to how well they schemed the whole ordeal, this doesn't bother to be likely in their mind. They carefully orchestrated a clear objective to their heist on Friday, that they no longer feel nervous about what they are going to do. Having all of their tools ready and available, and having enough men to carry out the job as well. There is no need to go over anymore preparation.

The men go back to the office building, and resume their cleaning responsibilities. Yet the thought of the heist floats in their mind. Over the course next few days, the men continue to work as normal, waiting until Friday approaches. The heist remains only a short while away. The days leading up to Friday, pass on rather quickly. The men stick to their regular routine. Keeping a low profile to themselves. Not getting into any trouble or doing any bad deeds. The men are currently holding two different faces to themselves. One face puts on a normal act. They go to work and clean the buildings regularly, without any hassle. The other side shows a vindictive evil passion to themselves. So powerful, it causes them to want to commit a bank heist. Mentally, these guys know how to make their motives ambiguous, and to trick others into thinking they don't have cruel intentions. These men are currently under heavy mental instability. Their choices are not very logical ones, but choices made on personal vindictiveness.

Their planning stage is finished, and they now wait until the day comes for them to act on the heist. The men are all come into the heist with different thoughts, but generally everyone has the same feeling of wanting to accomplish the bank job. Working together for this particular event. An event, which to many people would be considered very heinous. These five men are here for each other, and they wouldn't dare betray themselves to the group. They have come much too far to do that. These men desire success. Being with four other men who also feel oppressed towards how the world operates, it enables them to pursue their hidden dreams.

The wait is perhaps about to pay off. The day of the heist, happens to be today. It is finally Friday, and all of the guys are ready for the heist. All the events which lead before today, will come together at this very moment. The time has definitely come for everyone involved to perform well. It would be unfortunate that despite all the plans they hatched, for things to not go as planned. These men have no choice but to work in harmony towards each other. It is vital and crucial for them to not make any mistakes, and to give their absolute best. However dangerous and chilling their actions may be, especially considering the fact they are about to rob a bank. They must not buckle under the pressure. All of the men involved with this heist serve a purpose, and serve a meaning to complete the goal. Realizing their full and absolute potential, is the key for them to reap success. Every single one of the men, start to profile himself.

Russell feels secure between himself and the rest of the guys. He was a past bank manager, now about to turn the tables on his past professional life and rob a bank. The man who devoted his whole life to the professional word of finance, now no longer gives a damn, and turns his self-pity, into desire and power. The day to commit the heist has approached, and they must do what they have to do. Russell already has his agenda made up, and he is going to get what he wants.

One of his main priorities and goals, were to establish and get together a team that he trusted enough. Now that he was developed that team, the rest he feels should come very simple and easy. This was originally just a thought and suggestion that he had, now coming into immediate effect. His emotions were most likely broken from that day at the "Sunset Credit Union", and Russell no longer feels ashamed. He beats a different drum towards life.

He has done all of the preparing and planning leading up to it. Russell understands the potential chance of dangerous results and consequences this heist may bring, but his confidence makes him forget about those potentials. He doesn't wish to consider himself the leader or captain of the group, but this was originally his own idea. In an act to rebel, going forward with the heists. Honestly, it was a mere comedic suggestion he had, a coping skill to use after his traumatic experience at the "Sunset Credit Union". That idea became a quick ambition towards his. A possibly dangerous aspiration he thought about, that he is soon about to make reality. Russell is strong enough to deal with this madness, or else he wouldn't' have taken it to this level. This is something he wants very badly, and he refuses to give up. Russell right now, believes the sky is the limit and if they put their minds to it, they will win.

Kevin feels energetic towards the heist. He's a guy that is simply into computers and technology, using that to gain an advantage over others. Especially when it comes to criminal activity. Being Russell's best friend, he wants to do his very best towards this mission they are on. His computer skills should come in handy, and offer a boost towards their heist. Kevin has a humorous personality about himself, but when the action finally presents itself, he morphs into a completely different persona. He stays concentrated and motivated. This can be a good and also a bad thing for Kevin, as his personality adapts to whatever decisions he wishes to make. Kevin not only wants to make himself happy, but Russell happy as well. This moment is his chance to do his part, and make the team thrive towards completing the heist.

Kevin does have doubts, but he is doing a good job of concealing and hiding them. Using his wonderful sense of humor, to level out any stress he may be approached with. Laughter after all is the best medicine, especially under thrilling circumstances such as this. Kevin's will and bravery is his biggest trait to gaining victory towards the heist.

Jesse feels at times he's misplaced between himself and the rest of the guys, yet understands that he is welcomed. Being a bank teller who was involved in a violent bank heist, being blessed that Russell is the man he found salvation towards. He has self-worth issues, to where he feels he's not good enough. Jesse starts to compare himself to the other guys. Being a gay black man, Jesse feels he needs to try twice as hard to earn his position as a member of the group, and to prove not only himself wrong, but others wrong as well.

What makes Jesse continue, is if the other guys accept his wild personality, he should be proud and accept himself as well. Jesse is scared somewhat, as he's going against the grain of society. He's using all of his hardships he was presented with in his life, to move forward. Jesse believes in himself, and starts to appreciate how he's unique in his own right. His purpose is very meaningful towards the group. Jesse tries to break the barrier between what people expect for him, and what he actually wants to accomplish. He believes he is neglected in life. Not knowing where he belongs at times. Jesse feels he is owed happiness in his life. He wants to be powerful.

Brian feels that he has a competitive edge towards himself, mainly due to his experiences that he has faced in his life. Although he has robbed two banks before, that's not the person he actually is or wants to be. He's only agreeing to do heist, to offer his services to Russell. Turning to crime for opportunity, to better his personal life. Brian enjoys finding ways to mastermind others, like how poker players do. He acts on impulse very much, and his impulsivity can lead to negative effects. Brian feels remorse for his actions, as he isn't a violent man. He is a man that acts on ambition and opportunity. Being part of this group, he's adapting himself to become a more team oriented person. Brian wants to show that he's a kind heart, not letting his persuasive ways fool or trick other people into thinking he's evil.

He is definitely a changed man. Brian wants to immerse himself in more positive situations and interactions. Straying himself away from positions with negative people. Brian has found peace in this group. He has a gentle and positive heart, yet makes the mistake of being surrounded by ignorance and negativity. Brian believes that he can triumph over all of that, and dominate.

Victor feels unsure and insecure of himself, but he doesn't wish to let any of that destroy or break him. Victor wanted to rob a bank to better himself, and to find an easy way for him to be happy. He never envisioned that he would find a group that supported him. The bullying and teasing he has been faced with in his past, agitates and fuels his fire for him to act the way he currently does. He is tired of not being included or understood, and it takes a toll on his lifestyle. Victor turns to reckless behavior to distract the isolation he's always seems to encounter. He struggles talking to other people and expressing his actual feelings in a proper manner.

Victor then surrounds himself towards a vortex of self-hate. This heist is basically all he has left in his life, regardless of the outcome, or what what may come after. Victor feels he doesn't deserve anymore of that foolishness in his life. Sick of being labeled as a freak or creep or a horror movie monster. This seems to be a chance for him to shine, and turn all of the terrible perceptions of him around. Victor has nothing to lose, but a lot to gain from being in this group, so he moves ahead with all of that in mind.

The day of the heist is here, and these five men are about to do something very criminal and sinister. To others, this is just a typical Friday afternoon. The sun is shining bright, and the sky is blue and clear. The weather is fair and warm; this is perfection as far as climate is concerned. To these five men, this is not a typical Friday. Today will be one of those days that they will remember quite well in their lives. The day they all banded together as a group, and ventured out their first heist. This morning, they all woke up with a burst of energy. They are going to need a lot of it for today, as they are about to approach a crucial situation. Today will be a day in which they outlaw the world. The guys do not wish to turn violent at all. They are going to be using guns, which are going to be loaded. However, this is for their protection, and to be used as a scare measure.

They don't plan to shoot or hurt anyone at all. They also understand that if they are to get accosted by police or law enforcement, whatever a certain guy does, is strictly on him. If they are smart and clever enough, they won't get caught. This heist isn't necessarily for the money or financial gain, but knowing they beat the government in successfully carrying out this task. The money is typically an added bonus towards the end results. This is more of a crime for power and achievement. The thrill of knowing they completed something so dangerous.

It is now 2 P.M. Friday afternoon, and reaching closer towards the time for them to commit the heist. All of the guys are at the unit outside of "Home Base". They are all situating themselves for the heist, and are in the final stages of getting themselves ready. The men have already put their disguises on. Their disguises are identical to each other. They are wearing all black combat gear. Their tops consist of heavy dark black windbreakers. Their bottoms consist of black cargo snow pants. They are wearing heavy black ski caps, in which their mouth is covered by plain black bandanas. On the ski cap, it looks as if it's a makeshift mask. There is a hole in the eye area, and all the guys wear sunglasses to conceal their eyes. The guys are also wearing thick black gloves on their hands. For their shoes, the guys each wear a pair of black snow boots. The guys equip themselves each with a machine assault rifle.

Russell and Brian grab themselves two large canvas bags from inside the unit with all of their supplies. The guys each put their guns in the back of the black getaway van parked in the unit. Russell and Brian put their bags in the back of the van in addition to that. Kevin then immediately puts his laptop case in the van. The guys at this point proceed to huddle up and form a big group hug in solidarity and in love. Max approaches the guys. He smiles at all of them and starts to speak.

"Well, well, well. So it seems that it's time. I want to wish all of you luck before you go. I still think you all should have waited a little longer, but if you feel that now is the right time, I'm not going to stop you. Again, I want nothing to do with any of this. A part of me is worried for you guys, the other part of me knows you're going to do a bang up job. Be safe boys."

Russell while dressed in his disguise, nods his head to Max and responds to him.

"Yes. All of us are set, and if we don't do it today, we won't get the chance to do it ever. We did an extensive job of planning the events for today, and I have zero doubts. I know your gonna hate me for this and you don't feel the need to be thanked, but thank you again Max."

Russell pats Max on his shoulder. Max then smiles at Russell and speaks.

"Okay gentlemen, I'm going to leave you all to attend to your business. I'm hoping and praying you all return back here safe. I am going to put all my faith towards each of you. I will say one final time; I want you all to be safe. Good luck gentlemen."

All of the men nod towards Max, and Max then leaves the area. Russell then unlocks and opens the driveway door of the unit, he then starts to brief all of the men.

"Listen up, we're gonna leave in literally a minute from now. So we are all clear. Kevin, I want you to drive the van. I'm going to sit in the passenger seat. Brian, Jesse and Victor, I want the three of you to be in the back of the van. I don't want to waste any more time. Let's move."

The guys then all get into the black van. Kevin sits in the driver's seat and starts to turn on the ignition. Russell takes a seat on the passenger side. Brian, Jesse and Victor then sit in the cargo area behind the van. Kevin then pulls out of the unit, but stops the van right outside the driveway door. Russell runs out of the van to close and lock the driveway door of the unit, and runs back inside and takes a seat. Kevin then continues to drive out, heading towards the "United Farmers

Savings" bank. He gets on the highway, which currently has moderate traffic. Even though they are still a great distance from the bank, the guys start to feel anxious at this time. Kevin pays attention to the road, never occurring that he would ever drive himself to a bank robbery. Russell sits on the passenger seat, staring straight ahead. Brian, Jesse and Victor remain in the back of the van, looking out the front windshield as well. Kevin is driving at a regular speed, obeying the speed limit. They should know better not to draw any unneeded, or extra attention towards themselves. Russell cannot believe this situation is currently happening. There are no regrets, or changing his mind. Whatever happens from this point, happens. The men are completely quiet, and are not saying anything to each other. Brian however eventually breaks the tension, and speaks to all the guys.

"I need to bring this up. I want to tell you guys that I love you all no matter what happens. If we get caught, or if anything bad happens, I love all of you. I don't think anything is going to happen, but I still want to say that I love you all, and that's all I wanted to say."

All of the guys remain quiet in the van. Kevin continues to drive towards the bank. The men continue to feel anxious and nervous, slowly getting closer to the bank. Many of the guys start to open their mouths to speak, but then change their mind and remain quiet. It's hard to tell as all five are wearing disguises and you can't see their lips move.

The guys are keeping quiet, mainly due to the stress each of them feel right now. Being too anxious to get words out, so they continue to keep silent. Russell very briefly turns his head, and looks at Kevin. Kevin continues to be focused driving, paying close attention to the road. Russell then turns his head away from Kevin, and returns to looking forward. Brian, Jesse and Victor in the back of the van, are also motionless and still. They are not looking at each other at all. It has now been almost twenty minutes since they left "Home Base", with the bank being another twenty or so minutes away. At this point, Kevin starts to turn his head a few times towards Russell's direction. He is starting to feel a great deal of anxiety. Kevin has many thoughts inside his head.

He feels confident, yet on the other hand, he begins to feel scared, having doubts that a mistake might happen. Kevin's main worry is over mistakes, mainly due to acting poorly from the stress. The stress can be used to strengthen yourself, but it can also lead to carless actions, in which the careless actions might lead to failure. Kevin then begins to grasp the steering wheel very tight between his gloves. He then while looking straight ahead, nervously speaks to Russell.

"Russ, I'm going to be honest man. I'm starting to get butterflies in my stomach. I don't know why I feel nervous. We're not going to run into any problems at all, but I'm just feeling very nervous right now. Russ...I... I'm going to be fine Russ. Never mind all of that."

Russell turns his head to look at Kevin, and he softly responds to him.

"It's okay to feel nervous Kev. I'm feeling nervous too. What you need to understand Kev, is that you have to use those nerves for good. Use them as an energy boost to transform yourself to get through all of the pressure you get faced with. You can do it Kev. It's okay."

Although you can't see it because he's wearing a disguise, Kevin starts to smile at Russell. The van continues to go down the road, with the guys all staying extremely quiet. The men are now about fifteen minutes away from the bank. Russell looks at the clock on the dashboard of the van. It now reads 2:30 P.M. Russell then turns the radio of the van on, so the guys can start to feel more comfortable and relaxed. After turning the radio on, Russell raises the volume of the stereo up, so it plays loudly. Russell hoped it would make him feel more eased. The music is actually making him more nervous, as due sound level of the music, he can't hear himself think. Russell then a few minutes later turns the stereo off. He then sits back on the seat, and looks out straight ahead. Kevin turns his head towards Russell, and notices that he is nervous. Kevin tries to make them both feel calm, and speaks to him playfully.

"Russ, this is a lovely day isn't it? I don't see any clouds in the sky, it's so clear. This is such a nice afternoon Russ. Thank god it's Friday, right Russ? We're gonna do this, and we are all gonna party like fuck tonight Russ. Everything is going to go so smoothly man. Yeah."

Russell nods his head at Kevin. Under his mask, Russell has a very unsure face. Kevin's words should have helped him feel more secure, just like when he spoke to Kevin to make him feel better. However, Russell is not feeling at all confident after that. He's anticipating the heist very much, but at the same time, he's dreading it. Russell wants to believe they will have a flawless performance, but he can't be completely sure of himself. There are possibilities and chances that things won't go according to what they planned. The van continues to drive down the highway, with Kevin blending in with the rest of the vehicles on the road.

Victor at this time who is feeling anxious, thinks of a way to break the tension. He begins to laugh hysterically for nearly a whole minute. Victor's laugh sounds very evil, and sounds like it is coming from a clown almost. As Victor continues to laugh, this causes Brian to laugh uncontrollably as well. Coincidentally, Victor and Brian's laughs blend together, and they both produce a hilarious sound. Jesse who was trying to ignore both of them laughing, can't compose himself. He starts to laugh uncontrollably too. The sound of Jesse's laugh being included, makes the sound even more funny sounding than it already was. Kevin and Russell are on the brink of chuckling along with the rest of the guys due to the sounds of the mysterious and humorous laughter.

A few seconds later, Kevin and Russell at the same time, begin to laugh very loudly. All five of the guys in the van are now laughing together, creating an infectious laughter which will not stop. They continue to laugh, and are laughing at a louder rate. Kevin despite this, manages to stay focused towards driving. Eventually, the guys start to get themselves together. The laughter begins to subside as time passes on. Victor smiles under his mask, knowing that his attempt to break the tension worked. All of the guys now feel better about themselves due to the laugh attack they all just went through. Victor then speaks to the guys, letting the secret out.

"Hey guys, yeah I did that on purpose. We were all acting too rigid. I had to do something to get rid of that. So I decided to laugh for no reason. It was worth a try, and I felt that if didn't make you guys feel better, it would at least make me feel better. But I don't care, it seemed to work. It always works by the way. It works every time. Ha-ha."

Victor then starts to laugh for no reason again. This time, Brian takes his hand, and covers the mouth area of Victor's mask. He then quietly responds to him.

"Alright man, that's enough. We don't need any more of that. It worked the first time, and we're all set now. If you do it again, we're just gonna feel agitated. So that's enough."

Jesse who's feeling more relaxed, then starts to softly speak to all of the guys in the van.

"You guys, I want to thank all of you for working together. We are about to do something insane, and I'm so blessed that we are all getting along, and loving one another. It's nice."

Russell under his masks smiles at what Jesse said. Brian then responds to Jesse.

"Yeah, we are making a great time. We all have amazing chemistry. That's a plus for us."

Kevin while he continues to drive, starts to speak to the rest of the guys.

"That's the only reason why I'm here. If you guys weren't cool people, I would have said hell no to all of this shit. Russ, Jess, Brian, Vic, all of you are each awesome in your own way. I'm proud to have you as my teammates. We're about to kick butt and take names."

Right after this, Russell then turns his head towards Kevin who's still driving, and pats him on the shoulder. The men are now just a few minutes away from the bank. Kevin gets off the highway, and drives on the surface streets. Traffic for whatever reason, is a little tight. There isn't a traffic jam, but the streets are slightly packed. Once they are on the business streets, Russell turns his head and notices many business men with suits walking down the sidewalk with their briefcases. He then starts to have flashbacks to when that was his life. It wasn't that long ago, that he was one of those same exact men.

Russell finds it interesting how in a very short time span, his professional life changed drastically. He's now about to go and commit a bank heist. Upon reaching the surface streets, the other men in the van also begin to scan around. They are now only blocks away from their destination. In only a few short minutes, the heist will begin. Russell continues to look outside the window, observing many of the pedestrians on the sidewalk. Kevin who is becoming stressed due to traffic moving at a slow pace, makes an expected U-turn, directing them away to the bank. Kevin continues to head down the wrong direction for several blocks.

This causes Russell and the rest of the guys in the van to become puzzled, and confused as to where he's going. Due to the current anxiety they are under, none of the guys ask what his intentions currently are. As Kevin remains going in the opposite direction, Russell turns his head towards Kevin, and under his mask gives him an angry look. Russell proceeds to open his mouth, about to berate Kevin, yet at this moment Kevin quickly recovers. Kevin makes a right turn, which leads them back to the correct route. Russell then calms himself down, and turns his head back forward. Kevin continues, and is now only less than a minute away from the bank. All of the men start to feel pumped, being very close to the bank.

Kevin finally reaches the parking structure of the "United Farmers Savings" bank, and parks the van in a secluded area, adjacent to the entrance of the bank, located under the parking structure. Kevin turns off the engine, turns his head towards Russell, and starts to shake his head. Kevin then immediately opens his computer case, and powers up his laptop. While he's doing that, Brian grabs one of the large canvas bags, and quickly hands Russell one of bags as well. Kevin then starts to speak.

"Guys, I'm waiting for the alarm software to load up, and for me to figure out the correct hash sequence to disable the alarms. That way when they press the silent alarm, you guys won't be locked in, and the cops won't come. Problem is, it's gonna take a while. So, if you guys go in, and the software hasn't loaded, you all might be in trouble. They'll press the alarms, and I haven't jinxed them. But I don't want to disable them now that were here in the van. They might get scared, and decide to manually lock the doors. What do you guys want me to do?"

Russell turns his head towards Brian and stares at him in silence for a few seconds. Russell then looks out the windshield into the parking structure, then turns his head at Kevin.

"Well Kev, you know you have to use the alarm software accordingly right? If you disable the alarms too soon before we get in, the software sadly isn't foolproof, and it's going to signal that it's being tampered with. Worst case scenario is they lock the doors, and we won't get in because of that. But if you wait too long, they are gonna press the alarm and it won't matter at that time right Kev? Hmm. Why don't we just wait until you get it situated. Then when you have it all worked out, we'll then go in. Count ten seconds in your head Kev, and disable the alarms."

Kevin while he's still operating the software on the computer, responds to Russell.

"You're correct Russ, and I agree with that plan. I think the best thing to do is for us to wait here for a minute. By then the alarm system will work. I'll disable the alarms after about ten seconds from when you all bust away from the van. I don't see why this tactic wouldn't work."

Russell nods his head at Kevin, and they all continue to wait in the car while Kevin continues to work the alarm software. At this time, Brian hands Russell one of the rifles. Russell holds the gun in his hand, and for the first time ever in his life, he gets into beast mode. Holding that gun, knowing the exact details to what he's about to do. He uses this very little free time they currently have, to think about their routine once inside. While he's looking down at the gun, Russell then starts to speak to Brian about their plan of attack.

"We've already gone through this a million times, but I'm going to mention it a million and one times. Brian, we shouldn't be in this bank longer than three minutes. That's my goal. Brian, we're gonna deal with the tellers and the carts. Once all the tellers have emptied their drawers and the carts are also empty, we're done. We're outta there. Jesse and Victor, you guys just stay out on the main floor. That's our plan, and things should go fine based on that."

Brian while looking down, responds to Russell.

"Alright Russell. Sounds good to me. I understand everything, and if we all work together and work efficiently, we will be out of there very quickly with no issues at all."

Russell is still looking down at his gun, and he nods his head to what Brian said. Kevin continues to deal with the alarm software. Russell who notices that Kevin is still focused on the computer, still looking down, starts to talk to him.

"Kev, as soon as we get back to this car, I want you drive this van fast away from here. I don't want you to drive leisurely either, I want you to get away very quickly. Only until we reach far enough away from the bank do I want you to drive normal. Okay? You understand me Kev?"

Kevin with his head still facing the computer nods his head. He responds to Russell.

"Yeah Russ. You can count on me for that. I'll zip on out of here very quick man."

Russell continues to look down at his gun. They all continue to wait in the van for a minute. Kevin then turns his head towards Russell.

"Alright Russ. I'm all set. All I have to do is click that box, and the alarms are disabled. If I click it now, and you guys aren't in that bank in ten seconds possibly, they are gonna notice the silent alarm lights are on, because this software sucks like that, and they will manually lock the doors. So you guys need to hurry and get in there. You guys heading out right now?"

Russell then starts to choke up. This should be the moment he basks in his glory. It isn't at all, he's starting to freeze over being put on the spot and building up pressure. He's about to rob a bank, and now that's he's centimeters away from doing the job, he feels like concrete and cannot move. Of all times for Russell to succumb to all of the stress and pressure, now is not the correct time at all. This is the time for him to get into action, and to take charge. He needs to quickly find a way to get out of this block that he's currently in. Russell turns his head towards Kevin and stares at him blankly for a few seconds, feeling nervous. Hoping that Kevin will say something to motivate him and to make him calm down. Kevin is mistaking Russell starting at him, as a hint or sign for him to start to disable the alarm system. Kevin stares at him as well feeling nervous, and begins to whisper to Russell.

"Hey Russ, it's time man? Right now man? You ready Russ? Because I'm ready."

Russell continues to stare blankly at Kevin, and Russell turns his head to the rear area of the van, looking at Brian, Jesse and Victor. At this moment, he really needs something to snap himself out of this box that he's stuck into. Russell is unable to move, and he continues to feel frozen and stuck in his current place. Even though only a few seconds has passed by, to Russell it feels like a few years. Time is very crucial, and he doesn't have a second to waste on feeling nervous or anxious. The meaning of time has no bearing at this particular moment. Russell feels he's in some alternate area, and what's currently happening, isn't registering to him. Russell continues to stare at Kevin, holding the gun very tightly in his hands. Kevin then believes that Russell wants him to start the alarm. Kevin turns to his computer and clicks a button on the laptop. Russell then has an intense rushing anxious feeling crawl all over his body. Kevin turns his head again towards Russell, and starts to yell at him.

"You guys need to get out now! I just clicked the alarms! GO GUYS GO. NOW!"

Russell then raises his eyebrows from under his mask. He was not expecting Kevin to disable the alarms just yet. The anxiety he was feeling quickly evaporated from his body, but physically he still felt frozen in his position. Russell now had to somehow get himself out of the mood he was in, and to make himself get out the van. He immediately tries begins to snap himself out of it. He starts by trying to wrap his head around the current situation. By realizing that heist has now started. Russell becomes puzzled and confused on how to act, and mentally starts to clean his mind. From this point forward, he is now a bank robber, and they are about to commit a heist.

A couple seconds pass, and Russell continues to stare at Kevin, who is staring right back at him. These seconds in Russell's body feel like hours. He tries to react as fast as he can, but he still feels frozen solid in his place. Russell tries to clear his mind, and he finally strengthens his mental capacity to where he is now able to move. Brian, Jesse and Victor wait in the back for Russell's signal for them to leave. They wait in suspense as well, as they intended on following Russell outside of the van. With Russell not responding to them, they decide to wait in the back of the van until he instructs them to leave. Without any time to waste at all, Russell quickly turns his head to the back of the van and yells at Brian, Jesse, and Victor, while grabbing his gun and opening the door.

"Guys, we gotta go! We have to run guys! We have to go guys! Come on!"

Russell, Brian, Jesse and Victor, sprint towards the entrance of the "United Farmers Savings" bank. All four of them develop tunnel vision. Their minds are only on running, and getting inside of the bank. Each of them run on a horizontal line across from each other, as they continue to head towards the bank. Every step they take running, feels like ten tons, due to all the adrenaline rush they are experiencing. They have only been running in actuality for a few short seconds, but to the guys it feels like they have been running to the doors of the bank for much longer than that. They continue to run, heading directly to the front door of the bank. All of the guys during this particular time, start to wonder who is going to open the door first. They are all running in a straight, across from each other.

From the way they are running, someone will have to proceed ahead of the other three, and open up the doors. Russell is under much pressure, and looks around to notice that he and Brian are the closest to the entrance door. One of them will have to open the door to the bank very shortly. As all the men creep closer and closer to the entrance of the bank, and are inches away from the door handle, Russell starts to panic. He quickly sees shocked expressions from the patrons inside of the bank, even before he opens the door.

During this moment, he is reminded of that evening Brian and his partner went to rob the bank he worked at, and how they all had the same reactions. The men haven't even gone inside the bank yet, and

Russell is already feeling guilty of his current actions. This was something that Russell beforehand, would tell himself that he wouldn't let effect and bother him. It's not until he's put into that particular situation himself, that all of his previous rules and feelings change. The feeling of having someone afraid of you, makes Russell uncomfortable greatly. Brian as well begins to have a sudden wave of guilt. He witnesses all the expressions of fear on the patrons in the banks faces as well. The same faces he saw when he committed the heist against Russell's bank. Brian doesn't like to see people in pain, and this is the only part of robbing banks that he doesn't like. Jesse who's running behind Russell and Brian, then as well feels a great deal of guilt and pain from what they are about to do. He was a bank teller himself, at gunpoint being faced with fear. He's now bringing that onto other people. It made him feel upset. Victor then develops the same feeling, which made him choke up, from robbing the "Sunset Credit Union." He didn't like to bring this type of energy or vibe towards others. It wasn't a feeling that made him feel right at all.

The men continue onto the bank regardless. Brian opens the front door of the bank shouting.

"EVERYONE ON THE FUCKING FLOOR NOW. ON THE FLOOR NOW! I WANT EVERYONE TO HAVE THEIR FACES DOWN ON THE GROUND RIGHT NOW!"

Brian then waves his gun around to all the patrons in the bank. They begin to drop to the floor, with their hands behind their backs. Victor and Jesse stand in the lobby area, aiming their guns at all the patrons. Brian and Russell then walk straight towards the area of the bank tellers. There are three bank tellers present. One of them is a brunette female with curly hair. The other is an African-American woman with a bun hairstyle. The third bank teller is an older Caucasian woman with grey hair. Brian walks to the teller with brunette hair. Russell walks to the teller with her hair in bun. Victor and Jesse remain in the lobby, pointing their guns towards the patrons.

Brian starts to feel shocked at the current situation. As he was pointing the gun at the teller, he could see how scared she was of him. Brian started to feel bad for the woman for a short while, and it caused him to not be able to understand why he was there temporarily. He is now a part of a bank heist, and he doesn't have time to reflect like that. The teller continues to stand still in shock, with Brian aiming his gun at her. He tries to push out the words to tell her to give him the money from the drawer.

Brian continues to stare at the woman for a few more seconds, and he quickly begins to remember that he is doing a robbery, and he doesn't have time to choke up, like he's doing now. The longer he waits being locked in his thoughts, the higher the chance it becomes of them not succeeding in this heist. Brian toughens himself up, and shouts at the woman to empty her cash drawer. She raises her hands in the air. While aiming his gun, he throws the big canvas bag at her. He then proceeds to shout at the bank teller.

"Give me all the money in the drawer, and throw it in the bag! Empty it all, and throw it in the bag. Do it now and do it fast! Empty everything out, I want it all! Hurry! Hurry!"

The teller then rapidly starts to put stacks of money inside Brian's bag. Russell, remarkably is also choking up. He walks up to the bank teller and gives her eye contact. Russell starts to feel extreme empathy for the woman, that he's causing this much stress and turmoil towards her. The teller looks at Russell in fear of her life, and puts her hands up to him as well. Russell manages to quickly shake it off, and throws his bag at the woman. Russell then shouts at the bank teller.

"Open the drawer, put the money in the bag! Empty everything out of the drawer and do it very fast! Empty all of it out, and do it fast! Empty it all out!"

The teller starts to quickly put money inside of Russell's bag. At this time, Victor who's standing with Jesse in the lobby area, notices there is a third teller. He decides to take charge, and pulls out a canvas bag from his pocket. Even though Victor and Jesse were both instructed to stay in the lobby area as lookouts, Victor still in the back of his mind, has a feeling this might be a chance for him to take action as well. Against Russell's wishes and plans, Victor leaves Jesse alone in the lobby, and runs over to the third teller. At this same exact time, Brian unaware that Victor left the lobby, is now instructing the teller he was dealing with to empty her cash cart. While still aiming the gun towards her, he yells at the teller.

"Put all of that in the bag, give me all of it! I need you to put it all in their right now! Hurry! Put all of that in the bag now!"

The teller then starts to drop all the cash from her cash cart into Brian's bag. Russell is also unaware Victor left his assigned spot. Russell congruently, while still pointing the gun at her, shouts at the teller to empty the contents of the cash cart.

"Drop everything in the bag! Drop everything! Very fast! Drop all of the money in there into the bag! Do it fast! Drop it all! Drop all the money!"

At this moment, Victor then points his gun at the third teller with the grey hair, and demands her to empty the money from her cash drawer.

"Open the drawer lady and give me all the money now! Do it now! I don't have all fucking day sweetheart, give me all the fucking money lady! Do it now!"

The third teller begins to empty her cash drawer. Upon hearing this, Brian and Russell instinctively turn their heads towards Victor in absolute shock. They have no idea as to why he's doing, what he's currently doing. Brian's teller has emptied her cash drawer and her cart. Brian then walks over to the lobby area where Jesse is with his money bag, and turns his head towards Victor enraged. He then begins to shout at him

"Man what the fuck are you doing?! You are a fucking dumbass man! What the hell do you think you're doing?! Damn, you are such a dumbass!"

Victor ignores Brian, and the teller continues to drop money in Victor's bag. Russell's teller empties her cash cart. Russell begins to walk to the lobby area with his money bag, while turning his head towards Victor as he's running, he shouts at him.

"Man come on let's go! You're only costing us time man! Let's get the fuck out of here!"

Victor ignores Russell as well. The teller Victor is in front of, continues to empty her drawer. Brian loses patience. He begins to run over from the lobby area, to where Victor is. Brian attempts to forcefully drag Victor. Brian successfully drags Victor away from the teller, by grabbing the back of Victor's arm. Brian drags Victor towards the bank lobby.

However, the teller placed a dye pack in Victor's bag. It explodes loudly, the impact causing Brian to let go of Victor. Brian then runs towards the entrance. This also causes Russell and Jesse to run towards the entrance as well. Victor is badly stained with the bright red dye, and drops his money bag, from being startled by the explosion.

Victor then runs towards the entrance of the bank. All four men in a flash depart out of the building, and run to the adjacent parking structure. Kevin who the entire time was keeping an eye out for any trace of them returning, finally sees them approach the van. He unlocks the doors, and starts the ignition. Russell, Brian, Jesse and Victor all enter the van, and Russell shouts at Kevin.

"Kev, get us the fuck out of here now man! Drive this van very fast man! Drive!"

Kevin underneath his mask is grinning heavily, and turns his head to Russell while driving out of the parking structure. He then happily shouts at him.

"Russ! You guys actually did that shit! Fuck! Yeah baby, Yeah!"

Kevin continues to drive away from the bank, and gets on the highway.

Russell then looks down towards the ground, and shakes his head. Underneath his mask, he has a wide smile.

CHAPTER 14:

NOTHING UP, NOTHING DOWN

Now that the men have completed their first heist, they receive a confidence boost towards their morale. They were able to gain success towards something very risky and dangerous. The heist lasted for about a minute and forty seconds, keeping in mind the goal of them completing the job in a fast and swift time frame. Currently making their escape away from the bank, the men are still in rush of adrenaline and dopamine. It was only minutes ago that were able to rob a bank, and get away with the crime. The pride of knowing they successfully completed their first heist, brings a sense of gratitude towards their emotions. Russell who is now riding in the van back to "Home Base", starts feeling victorious.

Their first heist is now finished, with thankfully all of them safe. They remain in the van on their way back to their lair, still in shock. One thing that is for certain, they all worked together. Victor disobeyed their original plans however. A teller planted a dye pack in his bag, which exploded all over him. Even with that setback, they were able to get through the heist. All of their worries are now over, as they gloat themselves, for getting away with a perfect crime. At this point they do not know how much money they were able to snatch, but more importantly, they are satisfied of being done with the heist. Looking forward from this point, mentally the men feel proud and determined to use this opportunity as a way to not doubt themselves in the future.

While the men are in the van escaping, congruently back at the "United Farmers Savings" bank, the investigation towards the robbery begins. Five minutes after the guys completed their heist, the authorities are called to the scene. Everyone in the building remains in fear, and in shock from the events. The bank is barricaded and wrapped with crime scene tape. The police start to diagnose the incident, and gather as much evidence as they can. Detective Mike Henderson, who was also the detective in charge of investigation at the "Sunset Credit Union", arrives at the scene.

Even though Detective Henderson is a kind hearted man at times, he still is devoted to his job. When it comes to armed robberies and bank heists, he's especially conditioned to change his attitude more seriously. It is remarkable that he is appointed to investigate this bank as well. Likewise, with the "Sunset Credit Union", this bank also has security problems, which made it an easy target for the men to choose. The detective immediately asks to see the security surveillance video of the robbery. He is directed to the surveillance room, and watches in poor grainy quality the events which took place.

This particular bank has poor video surveillance cameras, similar to the setup at the "Sunset Credit Union." As he is watching the video, due to the fact the men kept their identity concealed wearing the black outfits and masks, he cannot make out who the men that robbed the bank are. He continues to watch the security video, being amazed at how fast the men were able to rob the bank, and how accurate they were with their decisions and actions. He knows that these men did careful planning beforehand, which explains why they had a near flawless execution towards the heist. They were in the bank for just a little over a minute, performing a very fast job in a short amount of time.

As the detective watches more of the security video, he becomes puzzled when he notices Victor, who along with Jesse were standing in the lobby area of the bank. All of sudden, he sees that Victor walks to one of the bank tellers. He takes more note, when the teller places a dye pack in the money bag Victor used. The dye pack detonated, with the ink getting all over Victor's arm and hand. The detective who has much experience with dye packs, knows that the ink used in dye packs, is extremely hard to clean.

They leave almost a tattoo like residue on the suspects clothes and skin. Despite the fact Victor was wearing a jacket, it is possible that the ink could have seeped through the fabric quite easily, due to the high power of force the ink exploded, and the material of the dye pack ink as well. The other two tellers were not planning on baiting dye packs in the robber's bags, but the third teller who is more experienced and has witnessed a lot of bank robberies, wanted to thwart the heist the best way she could at this point, and planted a dye pack in Victor's bag.

During the robbery, the bank had a moderate amount of patrons inside the bank. It was a Friday afternoon, so this is to be expected. The detective pays close attention to the robbers on the video, trying to see if he recognizes them at all from any past unresolved bank heists in the area. The disguises make this very difficult for him to tell, but he still finds possible ways of identifying who they actually are.

Detective Henderson, then had a feeling that he recognized Brian. He couldn't pin point exactly from what prior heist he could fit him into, he just had a feeling, and recognized his body shape from under the disguise rather well. He also noticed other features along with that. From the way the robber was holding his gun as well. The detective wasn't completely sure it was the same person, but it was a feeling that he was perceiving nevertheless. The detective then while he's observing the security video, wants to know how the robbers got to the bank.

Having concern of knowing what their getaway vehicle actually was. Unfortunately, there is no security cameras of the parking structure the guys came from. However, as the detective analyzes the security footage further, he can tell that the men came in and out of the same direction. This direction was the adjacent parking structure behind the bank.

The detective interviews the bank tellers about the robbers. Teller number one, which was the one that Brian used, explains that the robber was an average bodied man with an energetic voice. Teller number two, the one that Russell used, explained that he was a heavier set man with a deep beastly voice. The third teller, the one Victor used, said the man was slender, and he had a nonchalant calm but loud voice. She also mentioned that he kept shaking his arms nervously. The teller explained that she put a dye pack into the bag, as the robber seemed nervous and not as threatening as the other two were. The fourth robber which was Jesse, the bank employees weren't able to fully describe him at all. He stayed in the lobby area, and didn't speak. Because the men were all wearing heavy disguises and masks, witness were unable to describe their facial features.

The detective was frustrated that the men left very little incriminating evidence during this heist. It seems they may have gotten away with this one, and have completed a perfect crime. All hope towards his investigation isn't necessarily lost. His only salvation, was the fact one of the tellers used a dye pack towards Victor. This would cause his skin to stain from the dye pack very badly, offering a great deal of proof towards the robber's identity. Also due the explosion, Victor dropped his canvas money bag. This could be a big break for the detective, as far as him collecting evidence from the heist is concerned.

The detective walks over to the stained money bag, and starts to examine it. It was identical, to the same ones that Brian and Russell used. The tote bag doesn't have any particular designs on it, or any other factor to show where it came from. Victor and the rest of the guys were wearing thick gloves. The chances of fingerprints being left on the bag aren't very probable. In any case, Detective Henderson asks for the bag to be sent in for fingerprint testing regardless.

The detective then walks outside the entrance of the bank looking for any shoe prints. He luckily does find a solitary shoe print, that was left behind. The shoe print was caused from one of the guys walking through the car oil slicked pavement in the parking lot. All of the guys were wearing the same type of shoes, which were snow boots.

The particular print belonged to Victor. The detective asks for the shoe print to be taken into evidence. If the print doesn't come up as match, it can only be used for future reference. At this point, the detective is told that the silent alarms in the bank have been tampered with, after more investigation. Someone using a forbidden software system, disabled the radio frequency of the silent alarm, causing it not to go off. Detective Henderson then understands the robbers were extremely clever messing with the silent alarm system, and timed their execution to use it quite well. Part of him believes there were more parties involved outside of the bank controlling this.

Detective Henderson returns to watching the security video one more time in the surveillance room. Looking at the body language of the robbers, he can tell that the third man who approached the bank teller, was not supposed to do that. From the way the other two robbers; Russell and Victor; looked at him, and the way Brian tried to grab him away, was proof that wasn't what they originally planned. He takes more notes of the types of guns they used in the robbery.

Not able to come up with the exact type, he takes an educated guess and assumes they were using R4 type assault machine rifles. The detective glances through the video, trying to take anything else noteworthy from the situation. He notices one final thing about the robbery. The detective realized that the third robber reached into his pocket to pull out a canvas bag. This seemed very peculiar and odd to him, and gave him further proof to believe this robber didn't intend to approach the teller.

The detective finishes watching the security tape, and the tape itself is submitted into evidence. He walks around the bank, still in much disbelief as to how perfectly structured this heist was.

More more police officers begin to leave out of the building, as the investigation starts to conclude. The bank will remain closed for the rest of day, and reopen tomorrow. Detective Henderson, minutes later heads back to the police station nearby to review all of the evidence. The tote bag did not pull up any fingerprints as suspected, but the bag remains in the evidence in case for future reference. The shoe print that the detective was able to get from outside the entrance, did not show up as a match either. However, this as well taken into official evidence for future investigation purposes. Detective Henderson although not satisfied that he wasn't able to get much information towards the identities of the robbers, was thankful that innocent civilians were not harmed during this incident.

The robbers did have guns, but they were not used, and everyone involved thankfully went unharmed. Detective Henderson still had a feeling that he knew one, or possibly several of the robbers from their body shape under the disguises in the security video. For now, he cannot correctly put the pieces of the puzzle together. This particular case will remain pending, as he has done all the investigating he can do at this point in time. He has other cases to solve, and let's this one rest for now.

Back at the van, the men are still on the highway heading towards "Home Base". They virtually got away with the crime. Victor's mishap aside, the men continue unnoticed down the highway, without anyone assuming at all they just robbed a bank. The police are not in pursuit of them. They do not know which vehicle the robbers used, so they have no way of tracking them. All of the guys, Russell especially, notice the police are not following them, and feel more comfortable over that. Although, Kevin continues to drive down the highway at a somewhat high speed. Russell doesn't want them causing unwanted attention, and feels anxious over Kevin speeding. Russell removes his mask, and turns his head in Kevin's direction. He begins to speak to him softly.

"Kev, it's okay now. You can slow down. I think we're good now. You can slow down man. It should be smooth sailing from here. Alright Kev?"

Kevin with his vision still directed forward, nods his head. He decreases his speed and drives at a more moderate pace. Kevin while driving then starts to speak with Russell.

"I can't believe we really did it Russ. We robbed a fucking bank. I wonder how much we got? I knew we could do it, but we actually did it. I'm speechless Russ. I am."

Russell laughs, and playfully punches Kevin on the shoulder. While he's still holding the steering wheel, Kevin begins to take off his mask, dropping it center console of the van. Jesse then removes his mask, and Victor follows as well. Brian after realizing that the rest of the guys have removed their masks, begins to take off his mask as well. They all sit in silence heading towards "Home Base" for a few minutes. Brian then can longer keep quiet, and starts to shake his head. He then angrily expresses how he feels towards Victor.

"Victor, you're such an idiot man. I'm sorry, but you are. We all planned for you and Jesse to not leave that area. When you did that, that was only costing us more time, and making the situation branch out to be more complicated than it needed to be. What's worse is that you got dye packed. Look man, it's all over your jacket. Lift your sleeve up man."

Victor looks down on his jacket and notices bright red dye on the sleeve of his jacket. He pulls up his sleeve, and notices that his arm is stained with bright red dye. Jesse and Brian then gasps in shock and horror, and they start to shake their heads. Russell turns his head towards the rear area of the van and looks at Victor's arm. He has an expressionless reaction to it, and turns his head back forward, looking out the windshield. Victor looks down towards the ground feeling humiliated and embarrassed at himself. He then speaks under his breath.

"I'm sorry guys, I felt that we had extra time, and I wanted to get in the action. I was bored I guess. I learned my lesson, and I won't do anything like that again. When the dye pack exploded, I dropped the money bag. I'm so fucking stupid. I'm sorry guys."

Brian stares at Victor sharply, and continues to lash out and attack him.

"Victor, it's gonna be a bitch to clean all that shit off. You do understand that right? Now they are possibly gonna know it's fucking us that did it. That ink doesn't come off easy at all. I think maybe if I rub some 'WD40' on it, it might, but shit man. You just had to do that didn't you? Fuck. You shouldn't have done that man. You should not have done that."

Victor continues to keep his head down towards the floor. Kevin who is driving, starts to speak towards all the guys.

"Wait, what? Victor got hit with a dye pack? Why didn't you guys tell me this? I thought only Russ and Brian were supposed to be at the tellers? Why the fuck was Victor there? Maybe that was nature's way of teaching him a lesson for not following what we agreed on? Ha-ha."

Kevin then continues to drive the car, laughing to himself. Russell shakes his head at Kevin. Brian continues to give Victor a cold sharp stare, and returns to badgering him badly.

"When we go back to work, you have to wear long sleeves or something. That ink isn't going to come off, and you walking around with bright red paint on your arm is going to get us all in fucking trouble man. I'm gonna try my best to get that shit off you, but from what I heard, dye pack is very permanent almost. You didn't see her reach for a dye pack man?"

Victor starts to feel guilty towards the robbery. He feels ostracized by the other guys, and starts to feel depressed over his actions. He knew he wasn't supposed to act the way he did, but wanted to take advantage of the moment to include himself. He keeps his head down towards the ground, and under his breath responds to Brian.

"Brian, leave me the fuck alone. No I didn't see her put the dye pack in the sack. I didn't know she was going to do that. I screwed up, alright? I always fucking screw up. This is the last heist I'm gonna do with you guys. In fact, this is the last time I'm going to be involved in this group period. You guys clearly don't like me. Once we get back, I'm going to get changed, get in my car and leave. You'll never see me again guys, since I'm such an idiot and a dumbass."

Victor finally raises his head and scrunches his face at Brian giving him an evil look. Jesse feels empathetic towards Victor, and starts to speak to the rest of the guys.

"It's not his fault. How was he supposed to know a dye pack was going to go off? He was fired up in the moment, and he made a mistake guys. Let it go. It's all over. Let's move on."

Brian turns his head towards Jesse and frowns at him. Brian then softly speaks.

"Maybe you're right Jesse. I think I'm being a little too rough on him. I'm mainly mad because the dye pack exploded all over him, but I don't know. Victor, I'm sorry man. I don't like it when you make stupid choices like that, but you are valuable to us and we need you man. So don't feel like we don't need you. We don't need your stupid choices, that's all."

Victor then starts to smile at Brian. Victor raises his arm up, and talks to him.

"Brian, I guess it's not too bad. I'm gonna look at the bright side of it. I at least got a free tattoo from it. Red is not my favorite color, but I can live with it."

After saying that, Victor then begins to laugh at himself very loudly. This causes Brian, Jesse and Kevin as well to laugh at him. Russell however does not laugh, and he is keeping quiet. Russell is slightly disappointed at Victor. Victor, Jesse and Kevin continue to laugh together for a couple minutes. Kevin while he's still driving, then responds to Victor.

"Victor, don't feel bad man. We need you okay? I know I've said some pretty shitty things to you, I know. Forgive me on all of that, but you made a mistake and it's okay. We all make mistakes. The important thing is understanding your mistake was due to a risk you wanted to take. You didn't ask to be hit with a dye pack man. It's going to be okay."

Victor starts to smile to himself, and begins to cheer up. The men continue to proceed down the road towards "Home Base". Kevin still driving, starts to whisper to Russell.

"So Russ, you forgive Victor right? You're not mad at him are you? I mean, if you don't factor all of that in, you guys did a good job right? You're gonna forgive him right?"

Russell turns his head towards Kevin and starts to smile. Russell then looks behind him towards the back area of the van, and he makes eye contact with Victor. He then talks to him.

"Victor, from now on, do what we planned man. You'll be fine. Yeah that dye pack ink isn't going to come off. We can make it fade kind of, but…"

Victor interrupts Russell, by laughing hysterically at him. Russell is not amused, and fires back at Victor.

"Damn it. Victor, never mind."

Russell gets agitated, and looks out the windshield with his hand over his forehead. Due to Victor laughing, Russell doesn't finish what he was going to tell him. After a minute, Victor stops laughing. The van is then completely quiet. Brian at this point then starts to speak to everyone.

"We still did an amazing job you guys. Yeah Victor fucked up, but we didn't get caught. Nobody got hurt, everything for the most part went well. I don't know what our loot us, but I'm happy that we finally did our first heist. Because we planned this one so well, I say we do one more, then that's it. We'll do another next Friday, just like we did today, but that will be our last. But for the next heist, let's go bigger and better. Go out with a bang. I…"

Brian is interrupted when Victor begins to laugh loudly, causing Brian to be irritated and annoyed just like Russell was. Victor still laughing, responds to Brian while looking at him.

"Go out with a bang. Ha-ha. That's what happened, we all went out with a bang. The dye pack exploded on me, and it went BANG! Ha-ha. Good one Brian. Go out with a bang."

Brian looks at Victor in disapproval. Victor continues to laugh very loudly, and the rest of the guys are getting fed up with it. The men try their best to ignore him, but due to how loud he's laughing, and how distinct his laughter is, it's causing a lot of annoyance to them. Russell then loses his patience. He turns his head towards Victor, snapping at him.

"Victor, shut the fuck up man. God. That's quite enough of all of that. Shut up."

Victor smiles at Russell and halts his laughter. Kevin then while driving, turns his head towards Russell shaking his head at him. All of the men seem to be irritated by the way Victor is acting. A minute later, Kevin decides to speak to Russell.

"Hey Russ. As to what Brian said, we're only going to do one more heist right? Then that's it? I know you said you only wanted to do one, but yeah Victor got exploded with a dye pack, but if you never mind that, we all worked pretty well. I can do one more of these. I'm here if you need my help Russ. Then after that we all call it quits, no more robbing banks. Ha-ha."

Russell still looking out towards the windshield, responds to Kevin softly.

"Yeah Kev, we'll do one more, and I'm done. I'm only doing these to get back at the industry that fucked my life over. I think if we do one more heist, and pick a bigger bank, I'll be satisfied. Even though we won't be robbing banks anymore, we'll all keep in touch with each other, and move on with our lives as normal as we can. It will all be good."

Kevin continues down the road, and up turns the stereo in the van.

"It's too quiet in here Russ, I had to turn the music on. Everybody is acting all tense and shit. We should be celebrating and having fun. Speaking of celebrating, Russ when we get back and we all change, let's get so shitfaced drunk tonight. Let's get some Chinese food, and all the booze we can all drink. Let's get so wasted. We all robbed a bank together, we deserve it man."

Russell turns his head towards Kevin and laughs at him. He then responds.

"You want Chinese food Kev? You can have whatever you want. You want all the beer you can drink Kev? You can have that as well. I agree, it's time to celebrate."

Brian then snaps back at Russell.

"Wait, before we do any celebrating, we count everything we got. I want to know how much loot we have. That's my main thing. After that, we can party and do whatever the fuck we want. I first of all, want to know what our total take was. I have to know, I'm so anxious."

Kevin continues to drive, and agrees with Brian, directing his comments to the group.

"I agree. Let's count all the money first, then we can have a fiesta, and get drunk, and do whatever. We robbed a bank. I still can't believe any of this shit. Everyone in this van is batshit crazy Russ."

Russell looks down towards the floor and shakes his head. He then responds to Kevin.

"You can say that again Kev. Isn't that the fucking truth? We are all a bunch of loonies."

Kevin laughs at Russell, and continues to drive. The men listen to the car stereo in silence for several minutes. As they get closer to "Home Base", they each feel more calm. However, Victor then starts to laugh again for no reason, causing Brian to become irritated over this. He reaches over and pops Victor in the back of the head very hard. Victor shuts himself up, and suspends his laughter after being hit by Brian. Jesse starts to shake his head, feeling more empathy towards Victor. Kevin and Russell who heard Brian hit him, both start to chuckle to themselves. Following this, Brian starts to speak to all of the guys.

"As I was saying before, we did relatively well this time. For the next heist we should go bigger and badder. We don't have a choice, we have to. This shows we have the potential to work tougher and accomplish anything we set out minds to. Following the next heist, we take our money, and we all go our separate ways; still remaining friends. That's going to be the plan."

The rest of the guys do not respond to what Brian said, but mentally they are in agreement towards him. The van continues down the highway, now only a short distance from "Home Base". Traffic becomes loosely tight, until all of the cars become slowly packed together. Eventually cars stop moving altogether, and the guys then become stuck in traffic. Kevin starts to grunt and feel aggravated over this. His turns to Russell, and angrily chats with him.

"There must be an accident or something up ahead Russ. None of the cars are moving. I hope we aren't here all night. Damn it, I hate it when traffic gets like this Russ."

Russell looks down towards the ground, and speaks to Kevin in a quiet manner.

"Kev, these things happen man. Just try not to let it get to your head alright? We shouldn't be in this mix for that long hopefully. Listen to the music Kev. Relax. Alright?"

Kevin nods his head towards Russell, and turns the stereo in the van up. The rest of the cars then little by little start to advance in the highway. The traffic jam is beginning to subside itself, and traffic is beginning to come to a faster flow and rate. Eventually, the highway returns to its normal condition, and to its regular custom pace. Kevin finally approaches the highway exit, leading towards "Home Base".

A few minutes later, they finally reach the safe house area. Kevin stops the van right outside the driveway to the second unit, which is outside of "Home Base". Russell gets out of the vehicle, and starts to unlock the unit door. After opening it, Russell gets back into the van, and Kevin pulls up inside the unit. He then turns the ignition off and grabs his laptop case. All of the men get out of the van. Russell walks towards the unit door he opened, closing and locking it. The men at this point, start to take off their jackets, and their boots. Brian takes Victor's stained jacket, and puts it in a black trash bag, tucking it in a deep corner of the unit, hidden away from view.

All of them each proceed to change into their regular clothes they all put aside before they left for the heist. Kevin puts on a T shirt and jeans. Jesse puts on a tank top and shorts. Victor puts on a plain white T shirt and some khaki pants. Brian puts on a blue button down shirt and some jeans, and Russell puts on a black polo shirt and some jeans. Once they have changed, Brian takes all of the guns they used during the heist, and empties all the bullets and magazines. He places the guns away in the unit. Brian then takes two black trash bags, and puts each canvas tote bag that contains their looted money inside the black bags. Brian gives one of the black trash bags to Russell, keeping the other one to himself. Immediately following this, the men then walk towards the "Home Base" unit.

Brian reaches the gate of the unit, and starts to unlock it. As the door opens, the men all go inside. Brian locks the gate, and sets his trash bag over by the sofa areas. Russell then sets his black bag right in that same area. Brian then goes over by his bed to get his phone, and he begins to order some Chinese food. While Brian is ordering the food, Kevin sits down on the sofa, and turns the television on, which is showing "Family Feud". Jesse then sits down on the sofa next to Kevin, and watches the program. Victor during this time walks over to Brian's automotive tool area, looking to see if he has any "WD40", so he can conceal the dye pack paint on his arm.

Russell takes the black bag he set down, and dumps it all on the table in front of the sofas. Russell looks at all the loose cash that has formed a big pile, and starts to shake his head for a few seconds. He then starts to laugh to himself, while still looking at all the money. Kevin stares at Russell and proceeds to laugh at him, while Jesse gives Russell a puzzling look. Russell who's continuing to laugh to himself right after that, takes the bag that Brian set down, and dumps the contents of that bag on the table as well. He looks at the even bigger pile of cash, and laughs out loud. Russell then starts to speak to both Kevin and Jesse.

"That's a lot of money you guys. Shit. It belongs to all of us too. I don't know how much it is, but damn that looks like a substantial amount to me."

Coincidentally as Russell finished talking, the program went to a commercial break. Kevin looks at the large pile of cash on the table, and starts to shake his head.

"Well, we have to count it all Russ. Jesse and I can do that right now. I'm curious to see how much all of it is. It seems like a lot of fucking money Russ. I agree."

Russell smiles at Kevin, and walks over to where Brian is. Brian is still on the phone ordering Chinese food. Kevin turns off the television set so they can be totally focused, and he Jesse then begin to count all of the money they plundered. Once they count to a specific amount, they put the bills in separate piles on the table, counting only to one thousand for each. Victor finally is able to find a can of "WD40", and begins to rub some of it on the area of his arm the dye pack hit him.

The paint although not coming off completely, does begin to vanish itself away slightly. Kevin and Jesse continue to count all of the money, being focused on this tedious and repetitious task. Taking note, the large amount of bills they have to go through. This more than likely will take quite some time for them to finish. Brian gets done ordering the food and starts to speak to Russell.

"You want to go to the market with me and get some booze and to pick the food up? By the time we leave out the store, the food should be ready and we can head back?"

Russell nods his head to Brian. Russell then walks to the sofa area and starts to speak to Kevin and Jesse.

"Brian and I will be back shortly. We're gonna get pick up the food, and get something for us to drink. I want all this money accounted for by the time I get back. Understood?"

Kevin while he's still counting all the cash with Jesse, responds to Russell.

"Yeah Russ, we'll have all of this taken care of. See you when you get back man."

Russell shakes his head at Kevin. He along with Brian, both walk out of the unit. Russell and Brian leave in Russell's car. As soon as they leave, Victor walks over to the sofa area where Kevin and Jesse are counting all of the cash. He takes a seat down on the sofa, and looks at them grinning heavily. Kevin turns his head towards Victor, giving a disgusted and annoyed expression towards him. Victor then starts to laugh at Kevin. Kevin tries to ignore him, but Victor continues on with his silly antics and quirks. Jesse is also being bothered by Victor's behavior. They are trying to count the money, but Victor is causing a lot disturbance to the both of them.

Victor then starts to pick up stacks of cash off the table, throwing it the air. Unable to take much more of it, Kevin begins to have a temper tantrum. Kevin throws all the cash off the table, onto the floor. Victor starts to laugh loudly because of this. Kevin then pins Victor down on the sofa, pressing his knee to Victor's abdomen area. While doing that, Kevin angrily shouts at him.

"Victor, I need you to not bother us right now. We're trying to count all this money up. I don't like being this type of guy, I don't. However, you're annoying us right now. We have to start all fucking over again, so thanks a lot man. Shit. You're doing this on purpose too. Ugh. Victor if you want to help, all you have to do is say that you want to help. It's not hard."

Kevin shakes his head at Victor, and starts to pick up all the cash on the floor. Jesse starts to feel upset, and picks up the cash Kevin threw. Victor joins both of the men, and he picks up the money as well. While he's putting the money on the table, Victor speaks to them.

"Can I help you guys out with counting all of that? I'm sorry, I guess I'm bored and I get like that. I didn't think you would get all mad and stuff. So I can help you guys?"

Kevin turns to look at Jesse who nods his head. Kevin then takes a deep breath, and turns to look at Victor. Under his breath, Kevin starts to talk to Victor.

"Alright man, you can help. Don't bother us anymore though. Count the money, and only do that. Don't laugh, don't do any silly shit. If you do anything silly again, you're gonna have to go away. I'm not going to tell you again. We have to count all this money up man."

The three of them sit down on the sofa, and start to count the money. However, Victor continues his silly charades, and starts to giggle and snicker to himself. Jesse starts to frown, and Kevin who has already warned Victor, cannot contain himself towards the way he's acting.

"Victor, get up. I said if you did that shit again I was going to remove you man."

Victor then starts to get himself together, and cries out to him.

"Kevin please? No I won't do any of that anymore, I swear. Hey, do you have any weed man? We all can smoke some. I'm feeling kinda hyper right now, and that will chill me out. I need some weed to calm down."

Kevin gives an angry look to Victor.

"Will you stop acting silly then?"

Victor nods his head to him. Kevin with the same look on his face, deep breathes and shakes his head. He then turns his view over to Jesse. Kevin then speaks to Jesse in a bothered tone.

"Jesse, go over to where my laptop case is, and get that bag of herb please. Thanks."

Jesse grabs the bag of marijuana, and hands it to Kevin. Kevin then begins to roll a marijuana joint. Victor then hands Kevin a lighter, and Kevin starts to light the marijuana joint, taking a hit of it. He then hands Victor the joint, and he takes a couple hits from it. Victor hands Jesse the marijuana joint, and he as well takes a couple hits. The men each take a couple more hits from the marijuana joint, before Kevin puts the marijuana joint out.

"Alright that's enough, now we need to get back to this. We should all feel mellow now. We have to count this money up before they get back, so come on now."

They each start to count all the money, without any further hassle or issue. Meanwhile, Russell and Brian are at the supermarket, buying beer for them all. They head over to the liquor section. As they are deciding what to pick, Brian starts to look around the area of the store they are in. He then walks closer to Russell, leans towards him, speaking very quietly.

"Hey, I want to say that you did a good job today. I'm amazed at how well we did, and I want to thank you for that. You did such an amazing job. We really did it."

Russell while he's still looking at the liquor and beer selections, starts to smile. While he's looking at what to purchase, he responds to Brian, also speaking in a hushed tone.

"We did do well, and I want to thank you too. I don't want to believe it, but I have to believe it. Now, I want to have fun, and kick back and enjoy the hard work we did."

Brian looks at Russell and smiles at him. They eventually decide to get two cases of "Pabst Blue Ribbon", with Russell carrying one, and Brian carrying the other. They then walk towards the checkout stand to purchase the beer. After that, they head over to the Chinese restaurant to pick up their food order. They get their food, and they both then proceed to head back towards "Home Base". Kevin, Jesse and Victor, are getting towards the end of the stacks of cash they are counting. They continue to set piles on the table, evenly grouping them by one thousand each. Finally reaching the end of the pile, they can now figure out the complete amount. The men were able to get a total of ninety-two thousand dollars. Dividing the money evenly between them all, each man will get eighteen thousand, and four hundred dollars each. Right at the same time when they completed counting the money, Russell and Brian walk into the unit. Brian walks over to his kitchen area, setting the Chinese food down on the counter. Russell puts the cases of beer also on the kitchen counter area. He then sees that all the stacks of cash are piled evenly on the table. Russell walks over to the sofa area, and starts to speak with Kevin.

"So, did you guys finish counting everything up? How much is it."

Before Kevin can respond, Brian has a puzzled look on his face, and turns to Kevin.

"Kevin, were you smoking weed? I smell weed? If you were smoking, please be honest, and don't lie to me. I can smell it, and I know you did, so tell the truth."

Kevin begins to laugh, and then responds to Brian.

"Well okay, I'm going to answer your question first Brian. Yes, we were smoking pot. Only because Victor wouldn't calm the fuck down, so I had no choice. To answer your question Russ, we counted everything, and it came out to ninety-two grand. So every guy is going to get about eighteen grand each. That's not bad at all. I was expecting more, but that's still good."

Kevin then puts all the money in five separate piles on the table. Russell feels disappointed at the amount. Along with Kevin, he was also expecting to take out a bigger amount. Jesse feels indifferent about how much they were able to get. Brian who had heard Kevin say the amount they had, also thought their take would be higher than that. Jesse and Victor however seem to accept what they have, and are neutral towards this. Kevin then starts to hand a stack of the money to Victor, and then another stack to Jesse. Kevin then starts to hand Russell a stack of cash. At this moment, Brian walks over to the sofa area very angrily. He snatches the stacks of cash from Victor, Jesse, and Kevin. Brian then snaps back at all of them.

"Hey wait a minute, is everyone in agreement that we all should take our money now? I'd say we wait until we finish the next heist, then we add that amount to this one. I don't know, I mean if you guys want your cash now, you can take it. But I say we wait. What do you guys think?"

There is a long silence after Brian speaks, and all of the guys stay silent. This is a very interesting conundrum they are in. Either decision they make is logical, and neither is right or wrong. It all depends on what choice the group as a whole is comfortable in doing. If they take their money now, they can use it and spend it however they want. On one side, they feel deserve their money, and the guys did work hard in order to achieve it.

However, this might cause suspicion, and could possibly cause tension within the group on how they spend their cash. They also however could decide to wait until they finish their last heist a week from now. They can take their money from the first heist, and add it together, and they each will have their money for themselves. This causes no suspicion towards the group, as they aren't spending the money they received quite yet. The only problem is the guys must wait, and be patient to not feel greedy. The men all stay silent as they contemplate on what choice they wish to make towards this situation. Brian then speaks.

"Okay guys, we need to take a vote now, and decide what we are gonna do. Everyone who wants to get their money now, raise their hands."

Shockingly, none of the guys raise their hands. At this point, it's best they wait to get their funds, until they are finished with the last heist. If they spend all of the money during this time, it might cause issues within the group, and they could possibly stray away from each other. They all agreed to do one last heist next Friday. It seems more comfortable for all of them to have their money, once they are finished with the next heist. Kevin then responds.

"Well, Brian your idea makes more sense. We can wait and not be greedy about it."

Brian nods his head towards Kevin to agree with him. Brian then takes all the cash and puts it in a large black duffel bag. He sets the duffel bag over by his work station. Russell who was looking down at the ground, then responds to Brian's idea, bringing up an interesting point.

"Brian, I agree what we shouldn't spend any money right now, but the part I don't get, who's gonna be in charge of the cash. So you're just gonna leave the bag right there. How do we know you're not going to spend it? Who can we trust to not touch any of the money?"

Brian looks at Russell with a confused face, and at that moment someone begins to knock on the door of the unit. Brian walks over and looks through the peep hole, it's Max. Brian then begins to unlock the door of the unit, and Max then proceeds in. Max talks to all of the guys.

"I was watching live at five news a few minutes ago, and I saw that the bank you guys said you were going to hit, was a breaking story. I thought to myself, hey that sounds like my guys. I'm completely stunned that you guys were able to do it. I have to give it to you."

Max then starts to clap and smile at all the guys. Russell while looking at Max, then hatches an idea to himself. Moments ago, the men all agreed that they would wait to spend the money they got, until they completed the next bank job. Brian then took all the money, and kept it in a bag over by where he works on his cars. Russell doesn't fully trust Brian that he won't open the bag. He then realizes that Max is the perfect person to trust, and he won't mess with the money. Russell then walks over to the bag grabbing it, and begins to ask Max a favor.

"Max, can you hold onto this bag for us please?"

Russell then hands Max the black duffel bag. Max looks at the bag very puzzled. He turns his head towards Brian who stays silent. Max then looks at Russell asking him a question.

"I'll hold onto the bag, but you have to tell me what's in it first. If it's anything I'm not comfortable holding onto, I don't want anything to do with it. So tell me what's in the bag."

Russell turns his head towards Brian, and he responds to Max.

"Well, we counted all the money we got from the bank job. After that, we divvied all of it up. We each were about to take a pile of the cash, before we decided not to spend the money at this point. We're gonna hit one more bank next Friday, then after we hit that bank, we'll take that total from both of our heists, and then everyone gets their share of the money."

Max puts his hand under his chin, he continues to look at Russell who carries on.

"So in that bag is our take. The favor I ask of you, is to hold onto that bag. All five of us trust you, and not that we don't trust each other; we're just a bunch of young crazy guys. You're an older, more mature trustworthy man, and we all trust you to hold onto it. I appreciate it."

After Russell finishes speaking, Max begins to open the duffel bag. He notices the large amount of cash inside the bag and quickly zips it back up. He raises his eyebrows and speaks.

"Oh my. That is quite a lot of money. I understand everything completely now. I will hold onto this bag, and you can count on me. I find it very lovely how each of you are working together to resolve issues like this. I am proud of all of you."

Brian then smiles at Max and starts to open the beer case.

"Max, do you want a beer man? Incidentally enough, we're all celebrating the shit we just pulled today. I got some Chinese food too. Come on Max, stay with us."

Max laughs at Brian, and then responds to him in a very rough way.

"Okay, I'll hang out for a bit. Only because you guys robbed a bank today. Ha-ha."

Russell laughs and smiles at Max. Brian then hands Max a beer, and the rest of the guys a beer as well. All six of them start to celebrate and enjoy themselves. Russell is happy that they are all embracing in joy at this point. He seems happy that all of the guys unanimously decided to not touch any of the money now. Although it would be nice for them to spend some of it, for right now, the best choice for them would be to wait until they complete their final heist next Friday, before getting to the money. Russell knows that Max is a very trustworthy man, and they are thankful they can use him for support. Brian knew his idea was the most sensible to make, and would cause the least amount of issues. Kevin, Jesse and Victor also believe it is better to wait, than for them to have access to all the money now. The men have equal chemistry towards their decision making skills. Working together as a collective and agreeing with each other is a good sign. Brian plays some music, and they all eat, drink, and unwind. They feel glad to celebrate right now. They are outlaws, and feel good to consider themselves as such.

Several hours later, at 10 P.M., Max dismisses himself from the group.

"Okay gentleman, it's been lovely, but I must go now. I appreciate you inviting me to your party, I do. I have to leave, and I want you all to have a good night."

The rest of the guys then say goodbye to Max. Brian then walks over to him.

"Hey Max, I'll walk with you home man, it's kinda late. I don't mind walking you."

Max allows Brian to walk with him, and they both leave the unit, with Max carrying the black duffel bag with him. Kevin, Russell, Jesse and Victor are all sitting on the sofa area watching "Kindergarten Cop". Kevin reaches into his pocket and takes out his bag of marijuana. He then starts to roll a marijuana joint. Russell watches him do this and starts to smile. As soon as Kevin finishes rolling the joint, Russell snatches it away from him, and lights it. Russell takes several hits from the marijuana joint, then passes it to Kevin. The men continue to pass the joint around to each other taking hits from it. Kevin starts to take a hit, but is stopped by Brian, who at this point walks back into the unit. He talks to all the guys very angrily.

"So Kevin, that's now the second time you're smoking reefer up in here, when I'm gone. What the fuck is up with that man? I want some of that too. Hey, let me see that."

Brian snatches the joint from Kevin's hand, and takes several long hits from it. He hands the joint back to Kevin, and Brian goes over to the area where his cars are, and starts to wax them. An hour passes, and some of the guys begin to feel slightly tired. Brian continues to detail his cars; however, the rest of the men remain at the sofa. Jesse stretches across the sofa, and puts his head on Russell's lap, and closes his eyes. Jesse then starts to slowly fall asleep, while using Russell's lap as a pillow. Russell then takes one of his hands, and starts to rub Jesse's hair. Victor then who is feeling very tired, gets up from the sofa area, and goes to fall asleep on Brian's bed. Brian watches Victor do this, and laughs. Brian then goes back to detailing his cars. Kevin starts to roll yet another marijuana joint, lighting it. He takes a hit from it, and then hands Russell the joint, who takes a hit as well. Kevin then starts to talk to Russell.

"Hey Russ, isn't it funny how things go full cycle? I mean, take you for example. You were a manager of a bank. You were this epitome of this working man profile. Everything you did was pretty much by the book, and everything had to be prim and proper with you. These two jerks rob your bank, one of the jerks is over there on the other side of room. Then that whole event transformed you Russ. You robbed a fucking bank today Russ. What happened? Ha-ha."

Russell while still rubbing Jesse's hair with one of his hands, uses his other hand to take another hit of the marijuana joint. He then hands the joint to Kevin, and responds.

"Well Kev, that's interesting that you brought all that up. Maybe this was my destiny, maybe not. We all have choices, and I could have easily said hell no. If I wanted to right now, I could call the cops on Brian, for being an accessory to the robbery that killed two of my close friends. I'm not going to though. Because, Brian is a good guy. All five of us are good guys. We sadly are all misunderstood, and because we're misunderstood, we get tired Kev."

Kevin takes more hits of the marijuana joint, while watching the television. He then starts to laugh very loudly from what he's watching. Kevin hands the joint back to Russell.

"This movie is so funny Russ. I remember I was in elementary school when I first saw it. Thinking it was just going to be some stupid kid movie. It's not. 'Kindergarten Cop' is really something Russ. There are so many internet memes from this movie as well man."

Russell takes one last hit from the joint. Russell then hands the joint back to Kevin. Russell then leans his head back on the sofa and closes his eyes.

"I'm good Kev, you can finish it off. I've had enough man. Thanks man."

Kevin takes more hits of the joint, and he responds to Russell.

"Anytime Russ, you know you're my main man Russ."

Russell closes his eyes, and listens to Kevin laugh, and quote sayings from the movie playing on the television. Russell then eventually falls asleep.

CHAPTER 15:

NOTHING SLOW, NOTHING FAST

The next morning, Russell awakens on the sofa area at "Home Base", where the rest of the men also are. It is now Saturday morning, and the day succeeding their first bank heist. The previous night, the men all celebrated their heist by throwing an extravagant party. From all of the excitement, the men bonded towards each other at a high point and level. Russell stretches his arms out, and begins to sit up on the sofa. He looks down, and notices Jesse is still resting his head on his lap, however due to Russell's movements as he was waking himself up, Jesse is now awake. He however still has his head on Russell's lap resting. Jesse then shortly after that falls back asleep again.

While he's still sitting on the sofa, Russell looks over to the other side of the sofa, and sees that Kevin is asleep. He continues to look around the area, and sees that Victor is sitting down at the kitchen area eating a bowl of cereal, watching a video on his phone. Russell looks around more, noticing that Brian is working on a car. Brian has music playing on his phone, while he's working. He is modifying a black sport utility vehicle with tinted windows that Russell has never seen before, at his work station. Russell sees that Brian has added brand new traction tires, with the old tires discarded to the side. He also sees that Brian has removed the license plates as well. Although Russell is not a mechanic, he is moderately familiar with cars, and how they operate.

He can tell that Brian is now doing an oil change on the vehicle. Russell then moves his head back and closes his eyes. He decides to rest on the sofa for a few minutes.

While he's resting his eyes, Russell updates himself on all of the recent events that have happened. Yesterday, for the first time in his life, he successfully managed to operate a bank heist. One that he spent careful time and energy planning. He was only able to reign victorious, with the help of his comrades. They all were able to plunder a large sum of money, all for their taking. At this time, each of the men mutually agreed to not spend any of it yet.

The men want to commit one final heist on Friday, one which will be at a much larger bank. Once they have successfully completed that heist, the men will share the complete total of their money, and be comfortable with themselves. The men at this point, have not yet planned this heist yet, but come the time Friday approaches, they should be ready. Using their prior experience and desire from the first heist, it shouldn't be difficult for the men to go into their final heist. They were able to perform their first heist nearly flawless. Victor was hit with a dye pack, but aside from this, they still managed to work remarkably well.

Russell continues to backtrack himself mentally of everything which came together yesterday, and also brainstorms their future endeavors to their heist on Friday. He has many ideas he is considering, and he is optimistic about each of them. For right now though, Russell doesn't wish to explain his plans until a little later. In his mind, he wishes to return to the building they clean at, and do their briefing there. Russell feels drained and hungover from all the partying and celebrating the night before, and he can't bring himself to discuss heist plans at this current time.

Russell then opens his eyes and stares at the ceiling. He then becomes curious on what Brian is currently doing, and gets up from the sofa. Without trying to bother Jesse that much, he gets up very gently, and positions Jesse on the sofa, so he's not disturbed. Kevin still remains asleep on the other side of the sofa.

Russell while feeling slightly tired, waddles over to where Victor is with his hands in his pockets, and unintentionally starts to look at the screen on Victor's phone. Victor by the expression on his face, looks depressed and upset, and this causes Russell to be concerned over him.

Victor is watching a video news podcast on his phone, and seems to be bothered by the content. Russell assumed that Victor would be alerted by his company, but he isn't. Victor is well aware that Russell is standing by him, but he is much too enthralled on the podcast on his phone, and doesn't with to deal with him right now. Russell then starts to rub the back of Victor's shoulder. Victor then decides to be cordial and pauses his podcast, and turns head away from his phone to look at Russell who's smiling at him.

Victor then very reluctantly grins back at Russell, quickly turning his head back to his phone, resuming the video podcast directly after that. Russell then leaves Victor to himself, heading over to the area Brian is at, and starts to observe him.

Brian is disassembling many aspects of the vehicle, and is extremely focused. He is amazed at how efficient Brian is skilled at working with automobiles. Russell doesn't speak to him at all, though he has many thoughts on his mind concerning this particular situation he's in. Brian while continuing to his current task, senses Russell standing by him. Brian looks up at Russell, and laughs at him. Brian then immediately returns to the work he was doing. Russell keeps gazing his attention towards Brian, being very puzzled over his actions. Russell then walks closer to Brian, who's working under the hood of the car. He then whispers to him.

"What's with the car man? When and where did you get it?"

Brian as he's continuing to deal all his attention towards the car, responds to Russell.

"I figured that there is no time like now to be prepared and ready for our final heist on Friday. The van is nice, but as it's our final heist, I want us to do the job in a more sophisticated way, by having two more getaway cars. I was thinking ahead that way."

Russell then raises his eyebrows. Brian proceeds to explain himself to Russell.

"I managed to work my magic, and snag this Chevy Tahoe this morning from this car dealership about an hour from here. Don't worry, the guy who runs the lot is an asshole, trust me. I only steal from corrupt dealerships, that screw their customers. Look at my progress, not bad right? I'm only doing some minor modifications to it, so it can be a good getaway vehicle for us. Kevin can drive the van, someone else can drive this one, and there's another car I also was able to get, which another guy can drive. It's a black Ford Expedition parked at our other unit."

Russell continues to be intrigued at Brian. This was an idea which he seemed to be indifferent towards. The dangers of all of the guys leaving the bank in different vehicles, include the fact they may separate and get split from each other. Russell plans for all of the guys to stay together, and to not drift away. By acting as a team in unison, it may offer greater success to them all. However, Russell believes that by each of them having separate getaway vehicles, it will offer a better chance of them escaping the heist better. Instead of all of them ramming themselves into one vehicle, by using multiple vehicles, it will offer a smooth operation towards the heist. Russell then starts to understand that Brian has a knack to steal cars so well.

This is something that ordinarily shouldn't be ruled and considered a talent, but Russell couldn't help being impressed over the way Brian is able to accomplish all of that. Brian is able to be multi-faceted in that regard. Not only being skilled with his extensive knowledge on how cars operate, but being able to get any vehicle that he wanted. Stealing is very immoral, but as of late, Russell has thrown all his morals away. He looks at life at a different perspective, his oppression has taken over any sense of morality he had in his body.

Russell does admire Brian's abilities, but feels he's probably not approaching what he's capable of, in the correct manner. Gaining a more open mind towards agendas he didn't use to respect or understand at all, Russell changes his attitude to these topics. Russell remains curious about Brian nevertheless. He continues to watch him closely for several minutes, with Russell still having a puzzled expression on his face. Brian glances at Russell for a few seconds, noticing how perplexed he looks. Brian then responds.

"Russell, is everything alright man, do you need me to get you something?"

Russell shakes his head at Brian, and starts to look down towards the ground. He then crosses his arms, and walks closer to Brian. Russell then leans in and whispers to him.

"I'm glad you're trying to help Brian. I only want to ask can you let me and the other guys know when you're gonna do stuff like this please? I appreciate it. I mean, all of us more than likely would have all been fine with this, but I want us all to work together; and not make choices like this without consulting the whole group first. You understand right?"

Brian then looks at Russell, and he smiles at him. He then responds.

"Sure, no problem Russell. I understand man; I should have talked about this with all of y'all first. You're absolutely right man. I just wanted to act fast I guess. The idea was so hot for me not to go on ahead and do it. But you're totally right Russell. From now on whatever I do, I'll lay it down with you guys first."

Russell laughs at Brian, and pats him on the back of his shoulder. Russell wants each of the men to make decisions and choices that are discussed about with the whole group. If one person acts in a way ahead of the others, this possibly could lead to their solid team unit being wrecked and tarnished. One positive thing to consider through all of this, is the men are working in harmony of each other, and they must continue to do so. Russell continues to speak to Brian.

"I have two banks in mind. These are high profile though; big time. This is our last heist, so I want to pick somewhere that's gonna give us the best results. But I'll talk about all of that on Monday, right now I'm still kinda hungover from last night man. Shit."

Brian while still working on the car, briefly turns his head towards Russell and laughs at him. In this moment, Brian then shuts the hood of the car, and responds to Russell.

"Take it easy man. I'll take a break from this for now. I have to still work on the other car, but don't you worry. I get everything ready by Friday."

Russell then smiles at Brian and walks towards the sofa area. Brian starts to put his tools away. By now, Kevin and Jesse have each woken themselves up. They sit at the sofa area and watch the television, which is playing "Mythbusters". Russell then while he's standing in front of the sofa, starts to rub Kevin and Jesse's heads with his both his hands. He then speaks to both of them in a playful way.

"Good morning you two. I know you guys had fun last night."

Jesse nods his head at Russell, with Kevin looking up at Russell, but quickly turning his view back to the television. Russell then takes a seat on the sofa, positioned in the middle of them. Kevin while watching the television, talks to Russell.

"Russ, I have a really bad hangover man. I know you're hungover too Russ. I can tell. You can lie to me and say you're not, but I know that you are man. Let's all go and get something to cure it. You can pick the place Russ, I don't care. I just want to get some food."

Russell looks down at the floor, ignoring him. Jesse then angrily glares at Russell, and slugs him on his back. Russell looks over at Jesse with a confused face, and he grins at him. Russell turns his view back towards the ground, and Jesse then speaks to him.

"Russell, I agree with Kevin. I'm hungry, and I could use a bite to eat."

Russell continues to have his head towards the floor momentarily. He then lifts his head up, and stares at Kevin who's watching the television. He pats Kevin on the leg, smiling at him.

"Okay Kev. If you're hungry, I can take you out to eat man. I'm sorry about that man."

Russell then gets up from the sofa area, and walks over to Brian, who is still gathering all of his tools together. Russell then speaks to Brian.

"Hey man, do you want to go get something to eat with us?"

Brian who has his attention directed towards all of his car tools, responds to Russell.

"Thanks, but no thanks. I already ate earlier. I'm fine, but thanks for the invitation man."

Russell then nods his head at Brian and walks over to Victor, who is watching a podcast on his phone. Russell stands next to him without speaking, under the pretenses that Victor overheard his conversation with Brian; which Victor in fact did, and he would quickly give Russell his answer. Victor for whatever reason refuses to acknowledge him. Russell then taps him on the shoulder. Victor gives Russell a cold stare, and Russell talks to him.

"Victor, we are all gonna go and get something to eat. Do you want to go out with us?"

Victor while he's watching the podcast on his phone, quickly snaps back at Russell.

"Yeah, I heard you talk to Brian. No I don't want to go, but thank you for asking."

Russell laughs at Victor, and walks away from him. Russell then walks over to the area Brian is in. Brian has finished putting all his tools away, and he looks up at Russell.

"Is everything good? What do you want to tell me Russell?"

Russell pulls out his phone and car keys. He then responds to Brian's concern.

"Well. Brian, I think me, Kev and Jesse are going to go home after we eat. We feel kinda worn out from last night. So we'll see you and Victor, Monday morning then. You know you can call me whenever you need to Brian. Alright then, catch you later man."

Brian extends his hand out for Russell to shake it, and he does. He then says goodbye.

"Okay Russell, I'll see you Monday, and we'll take it from there. See you."

All of the men begin to say goodbye to each other, and Russell, Kevin and Jesse grab their belongings, and put their sunglasses on. They then walk out of "Home Base". It is partly cloudy today, giving off a slight breeze. Russell starts to walk over to his car, and unlocks the doors. During this time, Brian rushes out of the unit, and proceeds to spring over to where Russell is. Brian who is slightly out of breath, converses with Russell.

"On second thought, me and Victor will join you. I'm not really hungry, and neither is Victor, but we are still a little hungover. So why the fuck not? It's not like we're doing anything. We can go to a restaurant with you guys."

Russell smiles at Brian, and nods his head. Russell, Kevin and Jesse then wait in Russell's car, as Brian and Victor get themselves ready to join them. While they are in the car, Kevin turns on the car stereo, and the song that's playing is, "The Way She Dances", by N.E.R.D. The three of them continue to wait in the car, listening the music. They listen to a couple more songs on the radio, until Kevin reaches in his laptop bag. He takes out a bag of marijuana, and quickly begins to roll a marijuana joint. Russell watches him silently. Kevin finishes rolling the joint, and puts the marijuana bag back in his laptop case. Congruently, Brian and Victor then walk out of "Home Base". Kevin turns his head taking note of them walking out, and cuts the stereo off. He then puts his hand on Russell's shoulder, and softly speaks to him.

"Russ, I figured we could all smoke a little before we head out. Come on man."

Russell shakes his head at Kevin and cuts the ignition off. He along with Kevin and Jesse walk out of the car and stand outside of the "Home Base" unit. All five of the men gather around, as Kevin starts to light the marijuana joint. Kevin takes a couple hits from it, and passes it to Russell. As Russell is taking hits from the joint, Kevin asks him a question.

"So Russ, where are we going to go eat at? I'm hungry for anything really?"

Russell hands the joint to Brian, and he responds to Kevin very lightly.

"Kev, why don't you pick the place man. We'll go wherever you want to go Kev."

Brian passes the joint to Victor. Kevin then rubs his hand behind the back of his head.

"Well Russ, we can go to 'Applebee's' I suppose. There's one not that far from here."

Kevin pulls out his telephone and begins to reaffirm himself. Kevin then starts to place a reservation for all five of them with his phone.

"Alright Russ, I saved us all a table. I have a feeling it's gonna be crowded."

Russell looking down at the ground, nods his head at Kevin. Victor hands Jesse the joint. The men continue to smoke for a few minutes more, then they proceed towards the restaurant. Russell gets into his car, with Kevin and Jesse riding with him. Brian and Victor follow right behind them. They continue driving to "Applebee's". As they reach the restaurant, the men walk into the building. Being that it's Saturday, the restaurant is quite crowded and busy. Luckily, due to the fact they made a reservation beforehand, they are attended to rather quickly, and are seated by the waitress at a table. Brian sits at the head of the table, with Russell sitting on the other head of the table. Kevin sits next to Russell on the corner side of the table, with Jesse seated right next to Kevin, adjacent to Brian. Across the table is Victor, who is sitting near Brian's corner of the table.

This was the first time that all five of them are seated at a restaurant together. Russell then feels happy because of that, being glad his whole team is present. After they are all seated, the waitress then asks all the men for their drink orders. Russell, Kevin and Brian order a Heineken beer. Jesse orders himself a Cadillac Margarita. Victor orders a double shot of gin and tonic. The men converse towards each other at the table, not revealing or discussing any information that they shouldn't be.

The restaurant they are currently in has other people present inside, and they should know better than to do that. Minutes later, the waitress returns to the table with their drinks. She then begins to take their food orders. Russell orders a steak and a baked potato. Kevin orders the barbecue ribs with mash potatoes. Jesse orders a grilled chicken Caesar salad. Brian orders a small order of hot chicken wings. Victor orders a chicken fried steak, with potatoes. The men sit and exchange in friendly conversation with each other, while they are waiting for their food.

The waitress shortly returns to the table with their plates. Each of them begin to eat, being satisfied with the way the food came out. The men proceed to talk to each other in friendly banter. As they are comfortable around each other's company, they all continue to talk among themselves. Russell however, is doing the least amount of conversing. He is having a one sided conversation with Kevin, listening to him ramble excessively. Russell can't stop thinking about their final heist on Friday. He takes more bites of his food, still realizing that this same exact group he's currently dining with, is the same one that is going to help him rob another bank. Russell looks around at all of the men on the table, and smiles to himself. He continues to pretend to be attentive towards Kevin's ranting.

Russell then looks up at the television located in the bar section, which is showing an NFL game. He feels the match isn't that exciting, as one team is clearly overpowering the other, and Russell turns his view back to Kevin. The men eventually start to wrap up their meals. During this time, the waitress returns to the table with the checkbook. While the other four men are talking amongst themselves, Russell grabs the checkbook, and reaches into his wallet. Kevin who was having a deep conversation with Brian, notices Russell doing this, and immediately snatches the checkbook from his hand.

"Russ, it's okay. Don't worry about it. I'll take care of it Russ."

Kevin rubs Russell's shoulder, and smiles at him. Kevin then takes out his wallet, and turns his head towards Brian, and resumes the conversation he was having with Brian. Russell then shakes his head, and looks at the television at the bar again. The football game is now nearly over, with one team dominating against the other. The waitress returns to the table, and Kevin hands her the checkbook with his credit card inside. While Kevin is still talking with Brian, Russell and Kevin unintentionally give each other eye contact, and smile at each other.

The waitress returns to the table with their receipt. Kevin puts it in his pocket, and takes out some cash bills and sets them inside the checkbook as a tip for the waitress. Brian who is noticing that Russell is watching the football game on the television, looks at the screen as well. The game ends a few minutes later with the team who was annihilating the entire game, winning. All of the men then get up from the table, and start to head out to the parking lot. They each say goodbye to each other, and Russell, Kevin and Jesse get into Russell's car. Brian and Victor carry on to "Home Base" riding with each other, going in their own separate way.

While in Russell's car, all of the men put their sunglasses on. Russell turns on the ignition, and proceeds to drive Kevin home. Kevin turns the car stereo on, and looks out the window quietly. As he's driving and paying attention to the road, Russell is very thankful and blessed to have Kevin as a friend. There are certain times to where Kevin does aggravate him and get on his nerves, though he is very thankful and glad to have him in his life.

Kevin as well feels safe around Russell. They both have had a distant friendship, only recently touching base with each other again. Kevin is well aware of Russell's intentions and attitude. His personality fits together along with his, which explains how easy it is for the both of them to work together. No matter how inane or unconventional their agendas may be. Kevin understands how Russell thinks, and believes that he can accept whatever shall come between the both of them. During this car ride, Russell and Kevin do not talk to each other, and they remain silent. The only sounds are coming from the car stereo.

Russell approaches Kevin's building, and pulls the car over to the curb. With the car stereo still playing, Kevin grabs his laptop bag. He looks behind him towards the rear seat and rubs Jesse's hair. Kevin then playfully fixes Russell's collar, and laughs at him. Kevin then nods his head towards Russell and walks out of the car. Jesse climbs up to the passenger seat as soon as Kevin gets up. Russell and Kevin then silently salute each other, and Kevin walks into his residence.

Russell then heads straight to his apartment. As he and Jesse walk in, Russell starts to feel lethargic, and heads straight to the bedroom. Jesse during this time, slips off his shoes and walks over to the living room and lays down on the sofa, watching "Happy Gilmore", on the television. Russell takes off his shoes and socks, and immediately curls up on the bed. Russell starts to feel drained, and as he's laying down with the covers over his head, he angrily screams out to Jesse.

"Jesse, can you close the fucking door please?"

Jesse gets up from the sofa, and closes Russell's bedroom door. Russell then seconds after that falls asleep. Russell didn't know why he felt so tired like this. He didn't feel sick at all, he just needed to rest. Russell continued to feel tired for the rest of the day.

The following day, Kevin stopped by Russell's apartment surprisingly. He virtually spent the entire day at Russell's place. Russell wasn't at all bothered that Kevin choose to come over. Russell and Kevin then started to play "Call of Duty", on Russell's PlayStation console. Kevin was clearly beating Russell very badly in the game. Kevin was an ace at video games, and mastered them extremely well. Jesse watched the both of them play, while he read his magazines on the sofa. He was happy that Russell and Kevin were playing video games together. Kevin liked the fact Russell enjoyed video games as much as he did, and it only made their friendship more solid in that regard. Russell didn't mind that he was being punished by Kevin at the game. As long as he was spending time with his best friend, and as long as Kevin was happy, none of that was an issue to him.

Russell prepared some spaghetti for all of them for dinner, which they ate. Later that night, Kevin dismissed himself, and said goodbye to both Russell and Jesse. Russell and Jesse soon after that went into the bedroom, and went to sleep.

The next morning, being that it's Monday, Russell and Jesse customarily got themselves ready for work. As they leave out the apartment complex, Russell notices the overcast and gloomy weather. It almost looks as if it's going to rain. The sky has an intense haze, filled with dark gray clouds. Russell heads over to Kevin's residence to pick him up. Kevin takes a seat in the passenger side, and before he continues driving, Russell texts Brian to let him know that he, along with Kevin and Jesse are heading towards the "Wittberg Law Offices". He then starts the ignition and heads towards the building. Russell arrives early, and they wait in the parking structure. Jesse looks at a news app on his phone, with Russell leaning his head against the door window with his eyes closed, as he's slightly tired.

Kevin then plugs in an auxiliary cable through the stereo connecting to this phone. He turns on a "This American Life" podcast, which Kevin likes to listen to. Much time later, Brian and Victor arrive at the parking structure. Once it's time for them to start working, all of the men then walk into the building, and begin their cleaning duties. The men stay focused towards their work, not wasting any time. At this point, they are well aware of the routine and protocol, and what tasks they need to do. The day carries on, with nothing irregular, or out of the ordinary commencing or happening.

When break time approaches, Russell puts away his cleaning supplies, and heads to the outside roof area of the building. As he's walking up the stairwell, Russell puts on his sunglasses, and takes out his pack of cigarettes. Reaching the roof area, he is not at all surprised to see the other four men smoking a cigarette as well. The sky is still extremely hazy and overcast. There is also a slight chilly breeze in the air. This isn't sunny California weather, and it is a unique change of climate.

All of the guys are quietly taking their break, with Jesse and Brian listening to music on their phones, and Victor reading the newspaper. Russell looks over at Kevin, and sees that he's smoking his cigarette, while he's leaning across the ledges of the building. Kevin takes puffs of his cigarette, looking down at the cars rushing down the streets. It is now rush hour traffic time. Even though the men have to work, various other people in the city are now returning home from their jobs.

Kevin who has his sunglasses on, looks over at Russell and smiles at him. Russell then tells all the guys very silently, that he wants them to all meet him in the same room they met last week, once they are done with all of their tasks for the day. The men all nod their heads to agree with him, and they each continue to enjoy their break. Upon time for them to resume work, they all leave the roof area, and return to completing their tasks. Each of them stay focused on what they have to do, without any complaints or problems.

The men finally wrap up all of their itineraries. Russell starts to head up to head up to the board room they used last week. He, along with the rest of the guys meet him up there. Russell unlocks the door to the room, and once all the men are inside, he locks the door behind him. Russell then opens the curtains of the room, and turns on the lamp by the table. The guys all sit and look at each other for a short while, then Russell starts to speak.

"I'm going to keep this short, sweet, brief, and to the fucking point. We all know what we have to do, and so I'm not going to take up the little time we have to explain each and every thing. With that, I want you all to listen carefully, and listen well."

The men keep their attention focused to Russell, and he continues.

"I've had two banks in mind, and both of the banks are about the same layout and experience. I had "First Savings and Trust" on Main St., and "First Federal" on Grand. I can't make my mind up, so I'm going to flip a coin, and that's the one we're going to take. Heads, we do 'First Savings and Trust. Tails, we do 'First Federal'. Alright, here I go."

Russell reaches into his pocket and takes out a quarter. He flips it, and it lands on heads. He shows the coin to the rest of the guys, and then puts the coin back in his pocket.

"Alrighty then. For our final heist, we're gonna do 'First Savings and Trust'. It's a slightly bigger bank than 'United Farmers', but don't worry guys. We're gonna go check it out tomorrow morning. Again, I don't want to waste any unneeded time. We know the drill. Victor, this time stick with the plan please. Oh shit, I almost forgot."

Russell then turns his head towards Brian, and he continues.

"Brian managed to get us two more getaway cars. Kev is going to drive the black van, I'm going to drive the Expedition, and Jesse can ride with me. Brian is going to drive the Tahoe, riding with Victor. We should be able to escape very easily this way, no problem."

Russell then turns his direction towards Kevin, and carries on with the plan of attack.

"Kev, only because this is going to be our final showdown, I'm going to allow you to use those detonation devices this time. However, be careful man. Only use them if you know exactly what you're doing Kev. Do you understand me?"

Kevin nods his head at Russell. Russell then gets up from his seat and looks out the window. As he's observing the surrounding buildings, he then wraps up the meeting.

"Okay gentlemen, that's about it. As I said, I don't want to waste any time, we all know the drill and how everything is going to go. So with that, I have nothing else to mention."

Following that, all of the men get up from the table, and start to walk out of the room. Russell and Brian then proceed to lock the entire building. The men head towards the parking structure, and leave out the building.

The following morning, after Russell and Jesse wake up and get themselves ready, Russell calls Brian and explains that he along with Kevin and Jesse are on their way to the "First Savings and Trust Bank". He tells Brian to meet him a couple blocks away from the bank, and to look for his car. Russell and Jesse then leave, and Russell picks up Kevin who has his laptop case. Russell then directly heads towards the vicinity of the bank. He parks at the area nearby, where he told Brian to meet up him at. Kevin immediately opens up his laptop case, and likewise as he did with the first bank they examined, he pulls out all his tools. He takes out the spy glasses, and opens up the feed software on his computer.

Kevin then opens up the alarm software so it can load, as he also intends to use that as well. Minutes later, Brian approaches the area, and parks directly behind Russell's car. Brian and Victor then walk to Russell's vehicle. Victor sits in the rear area of Russell's car with Jesse. Brian walks over to the passenger side door, and Kevin then starts to place the security glasses on him. Kevin also puts the earpiece in Brian's ear, so he can hear everything that is coming from Russell's car. Kevin then starts to speak to Brian.

"Okay Brian, you're the test dummy again. Make us proud man, do your thing buddy."

Brian laughs at Kevin, and starts to walk towards the direction of the bank. The feed software on Kevin's computer immediately captures everything the glasses pick up. The "First Savings and Trust Bank", is a high profile bank located in Downtown Los Angeles. It's positioned on a highly populated spot on Main St. however directly behind the bank is an indoor parking lot, which extends to Broadway Road. This gives an amazing secret route for the men to escape out of. The bank is one of the oldest in Los Angeles, along with 'First Federal', the bank they did not end up picking. It has both an old exterior and interior.

Having a classic theme and design to the bank. Brian continues to proceed to the bank, with the rest of the guys watching what he captures what the glasses pick up, on Kevin's computer screen. As Brian is walking to the bank, the alarm software that Kevin uses, is now finished loading, and he starts to scan their alarms. Russell looks at Kevin type heavily on the program, shaking his head. He cannot believe how much Kevin is skilled in this particular category. Using black market hacking software such as that, only makes Russell more optimistic on how society and the world can be oblivious to things such as that. Humans are truly evil, and can accomplish whatever they want to overthrow the natural order and flow of things. Using knowledge, to benefit whatever you want to scheme.

Russell continues to think to himself, and understand harsh truths. Criminals, like magicians, can trick and fool in a variety of ways, it's amazing how everything is structured the way it is. Intelligence can be used in multiple ways, and sometimes people overestimate what people are actually capable of. Russell can understand Kevin's desire to overthrow the boundaries of the entire infrastructure and and how things are running. Russell himself also has similar thoughts and agendas, and how he can use that for his own personal gain and success.

Kevin continues to operate through the computer software. He then reassures Russell.

"Okay Russ. Give me just a minute, and I'm going to see what this bank is made of."

Russell nods his head, while still looking at the screen. Brian then opens the door to the bank, walking through a lovely vestibule lobby area. There is an array of plants, and the way this area is setup, it looks like it's a rainforest.

The bank does not have a security guard duty, so already Russell begins to feel extremely confident over that. Russell has a well adverse knowledge to practically every bank located in the Los Angeles area. When he considers banks for them to hit, he narrows down the ones which he feels are the most vulnerable, and the easiest for them to target. This particular bank does not have an updated security system. For a bank this size, that is unacceptable, and that really shouldn't be the case. However, for the sake of this bank being the location for their next heist, this is considered an advantage.

Brian continues to walk through the bank, and Russell becomes slightly agitated when he sees that there are a large number of patrons inside the bank. Brian waits in the long tine extending to the teller. As they did previously, Brian is going to ask for change for the teller, so he's not drawing attention to himself by casing the bank. When he gets to the teller area, the guys will have a clear picture as to how the bank is setup, gaining a better knowledge of the entire layout.

As Brian waits in line at the teller, Kevin continues his attention towards the security alarm software. As he's going through it, Kevin then finds an amazing discovery on the alarm software. He laughs very loudly, and updates Russell and the other guys on the alarms.

"Holy shit Russ, this bank has shitty alarms. You would think they would have everything updated and everything well secured. Nope. These alarms aren't going to take any time at all to silence, and this is wonderful Russ. I can't believe how lazy people are nowadays. I know, assholes like me that are smart and have access to this is rare, but despite all that shit. There is no excuse for this bank to not be secure like this. Wow man. Ha-ha."

Russell softly punches Kevin on the chin, and looks back at the camera feed of the bank. Kevin then closes the alarm software, and starts to open the detonation software. Being that this is their last heist, Russell is allowing Kevin to use this software, should he choose to. This software is highly dangerous though, and requires someone to know exactly how they work. Kevin only has a very little understanding of the software, yet fully believes he can figure out how it all constructs itself.

When Brian gets closer to the teller, and starts to move his head around the area; knowing the camera inside the glasses will pick everything up. Russell then starts to see the vault area. It's located in a close proximity to the tellers. Being that this is going to be their last heist, Russell is heavily contemplating using an industrial drill, to gain access to the vault. He hasn't currently made his mind up on this yet, however he is strongly urged to go along with it. This is a thought that come Friday, he needs to make his mind up on. Brian continues to scan his head around the building, taking note at the lack of security cameras.

Russell noticed during his time working in the banking industry, that most banks used obsolete security cameras. This was something that always puzzled him, but there wasn't much that he could do to remedy this particular problem. Internal security affair departments of the bank are the ones that are in charge of this issue. Brian continues to wait in line behind the tellers. Kevin continues to go through the detonation software, researching it very carefully. He then starts to talk to Russell.

"Russ, I'm going to be honest, I'm not that familiar at all with this stuff, but that's quitters talk. I'm going to figure this out Russ, and this is going to help us a lot. There's a courtyard about a quarter mile from here, it would be the perfect spot to put the diversion at. I'll drive over there right before the heist, and place the detonators very carefully. Before you guys head into the bank, I'll set them off, and It will cause a loud bang, and everyone is going to be all worried, and distracted about that. This is going to be so good Russ."

Russell puts his hand under his neck and continues to watch the camera feed. By this point, Brian has finally reached the teller area. As suspected, Russell is glad the teller area is not secure in the slightest. It will grant them easy access to do the job efficiently and quickly. Russell also takes a closer look at the vault area. By using the industrial drills, they could possibly break through the vault barrier if they wanted to. Kevin continues to mess with the detonation software. He then talks to Russell.

"Russ, I'm also thinking of using the spare detonators to troll the people of the bank. You guys can drop them off at the entrance before you walk in. As you guys are coming out, I can set them off, causing a loud explosion. What do you think Russ, sounds good?"

Russell turns to look at Kevin with a disappointed face. He then responds to him.

"No Kev, don't do that. That's not our style. I'm all for you using the detonators as a distraction, as long as nobody gets hurt by that, but by doing extra unnecessary stuff, I don't think so Kev. I'm going to ask you not to do it Kev. Alright?"

Kevin with his vision still directed at his laptop, laughs and shakes his head at Russell.

"I was just fooling around Russ. You know I would never do something like that man. I was only joking Russ. But say if I did do it, that would be awesome and crazy right? Ugh, anyways Russ, I'll practice more on this later back at "Home Base" man. That whole area outside the unit will give me more than enough space to practice the detonators."

Kevin then shuts down the detonation software, and he then focuses his attention on Brian's camera feed. Russell looks down towards the ground and shakes his head. He then returns to watching the camera feed on the computer. Brian then starts to head back to Russell's car. Russell is comfortable heading towards Friday. Even though this is a much larger bank than the one they took on previously, it is still poorly operated and not secure. When it comes to a bank heist, performing one at this bank shouldn't be difficult at all. The problem Russell now must think about, is whether or not he wants to try to open the vault. Something he wasn't originally thinking about, which now lingers on his mind. If he does decide to go through with that, his whole plan might have to be slightly changed. Going for the vault means a bigger reward they will receive. He also wants Kevin to be well prepared when using the detonators. It is very important that Kevin has his safety in mind. Working with explosives, no matter how experienced or informed the person dealing with them is, still has a risk factor. Russell can only think positive towards Friday. He trusts all the rest of the men, and that seems to be enough.

Brian reaches the passenger side door, and takes off the camera glasses handing them to Kevin. Kevin puts the glasses, and his computer inside the laptop case. Brian then returns to his car, and all of the men head towards work. They are now finished with this task, and they have gathered enough information that they need. The men feel ready to take on this bank. Kevin will now use the time they have until Friday, to educate himself more on how the detonators work. For now, they do have to return to work. Russell and Victor arrive at the building, and they go inside. Without hesitation, they get their cleaning supplies and start working. As they do with any other day, keeping the fact they cased a bank earlier out of their minds. They strictly keep their minds towards their work.

When break time approaches, the men head up to the roof and smoke a cigarette. The sky is still overcast as it was the day before. Russell seems to be indifferent towards this cloudy overcast weather. When standing up high on the roof, the sky gives off an interesting feel. The men take their break time to relax, as they have been working hard the entire day.

They keep silent towards each other, not saying a single word. Not at all mentioning anything about the heist on Friday. They know that this is not the time and place to do so. Russell looks over at Kevin who's looking down the ledge of the roof as he usually does. He walks over to join him and looks down at all the cars and people below. He rubs Kevin's shoulder, and he then sits down at a benched area next to Jesse and Brian, who are also smoking their cigarettes. Victor sits on the side of the bench reading the newspaper. The men finish their break, and head back inside the building. Come evening time, it is significantly harder for them to do their tasks.

There are more tasks which need to be completed, and more office rooms that need to be covered, as employees have now gone home. The men struggle through the remaining hours they have left to work. All of them using all of their energy and strength to muscle through their objectives. Doing trash runs is also exhausting. Having to take their trash carts in the elevator, and go down to the parking lot dumpster every time their trash cart becomes full. It's a repetitious task, but it has to be done. Brian starts to deep mop the first floor. A task which arguably is the most tiresome to do.

Russell as he's cleaning, cannot stop thinking about the heist, and how well each of them are working together with this crusade. He finds it fascinating, that they all can be attentive towards planning criminal activity, yet be obedient enough to stay committed towards the work they have to do. Russell would never imagine he would be cleaning buildings. He would never imagine that he would ever rob a bank, but his life has been though many different changes lately.

The men finally finish all of their tasks, and start to put all the cleaning supplies away. Russell and Brian then start to lock the entire building up, shutting off all the lights as well. The men then exit out of the building, and head towards the parking structure. Russell, Kevin and Jesse say goodbye to Brian and Victor, and they all leave out of the parking structure, and head on about their way; with Brian and Victor going towards "Home Base". As Russell is driving down the road, Kevin pulls out his phone, and begins to speak with Russell.

"Hey Russ, I'm hungry. Can you stop at 'Del Taco'? I'll pay for whatever you and Jesse want. I haven't had anything to eat all day Russ."

Russell looks over at Kevin and and smiles. He then responds to him.

"Yeah Kev. I can take you wherever you want to go man."

As Russell is driving down the road, Kevin opens his laptop bag and takes out a bag of marijuana. Even though Russell is driving and has his mind on the road, he knows exactly what Kevin is doing. Russell starts to grin to himself due to that. Kevin quickly starts to roll a marijuana joint. After Kevin is done rolling the joint, he grabs a lighter from his laptop bag. Kevin puts the joint in his mouth, and turns to Russell who is still driving. Kevin then asks Russell a question.

"Russ, you don't mind if we smoke this in here do you?"

Under regular circumstances, Russell would not allow for this. However, Russell as of late is bending every single rule and agenda he used to follow. Russell replies to Kevin.

"Kev, I don't give a fuck man. You can do whatever you want."

Kevin laughs at Russell, and lights the joint. He takes a hits from it, before reaching behind him and passing the joint to Jesse. Jesse takes a hit from the joint, and passes it back to Kevin. Kevin then takes another hit of the joint, and passes it to Russell, who takes a hit of the joint while he's driving. The men continue to smoke the rest of the marijuana joint. Kevin puts the tip of the joint back in his marijuana bag, and puts the bag into his laptop case. Russell then playfully punches Kevin on the chin, before playfully arguing at him.

"Kev, you got my car smelling like weed man. What the hell?"

Russell Kevin, and Jesse all laugh at each other, and Russell continues down the road. He eventually reaches "Del Taco". Kevin orders a California Burrito, a side order of fries, four tacos and a Coke. Russell orders a Supreme Burrito, a bean and cheese burrito, and a Sprite soda. Jesse orders a chicken quesadilla, two fish tacos, and a Root Beer. After getting their food, Russell gets on the highway, heading towards Santa Monica. Not alerting the rest of the guys of his destination. Kevin and Jesse are at first puzzled at where Russell is going, but then they immediately accept the suspense and surprise. Kevin turns up the volume on the stereo, being pleasured by the music.

Russell soon gets off the highway, and heads towards the beach and pier area. He parks the car, in the parking lot facing the ocean. Getting a clear view of the "Pacific Wheel" Ferris Wheel, at the Santa Monica pier. As it has been cloudy all day, the night gives off a lovely bright orange color in the sky. This causes the night sky to have a unique glow and hue to it. Giving a very warm and interesting display. The smell of the ocean is also lovely, and the sound of the waves and tide coming though are peaceful to hear. All three of men gaze at the beauty of this scene. The men then eat their food, while looking at the view. Kevin while taking bites of his food, starts to talk to Russell.

"Russ, thanks man. I haven't been to the beach in ages. I can't believe I live in LA, and I never come to the fucking beach. I don't understand that at all."

Russell eats some of his food, and responds to Kevin.

"I figured you would like this Kev. It's been quite a while since I've been here too. I come here from time to time. During nights like this, it's nice to sit and watch everything."

Kevin continues to eat his food, and nods his head at Russell. He then continues.

"Yeah Russ, this is really something. That Ferris Wheel is cool too. I like the lights. The patterns, and how it changes like that. I can probably figure out all the mechanics they use to make it go like that. I like how the LED lights go with the night sky and the ocean."

Jesse who's sitting in the back, then talks to the rest of the guys.

"This is one of the few things I like about California. The beaches, and this whole aesthetic and vibe. It's only a handful of places you can get a scene like this. Los Angeles is one of them. This is remarkable, and I'm happy to be able to see something like this."

Kevin then quickly responds to Jesse, as he's eating his food.

"I have to agree with you man, interesting observation Jesse. California does have hidden gems such as this, you have to admit that."

Russell nods his head at Kevin, and eats more of his food. He looks over at Kevin looking out the windshield towards the ocean. Russell smiles to himself, and continues to eat. Kevin then takes more bites, and continues to talk to Russell.

"Russ, do you know how to surf man?"

Russell while looking out towards the ocean, responds to Kevin.

"Uh, no Kev. I don't surf. I play football and hockey. I'm Russian, not Hawaiian Kev. I don't surf. But I appreciate you asking me if I did. Ha-ha. Do you surf Kev?"

Kevin laughs to himself, and while he's taking bites of his food, responds to Russell.

"Oh no Russ. I'm way to stumpy and short to surf. I mean it seems fun, but I don't know. I wouldn't be able to keep my balance like that. Usually surfers look like Matthew McConaughey, and not like me Russ. So no, I don't surf."

Russell laughs, and shakes his head at Kevin. Kevin then speaks to Russell softly.

"Thank you again Russ. I know you get tired of me saying thank you, but oh well."

Russell while looking ahead towards the ocean, smiles to himself. The men start to finish eating their food. Russell grabs all of their trash, and throws it away in a nearby trash can. He then gets back into the car, starts the ignition and drives towards Kevin's residence. During this ride back, all of the men in the car remain quiet. Russell when he approaches Kevin's building, pulls up to the curb and cuts the ignition off. Kevin then begins to grab his laptop bag, and opens the passenger door. Kevin without saying a word, then starts to walk towards his building. Jesse then gets out of the car, and starts to hug Kevin very tightly. Kevin who wasn't expecting that laughs, and starts to speak to Jesse, while he's still hugging him.

"Ha-ha, Jess. I love you too. You'll see me tomorrow man. Okay?"

Kevin kisses Jesse on the cheek. Jesse then responds to him.

"Good night Kevin. See you later man."

Russell who was watching all of this, gets out of his car and hugs Kevin. Once they finish hugging, Kevin then takes his laptop case, smacking Russell in his rear with the case, and laughs. Russell then immediately takes Kevin's glasses off, teasing him. Waving them up in the air for Kevin to grab them. Russell slaps Kevin on his rear, laughing as well.

"Good night Kev."

Russell hands Kevin back his glasses, and Russell gives Kevin a kiss on his forehead. Kevin then takes his hand and smacks Russell on his rear, and laughs. Kevin then responds to him.

"I love you Russ. See you in the morning man."

Russell and Kevin, hug one final time. Russell, Kevin and Jesse all wave goodbye to each other, as Kevin walks into his building. Russell and Jesse then get back into the car, and Russell drives home.

CHAPTER 16:

NOTHING GOOD, NOTHING BAD

During the days leading up until the heist, the men feel safe and confident. They have already accomplished success with their first heist, so this shouldn't be any different. Nothing should come strange, or out of the ordinary for them to manage or deal with. The men have already scoped out the bank they are going to target, likewise as they did with their first bank they hit. For this heist is their last, every one of the men want to leave out of it feeling victorious. Confidence is very beneficial at this point, as if they don't believe in their actions, they won't be able to gain anything positive from their adventures. From the time they have spent around each other's company, the men developed a close bond. In order to pull off a bank heist, you need to have a core team that works well under pressure. With their first heist, they did have some slight mistakes. They hesitated going into the bank originally, and one of their men was attacked with a dye pack. Besides that, they had a flawless performance. Due to that event, the men now feel they have received enough experience to carry on with the next heist.

The men agreed to do only one more heist, to stick it to all the oppression they face in their everyday lives. Using this agenda, they picked a much larger bank than the one they previously used. Being this will be the last time they will be doing this criminal act, they want to finish it with style. Once this heist is completed, the men will continue on their lives, going about their separate lifestyles. However, keeping their friendship together still. These men don't consider themselves career criminals or violent people. From all the harsh situations they have been approached with, they are simply misunderstood creatures; feeling unwanted in general society. There is only so much that a man can take mentally, before he starts to feel completely outcast from others.

These five men under immense pressure and high energy, act in the way they wish to. Acting in a way they were conditioned to, and in a manner that they feel is the only option for them. Taking on this unusual method of behaving and plotting, believing nothing really is to lose or is at stake. Honestly, the men need to realize how in over their heads they actually are. They are taking on a violent rush of activities, and this is sadly brushed away by each of their mental instabilities. Illogical thinking is running rampant in all of their minds.

Living in the moment, and not seeing the full spectrum of the issues and consequences they might be approached with. A major mistake these men are making, is possibly acting fast and swift; and not acting slow but accurate. Not wasting time is an important mindset to have, but when it comes to crucial situations such as committing bank heists, there is not any room at all for error or mistakes if they can be avoided and blocked.

With the days looming towards the heist, the men continue their cover job without any hassle. They don't want to doubt themselves by feeling anxious. They have already gotten away with one heist, and now going towards their second and last heist. As they are working, a policy they secretly seem to keep to each other, is that none of the men talk or brag about the heist. It is important for them to feel confident at this stage, however they don't want to over embellish themselves with any unwanted emotions and expressions. The men are travelling across highly classified and personal and criminal waters. They cannot risk being too careless with the way they present themselves towards the rest of the world. Anything they can do to conform their agendas publicly away from others, is necessary. The cleaning job allows for all of the men to come together, and hide their true selves from ordinary people. Despite the fact they gather around during the week and clean buildings together in peace, it doesn't cover the fact these men are criminals. They have dangerous agendas running all across their minds. Keeping in mind, any mental difficulties each man is trying to battle in his own right and conscious.

It is now Friday; the day the men have all set aside to do their last heist. This will be the final curtain call for all the men. Following today, the men will no longer consider themselves outlaws, and will have proven their point enough to be happy and satisfied from what they were able to complete. Each of the men are gathered outside of the "Home Base" unit. It was this same time last week, in which they all prepared for their previous heist. It is now 2 P.M. The same identical time they all branched out the week before.

The men have done all of this before, yet nothing is guaranteed to go completely as planned in life. Original intentions are likely to be changed, especially when you factor in the nature of the situation. A bank heist brings much pressure, and stress towards all of the men. Mentally as they did before, they all begin to offer minor self-reflection, before they head off and commit another dangerous heist.

Russell is well aware of the magnitude of this current setting. All of this was originally his idea and plan. Russell from the beginning wanted to pull off a bank heist, as the ultimate rebellion of his original lifestyle. Russell was simply an ordinary man, living by ordinary standards. That is not the case anymore, he is now permanently mentally scarred from events he didn't ask to happen, or be included in. On the outside, you would never assume a man like Russell would dare risk his profile and reputation to continue with activities such as this. Russell being on the edge of losing hope with following the rules he's suspected to do, is no longer mentally concerned about any of that.

This is his lifestyle now, and this is the one that he's choosing to live by. The consequences he may face from his choices; are simply those he's going to have to accept. His newly found vindictive personality, is one that he feels people should understand and relate to.

Going into this last heist, Russell wants to move ahead with both sides of what makes him who he is. The side that is the more professional Russell, and the person he used to be. The guy who always followed the rules, and went by the book and codes he was meant to follow and obey towards. Then the other side of Russell, who is more willing to act more dangerously and on unpredictable impulse. Following whatever thoughts or plans he wants to follow, and acting in a way to which the reward is only given by immersing yourself under irregular objectives.

Like with the previous heist, Russell sets himself in position to become the bad guy. He doesn't enjoy breaking the law, but it's at the point to where doubting yourself doesn't much any sense at all. Russell realizes that he must adapt himself one final time, to accomplish all the dangers that this heist will bring. He is confident with his participation, and the help of the rest of his men, they will once again leave out of this event successfully. Russell is completely ready to proceed towards their mission, and commands his feelings to a more relaxed state.

Kevin being a kind hearted man, always tries to see the positives in every person. Coming into this heist, not being directly related to the "Sunset Credit Union" incident at all. He latches himself onto others, which he feels he can relate a higher regard to. This however can make Kevin an easy target, as he is quick to not judge others. He sees the world in a different light and tone, willing to give people the benefit of the doubt even if they truly don't deserve to.

Kevin also has a hyperactivity issue. If he's determined to go along with a particular subject or plan, it's going to be difficult to convince him to move away from it. Kevin being skilled in computer hacking, makes him believe that he's invincible to any category related to that. Kevin believes that using both man power, and artificial technology power can lead to a winning combination.

Feeling out of place and mismatched compared to other men, he immerses himself with computers to make up for all of his errors that he faces in the typical world. His friendship and connection with Russell, is something that is a key point towards all of these ordeals. He thrives on knowing that he's making others happy, also finding a place and position to belong to. Going into this final heist, he will give his total best. Kevin realizes that he is being an important member of the team, along with the other guys.

Jesse approaches all of these events in shock. Wanting to feel included and accepted, he goes along with choices and plans he shouldn't be agreeing with. His submissive attitude, allows him to deal with any pain or issues he encounters. Jesse has never had a supportive system growing up, he uses his experiences with the rest of the guys as his second family. He wants to use this current time, to think of it as a method to vent all of his turmoil's over. He doesn't know why things happen the way they do. Jesse is not proud to be attaching himself towards criminality, but he is acceptance towards it. The feeling of wanting to be included, even if this inclusion is surrounded by negativity.

Jesse simply wants to find his own meaning in the world, and he does not find it easy to deal with being secluded. Jesse feels like he was born to be someone, that he doesn't wish to be. Being underprivileged for most of his life, and being rejected for no reason in situations. Jesse finds it very unfair. Finally, being around a group of men he feels glad towards. Having a strong support group with the rest of the guys, allows Jesse to forget about all of that. That's all he wanted in his life, to be accepted and loved despite his social status and personality. Jesse is safe and secure around them, and advances through this final heist eager to perform well.

Brian has the most criminal experience out of all the guys. He isn't a violent man at all, but he has much experience towards living his life against the law. Including himself with many groups, some of which aren't positive environments to be dealing with. Brian at first didn't want to join the group, and was on the path to leaving these types of behaviors and actions behind him. Understanding that he's not dealing with a typical group of outlaws, and all of the men himself included, don't quite fit into the regular mold as to what a criminal consists of.

He makes a large exception to his traditional values. Trusting the other four guys, he is aware that each of them has a lot to prove to themselves. Their mental struggles each of them deal with, causes them to fight back. Even though he has great knowledge towards his kingpin like lifestyle, and working around situations such as that. Robbing banks, isn't the only thing he likes. Brian enjoys his hobby of cars, and that's his main ambition. Getting sidetracked and including himself with the dangers of unrelated agendas and tasks, makes him more agitated towards his own personality. Brian walks into this last heist, optimistic of his future endeavors. For this one last time, he will offer his help. He is strong minded, and his attitude is powerful. Brian has to spring into action, in this pivotal moment.

Victor uses his eccentric personality to his advantage usually. As much as he hates the seclusion he deals with from other individuals, part of him is glad that his personality causes fear and ambiguity towards outsiders. Being a man of mystery when it comes to outwitting yourself to social standards, is a positive trait that Victor at times is thankful and glad about. Victor is being rewarded with his unique personality in this case. The rest of the guys put up with the way he deals with his life. He is a man that generally means no harm. Exterior wise, Victor does give off a beastly threatening profile. However, this is not truly the case always. Victor is very much a misunderstood man that like the other four, views life from an entirely different lens and scope. His mind is more directed and geared towards opportunity.

The rejection he faces, gives him the opportunity to reject himself from others as well. Why should he mold himself into this ideal person, if others won't respect him? Doing these heists give many perspectives towards Victor's opinions. The dye pack exploding in his arm, in which you can still see the paint stain, makes him think about this entire venture. Proceeding towards this final heist, Victor takes in all the experiences he's learned. The time he's spent around the other men. Victor decides to keep being himself through it all.

With it now being the day of the heist, it all comes down to this. The weather is perfect, and warm. The skies are a typical shade of blue. Regularly, this would be a typical afternoon. The men are approaching their final heist together. With tensions becoming high, they continue to psych themselves up for all that is going to occur. They have no idea what is to come. Despite the fact they carefully planned and mapped their whole situation out clearly, the unpredictable still has a way of revealing itself. Russell's main concern was whether or not to use the special industrial power drills, to gain access to the vault.

Another concern Russell was having, was allowing Kevin to use the detonation devices and software. For the past two days, Kevin has been doing practice runs with the detonators outside the unit at "Home Base". Even though Kevin has gained much practice with how the detonators are setup, he still is not completely sure on how they are implemented. Russell must believe in all the strengths his men can exhibit. He knows they all have the potential to persevere towards anything. The men are also slightly afraid of being captured by the authorities. This was something in their first heist they also felt much worry and concern over. Keeping in mind their careful planning beforehand, they do feel the chances of them being captured and caught aren't that high.

Making the right decisions under pressure, and working together will cease any of these thoughts. Not wanting to feel over confidence to the stress, the men were able to finish the heist a week ago successfully. It doesn't make them completely calm with their nerves, however they do feel slightly sure of themselves. As this is their final heist, the men will take whatever situations thrown at them, and push their limits to full capacity. The rewards they gain from this heist, will be enough for all of the men to perform with great accuracy as a team. Making any type of mistakes isn't acceptable at this point, they need to achieve victory. Using every advantage and tactics to give a perfect performance.

Upon completing this heist, the men will rejoice in happiness. Their agenda was fulfilled, by rebelling against their feelings. Having the wit to pull of their last heist. Each man knows his own position towards their main goal. This is probably the main motivation they all have in their minds. The feel of finishing this heist together. Putting all the energy they have from being mistreated by the world, and using that as fuel to push through all the boundaries and obstacles. With only a short time until the heist commences, anxiety is starting to boil within all of the men. It is time for them to get into action, and to position themselves for this heist.

The thrill on all of their minds is only natural and suspected. In order to do something like this, your mind must be adapted to handle the stress of it all. Switching your attitude into that particular moment is key. As with their last heist, they cannot succumb or give into the pressure they are feeling. If they give into the pressure, they can make careless mistakes, and disaster might approach. With the men being confident upon each other, and figuring out how to proceed with the heist as a team, they need not worry about such things. The confidence that each man holds within, is all that should matter.

The men are now standing in the unit at "Home Base", and looking at all of their tools and accessories they will use for the robbery. Brian takes all of the guns, checking to see if they are properly loaded and locked. He then sets all the guns down on a counter located inside the unit. Using the guns strictly as an intimidation factor. Identical as they did in the last heist, the men begin to get into their disguises. They are wearing the same exact setup they wore previously, which consist of all black combat gear. This includes them each wearing the same heavy black windbreakers. Victor however is wearing a different one, as his past windbreaker is stained from when he was hit with the dye pack. Other aspects of their disguise, include black cargo snow pants, and thick black ski caps. With the ski cap, the men wear dark sunglasses to cover their eyes, and black bandanas to cover their mouth region. This forms a mask, making their facial identity hard to detect. All of the men are wearing thick gloves on their hands as well, they are all also wearing black snow boots in addition to that. The men are now all suited with their disguises on.

For this heist, the men are going to be using three separate vehicles. All of the vehicles contain dark tinted windows, so the identities of the people inside cannot be seen. Two of the vehicle's, Brian was successfully able to steal from a crooked car dealer. Brian also modified these cars during the past week, so they can be fast enough to be evade the authorities easily, offering an excellent plan of escape. Russell and Jesse will be riding in the Ford Expedition. Brian and Victor will be riding in the Chevy Tahoe. Kevin will be using the black van from the first heist. Russell for this heist is planning to use the industrial drill to gain access to the vault. He will take the biggest drill located in the unit, to which he feels is the most powerful. Russell puts that drill in a large duffel bag. Russell will use another large duffel bag to put inside whatever money he gains from the vault. Brian will take two large duffel bags, and take whatever he can from the tellers, and the cash carts behind them. Victor and Jesse will be positioned out on the lobby floors as backup.

Kevin will drive to the diversion location to set the detonators. After setting the detonators, he will then drive to the outside end of the bank disabling the security alarms. He will stay outside the entrance of the bank on the surface streets, as a lookout. Speaking to the rest of the men through their headsets. He will wait until the guys leave the bank, heading towards their own separate getaway vehicles in the parking structure located directly behind the bank. Kevin will then leave after the rest of the men exit out of the bank.

The men are all in the unit, looking over all of their tools and supplies. In only a few short minutes, they all will leave to the bank. Brian then gives the keys of the vehicles to Russell and Kevin. Following this, the men grab all of their essentials. Russell and Jesse begin to set their guns in the back area of their getaway vehicle. Russell sets the bag containing the drill inside the back, and also sets the empty duffel bag right next to it. Brian and Victor set their guns in the back of their vehicle as well. Brian then puts both of his large empty duffel bags in the back of the vehicle along with that. Kevin gathers all of the detonation devices, and gets his laptop case. He sets them in the black van.

The men are virtually about ready to proceed towards the bank. At this moment, as they did in the previous heist, the men huddle together for nearly a minute. They wrap their arms in a circle, and hug each other, showing love and affection among each other. With this particular heist, the men are going to be separated from each other during the majority of it. It is a scary thought knowing all of them are going to be in separate cars. However, this is a more accurate way of executing the heist. It should allow for a smooth escape, once they have finished the heist. While the men feel anxious due to the pressure of splitting up, they understand it's the nature of the heist. They each care about one another, and try to be brave and strong, so they can finish the job well. Once the men finish their embrace, they immediately begin to prepare to depart from the unit.

Kevin then gives each of the guys a headset earpiece. The earpieces only allow for Kevin to speak to them, they cannot respond. Russell then stands in front of all the men, and runs the entire plan through.

"Listen guys. This is how we are going to approach this. We are all gonna head out and head back in separate cars. That's how we're gonna do it. Kev is going to take the van, and plant the diversion a few blocks away from the bank. The rest of us are going to head straight to parking lot behind the bank. Once we are there, we will wait for Kev to tell us he's disabled the alarms. Kev will stay across the street as our lookout, as we run from the parking lot, to the bank. Once we get inside the bank and walk through the doors, Kevin who's watching us, then will set off the diversion. Do you understand me so far?"

All of the guys nod their head in agreement with Russell, and Russell continues.

"Once in the bank, Brian I want you to take care of the tellers and the cash carts. I will start to drill in the vault. Jesse and Victor, I want you guys to remain in the lobby. Do you understand Victor? Remain in the lobby, I don't want you doing anything else man. Then once we are all done, we head out. Kevin will see us run away, then he will drive back here along with us. If we all work together and work quick and fast, we'll be out of there very fast. Now let's do this, I have faith in all of you men. Let's get this done."

The men nod their heads to agree with Russell. Brian heads over to the garage gate, and proceeds to unlock and open it. Once he is able to get the door open, on the other side, he notices Max. Max walks into the unit and starts to speak to all of the men.

"What timing, I caught all of you right in the knick of time I see. I said to myself, if I came over here and they were already gone, then oh well. Luckily, you guys are still here. It was meant to be I suppose. Anyways, I want you guys as always to be careful. I am hoping the best for each of you. Please stay safe you guys. I care about all of you."

Brian opens the garage gate, and walks over to Max to speak to him.

"Yeah, we were just about to get going. You caught us in the right time indeed man, how funny. Everything is all set, and we're ready to go. As you're here, I do want to say how grateful I am to have you assisting us like this. Max, thank you for all your help. Thank you for being here, and just you supporting us man. We're going to do alright, and do better than we did last time. We all know what we have to do, and we all planned it well. It's now executing it fast and well. That's not a problem at all. We got this, piece of fucking cake."

Russell walks over and talks to Max.

"I also want to sort of ditto what Brian got through saying. I am glad that you've decided to give us a chance and trust us. We wouldn't be able to accomplish any of this without your help. I'm thankful, and the rest of the guys are thankful as well. Thank you."

Kevin walks over to Max and talks to him as well.

"Your detonation software is really something Max. I've been studying it all week, and I think I got it down. There are still some minor kinks I'm not entirely sure I've managed to fix. That's okay, as I basically got the general idea on how they work. They are going to be a major help with this heist, and I'm so glad to use them."

Max puts his hand over Kevin's shoulder, and softly responds to him.

"Be extremely careful with those. They are wonderful gadgets yes, but they can also be dangerous to work with as well. I don't want you to get hurt by using them. I'll take your word that you have studied them enough to properly manage them. Please be careful."

The detonators are an interesting tool to use for a bank heist; causing a distraction and diversion, however they are in fact risky to use. Even the slightest error when trying to connect the computer software to make them explode, can cause unfortunate results. The detonators can go off for no reason if they aren't calibrated correctly. Kevin does have complete control to if, and when the detonators go off by computer. However, they can also explode without being controlled to by the computer program. If someone moves by the detonator, and it wasn't properly coded by the computer, it will explode and go off in that case. Despite all of this, Kevin feels he has enough knowledge to deal with these detonators. He feels comfortable enough to use them in the heist, as a major advantage to their tactics. Kevin replies to Max.

"Don't worry, I have it under control and I know the risk factors. I appreciate your concern, but please don't worry about any of that. I have it all under control, and everything is going to plan out fine. That's why I did many practice runs with them. I wouldn't be using them if I wasn't sure I could plant and code them right."

Kevin then pats Max on the shoulder, and Max smiles back at him. Russell then starts to slightly worry about Kevin. He walks over to him and puts his hand on his shoulder.

"Kev, listen to me. If you don't want to use the detonators, you don't have to. I know I said you could use them, but if you don't feel safe about it, you can leave them alone, and it won't bother me at all. It's your choice Kev. Whatever you do, I'll be okay with. I only care about your safety, and I don't want to see you get hurt man. Be careful Kev, alright?"

Kevin starts to walk towards the van, while talking to Russell.

"Russ, this is my specialty man. I know all about computers, and all this fancy stuff. This is where I come in and offer my skills, over stuff like this. If this is going to be our last heist, why not do it in style Russ? You said it yourself, which is why you have the drill. So you can use the drill to open the vault, but I can't use the detonators? Come on Russ, you know that's not fair at all. I should be able to have fun as well. Come on Russ."

Russell looks down towards the ground, and then starts to hug Kevin.

"Kev, I only want you to be careful man. I love you too much, and care about you."

Brian walks over to Russell and Kevin, and angrily speaks to them.

"You guys, we are gonna have to move out of here. I appreciate all the sentimental shit, but we don't have any time for that. We have to get going, like, now. Come on guys."

Max then proceeds to walk away from the unit, saying goodbye to the men.

"Again, I want you guys to take care and be safe. I was scared the first time you guys went out. This time I'm not as nervous, but I still care about all of you. Work together, and please be safe. I want to see all of you later celebrating, and I'll celebrate with you. For now, I'll wish you guys goodbye, and I shall see you later. Take care you guys."

The men then wave goodbye to Max, and he leaves the area of the unit. They each then get inside of their vehicles. Kevin gets inside of the black van and starts the ignition. Directly to the right of the van, is the vehicle Russell is driving, with Jesse sitting in the passenger seat. Russell turns on the ignition and waits. Right behind Russell is the vehicle Brian will be driving, with Victor in the passenger seat. Kevin then tests the earpiece system.

"Alright. I'm going to head out now guys. Before I go, if you guys can hear me, I want all of you to honk your horns now. Once I hear the horns, I'll take off towards where I need to go and plant the detonators. As soon as I get to the bank, I'll let all of you know. I'm going now."

Russell and Kevin honk their horns, conforming they can hear Kevin through the earpiece system. Immediately after that, Kevin drives out of the unit, and heads straight to the location to plant the diversion detonator. Directly behind Kevin, Russell drives out of the unit, and heads towards the "First Savings and Trust" bank. Brian creeps out of the garage door of the unit, and gets out of the vehicle. After shutting and locking the gate, he gets back into the car and heads towards the bank. Each of the men are now on the highway, heading towards the same area following each other. The highway has slight traffic, which is very custom for Los Angeles. The men are all keeping a moderate speed, trying act as normal as they can. Russell is driving directly behind Kevin in the same lane on the highway. They are not going to the same destination though. Russell along with Brian, will be going to the bank. Kevin will be heading towards a courtyard area nearby, to plant the diversion. Russell while he's heading towards the bank, starts to feel slightly worried about Kevin. He honestly feels that Kevin shouldn't be dealing with any of the detonation software. They are far too dangerous to not take lightly, or without great concern and care. Russell at this point can only trust Kevin's expertise towards things such as that. Russell also starts to feel scared, as he cannot keep in contact and talk to Kevin. He again, can only trust Kevin's own behavior and actions.

Russell then is beginning to slightly regret planning for the guys to split up on the way to the bank. In the first heist, he was more secure and felt comfortable, because all of the guys were in the same van. The fact they are split up and travelling in different directions, causes Russell to be anxious somewhat. He does however still believe that this can be a satisfactory method for them to finish the heist in an orderly manner. Brian who's briefly speeding, is able to catch up to Kevin and Russell. The men keep a straight single file line on the lane. Brian along with Russell, for some reason is starting to worry about Kevin as well. Brian now starts to also believe that separating and splitting up wasn't such a good idea, despite it being a swifter way for them to travel to and from the heist. It's interesting how when they were planning the heist, it seemed it was a good idea. Now that the action has started to commence, and they are on the spot, they start to have second thoughts about it. Jesse who's sitting next to Russell in their vehicle, remains quiet, submissive and relaxed. He trusts Russell, and he understands that they are now committing a heist; he needs to be completely focused. Victor is also keeping calm at the moment. He is sitting beside Brian in their vehicle. Victor is under a great amount of stress, but he is managing to get his emotions in order.

All five of the men in separate vehicles continue down the highway, anticipating all the events they are about to commit. The men stay in very close proximity, making sure not to lose track of each other.

As they stay on the highway, the traffic starts to dwindle down, and the men instinctively speed up at that point. The bank is not far from the distance the men at currently at. Staying on the highway, the men still form a single line together on the lane, one right behind the other. Russell then starts to notice that Kevin is starting to pick up speed. He is very puzzled as to why Kevin feels the need to drive that fast. They are still on the highway, so there is no need for Kevin to separate and distance himself at this point. Russell shakes his head, as Kevin starts to speed up even more, and stray away farther down the lane. Russell has no choice but to speed up as well in order to stay in Kevin's distance. Brian who was right behind Russell, increase his speed too, so all the men remain together. Russell can only assume that Kevin is possibly nervous and anxious, and that explains his sudden burst of erratic driving. He doesn't want them to cause any attention to themselves if they can avoid it. If they are speeding down the highway at high speeds, it will alarm the other drivers on the road. Something like that will have people assume they are up to no good, and that isn't what Russell needs at this point.

Kevin continues to keep a high speed down the highway. Russell wishes he could speak to Kevin, and tell him to decrease his speed. The men are trying to be inconspicuous, and are trying to blend in as much as they can. Driving fast, is putting an unneeded target on their back. Brian can tell that Kevin is speeding as well. He knows that Russell wouldn't be increasing his speed that fast, unless Kevin who was travelling in front of him was speeding. Brian like Russell, doesn't understand why Kevin is driving the way he is either. Only guessing that Kevin is under stress and doesn't realize what he's doing. Russell tries to think of a way to signal to Kevin to slow down. Russell thinks to himself for a minute, and wonders if he uses his windshield wipers, would Kevin get the hint or not. He then decides not to do it, as he's not sure Kevin would understand the message or point behind that. A few minutes later, Kevin does return to a normal speed down the highway.

Russell then begins to feel more calm, and not as tense as he was; knowing that Kevin is no longer speeding.

The men stay on the highway, until the reach the exit heading towards the surface streets. After getting off the highway, the men continue to keep close towards each other. Being only a few blocks away from the bank, Kevin begins to make his turn, towards the diversion area. Russell and Brian continue through a separate route to the bank. The men are separated at this point. With Russell driving, he starts to have an unwanted anxious feeling course all through his body once more. They did agree to split up at this point of the heist, but Russell still feels uncomfortable. Again, when the men were planning all out of this out, it seemed easy to understand and accept. With the fact they are now sticking to the plan and living it out, it's a different feeling.

Deep regret is now starting to flow all throughout Russell. He begins to completely feel that perhaps made a mistake by allowing Kevin to separate from them. Despite his methods of trying to self-assure himself that everything will go according to how they mapped it out, it's still not enough to calm Russell down. Russell tries his best to ignore all of these doubts that he's feeling, and continues to head towards the parking structure of the bank. Brian starts to feel apprehensive. He along with Russell, is worried about Kevin. It's too late for them to go back on their plan, and these feelings they are experiencing, have to be ignored. The heist is going to go through in only a couple minutes or so. They have to proceed, and stick with the plan. Being worried and anxious isn't going to help them any. As Russell and Brian are seconds away from pulling up to the bank, Kevin finally reaches the diversion area.

Kevin pulls up to the curb, and parks the van outside of a courtyard, located a couple blocks away from the bank in front of a commercial office building. From the way he's parked against the curb, there is an array of bushes and shrubbery to where he's going to put the devices at. He's offered enough ambiguity, to where outsiders cannot detect what he's doing. While he's parked, Kevin gets his laptop case, and quickly turns on the computer. With the computer on, he navigates over to the detonation software. It takes a minute for the computer load the program up. After the program loads, Kevin carefully enters in the correct coordinates to operate the detonators. Once he's finished processing all of the information into the computer, Kevin then grabs two of the detonators. He grabs two, only in case if the first one does not explode. There is a chance that the detonators might not explode due to a rare chance of malfunction glitches. If he uses two of them, if one detonator doesn't go off, the other should without any issue. Kevin has two more spare detonators that he is not going to use. He sets them in the back of the van. Kevin reaches across to the passenger side door of the van, and briefly cracks it open. He tosses both detonators into the bushes in the courtyard.

Kevin quickly closes the door, and starts to set the detonators, using the program on the computer. They detonators are now set, so all Kevin has to do is click on button on the computer when he's ready, and the whole area will give off a powerful distraction explosion. It should cause the authorities to head over to that area, instead of heading towards the bank. Kevin then starts to drive over to the bank. Russell and Brian finally reach the parking lot of the "First Savings and Trust" bank. They park on the end of the parking structure, so then can quickly get in and out of the area quickly. Russell reaches behind him and grabs his gun, the duffel bag containing the drill, and the empty duffel bag. Jesse also grabs his gun from this section as well. Brian grabs both of his duffel bags, and his gun. Directly following him, Victor reaches back and grabs his gun. All four of the men wait for Kevin to arrive across the street, so he can disable the alarms inside the bank. During this time, the men are starting to feel the same exact way they felt during their first heist. This feeling shouldn't be happening at all. If anything, they should be feeling confident of themselves. They have done a bank heist before. This is going to be their final heist, and they should not have any doubts running through their minds.

Kevin at this time finally arrives across the street from the bank. From the position that he's parked, there is a fenced barrier blocking the other side of the street, where the bank is located. Kevin then starts to disable the alarm system of the bank. He is able to do quickly, and soon as he's done with that, he alerts the other guys to head inside the bank through their earpieces. Right them, all four of the men get out their vehicles, and lock them. Russell is carrying his gun in his hands, the duffel bag containing the drill, is strapped around his shoulder. Also carrying another duffel bag, containing the drill. Brian is carrying the empty duffel bag around his shoulder, with his second bag also stuffed inside. Victor and Jesse are carrying their guns.

The men continue to race through the parking lot into the "First Savings and Trust" bank. As they are running, they feel extremely heavy with all of their steps. Time is passing by slow, and it seems like minutes have passed since they left their vehicles, even though it has only been a few seconds so far. The men are continuing out of the parking structure. Victor is ahead of all of the men, so it seems that he is going to be the one that is going to open the door. They are only a few steps away from leaving out of the parking lot. Getting closer and closer to the front door of the bank, they feel like they are walking through quicksand. They exit out of the parking structure, and head into a courtyard on the side of the bank.

Being that they are now visible to pedestrians and other civilians on the street, this doesn't seem to matter. Others on the street are not able to notice them from how fast the men are running, and they shockingly going unnoticed. With every second counting, wanting to finish the heist as quickly as possible; trying to get in and out of the bank with fast time. The men finally make the turn from the side courtyard, and make their way to the front door of the bank. Feeling as if they are moving in extreme slow motion, the guys start to slightly freeze for a half a second upon reaching the front door. They start to put their game faces on. They are about to go inside the bank, and there are now at the ultimate point of no return. Inches away from the door, the men position themselves to strike. Victor reaches his arm out for the handle, and opens the door. All of the men enter the bank, and rush inside. They continue running past the entrance, going through the vestibule, leading themselves into the lobby. Victor then aims his gun and then begins to shout very loudly.

"DOWN ON THE FLOOR, GET DOWN ON THE FUCKING FLOOR NOW! EVERY BODY GET DOWN ON THE FLOOR. I WANT TO SEE EVERYBODY DOWN NOW!"

Kevin across the street from the bank, sees the men are now inside, and quickly disables the alarm system. He then immediately sets off the diversion a few blocks away. Kevin correctly calibrated the detonators to cause a slight explosion, leading to no injuries to people in the area. However, it does act a distraction towards their heist, as many people did notice the explosion, and immediately start to call the police over that. Kevin then keeps his view towards the front door of the bank. The men act accordingly to their plan, and get down to business. All of the patrons in the lobby are immobilized on the floor and in fear. The tellers who are in shock, quickly raise their hands up, as Brian aims his rifles at the both of them. There are currently two bank tellers working currently. Brian who is going to take care of them all, walks over to the first teller who is an attractive blond female. He then points his gun and loudly screams at her.

"Give me everything in the drawer and put in the bag! Empty the drawer!"

The teller immediately begins to drop cash from inside her cash drawer, inside the duffel bag Brian has. Victor and Jesse stay in the lobby. At this point, while Brian is taking care of tellers, with Victor and Jesse being his backup, Russell heads over to the vault. He clips his gun across his shoulder, and takes out the drill from the duffel bag. Russell using all of his strength, begins to drill through the lock on the vault. Pieces of metal shrapnel from the vault are flying everywhere. Sparks are also coming out of the lock, from the force Russell is giving it. The drill is powerful enough to withstand all of the punishment Russell is currently using. As he continues to thrust the drill into the lock, Russell starts to hear faint clicking sounds meaning he's getting closer to destroying the lock on the vault. Meanwhile, Brian tells the teller to empty her cart.

"I need for you to give me all of that! Put it all in the bag right now!"

The teller empties the cash cart behind her teller, dropping all of the cash from it, inside the duffel bag that Brian is holding. Brian then goes behind to the area the teller is in, and grabs her back and brings her to the lobby area. He then starts to shout at her.

"Don't you fucking move! Stay down on the fucking floor! Stay down!"

Victor and Jesse remain in the lobby aiming their guns at everyone in this area. Russell over by the vault area, is starting to tire. He did not expect to struggle with the lock this badly. He then decides to ram the drill inside the lock in a zig zag pattern, nearly damaging the end steel bit of the drill. This remarkably seemed to work to his advantage, as the lock of the vault has now been jimmied enough for him to open the gate. However, the drill bit is stripped, and unless he's extremely careful, the entire drill will possibly break. Russell opens the vault, and starts to drill a safe box, making sure he doesn't damage the drill further than it already has been.

Kevin who's keeping his eye on the front door of the bank, notices that the detonation software on his computer, is asking if he wants to set off a round of detonators. Kevin is puzzled, as he already set off the diversion, and doesn't understand why the program is asking for him to do it again. He ignores this warning. During this time, Kevin begins to feel hot and uncomfortable with his mask and disguise on. He feels he no longer needs it, as the men are more than likely going to be running out of the bank within the next few seconds. Kevin quickly starts to undress himself, wearing his regular clothes under the disguise. Kevin then turns his head back to the bank entrance. Back inside the bank, Russell is able to open up a safe box, which contains quite a bit of cash inside. He doesn't hesitate at all, and empties stacks of cash from it inside the other duffel bag quickly. Russell then decides to open one more box, before running out of the vault. Brian is now heading over to the second teller. She is a female with long curly red hair. He starts to yell at her.

"Empty your drawer right now! Empty everything out of it into the bag now!"

The teller out of fear and shock, immediately begins to take out all of the contents of her drawer, and places it into Brian's bag. Once the teller has emptied her drawer, Brian continues to aim the gun at her, and threatens the teller with more instructions.

"I want everything from the cart! Empty everything and put in the bag! Empty it!"

Brian aims his gun at the teller, who is now dumping all the cash from her cash cart, into the duffel bag that Brian is holding. Victor and Jesse stay in the lobby as backup to both Brian and Russell. Russell who is in the vault, opens up the second safe box. He empties it, and there is nothing inside. Russell then becomes angry over that, and decides this time for sure, to only open one more box. If the box is empty, then he will leave out the vault regardless. Russell takes the drill and sticks it into another safe box. Kevin who's in the van, acts as a lookout outside of the bank, checking to see if there is anything he should alert the guys inside about. Kevin looks at his computer screen, and notices the same message he disregarded before, is again resurfacing. The message is telling him that there are active detonators ready to fire. Kevin still is confused over this. He is not remembering the discarded detonators located directly right behind him. Kevin brought four detonators to the heist. Two of which he used as a successful diversion at the courtyard, located a short distance away from the bank. The other two, which Kevin was going to calibrate so they gave off a very mild smoke explosion. He was originally planning to give them to the other guys, to plant inside the bank to scare the people inside. Russell later told him not to, so he never used those particular detonators. Kevin is forgetting that these detonators are behind him in the van. He is mistaking this message, as a glitch directed at the diversion at the courtyard. In actuality, the detonators behind Kevin have somehow been activated by mistake. Due to Kevin's lack of knowledge on how the software operates, he accidentally set off these detonators. Kevin also didn't calibrate these discarded detonators. If they were to go off, they would give off a powerful explosion. Kevin closes the program, and ignores it.

Back inside the bank, the teller has finished emptying her cash cart. Brian aims his gun at her, and as he did with the first teller, grabs her back and directs her to the lobby.

"Stay down! Stay down on the ground!"

Russell is able to get another safe box open with the drill. He opens the safe up, and it contains a moderate amount of cash inside. He sticks the money inside the duffel bag quickly. Russell notices that one of his duffel bags is full, so he uses the drill bag to put the rest of the cash in. He stuffs the drill inside the other duffel bag, and runs out of the vault. Russell continues to run to the lobby of the bank, and Brian, Victor and Jesse run along with him. When they exit the lobby of the bank, heading into the main vestibule, Russell and the rest of the men hear a loud explosion coming from outside the bank. Upon hearing this explosion, Russell who is still running, feels as if his heart has stopped beating. He doesn't know where this explosion came from, but the sound made his heart immediately stop. The men continue running out of the vestibule, and Victor opens the door to the bank leading outside. Something inside Russell's head told him to look across the street. Russell for a split second turns his head across the road, and notices that the black van Kevin was in, has exploded. The detonators located inside the back of the van somehow went off. The explosion killed Kevin instantly.

Russell stops outside the entrance of the bank for a couple seconds. The rest of the men instinctively look at the demolished van, and the flames surrounding it. They are all fully aware of what happened, but cannot afford to stop and lament over it. Brian then screams at Russell.

"Man, fuck! We have to go now! We can't just stand here! We gotta move!"

The men continue to run towards the parking lot behind the bank. As they reach their vehicles, they all get inside, and speed off. Russell and Jesse take their masks off, and Jesse notices Russell crying; he notices how red Russell's face is, and Jesse begins to cry as well. Russell then starts to laugh. Jesse who is continuing to cry, stares at him. Russell proceeds to drive, laughing and crying.

CHAPTER 17:

NOTHING EMPTY, NOTHING FULL

The completion of the second heist brings much disappointment and sorrow; and many answered emotions and questions as well. With this intending to be their final heist, the men gave a more daring performance than they did previously. This was supposed to be the final curtain call, and the men were going to finish this heist with impeccable style. Inside the bank, the men were able to exhibit a stellar job. They acted very swiftly, using techniques and tactics that they didn't use during the original heist. In the case of Kevin, some of these decisions have left them with disaster consequences. Upon exiting the bank, the men saw the van Kevin was in explode. Not fully understanding why that happened, and whether or not Kevin was sitting inside. With Kevin being killed by the explosive devices, the men have to now deal with the results from that.

The men assume that Kevin was killed by the explosives, but they are not entirely sure. At this point, not to undermine Kevin's position, they need to escape from the heist. Although they completed the heist without any issues, the men can't help but feel tense and concerned over Kevin. They begin pondering that one of the worst things that could possibly happen during a heist, has most likely happened. Having to fully understand that a member of their group is possibly dead, this is something that none of them would ever imagine to occur. This is something that many of them would refuse to accept or agree with. A situation such as this sprouting out, is not anything they wanted. With the men not entirely sure if Kevin was inside the van when it exploded, they need to carry on and exit themselves away from the vicinity of the bank.

With a multitude of thoughts running in their minds, the four men drive back to "Home Base". Not knowing whether Kevin is alive or dead. The men, especially Russell have a feeling that Kevin sadly did not exit out of the vehicle. Russell feels extremely hurt at this current time. He is hoping that Kevin is safe, but is already preparing himself for the worst. He knows that the explosive devices were the reason the van exploded. Russell feels guilty, as he egged Kevin on to use them during the heist. The men are all quiet, under too much high stress to talk or speak. Their main objective for right now, is to head towards "Home Base". They will then direct their attention towards Kevin, once they have all settled back at their hideout. Russell looks in his rear view mirror, and sees that Brian and Victor are right behind him. Both of the men are travelling at a normal rate of speed at this point.

As they are getting closer to the unit, the men become more worried over Kevin, and they are curious as to what exactly happened to him. Russell continues to cry as he's driving. He cannot control his tears or emotions. Jesse is also crying, due to being concerned over Kevin as well. Brian and Victor in their vehicle, are crying as well for virtually the same reasons as the rest of the men are. They stay on the highway heading towards "Home Base"; evading the authorities once again, and having a clean getaway.

The police investigation towards the heist, now begins. A string of 911 calls over the explosion at the diversion point, witnesses who saw the robbers run out of the building, and those who saw the van explode. Police officers and investigators swarm the "First Savings and Trust" bank, the area over at the diversion point, and the area at the van. Each of the areas are heavily barricaded by police. News outlets are also swarming these settings in addition to that. Civilians are also observing all the proceedings. At the diversion area, the impact of the detonators didn't cause any immediate or heavy damage. According to all of the witnesses, thankfully there wasn't anyone that was hurt as a result from the diversion. It only caused a loud distracting bang to those that were around when the detonators went off. The investigators ask individuals that saw the explosion, if they were able to catch anyone suspicious looking in the area. Unfortunately, the witnesses could not give any details in this regard.

The investigators do not have any details as to who planted the detonators. With there not being any security cameras located outside of this courtyard, the identity of this person remains difficult to achieve. Investigators are at first puzzled over a motivation as to why someone would do a thing such as this. They continue their investigation in the area, until they finally come across the partial remnants of the detonation devices, which caused the explosion. The investigators using their expert logic, are correct by assessing that these were the detonators used.

Following this, the investigators all gather the detonators from inside the shrubbery, and add them to the collection of their evidence. While they are still searching for a motive for this situation, many of them have a strong possibility that this has much to do with the heist over at "First Savings and Trust". With there not being anything else to examine at this setting, the investigators move on.

The black van which was engulfed in flames due to the explosion, is extinguished by the fire department. The van is completely totaled and wrecked. Only a few pieces of the vehicles frame exist. Firefighters as they clear the vehicle, notice Kevin's body sitting in the driver's seat. The coroners quickly arrive and take him away. Most of the evidence inside of the van, except for the detonators, have all be incinerated. This can make the investigation quite difficult, as the materials that Kevin used in the van, are burned from the explosion.

Kevin's computer case with the software used to control the detonators is destroyed. The disguise Kevin was wearing is burned to ashes as well. Detective Mike Henderson arrives, as he is called to investigate the robbery. Other investigators join him as well, and he is informed on the findings at the diversion area. Detective Henderson starts walking towards the area the van was in. The power of the detonators severely damaged two other vehicles that were in front of, and behind the van. Luckily, there wasn't anyone inside the vehicles. The explosion also caused damage to two street lights, and a palm tree in the same area. The detective carefully scans through the destroyed van for evidence. He then notices remnants of the detonation devices, and talks with the other members of his team. They piece together the detonators from the diversion point, and they match. He at this point knows the explosion which happened at the diversion point, and explosion which happened towards the van, are connected. The next order of business, is to find out how they were. The detective continues to stay in this area putting together both of the events.

His original theory, is that the bank robbers used the detonators to distract the police while they were in the bank. This was able to work, as a couple officers did report to the diversion area, and were not aware at all of the heist that was congruently taking place at the "First Savings and Trust" bank. However, he couldn't exactly explain the detonators exploding the van, and the deceased body located inside of it. Witnesses couldn't explain exactly when the van pulled up to the corner. Likewise, with the area surrounding the diversion point, there are no security cameras which can display this particular information. However, witnesses explain that at the same time which the van exploded, they noticed several men running outside of the bank across the street.

Detective Henderson then believes the robbers inside of the bank, were aware of the van exploding, and perhaps intended for it to explode. The events happened too close from each other for this to not be the case. He believes the detonators in both of the areas, were controlled by an unknown outside source.

Another theory that the detective has, is the deceased person in the van, was a possible hostage victim. The van was possibly used as a getaway vehicle, with a hostage inside. The detonators have either accidentally or purposefully went off, killing the hostage inside. With the possible hostage being killed as a result of the robbery, the detective doesn't understand why that had to be the case. He becomes extremely saddened that a life had to be lost during this ordeal. Detective

Henderson however, is completely unaware that this man wasn't a hostage at all. This man was one of the individuals involved with the heist in some shape or form. Due to the lack of evidence they have, any theories they can think of which slightly make sense, are the ones they will use at this particular point and time. With many plausible theories on the table, the detective is still not ready to give any concrete accusations.

Detective Henderson puts the detonation remnants from the van, into their evidence collection. He stays in this area, trying his best to come up with reasons explaining all the events which took place. Detective Henderson fails to come up with any additional evidence at this scene, and it causes him to become frustrated. He decides that there isn't anything else for him to examine, and he proceeds to walk inside the "First Savings and Trust" bank.

As the detective enters the bank, he quickly spots muddy shoeprints in the vestibule area. One of the robbers stepped into a dirt patch right outside the entrance. From the heavy snow shows they were wearing, it made a clear impression towards the freshly mopped floor of the bank. Something like this, is a big break towards the investigation. The shoe prints look familiar to Detective Henderson, as they should. The shoes the robbers were wearing, were the same kind they used in the previous heist. Detective Henderson takes the print of the shoe into evidence, so it can be compared to the others in their evidence collection. He continues to walk around the bank, as the patrons inside are being cleared to leave. The employees then give accounts to the events which conspired.

Looking around the bank, the detective angrily takes note of the poor security layout of the bank. The banks which display horrible security, are the ones most at risk of being robbed. The "First Savings and Trust" bank, is quite an old building. It continues to use older methods of bank security. Many areas inside the bank are not secure as they should be, and he's surprised this bank and many others, are able to pass federal security regulations. The bank doesn't have a security guard hired either, this is something he also thinks is odd. As he looks up towards the ceiling, the detective sees very few security cameras; he is fearful that the surveillance system will yield him from getting any positive results.

From the witness statements in the bank, there were four robbers that were present. Two of the robbers remained in the common lobby area of the bank. One robber was taking care of the bank tellers. The remaining robber used a powerful drill to break into the vault and safe boxes. None of the witnesses know which direction they came from to enter the bank, and which direction they left out of. The men entered and exited the bank, by leaving the parking structure located behind the building, and running through the courtyard on the side of the bank, making a sharp turn towards the entrance.

However, the investigators cannot be sure this was the exact method they used. There are no cameras situated in the private parking structure behind the bank, and there aren't any cameras located in the courtyard next to the bank either; which the men were running from. With the evidence they have, they are more leaning towards that the robbers arrived at the bank using the van which exploded, and ran across the street. The men were present in the bank, for two minutes and ten seconds. A slightly longer time than their first heist, but they still managed to get in, do their job, and leave without any hassle or issue.

Detective Henderson was adamant that the individuals behind his heist, have done this before. The detective was glad to find out that everyone present in the bank, was unharmed; despite the fact the robbers used guns. From further investigating, the security alarms in the bank were disabled and hacked from an outside source as well. Based on this evidence alone, he knew very well the "United Farmers Savings" heist, was connected to this one. Detective Henderson was hell-bent that this was the same group of men involved with this heist. No matter how obsolete the alarm systems in banks are, it's is uncommon for people to have knowledge and resources to disable the alarms. He also knew that they carefully planned how they would execute everything as well, down to every detail and movement.

Detective Henderson requests to see the surveillance video immediately. As he already suspected, the video quality makes it difficult to view certain elements of the heist. But Detective Henderson is ninety percent sure, the same group of men who pulled the "United Farmers Savings" heist, are the same group involved with this heist. Only going by their body types from this surveillance video he's watching, he has hunch that they are the same men. He wouldn't have a correct guess to this until he puts the evidence together, but he is positive towards his observations so far.

The men are wearing the same disguises as in the first heist, and their identities are impossible to figure out. The detective finds it remarkable how one of the men was able to break through the vault. The camera view inside the vault isn't clear, but gives an accurate portrayal nevertheless. As he watches the video of Russell breaking into the vault, he is astonished as to how easy he made that seem. He observes by the video, how well the men worked together during this heist.

Detective Henderson has seen many robberies, and this would top the chart, if he had a list of the ones which were done perfectly; this would be number one without any doubt. He continues to watch the video, to the point where the men are running out of the building. Despite the picture quality being poor, the camera was able to pick up that the men stopped for a couple seconds at the entrance of the bank. Detective Henderson believes that this is the exact moment the van exploded across the street. The men then make a left turn and run away from the bank. Detective Henderson believes the men more than likely ran inside the parking structure behind. Being that there are no security cameras in that area, this is only a logical assumption he can use. The detective is given a copy of the surveillance tape, and it is entered into evidence. He walks through the bank, and proceeds towards the vault area.

The detective notices drill bit pieces on the ground, from the drill Russell used. These are taken into evidence as well. Detective

Henderson then wraps up his investigation, and quickly heads to the police station, to go over all of the evidence obtained.

At the station, Detective Henderson in a side by side comparison, watches the security surveillance video of the "United Farmers Savings" heist, and the "First Savings and Trust" heist. Because all four of the men are of different body shapes, it is easy to tell whether or not the men are the same in both of the robberies.

The robbers are wearing the same disguises in both events, and the guns used are the same as well. So that already is a major sign of relevance. The two men that are positioned in the lobby area of the bank, are the same stature and profile in both heist videos. The body type and profile of the other two robbers, are a match in addition to that. Even though the men are hiding every aspect of their identity, Detective Henderson is satisfied that he was able to put the same group of men, towards both of these robberies.

The shoe prints that were gathered from outside the entrance of both banks during the heists, turned out to be a perfect match. With it now being official, that both of these heists were in fact done by the same group of individuals. Detective Henderson although wasn't able to identify exactly who these men are, can settle with the fact he knows that these are the same men, and that they are dealing with possible professionals.

Detective Henderson dubs them the "Snowman Bandits", due to their disguises being composed of ski masks, heavy jackets, and snow boots. Detective Henderson gives a conference meeting to all the other chief investigators at the station, and considers these particular cases high risk. He is fairly sure that the men will strike again soon. Detective Henderson then moves onto other cases.

Russell, Brian, Jesse and Victor remain on the highway, heading towards "Home Base". Each of them remain quiet, and are in an opposite mood than they were from the first heist. Despite the fact they orchestrated the heist as planned, seeing Kevin's van explode, squashes any type of pleasant victorious feeling they should be expected to have. The men are too afraid to talk about the possibility of Kevin being killed from the explosion. Russell continues to sob as he's driving, wiping his tears away with his hand. All he can think about is Kevin, and starts to regret the fact they all separated from each other during this heist. The anxiety they all have over Kevin could be avoided, if they didn't stray away as they did. Russell thought by having them all split up, it would make the heist flow easier. Escaping the heist in separate vehicles, would allow them to exit out of the heist faster. He is now starting to believe that idea wasn't worth it at all. The benefit from plotting an idea such of that, wasn't a positive gain to them. Especially considering the fact that one of their team members were killed during this heist.

The men do have a short glimmer of hope, that Kevin maybe managed to run out of the vehicle and is safe. That is merely a small amount though, as most of the men are preparing themselves for bad news. As they continue to drive down the highway, the men as much as they want to be happy they have gotten away with another heist, cannot get over the fact that Kevin is not with them. The men are in separate cars, and can't see or talk to each other, but they can almost read each of their minds.

All four of them have a mutual wave of emotions going through their bodies. Russell and Brian look forward out of the windshield of their vehicles, with Jesse and Victor who are sitting in the passenger seat of both vehicles, looking forward as well. The men try to be strong, and start to calm themselves down during the ride back. One thing that is for sure, is that they completed their final heist as they intended to. The van Kevin used did blow up, but they did not harm anyone inside of the bank. Russell was amazed on how his plan to use the industrial drills to break into the vault, actually worked in his favor. Brian, Jesse and Victor, worked together under the pressure of the heist as well.

Kevin did manage the help the guys during this heist. He disabled the bank alarms, which allowed the men to have an advantage towards not being detected during the heist. He also successfully planted a diversion which caused the authorities to direct their attention towards that area, and not the heist. It can also be considered a complex development towards the heist investigation. Kevin who was just as guilty as the other men towards the heist, is now being billed as a hostage due to how much the detonation diversions caused a loop towards the investigation; both at the courtyard located a few blocks away from the bank, and sadly the same detonation which killed him in the van. The men at this point, are completely unaware of these facts and theories. As the only thing that remains on their mind, is they saw the van explode upon leaving the bank. It is natural for them to be concerned over Kevin, and it destroys the overall mood. Having this scene in their memory as they escape from the heist, is one that brings a million thoughts inside their heads. Completely unsure as to how events will come together from this point on, their only choice is to head towards their safe house, and figure out those details later.

The men reach the exit of the highway leading towards "Home Base". Russell continues to drive, and pulls up to the area outside of the unit. He parks the car away from the gate, and turns off the ignition. As Russell is waiting for Brian to unlock the garage gate of the unit, he tilts his head down towards and ground, takes his hands and covers them over his face, sobbing heavily. Russell starts to feel upset and tense over the current affair of events. Jesse who's watching Russell cry, attempts to console and comfort him, and rubs Russell's shoulder. Russell violently pushes Jesse's hand away. Jesse continues to look at Russell with a sad face. Brian pulls up to the unit, and parks right outside of the unit. Brian gets out of the vehicle, and starts to unlock the door. After this, Brian gets back into the vehicle, and parks it inside of the unit. Russell who heard Brian drive into the unit, looks up and turns on the ignition. He directs the vehicle inside of the unit, parking it. Russell then turns the ignition off.

All four of the men get out of their vehicles. Brian walks over to the garage door of the unit, closing and locking it. While keeping quiet and not giving eye contact towards each other, the guys start to undress out of their disguises. Brian then collects all of their guns, emptying out the magazine cartridges. Brian places the guns down on a counter in the unit. Russell walks to the getaway vehicle he used, and grabs both of the duffle bags. He puts the duffle bag containing the money from the vault, around his shoulder. He then takes the industrial drill out of the other duffel bag, however the duffel bag the drill was in, has looted cash inside as well. He sets the drill right next to the guns on the counter. Russell then walks to the vehicle Brian used, and grabs two more duffle bags containing money. He gives Brian, Jesse and Victor a bag each. The men then start to walk over to "Home Base", each of them carrying a duffel bag around their shoulders.

Brian walks up to the unit door and unlocks it. While walking inside of the unit, the men all walk over to the sofa area. They set their bags down next to the coffee table, and sit in silence. During this time, they all do not know what to do next; due to the anxiety they are each feeling. It feels awkward with Kevin not being with them. From how exuberant and lively his personality and attitude was, compared to the other four. Kevin not being with them, is the main reason for the pressure they are feeling, and being unknown to his current condition.

The rush of completing the heist, in addition to what they witnessed as they were running out of the bank, is causing a great amount of fear in their minds. The men are too afraid to speak at this moment, as they sit on the sofas, with their stolen cash under the coffee table. Victor briefly gets up to grab a glass of water, then returns to the rest of the men, staying completely quiet. Brian gets up as well; he heads over to the area his bed is in, and pulls out a liquor case. Inside of the case, contains a large unopened bottle of "Jack Daniels" whiskey.

Russell, Jesse and Victor watch Brian in silence. Brian with the bottle still in his hands, grabs several shot glasses. He brings the bottle and the shot glasses over to the sofa area, and sets them down on the coffee table. Brian then takes the remote, and turns the television on, switching it to the local news station. This was intentional, and he was assuming the stunt all of the men pulled shortly ago, would be featured on the news. Brian then takes a seat on the other side of the sofa, and watches the news program. Jesse and Victor look at the news on the television as well.

Russell however looks down towards the ground with a smirk on his face, and starts to rub his hand under his chin. The news is covering an array of stories, but isn't mentioning the event the men were involved in. The guys continue not to speak to each other, and sans

Russell, continue to watch the news. Finally, the men all start to feel anxious when an anchorwoman starts to speak, with the surveillance video of the men during the heist, playing during the coverage of the story.

"A bank in the downtown area was targeted this afternoon in an armed robbery. Investigators say four men walked into the 'First Savings and Trust' bank on Main threatening those inside, and quickly escaping. Investigators have labelled them the 'Snowman Bandits', as they believe they are connected to another recent unsolved robbery."

The anchorwoman continues, with all of the men listening closely to the news report.

"A man who investigators strongly believe to be a hostage, was sadly killed across the street from the bank, when an explosive device said to be used by the suspects, went off inside a van he was in. The identity of the hostage, is being withheld. If you have any information on the identities of the suspects, please call the Los Angeles Police Department."

Brian out of shock, quickly cuts the television off. This news, the men were all sadly readying themselves for. It is now official to them, that Kevin was killed during this heist. The men are still unable to talk to each other. Being in extreme shock from this, any thought or action inside of their mind is frozen. They all remain seated on the sofa areas, in their own world; afraid to proceed into the future. Grieving is turning out to be strange, as the men take in Kevin's death in an interesting way. Perhaps out of a coping mechanism to deal with the depression, the guys go into a denial mode. Brian then with a stoic look on his face, starts to pour the whiskey into the shot glasses. After all of the glasses are full, Brian takes one of the glasses, and swallows the liquor in one gulp; shaking his head due to the taste of it. Jesse and Victor watch as Brian pours himself another shot and drinks it. Russell keeps his head down towards the ground, and continues to have a smirk on his face.

Jesse and Victor then both grab a shot glass, and start to take sips of the liquor. Brian then takes one of the full shot glasses on the table, and waves it under Russell's face. Russell ignores Brian at first, but when Brian continues to hold the glass by his face, Russell while still looking towards the floor, grasps Brian's wrist very tightly, and Russell with much force, thrusts and controls Brian's arm, to set the shot glass back on the table. Russell then starts to laugh while still looking down, and begins to finally softly speak.

"Jesse, Victor. Count all the money in the bags. Right fucking now please."

Jesse and Victor grab all four of the bags, and proceed to walk over to Brian's bed. They immediately begin to unzip the duffel bags, dumping all of the cash out. Brian who is deeply afraid of Russell right now, decides to give him some space. Brian grabs a chair from his kitchen area, and walks over to join Jesse and Victor at the bed. Russell stays seated at the sofa area with his head still pointing down. Jesse and Victor sit on the bed, and begin to put all the cash in stacks on top of the bed. Separating them in groups of one thousand. The amount of cash they were able to obtain, is greater than the amount they received in their previous heist.

As Jesse and Victor continue to count the cash, Brian looks over at Russell, who still looks petrified and upset. Brian then looks across the bed, and sees that they have now over a hundred different stacks of cash. The men then begin to count the final amount of bills they have left, piling those up as well. When they are finished counting all the money, Jesse and Victor to be certain, once again count all the money they were able to steal a second time. Their official grand total came out to be, one hundred and thirty-seven thousand dollars.

Russell who heard the men reveal the amount of money they had, remains silent and motionless on the sofa area. Jesse and Victor then look at each other, feeling confused as to what to do next. Brian then takes all the stacks of bills, and stashes them in the duffel bags. The men all return to the sofa area, and Victor begins to pour himself a shot of liquor. Brian then starts to feel annoyed over the way Russell is acting, and takes another shot of liquor, shaking his head at Russell. Russell then starts to lose control.

Russell takes his shot glass, and swallows it very quickly. He then takes the bottle of whisky, and pours himself four more shots, consuming them rather fast. Brian, Jesse and Victor watch Russell the entire time. Russell then gets up, and throws a tantrum. He walks over to Brian's work center, and begins to throw all of Brian's wrenches and tools on the ground. Brian who is aware that Russell is under much depression and grief, doesn't go up to Russell at all. Russell continues to throw many items across the floor. He walks back over the sofa area briefly, and pours himself another shot of whisky, and gulps it down. Russell sets the glass down on the table, and then walks around the unit with his head down on the ground, shouting and ranting.

"I'm gonna miss Kev! Shit. I don't know what to fucking do you guys! None of that money means shit. Nothing we did today means shit. Kev is fucking dead! KEV IS FUCKING DEAD. HE'S NOT COMING BACK, AND YOU GUYS DON'T CARE?!"

Russell starts to cry, and Brian walks towards Russell to comfort him. Russell shoves Brian away from him, and Brian nods his head and walks away from Russell, responding to him.

"Russell, it's not that we don't care, we're in shock man. Me, Jesse and Victor can't believe Kevin was killed either. We saw it happen, and we all knew what the fuck happened. Russell, take all the time you need man to let this sink in. I'll leave you alone if you want me to."

Russell continues to look down, and carries on with his rambling.

"I had a feeling those fucking detonators would be the death of him. I just knew it, turns out it was. This was going to be it, our last heist. So I let him use the damn detonators, knowing that he shouldn't be using them. I should have told him no. I should have told him, hell no."

Brian walks to the coffee table, and pours Russell another shot, and hands it to him.

"Hey man, you didn't know. That's the thing you need to realize with all of this. You didn't know. What happened was a freak accident somehow. I totally understand you're feeling guilty about it, but Russell, calm down man. We're all here dealing with it too."

Russell takes the glass from Brian and quickly swallows it. Max then approaches the unit, knocking on the door. Brian walks over and lets him in. Max then starts to speak.

"I already know what happened. I want to tell each of you something. My older brother was drafted into the army when he was eighteen for the war in Vietnam. I was twelve when he went away. My brother was my best friend, and I never saw him again. He was killed on the battlefield, and it was something that I always thought was unfair."

Russell turns his head towards Max, and Max continues to speak.

"But you know, life is unfair. I don't think it's fair that I don't have any legs, but it is what it is. Things happen unfairly like that sometimes. Russell, I'm not only sorry for the loss of Kevin, but for the loss of all of your family and friends. You've had a tough life, and you have all my sympathy and empathy for being mad at the world."

Brian walks over to the duffel bags containing the money they had gotten for the heist earlier, and grabs them. He then hands the bags to Max, and starts to talk to him.

"I don't know where we are going to go from here. But for right now, Max can you hold onto this for the time being? Like with Russell, I don't know what the fuck to do right now, and I'm starting to feel woozy from seeing Kevin blow up like that. I just don't know."

Max grabs the bags, and starts to head towards the door of the unit.

"I see that this possibly is a very delicate time right now, and I'd better go. I want you all to know that whatever you decide to do from this point forward, remember to always listen to your heart. I care about, and love each and every one of you. I'll shall see you later. Take care."

Max then leaves out of the unit, and Brian walks over to close and lock the door. Russell then walks over to the coffee table near the sofa area, and pours himself another shot.

"I..., I forgot what I was going to fucking say. I'm done. Kev is dead, and I don't see the point of living anymore you guys. Everybody close to me is fucking dying. This is bullshit, and today was supposed to be a happy day, where we all celebrate our final heist. There is nothing to fucking celebrate. Kev is gone, and he's not coming back. That's the fucked up part. Ugh."

Russell starts to feel depressed over the death of Kevin, more than we was already. He is beginning to miss his best friend, and feels partly guilty of his death. He feels if he didn't allow Kevin to use the tools in the heist, he might possibly still be here. Russell starts to feel bad for allowing the guys to split and merge away from each other, during the heist as well. So many events running through his head, that he feels shouldn't have gone the way they have. Russell is in some type of depressive vortex right now. Kevin isn't present to act as the comic relief in the group. Russell is unaware as to how to proceed, and how to keep going through all of this. The rest of the men feel just as depressed as Russell does, though they are trying their best to deal with the pain in different methods. Brian watches as Russell stays in his depressive mood, walking around the unit. Jesse is currently crying, and understands the sorrow Russell is having. Victor has a sudden mood swing, and starts to pour himself several glasses of liquor. Russell then returns to the sofa area, and sits down. He then takes his phone out and goes through it.

"I think I have an old picture of me and Kev from years ago. We were at this party, and Kev took it, and he texted it to me, and something told me to save it. I know it's in here somewhere. Damn. I just have to accept Kev is gone, and deal with it. Damn."

Jesse wanting to console Russell, walks over and sits the sofa; resting his head on Russell's shoulder. Russell then shoves Jesse off him, and violently snaps back, causing Jesse to walk away from him in fear.

"Get your fucking hands off me Jesse. Get the fuck off me. Don't fucking touch me. Nobody fucking touch me right now. I'm not in the fucking mood right now. Do not touch me. I don't mean to be like that, but don't be feeling on me like that right now. Step off."

Russell continues to go through his phone to find the picture. A couple minutes later, he is able to locate the picture, and lifts up his phone to show it to the rest of the guys.

"Oh man, I can't believe I still have this picture. This was me and Kev from ages ago at a university party. Kev took this picture, and I don't know why, but I kept it after all these years. I remember this party too; it was pretty bad. What's funny is I think we crashed this party, and we weren't even supposed to be there. Damn. Fuck, I'm going to really miss Kev."

Jesse who's now laying on top of Brian's bed, speaks to the rest of the guys.

"Kevin was a funny guy. It's not going to be the same without him. I'm remembering all the good times I've had with him. I've not been able to get to know him as long as Russell has, but he was a bundle of joy. He will be missed, and it's tough dealing with the fact he's gone."

Brian then pours himself another drink, and responds to Jesse.

"Yeah, he was a funny guy. Ha-ha. I can't relate to the level Russell has with him, but from the time I did spend with him, I do miss him. I remember all the jokes he used to say and shit. It's fucking crazy how he's not here anymore. This group is now incomplete, and it's not going to be the same, it's not. He was our friend, and he's gone now."

Victor starts to panic and feel uncomfortable. The way he deals with traumatic events is quite different from the rest of the men. Russell approaches things originally with a violent outburst and tantrum, and slow begins to accept the way things are. Brian uses an optimistic approach. He starts to see the good in the situation, and wishes to stay quiet on his emotions. Jesse turns to a more observant approach, taking in as much information he can towards the traumatic event, and in his own time settling himself towards his reactions.

Victor however, has a strange combination of all of the above. He at times can have a violent approach towards the way he handles himself, at the same time refusing to fully express himself. Victor remembers the strange relationship he had with Kevin, and how Kevin originally made fun of him and bullied him. Victor pours himself several drinks and remains quiet. Russell while still staring at the picture of Kevin and himself on the phone, continues to reminisce about his memories of Kevin.

"Kev always said things that I was scared of saying. That's what I liked about him. He had no filter on him, at all. Whatever was on his mind, he would say. He was such a fucking chatterbox though. He would not stop talking at all. Sometimes I wouldn't even know what the fuck he was saying, I would just nod my head and say 'you're right Kev'. Ha-ha. Damn."

Russell continues to stare at the picture, and starts to smile. Victor who's sitting on the other side of the sofa, then starts to feel anxious and apprehensive. He starts to scratch himself very vigorously, and screams to the top of his lungs loudly. Victor makes himself several drinks, one after the other. Brian watches Victor continue to pour himself multiple drinks, and he walks over to the area and snatches the bottle away from him. Brian then scolds Victor.

"Alright, you've had enough man. Slow down. Take it easy alright? I saw you pour like ten fucking drinks man. I don't know how well you handle liquor. Hell, I really don't know you period. Ha-ha. Slow down okay? This is a tough time for all of us, I understand. But you've had enough man. No more drinks for you. Chill out, alright?"

Victor gives an angry look towards Brian, and flips him off. He then runs over to the kitchen area, and goes through his toiletry bag. Victor pulls out of can of black shoe polish, and rubs nearly the entire contents of it over his forehead, cheeks, nose and chin. Immediately after that, just as like Russell did, Victor runs over to Brian's work station and begins to throw Brian's tools over the place. Russell and Jesse watch Victor, and start to feel concerned and worried by his actions. Unlike with Russell, who Brian understood was going through emotional turmoil; Brian felt unsure of Victor, and feels he's playing some type of mind trick or game with the other guys, that could lead to ugly effects. Because of his unpredictable mood swings, Brian knows exactly what Victor is capable of.

Victor goes through one of Brian's tool bags, and pours an entire bottle of transmission fluid on the floor. He then starts to take Brian's automotive tools, and throws them against the wall. Victor continues to lash out his rage, and throws more of the tools at the wall. Victor then takes his fist, and punches the wall very hard, which forms a big hole. The rest of the men stare at him in shock, not knowing how to react to the way he's behaving. Brian starts to become angry, and shouts at him.

"Hey, what the fuck?! Are you fucking serious right now?! Dude?!"

Victor walks away from the workstation before Brian gets there, and Victor then walks into the kitchen area, pulling out a large butcher knife from the drawer. Victor then takes the knife, and swipes his forearm with it, expelling a large amount of blood. Russell and Brian then immediately run over to Victor, confiscate the knife, and pin him to the ground. While Russell and Brian have him tackled to the floor, Victor then starts to scream at the both of them.

"Get off me, get off me. Why are you guys doing this to me? Get off me."

Russell and Brian continue to restrain Victor to the floor, and Jesse who's watching the three of them, starts to cry and feel scared. Brian then responds to Victor.

"Victor, you are drunk, crazy, insane, psycho and out of control. You doing all of that, isn't helping us right now. Victor, me and Russell are going to let you go, but you have to calm down man. I know you're upset, everybody in this fucking building is upset man, but you gotta calm down. What you're doing right now is going to get us all in trouble, especially you."

Russell and Brian then lift Victor up, and direct him to the sofa area. Victor then sits down and starts to laugh to himself. Victor's arm is bleeding heavily. Brian pours rubbing alcohol on his arm, and gives Victor a warm towel to cover it. Brian then speaks to him.

"Damn, I don't know why the fuck you did that man. What was the point of that? You're only making things difficult and worse for all of us Victor. Damn."

Victor presses the towel over his arm, and continues to laugh. He then starts to speak.

"I remember Kevin used to always call me the scarecrow. He thought I looked scary and weird. It's true, I do look like a fucking scarecrow. At least he's right. That guy was really something else, and it's sad he's not going to be around anymore. He was really something."

Russell looks at Victor with an angry expression, and shakes his head at him. Russell then turns to look at Jesse who's continuing to cry. Russell then looks at Brian who's over at his workstation on his hands and knees, cleaning the mess that Victor just made. Russell then with his hands in his pockets, walks across the unit, and begins to speak under his breath.

"All you guys are fucking crazy. This is some straight bullshit; I don't know how I got this fucking involved. I wish I never met any of you. This is it, I'm outta here."

Russell then grabs his car keys and roams around the unit with his head down on the ground, laughing to himself. He walks over to the sofa area, and turns to look at Victor, who's continuing to laugh holding the towel on his arm.

"I wish I never met you. You're the craziest, sickest, most looney tunes man I've ever met. I really feel sorry for you. I'm as equally sadistic for giving you the benefit of the doubt. I can't believe you're an actual human being. You're like some lab experiment gone wrong. Both physically and mentally. You look like a fucking weirdo, and act like one too. I don't know what else to say, except you're a really scary, freaky, creepy guy. Good riddance."

Victor stops laughing and looks at Russell with a cold stare. Russell gives an identical stare to Victor, and sadistically laughs at Victor. Russell walks over to Brian's bed, where Jesse remains crying. Russell smacks Jesse hard on the face, and starts to yell at him.

"I want you to get your shit, and get out of my house. You're such a whiny nigger faggot, that acts like a damn woman. Be a man and quit crying, or I'll give you something to fucking cry about you fag. I've been patient with you this entire time, and I was silly enough to ignore it and not say anything until now. I felt sorry for you, because you're the worst of the worst, being black and gay. I don't give a fuck about you, so you can cry about that. Goodbye."

Jesse still crying, quietly looks at Russell. Russell smirks and walks away. Russell then proceeds over to Brian's work station. Brian is continuing to clean up the mess Victor caused. Russell turns to look at Brian, and starts to admit his harsh truths about him.

"I wish you and your friend never robbed my fucking bank. It's because of you, we're all fucking here. It's all your fucking fault. You're the one that ruined my life, so thanks a lot. So I thank you for that. I had a good job, and a good life. I had Peter. My life was perfect. You came and fucked up everything good I had. I can't believe I gave you a second chance, I should have called the cops on you when I had the fucking chance. You fucking loser. See you never."

Brian keeps his attention towards cleaning the floor, and Russell walks away. Brian while he still has his vision towards cleaning the floor, responds to Russell.

"Why the fuck are you still here then asshole? The door is that way. If we mean that much to you, why the hell are you still here man? What are you still doing here then?"

Russell then reaches in his pocket and grabs his car keys, and walks towards the door. As he's walking away, he kicks the cleaning materials Brian is using, and mutters under his breath.

"I'm on my way out asshole, don't even trip or worry about it."

Brian shakes his head, and continues to scrub the floor. As Russell is heading towards the door, Victor runs over to his toiletry bag, and pulls out a handgun. He runs back over to Russell and aims the gun towards the back of Russell's head. Russell immediately stands in shock, with his back turned to Victor, as Victor continues to press the gun against the back of Russell's head. Brian and Jesse watch in shock, as Victor starts to speak to Russell under his breath.

"So I'm a creep right? Being that I'm a creep, if I were to pull the fucking trigger, that wouldn't be so out of the ordinary for a creep to do, now would it? I bet you're feeling scared aren't you? Well, you should be. After all, I'm a creep, that's what creeps do right? Scare people. Now, I want you to apologize not only to me, but to Brian and Jesse as well."

Russell then starts to laugh, and with Victor still holding the gun to his head, Russell with his back still turned, responds to Victor in an amusing cynical tone.

"I'm not apologizing for Jack Sprat. I meant what I said, and I'll say it all again verbatim if you want me to. All of you guys are insane, and this shit you're currently doing is only proving my point. You're not going to shoot me, so quit all of that."

Victor laughs and shoves the gun harder into Russell's head. He then responds to him.

"I'm not going to shoot you huh? What makes you feel so sure of that?"

Victor quickly removes the gun from Russell's head, and Victor aims and shoots it at the wall, nearly missing Russell by a foot or so. Russell then tries to snatch the gun away from Victor, and they wrestle on the floor. Brian walks over, and he helps Russell tackle Victor. Brian is able to successfully grab the gun away from Victor, and Russell holds Victor to the floor. Brian hides the gun away near his workstation, and walks over to where Russell and Victor are.

"You can let him go Russell, he's not going to do anything. Trust me."

Russell stops restraining Victor, and Victor then runs towards the door.

"That's okay, I'm going to go to my car and get my other gun. Don't worry, I'm not going to waste any bullets on you guys. I'm going to kill myself. I can't deal with this anymore, and it's time for me to go. I can't deal with this shit anymore, and I've had enough. It's time for me to die, and I don't deserve to live. Don't any of follow me. If you guys do follow me, I will kill each and every one of you. Do not follow me."

Victor then runs out of the unit, and Russell, Brian and Victor then immediately chase after him. Victor jumps into his car, and proceeds to start the ignition. During the same exact instance, Russell runs towards his car, and starts the ignition, with Jesse running right behind him. Jesse gets in the rear seat. Brian swiftly locks the unit, and sits in the passenger seat of Russell's car. At this time, Victor starts to speed away from the unit, and Russell stays right close behind him.

Victor gets on the highway, and Russell continues to stay on his trail. Victor increases his speed to a high level, and weaves in and out of lanes on the highway. Russell maintains to keep close distance to Victor, and speeds up as well. Russell is determined not to let Victor out of his sight. He holds onto the steering wheel firmly. Russell shakes his head and unintentionally laughs.

CHAPTER 18:

NOTHING UNDER, NOTHING OVER

Russell continues to follow Victor down the road. Despite the fact the men seem to be under a great deal of stress and depression, also having to grieve in their own way. With Victor threatening to kill himself, it caused for the rest of the men to snap out of whatever slump that they were in. At this current time, the men feel that Victor's mental state needs to be properly attended to. Even though all of the men in their own way deal with mental issues at a separate level and degree, they still owe it to Victor to help him out during this difficult situation the men are faced with. Forgetting all of their criminal activity that they have recently done, and adapting their minds towards giving care to someone who needs it.

The men are only minding the fact that Victor is clearly not taking the recent news as well as the other men are. When Victor rushed out of the unit as he did, the rest of the men could have chosen to leave him alone, and not have followed him. That seems out of instinct to be the incorrect choice to make, as they all know Victor's personality, and feel they need to act fast. Not omitting the fact of high tensions and impulse reactions from what they witnessed all throughout the day. Also, not allowing that to be their immediate reaction and judgment towards the decisions they make. Based on everything that they have been through together over the past weeks, it's hard for them to ignore what just happened. Fact of the matter is, Victor has threatened to take his own life. The rest of the guys feel that it does not matter if they like him, hate him, or if Victor is a complete stranger to them, it is their duty to protect and look after his mental health. If something were to happen, the rest of the guys would be overthrown with guilt. Strange that despite the men each beginning to feel distant from each other, when under the pressure that someone in their group is in need of help, they quickly step into action. They understand this is Victor's method of crying out for the rest of them to heal him and to stand by him. Everything else unrelated to that, perhaps needs to be put aside, and discussed later. Victor is clearly not well, and the men need to access him expeditiously.

Not having any idea as to where Victor is going, Russell, Brian and Jesse stick to following him regardless of that. Victor remains on the highway, travelling to a distant location and setting. It has now been close to an hour since they have been following Victor. Looking around the horizon, the sun is starting to set, and it's becoming dark. The men who are following Victor, are now starting to become extremely scared at the situation. Their biggest concern is Victor ramming himself into another car, or driving off a cliff, or anything to that extent. Although, the men don't truly feel that Victor is planning or intending to do that. Most of their assumptions wrap around the idea that Victor is most likely asking for attention.

Victor starts to lower his speed, and Russell feels slightly comfortable over that. He realizes that Victor is planning to pull over and stop his car possibly very soon. The thrill of Victor's current mental state, in addition to his outrageous behavior, makes the men question many things to themselves. What will happen as they continue in this particular scenario? Is it worth it trying to pursue Victor, despite the way he was behaving before he stormed off? Are there any chances of this being some type of setup or trick that Victor is orchestrating? These possibilities are unknown, but the men still strive towards having positive intentions reinforced at Victor.

Russell is feeling regretful for his rant that he gave earlier towards each of the men. Dealing with the death of Kevin, Russell acted on strong impulse feelings he had. He was only saying what was on his mind, and shouting out expressions he kept hidden. Russell is feeling distant from the group. Most of the things he mentioned, he actually meant, but regrets saying it out loud. The way he went about it, Russell feels wasn't the appropriate way to do it. As of right now, he wants to give his focus towards Victor's health and wellness. The guilt Russell is experiencing, from the rant he directed at the other guys, is pressuring him to act on redeeming and changing his attitude.

Also realizing that he doesn't have to be friends with Victor, but it's not in Russell's character to not help someone out who's under dire depression that Victor is in. Russell ignores the fact that Victor pointed a gun at his head shortly ago, understanding that is due to the stress and sadness that Victor is having inside his mind. Russell locks his eyes towards Victor's car, not saying a single word. Brian and Jesse remain in the vehicle with him, not speaking. Their vision remains looking forward ahead at Victor's vehicle. All three of them in complete suspense as to what Victor is thinking, and to what he plans to do next.

Victor continues to drive down the highway, still feeling a great amount of depression. He is hurt mainly due to what Russell said to him before he ran out the unit. Dealing with the death of Kevin is proving to be difficult for Victor, as he doesn't deal with sorrow in the same manner than the rest of the men do. Victor was trying extremely hard to cope with the chain of events that happened earlier, but it caused too much strain for him to handle. He doesn't realize that he isn't the only one dealing with this particular issue right now. Inside Victor's mind, he feels like an outcast and isolated with his feelings, when this isn't the case at all.

The other three men are at an equal playing field as far as their emotions are concerned. They are going about it in a completely different method than Victor is approaching it. This is causing Victor to become confused with the way he is presenting his attitude and emotions. Victor has always had suicidal ideations since he was young. Being bullied in school didn't help towards any and all internal depressive agendas Victor was keeping inside to himself. There are several times to where his depression gets to an out of control state, and he takes on suicidal thoughts and actions. Victor becomes confused, and doesn't fully understand the severity of his actions when he's depressed. Turning to suicide and self-harm, Victor truly believes that it's his last and only resort towards escaping this mental trap he is battling. Victor intends to drive himself to a distant location to possibly take his own life. Under immense mental pain, he is fed up with the way things are currently being handled.

These strange occurrences and actions that he's offering and also displaying not only towards himself, but to the rest of the guys as well are interesting to note. Victor is aware that Russell is following every single move he makes. Not minding that he told the rest of the guys not to follow him, he knew that they were going to come after him regardless. Victor is feeling depressed, and is using them perhaps as an audience to fuel whatever mania he's battling with mentally. Whatever actions or plans he is thinking about doing, shall remain ambiguous and unknown, even to Victor himself.

The depression generally is being masked with an energetic rush, one that is going all through his body. Making him want to participate in this chase that he's currently in with Russell on the highway. It's a complex mixture of Victor experiencing multiple levels of sadness, and also facing an energy boost from the inane behavior he's portraying. After all, Victor sets himself away from the rest, and has an unusual profile unlike some. Quite frankly, he's a difficult man to manage and research, and this is entirely his own personal agenda and plot to make it seem that way.

Russell keeps his distance right behind Victor, still in deep suspense as to what location in particular that Victor intends to finally pull over and stop at. He knows that Victor is going to stop sometime, perhaps very soon. Russell can tell, due to the way Victor isn't driving as fast as he was originally, that he's starting to tire. The probability is relatively high of Victor arriving soon, at whichever destination he plans on going to. While Russell keeps his attention towards the road, he repeatedly goes back, and thinks about the tirade he gave towards each of the men back at the unit. The pain and guilt is causing his entire body to turn into stone. Russell starts to realize that under this intense scene of pressure, feelings can easily change. During that particular time, Russell was holding onto honest opinions, and decided to let his opinions be publicity heard. That was then, and knowing the present while he's driving on the highway, Russell now starts to regret mostly every single bit of what he expressed towards the men. He wishes he could take everything that happened in that instance back, as he acted only on his own impulses due to the high tensions he was feeling.

Russell hates being that type of man, to reveal ugly, harsh and hidden truths to himself. Russell understands that he's not a perfect man by any means, but his own temper and attitude overtakes his own good judgment and conscious sometimes. It turns him into a man that he doesn't wish to be, and more of a man that he feels people assume that he should be and act. Russell deeply misses Kevin, and this is something that as much as he's struggling to continue on and accept, it's always going to be a major focal point in his mind. Russell simply does not think it's fair in the slightest that Kevin is gone, it doesn't make any sense. Most of this frustrations and sorrow, is centered towards that. Russell due to the hurt, is transforming into an angered monster, to cope with the grief he is having.

Russell looks out in the night sky, and stays completely quiet driving. Russell puts his hand under his chin, and takes a quick peek over at Brian, who's looking out the windshield. He ponders whether or not he wants to open his mouth and speak to Brian, but ultimately remains quiet. Russell can tell that Brian is upset and disappointed at him. Brian has every reason to be, as Russell did say disgusting and nasty things not only to him, but the rest of the men as well before they left to chase after Victor. Russell feeling regretful from the way he treated Brian, finds it awkward that he's refraining from speaking to him. Russell has faith that he will eventually make amends with Brian later. Russell also starts to feel bad at the way he not only hit, but said unacceptable things towards Jesse. He didn't mean to hurt Jesse in that way at all. Russell sadly cannot help the fact he's an honest man, and the truth does hurt sometimes. He said what he felt he needed to say at that present occurrence. Russell is sure that Jesse will also eventually forgive him. Mainly Russell is focused at Victor. Victor held a gun towards Russell's head, and it was something that really made Russell attentive. He understands that Victor is not an ordinary individual, and his well-being needs to be rectified immediately. Russell shakes his head, and directs his view back forward, remaining right behind Victor's vehicle.

Brian congruently scans his eyes over at Russell. Doing so with an identical fashion as Russell, he also puts his hand under his chin, and shakes his head at him. Brian is extremely hurt by what Russell said to him back at the unit. He feels betrayed and punished by the way Russell spoke to him. Brian is not sure if he can ever trust Russell again, mainly because of how quick Russell snaps, and becomes too out of control with his anger. He feels that Russell is not appreciative of all the help he has given him. If it weren't for Brian's help, they would not have had access to all the tools which allowed them to complete all of their heists. Brian thought the best thing to do, is ignore Russell.

He doesn't understand the sudden mood swing that Russell gave to the guys. Brian deeply felt that Russell needs to be left by himself, if he's going to quickly alter his attitude such as he did. Brian didn't appreciate the way Russell spoke to Jesse and Victor. Ordinarily, Brian's cool and laid back personality can only go so long. He was seconds from turning violent towards Russell. They have got into a physical fight before, and Brian was not at all afraid or hesitant to stand his ground towards Russell. He is not afraid of him, nor is he intimidated of the way he is displaying his emotions, his overbearing attitude and his fiery anger and temper.

Brian is actually scared of wrecking his friendship and relationship, that he was able to have with Russell. He has enjoyed the support and bond they felt towards one another, and doesn't understand why Russell is willing to suddenly give all of that up. Brian is well aware that Russell is hurting from the death of his best friend, but there is no need for him to take it out on the rest of the guys as he did. Brian cannot stop thinking about Victor. His feelings towards Russell are not as important, as the painful concern that he has directed at Victor. Brian has witnessed firsthand many interesting aspects, traits and signs that Victor himself has revealed. These all support the fact; he is someone that has been through hardships in his life. Brian holds onto much empathy towards Victor, and values his personality and self-worth. He cares a great deal about him.

Jesse sits directly behind Russell in the rear seat, staying quiet likewise with the other men in the vehicle. His head and vision is positioned down towards the ground, and he refuses to lift his head up. Jesse's body is completely motionless, except for when he wipes tears from his face with his hands intermittently. He silently sobs and cries, thinking about various things inside his head. Thinking is all he can do right now, and Jesse has always been a more observant thinker, especially when it came to depressing times. Feeling too ashamed to say anything, he remains seated, and keeps completely to himself. Jesse has never felt this depressed and upset in his life. Recently, he has been keeping many of his emotions to himself, and now he's in the process of letting all of his sadness out. He starts to wipe more tears from his face. Feeling emotional, due to how everything is currently panning out. Jesse having a list of things he's confused and bothered about. Originally being crushed by what Russell told him back at the unit.

All throughout his life, Jesse has always been rejected and neglected by many people. Having Russell essentially shun and push him aside, broke Jesse's mental spirit. He can't begin to think or put together why Russell held onto those sentiments and opinions. Not only that, but the way he expressed and presented those thoughts as well. Jesse for now has to distract his mind away from any animosity he has towards Russell. This is not the only thing that is bothering him. Jesse like Russell, is also trying to grieve over the loss of Kevin. He was an important member of their group, and Jesse developed a close friendship with Kevin. Jesse understands that Russell compared to the rest of the guys, had the closest history with Kevin, so therefore Russell is going to take Kevin's loss in a different method, as the other men would. Jesse does not understand Russell's harsh temper, and his disrespectful and violent attitude. He believes it only makes the situation the men are being placed in currently, much more difficult to withstand. Jesse is scared of Victor's impulsive depression, and his suicidal tendencies. From noticing Victor's self-harm scars on his arm the first day he met him, Jesse kept a special place in his memory to be concerned and empathetic towards the safety of Victor's mental health.

Victor is slowly starting to calm himself down. The speed he's travelling down the road at, is at a much lower pace and rate. Victor continues to feel tense and agitated, but he is adapting a much calmer expression and impression than he had previously. However, his depression is still creeping itself. The suicidal ideations he's experiencing, have not completely vanished from his body. Victor has a grin on his face, as he keeps his eyes looking out his windshield.

Despite the fact he's grinning, there are a thousand different emotional traits that he currently has. Victor starts to think of the other three men. He knows exactly what they are all thinking, and can tell how they are feeling as well; which are the same exact thoughts and feelings that he currently has in his mind. Victor is angry at Russell, and is not finding it easy to realize that Russell possibly was acting under pressure, and that Russell feels bad for what he said. According to Victor, none of that matters at all. Russell's words did have much power, and they were powerful enough for Victor to feel less than.

Victor isn't blaming Brian or Jesse at all, in fact he's grateful and blessed to have the rapport he has with them. Russell on the other hand, Victor is not pleased to deal with, and he holds great disdain hatred towards. Victor is aware that Russell is depressed over Kevin, but that however simply isn't enough to cover up Russell's strict attitude and disrespect. Victor just like the rest of the guys, had a unique, special bond and relationship with Kevin. He as well is finding it tough to deal with Kevin now being gone. Victor however cannot excuse this from the way Russell blatantly disrespected him. Victor had no intentions to pull the trigger when he held the gun to Russell's head, but he did it to show how upset and fed up he was at the way Russell was acting. Already feeling worthless and down, hearing Russell relay everything he mentioned to him, only made the situation worse than it was. Victor is particular with the way he acts, and the way he associates and socializes with other people. He can only take so much, especially during times in which tensions are high, and emotions are out of control. Victor doesn't wish to make this time directly about him, but he was left without any choice to do anything otherwise.

The men stay on the highway for another twenty minutes. While they are driving farther and farther, Russell, Brian and Jesse become more anxious and nervous. Anticipating the time when Victor will officially stop the car, and reach wherever he is trying to go. Around this area, consists of an industrial coastal area, with many factories and warehouses. Victor knows exactly where he is headed, however the rest of the men have no idea what any of his moves are going to be. The night sky continues to shine throughout the area. Headlights that are coming from other surrounding vehicles, reflect against the landscape of the road. For a Friday night, traffic seems to be not as active as it usually is.

As the men keep on the highway, the headlights seem to dissipate, and there are less vehicles travelling in this area. This causes the men to have an intense anxious feel; one which is completely different than they were previously feeling. What makes this feeling different, is that the men begin to feel unsure as to what will follow while they are in this current setting.

A few minutes later, Victor finally reaches the exit he wishes to take. Russell stays right behind him, and follows by exiting off the highway as well. Victor proceeds into a commercial back roadway, adjacent between various abandoned warehouses and factory units. Victor is driving at an usually low speed, and Russell continues to caravan right behind him at the same rate. Minutes later, Victor eventually increases his speed, and he now swerves into more side business streets. Despite it being Friday night, these buildings contain various closed outlets, office buildings and strip malls. Eventually, Victor branches out from this area. He directs himself towards Pacific Coast Highway, a populated street with much activity. The men are now in Huntington Beach, a city located in Orange County. An area which is south of Los Angeles. This is a high activity location, with high entertainment value. With several patrons standing outside nightclubs, shopping centers and restaurants, and there are many people walking on the sidewalk. As the men continue to travel down this road, they start to truly feel more comfortable. Towards the right of the street, you can get a great view of the beach. Victor stays on this road for several minutes, as the booming entertaining crowds creep away into a quieter industrial area of Huntington Beach, where there are not many people present.

As he's driving, Russell looks out towards the ocean, at the waves crashing onto the shore. He feels captivated by the surroundings he's in, and embraces every bit of it. Victor suddenly positions his vehicle to the far right lane, and puts on his turning signal. He immediately pulls into an isolated shelter, featured on the far side of the beach, facing the shore. The area is nearly completely dark, with only the moonlight, and a couple outdoor lights perched, giving out very little illumination. Off to the side, there are many ledges to where people can sit down if they wish to. There are also many boats and ships out in the distance of the water. Victor parks in the small parking area, located adjacent to the shelter, and turns off the ignition. Russell then pulls up to a spot to the right of him, and turns off his car as well. As he's looks out towards the ocean, Russell starts to wonder why Victor chose this particular area to finally pull over at. The men remain in their vehicles for a few minutes, and observe the ocean view, and the sound of the waves pulling in.

Victor while he's still in his car, opens up his glove compartment, and takes out a box of Marlboro cigarettes. He becomes frustrated when he cannot find his cigarette lighter. Victor walks out of the car, and rummages through his trunk. Russell, Brian and Jesse, nervously watch every move he makes, not knowing exactly what he's looking for. Victor after ransacking his trunk, cannot find his lighter and feels frustrated. He closes his trunk and locks his car. Victor then looks out towards the ocean, sticking a cigarette inside of his mouth. He turns his head over to Russell's vehicle, hesitating to walk over. A few seconds later, Victor reluctantly walks over to Russell's car, and knocks on his window. Russell rolls down his window, and Victor speaks.

"Any of you guys have a lighter? I can't find mine."

Russell while he's starting at Victor, unintentionally laughs at him, and congruently Brian reaches into his pocket and pulls out a lighter. Brian then walks out of Russell's car. He hands Victor the lighter, and Victor lights his cigarette. Russell right after this, walks out the car. Jesse immediately follows him, and Russell locks his car. Victor then takes a couple puffs from his cigarette, and he reaches in his pocket to grab his pack of cigarettes. He waves them in the air, hinting if the other men would like to have one. Russell, Brian and Jesse each take a cigarette. All four of the men sit down on the ledges facing the ocean, remaining quiet. The only sounds are coming from tides of the sea. Russell as he's looking out towards the water, starts to softly speak to Victor.

"Hey, Victor. I'm sorry about earlier man. I know that you probably don't want to hear me say that, but I feel bad for what I said to you. I'm so sorry, and I want you to forgive me."

Victor takes a puff from his cigarette, and looks down towards the ground and responds.

"It's okay. I get used to it. You're not the first to go off on me like that."

Russell shakes his head, and continues to look out towards the distance. Victor continues.

"I grew up not that far from here. When I was a teenager, I would always come to this beach, and read quite a lot. I would ditch school quite often, because the other guys at my school would always call me 'Creature Feature', and be scared of me. Only because I look like a movie monster, I got treated like shit, and was always bullied. It was so tough for me to deal with that."

Brian stands up from the ledge, facing behind the rest of the four men. He takes a puff of his cigarette, and then starts to stretch his body. Victor then carries on, talking softly.

"If you want me to tell the truth, I had intended to go somewhere else to kill myself at first. Where exactly? Well that's none of your fucking business. I decided to change my mind, and go somewhere I knew was a special peaceful spot to me. I believe I made the right choice."

Jesse then with his cigarette in one hand, gets up, and walks over and stands behind where Victor is sitting. Russell notices Jesse walk over, but he keeps his head facing forward. Jesse then starts to massage Victor's back with his other hand. Victor doesn't emote or respond at all to Jesse's actions, but Victor does take a puff of his cigarette. Jesse then talks to him.

"Victor, I know exactly how you feel. There are times to where I get into this deep level of depression. Usually brought on from feeling excluded from everyone else. We all care about you, and we love you man. We are all dysfunctional rejects, so it's going to be alright."

Victor doesn't respond to Jesse, but he does mentally agree with him. Jesse continues to massage Victor's back, and Brian pulls out his phone turning on some smooth electronic music. Brian sets his phone down on the ledge, and takes another puff from his cigarette. Brian then starts to speak to Victor, while looking down towards the ground.

"Yup. You're stuck with us man. That shit Russell tried to pull was epic fail. He's just an asshole, so don't worry about him. Victor, it's alright buddy. We're here for you man. Okay?"

Russell laughs and shakes his head at what Brian said, and continues to keep his vision out towards the ocean. Victor doesn't react and keeps stone faced. Like Russell, he looks at the waves of the ocean as well. Victor then takes another puff of his cigarette and carries on talking.

"But, you guys are at least somewhat normal. I'm this scary freak nobody likes, and there is nothing that's going to make me think otherwise. That's very kind of all of you to think of me like that, but the truth is, compared to you guys, I'm on a different category, and you guys simply do not understand how much more difficult it is for me to deal with all the bullshit."

Russell laughs to himself for a bit, and while facing ahead, Russell responds to Victor.

"I'm going to tell you something Victor, and I want you to listen. You don't have to like me. I know you think I'm an evil wicked man. That's okay, because it's somewhat true. Ha-ha. But seriously man, listen up. If everyone was the same, this world would be boring as fuck. You are special Victor; you matter to us. Forget what I said earlier, that should show you that I'm not perfect either. I'm human, and you're human as well. Cheer up man."

Victor shakes his head, and responds to Russell while he's looking at the ocean.

"I suppose you're right Russell. Maybe I am letting myself down a bit too much, and not understanding how much me being unique, makes me a special in that way. I'm sorry for pulling the gun on you man, but I don't regret doing it. You're an asshole, and you needed that. I wasn't trying to hurt you, but I didn't like the way you were talking to me and the rest of the guys."

Russell takes a puff from his cigarette, and shakes his head. He then looks down towards the ground and begins to feel guilty. Under his breath, he speaks to all the men.

"I am an asshole yes, and I'm sorry. I'm sorry Victor. I'm sorry that I caused you to feel depressed and upset. I'm sorry Brian for disrespecting you, and getting in your grill like that man. I'm sorry for hitting you Jesse, and also saying those harsh horrible things to you."

Victor, Brian and Jesse, do not respond to Russell, but they believe that he's being honest with wanting to apologize for his previous behavior. Victor then responds to him.

"It just doesn't feel right at all. I have to accept that Kevin isn't here with us, and he's never going to be with us ever again. It's not fucking fair. Why him? There's nothing we can do, and that's the part that's so fucked up. I know he was your best friend Russell, and that's one thing we both currently share, is that we are dealing with coming to terms on Kevin. It's so sad."

Russell looking down on the ground, responds to Victor in a quiet tone.

"I don't know man; I can't answer any of that. Of course it's not fair, life isn't fucking fair at all man. Kev didn't deserve that at all, and if I have to deal with it, you have to deal with it as well. We all have to support each other, and stay strong about it. Kev would have wanted us to be happy, and not hold onto feeling depressed and sad. But yeah it's not fair that Kev is gone."

Brian takes a puff from his cigarette and looks at the ocean, responding to Russell.

"Russell, you didn't have to go off like you did though. You know that was fucked up, and acting like a jerk and turning your back on us like you did wasn't right. All of us miss Kevin, every single one of us, but there is nothing we can do about it. I'm sorry Russell."

Jesse picks up Brian's phone, to find out what song is playing. While he's still looking at the screen of Brian's phone, Jesse then and responds to all of the guys.

"I don't want us to fight, and to act this way. It's not worth it. We need to stick together."

Russell continues to look out at the ocean, and feels guilty. He then speaks to the men.

"Nothing at all can excuse what I've done. I do want for us all to stick together as friends. We've gone through so much to distance apart now. With Kev gone, I'm still not accepting he's not here. I keep thinking about him, and his sense of humor. Ugh... I'm sorry guys. I mean I hope you all understand why I acted that way, and you forgive me for all of it. Please."

Victor immediately starts to laugh out loud to himself. Everyone else ignores him, and following that, while he's facing the ocean, Victor responds to Russell.

"Russell, I'll only forgive your apology if you do two things. One, I want you to take us out to eat. Me, Brian and Jesse, I want you to to treat all of us. You don't have to worry about where to go, because it's my decision. I want Japanese food. The next thing, I want you to take us all to 'Knott's Berry Farm' tomorrow. I haven't been since I was young, and I really want to go. We all deserve a day to have fun together, so why not? Is this something you can do?"

Russell stands up from the ledge and takes another puff of his cigarette. He then responds.

"You want me to take you out for Japanese food, and you want us to go to an amusement park tomorrow in addition to that? Well...alright, I guess it's the least I can do to make up for what happened earlier. Okay Victor, I'll grant both of your wishes man. If this is what will make you happy. Only just this one time though, don't press your luck with me anymore. I'm not normally this nice of a guy, so understand this is uncommon that I'm doing this."

Victor then turns his head towards Russell, and stands up from sitting on the ledges. He immediately stands up and walks over to Russell, giving him a tight hug. Russell then smiles at him, and returns the favor but embracing him in the same way. Victor then walks over to Brian and Jesse, and hugs them both also very close, like he did with Russell. Feeling pleased that he was able to make peace with Russell, Victor now no longer feels depressed, and is glad that he is being appreciated. They all remain standing close to each other for a while, then Victor walks towards the ocean; staring out in the distance for a couple minutes, observing the scene. With a wide grin on his face, Victor starts to speak to the other men.

"Thank you guys for helping me. I was scared that I was going to do something really scary tonight. I was so depressed, and was so low. I wanted to give up that badly. I don't like being pushed aside, and being neglected and rejected. It's a terrible feeling to have. But I do feel special, and I know that I belong with all of you, and you guys belong with me. I'm happy."

Brian nods his head and walks over to Victor and rubs his shoulder. He then talks to him.

"Yeah, calm down man. It's going to be alright. We're here, and we are always going to be here for you. No more feeling suicidal, okay Victor? Can you promise me man?"

Brian then kisses Victor on his forehead, and rubs his hair. Victor laughs to himself, then in a flash second, Victor grabs the back of Brian's head, and kisses him on the lips passionately. They kiss for a few seconds, and Brian pushes himself away from Victor. Russell and

Jesse watch the both of them in amusement. Brian then shakes his head, and smiles at Victor.

"Okay, okay, you feel better now? Did that cheer you up? You're such a bag of tricks."

Victor stares deeply and smirks at Brian, and laughs to himself. He then responds.

"My god, I never noticed how handsome you are. You're a very handsome man Brian."

Brian rubs the back of his head, and smiles at Victor. Brian then replies to Victor.

"I don't want to brag, but yes I'm a good looking guy, and I'm also the best looking guy. But all of us are handsome in our own way. Russell is handsome. Jesse is handsome. Kevin was handsome. Even you Victor, you might not realize, but you are also handsome in some ways. Ha-ha. Let me get that junk you wiped on your face off."

Brian takes a clean cloth from his pocket, and starts to wipe the shoe police Victor rubbed on his face, off. Victor smiles at Brian, and then turns his view back towards the ocean. Brian shakes his head, and takes a puff from his cigarette. Jesse watches the other three men, observing their behavior. Russell during this time, takes out his phone and starts to look up nearby Japanese restaurants. He ends up finding a restaurant, and taps Victor on the shoulder to get his attention. Russell asks if the restaurant is okay, and Victor agrees. Immediately following that, Russell makes a reservation at the restaurant for all of them. After placing the reservation, Russell goes back to watching ocean, listening to the roaring sound of the waves, as they flow through the sea. Once all the men have finished their cigarettes, Brian grabs all the butts, and throws them away in a nearby trashcan.

Victor then stands up, absorbing one final glance at the ocean, and reaches inside his pocket taking out his car keys. He then proceeds towards his car. The rest of the men then take this as a sign for them to leave, and they as well take one last look at the beach. Russell, Brian and Jesse then walk towards Russell's car. All of the men then drive away from the scene, heading towards the restaurant. Victor follows

Russell on their way to the destination. They proceed back towards Pacific Coast Highway, where the restaurant is situated on. As it being Friday night, there are people standing outside various restaurants and clubs, and there is a high profile of activity going around. Russell reaches the restaurant, and he along with Victor, park in the designated area behind the building.

The men exit out of their vehicles, and walk inside. The restaurant has a space age artistic and futuristic theme, with many vibrant colors and lights being assorted around for decoration. Many modern and contemporary patterns are placed all around. The restaurant has a bar and lounge associated with it, adding a more intimate and personal feel. As the men are escorted to their table by the waitress, they are seated at a booth. Russell and Jesse, and Brian and Victor sit adjacent to each other on both sides of the table. The men give their drink orders to the waitress. Russell and Brian both order a pint of beer, Jesse orders a Tequila Sunrise, and Victor orders himself a Sake to drink. Once the waitress leaves the table, the men all begin to read over the menu. Victor then compliments the makeup of the restaurant.

"This place is really something. I never seen a restaurant this abstract and innovate such as this before. Very lovely and nice. Had no idea places like this existed. I'm so embarrassed to admit this, but I never eat out really, because I'm by myself all the time. Meh."

Russell looks at Victor for a second and raises his eyebrows, and responds to him.

"Well, I'm happy that you're getting a chance to experience this new opportunity."

The waitress returns to their table, giving the men their drinks. She asks if they are ready to order, and as they are having a difficult time deciding what to get, they ask her to give them a little more time. When she leaves, Victor thinks of an interesting plan, and speaks to the guys.

"I wonder if we should get the sampler plate. That seems to be a good choice. It's a little of everything, and we can just share it, and take what we want. Yeah, let's do that."

The men quickly agree towards his idea on ordering that. When the waitress returns once again to their table, they order the sampler plate. It consists of several special dishes, including a large order of different sushi varieties. California Roll, Sashimi Sushi Roll, Tuna Roll, and Spicy Wasabi Roll. It also comes with a large order of pot stickers, shrimp tempura, beef dumplings, and chicken teriyaki and rice. Along with that comes miso soup, and salad. While they are waiting for their order to arrive, Victor starts to speak to all of the guys.

"You know what's funny, I'm half Japanese, and don't really get to eat Japanese food that much. So this is nice that I'm getting to honor my culture and heritage this way. Ha-ha."

Brian is on his phone watching a live mixed martial arts fight. Jesse is playing a trivia game on Russell's phone. Russell who is the only one who has his attention undivided, takes a sip from his beer, and nods his head in agreement with Victor. Victor then continues to have a one sided conversation with Russell, who's listening to everything Victor says, nodding his head for quite some time.

When their order finally arrives at the table, the quantity of food is much larger than they anticipated. They men are all in shock, not expecting for the order to be that large. However, they don't see this as a negative aspect at all. They each enjoy the food, and eat all of the contents. Once they finish their food, Brian returns to watching the fight on his phone, and Jesse goes back to playing the game on Russell's phone. Victor then continues to ramble on about miscellany topics to Russell; which Russell simply nods his head in return. The waitress soon comes back to the table with the check. Russell takes out both his wallet and credit card, and places the card inside the checkbook. Russell then looks at Victor.

"Did you want something for dessert? You can have whatever you want, I don't care."

Victor nods his head at Russell, then responds to him. Victor then pulls out his phone.

"I like 'Cold Stone' a lot. I haven't had it in a while. There's one right around the corner."

Russell nods his head, and finishes his beer. The waitress collects Russell's credit card and leaves the table, and Brian shows the fight on his phone to Russell, commentating on it.

"That guy got creamed, damn. He got pulverized, he's bleeding all over the place. Shit."

Russell shakes his head and laughs. He looks down at the table and responds to Brian.

"Conor McGregor is a beast, what can I say? Unfair fight if you ask me. I don't know."

The waitress returns to the table one final time, giving Russell back his credit card, and the receipt of the bill. Russell reaches into his wallet and takes out several cash bills for a tip. The men then walk out of the restaurant, and head towards the ice cream store. Once arriving there, they each order whichever ice cream they care for. After getting their ice cream, all the men sit on a bench directly outside of the store, and eat. Brian then starts to speak to Russell.

"Russell, you and Jesse can leave together, I'll ride back with Victor. It will be alright. That way you don't have to drop me off, then head to your place. It's easier that way."

Russell doesn't respond to Brian, but Brian can tell that Russell agrees to this. When the men finish their ice cream, they all hug and say goodbye to each other. Victor and Brian drive away towards "Home Base", with Brian sitting in the passenger seat. Russell and Jesse then drive away together. As Russell is driving, he quickly remembers something he forgot. Russell reaches into his pocket for his phone; dialing Brian's number. He then hands Jesse his phone.

"Shit, I forgot. Ask Brian what time Victor wants to meet up at tomorrow, please."

Jesse speaks to Brian over the telephone, asking him what Russell instructed him to tell. Brian responds that Victor wants to arrive to the amusement park as early as possible, and they want to meet up at 9 A.M. tomorrow. Jesse hangs up Russell's phone, and sets it under the center console. While Russell is driving, Jesse turns his head over at him, and speaks.

"Russell, can I still stay with you? I know you said you didn't mean what you said earlier, but I still want to make sure it's okay. Because if you want me to go I will. It's okay."

Russell while keeping his view towards the road, smiles and reaches over to rub Jesse's hair. Jesse smiles at Russell, and he turns the stereo volume up. Russell then heads immediately to his residence. As he and Jesse are walking inside, Russell walks over to the refrigerator, and ruffles through the items resting on top of it. Russell pulls out a small bag, waving it at Jesse. Jesse walks over to him leaning his head on Russell's stomach, and Russell wraps his arm around Jesse's back. Russell while he's holding the bag, starts to whisper to Jesse.

"Aww, Kev. I had a feeling he left this here by mistake. Wanted to check and make sure. We're not going to smoke all of it no, but I do want all of us to smoke some of it in honor of Kev. He would have wanted us to enjoy this, I just know. The rest I want to probably lock away forever, so it's something I'll always have from him. Damn, I'm gonna miss that guy."

Russell and Jesse embrace each other for a couple minutes, then they separate from each other. Jesse walks into the bedroom, and starts to undress into his sleepwear. Russell takes of his shoes, and sits on the sofa to watch "Law and Order", on the television. Jesse then walks over to Russell.

"I'm going to go to bed. I'm really tired, so I'm going to go to sleep now."

Russell while still looking at the television quickly snaps back at Jesse.

"You can do what you want. Shit I'm not even tired, I might not even sleep tonight, or I may rest my eyes here for like an hour or so. I'll see you tomorrow then. Sleep tight."

Jesse with an unsure expression on his face, crosses his arms and walks back into the bedroom closing the door behind him, and crawls into Russell's bed. A few minutes later, Jesse falls asleep. The following morning, Jesse wakes up at 8 A.M. He gets out of bed, and arranges the outfit he plans to wear at the amusement park, which is a red patterned button up shirt, and some denim shorts, with red Vans sneakers. Jesse heads out the bedroom towards the bathroom to shower, and he notices that Russell is sitting on the sofa, already fully dressed. He's wearing a black polo shirt, with blue jeans and black Adidas shoes. Jesse walks out the shower and into the bedroom to dress himself, and once he's finished with that, Russell and Jesse put their sunglasses on and walk out the door. While Russell is backing out of the parking structure, he talks to Jesse.

"I already spoke with Brian, and he said to meet him and Victor there. So we're just going to head straight there. I haven't been to Knott's Berry Farm in ages though. So random."

Jesse nods his head, and Russell gets on the highway; proceeding straight to the amusement park. As they arrive, Russell is aggravated due to there virtually not being any available parking spaces in the parking lot closest to the entrance. It is after all a Saturday. Quite arguably the most populated day to visit. After understanding that the parking lot is full, Russell drives farther away to another parking structure, a mile away from the entrance. Luckily, this particular lot does have available parking spots. Russell parks his car, and he and Jesse start to walk towards the amusement park. "Knott's Berry Farm", is California's oldest amusement park. It was once a Berry Farm operated by Walter Knott. Over the years, it has later been converted into its own special theme park. It is mostly frontier and western themed, and contains not only Roller Coasters, but several Californian gold rush, and pre civil war United States themed exhibits, and also many Native American homage entertainment attractions as well. Russell and Jesse reach the entrance of the theme park, and notice the ridiculously long lines queuing up outside the front gate.

The park doesn't open until 10 A.M., another fifteen minutes or so. It is a perfect day today, with the sun shining very bright. The temperature despite being early in the day, is already quite warm and humid. There are light clear blue skies, making this a wonderful day to visit an amusement park. This is extremely immaculate weather. As Russell and Jesse wait outside the gate, Russell starts to text Brian, trying to find out where exactly he is at this time. Brian responds back to Russell, that he and Victor are remarkably standing outside the gate as well. Russell and Jesse then try to see if they can spot where they are, but due to high volume of people waiting outside the gate, it is impossible to spot them out. Russell and Jesse decide to remain in line. Once they are inside the park, they will wait near the entrance, so they can gather together. Minutes later, the park does open, and Russell and Jesse walk through the gates.

All of the men shortly after that, eventually reunite with each other. Victor is wearing a blue graphic t-shirt and jeans and white tennis shoes. Brian is wearing a black buttoned up shirt, also with jeans and sneakers. The men quickly wait in line for the "Ghostwriter" rollercoaster, positioned right beside the entrance of the park. After riding the rollercoaster, the guys then go look at a wild west performance show. Following that, they go and check out several gift and hobby shops located all around the park.

The men get on two more ride attractions, the mine cart underground ride, and they also get on the log flume ride. Even though the men are having a nice time, most of their day is being spent standing in line for attractions. The park is extremely crowded on this particular day, so the que times to get on the rides will be quite lengthy. While they are waiting in line for the rides, the men engage in banter and friendly talk. Using these opportunities to chat with each other and expand socially; finding things about one another that they didn't know beforehand. The day continues onto the evening, with the men practically checking out every ride and attraction the park has to offer almost. One of the last attractions the men all witness together, is a Native American 3D animation presentation called the "Mystery Lodge".

The show tells a story about Native American lifestyle and nature. Once they leave the show, it is now late in the evening. Russell and Jesse wish to go to the video arcade. Brian and Victor decide to revisit some rides they have already been on. The men all agree on separating from each other for the rest of the day. Russell and Jesse say goodbye to

Brian and Victor, and they all go on about their way through the amusement park. Russell and Jesse once inside the arcade, play several games. Russell plays one of Kevin's favorite games, which is "Time Crisis". Russell although not as skilled as Kevin was at it, does rather well in the game. Russell and Jesse then go to the air hockey tables. Russell notices that Jesse is not that great at the game, and lets him win several times, with Jesse quickly deducing what Russell is doing. However, they are having a great amount of fun while playing.

Russell and Jesse leave out of the arcade, and then decide to take a risk that it being so late in the evening, that the whitewater rafting ride won't have a long line. Sure enough, the line for the ride isn't long at all. They get on, and they get moderately wet, as suspected. Due to the night still being quite humid, they are able to dry off fast. Russell and Jesse then walk through many prize redemption skill games. Russell asks Jesse if he wants to win a prize for him, and Jesse says no. Russell doesn't listen to him, and plays a game anyways. In order to win a prize, Russell has to throw darts at balloons to pop them. Russell successfully does on his first try, and Jesse picks out a big "Snoopy" doll to take. They both then get on an elevator gentle ride, and then on the train attraction which takes you around the park. Russell and Jesse then decide to go home, as it's now almost 9 P.M., and the park closes in an hour. Before heading home, Russell and Jesse stop at the "Knott's Berry Farm" fried chicken fast food restaurant still attached to the park.

While they are waiting in line to order, Yvette surprisingly taps on Jesse's shoulder.

"Oh my god, Jesse!? Is that you? This is a small world. How have you been sweetheart?"

Yvette didn't notice Russell standing in front of him. But Jesse turns arounds to her.

"Yvette! I'm doing fine. It's good to see you girl! Oh god!"

Yvette and Jesse hug, and from hearing Jesse acknowledge Yvette, Russell turns around and reveals his face to Yvette. She has a complete opposite reaction to him, and responds.

"Oh, hey Russell. How are you hun? You doing good?"

Russell simply nods his head and smirks at her. Russell and Yvette then hug each other. Yvette is with a male companion of hers. He is a forty-year-old bald Caucasian man with a hockey beard and mustache who's extremely quiet. Yvette then introduces him to both Russell and Jesse.

"Matt, these were my coworkers from the bank I worked at. I don't think they have ever met you. You guys, this is Matt. I've been dating him for a while. He's never been to 'Knott's Berry Farm', so I thought I would take him here. My kids are with my sister, and they are out in the park somewhere having fun. I wanted to get a quick bite to eat. Nice seeing you both."

Matt shakes both Russell and Jesse's hand. Jesse then engages in small talk with Yvette, while waiting in line. Jesse quickly comes up with a fib, that he and Russell are at the park, because Jesse asked Russell to take him there, due to Jesse's affinity for amusement parks. He also explains to her that he and Russell are now close friends. He of course is not revealing any of the recent antics and shenanigans that he and Russell have been involved in. Not explaining to her anything about Brian and Victor. Yvette based on her past relationship with Jesse, has no doubts at all to what he's explaining to her.

Yvette explains that she now has a job at Matt's tow truck company as a receptionist. Russell due to his difficult relationship with Yvette, decides not to speak to her at all, keeping his head forward, eavesdropping at Jesse's conversation with her. He does however smile to himself, that Jesse is clever enough to keep everything a secret. Russell reaches the counter, and orders food for himself and Jesse. Yvette and Matt then place their order. When Russell and Jesse's order is ready, Yvette and Jesse hug once more, and say goodbye to each other. Yvette then smacks Russell on his shoulder, and she gives him a disappointed look, and quickly gives him a hug.

She and Matt then walk away. Russell and Jesse then walk the long distance back to Russell's car, staying silent of each other. Jesse holds onto the large stuffed "Snoopy" dog that Russell won for him. Once inside the car, Russell takes out his box of cigarettes, and gives

Jesse one. He lights his cigarette, and lights Jesse's cigarette as well. Russell takes puffs of his cigarette, while he's driving. Jesse turns up the stereo which is playing hip hop music. Throughout the car ride home, Jesse and Russell remain quiet and don't speak at all.

When they both arrive to Russell's home, Jesse places the stuffed animal in the corner of the living room, underneath Russell's framed sports jerseys. Jesse then slips off his shoes and takes one of his fashion magazines, and walks inside Russell's bedroom. Jesse lays down on Russell's bed, listening to music while reading the magazine. Russell takes off his shoes and socks, and sets them under the coffee table. He then walks over to the kitchen, and opens the freezer. He takes out a bottle of vodka, and pours it into a glass taking a sip. Russell then walks out to the balcony connected to his kitchen, and walks over to the side connecting to his bedroom.

With the curtains slightly open, Russell notices Jesse is unaware that he's standing outside, due to the night sky, and Jesse having his headphones on. Russell knocks loudly on the glass, scaring Jesse greatly. Russell then laughs at him, and Jesse gives him a disgusted expression. Russell signals for Jesse to unlock the balcony door and he does. Russell stands in the doorway, and raises the vodka glass in front of Jesse and grunts, signaling him if he wants a sip. Jesse takes a swallow of the vodka and they both smile at each other.

Russell then pecks Jesse on the cheek. Jesse then returns to Russell's bed, puts his headphones back on, and returns to his magazine. Russell shuts the balcony door, and looks out towards the city and the night sky. Taking sips from his glass of vodka, smiling to himself.

CHAPTER 19:

NOTHING SMOOTH, NOTHING ROUGH

The following morning, Jesse awakes in Russell's bed by himself. He is staring outside the balcony window, looking at the sun and sky. Still feeling slightly tired, Jesse turns his head over to the alarm clock on the nightstand; it is showing that it's 11:30 A.M. He comes out of the bedroom, and walks to the living room where Russell currently is sitting down on the sofa watching a football game. Russell is wearing a white hoodie, and some black sweatpants with sneakers. Jesse takes a seat down on the sofa beside him, and watches the television screen showing the sports game. Russell is eating a bowl of corn flakes, and drinking a cup of coffee as well. A few minutes later, Jesse walks back into the bedroom, and picks out a pair of clothes to wear, and then heads into the shower. While Jesse is in the bathroom, Russell receives a text message from Brian, to come to "Home Base" immediately. Russell informs Jesse of the text message, and after Jesse dresses himself in a t shirt and shorts, both of the men leave, and head out towards "Home Base". Russell starts to wonder what the problem is, as he can tell that Brian wouldn't have asked him and Jesse to show up otherwise.

Russell then from all the anxiety from their final heist Friday, and Kevin sadly being killed as a result of it, starts to remember that they never actually officially discussed what they all plan to do from this point on. Also, they haven't divided the money they received during the heist between the men yet. What they were able to get from the final heist, was once again given to Max to hold onto temporarily, who is also keeping the cash from their first heist. Even though Kevin is no longer here, Russell is confused as to what will happen now between him and the other men. He has a feeling that Brian calling them to all meet up, might have something to do with that, and a major development has been newly discovered somehow.

Russell is glad that for the most part, he has accepted Kevin's fate, and is going through the grieving process. He is happy that yesterday the men went to an amusement park, to have fun and get together in an exciting and joyous situation such as that. He found it odd and pleasing that he ran into Yvette, and being glad she is taking what happened in the past well. Russell has all of these thoughts in his head, as he drives to the unit to meet up with Brian and Victor. Once he parks his car outside the unit, Russell with Jesse proceeds over to the door of the unit, and unlocks it. As they both walk inside, Brian is pacing all around the unit looking down towards the floor, with his hand behind his head looking very nervous and anxious. Victor is sitting over at the sofa area, making doodles of landscapes on a piece of paper. Russell walks over to Brian and talks to him.

"So, what's going on exactly? Is something wrong? Tell me what happened, I'm not going to get mad. If something happened, just tell me man."

Brian continues to pace all around, looking unsure of himself. He then stares at Russell for a few seconds, and gives a menacing expression at him. Brian responds, and snaps back at him.

"That's a lie, you always fucking get mad at the slightest shit Russell. Everything is a huge fucking big deal to you. You always overact to stuff. So, you will get mad. I just know."

Russell smirks at Brian, and shakes his head. Jesse during this time walks over to the sofa and sits next to Victor, and watches him as Victor is continuing to draw. Victor looks at Jesse, and they both smile at each other. Jesse then picks up completed pictures Victor drew, and is amazed at Victor's talent. The pictures are of parks and other nature themed settings of trees, buildings and birds. Brian then walks to the kitchen area, and pulls out two Budweiser's, giving one to Russell. They both open their beers, and Brian takes a sip of his. He then continues to speak to Russell.

"Victor was reading the paper today. You never mentioned that Kevin had a family. But they are holding a funeral for him on Wednesday. That's what I wanted to tell you."

Russell takes a swallow of his beer, and shakes his head. During the investigation of their last heist, Kevin's body was properly identified a few hours after his body was sent to be examined. The authorities ruled that Kevin was a hostage during the heist, as he has no criminal ties, and has no prior criminal records either. Russell creeps over to Brian's workstation and gazes at the classic cars Brian has parked. One of which is the Oldsmobile convertible. Russell starts to move his hands around the convertible. He then replies to Brian while looking at the car.

"I never mentioned he had a family, because I didn't even fucking know he had one. Kevin told me his parents both died, and the rest of his family forgot about him. He always told me he was the Black Sheep, and was never appreciated or understood. I don't know."

What Russell mentioned to Brian was correct. Kevin has a complex family situation, and his parents are both deceased. Kevin must have had distant family which live in the area as well, that he never revealed or made notice to Russell about. His family members were told that he was killed, and have quickly arranged a funeral service for him to take place in a few days. This news comes as quite a shock for Russell. The last funeral he went to a few weeks ago, was for Peter and Jennifer. It was during this funeral that he found out about Brian being the robber who escaped during the heist at the "Sunset Credit Union", and Victor being the guy who originally was supposed to rob the bank, but stood outside and watched the entire time.

Both of these men, whom were present at the funeral. As Kevin was someone who was very close with him, Russell feels obligated to attend, and has many conflicting emotions. One part of him feels secure in attending the funeral to respect Kevin, and to say his final goodbye to him. The other side of Russell feels guilty that he is the reason that Kevin was killed. If he was never reintroduced to Russell's life, Kevin most likely would not have gotten involved with the rest of the men. It was because of his actions of playing a part in the bank heists, which was ultimately the death of him. Russell feels strange that he will attend the funeral, and people would be curious as to who he is. He has never met Kevin's family, and they have no knowledge or recollection to him either.

Russell takes another swallow of his beer, and continues to run his hands around the convertible, being very attracted to this particular car. Jesse who was eavesdropping on Russell and Brian's conversation, turns his view over at Russell, and looks at him feeling concerned. Russell opens his mouth to begin to say something to Brian, but is interrupted at a knock from the front door of the unit. Brian walks over, and opens the door to find Max on the other side. Max walks into the unit, and directs himself to where Russell is. He then starts talking to Russell.

"So. I heard that there will be a funeral service for Kevin on Wednesday. I would like to attend, so if you all could help me get there it would be nice."

Russell turns his head over to Max and takes another swallow of his beer. He laughs to himself, and looks back at the convertible. Russell under his breath responds to Max.

"What's funny, is that I didn't even decide if I was going to go yet. Part of me wants to, and the other part of me doesn't. I feel guilty for showing up, knowing that I put Kevin through this, when I didn't have to. I guess now I don't have a choice. Max if you wish to go, then that settles it. I'm going to go as well. All of us are going. We owe it to Kevin to pay him respect."

Brian nods his head, and takes a swallow of his beer. Victor suspends his drawing, and walks over to where Russell, Brian and Max are. He was listening to everything they were talking about. Victor leans in close to Russell, and asks him a special request.

"Hey Russell, I was wondering if I could borrow a suit. I don't have one. I want to wear a suit at Kevin's funeral. I could ask Brian, but

I don't want to. I'm asking you. The rest of you guys know how to dress nice, and I could go to a suit shop and get one but again, I don't wish to. I would rather ask to borrow one from you. So can I please, if you don't mind?"

Russell smiles and shakes his head at Victor, and laughs to himself as well. He puts his hand on Victor's shoulder and responds to him in a soft quiet tone.

"Yeah I have a suit that you can wear. It's okay, you don't have to worry about not having anything nice to wear. I can cover you this time. Wednesday morning, you and Brian can stop by my place before the service, and I'll give you a suit. Don't worry about it."

Victor smiles at Russell, and returns to the sofa area, and carries on with his drawing. Max then starts to exit out of the unit. He says one final thing before leaving.

"I want for you each to know, that you guys are still contracted to clean buildings. This is your final week though, and then you guys are free, and won't have to do it anymore. As next month the contract expires. It's unfortunate that Kevin is no longer here, but I still need you guys to clean this week. You guys can take Wednesday off, but I need you to work this final week."

Russell looks down at the ground and nods his head. He for a while, forgot that he and the rest of the guys have been scheduled to clean buildings for the past weeks. With Kevin no longer being here, these thoughts have erased completely from his mind, and he wasn't even aware of the fact. As it's the last week they must do this job, Russell would rather get it over with, and finish it. Brian walks over to the door where Max is, and quickly responds to him.

"We will all be there, no problem. We will get the job done, and get to work no problem."

The rest of the guys say goodbye to Max. Brian then offers to take Max back to his unit, and they both walk out. Russell heads over to the sofa area where Jesse and Victor are, and takes a seat. He looks over and observes what Jesse and Victor are doing. Jesse is reading a fashion magazine that he brought with him, and Victor is drawing a picture of a tropical rainforest, showcasing exotic trees, waterfalls, birds, jaguars and monkeys. Russell picks up one of Victor's finished drawings, gazing at it with much fascination. This particular drawing Russell is holding, is of a peaceful countryside farm. With animals such as cows and pigs, standing next to trees and a sunflower field. As he's looking at the drawing, he speaks to Victor.

"These are really good man. You drew all these yourself? This is a really good talent man that you shouldn't waste. I'm amazed how easy and simple that you make it seem as well. This is dedication to draw like this, and there is potential for this type of talent you have. So many possibilities, you could get a job doing cartoons, or comic books and shit like that."

Victor doesn't immediately respond to Russell, and concentrates heavily on his drawings. Russell picks up another one of the drawings, observing every detail of it. He had no idea that Victor had the ability to construct a hidden gift such as this. Victor looks up quickly from his drawing, and notices that Russell is captivated by his art. He then replies to Russell.

"Believe it or not, I had a brief stint at 'Los Angeles Trade Tech' on Grand for a while, teaching art to people. It was nice that I was teaching people that had my same passion. The whole story is none of your fucking business, as things didn't work out. This is simply a passion I have. Nothing more or less at the moment. But thank you for the kind words on my work."

Russell stares at Victor, and shakes his head. He turns his view back to the drawing of the farm Victor drew, and Russell notices more things about the piece he didn't see before. Victor then continues to talk.

"I think I'm good, but I don't think I'm great or perfect, or at the same level of talent such as Van Gogh and Da Vinci are. The one which you're holding now, it might seem perfect to you, but to real artists, I've made at least ten mistakes, and several other things which could be improved. The tree trunk I feel I could have done better on, but art is like that sometimes."

Russell continues to look at Victor's drawing, and offers encouragement to Victor.

"Well you do have a talent man, and I don't know why you beat yourself up about it. You have great potential, and you have to be proud of these potentials that you possess you know?"

Victor nods his head at what Russell said, and continues to draw. Brian at this time arrives back inside the unit, and walks over to where the rest of the men are, and sits down.

"Hey Russell, I figured I would make this clear for you. On Wednesday, Victor, Max and I will arrive at your place. Victor can change, and then we'll leave. As the funeral is closer to where you stay anyways. We'll all ride there together. This is fine with you right?"

Russell takes another swallow of his beer while looking down. He responds to Brian.

"Yeah sure, whatever. That is fine by me. You know what, I think me and Jesse are going to head out. We'll meet you guys at work tomorrow, okay? We'll see you guys later."

Russell finishes the rest of his beer, and hands Brian the empty bottle he was drinking. All the men say goodbye to each other, and Russell and Jesse then walk out of the unit, and head to his car. When Russell arrives back at his residence, he quickly proceeds towards the living room. He grabs the box directly underneath the television, which contains his yarmulke. Russell opens the box up and holds his yarmulke in his hands for a short while. Jesse walks over to where he's standing, and Russell then starts to become sad. He then starts to whisper to Jesse.

"I'm fairly sure that Kev's family is going to be Jewish. He said he wasn't that serious about it, but I want to honor him in the best possible way. Even though his family don't know me, I still want to give a eulogy to him out of respect. I cared about him a great deal."

Jesse then reaches under the television set and grabs Russell's Tanakh. Russell quickly snatches the book away from Jesse and gives an angry look towards him. He then snaps at him.

"Did I ask you to touch that? I didn't right? So why did you do it? Don't touch what's not yours okay. That book is very special to me. It's hundreds of years old. Don't fucking touch it."

Russell places the book back under the television, and Jesse angrily fires back at him.

"I'm sorry for touching it yes, but I'm not sorry for your rude ass attitude. You didn't have to react that way about it at all. I only wanted to look at it. I'm sorry, but not sorry."

Jesse then takes a seat on the sofa, reading his magazine. Russell then responds to Jesse.

"Well, don't touch this book, ever. I don't want to see your fucking hands on it ever again. Am I understood? If I see you touching it again, I'm going to get mad. Don't touch it."

While he's reading the magazine, Jesse nods his head at Russell. Russell puts his yarmulke away back in the box, and sets it under the television set. He walks over to the kitchen area, and opens the freezer to pour himself a glass of Vodka. Russell then walks back to the sofa area, and turns on the television, which is now showing a basketball game. They both remain quiet for several hours as Jesse reads his magazine, and Russell watches the game. Later in the evening, Russell walks over to the kitchen and reheats the leftovers from the food they got at the amusement park the day before. Russell makes himself a plate, and Jesse joins him in the kitchen, and makes a plate of food from the leftovers as well.

They both return to the living room, and eat together. Immediately after eating, Jesse starts to feel tired. He walks inside Russell's bedroom, and changes into his sleepwear. He lays down in the bed, and drifts himself off to sleep. Russell walks over to the bedroom door, and shuts it. He returns to the television, now watching a football game. Russell a couple hours from this, feels tired and turns the television off. He then immediately falls deep asleep, while he's laying down on the couch.

Russell wakes up the next morning at around 9 A.M. He gets up from the couch, and walks inside his bedroom, where Jesse is still asleep. Not trying to wake him, he grabs the clothes he wishes to wear for the day and sets them in the side of the closet. Russell then directs himself to the bathroom to shower. Once Russell is finished bathing, he returns to the bedroom and dresses himself. While he's getting dressed, Jesse who at this point as woken up, pretends to still be sleeping, watches him. Russell has no idea that Jesse is awake, and tries to make as little noise as possible. When he finishes putting his clothes on, Russell returns to the sofa area, and watches the morning news. Jesse then walks to the closet, and gathers his outfit for the day. He walks into the bathroom and freshens himself up. Upon leaving the bathroom, Jesse proceeds to put his clothes on, and returns to the sit on the sofa with Russell.

Back at "Home Base", Brian and Victor start to prepare themselves for the day. Brian is in the bathroom in his underpants, trimming his face, with shaving cream being lathered on his face. Victor who has just woken up minutes ago also wearing his undershorts, watches him. Brian ignores him, and carries on with shaving. Victor then grabs the razor Brian is using, and playfully runs it over Brian's face a few times. Brian gives an agitated smile to Victor, and snatches the razor back from him, and continues to shave his face. Victor laughs, walks into the shower, and bathes himself. While Victor is in the shower, Brian finishes shaving, and gets dressed. He goes to the kitchen area, and makes himself a scrambled egg sandwich, and starts to eat it. When he's finished eating, Victor right after leaves the shower, and gets himself ready as well. Victor returns to the kitchen area, and makes himself a bowl of cereal. While he's eating, he reads a news website on his phone. Brian walks over by his bed, and gets his hair gel. He proceeds back into the bathroom, and styles his hair.

Russell and Jesse put on their sunglasses, and leave Russell's apartment to get to work. While he's driving, Russell who's feeling hungry, realizes they have spare time before they have to start working, stops at a "Jack In The Box" drive-thru. He orders a ham and cheese croissant sandwich and a coffee, and Jesse orders an orange juice and French toast. After getting their food, Russell drives straight to the "Wittberg Law Offices." He parks in the underground parking structure, and he and Jesse start to eat their breakfast. Russell pulls out his phone, and listens to Kevin's favorite news podcast, "This American Life", using an auxiliary cord to stream the audio through his car stereo. After they finish eating, Russell takes their trash and throws it away in the trash bin nearby where he is parked. Getting back into the vehicle, Russell takes a sip of his coffee, and tilts his head back in the seat. He listens to the radio show with his eyes closed. Jesse sits quietly listening to the podcast as well, keeping his vision forward. Russell and Jesse stay in the car, waiting until their work shift begins. Eventually, Brian and Victor arrive at the scene as well. The men only have a few minutes before work starts, so without wasting any time, all four of them go inside the building to commence their work duties.

Being that previously all of the men had a solid system and structure as to how the tasks were carried, things have to be done quite differently now that Kevin is not here. Not only the physical aspect of the men having to do considerably more work with it being only four of them, but mentally as well.

With Kevin not present, even though they aren't mentioning it out loud, it is still tough for them to go about the day without him. Following this week, the men no longer have to clean, so putting in mind that this will be their final work week, makes things slightly easier to deal with. Their performance towards their tasks, go by flawless. The men all find a way to equally work together to make up the tasks which need to be completed on Kevin's floor.

At intermittent times, they would run into each other while working, yet they aren't stopping to talk or chit chat. As they are all cleaning, they think about all the situations they have been faced with until this point. Realizing that they committed not one, but two separate heists. One of which have killed one of the members in their group. It's amazing how they are able to focus on work so well, never minding any of the previous events.

When Russell is mopping the floor, he starts to have flashbacks of how his life got to this point. He understands all of the actions and reactions, which made him be in this current position. Yet, he doesn't understand that why he was the unlucky one to be picked for all of this.

Russell thinks about his life working in banks, and how that was something he always aspired himself on doing. Wanting to rebel against not only his childhood and upbringing, but all the things which happened when the "Sunset Credit Union" was targeted. He's now a two time armed robbery culprit, and has had one of his close friends killed during these newly found hijinks that he decided to plan and orchestrate. Shockingly, this isn't enough.

Russell still has much vindication on his mind, and isn't close to feeling satisfied. The death of Kevin has possibly turned him into this unpredictable monster, that acts entirely on his impulses, whether they are logical or not. The other men strangely have quickly forgotten about all of the heists, and most of them still dealing with Kevin being killed. The past weekend was filled with mixed actions and reactions. Now, they must attend the funeral of Kevin, and it's something they never envisioned or imagined. Russell continues to work, still having bouts of flashbacks and distant memories running in his head.

Break time finally approaches, and the men start to put away their cleaning supplies. They all then walk up to the roof to start their break. Russell tells the rest of the guys that he wants to treat them to a snack. He puts on his sunglasses, and decides to drive to a fish taco restaurant nearby, while the remaining men wait outside on the roof of the building. As Russell arrives at the restaurant, he sees an extremely long line. The food at this restaurant is liked by many, so the long crowds are not uncommon. Russell being a man who at times cannot control his patience, starts to become aggravated over this. Feeling bored, he pulls out his phone and plays a bowling game. He continues to wait in line for several minutes, as he slowly gets closer to the counter. Russell is unaware because his head is down on his phone, that someone he knows just walked into the restaurant, and is standing right behind him. Russell has a strange feeling that something isn't quite right. His intuition is correct, but he simply ignores it and doesn't look around him. Russell with his head still focused on his phone, hears a voice shout out to him.

"Russell! Hey, Russell!"

Russell turns his head behind him, and notices that it's John calling out to him. Russell without making any expressions or gestures, scans his head back down to his phone. John who has sunglasses on as well, feeling angry that Russell is ignoring him, walks out out line from behind him, and gets about half a foot away from Russell's face. He shouts out to him again.

"Russell, I know that's you. So you can knock all that off. I have something to tell you."

The line moves, and Russell continues to ignore John, keeping his head down. John remains in Russell's personal space area, and when John pushes Russell's chest, he responds.

"If you fucking do that again, I will knock you the fuck out. What the hell do you want?"

John smirks at Russell and rubs his hands together. Russell stares at him angrily. John walks back in line, and mutters several words out to Russell while he is doing so.

"I'll let you order your food first, then I'll tell you what I have to say."

Russell shakes his head and continues to play the game on his phone. He eventually minutes later makes it to the counter, and places his order. Russell feels scared, because he is going to have to deal with John shortly. Russell returns to playing the game on his phone. John finishes placing his order, and walks over to Russell, who still has his head directed towards his phone. John stands in front of Russell for a few seconds, and proceeds to speak with him.

"Russell, I don't work at Sunset anymore. I now work at First Federal around the corner. I decided to take an assistant manager position there. I know that must hurt to hear."

Russell slightly smiles to himself, while he's still playing the game on his phone. John continues to torment Russell, and creeps closer to him, being only inches away from his face.

"I know you're still unemployed. Nobody will hire you, because you're pathetic Russell, and always have been. Peter felt sorry for you, and that's the only reason you got that manager job at Sunset. I don't understand why that man gave you a chance. I feel sorry for you."

Right after John finished saying that, Russell's order is ready. He walks to the counter and grabs his food. On his way out, he is stopped by John, who ruffles though Russell's hair.

"Where you going Russell? I hope it's to find a job, I know you don't have one."

Russell stops walking and turns back to where John is. He looks around the restaurant, and notices that everyone else is minding their own business. Russell then sets his food down on a table, and rushes over to John, grasping his collar very tightly. John grabs Russell's collar as well. Russell and John both grin at each other, not feeling intimidated at all. The other patrons in the restaurant watch the both of them. Both men let go of each other, and Russell grabs his food. He starts to walk out of the building. Not before John issues one final remark towards Russell.

"Bye Russell. It sucks to be you. Sucks to be you. You still look like Satan by the way."

Russell ignores John, and walks out of the restaurant. As he is going towards his car, Russell takes note that John said he is now working at the "First Federal Bank". Incidentally, this was the bank the men were going to choose on the last heist, based on a coin flip. In which they ended up choosing "First Savings and Trust" instead. Being that John is at that bank, Russell starts to feel sinister at this time.

He wants to rob one final bank, this being the absolute last time for sure. This will not only satisfy this current feeling of being incomplete, but will rectify whatever feelings he has for losing Kevin in their previous heist. John, who he considers his mortal arch enemy, is manager at that bank. Hitting just one more bank, would be the cherry on top, to make all of his oppression complete. The men who targeted his bank that day, that was also their third heist as well. Third time should be the charm. Russell gets in his car, and drives back to the other men still on break. He starts to wonder how he's going to relay this information to them, and if they are going to be supportive of it. Russell starts to feel scared that the other men might not agree to go along with it, especially considering the fact Kevin was killed in their last effort.

Russell sees it in a unique unconventional way. He wants to use this heist to avenge Kevin, and for them to go out and strike, only one more final time. Russell arrives back at the building, and walks up to the roof area meeting with the other guys. Not mentioning what just happened at the restaurant to the other men. He hands each of them their food, and doesn't reveal his latest scheme and plan quite yet. The men all eat their food, and talk about several petty things together. When they finish their food, they remain on the roof until the rest of their break is over. They quickly get back to work after their break, and stay focused completing the rest of their tasks. Russell cannot stop thinking about planning another heist. It wasn't strictly the confrontation he had with John earlier that set him off, but adding that situation with Kevin's death, makes him more determined to take charge with his thoughts.

As Russell continues to clean, he cannot keep his emotions calm any longer, and feels he has to explain this to everyone else. The men wrap up all of their work duties, and all meet up on the first floor. Russell then asks for all of them to meet him on the top floor, like they have a couple times before. Only this time, they are without Kevin. The men reluctantly unsure of what Russell wants, agree to follow him up there. After they walk inside the board room, Russell closes and locks the door behind him. He then opens the curtains in the room, as he customarily did all the times before they were in there; revealing the night city scape of Los Angeles. Russell then turns on the small lamp in the corner of the room, revealing a small source of light. Brian, Jesse and Victor sit around the table, and look at him in confusion, scared of what he has in store. Russell creeps over to the window and looks outside for a few seconds. He looks around at the surrounding buildings. With his vision pointing out the window, Russell lays it down to the men in a direct and swift way.

"Guys, let's do one more hit. This will for sure be the last and final time. We have to hit 'First Federal'. We were going to do it anyways, so might as well right? What do you guys say?"

Brian, becomes immediately irate; he jumps up from the table, and tackles Russell to the floor. Jesse and Victor try unsuccessfully to break them up, however Brian gives in, and lets Russell go. They both get off from the floor. Russell grins in an evil way to Brian, and Brian shakes his head. Brian unlocks the door to the room, and before walking out, yells to Russell.

"What do I say? I say you're a sick man. I'll see you tomorrow. Victor come on, we're leaving. Jesse, do you want to come with me, or are you alright?"

Jesse looks over at Russell who's grinning at Brian. Jesse then responds to him.

"No Brian, I'm okay. I'm going to go with Russell. I'll be fine. Thank you though."

Brian nods his head, and he and Victor say goodbye to Jesse, and walk out, with Brian giving one final angry glare at Russell, as he shuts the door. Russell then returns to looking out the window, and starts to whisper under his breath to Jesse.

"I fucking ran into John today at a restaurant during break. He works at 'First Federal' now. I didn't say anything to him, but he kept bothering me. Me and him fought, it's okay."

Jesse then covers his mouth, and walks over to Russell, responding quietly.

"Holy shit. No wonder that's why you want to do another heist. I normally would say no, but at this point, I seem to trust you. If you explain that to Brian, I'm sure he will change his mind and agree to do it. John, ugh. I fucking hate him, I believe he's racist and homophobic. I told you that right? Victor will do whatever we decide to do. I trust you Russell. I feel you."

Russell nods his head at Jesse, and continues to look out the window. A couple minutes later, Russell closes all the curtains in the room, and shuts off the light. He and Jesse walk out the room, and Russell locks the door. Russell makes sure all the rest of the doors in the building are locked, and he and Jesse head to the parking structure, and leave. As he's driving back home, Russell seems to not be too concerned over Brian's initial reaction towards doing one more heist. Brian since the beginning, has always been on the fence for going along with committing heists. He feels Brian's reaction was only natural, considering what they have been through. Russell reaches his residence, and parks his car. He and Jesse walk inside his apartment, and Russell proceeds over to the sofa, and takes a seat. Russell turns on the television, and watches "Shark Tank". Jesse feeling sleepy, then proceeds towards Russell's bedroom, lays down on the bed and rests. Russell runs over to the bedroom door, and shuts it, returning to watch the show. Russell continues to look at the television for a couple more hours, watching "The Late Show" as well. Eventually, Russell does pass out on the couch.

The next morning, the men all wake up and do their regular routine. The men arrive at work, and stick with their tasks, not acting out of the ordinary. With tomorrow being the day of Kevin's funeral, they will not have to work. Even though the men are working together to get their objectives done, Brian and Russell are refusing to look at each other. Both of them keeping the incident which happened last night in mind. Brian does not want to do another heist, and finds it slightly ridiculous that Russell wants them to. He feels that the men all decided that the heist they did previously, was the final one they would commit. The plans for them to take on yet another bank, Brian felt wasn't even in the order of business. When break time finally arrives, and the other employees have left the building, Russell takes Brian inside an empty room on the top floor. He closes and locks the door behind them. Russell then whispers to Brian.

"Hey, about last night, I want to apologize. I'm sorry for the way I went about that. After thinking about it, that wasn't cool at all. I totally understand your reaction. But listen to me, we have to take 'First Federal.' The guy who is the worst enemy in my life, is manager at that bank. I worked with him at Sunset, he is a horrible man. Please work with me Brian, one last time."

Brian looks down towards the ground, and frowns at Russell. He then responds to him.

"I'm going to hell, and I feel I might possibly regret this, but let's do it. This is it, after this, no more. Three is enough, and if it weren't for the fact you have personal beef with this bank, I wouldn't go along with this at all. You can count me in Russell, I can't believe this."

Brian laughs to himself and shakes his head. He and Russell hug, and they embrace each other for several seconds. They both exit out of the room after that, locking the door. When break is over, all of the men immediately return to work. As the work shift ends, they all meet on the main floor of the building. Russell whispers something into Victor's ear, and Victor nods his head. All of the men then head up to their meeting spot on the top floor. They all walk in, and sit down around the table, and Russell looks at the rest of the men, smiling. He then speaks.

"Alright, so everyone is in agreement. Friday. 'First Federal'. Need I say more?"

The men all nod their heads at Russell, and support his final plot. Russell and the rest of the guys, remain at the table as Russell explains more information about the bank. He explains that he wants them all to case the bank Thursday morning. Even though they do not have the help of Kevin and his technologic tools, they are going to have to still proceed somehow. They all agree to discuss more about their plans on Thursday. For now, they have a funeral to attend tomorrow, and they need to get prepared for that. The men all exit out of the room, and Russell locks the door as they leave. After locking the building, Brian and Victor drive away. Russell and Jesse then drive away as well. When Russell reaches home, he heads directly to his bedroom closet, and pulls out the suit he wishes to wear to the funeral. Russell also sets aside a suit for Victor to wear as well. Jesse follows him into the bedroom, and watches as Russell goes through the closet. Russell as he's going through his closet, speaks to Jesse.

"I'm particular with the way I have all this arranged, it has to be in a proper way. I don't like my clothes all mismatched. Formal wear and casual wear, and everything else is in order."

Jesse nods his head, then closes his eye and lays down on the bed falling asleep. Russell looks over at him and smiles. Russell walks out of the bedroom, and shuts the door. He then goes to the living room, and starts to practice his eulogy for Kevin. Once he's done, Russell sits down on the sofa, and turns on the television, watching the local nighttime news. Russell must have somehow feel asleep sometime, as he wakes up hours later. Upon rising, he looks at the time on his phone, and sees that it's now morning time. He now only has a couple hours before the funeral stars. In panic, he runs to the bedroom and pulls out his suit. He looks over at his bed, and notices that Jesse is still sleeping. Russell forcefully wakes Jesse up, and snaps at him.

"We're running late, get up. You can go into the shower first. We have to hurry. Brian, Victor, and Max could be here any fucking minute now. Damn, I don't like being late."

Jesse quickly gets up obeying Russell, and walks into the bathroom. As soon as Jesse walks out of the bathroom, Russell quickly proceeds in, and gets himself situated. Jesse starts to dress into his outfit for the funeral. He is wearing a black vest, with a grey shirt and black tie. He has on brown dress pants on, with black shoes. Jesse sits down on the sofa area, and at this time Russell's phone starts to ring, with him still being in the shower. Jesse picks up the phone, and it is Brian informing Jesse that he, Victor and Max are outside the building, and cannot find a place to park. Jesse struggles to find a solution, and luckily at this time Russell leaves the bathroom with nothing but a towel on. Jesse hands him the phone without explaining anything, and Russell answers. Brian relays the same exact situation to him, and Russell responds by quickly giving Jesse the key card to the parking structure, so Brian can park in the guest spot.

Jesse runs out of the complex, and runs outside to look for Brian. Russell in the meantime, quickly gets dressed. Outside, Jesse and Brian spot each other, and he hands Brian the key card. Brian swipes the card at the gate of the parking structure, and hands the card back to Jesse, and Brian drives in. Jesse then walks right behind Brian's car, as he advances to the guest parking spots. As soon as Brian parks his car, Jesse helps grab Max's wheelchair from the trunk of Brian's car, and they put Max in his chair. All four of them get inside the elevator, and proceed up towards Russell's apartment. Russell who is now fully dressed, lets them in. Brian, Victor and Max start to observe Russell's home. Russell quickly grabs his yarmulke from under the television and puts it on. Max compliments Russell's apartment.

"This is a nice pad. I love the way you have everything designed. It's looks like a 'Hooters' or some other sports bar in here. I'm liking the fish aquarium as well. Pretty nice."

Russell ignores Max, as he runs into the bedroom, and grabs the suit Victor is going to wear. He hands the suit to Victor, and silently points towards the bathroom so he can change. Victor directs himself there, and gets dressed. Russell, Brian, Victor and Max are all wearing the same exact suit. They are wearing black suit jackets, with black pants, and white shirts with black ties. Russell grabs his Tanakh, and sets it on the coffee table. Brian then talks to Russell.

"I'm not Jewish, I'm Catholic. I find it interesting how committed you are. That's good."

Russell cannot find his car keys, and searches all over the living room to find them. Brian then grabs his Tanakh, and Russell snatches it from him, staring at him angrily. Russell continues to look for his keys. He responds to both Brian and Max, in a very passive aggressive manner.

"I didn't ask for your opinion on that Brian. Thanks Max, I try to keep my place nice."

Brian and Max then hint that Russell at this time isn't in the mood to talk, so they let him be. Victor comes out of the bathroom at this time, and Russell grabs his discarded clothes, putting them in a black bag. He sets the bag on top of his washing machine, located in a small room in the other side of his apartment. Russell finally is able to locate his keys, and puts them in his pocket. He turns off the television, and closes all the curtains in his apartment. Russell then signals for the rest of the men to follow him out.

All of the men exit out of Russell's apartment, and put on their sunglasses. They all head to the parking structure. Russell and Brian, help Max out of his wheelchair. Max is situated on the passenger side of Russell's car. Jesse and Victor help store his chair in the back of the car. Brian, Jesse and Victor all sit in the rear seat area. Russell backs out of the parking structure, and drives to the funeral procession. He looks and observes the weather, noticing that it's a gloomy cloudy day.

Russell find it's odd that the last funeral he attended, also had similar weather. It doesn't make the already depressive mood that he is in, any better. Russell doesn't care for funerals, and finds them uncomfortable and upsetting. He does want to pay respect to his best friend, and attend. During the ride, the men stay quiet and do not talk to each other.

This is a delicate time, being that it is a funeral. It is not the time for any of them to engage in any trivial discussions or behavior. Russell continues to drive to the funeral, only now being a few blocks away. He starts to feel nervous, as for the first time he's going to meet Kevin's family. Russell has already decided that he isn't going to make a big deal of his presence. He is going to say a eulogy, but he isn't going to introduce himself to any of the guests. Basically, he originally had no intentions of showing up at the funeral in the first place. Funerals are something he rather not be at, but Kevin was his best friend, so Russell wants to honor and respect him. Russell finally arrives at the funeral service.

Russell parks his car, and while he cuts the ignition off, he quickly scans the setting for a few seconds. Like with Peter and Jennifer's funeral, the proceedings are being held outside in a graveyard. There are lovely flower arranges around Kevin's closed coffin. The coffin is located on a raised platform in the front of the area. Right behind the coffin is a pulpit, which is also decorated with a flower arrangement. There is a considerable amount of people present at the funeral. Russell sees many people whom resemble Kevin, and he deduces that these people are his close relatives. At this time, Russell cannot see anyone he personally recognizes.

Russell gets out of the car, and Jesse and Victor grab Max's wheelchair. Russell and Brian help Max into his chair. The men then start to walk to the funeral procession. They all sign the guest book, and start to decide where they want to sit. Russell is pushing Max's wheelchair, and he decides to sit in the front row, positioning Max right next to him. Brian whispers something to Russell, and Russell nods his head. Brian then forcefully grabs Victor and Jesse by the arms, and he sits them down with him in a back row away from Russell and Max, so they don't draw attention to each other. From the position from which they are sitting, they cannot see Russell and Max, nor the front row at all. Russell then starts to feel nervous and uncomfortable at the funeral. He wonders if he is going to choke up, as he did at Peter and Jennifer's funeral, when he gives the eulogy towards Kevin. Russell feels uneasy, as none of Kevin family members know who he is. He's refusing to make eye contact with anyone at the funeral, and stares only ahead. As Russell is sitting in the front row, he has a good look at Kevin's casket. It's black with steel streaks across the surface of it. He also takes note of the lovely flowers set on top as well.

Russell starts to uncontrollably cry while he's looking at Kevin's coffin. Russell pulls out his handkerchief, and starts to wipe his face. Max glances over at Russell and notices him crying. Max then reaches over, and starts to rub the back of Russell's shoulder. Brian, Jesse and Victor are also starting to feel upset at the funeral. This is a special time to remember and honor Kevin, and it's upsetting that despite all three of them were close with him, most of the people attending, do not know who they are. The three of them have also met Kevin under strange circumstances, and over circumstances which ultimately killed him.

They are holding onto a heavy burden of guilt. Jesse and Victor both begin to cry, and Brian feels upset himself. Russell continues to stare straight ahead, when he notices a young curly haired woman who looks similar to Kevin, sit right next to him. Russell soon realized that this same woman was standing by the entrance of the procession, and saw him and Max come in. Russell is not looking at the woman at all, but she is profiling Russell, trying to figure out who he is. The woman looks away for a couple minutes, but then returns to staring him down.

Russell begins to feel nervous, and his biggest fear is this woman wanting to talk to him, and wanting to know who he and Max are. He is certain that she is a family member of his from the resemblance, but that's where the perceptions end. The woman then taps Russell on the shoulder. Russell feels frozen, and struggles to turn his head. He does, and stares at the woman for several seconds. The woman then starts to speak to him.

"My name is Katrina Peterson. I'm Kevin's aunt. I'm his father's younger sister. I came from Chicago to see him. Me and Kevin were the same age. If you don't mind me asking, can I ask how you knew Kevin?

Russell starts to feel anxious, and is unable to react at first. He is able to calm himself down, and he quickly thinks of a reasonable fib, with some elements of truth to tell her.

"Well, I'm Russell McCoy. I was a close friend to Kevin. He was my classmate. This is Max Newman. You know how Kevin was into computers? Max was one of his teachers. Kevin was really dear to both of us, and we are here to pay our respects."

Katrina smiles at Russell, and she shakes both Russell and Max's hands. She then quietly faces forward. Russell is relieved that the woman bought his fib, and accepted everything he told her. Russell faces forward as well, and at this time the procession begins. As the memorial service goes on, several of Kevin's family members including Katrina, walk up and say their remarks towards Kevin. Russell patiently waits for the time for open remarks, so Russell can give his eulogy. Russell starts to feel more nervous as time progresses. Max once again comforts Russell, as he can tell he's under a lot of pressure. Brian, Jesse and Victor can't see Russell, but they know he is nervous. The time finally comes for those who wish to say their final remarks, to do so.

Russell takes several deep breaths to himself, and he starts to grab his Tanakh. Katrina rubs on his leg, and smiles at him. Russell smiles back at her, and walks towards the pulpit. Every step he takes, feels like his feet are made of stone. The pressure and anxiety which are surrounding his body, is about too much for him to handle. He reaches the pulpit, and uncontrollably starts to cry. Russell takes out his handkerchief and wipes his face. Russell gets himself together, and then opens up his Tanakh. He starts to give his eulogy to Kevin.

"My name is Russell McCoy, and Kevin was my best friend. Kevin, I love you."

Before he continues, Russell remains standing at the pulpit, silent for a short while. He keeps his vision down, not saying a single word. Russell begins to feel extremely depressed, and tries to compose himself. Russell is currently unable to continue, due to the current state of events. Brian, Jesse and Victor watch Russell at the pulpit, understanding his emotions; having an identical feeling of sorrow themselves. Russell quickly manages to recover himself, and to deal with the hurt he's feeling; he proceeds to recite the Psalm of Comfort in Hebrew, in honor of Kevin.

מִזְמוֹר לְדָוִד: יְהוָה רֹעִי, לֹא אֶחְסָר.

בִּנְאוֹת דֶּשֶׁא, יַרְבִּיצֵנִי; עַל-מֵי מְנֻחוֹת יְנַהֲלֵנִי.

נַפְשִׁי יְשׁוֹבֵב; יַנְחֵנִי בְמַעְגְּלֵי-צֶדֶק, לְמַעַן שְׁמוֹ.

גַּם כִּי-אֵלֵךְ בְּגֵיא צַלְמָוֶת, לֹא-אִירָא רָע-- כִּי-אַתָּה עִמָּדִי;

שִׁבְטְךָ וּמִשְׁעַנְתֶּךָ, הֵמָּה יְנַחֲמֻנִי.

תַּעֲרֹךְ לְפָנַי, שֻׁלְחָן-- נֶגֶד צֹרְרָי;

דִּשַּׁנְתָּ בַשֶּׁמֶן רֹאשִׁי, כּוֹסִי רְוָיָה.

אַךְ, טוֹב וָחֶסֶד יִרְדְּפוּנִי-- כָּל-יְמֵי חַיָּי;

וְשַׁבְתִּי בְּבֵית-יְהוָה, לְאֹרֶךְ יָמִים.

Russell finishes his eulogy. He returns to his seat, and Katrina starts to rub the back of Russell's shoulder. Soon after that, the procession ends. Russell stands up, and Katrina hugs him. She then immediately walks away. Russell then starts to push Max's wheelchair, and they start to leave the area. As he's leaving, Russell notices Detective Henderson who's wearing a fedora hat, walk away from the procession and drive off. He is surprised to see him there, and starts to slightly feel scared. Russell did stand in front of all the attendees, and Detective Henderson has met Russell before. At this time, Russell ignores this. Russell continues to push Max to the car. When Russell gets to his vehicle, Brian, Jesse and Victor have all reunited with him.

They help Max out of his wheelchair, and into the car. Russell then drives back to his home. When they get back, Brian informs Russell that he can drive Victor and Max back to "Home Base". Russell helps Max into Brian's car, and Jesse and Victor put Max's wheelchair in Brian's trunk. The men all say goodbye to each other. Russell and Jesse walk back into Russell's apartment. As they walk in, Russell heads towards the freezer, and takes out a bottle of Vodka. Jesse walks over to the sofa, and takes a seat. Russell takes out two glasses as well, pouring the liquor into each glass. Russell directs himself over to the sofa where Jesse is sitting, and brings the bottle and both of the glasses. Russell gives Jesse one of the glasses. Jesse takes a sip of the alcohol. While taking a sip of the liquor, Russell starts to feel depressed. He starts to cry, and wipes his face. Jesse watches him, and feels upset as well. Jesse moves in closer to Russell on the sofa, and tries to console him by petting his cheek. Russell however physically pushes Jesse away, and screams at him in return.

"Why did you touch me? Don't touch me. I don't want you touching me. Don't ever touch me again. You keep your faggot hands away from me. Don't touch me ever again."

Jesse looks at him puzzled. Jesse finishes his glass of vodka, and walks towards the bedroom, responding to Russell.

"Bullshit, you always say that crap, then an hour later, it's a whole different dance and tune. Russell, you're such an asshole. I'm going to touch you whenever I feel like, because I can. I don't give a fuck what you say, because it's all shit. I'm going to take a nap, I'm tired."

Jesse closes the bedroom door, and starts to undress himself into a T Shirt and undershorts. Jesse then lays down on the bed, and proceeds to rest. Russell still has his suit from the funeral on, and is in the living room. He takes more swallows of the Vodka. The television is not on, but Russell has heavy metal music playing on his phone. At this time, he's feeling out of control, and under a heavy depressive episode.

Russell is also extremely inebriated as well. He makes himself several drinks with the vodka. Hours pass, and it is now nighttime. Russell is still drunk on the sofa, listening to rock music. He is highly intoxicated, and smiling to himself on the couch, moving to the music. Minutes later, the music on Russell's phone all of a sudden stops; his phone has run of battery. Russell is angry at this, and breaks the glass he's drinking by squeezing it in his hand, with the shattered pieces causing his fingers to slightly bleed. Russell laughs to himself, and licks the blood from his fingers. Russell then stumbles over by the television, and charges his phone. Jesse wakes up from his nap, and walks out of the bedroom. He notices the broken glass on the floor, and Russell's bleeding hand. Russell and Jesse make eye contact, and Russell laughs at him. Jesse frowns at Russell, shaking his head. He then takes the vodka bottle.

"Russell, you're way too drunk. You don't need to drink anymore."

Russell then snatches the vodka bottle away from Jesse's hand and opens it. Russell unscrews the top, and tips it over to Jesse; motioning for him to take a drink. Jesse laughs at him, and Jesse takes a couple of swallows of the liquor. Russell then takes several big gulps from the bottle. Jesse then snatches the bottle from him again.

"Okay big guy, that's enough of that. You're gonna get yourself killed if you drink anymore. No more. You don't need to drink anymore Russell. You're drunk as a skunk."

Russell then lifts his hands up in the air, and shrugs his shoulders. He then takes a seat on the sofa. Jesse places the vodka bottle back inside the freezer, and joins Russell. Russell then laughs to himself, staring into space. Russell then stands up. He grabs Jesse by his hands up from the sofa. Russell leans close to Jesse, and kisses him passionately. Russell then hugs Jesse tightly. Russell then silently and softly speaks to him.

"How much do you love me? Because I don't love you at all. I'm just curious on how much you love me though. You're the desperate one, not me. How much do you love me?"

Jesse looks at him, and laughs over Russell's drunken behavior. Russell then snaps back.

"How much do you fucking love me?! Say it! I'm waiting! How much do you love me?!"

Jesse starts to rub Russell's face, and he whispers in Russell's ear.

"I don't know how much I love you. I do know that I can't get enough of you."

Russell laughs at Jesse, and immediately lifts Jesse's whole body in the air, with his arms. Russell then whispers out to Jesse, while still lifting him in the air.

"Would you die for me? Do you love me that much to die for me?"

Jesse while still being lifted by Russell, simply laughs. Russell laughs as well, and runs to the kitchen area carrying Jesse on his back; stopping at the balcony door. Before he opens it, he whispers to Jesse.

"Don't say a fucking word. Shut your fucking mouth. Don't say anything at all. If you say one syllable, I will fucking drop you. Shut your fucking mouth."

Russell opens the balcony door, and shuts it behind him. He stands on the balcony, cradling Jesse in his arms. He reaches across the edge of the balcony, and completely dangles Jesse's whole body over it. Jesse stays silent, as Russell has a wide grin on his face laughing.

Russell starts to loosen his grip from Jesse, and Jesse simply looks at him stone faced. Russell then starts to snap out of it, feeling guilty, He quickly carries Jesse back inside. Russell closes and locks the balcony door, and he stares at Jesse for a few seconds. Jesse then punches Russell across the side of the face very hard. Jesse runs into the bedroom, slamming the door behind him. Russell laughs, and stumbles across to the sofa area, smiling to himself. Jesse opens up the bedroom door, and peeks over at Russell. He walks over to him, and takes his suit jacket off and removes his tie, setting them both behind the sofa. He then takes Russell's shoes and socks off, and sets them under the table.

Russell steadily laughs while Jesse is doing all of this. Jesse walks over to the freezer and grabs some ice cubes, putting them in a Ziploc bag. He sets the bag of ice over the side of Russell's head, and lays him down on the couch. Jesse kisses him on the forehead, and turns out all of the lights in the room. Jesse then walks into the bedroom, and shuts the door, falling asleep seconds after that. Russell eventually drifts off to sleep as well.

CHAPTER 20:

NOTHING HIGH, NOTHING LOW

Detective Henderson pours himself a cup of coffee at a convenience store nearby the Downtown Los Angeles Police Precinct. He has been running on very little sleep; trying to crack the case on the heists the men have done over the past couple weeks. They have been dubbed the "Snowman Bandits", by police. Detective Henderson is frustrated that he hasn't been able to get any solid leads or hints in any of the heists. The only thing he has been able to figure out, is that the men always strike on Fridays. Based on that information alone, he has a strong suspicion that the "Snowman Bandits", are going to hit a bank tomorrow. It so happens that Detective Henderson is holding a meeting with other officers and investigators at the station; discussion being focused on the "Snowman Bandits", and figuring out their tactics and plans.

Detective Henderson gets inside his car, and drives to the station. When he arrives, before he gives his meeting to his other colleagues, he heads over to this office. He watches over the surveillance tapes from both of the heists. He tries to spot any key details out, that would aide towards solving this investigation. He studies the tapes very carefully, and is not able to find out any new information that he wasn't already aware of. Detective Henderson shakes his head out of aggravation, and takes the surveillance tapes with him. He continues onto a private meeting room. As minutes pass, more people gather inside of the room. Detective Henderson then decides to start the meeting. He plays the surveillance footage, from the heists the guys participated in.

"Good morning ladies and gentlemen. The reason to which I have called you for this meeting, is that we are dealing with serious bank robbers. These guys are professionals, and know exactly what they are doing. They are extremely armed and dangerous, and they need to be taken off the street and caught. Sadly, we have nothing on them, as that's how swift they are."

Detective Henderson's fellow officers and detectives listen as he continues to explain.

"These men are a group of four. It seems that two of the men act as the ones that do most of the action, and are the ones that gather all of the money. The other two are usually kept as lookouts on the floor. This is an interesting setup they have planned out. Even though these men have done a good job, and have also kept their identities concealed, I believe we can crack this case."

Detective Henderson takes a swallow of his coffee, and carries on with the meeting.

"We have to take a stand against these men; we cannot let them get away again. Because of this, on Friday, every major bank in the downtown area is going to have an armed security guard present. This includes 'Union Bank' on Wilshire, 'First National' on Western, and 'First Federal' on Grand. The possibility of them taking one of these banks, are extremely high."

Detective Henderson fast forwards the security tape, to the point where the men run out.

"These guys have some type of getaway vehicle located away from the bank. I don't understand how they can run out so fast without being recognized or stopped. Whatever system they have, we can beat it. It's important that we find out the method they escape in. If we know their getaway vehicle, we can get the helicopters, and the whole nine yards to track them down."

An officer listening into Detective Henderson's meeting, raises his hand to speak.

"I have a slight suggestion and idea we could implement. Maybe we can have an officer stand outside the possible targeted banks in an unmarked car, waiting for the men to come in. He can also call for backup, while he goes in to deescalate the situation. It's a suggestion I have, and I feel it definitely could work."

Detective Henderson takes another swallow of his coffee, nodding his head in agreement.

"You know what, that is a great idea. I love it, let's do that. In addition to making sure armed guards are present at every major bank on Friday, I also want a peace officer car to hold outside every bank, waiting for the men to go in as well. Better safe than sorry."

The detective continues to analyze the surveillance tapes, and present other key details to everyone in the meeting. Detective Henderson points out how fast the men plan out their actions.

"Remember, these men are quick. They are in and out of these banks in a flash. If we don't act a step quicker than they do, they will once again flee. That will not happen this time. Fool me once, shame on me; fool me twice, shame on you. You can't fool me three times."

Detective Henderson takes yet another sip of his coffee, and sits down on the surface edge of the table. He runs his fingers through his spiked hair, and shakes his head.

"Yesterday, I went to a funeral of someone who I truly believe, was an innocent hostage in their last hit. This man had a loving family, and it's sad they had to see him go the way he did. I don't want to see anything like that ever again. These guys have to be stopped."

At this time, Detective Henderson begins to wrap up, and says his final remarks.

"Alright people, that will do it. Our plan is to have guards set up at all the banks, and to have a plain patrol car outside the bank, waiting for them to run in. Take care everyone."

Individuals begin to walk out of the meeting room, and Detective Henderson starts to gather all the evidence and surveillance video tapes related to the heists. He puts them in a large cardboard box. Once everyone else has left the room, Detective Henderson closes the door. He starts to feel an uncontrollable anger, which makes his blood boil. Under normal circumstances, Detective Henderson can solve armed robbery cases quite easily, and he always finds a hint, or something which gives him a big break towards the investigation. With this particular case, he feels that due to the lengths the men are taking to execute their heists flawlessly, he starts to feel hopeless. He starts to question that he isn't good at his job, which is to protect the civilians against cases such as this.

The detective plays the surveillance videos of the heists one final time. For some strange reason, he feels as as though Russell and Brian's bodies are familiar to him, and that he has met them before. He cannot put the pieces all together, as the men are wearing heavy disguises. This feeling that Detective Henderson is experiencing, is causing him to be even more upset than he already was. He feels confident that he recognizes the body types of two of the men, but that simply isn't good enough when it comes to a bank robbery investigation. Sadly, he cannot figure out who these men actually are, as the ski masks and snow outfits make their identity nearly impossible to tell.

Detective Henderson becomes furious, and runs over to a wall in the room. He takes his fist, and starts punching the wall very roughly. From hitting the wall, his knuckles start to bleed badly. Detective Henderson wipes the blood from his knuckles with his handkerchief, and sits down at the table in the meeting room. Detective Henderson being Catholic, reaches in his pocket, and takes out a wooden cross. He closes his eyes and looks up at the ceiling, and starts to pray that his sanity will be healed. The immense mental pain he's under, is too much for him to deal with. Detective Henderson plans to retire from being a criminal investigator soon, as the job is causing too much stress for him. He hopes that he is able to gain some closure to this particular case, before he actually does withdraw himself from the police force.

Detective Henderson finishes praying, and puts the cross back in his pocket. He grabs the box of evidence belonging to all the heists, and leaves out the room. When returning to his desk, Detective

Henderson swallows a couple Tylenol pills, and then starts his break for the day. He gets in his car, and drives to a nearby shooting range, where police officers are allowed to have target practice. The shooting helps him express his anger better, and allows him to be more calm and collect with how he's feeling. While he's shooting, he cannot stop thinking about the heist investigation, and how bad he truly wants more answers surrounding it. He fires away at more targets, with near perfect accuracy.

Detective Henderson then has to report back to work, as his break is now over with. The target shooting definitely was the correct solution to the slump he was in. He gets back into his car, and drives back to the precinct, to get started on other active cases. Yet, he is more focused on getting to the bottom of the "Snowman Bandit" heists. On Friday, he feels that if they are prepared enough, they can possibly crack this particular case.

Meanwhile at Russell's residence, Jesse wakes up, crawling himself out of the bed feeling lethargic. After looking at the alarm clock which is stating that it's 9 A.M., Jesse wasn't expecting for it to be that late. The men have all agreed to case the bank this morning, for the heist tomorrow. Looking at the clock, Jesse knows that they are running terribly late. Jesse begins to panic, and runs over to the closet to pick out his clothes, throwing several articles of clothing all across Russell's bedroom. Jesse also starts to have flashbacks on last night, after they came home from Kevin's funeral. Russell almost killed him, by dangling him across the balcony. He ignores all of this, and keeps his mind focused towards getting ready. Once Jesse picks out what he wants to wear, he heads into the living room.

Russell who was completely drunk the night before, is now badly hungover. Jesse tries to push at him to wake him up, but Russell doesn't wake. Jesse then grabs a glass of water, and throws it at Russell's face. Russell starts to reluctantly wake up. Jesse then walks into the bathroom to get himself ready. Russell is now slightly awake, and sits himself up on the sofa. He has a really bad headache, and the last thing he remembers is coming home from Kevin's funeral the day before. Everything else is a blur at this time, and he cannot recall or remember any of it. Russell then realizes that it's Thursday, and he has a lot to do. He still has on his clothes from yesterday's funeral. He staggers inside his bedroom, so he can get himself some clothes to wear.

Russell is too hungover, and strugglers to get undressed. Without removing any of his clothes, he lays down on the bed, and falls straight back to sleep. Jesse who has finished getting ready, notices that Russell has fallen asleep. Jesse does the same thing as he did previously, and throws a glass of water on him. This causes Russell to awaken once more, and Russell sits up on the bed. Jesse walks out to the kitchen, to make Russell a cup of coffee. Russell then remembers that he needs to get himself ready, and tries once more to undress himself. He fails yet again, becoming too tired and hungover, and drops himself back down to bed once more. Jesse returns to the bedroom with a cup of coffee for Russell, and becomes irate when he sees that Russell is asleep again. He has had enough. Jesse sets the cup of coffee down on the night stand, and starts to slap Russell on the face repeatedly.

"Russell, get the fuck up. That's what you get for fucking drinking too much. We have a lot of shit to do today. You gotta get up now. Here, drink some of this, it will help you."

Jesse hands Russell the cup of coffee, but Russell squints his eyes, and shoves it away. Jesse feeling angry, then tries to force the coffee down Russell's lips, and Russell takes very small sips of it using this method. Jesse continues to do this until half the cup is empty.

When Russell still doesn't wake himself up, Jesse reaches his limit, and starts to undress Russell. He removes Russell's shirt, and then he takes of his pants. Russell is now only in his boxer shorts on the bed, still with his eyes closed, about to drift right back to sleep once more. Jesse picks out a white polo shirt, and some black sweatpants for Russell to wear. Jesse struggles to dress him, as Russell is quite a heavy man. Jesse luckily is able to have Russell nearly dressed. He puts Russell's socks and sneakers on as well. Jesse then grabs Russell's deodorant and cologne from his dresser, and he freshens Russell up. Russell starts to slowly compose himself, and begins to speak.

"Hey? What's going on? What the fuck are you doing? How did you get my clothes on?"

Jesse and Russell then stare at each other, Jesse observing how tired Russell is. Jesse returns an angry and disappointed face to Russell. Jesse then tries to lift Russell off of the bed. Due to Russell's heavy weight, this is not easy to accomplish. Jesse is able to lift Russell up, and he walks him over to the bathroom. Jesse then starts to brush Russell's teeth. Once he's finished doing that, he sets Russell down on the sofa. Russell not even a second later, is deep asleep. Jesse had a feeling Russell would do just that, and doesn't seem that agitated over it.

Jesse grabs Russell's keys and wallet, and sticks them both in Russell's pockets. After that, Jesse picks up Russell's phone from under the television set, and starts to text Brian. He explains to Brian that Russell is hungover, as a result of feeling depressed after returning home from Kevin's funeral. Jesse asks if Brian can come pick himself and Russell up. Brian understands completely, and does agree to help out.

After talking with Brian on the phone, Jesse starts to slap Russell on the face again to wake him up, and Russell does wake up. Jesse then grabs the coffee cup, and tries to get Russell to drink more of the coffee, by forcing it down his throat. However, Russell is doing a good job of persisting the coffee. Russell gets the entire rest of the cup of coffee down, and Jesse wipes Russell's mouth, as he starts to regurgitate a small amount of it. Russell then falls asleep yet again. Jesse sits on the other side of the sofa, and places his hands over the side of his face, feeling defeated.

Jesse looks down towards the ground for several minutes, looking up when Russell would wake up for a few seconds, then immediately he would result back to sleeping. Jesse sits back on the sofa, and looks above.

Jesse then starts to flashback one more time about last night. He didn't know how intoxicated Russell actually was, but he couldn't believe that Russell was very close to killing him. Jesse was scared that if he said anything or screamed, that Russell would throw him off the balcony. He wasn't expecting for Russell to do any of that. As much as he doesn't want to blame it on the fact that Russell was just strictly drunk, sometimes that excuse isn't enough. Jesse begins to worry deeply, as of all the days for Russell to be under the weather, today is not the correct day. Jesse is also aware that Russell probably has no idea of what he did the night before. He was that drunk, it caused him to black out. This means he will not remember any of the events he did while he was intoxicated, the day after. A half an hour later, Jesse while he's looking up at the ceiling thinking to himself, Russell's phone rings.

Jesse looks at Russell, who is still very much out of it, and he goes to pick up Russell's phone. Brian is on the other line, wanting to get inside of the complex. Jesse quickly tries to find where Russell put the card key, as Jesse searches for it in the kitchen. Russell has placed the card key on the other side of the counter. Jesse grabs it, and he runs outside to Brian to hand it to him. Brian pulls into the parking structure, and Brian, Jesse and Victor all walk into Russell's apartment. Brian notices how out of it Russell is, and tries to get Russell to return to his normal self.

"Russell, hey. You okay man? We have to leave okay? Come on Russell, get up man."

By hearing Brian's voice, Russell for the first time this morning, starts to come back to reality. He looks around the room, and responds to the other men.

"I'm sorry guys, I had too much to drink, my head is spinning all around, and I can't really see that much. Everything is all dark. I can't drive, but we can go now I guess."

Brian nods his head, and the four men walk out of Russell's apartment, and get into Brian's car. This particular day is quite cloudy, but the sun would intermittently pop itself out in the sky. Every half hour the sun would appear, giving out a nice gleam of rays and light. A warm humid sensation in the air, floats all around. Then for the next half hour, the sun would hide itself back into the clouds, and the sky would become dark and cloudy; giving a moody and gloomy atmosphere. It becomes colder when the sun is not visible and behind the clouds as well, giving off a slight windy breeze. With Russell now fully awake, he looks out the window of Brian's car. Russell still has a really bad headache. He has no recollection of what exactly made him drink as much as he did, and he is so tired; he has to keep reminding himself to stay awake.

The men are currently driving to "First Federal Bank", to examine the bank for the heist tomorrow. Something which they have done twice before with other two heists they have committed. The only issue is; Russell is ill at the moment. With the men thinking of him as their leader towards all of these crusades, it could possibly make the planning stage much more difficult.

The men have several things that they need to get done on their agenda for the day. Casing the bank they will hit tomorrow is one, and going to their last work shift is the other. This will be the first heist, to where the men will not have any assistance or help from Kevin. Any electronic devices that they have used in the past, none of those tools can be implemented now. They will go with this last heist, the old fashioned way. Using quick thinking, and fast judgment. Russell starts to conform himself the longer Brian drives, and the closer they get to the bank. He now is starting to remember getting insanely drunk after Kevin's funeral.

Although his memory of it is still very much scattered, he is now remembering picking Jesse up, and dangling him off the balcony. Russell takes his sunglasses off, and his eyes are bloodshot red. He begins to produce tears, due to how irritated his eyes are. He looks towards the floor of Brian's car, and shakes his head; his vision is poorly, but it's slowly starting to come back. Russell's headache has not gone away, but it's not as severe as it previously was. Brian gets closer to the bank, and Russell starts to talk.

"I'm sorry you guys, I got too carried away. Usually we Russians are good at holding down liquor, but I'm being such a pussy right now guys. I feel so ashamed, I'm sorry."

Brian while driving, understands where Russell is coming from, and responds to him.

"You don't have to apologize Russell. You're absolutely right though, you got carried away, and you have now learned your lesson. Now you have to be a man and get yourself together, as we have to go into beast mode right now. It's very important you stay alert now."

Russell bites his nails, and shakes his head while looking down. He pulls out his phone, he turns his head around to look at Jesse, and he asks him a question under his breath.

"Did you get me dressed? Because I would know if I put clothes on, and I don't remember getting dressed. If you dressed me, that's impressive. Crazy you did it so well."

Jesse while looking out the window, scoffs at Russell, and answers his question.

"Yes Russell, I got you dressed and it was not easy. But I had to do it. Okay? Ugh."

Russell takes off his sunglasses again and rubs his irritated eyes with his hand. He looks out the window, and starts to grunt and complain to himself. Victor then looks behind, at profiles Russell. After seeing how bad his condition is, Victor reaches in his pocket, and gives Russell some aspirin pills, and eye drops. Russell quickly grabs both of them from Victor. The men are happy that Russell for the most part, seems to be getting back to his regular self. Being that the heist is tomorrow, all of them need to be in proper condition to do the job right.

Russell now sobering himself up and getting out of his hangover, now has a more perfect recollection of the incident last night between himself and Jesse. He distinctively remembers grabbing Jesse, and becoming insanely close from dropping him high above from his balcony. Russell however doesn't know why he would ever think of doing such a thing, but is able to recall doing the action. Russell starts to have a sudden uncomfortable feeling of guilt over that. Wanting to get a clearer picture as to what when down when he was drunk the night before, with Jesse being the main witness to all of his actions. He turns his view over to Jesse who's looking out the window. Russell hisses at Jesse to get his attention, but Jesse is ignoring him. After Jesse doesn't respond, Russell shakes his head and doesn't worry about it. Victor plugs his phone into the car stereo; he is playing a bunch of old Beatles songs. Victor despite being young, always seemed to prefer music from way before his time. He is able to recite all of the lyrics perfectly to nearly every single song. Brian looks at the clock on his dashboard, and it is now showing 10:45 P.M. They men have to be at work by noon, so they do not have much time at all. Thankfully, they are not that far away from the bank from the position they are at now. Brian proceeds down Grand St.; one of the major streets located in downtown Los Angeles.

As he's riding in the rear seat, Russell once again takes note of all of the high profile business men in highly tailored suits, walking with their briefcases down the street. Russell as he's starting immensely out the window, starts to rub his goatee slowly, and smiles in both amazement and in shock, mainly because this used to be the exact same lifestyle he had. Going from being professional such as that, now planning his third bank heist. Coming to terms that his life has completely changed, and he is now a totally different person. Russell shakes his head and looks down at the ground, resting his hand on his forehead. He then takes the bottle of eye drops Victor gave him, and carefully uses the eye drop liquid to heal his eyes. Russell squints and grumbles due to the irritation of the formula going into his eyes, and hands Victor back the eye drop bottle. Brian mistakenly drives right past the bank at this point, as the "First Federal" bank has a slightly confusing entrance towards it. Russell quickly notices this, and shakes his head. He slightly snaps at Brian for doing so.

"Brian, you just went by 'First Federal'. That big building with the glass doors, that was the bank right there. I thought you knew where it was man? Ugh. Don't feel intimated though, it is the biggest bank we've seen so far. We can take it. Go back, and don't miss it this time."

Brian proceeds into the turning lane, and shakes his head. He responds to Russell.

"I'm sorry man, you should have told me. How the fuck was I supposed to know? Can you chill Russell? Damn. You've been unconscious all morning, now that you've woken up, you want to start pushing us around like that. I'm the driver, and that's now how to talk to people, especially people that are your friends, and are supposed to help you rob a fucking bank. Shit."

Russell looks down towards the ground once again, shaking his head and laughing out loud. Brian is puzzled by Russell's reaction, and makes a U-Turn, back to the correct direction. Russell pulls out his phone, and starts to respond to Brian, chuckling out the words.

"Fuck you Brian, That's not even pushing you around at all. I only said that you passed up the bank which you did, and you took it as me belittling you. I wasn't. Forget about it man, you can park at this corner, the bank is behind this building here. You can part right here man."

Brian takes a deep breath, and pulls the car over to the curb. They are now facing an office building, and an underground parking lot. It is connected behind the "First Federal Bank". Likewise, with the previous two banks they have targeted, this bank also has a slightly obscure path outside of it. This will allow for easy access, when trying to escape from the heist. Russell also has a personal vendetta to this bank, as John is now a manager. The vindication he feels, only causes Russell to act more dangerously towards this particular heist.

With this being their absolute final heist, they are all ready to finally proceed with the plan. Unfortunately, the men have no idea that earlier this morning, Detective Henderson held an important conference at the police station. He is implementing tactics the that they have never reinforced in the past, to catch them. These new plans that they plan to use to defect the men, could perhaps make this their most difficult heist yet. Using all of the desire they have gathered up from all the heists they have done, confidence is the major thing which keeps them going, and allows them to feel confident. As the men are parked right behind the bank, Russell starts to explain several things to them.

"Alright guys. I know I said this bank was similar to 'First Savings', well, I lied. This one is slightly bigger and better. It's one of the biggest banks in downtown LA. Which is why I really wanted to hit this one last time, instead of doing 'First Savings'. Don't feel intimidated guys, this bank is going to be simple, if not easier than the last."

The men all nod their head to agree with what Russell is saying. Russell then rubs the back of his head, as he's examining the parking structure located right in front of them.

"It's a good thing this parking lot is here, it is going to make getting out a breeze. I don't know why all these banks have these lots close together to the buildings like that. It's almost as if these banks want people to find and spot ways to outsmart them. I don't know; I don't get it. But, we will each park own own separate getaway vehicles through there, and the same way we left from 'First Savings', is the same way we are going to leave here. It's not any different."

Russell then taps Brian on the shoulder, and gives him a one-hundred-dollar bill.

"Brian, I need you to go study as much as you can with the bank. Victor and Jesse don't need to walk in, it's fine. They are only going to be lookout. I already know this bank well enough, but you don't. So try to get a feel of how everything is setup and situated for tomorrow.

Unlike in the previous heists, this time the men cannot use Kevin's technology tools. Most of which were able to help them achieve success towards the heists. They do not have to implement things like that to pull off a successful heist, but it would allow for things to blend at a smoother rate. On the other hand, it was from using these tools, which caused the disastrous and unfortunate result between Kevin. Now that the men can only use their common sense, and strategic planning in this heist, they must work together at an even harder level. Brian starts to exit out of the car. Russell watches Brian walk towards the bank, and runs his fingers through his hair with his head, pointing down towards the ground. Even though Russell is more alert at this point, he is still quite hungover and tired. He is trying his best to not drain himself in front of the other guys. Russell looks over at Jesse, who is reading a "Cosmopolitan" magazine. He also watches Victor listen to several Beatles songs in the car stereo, perfectly singing along to the words; using the dash console as a drum to beat against the music.

Russell is happy that the other men are feeling well, but he currently isn't. He feels tired, lightheaded and disorientated. You would never assume this though, because Russell is being strong with his outward expressions. The last thing he wants, is for them to feel scared because of how he is acting and feeling.

Russell has a terrible headache, and the pain is becoming much too difficult for him to bear. He reaches in his pocket, and grabs the aspirin that Victor gave him shortly before. Russell scans across the area, looking for a convenience store, drug store, bodega, or something similar to that. There are many commercial office buildings, but not that many corner stores in this particular area. Russell feels there has to be one, and finally locates a place down the street. He feels satisfied and plans to quickly run over there, getting back before Brian returns. While Brian is inside casing the bank, Russell plans to go and get himself a bottle of water, so he can take the aspirin pills. He positions himself to get out of Brian's car, and opens the door. Before he gets out, he speaks to Victor and Jesse.

"I'm going to go to that store over there, do you guys want anything at all?"

Victor and Jesse both shake their heads at Russell, and Russell gets out of the car. As he is walking to the store, Russell shockingly sees Detective Henderson, walking with a female investigator. The detective is simply on his lunch break. Russell hides behind a column, not wanting to be noticed by him. Russell remains hidden behind the column staring at the Detective, and observing his every move. Russell knows that Detective Henderson is in charge of investigating bank heists, and although Russell is not in Detective Henderson's radar at all with possible suspects, he starts to panic nonetheless. Detective Henderson walks away from the scene with his colleague, a minute after that. Russell once he no longer sees the detective, stops hiding himself from view.

Russell then proceeds to walk towards the convenience store, to get himself some water. Once he's inside the store, even though Victor and Jesse said they didn't want anything, Russell wants to surprise the rest of the guys anyways. He sees a bag of "peanut M&Ms.", Victor's most liked candy. He also sees a bag of "Flaming Hot Cheetos" chips, and he knows that they are Jesse's favorite. Russell as he continues to walk through the store, grabs some "Skittles" candy. These happen to be Brian's most liked confection. Continuing to walk around the store, Russell sees a bag of "Famous Amos" cookies. These particular cookies were the ones Kevin favored the most. Russell decides to get these for himself. Finally, he walks over to the refrigerators of the store, and gets four water bottles. Russell then pays for all of the items, and departs from the store.

Brian is inside the "First Federal Bank of Los Angeles". Like with "First Savings and Trust", this bank is relatively old as well. Inside the bank, you can see gothic and colonial inspired designs around the walls, and the architectural theme is also quite detailed. The building has a contemporary classic feel, and you would think the bank came straight out of the Victorian era. This bank along with practically every bank the men have hit, does not have the most modern options available when it comes to security. The bank is setup in way, that the tellers are completely exposed, and can be targeted from the way their terminals are positioned. In addition, if carefully planned, the vault can easily be accessed from the way it's positioned as well.

The bank has a somewhat ambiguous entrance of mirrored glass doors, being positioned on the far end of Grand Ave. The entrance gives an illusion of not being noticed by others. The entrance is also adjacent to a large unrelated public parking lot; someone who is clever enough can make a fast escape. Brian notices how the bank has only one way in, and one way out. His knowledge of banks doesn't come close to Russell's, but he feels that a bank large as this, should have at least two entrances on either sides of the street. The area facing the parking lot which they plan to escape in, is obstructed by a decorated wall in the bank. If it weren't for this wall, getting around this bank for a heist, would not be as simple. Brian doesn't see a security guard on duty either. What he doesn't know that come tomorrow, there will be an armed guard standing at the door. The men are going to have to find some way to work around this obstacle and hurdle, the best way they can. Brian sees that the few security cameras look worn out and old, and they are also no cameras in areas that they should be in. From this current value he's able to observe, this heist shouldn't be any problem for them to manage.

The line inside the bank isn't that long, and Brian makes his way to the bank teller. He hands the woman the money Russell gave him, as she proceeds to open her cash drawer, to give him change. Brian gets a test run of the area he's going to be at the following day, and is comfortable with how the layout of this area is. As the teller hands Brian the cash bills, he notices that there is a red button on the side of the cash terminals. This happens to be an obstructed silent alarm, which from the way it's placed on the terminal, is not easy to recognize at first. This was something he hasn't noticed the other banks they were at, implement. Feeling happy that he was able to catch this important detail, Brian exits out of the bank, and returns to the car with the rest of the men, around the corner.

Russell is now walking back to car as well, with the items he purchased from the convenience store. He gets into the car, and hands Victor the bag of "M&M's" and a bottled water, and hands Jesse the bag of chips and a bottle of water, which Jesse takes from him reluctantly, and angrily stares back at Russell. After opening the package of aspirin, Russell pops both of the pills in his mouth, and drinks some water. Russell then starts to eat some of the cookies he bought. Shortly, Brian returns to the car. Once Brian is inside, Russell hands Brian a bottle of water, and the candy which he had gotten for him. Brian grabs both of the items, and begins to eat some of the candy. They men all quietly sit in the car for a few minutes, and Brian as he's eating the candy, starts to explain to Russell what he noticed while observing the bank.

"You were right; this bank is good. It's a big bank yes, this is definitely the largest one out all the ones we've been at. That doesn't bother me though, as we got this. Hey guess what, when I was at the terminals, I saw these very small red buttons. They are silent alarms attached to the terminals. It's a good thing I was able to catch that, so I know to tell them not to push it."

Russell nods his head at Brian, and eats several of the cookies. He responds to Brian.

"I know John is going to be working tomorrow too. I can't wait to see how he's going to react to this. He always feels indestructible to everything. He's not, this is going to show him. This heist will be for Kevin, and this time for sure will the final countdown. I'm ready."

Brian laughs at Russell. Brian looks at the clock on the dashboard of his car; the men are running slightly late for their last day of work. Brian starts the ignition, and beings to drive them all to work.

As this happens to be a Thursday, the men have to clean the "Porter Professional Building." Being that both this and the "Wittberg Law Offices" are run by the same company, and were also built by the same engineers, the layouts of all the buildings are nearly identical and the same. When he gets to the building, Brian parks in the underground parking structure, and the men immediately get out the car, and walk inside. The last day of work, is somehow feeling like the first day of work. The men are excited because this is their last day, and they do not have to come back. But not slacking off with their work because of that either. For some particular reason, it is much harder to finish the tasks today. It's is indeed interesting how their final day working, is proving to be the most difficult and hardest day they have worked. The aspirin that Victor gave Russell, seemed to be what he needed. Russell now feels energized, and his head is no longer bothering him. While Russell is mopping the floor, he can't stop thinking about how around this time tomorrow, the men will be doing their final heist.

Russell is glad that he will no longer have to clean buildings anymore. The other men in addition to that are also feeling glad this charade is about to come to an end. For the past few weeks, they have cleaned buildings, and have organized a couple different heist plots.

Unfortunately, Kevin had to be the odd man out, and they are doing this one final time to avenge him. The men finally make it to their break time, and they all head up towards the roof to smoke a cigarette. Russell sits down on a bench, looking at the cloudy overcast sky, feeling calm. Brian, Victor and Jesse are feeling calm and confident as well.

They continue relaxing for several minutes on their break, being quiet to each other. Their break comes to an end, and the men promptly return to their final work day.

Russell begins to clean all the office buildings one last time, and makes sure he does the best job he can do. He won't return to cleaning this building ever again, so he wants everything to be spotless. Brian, Jesse and Victor have the exact same agenda. This is their last day, but it doesn't mean they shouldn't treat this like any other day they are scheduled. All of their tasks still have to be done, and their work must still be done properly. Brian power mops the floor for the last time, and makes sure the floor is the cleanest he's ever had it. Jesse and Victor give out the same results. For the last time, the men start to wrap up all of their tasks, and finish their work day.

Russell returns to the main floor, and sits down on a chair in the lobby feeling tired. He watches Brian who is exhausted as well from power mopping the floor. Brian finishes the task, and starts to put the power mop away in the supply closet. When Brian returns, he walks over to the lobby where Russell is sitting, and sees that Russell has closed his eyes, and has taken a nap on the chair. Brian begins to play with Russell's hair and goatee, and this causes Russell to awaken. He gives an agitated glare towards Brian, and Brian laughs and walks away. At this time, Victor and Jesse have finished their tasks, and join the rest of the men in the lobby. Russell quickly gets up from the chair, and signals the men to follow him. They walk towards one of the rooms in the top floor of the building. Once they have all gotten inside, Russell locks the door, and opens the curtains. As it was cloudy earlier in the day, the night sky gives out an interesting bright red color. The city lights go against the clouds, and a lovely glow shines through. While Russell is staring out the window at this fascinating view, he smiles to himself. He then speaks to the rest of the men.

"This is it, this time tomorrow, all of us are going to be done with all of this. This whole entire experience was really something. Ordinarily, I would never in my life think I would ever work with a bunch of guys like you, but here I am. I wanted to see this one last time."

Brian gets up from the table, and stands right by Russell. He also glares out the window as well observing the panoramic view. He pats Russell on the shoulder, and starts to whisper.

"Might as well right, if this going to be our last day, might as well take all of this in."

Russell nods his head, and they both continue to look out the window. Brian then speaks.

"Hey, I want you and Jesse to sleep over with at my place tonight. I don't want a repeat of this morning, and you acting the way you did. I don't know what happened to you, and don't care. I just don't want to do any of that tomorrow morning. I want to be safe and watch you, so you and Jesse can stay with me. That way when tomorrow morning comes, we will be ready."

Brian pats Russell on the shoulder again, and Russell laughs to himself. Brian then starts to walk away from the window, and Russell whispers something out to Brian.

"Can I stop and get something at my place first? It will only take a minute. I have to grab something really important."

Brian silently nods his head, and starts to walk towards the door. Russell then walks away from the window. Victor and Jesse for a minute look out the window as well, observing the view for the final time. All of the men then leave out of the room, and Russell locks the door. Brian and Russell for the very last time, lock up all of the doors inside the building. Russell hands Brian his set of keys to both of the buildings, as he no longer needs them. Brian locks the front door of the building, and puts his and Russell's keys, inside a plastic bag to give to Max later. They all proceed into the parking structure, and drive away. Brian immediately heads to Russell's residence, and Russell hands him the card key to get inside the parking structure. Once Brian is parked, Russell steps out of the car.

"I'll be right back you guys. Jesse you stay here; I'll only be just a minute. Hold on."

Russell runs inside the complex, and heads straight up to his apartment. As he gets inside, he walks over to his kitchen, and grabs

Kevin's bag of marijuana. He then locks his apartment up, and runs back down to the parking structure. Russell doesn't explain what he exactly grabbed from inside his apartment, and the men don't pester or bother him about it either. Brian then drives away from the complex, and heads to "Home Base". Right before stopping there, Brian goes to "Carl's Jr.", a hamburger drive-thru located not far from the unit, and gets food for all of the guys. After getting the food, Brian then pulls up into the unit, and parks his car outside.

Brian walks to the door, and unlocks it. When all the men are inside, Brian sets the food down on the table in front of the sofa area, and Victor and Jesse take a seat. Brian then walks over to his bed, and Russell taps Brian on the shoulder, waving a bag of marijuana in his face. Brian gives a disappointing looking smirk towards Russell, and rolls his eyes. Brian then snatches the bag from Russell. Victor and Jesse watch them both this entire time. Russell grins at Brian, and Brian hands Russell back the bag. Russell then walks towards the sofa area with Victor and Jesse. He takes a seat, and starts to open the bag of marijuana. Russell then struggles to roll the joint.

"I can't do this as well as Kev. He would do this like nothing. He could roll these in like five seconds. It's taking me a minute to get everything all together, I'm not even at the rolling part. I believe this is how you do this. I don't know everything, but I do know some stuff."

Victor laughs at Russell, and takes the bag away from him. Victor then asks to see the tabloid magazine Jesse is reading, and Victor sets it on this lap. He then softly speaks to Russell.

"You're doing that completely wrong. Watch and learn."

Russell hands Victor the bag of marijuana, and Victor begins to roll a joint. He licks the rolling paper and folds it halfway, and starts to put marijuana inside of it. He lays the joint on top of Jesse's magazine. Victor then asks for a pair of scissors, and Brian hands them over. Brian then turns on an internet radio station on his phone, and connects it to the stereo system hooked up in the unit. Victor uses the scissors to cut through the marijuana, so it fits nicely in the paper. Russell smiles and shakes head while watching Victor, amazed at what he's doing. Victor then carefully rolls the joint together. He hands it over to Russell, and

Victor immediately begins to roll a second joint. Victor very quickly assembles the second joint even faster, and this one he hands to Jesse. Brian hands Russell a lighter, and Russell lights his marijuana joint. Jesse uses the same lighter, and his joint is lit as well. Once they both take hits from it, Russell passes his joint to Brian, and Jesse passes his over to Victor. Brian then walks over to the refrigerator, and pulls out several "Bud Light" beers. He gives one to each man, and takes one for himself. The men all sit with each other, relaxing and feeling comfortable. Tomorrow, this whole attitude needs to be quickly changed. Going onto the heist, with this being the heist strictly based on revenge. The heist they will take to make up for losing Kevin. Russell using this heist to get back at all the mistreatment that John who is manager of the bank they are targeting, gave to him. After tomorrow, each of them will return to their regular lives, and no longer be considered outcasts. Still remaining friends, and keeping in touch. Brian takes a hit of the joint, and starts to talk to the men.

"So. I'm very curious. What are you guys doing to do with your share of the money? I'll guess I'll start. I don't know. I kinda want to start my own luxury car modification business. I know what you're thinking, I do all that shit now. Correct, but more like the real deal though. Doing high profile stuff, like Lamborghini's, Ferrari's all that shit. Yeah, that's what I want."

Victor takes a hit of the marijuana joint, and passes it to Jesse. He waits a couple of minutes to come up with his response, and he then in a soft manner, answers Brian's question.

"Well, I don't want to you guys to laugh. I was thinking about what Russell told me a few days ago about my art. I was thinking of maybe moving to Japan. I can start my own outsourced animation company. Doing anime and manga, it's a competitive business, but I know I can do it. Fuck, that would be my dream. Looking at Mount Fuji too for inspiration. Aww, yeah."

Jesse takes hits of the marijuana joint, and thinks about his response as well. Jesse doesn't have a complete and precise answer at this point, but he does answer Brian's question.

"Hmm, well I don't know. I'm not really a materialistic person, and I don't have any dreams or aspirations right now. Money is nice yes, you can accomplish a lot with it, don't get me wrong. But, I don't know what God has in store for me. I do think that Brian your plan is lovely, and yours is too Victor. I have to be honest, and say I don't know guys. Sorry."

Russell takes a couple hits from the joint, and passes it to Brian. Russell then rubs the back of his head, while he's looking down towards the ground. The rest of the men look at him in suspense, expecting his answer like they all gave, and then Russell gives his response to the question Brian asked.

"This is something we haven't really talked about huh? I never did this for the money, this was all based on me going against the world. The money was an added bonus I guess. I do have to agree with Jesse, and say I can't say I want to do 'X' or I want to to 'Y' or 'Z'. I want to see what happens, and be optimistic on the future. I'll take it from there, and that's my answer."

All of the guys nod their head at Russell, and they continue to smoke together. Once they have finished all the joints, Russell takes the bag of marijuana, and tells Brian to keep it in a secure place. This bag, strangely is the only thing Russell has left to remember Kevin by. Brian walks over to his work station, and hides the bag in one of his storage compartments. The men then start to eat their food. Brian turns on the television, and the show "24", is playing on the screen. Brian then sits down in his chair facing the other men on the sofa. Russell finds it interesting how fitting the television program is, considering in only a short amount of hours, they are going to take on yet another daring escapade.

As they are eating their food, Russell starts to feel scared for the first time today. He wonders if this will be the last time they will all eat together. The confidence going into tomorrow's heist is quite high, but these doubts still creep themselves, and find a way to intermittently enter into Russell's thoughts. It is normal for Russell to feel scared about proceeding, as tomorrow is the big day. It is where everything will all come to an end. The events which have changed his life permanently and completely, will all suspend themselves, when they take on the heist. The men all finish their food, and Jesse and Victor begin to feel tired. Victor walks over to Brian's bed, and quickly makes himself comfortable and rests. Jesse lays down across the sofa, and rests his head down on Russell's lap. Russell is uncomfortable by Jesse laying on him like that, but he ignores it; softly stroking Jesse's hair.

Russell originally wanted to push Jesse off him, but considering the current situation, he leaves Jesse alone. Russell shakes his head, and grabs his beer from the table. Brian is not watching the television, but he is instead staring at the floor, thinking to himself. Russell takes a swallow of his beer, as he's watching the television screen. Victor and Jesse at this point, have fallen asleep. Brian and Russell are not tired at all, and begin to converse with each other. They end up staying up for several hours, late into the night. Brian then whispers out to Russell.

"Hey Russell, I'm starting to feel nervous man. I just have a strange feeling. I know I'm acting all paranoid, but I just have a feeling. You know, that feeling you have when you know that you forgot something on your way out of the house? Sometimes it's a phantom feeling, and you didn't forget anything at all. Other times, sadly the feeling is true. You know what I mean?"

Russell takes another swallow of his beer, and nods his head. He responds to Brian.

"I do. I have that feeling too. There's nothing I can do though; we have to do this. It's the last time, so we have to stick it through man. I know we can easily forget about this, and take what money we have, but the fact we hit three banks, think of the feeling that would bring. I have to do this not only for Kevin, but I have to do this so everything is clear and complete."

Brian nods his head, and looks over at his workstation. He realizes that it is a mess. Without making too much noise, Brian cuts off all the lights, and starts to put away some of the loose tools that were scattered around. Russell keeps his view towards the television screen. He finishes his beer, and sets the empty bottle down. Brian saw Russell complete his beer, and grabs two more additional beers from the refrigerator; giving one to Russell. Brian then takes a seat down on his chair. They both think their beers, while they watch the television. When a commercial break comes, Brian looks down and he shakes his head, and carries on with his conversation he was having with Russell.

"Russell, I can't sleep. Not because Victor is passed out in my bed, and sometimes I do sleep with him, but, I don't want to bother him. I'll let him sleep in peace. But I'm not tired man. I guess you can say that I'm a fucking insomniac man. Too anxious to sleep, that's probably what it is. It's okay though, because I can work without sleep. I go without sleep all the time."

Russell takes another swallow of his beer, and points to Jesse sitting on his lap.

"This one keeps me up all night all the time. He sleeps on my bed, and I normally just stay up on the couch all night watching sports and shit. We're probably going to stay up all night Brian, I just know. It's going to be morning in a few hours."

Brian nods his head, and sits back in his chair. Brian takes another swig of his beer, and sets the bottle down on the table. Brian then talks to Russell once again.

"Well Russ whatever happens tomorrow, we're all winners right?"

Russell finishes his second beer, and sets the bottle on the table. Russell turns away from the television and looks down towards the ground, and responds to Brian.

"All of us are winners, and all we do is win. If you're not first, you're last right?"

Brian nods his head, and sits back in his chair. He closes his eyes, and listens to Russell. Russell then continues.

"The only thing you can do is win. Losing is not an option, we have to win."

Brian nods again. Russell then tilts his head back on the couch, and rests his eyes.

CHAPTER 21:

NOTHING OPEN, NOTHING CLOSED

It is now time for all of the action to commence. Everything which has been brewed and piled up over the past few weeks, must now all come together. This will be the final battle that the men will have to approach. They are all about to take on the last ever heist they will commit. Originally, the men had no intentions at all of doing a third heist. The oppression got to each and every one of them, and they were able to sway their minds to go ahead with doing it. From the success they were able to achieve from the first heist, allowed them to carry on towards the second. In the second heist, they approached this particular one, planning it to be their last heist. Wanting to gloat and celebrate after completing it. This was not the case at all, and things went differently than they suspected. Despite the fact they did manage to perform the heist well, they however were struck with an extreme tragedy. Kevin ended up being a victim in that heist; it difficult for all of the men to accept. It made them all turn against the core of the group, and they went into a big deal of defeat, depression and mental anguish. Once they were able to accept and grieve over Kevin in the proper way,

Russell then decided to plan one final heist. This heist partly being on behalf of Kevin, as he is no longer with them. Russell also feels the men have unfinished business. By doing this third heist, they will be complete, as far as their careers as outlaws are concerned. Upon finishing this heist, the men all hope to stay together as a group, and carry on with whatever choices and plans they have for their lives.

With it now being Friday, the heist will take place shortly. Emotions are running high, as they always customarily do between all of the men, right before a heist starts. They men are fairly sure that they will breeze through this heist, and give it their all. As the men are already aware of, there is a possibility of danger. Things could possibly turn for the worst with this heist, and results might not be pleasant.

One thing to consider, is that the bank they are going to hit which is the "First Federal Bank of Los Angeles", is currently being watched by the police now. Investigators strongly believe the men are going to attack this bank today. The authorities have taken extra methods and tactics, to make sure they thwart the robbery. A police officer in an unmarked car is parking right outside the entrance of the bank now, waiting for the men to run in. He will then call for backup to arrive at the scene. After a minute has passed, the officer will walk into the bank, and try to subdue the situation in the best possible way before the rest of the authorities arrive. There will be an armed guard inside the bank to watch over for any scenarios to occur as well. Due to these extra tools the police are using, it makes this heist much harder to deal with.

The men are going to work harder than they ever have, to come out victorious in this heist. From the looks of things, it seems this heist will be much harder than the first two were. Third time should be a charm though, as this would be a rematch of the second heist at "First Savings and Trust". Kevin being killed, almost makes their last heist not count. The rest of the men were able to do a satisfactory job and escape. Kevin was unfortunately caught victim by the detonators outside of the bank. He wasn't able to leave the heist with the rest of the men. The group now being incomplete with Kevin, that heist has many bad memories associated with it.

Russell and Brian did not get any sleep the night before. They stayed up practically the whole night talking to each other. Only managing to rest for a few minutes, if that. Perhaps the excitement and all of the anxiety they were feeling towards this heist, made it difficult for them to sleep. All of the guys are now walking outside of the "Home Base" unit. Feeling tough with their expressions and attitudes. Like with the previous heists, the men are now heading towards the other unit, which contains all of the tools they need to use to commit the heist.

With this now being the third heist the men are preparing for, everything seems so simple to put together. The men adapt their minds to not waste any time, and quickly get everything prepared for what they are about to do. However, this will be the last time they will get ready for a heist. After they finish this heist, they won't ever have to be faced with this type of pressure anymore. The men have no intentions at all of doing a fourth heist. This heist is strictly to make up for the previous heist, which killed Kevin. In a way, this heist is to avenge his death, and for them to perform even better.

This bank will be the largest one they will take. As it being the final heist, it's fitting that this bank is the largest, and possibly the most complex one to approach. The men are all past the doubting stage, and they know the heist must be done. None of them wish to back out or quit at this point; it's quite the contrary. The men want to stick together, and use all of the events which conspired over the past weeks to guide them through their lives. With this newly found brotherhood they have created for themselves, it makes them want to appreciate social interactions to a higher level than they have previously. Albeit the men are all committing bank heists, they are still able to attach themselves to work together as a team.

They men reached the inside of the other unit. Inside this unit, their disguises, weapons, and getaway vehicles are stashed inside. Getting right to the point, the men don't hesitate to get themselves ready for the heist. They of course, will be using and putting on the same disguises they wore in the previous heists. The police have dubbed them the "Snowman Bandits", from the fact their disguises are snow jackets and snow boots. Every man is thinking of something different in his head. They each have this unexplainable anxiety in their bodies. When you have to do a bank heist, you have to act quick, and you need to control your emotions. If you don't calm yourself down when you are faced with a daring event such as this, you could end up making a devastating mistake. The men strive on working together, to achieve the common goal. All four of them hold onto separate thoughts and feelings.

Russell is quite arguably the captain of the ship, and he has been calling all of the shots since day one. Whatever he wants to do, he expects the other men to do it. If there is a certain thing he wants done, the rest of the men in Russell's mind have to obey it. Russell being a bank manager at the "Sunset Credit Union", has caused him to take the lead throughout the events they all have been approached with. Going onto the third heist; something he never planned on doing. Heist number two was going to be the last heist. Kevin who was his best friend, and someone that Russell still misses dearly, was killed in that heist.

Russell feels this heist has to be done, to cover up the second heist. He is starting to feel much anxiety and excitement. As this is the last time they will do this, Russell wants to give a perfect performance. Russell orchestrated all of these heists, to rebel against the corporation and business that for lack of a better terms, screwed him completely over; both mentally and emotionally.

Russell has this strange feeling of something being incomplete. That incomplete feeling is being caused, because Russell wants to go straight ahead with this third heist. His mind has been made up, and feels that this is something that they have to do, and it's not something that can be changed at this point. The men never go back once they have gotten this far, especially with it now being the day of the heist. Russell importantly wants to use this to test John who is the manager of the "First Federal Bank". John quite frankly, is Russell arch nemesis, his rival, and his mortal enemy. Russell wants John to feel scared, and to feel humiliated by having his bank robbed. He wants John to experience that same type of humiliation that he gives to others. Russell feels that for this final showdown, and what he has at stake, gives him whatever boost he needs to turn into a beast. He only uses this beast character, when it comes down to the heists. Russell ordinarily doesn't like to get violent, or to cause pain to others. He would never hurt or harm anyone innocent like that. He simply wants to go against the same infrastructure that has rejected and oppressed him, and caused his life to go astray as it did. Russell no longer wants to follow the conformity rules, and deals with his own agendas and regulations.

Jesse was simply a bank teller before all of this began. That was generally what his lifestyle consisted of. He was a regular employee at the "Sunset Credit Union." His life as a gay black man, has been of much disappointment and struggle. Feeling out of place in the world, and having to deal with the fact he's different in many aspects from other people. While he was working at the bank, he was quite comfortable with all the other workers, except Russell. It wasn't until the day their bank was targeted, that Jesse developed an interesting relationship that he never would envision with Russell. It was unfortunate that an event such as that had to bring them together.

Jesse feels that he can relate to Russell completely, and understands his pain and oppression as well. This third and final heist means a great deal to Jesse. This will be the last time to take all his anger and hardships that the world has given him, towards committing this heist. He also understands the risks and cautions involved with these types of activities. Jesse feels sad that Kevin was killed during the previous heist. He has faith in the other men, that they will work together once again in this heist, and push through. Jesse has had enough, and is tired of being told no, and is tired of always being last. Advancing to this final heist, he keeps his mind attentive. This is the time and chance to turn everything in his life around. Jesse realizes that it's time for him to take charge.

Brian has always been the type of guy that was smooth enough to get whatever he wanted. Not only because he was attractive physically, but mentally as well. Brian is indeed a very handsome man. He also has a good personality about himself; with high swagger and attitude. It is also due to this, that Brian gets himself involved around people and situations he has no business being in. It was clear that during the "Sunset Credit Union" heist, Brian had no business, none whatsoever, working with Scott. He wasn't violent like that, and wasn't even planning on robbing banks. Brian is more of a carjacker, and someone who likes to hustle around cars and automobiles. Working with cars has always been Brian's main ambition in life not being an outlaw.

Although Brian isn't happy for the events which conspired the day he and Scott decided to rob Russell's bank, he understands how fate works. The fact that two innocent people were killed; from all the pain and guilt, Brian quickly ran away from the scene. He is however happy to have met Russell. Brian is confident that going into this third heist, they will all do well, but he's still slightly concerned. This concern is mostly due to the men feeling over confident of themselves, and not dealing with the pressure in the appropriate way. Brian believes that if they work well, and if they don't feel drained by their emotions, he and the rest of the guys can leave of this heist for one final time as champions, and win.

Victor does not think the way most other people do. He feels he is an alien from some strange planet, that is forced to live with other people. It's not only because of his unique exterior experience, but his mental personality and his internal attitude. It was last Friday that Victor had his mind made up, to take his own life. The depression from witnessing everything he has in the past weeks, made him lose all control. Although the men keep reminding him that his position in the group is needed, Victor doesn't feel he belongs at times. He starts to remember how he got involved in all of this.

Victor was a man who lived in his car, and never minded anyone else, because of how scary he claims he looks. He was desperate for money, and decided to rob the "Sunset Credit Union". Victor had no idea whatsoever, that there were already men who were intending to rob that same bank, at the same time he was. Victor simply watched the entire heist pan out, without doing anything. How would things be different, if Victor simply walked in the bank, and robbed it? Would he have met the other men? Victor would not have killed or hurt anyone, and would not have turned violent. This is something that always puzzles Victor, and will always puzzle him. Despite the fact this incident has passed, Victor still wonders about it. He is now concerned on the final heist. Victor knows that he needs to help out the rest of the guys, to finish this heist. Using this heist to be the cap on the jar, of all his hardships.

It is now crunch time for the guys. They do not have any time to waste at all, and they need to get ready for the heist. The men all begin to put on their disguises. Making sure their masks are concealed around their faces well. The men have on their snow boots, and put on their gloves as well. Again, this heist is practically going to be a repeat of the previous one they did. The second heist was originally supposed to be their last, and was planned out to be so. From the way how things panned out, the heist didn't turn out to be successful as the men have hoped. Kevin is now dead, and it's something the rest of the guys still haven't been able to fully deal with.

They are going ahead with this heist, as a tribute to Kevin. Showing that they aren't going to let the unfortunate events which happened in the previous heist, let them down. The additional fact that Russell has a personal vendetta against the manager of the bank, is truly dismissive. Really, that was simply a bonus to add fuel to Russell's fire. It only triggered him further to act on his impulses. The biggest mistake that each of these men have right now, would be the fact that they are feeling over confident. Understanding that they have done two heists before, and they have a good grasp of what they are doing. They still however don't see most of the consequences of their actions, and the effects it will have.

Detective Henderson during this same exact time, sits at his desk with a smirk on his face, staring at his blank computer screen. He takes a small sip of his coffee, and sets the cup down on his desk. He leans back in his chair, and folds his arms around his wide belly. The reason he is feeling nervous, is that he knows the "Snowman Bandits", are about to strike. He just doesn't know which bank in particular they have in mind. He only knows that they have hit a bank, for the past two Friday's. Understanding that he needs to take whatever precautions he can, to stop these men. Detective Henderson has asked that private armed security guards be present in every major bank that hasn't been targeted yet. This includes the "First Federal Bank", the men intend to visit. All of the details from this particular case, is bringing much agitation and anger towards him. Not only because of how the men plan all of the heists that they commit, but how quickly they move about them as well. Detective Henderson rubs his fingers through his spiky hair, and unclips his badge from his waist. He stares at his badge, and shakes his head. This particular job causes him much stress, as Detective Henderson plans to retire very soon from the police force.

One of his final wishes, is to get more answers and information regarding the "Snowman Bandit" case, before he leaves. He waits for the dispatch call, alerting him that they are at the bank. This is his cue to act fast, and to get to the bottom of the investigation before the men flee once again. Something like that would really destroy Detective Henderson's spirit, as he really hopes that today is the day he is able to bring more unanswered questions towards this particular case. The meeting he had yesterday, was his only effort in being one step ahead of these men. He knows that all of this will make a big impact towards the heist the men plan to execute.

Over at the "First Federal Bank", a police officer dressed in uniform, waits in an unmarked car positioned right outside the front door of the bank. He is waiting for the suspects to run inside. Once they are in the bank, with the help of the armed guard, the situation will easily be deescalated. There are officers outside of surrounding banks which are at risk of being targeted, as well. This is part of Detective Henderson's plan. If the banks are not taking the proper action to secure their buildings, then he feels he has no choice but to do the job himself. Detective Henderson takes another sip of his coffee, and leans back in his chair, staring at the ceiling tiles. He doesn't see why his plan will fail; from the way he has everything positioned, it should turn out exactly the way he anticipates.

The police man sitting outside of the bank keeps his vision towards the bank entrance. His name is Clyde Waker. He is a twenty-nine-year-old, baby faced bald man. He was previously in the United States army, and later became a police officer. Officer Waker has been a police officer for now three years. Being only with the "LAPD" for a year and a half. He is not married, and doesn't have any children. In his spare time, he likes to each Little League baseball to young men. Officer Waker was called to scene randomly, like every other officer at the surrounding banks have been as well. As far his personality goes, Officer Waker is generally a nice guy, and a quiet man at times. He is very patriotic, and enjoys sports and shooting. Officer Waker honestly hopes that the men choose a different bank, as his biggest fear is being obligated to get in the middle of a robbery. Although, he understands he has to do, what he has to do. It's the job he was sworn to take, protecting and serving civilians. But to be honest, he doesn't want to see the robbers run into the bank he was picked to patrol.

Inside the "First Federal Bank", is an armed security guard working for a third party company. Ordinarily, this bank doesn't hire security guards. Detective Henderson wants to make sure that all of the banks are secure, and instructs that one is positioned at locations which are at risk. The security guards present at each location are random as well, and were chosen by an outside company, not affiliated with the police department.

The security guard on duty at the "First Federal Bank", is a thirty-eight-year-old Caucasian man named Alan Richmond. He has brown hair, in a flat top hairstyle, and a bushy mustache. He has been a security guard his entire life, and has tried several times to get himself into the police force. Unfortunately, with every attempt he tried to become a police officer, not working out in his favor. He doesn't understand why this is so; taking in consideration his past military experience. For now, he remains a security guard. Only hoping that someday he will eventually become a police officer. The security guard doesn't feel like there will be any incidents or problems that will happen. His attitude is relaxed and calm, and he carefully scans all of the people inside of the building.

The security guard is ready if he needs to step in if a situation happens. He continues to stand right next to the entrance, noticing every single person that walks in and out of the bank. The guys are not expecting a security guard to be standing at the front door of the bank.

It is unknown as to what their tactics will be towards the heist as a result of that. The first two heists, the men did not have to deal with a guard present inside the bank. So this will be interesting to see how they are able to cope with an obstacle such as this, during the heist.

Detective Henderson takes another swallow of his coffee. All he can do is sit and wait, until he is told what bank exactly the men have picked. He knows they are going to strike; he just doesn't know where exactly they are going to strike at. Everything seems to be set perfectly for him to catch what he's looking for. Detective Henderson has set up several traps and methods to crack this case, and now waits patiently.

He sits far back in his chair, and closes his eyes for a second. He starts to relax, and clears his mind of any negative thoughts. Detective Henderson spent a great deal of time trying to find patterns in the case, that others weren't able to notice. This case is one that has bothered him constantly.

The possibility that only in a short while, he has the chance to make a development in the case, makes him excited. Detective Henderson is planning on retiring and leaving the police force. Putting an end to this case, will be the perfect way for him to finish his career. After taking one final sip of his coffee, Detective Henderson puts his hands on his forehead, rests his elbows on his desk, and shakes his head. Having a strong feeling, that he's about to receive some news.

The men are now all dressed into their disguises, still remaining at the unit. The game plan for this heist, will the same in the second heist. Russell plans on breaking into the vault using the power drill, while Brian takes care of the bank tellers. Jesse and Victor will remain in the lobby, giving backup to them both. This system worked well for them while they were inside the bank the last time, so they feel confident on using the same approach. Russell also feels that the men travelling in separate vehicles is something he feels that they should do again. Although he's not happy with it, and wants them all to remain together, it is more logical for them all to leave in separate cars. It allows for the escape to run by more smoothly. Russell and Jesse will be riding in a Ford Expedition. Brian and Victor will be riding in a Chevy Tahoe. Russell grabs two large empty duffel bags, and puts the industrial drill inside one of the bags. He then grabs one of the rifles. Russell puts both of the items in the back area of the getaway vehicle. Brian grabs two empty duffel bags, and one of the rifles. He places all of the contents in his getaway vehicle. Jesse and Victor then grab their guns, and they both set them inside their getaway vehicles. Following this, the men as they did in the previous heists as well, gather and huddle up and embrace each other for a minute.

This particular ritual has been custom, so it comes natural for them to do. It is tough with Kevin not being there with him. With this heist, they are going to have to act without the aid of his computer services. It will be difficult for them to go about everything without using help such as that, however the men feel they will still complete the heist, without having the need to use that. The sadness of Kevin being apart from them is upsetting. This heist will make the men test themselves in ways they did know they could bring themselves to.

Understanding feelings, thoughts, emotions, ideas, and expressions that never would have crossed their mind in any other instance. As individuals, they all have a different reason to be standing where they are right now. Each man feels a certain way, about separate agendas, for different reasons. However, when it comes to this heist, all four of them are equally feeling the same thing. They hold onto each other tight, in a big group hug. They support each other, and formed a brotherhood; now they need to get into action one last time.

Understanding whichever happens from here on out, they have to accept and deal with it. When they finish embracing each other, Russell stands in the middle of all of them, and starts to speak.

"We all know what to do. We get in, we get out, we come back here. We're done. We celebrate, and we go on with our lives. This was fun, but this isn't us. I know this is number three, but pretend this is number two. We're starting over mainly for Kevin. With this, everything will be complete, and we would have proven our point. We're not going to keep doing this. That was never our plan to rob three banks. Our plan was to stick it to man, and I believe we've accomplished all of that. I'm now ready to end this, one final time for certain. Let's go and get this started, and let's go and finish this men."

Like with the previous instances before, Max arrives at the scene right on time before the men all leave. He moves his wheelchair closer to the other guys and talks to them.

"I don't know why I keep catching you guys like this. I'm not complaining, it's good that you all plan to prepare yourselves and leave in a flash like that. I don't' know why I have bad timing, and nearly miss not giving a chance to speak to you. As always, I'm here to offer my support, and I'll be waiting for all of you later. I want to celebrate with you all later."

The men all appreciate Max dropping by before they depart for the heist. Russell gets closer to Max, and puts his hand on Max's shoulder. He then speaks to him in a hushed tone.

"Max, this is lovely that you care about us like this. If it weren't for you, I don't think we could be able to plan most of these out as thorough as we do. As much as you hate it, when I mention your acts of kindness, I'm thankful for it Max, and so are the rest of the guys. Thank you Max, I really mean it."

Max smiles, and the each of the men give him a hug. He then speaks to all the men.

"I love all of you, and come back safe men. Remember, that you guys have worked together through all of this, and have been through so much. I love you all. I'll see you later."

The guys all wave goodbye to Max, and Max has now left the unit. Brian then immediately walks over to the door of the unit, and unlocks it. Brian opens the door. Russell gets into his vehicle, and Brian gets into the other vehicle. Russell turns the ignition on, however, the car will not start. Russell begins to panic.

Of all the times for something such as this to happen, he didn't want it to be now. Russell tries to get the car to start, but the engine will not start. Brian turns the ignition on in his vehicle, and starts to drive out of the unit. Brian stops himself, when he notices that Russell hasn't started his vehicle yet. Due to the tinted windows both vehicles have, Brian cannot see inside; he assumes that the reason why Russell hasn't started the vehicle yet, is because he isn't ready to leave. Brian decides wait a while, rather than see if Russell is having any issues. Russell tries one more time start the vehicle, and it will not come on. Feeling frustrated, Russell slams his head against the steering wheel. Russell tells Jesse to get out of the car, and Russell and Jesse walk over to Brian's vehicle. When they reach Brian's vehicle, Russell bangs on the driver side window. Brian rolls the window down, and Russell looks down towards the floor, talking to Brian.

"The car won't fucking start. I kept trying and trying. It won't start. Ugh. Fuck. Shit."

Brian starts to shake his head, and gets out of his vehicle. He walks over to the other vehicle, and opens up the hood. Brian is puzzled as to what the issue perhaps is. Sadly, he does not have enough time to do a full diagnostic on the vehicle. It could be multiple reasons as to why Russell cannot start the vehicle. It could be anything as simple from the car needing oil, or the battery being dead. These issues could be fixed rather easily, and wouldn't strain any time for their heist. Or it could be something more complex, such as the alternator or transmission being shot.

The men currently cannot fix or attest those types of problems at this time. Brian starts to regret all of the modifications he has put towards this car. At the time, he felt it would give the vehicle a better chance on having a faster acceleration speed to get away easier. He now believes that he should have kept it simple with everything he added.

Brian starts to check the oil, it's fine. He checks the battery, that is alright as well. Brian then runs to "Home Base", and grabs his tools and his electronic error reader. He quickly plugs in his electronic reader in the car, which pulls up many error codes related to the engine; so that if an error is confirmed, all Brian has to do is find out what part is weakening the car for it not to start. Brian then using his tools, takes apart the car. Russell and the rest of the men watch Brian move about this very quickly, with his disguise still on. Brian believes the engine system in the car, is causing the ignition not to come on. Brian becomes slightly angry, and slams the car hood down. Brian has several conclusions as to what the problem could possibly be, but he isn't sure that he has the appropriate amount of time to replace the broken part in the vehicle. Brian turns his head towards Russell, and snaps at him.

"I don't know what's the deal. If I only had a little more time, I would know for sure. It could possibly be the alternator, or the radiator perhaps as well. If I knew this shit yesterday, I could have already replaced everything now. We had to find this out now? Ugh. Russell, we don't have a choice, we have to all leave in the other car. Come on man."

Russell nods his head; he and Jesse grab all the heist items, and store them in the other vehicle. They all sit inside, and Brian quickly drives out of the unit. Victor moves himself to the back rear seat area with Jesse, and Russell sits in the passenger seat of the vehicle. Brian gets out, and closes and shuts the door of the unit, and the men all finally leave "Home Base", and head to the "First Federal Bank". Brian starts to shake his head, and drives at a slightly high speed. While he's looking straight at the road, Brian angrily starts to speak to Russell.

"I need to ask you a question, and whatever decision you want me to do, I'll do it. Do you want me to jack another car before we get there? If you don't want me to Russell, I won't. I need your answer now though. There's a place nearby that has good getaway cars."

Russell turns his head towards the window, and responds to Brian very quietly.

"No Brian, we'll be fine. I don't want to talk about it, just go to the bank man. Okay?"

Brian shakes his head, and gets himself on the highway. Russell looks out, and sees that today is an overcast gloomy day, like yesterday was. Not compared to their previous heists, which all had immaculate sunny and warm weather. Russell doesn't know if this is a sign or not, that a terrible outcome is going to happen. He starts to worry over several things, and his confidence dissipates out of his mind. Russell is still upset that the getaway vehicle wouldn't start, and doesn't like it when things don't go smoothly.

The heist is already starting badly, and Russell is actually scared. His knees begin to shake uncontrollably, and he can feel his whole body start to become tense. Russell looks out towards the highway which Brian is driving on, and Russell's vision completely fades to black, and he starts to hallucinate. Russell sticks to the seat, and is unable to move his body at all. Hallucinations run in his head very quickly, in a thrilling way. The hallucinations are separate events from his past. Starting with many happy and upsetting memories from his childhood. He starts to remember the times he has spent with his parents, and all the fun he has had when he lived in Milwaukee.

Reliving some of these times in his mind, that Russell seldom thinks about. These include flashbacks of him playing in the snow with the other boys in the neighborhood, and other distance memories he has of being with his family. Russell doesn't understand why he is having these thoughts, and he doesn't know why he can't control them. The hallucinations continue with more recent events from his life. Russell thinking of Peter, and all the things they have done together.

Russell considered him like a father. Russell also thinks about Jennifer, and the time he has been with her, and how beautiful of a woman she was. He has more memories run in his head, as the flashback hallucinations continue to fly all around. Russell now starts to go back the first time he met Kevin. How Kevin was sitting by himself at study hall, stuffing his face with junk food, studying, and Russell introduced himself. Then all of a sudden, these images quickly vanish from Russell's mind. When this happens, he turns his head quickly, and this causes Brian to be concerned.

"Are you okay man? You're feeling okay right? Calm down, okay? It's going to be fine."

Russell is actually not feeling okay. He starts to have the same feeling he experienced the day the "Sunset Credit Union" was hit. Russell isn't feeling that confident about this heist, and is having many second thoughts. This is his absolutely his final chance to back away. Russell can either tell Brian the truth, and that's he's not feeling well, and doesn't want them to go along with it. Or, Russell can simply not care, and pretend that everything is going well. Russell then makes his choice, and turns his head over to Brian, responding to him.

"Yeah man. I'm okay. I'm tired I guess. Sorry for having you worry like that. I'm okay."

During this trip, the men generally stay quiet. There is no need for them to joke or around right now. They have a mission they need to focus on, and this heist means everything to them. All of what they experienced, needs to all mean something towards this heist. So therefore, they have to be focused, and ready to approach it in an appropriate way. Russell looks around at the highway, and notices that there are realistically no other cars on the road. It is unusually strange to him, that it being a Friday afternoon, there are not many cars driving. Brian keeps a somewhat high speed, as they are now not far from the bank. The men do not say a single word to each other, as they carry on towards the bank.

Brian reaches their exit, and they now are travelling on the surface streets. With it being only a few blocks from the bank, the feeling Russell has, continues to pierce through his stomach. He starts to wonder that he is perhaps making the wrong decision, and he should not proceed with this heist. Russell being a man who doesn't like to listen to his conscious, ignores this feeling. Brian continues to drive through the streets, and all of the men in the car position their minds to towards the bank heist. When they arrive at the parking structure, Brian drives in, and parks the vehicle near the entrance. Brian cuts off the ignition, and at this time, the world feels as if it's no longer turning.

Russell can feel his heart stop, and a feeling he had during their very first heist, starts to reemerge itself. The other men have this feeling as well, and it's a mutual wave of reactions going around. Several minutes pass, and the men remain silent and motionless in the vehicle. Without warning, Brian then reaches behind him, and grabs both his empty duffel bags. Following that, Brian opens the car door and runs out. The rest of the guys then snap out of it, and run out as well.

When the men are now running towards the bank, Brian locks the vehicle back up. All four of them are sprinting fast to the entrance, however this common feeling of them running through quicksand or thick mud, in addition to everything happening much slower than it actually is, starts to happen. This is most likely due to all of the pressure buildup they have. Even though the men have only been running for four seconds, this seems like several hours to them. They finally turn the corner out of the parking lot. The ambiguity of the parking lot, allows for a smooth entrance such as this. The men are now on the sidewalk to the entrance of the bank. Creeping closer to the bank, the men keep their vision only on the glass doors of the bank. Brian who's ahead of all the guys, reaches for the door handle, and opens it. They all race into the building. Officer Waker across the street in his patrol car, notices them right then, and starts to freeze. He starts to shake, as he picks up his radio receiver, shaking his hands rapidly.

"This is Waker, I have a 2/11 in progress right now. Suspects are inside 'First Federal.' I repeat, 2/11 in progress. Suspects have entered First Federal bank on Grand. Do you copy?"

Officer Waker starts to feel nervous and unclips his gun from his waist, as he stares through the double sided glass door entrance of the bank, which doesn't allow you to see what's happening from the inside. Officer Waker does not hear a response from his radio, and panics.

Inside the bank, the men continue past the main entrance area, and all four of them find a shocking discovery. There is a security guard standing in the lobby area. Russell does not know what to do, but they continue to run further inside the bank. They were not assuming a guard would be present, and didn't plan as such. Brian starts to freeze up, and he and Russell stare at each other in defeat, feeling scared and unsure of what to do.

During this time, a loud gunshot goes off, and several people scream. Russell turns his head to the direction he heard the gunshot from. While he's scanning around, all of the patrons inside the bank head to the floor, with their hands behind their head. Russell then sees the security guard is lying dead on the ground from being shot in the head. Victor fired his gun at the guard, when he noticed the guard takes his gun on his waist, and aim it at the guys. Victor is still pointing the gun at the now deceased guard. Russell, Brian and Jesse look at Victor in shock, not believing that he actually did that. Victor then runs closer into the lobby as he shouts out loud.

"EVERYONE STAY ON THE FUCKING GROUND! GET THE FUCK DOWN ON THE FLOOR NOW! EVERYONE GET DOWN ON THE FLOOR NOW!"

Victor then nervously speaks to the rest of the guys, as they stare at him confused.

"I didn't have a choice guys. What the fuck was I supposed to do? I'll explain later."

Russell shakes his head at Victor, and can't believe he actually murdered the security guard. This was the first time that one of them has killed anyone through these whole ordeals. The sad thing is, this is not the time or place for Russell to lament over that. Russell quickly grabs the industrial drill and heads over the vault area. Jesse is currently feeling tense, but minds his position in the lobby area with Victor. Brian shakes his head at Victor, and runs over to the bank tellers, pointing their guns at them. Brian approaches first teller who is a young attractive brunette woman. He notices that she is trying to push the alarm on her terminal.

"I don't fucking think so! Open your drawer and put everything inside. I want to see that fucking drawer empty now! Open it, and empty everything in the bag now! Do it right now!"

The woman takes her hand away from the alarm and empties her cash drawer, dropping the stacks of cash inside Brian's duffel bag. Once she has done that, Brian instructs her to empty the cash cart located behind her as well.

"Open that shit up right now! Empty it in the bag! I want it all now!"

The woman is able to quickly empty all of the money from that, dumping it into Brian's bag. Russell is finding it slightly difficult to break into the vault. Despite using a brand new bit on the drill, it starts to break. Sweat is running down Russell's forehead under his mask, as he rams the drill inside. The lock luckily manages to break unintentionally, and Russell then runs inside the vault, now drilling some of the bigger safe boxes. Brian then walks across behind the counter, and brings the teller to the main floor, still pointing his gun at her. John who is laying down on the floor near his desk, lifts his head up at this time, and watches Brian walk over to the second teller; an older African-American woman. John continues to watch Brian, and John starts to grab his handgun from underneath his suit jacket; waiting for the right time to spring into action. John conceals carries a gun sometimes to work, and had a feeling that he should bring it to work today. Brian points his gun at the teller, and shouts at her, when he notices that she as well is going for her silent alarm.

"Hey! Hey! Open up the drawer, and don't hit that fucking alarm! I dare you to! Open the drawer, put it in the bag, and you won't get hurt sweetheart! Drop the money inside now!"

The woman does not hit he alarm, and does exactly what Brian tells her to, and empties the money from inside her terminal, into Brian's duffel bag. Russell inside the vault, opens up one of the biggest safe boxes on the wall. Inside contains a large amount of cash. He drops all of it inside his empty duffel bag, and it fills completely up. Russell has a wide grin on his face, not expecting for the box to contain that much. Back in the main area of the bank, the second teller is told by Brian to empty the money inside the cash cart, and to place it all into the duffel bag. He continues to point his gun and shout at her.

"Yes! Give me all of that and set it in the bag! I need all of it now! Put it in the bag!"

When she finishes that, Brian like he did with the first teller walks around the counter, aims his gun at her, and brings her over to the main floor area. As Brian is walking towards the third and final teller, who is a young attractive Hispanic woman, John at cannot take being a victim and hostage anymore. He feels he can take charge in this current situation, and essentially save the day. John then gets up from the floor, and acts as a hero. He points his gun at Brian.

"You guys picked the wrong day, and the wrong bank. All of you go to hell."

Before John pulls the trigger, Victor immediately aims towards John's legs, and shoots him several times in that area. John screams out in pain and drops his gun. Victor runs over to John and confiscates his gun, and runs back to the main area of the bank shouting.

"Unless you want to be next, all of you stay the fuck down right now!"

Brian and Jesse are now completely stunned at Victor, and how out of control he's acting. Russell is currently in the vault and has no recollection of what just happened. He has no idea that Victor has shot John. Russell opens up his second cash box, which contains more cash. Russell empties all of that into his other duffel bag, and decides to force open one more safe box. Jesse remains frozen from where he is, and doesn't move. Brian shakes his head, and carries on to the final teller. John cannot walk from being immobilized, and shouts at Victor.

"You piece of shit; you're going to pay for this asshole. Go straight to hell. Ugh."

John then starts to crawl away from his current location, and Victor intentionally shoots the floor right next to John to scare him. Brian ignoring Victor, points his gun at the last teller.

"Open the drawer up, you already know. Drop all the money inside the bag!"

The woman starts to take the cash from inside her terminal, and drops it inside Brian's second duffel bag, which is already overflowed with cash. Back outside, Officer Waker notices that backup has not arrived yet. He at this time, decides to walk inside the bank. With his gun drawn, Officer Waker gets out of his patrol car, and runs across the street, heading in towards the bank. Congruently, Brian instructs the woman to empty her cash cart.

"I need you to give me all of that! Put it in the bag! Give me all that!"

Russell in the same time, opens his final safe box open. It contains a reasonable amount of cash; not as much as the first two, but Russell takes it anyways. He then quickly takes his duffel bags wrapping them around his shoulder, and Russell runs out of the vault. Russell is now in the main area of the bank, as Brian is walking the third teller out to the lobby area, and places her on the floor. Russell then notices John is bleeding heavily from his legs, with Victor still aiming his gun at him.

Russell immediately starts to feel empathetic towards John. Yes, John was someone that Russell didn't care for, but he didn't want the man to be physically hurt. As Russell stares at John on the floor, Officer Waker enters the bank. Officer Waker sees the dead security guard at the door, and starts to feel more serious on the situation. Officer Waker points his gun at Russell, who is standing the closest to him.

"LAPD, get down on the ground now! I want to see your hands! Get down."

Russell and the rest of the men start to give in and obey Officer Waker. They feel this is it, the game is up, and it is time for them to give in and accept defeat. Russell, Brian, Jesse and Victor all start to kneel face down on the ground. Russell, unfortunately while he was trying to move his gun which was wrapped around his shoulder out of the way so he can lay on the floor, causes suspicion to Officer Waker. The officer mistakes this as Russell trying to fire his gun at him, and shoots Russell several times in his upper left chest area near his heart, and his left arm.

Russell screams in pain, and falls down to the ground. Brian, Jesse and Victor then immediately stand back up, filled with horror. They stand still watching this scene. Victor then believing that Russell is dead, loses it. Victor aims his gun Officer Waker. However, Officer Waker shoots Victor in the neck several times, causing Victor to fall to the ground. Brian out of unexplainable impulse, then shoots Officer Waker in the head, killing him. Jesse stands frozen and still. Brian then rushes over to Victor. Victor is bleeding very heavily, and cannot move. He is however still conscious. Brian speaks to him.

"Are you alright man? Speak to me. Please tell me you're okay."

Victor nods his head at Brian. Brian then walks over to Russell.

"Hey man, are you doing good? Can you get up and walk fine?"

Russell struggles to respond to Brian, but he is able to stand himself up. He then responds.

"My fucking chest hurts, and my arm hurts like fuck. But yes I can walk. Ugh it hurts."

Jesse continues to watch both of them, still unable to react or move. Brian returns over to where Victor is, and this time, Victor starts to lose consciousness.

Loud police sirens are approaching from a couple blocks away, and the men start to feel pressured. Brian starts to pick Victor up to carry him, but Victor grabs Brian's arm tightly, and Victor shakes his head at Brian. He whispers to him.

"It's my time to go, I'm not going to make it anyways. I've lost way too much blood. I'm done. It's okay. You guys need to get out of here now."

Brian begins to cry, and partially lifts up Victor's mask. Brian partially lifts up his own mask, and kisses Victor on the lips. Jesse watches them, and Russell who's is in immense pain, watch all of this unfold as well. Brian then runs over to the rest of the men, and shouts to them.

"We have to get the fuck out! They are on their way here now! Come on!"

Russell who despite being under total excruciating pain uses his strength, and along with Victor and Jesse, they all run outside the bank. They proceed through the surrounding path leading into the parking lot. Without them being aware, one of the patrons inside the bank, does something daring and runs after them to see which vehicle they exit from. The man following them creeps behind them carefully, and notices that they leave in a Chevrolet Tahoe without any licensed plate, and tinted windows. The man then takes a picture of their vehicle with his phone, and heads back to the bank. They men all get inside the vehicle, and Brian speeds off. Russell screams in pain. Jesse tries to comfort Russell, who's sitting in the rear seat with him. As the men are speeding away, Russell continues to scream in pain.

"Aww, this fucking hurts! Damn, I'm going to die aren't I!"

Brian continues to drive feeling anxious, and Jesse continues to caress and comfort Russell who is under a great deal of pain.

At this time, the authorities arrive at the bank, just missing the rest of the men within about thirty seconds. Detective Henderson and other officers then rush in the bank, aiming their guns for any possible active suspects. As he's walking through the bank, Detective Henderson sees the hostages down on the ground, and notices the dead security guard, and Officer Waker's deceased body as well. Detective Henderson starts to feel disgusted at the sight of this.

"We have a couple officers down over here."

He walks through to where John is, and he is still alive.

"I need an ambulance now. We have an injured hostage. Sir, hang on in there, we're going to get to you the hospital. Ambulance is on its way; it will be here shortly."

John nods his head at the detective, as he remains on the floor in much pain.

Detective Henderson while still waving and aiming his gun, then notices Victor on the floor; he is still conscious. Detective Henderson puts his gun back in the holster, and screams out to the officers.

"I have a down suspect, but he's still alive! I need an ambulance right fucking now!"

Detective Henderson then removes Victor's mask, and holds his head up. Detective Henderson cradles Victor's head in his hands, speaking to him softly.

"Hey son, what's your name? Where are you buddies at? Talk to me."

Detective Henderson notices Victor is slipping out of consciousness and performs mouth to mouth recitation on him. This causes Victor to temporarily regain consciousness.

"What is your name, can you tell me your name?"

Victor smiles at Detective Henderson, and croaks out his response.

"My name. Ugh. My name, is Romero. I had a good life, I think. Goodbye."

Detective Henderson while still holding Victor's head, looks puzzled.

"Romero? Okay. Romero, you'll be fine, we're gonna take you the hospital. It's going to be fine. I need you to tell me who your buddies are okay? Can you tell me that?"

Victor then slips back out of consciousness. Detective Henderson performs CPR on him once again, however this time he is not successful with his efforts. Detective Henderson lifts up Victor's eyes, checking his pupils; he is now dead. He then cries out to the other officers.

"Suspect is gone; I need the ambulance here right fucking now. Do you hear me?"

Detective Henderson then rests Victor's head down on the grown, and walks back to the other side of the bank. He then takes his gun from holster and throws it on the ground. The other officers watch as Detective Henderson has a tantrum. He removes his badge from his waist as well, and throws it across the wall of the bank. Detective Henderson then unfastens his tie, sits down in the lobby area, and starts to cry out.

"That's it. I quit. I can't do this anymore. I can't. I quit."

Detective Henderson then gets up, and walks over to the water cooler in the lobby, and gets himself a glass of water. He then takes several gulps of his water. He returns back to his seat, muttering to himself.

"I'm done, I quit. I'm not doing this fucking job anymore. I fucking quit."

Detective Henderson looks around the current chaos of the bank, and then wipes his face with his handkerchief. He then sets his cup down, and folds his hands on his lap. He closes his eyes and raises his eyebrows. He leans his head up pointing at the ceiling with his eyes still closed, and remains quiet.

CHAPTER 22:

NOTHING EARLY, NOTHING LATE

With Russell, Brian and Jesse now on the run, they continue on with their escape; leaving a presumed deceased Victor at the bank. All three of the men continue to stay in shock, in much disbelief as to what actually happened during the heist. From the time that Victor shot and killed the security guard standing near the entrance of the bank, was when the heist took an unfortunate twist and turn for disaster. The entire situation did not go as expected. All of this has now developed and produced many strange and unprecedented effects and consequences. John was shot during the heist, which was also something drastic. Being violent, was never part of the plan whenever the men would do a heist. Victor shot not one, but two men; killing one of them which was the security guard. Brian has also shockingly killed someone as well, Officer Waker. This was only because Russell as he was walking out of the vault, was stopped by the officer, and was

told to surrender. Remarkably, all the men originally decided to give in and surrender. Being that they were involved in a tough and difficult spot from being corned by the police officer, it was decided at that particular point, the men would accept their defeat. They all proceeded to lay down on the floor, obeying whatever the officer instructed them to. Russell, who had his rifle wrapped around his chest, was trying to position the gun so he could get down on the ground. The officer thought that Russell was intending to fire his gun at him, so he shot Russell in the chest, and in his left arm with several rounds. From how badly Russell was shot, Victor began to panic and feel worried, and he pointed his gun at the officer. However, the officer quickly aimed his gun at Victor, shooting him in the neck multiple times. Brian out of heavy impulse, shot and killed Officer Waker right after that. Feeling betrayed by the officers' actions, the men then turned against their original plan to surrender, and have now ran out the bank. Before they ran out, Brian attempted to get Victor to come with him, but failed. Victor was far too weak to continue, and has already lost a great deal of blood. The men barely left the bank in time, before the authorities arrived. All three of them got into their getaway vehicle in the parking lot behind the bank, and are now escaping.

Brian drives the vehicle as fast as he can, trying to get back to "Home Base", which is still quite a distance from where they currently are. He, and the rest of the men have already accepted that Victor is now gone, and they are the only ones which remain. Brian is aware that Russell was badly shot, however he doesn't know the extent of his injuries. At this point, he can only head back towards the unit. Brian cannot chance taking Russell to a hospital, as that would only add more suspicion to them being there, and they would be apprehended by the authorities. Luckily, Max is a trained medical professional, and he could help them out in this particular case. Jesse is in the rear seat with Russell. Russell from being shot, is under much pain, and he isn't able to move. He is slouched over Jesse's lap, and Jesse is holding onto him tightly.

Jesse takes off Russell's mask, and Jesse removes his own mask as well. Jesse becomes mortified and shocked when he notices how pale Russell's face is. Russell is losing a great amount of blood, and his body is becoming weak because of that. Jesse places his hand over Russell's forehead, and it's cold. Jesse then starts to cry, from seeing Russell in this current status he's in. Jesse is scared and worried that Russell is very close from dying. Brian then moves his mask, and drives faster than he previously was. All of the men are not speaking to each other; they are under too much pressure to talk. This heist was eventful and thrilling to each of them, and the main focus is to get back to "Home

Base", as fast as they are able to. Russell then begins to groan and moan in pain very loudly, which causes Brian and Jesse to feel scared. Russell squeezes onto Jesse's hand with his right arm, as he not able to move his left arm. Jesse looks at Russell's face once again, and he is now becoming more pale faced, and his pupils are also dilated. Jesse then feeling depressed and hopeless at how things are turning out, looks out the window sobbing. From how fast Brian is driving, everything looks like heavy streaks, including the other cars and the buildings surrounding the highway. Russell continues to scream and holler from the pain he's in, and Jesse starts to rub Russell's hair very softly to comfort him. Brian who can hear Russell's cries, starts to worry. Because Brian is driving and paying attention to the road, he's not able to see how badly Russell looks in the face, like Jesse can. Brian shakes his head in total disbelief that everything is turning into disaster, and things are not looking good for them right now.

Back at the "First Federal Bank", Detective Henderson continues to sit in the chair with his eyes closed. More investigators walk into the bank, and notice how he is slacking off. They walk over to him, and ask why he's not investigating the robbery. Detective Henderson responds by saying that he's unable to contain himself at the moment, due to how heinous this particular robbery was. He explains to the other investigators, that three different individuals are dead, and some of the suspects, are still out on the run. He explains that he threw his badge across the building out of rage from feeling upset. Detective Henderson also explains that he plans to now retire from the force, and no longer wants to work in this field. This type of work is not for him anymore. This high pressure is not something he can manage or deal with any longer.

Detective Henderson is told that for now, he's still the chief investigator when it comes to armed robberies, so they need his help. Detective Henderson although already having his mind made up, and will be retiring and quitting very soon, understands that he took an oath to protect the people of this city. He needs to knock off whatever issues he's dealing with, and do his job, which is to investigate the robbery which took place. Detective Henderson decides to temporarily remain as a detective for now, and walks over to the area where he threw his badge. He grabs it off the floor, and clips it back on his waist. Right after that, the man who saw Russell, Brian and Jesse run into their getaway car, shows Detective Henderson the cell phone picture he took of their getaway vehicle. The detective immediately then orders for an all-points bulletin to be issued. Even though the vehicle doesn't have a license plate, due to the severity of this particular robbery, all of the police make this vehicle their prime concern. An APB is then sent out for the vehicle the men are in.

Detective Henderson then walks over to where John is. From being shot in the legs very badly, Detective Henderson tells him the ambulance will be coming soon, and that he's going to be alright. John is irate that the men have escaped, and he screams out in pain from being shot. Despite the fact he's badly injured, John must try to remember as much as he can from the robbery. With him being the bank manager, Detective Henderson needs to gather as much information on the incident as possible. John in an angry manner, explains everything which happened during the heist, to Detective Henderson. The detective takes out a notebook, and begins to jot down everything that Brian says.

John tells him that four men entered the bank, wearing heavy disguises comprised of snow outfits. As soon as they entered, one of the robbers shot and killed the security guard. John points to Victor's corpse on the floor, letting Detective Henderson know that he was the one who shot the guard. John then continues, and says that one of the men took charge of all the tellers, and other man ran out to the vault area. The other two men stayed on the main floor area, pointing their guns at everyone. John then explained that he was tired of being taken advantage of in his own bank, and wanted to save the others.

As he has a concealed carry permit, he took out his gun, and pointed it at the robber who was taking care of the tellers. John then points again to Victor's corpse, and reveals that he was the one who shot him in the legs. After he was immobilized, John explains that everything else he can't exactly recollect as he was laying on the floor, being held hostage by the robbers. John does say that a police officer came into the bank, right when the men were about to leave. He says the officer told them all to get down, and during that time, he heard several rounds of gunshots. After that, John says he heard the robber who is dead on the floor of the bank, tell the other men to escape and leave him there. John says that all of the men presumably ran out the bank after that. John then argues and screams from the pain he's currently in. He then complains once again, about how despite the fact a security guard, and a police officer were present to help deal with the situation, some of them still managed to escape. John is not happy at this fact at all. Detective Henderson agrees with him, and walks to other areas of the bank, talking to other patrons that were inside of the bank during the robbery, to gather more witness statements.

The ambulance finally arrives at the bank, and John is carried away by the paramedics to go to the hospital. At the same time, the coroner is now at the bank. Victor's, Officer Waker's and Alan the security guard's bodies, are all taken away as a part of the evidence for this case. Detective Henderson requests that Victor's fingerprints be immediately registered. With the fact he's one of the prime suspects in this manner, he is not yet identified. Detective Henderson explains the man only mentioned that his name was Romero.

The detective continues to walk through the bank, and out of habit he begins to nitpick at how poorly operated everything is. With the building being quite old, it's one of the oldest banks and buildings in Downtown Los Angeles. That shouldn't excuse the fact of poorly operated and constructed security systems, and the layout the bank has; it is a big target for robberies. The bank tellers shouldn't be at risk the way they are, and the bank is not safe at all.

He believes that the classic design the bank has, is being disguised and covered up from how flawed the building actually is. It scores well for attracting patrons, and it scores well for keeping a colonial architecture design. However, when it comes to bank robberies and safety, this bank doesn't score well at all. Detective Henderson is also upset that the vault for this bank is also poorly operated, that someone can easily hack and break through the lock with the correct tools. He looks at the ceiling, noticing the very few amount of surveillance cameras. By simply looking at these cameras, he knows well that the software used to capture these cameras are also not up to standards. Detective Henderson requests to see the surveillance video, and he starts to watch it.

The "Snowman Bandits" as they are dubbed and called by the police, are seen entering the bank, and most of the eyewitness accounts, support generally what the video already compromised of. Detective Henderson is more concerned at catching the other three robbers who are still currently at large. He walks outside the bank for a few minutes, and takes a cigarette break. All of the emotions he's feeling, are starting to make him feel uncomfortable and anxious. This is turning out to be one of the most sinister robberies and heists that he has ever come across. It was enough for him to make his mind up, towards retiring from this profession.

Detective Henderson takes puffs of his cigarette, as he notices news vans belonging to practically every single major station arriving at the bank. He knows that very shortly, he is going to have to hold a press conference of this robbery. Detective Henderson starts to finish up his cigarette, and throws the butt of it away in the trash can.

He walks back inside the bank, to where the investigation is still very much ongoing and still active. News reporters walk inside the bank, and question the detective, in an attempt to gain any information surrounding the heist as they can. He simply tells them that he in a few short minutes, will explain everything to them, letting the public know about this unfortunate event. The detective talks to some of his fellow investigators in the bank, informing them that the press is outside, wanting them all to explain the events to the public and media.

Outside the bank, the media begins to prepare and setup for the conference Detective Henderson will be holding shortly. A small crowd of civilians also out of curiosity noticing the surplus of police cars and news vans, stand and gather around the bank towards the podium where the detective will be holding his press conference.

Detective Henderson finishes his objectives inside the bank, and he then walks to the podium outside the entrance. He immediately starts to feel nervous from looking at all the cameras pointing at him.

For a short while, he is unable to compose himself and map out the words he wishes to explain. Knowing that many people are going to be watching this event, and it's important that if he wants these men to be caught, he must relay and explain to the viewing public as much information about the circumstances as he can. He stands at the podium and starts to scribble down notes, and his fingers shake rapidly, making difficult for him to write. Each time he attempts to write down notes, they come out sloppy and unsatisfactory. Detective Henderson then becomes frustrated. He breaks the pen he is writing with, and crumples up the paper he was writing on. He decides to improvise his statements. It might not be the most professional thing to do, but it's more comfortable for him at this time. All of a sudden, Detective Henderson is alerted that he is about to stream live on the news. He looks at the camera, giving his statement.

"I would like to inform the people of Los Angeles, that around 2 P.M. this afternoon, a group of men who we have called the "Snowman Bandits", have entered the 'First National Bank' right behind me here on Grand Ave., and committed an armed robbery. In the process, a hostage was injured with critical injuries. One of the suspects was killed, another suspect was injured, a police officer and a security guard were also sadly shot and killed during the event."

Detective Henderson for a few seconds, looks at the camera and becomes unable to open his mouth to express any words. His mental capacity after explaining that part of the event made him internally choke up. He looks down towards the podium, to give the illusion or façade that he's actually reading notes, when he doesn't have any. He then while still looking down, shakes his head and clears his throat. Detective Henderson looks back at the cameras and continues.

"Suspects are believed to be armed and dangerous, and they are currently at large. Two innocent people were killed, and these suspects will stop at nothing. A hostage that was present inside the bank, managed to get a picture of their getaway vehicle. It is a black Chevrolet Tahoe, without any license plates. The windows are tinted heavily as explained by the witness. Again, these men are armed and dangerous, so I ask that you please take caution."

Detective Henderson looks down once again to make it seem like he's reading notes. He decides to wrap up his explanations, and give out his final remarks to the press and news media.

"If you see these men, please alert us. This is very important that we catch these guys. These men are dangerous, and we need to capture them. At this time, I will not be taking in any questions, or any other remarks that the public wishes to know. I thank you all for your time."

As Detective Henderson steps away from the podium, many of the news outlets try to pester him for more information, but he ignores them and doesn't give into what they want. He walks back inside of the bank, and looks around the scene again. In great disbelief of how everything happened, and all of the tragic situations which have resulted from the heist. The only thing which is making him feel positive, is that he was able to find out the information around their getaway vehicle. Having all of this available for the public to know, will make it much easier for this investigation, and capturing the suspects. For one final time, he shakes his head and feels disappointed that his plan didn't go as expected.

Having a failed attitude, Detective Henderson no longer wants to work in the police field, and will always have this case in particular, as the main prominent reason as to why he gave this career up. It is causing too much stress that he is able to deal with and control, and he has had quite enough. Detective Henderson then lets the rest of the investigators continue their agenda, making sure they all know he's leaving the crime scene.

He walks out of the bank, and gets in his car, driving off. As he's driving, he circles around the surrounding area. Instead of going back to the police station, he remains patrolling the street. Mainly having a strange feeling that the men could possibly still be in the surrounding areas of the bank. Detective Henderson contemplates asking the department to set up road blocks to capture the men. He pulls his car over to the side of the road, and calls the police headquarters, asking to set up barriers in the highways and major roads, as there are active armed robbery suspects in the area. At that moment, in addition to information of the getaway vehicle the men are using, many major roads are being blocked by authorities. With all of these tactics on the line, Detective Henderson feels that his chances of catching these men are high.

Detective Henderson continues to roam through the downtown streets, wondering if the men have taken the vehicle to a chop shop nearby the bank, that many perpetrators in his past cases have used. The men could have possibly done this, to evade capture to get rid of their getaway vehicle. It is possible he could gather information on the men who dropped the vehicle off. This might turn out to be dangerous and risky, but it's one he's willing to take and gamble with that. A chop shop would be the most logical place in order to get rid of a getaway vehicle, without the authorities finding out.

Detective Henderson drives down several side roads and streets. He quickly arrives at a worn down factory building, a couple blocks away from the "First Federal Bank". This is a chop shop where people who steal cars, but the businesses is being fronted as a junkyard and scrap metal recycle factory. As he doesn't have a warrant or any probable cause, Detective Henderson cannot enter the building and search for the getaway van. He stares out the window, and questions as to whether or not he should leave. Also considering if he should approach the intimidating looking men that are standing outside the entrance of it. There are several gangsters standing outside the building, and again with Detective Henderson not having a warrant, it's going to be difficult for him to proceed. It seems unsafe for him to carry on. The detective ultimately decides to drive away and investigate elsewhere. He pulls around the back corner of the chop shop, and doesn't see a vehicle matching the one the robbers used.

Detective Henderson raises the volume on his scanner radio, and he is told that all the barriers are now set up on mostly every major street in the surrounding areas of the bank, and they are in the process of having highway roadblocks to question any vehicles that match the description, and any suspicious looking people. Detective Henderson readies himself to directly report to any roadblock location that updates him on new findings, so he can check out the scene himself as part of the investigation.

Russell, Brian and Jesse continue to escape from the police, trying to reach the unit as fast as they can; unaware that a witness caught their vehicle. Brian on the other hand, starts to panic that there is a chance that someone might have seen their getaway vehicle. He's not completely sure, but it's a feeling he has, and most of his intuitions are usually right. As he's going down the highway, Russell continues to holler and scream out in pain, from the bullet wounds located in his chest and in his arms. His face is extremely pale and white. Russell although conscious and breathing, is not blinking, and his eyes are completely still. He also loses the grip he had against Jesse's hand, as he has no strength left. Jesse starting to feel concerned about Russell, begins to take Russell's disguise completely off. Russell's whole body temperature is cold; he is also sweating heavily.

Jesse removes Russell's jacket, revealing his white polo shirt, which is completely bloody and the gunshot wounds are still actively bleeding. Jesse also removes Russell's disguise pants, in which Russell is wearing black sweatpants under that. Jesse lifts up Russell's shirt, and sees how terrible the bullet wounds look. Jesse then sits Russell up on the seat, and uses the snow jacket disguise, to wrap around his chest, shoulder and arm to stop the bleeding. Jesse then takes off his own disguise, to which he's wearing a blue t-shirt, and cargo shorts under. Jesse looks at Russell's face again, and is under immense horror and depression from seeing him in this condition.

Noticing that Russell is not moving his eyes, he takes the sunglasses used apart of Russell's mask, and puts them on Russell's face. Jesse then puts his own sunglasses on, to hide the mental pain he's feeling. Jesse takes the snow jacket he was wearing as a disguise, and rips it up, forming a blanket. He then covers Russell's entire torso up. Jesse is noticing the large amount of blood that Russell is losing. Jesse then holds onto Russell tightly, and starts to cry out to Brian very loudly.

"He's gonna die if we don't get him to a hospital now! He's gonna die! He has lost so much blood, and he's not even moving his eyes! He's is still breathing! What are we gonna do?!"

Brian who has removed his mask, but still has his disguise on, punches the steering wheel with great force, and continues to speed down the road. He fires back at Jesse.

"We can't take him to the hospital. If we do, they are going to know it was us, so we can't take him to the hospital. I know it's still far from here, but maybe Max can help him. I'm praying that he can. I'm sorry Jesse, I am doing all I can do. I hope that Russell can hang in there a bit longer. This is a tough spot were in. Shit. Nothing is going right at all."

Jesse looks down towards the ground, and shakes his head. Right then, Brian starts to gain an idea in his head, that he feels might make the current situation easier. In addition to feeling worried about Russell's condition, Brian has a feeling that they are somehow being followed. Most of it is him worrying too much, but it's still something that concerns him. Without telling Jesse any of this, Brian makes a sharp turn out of the highway, pulling onto a secluded underpass.

Jesse looks around puzzled, not knowing what Brian is currently doing. Russell continues to scream and yell from the pain he's in, and Jesse remains holding onto him. Brian drives down a stretch of dirt roads, next to many industrial buildings, and quickly pulls the car over; adjacent to a bunch of salvaged cars. There aren't any people present in this area, and it's a completely serene environment located on a dead end strip off the highway.

Brian opens up the glove compartment of the vehicle he's currently in, and takes out a slim jim tool, used to break into vehicles. Brian then runs out of the vehicle, and walks towards one of the more reliable salvaged cars. Brian struggles to break into an early 90s Mercedes E 500 using the tool. Jesse looks at him for a split second in the rear window confused, and Russell hollers and screams, punching

Jesse from the pain. Jesse then turns his view back to Russell, and rub's Russell's hair, and the side of his face. Jesse then cracks the car door open on the side Russell isn't laying on, and screams to Brian while he's comforting Russell, who is screaming out in pain.

"What are you doing?! Please tell me whatever you're doing is going to help us out!"

Brian successfully breaks into the car, and starts to hotwire the vehicle. Within a few seconds, he's able to start the car. After the ignition comes on, Brian walks out of the car and opens the rear door, and tries to grab Russell out of the car. Jesse is still puzzled, but gets out of the car, and helps Brian move Russell. As they lift him up, Brian speaks to Jesse.

"I think we're being followed. I'm probably over reacting, but in case I'm wrong, I want to do this anyways. I don't think Russell is going to make it, but if he does... I want you to take him to Max immediately, explain to him what happened, and if Max can't help Russell, then..."

Brian and Jesse then sit Russell in the back seat of the Mercedes, with his body still being covered by the snow jacket. Jesse sees that there is a wool blanket located in the rear seat of the car. He wraps that around Russell's body, making sure his arm and chest are still wrapped up by the makeshift splint he created using pieces of Russell's disguise. Jesse throws away the black jacket Russell was covered with before away in a nearby dumpster. Brian runs over to the other vehicle and grabs the duffle bags, and opens the trunk latch from inside the car. He sets the bags inside the trunk. Jesse cannot keep up with how fast Brian is moving, and continues to freeze up, currently in shock.

Brian then starts to undress out of his disguise, to which he is wearing a blue polo shirt, and denim jeans under. He throws his disguise, and the remaining articles of Russell and Jesse's disguises away into a nearby dumpster. Brian then reaches into the glove compartment, and throws at set of keys belonging to Max's unit, at Jesse. Jesse catches the keys, and looks at them with a puzzled face. Brian then opens the door to the other vehicle, and screams out to Jesse.

"You know the way back to the unit right?! I'm going to go down a separate path! Just

get him back as fast as you can! We'll meet up later! I trust you with the money, get him to Max quick, or else he's going to die! Make sure you keep the car running at all times, and you don't drive too slow! Just keep driving until you get there! I hot-wired it, so it might not start back up on if you drive too slow, or put it in park! I'm sorry, I have to go now! Good luck!"

Brian hesitates for a moment, standing at the door of the vehicle, and runs over to Jesse to hug him. Brian then within seconds, immediately sprints back to the other vehicle, gets inside, and speeds off from the scene. Jesse cries out in fear, even though Brian cannot hear him.

"Wait! Brian! What the fuck, don't leave me here! Shit! Don't leave me! Fuck!"

Jesse then looks back at the Mercedes Brian stole, and watches Russell continue to scream and holler from the pain he's experiencing. Jesse gets into the car, and starts to speed off back into the highway. At this point, Jesse tries to calm himself down, so he can get Russell back to "Home Base." From how badly he's crying, Jesse is having a difficult time driving, due to the depression and mental stress he's having. He's worried about Russell, not knowing if he is going to live or die. The fact Brian has separated from them makes everything scarier to deal with.

Jesse has too much to deal with. Having to direct Russell to Max before he bleeds to death, still trying to escape from the heist they were in, and having to keep the car in the drive gear at all times as it's hot wired. If Jesse drives too slow, it might cause the car to stall or cut off. He doesn't have the key to this car, so that would be an unfortunate occurrence. Jesse while he's driving on the highway, makes sure he's not speeding to cause attention, but drives fast enough so the car won't stop. As he's driving, Russell's screams and cries become even louder, which makes Jesse start to feel upset, and not focus on his driving. Russell is completely knocked out from the blood loss, and is very close from slipping out of consciousness. Jesse speaks to him.

"Russell, I know. Just hold on, I'm going take you to Max. Just hold on for a while."

A few minutes later, Jesse looks down, and sees a police barricade in the road. Officers are stopping every single car, and profiling all of the drivers and passengers. Jesse knows that they are the reason behind all of this, and cannot believe what is going on. In his mind, he knows he's going to have to fib about basically everything, and act as natural and he possibly can. Jesse's heart immediately beats a million rates per second, and he struggles to think of what he should do. Jesse is afraid that if he stops the car at the police roadblock, he won't be able to start the car again. That's also a trivial concern as well; they are currently fugitives at large, for armed robbery and murder.

Having to face the police scares Jesse. It seems that Jesse doesn't have a choice, and he is going to have to halt to the officers at the roadblock. Running away from the police, doesn't seem like the smart decision. Jesse pulls in closer to the barricade, and starts to pray that the car doesn't turn off as he speeds down. The car remains in drive gear, which causes Jesse to feel relieved and happy. He still however has to deal with this police roadblock, and has to idle his car; which Jesse fears will stall the car. He tries to stay calm and carries on. An officer signals to Jesse with his hands to creep up to a designated area, and to stop moving the car. Jesse reaches the correct spot, and the officer uses his hands to inform Jesse that he's at the correct position.

Jesse puts the car into park gear, and thankfully it doesn't stall. The car continues to remain in drive gear with the ignition on, and Jesse has successfully stopped the car moving, without the engine turning off. Jesse now has to think of how he's going to talk himself out of this current ordeal. He rolls the window down, as the officer walks closer to his car. The police officer then talks to him very softly.

"Good afternoon sir, we're currently doing a simple welfare check, and I can't go into all the details, but we're making sure that everyone passes by is not up to anything suspicious."

The police officer who stopped Jesse, is a bald young African-American man. The officer turns his view towards Russell who has his sunglasses on, and is wrapped with the wool blanket. The officer looks at Jesse again with a confused face, and Jesse already knows what the deal is.

"Yes officer, as you can see my roommate is ill. He has the flu, and he's been sick for the past several days. I'm taking him to the emergency room right now."

The police officer continues to profile Russell with a puzzled face. He then looks at Jesse.

"Sir, can I see your driver's license, proof of registration and insurance please."

Jesse even though he has sunglasses on, his eyes show nothing but fear. Jesse does not have his license with him. It's in his tote bag back at the unit. Jesse looks away from the police officer at the windshield for a few seconds, not knowing what to do. The officer then crosses his arms. Russell who is knocked out, screams and cries from the pain he's in. The police officer turns his direction back at Russell again, and Jesse then turns and responds to the officer.

"Why do I need to show you my driver's license? Am I being suspected of a crime? Am I being detained? I'm a legal American, and so is my roommate. We're not criminals. I'm only trying to take my roommate to the emergency room sir. That's all, and that's it. Am I free to go?"

The officer takes a deep breath, and while looking at Russell, responds to Jesse.

"Sir, I'm doing my job. As I said, we're just checking out suspicious activity. I'm looking at your roommate, and he's not looking that well. But you're taking him to the hospital. So as long as you promise me that you'll take him straight there, I'll let you go. You can carry on sir."

The police officer then signals his hand for him to go, and Jesse then responds to him.

"Thank you so much officer. Yes, I'm going directly to the hospital. Thank you officer"

Jesse then drives away from the roadblock, and continues on his way towards "Home Base." That could have turned out much differently than it did, and Jesse is glad that he caught a break that time. He begins to worry about Brian, and wonders how he's currently doing.

Brian is taking a different path down on a separate highway to get to "Home Base". The reason why he separated himself from both Russell and Jesse, is that he feels it's safer for them to split up. In case Brian is cornered by the police, he doesn't want to get Russell and Jesse involved. He is slightly worried on Russell's health, and to whether Jesse can make it to Max in time. Brian after all murdered a police officer out of impulse.

He has never killed anyone in his life, but being angered after seeing Russell and Victor shot, Brian took the officers life. Brian then realizes that he forgot to hide the guns from the robbery. He was able to think fast enough to put the money bags into the vehicle Jesse is driving, but completely forgot that the guns are still in the vehicle. Brian drives down the highway, hoping that he isn't stopped or accosted by the authorities. Driving as fast as he can, heading towards the unit.

However, Brian soon runs into the same dilemma that Jesse did. Brian notices a large police roadblock in the highway. Brian also starts to feel scared, as he's using the same vehicle the men have used in the heist, and that automatically will bring suspicion to the police. Brian starts to shake his hands across the steering wheel, and is in complete fear from not knowing what to do, and how to act. The police officer, who is a silver haired Caucasian man, signals for Brian to stop at the barricade. The officer notices the vehicle matches the description that they are looking for. A black Chevrolet Tahoe with tinted windows, without any license plates. However, the police can't go on this alone.

They need to make sure everything is tied exactly to their investigation, so an innocent person isn't framed. Brian stops the vehicle where the officer tells him to. While the officer is walking to the window of the vehicle, Brian quickly thinks of a way to get out of this. He then starts to blame himself for choosing to stay in this vehicle. He could have easily gotten himself another vehicle, likewise as he did with Jesse. Hindsight is of course twenty-twenty, and Brian simply wasn't thinking at that particular time. Brian then notices something that seals his fate. The guns the men used during the robbery, are clearly visible from the driver's side window. Brian rams his head to the back of the seat, realizing how much in trouble he is in. His only hope is that the officer doesn't notice the guns that are positioned in the back of the vehicle. The officer tells Brian to roll down his window, and he does. Before the officer can speak, Brian then pleads and cries out to the officer.

"Officer, I'm a cable guy and I'm late for work. I have a wife and kid, and I need to get to work. I bought this car from a guy off craigslist a few days ago, so I don't have my plates, and I didn't go down to the DMV yet to clear it off. I gotta get to work officer, so I need to get going."

The police officer looks at Brian, as if he can tell he's lying and not doing a good job at it. When he notices the officer look at the guns in the back of the vehicle, Brian responds.

"In my spare time, I like to go to the shooting range. I have a permit for those guns, I left it at home though. It's my constitutional right to have guns' sir. Like I said, I'm a cable guy, I need to go to work which I'm actually late for. So if you can let me move ahead please. I..."

The officer raises his eyebrows at Brian, and stops him by waving his hand at him.

"Sir, I need for you to get out of the vehicle right now please. Step out the vehicle sir."

Brian looks down at the ground, and starts to feel scared. He knows that his only choices are to be honest and fess up to everything, to continue to coax the officer to believe his fib, or to run away. Brian looks back at the officer, and tries to continue to fib and sweet-talk him.

"Officer please, I need to get to work. I'm not a bad guy, I'm late for work. I'm only a cable guy, don't make me go through this. Please let me go, I'm not a bad person, I..."

The officer then reaches for his gun on his holster, which causes Brian to stop talking, as he doesn't believe the officer is buying what he's saying. The officer is fairly confident that Brian is one of the robbers involved in the heist. The vehicle matches completely, and Brian being a terrible liar and manipulator, is not doing a good job of convincing him otherwise. Brian then looks down towards the floor, and is silent for nearly a minute. The officer then screams at Brian.

"I said get the fuck out the vehicle! Sir get out right now, or I will make you get out!"

Brian upset that the officer spoke to him in that matter, now understands his only options are to be honest and exit out of the car peacefully; or he can simply speed away. If it weren't for the fact of the police officer talking to Brian in the disrespectful tone he did, it would have made his decision much easier. Brian doesn't respect the law, and has at this time given up hope of being respectful, and wants to exhibit as much defiance as he can. However, he also can tell that now would be a good time to give up, and accept whatever happens. The officer becoming extremely impatient with Brian, continues to hold his hand on his gun holster. Brian then unfastens his seatbelt, and reaches for the car door.

In a flash second however, Brian flips off the officer, laughing at him, and quickly speeds away from the scene. The officer fires several rounds at Brian's vehicle, missing every single one. After noticing him fire rounds, the other officers at the barricade are alerted.

The officers, including the one who pulled over Brian, run to their patrol cars, and follow after him. The officer that stopped Brian, is a forty-eight-year-old veteran of the police force. He is married, and he has two young children, a son and a daughter. His name is Flynn Livingston, and has been a police officer for nearly all of his life. Officer Livingston, then reaches for his transistor radio, and explains all of the details.

"This is Livingston, I'm currently on a pursuit with one of the 'First Federal' suspects. We are on the 110 going southbound. I'm on pursuit with the suspect. Units please be on alert."

Officer Livingston and other officers, continue to chase down Brian, as he speeds down the highway. Brian is currently heading towards the direction facing "Home Base". Detective Henderson heard Officer Livingston give out that message, and he immediately turns on his siren, and follows over to that area. He is glad that his bulletin has worked, and one of the suspects were caught because of it. While Brian is still chasing the police, he begins to feel empathetic. Brian understands that if he continues on towards "Home Base" and Max's unit, he's going to only get Russell and Jesse into trouble. Feeling scared and guilty, regretting leaving Jesse by himself, and that Russell is possibly near death, he doesn't want to make that situation any more difficult. Brian also feels he has a greater chance to avoid the police, he if routes himself to a different area.

While the police are still pursuing him, Brian makes a sharp exit of the highway, and gets back on the highway towards the opposite direction. He is now travelling northbound on highway 110, heading directly towards the "Angeles National Forest". Brian feels he can possibly lose the police, if he manages to hide in the forest. This is his current plan at this point. Brian feels this is what he has to do, in order to get away. Brian speeds down the highway, nearly missing several cars and avoiding collisions. The adrenaline he's feeling during this police pursuit, makes him more determined to continue along with it. Brian is enjoying that he's being chased by several police cars, and feels confident that he can outrun each of them.

This is like a game, or a fun race for him. Unless he runs out of gas, Brian feels that he can do this all night, as the forest is still a large distance from where he currently is. He has nothing to lose, as he's already wanted for armed robbery and murder, so this police pursuit isn't anything to be that concerned or worried about. Brian feels guilty that this is something he deserves, and he brought it on himself to get caught. He could have easily gotten another getaway vehicle, but he for whatever reason decided not to. This situation that Brian is faced with, is one that he has to manage and deal with for himself, and find a way out of himself.

Brian as he's speeding in this hot pursuit, can't believe how this entire heist turned out. Everything was meant to go completely opposite than it did. By now, all four of them should have been back at "Home Base", celebrating and being happy with finishing the heist. Now, it seems that there is nothing but total and complete disaster going around. They are now killers, instead of robbers. Not ever being in their agenda to kill any innocent people. Victor is dead, and Brian starts to feel scared over Russell. So many thoughts he's thinking about, and the only thing he can do at this point is run. He's back to where he was before getting involved with this group, running from all his problems. Brian then starts to feel bad for killing Officer Waker, and doesn't like the feeling of knowing that he shot and killed a police officer.

Brian then went back to how he originally was hesitant on agreeing to join the group. All the other men had no problem going along with the inane and crazy heinous ideas, but Brian was adamant ever since the beginning. He only agreed to do it, feeling guilty from the mental pain he gave towards Russell. It was because of Brian hanging around the wrong crowd, that got Russell's close friends killed. Brian finds it fascinating how things go full circle like that, and relate towards each other.

Continuing down the road, Brian smirks to himself, as he takes a peek in the rear view mirror. He sees at least five police cruisers inches away from his vehicle. Brian laughs to himself, and is now travelling at over a hundred miles per hour. Weaving through cars, coming extremely close from crashing into them. His intention still being to direct himself to the forest to hide from the police. The officers following him, have no idea where exactly he's going, but remain close to follow his every move. Brian then reaches in the glove compartment and takes out a cigarette, lighting it. He laughs to himself more, enjoying this situation he's in.

Taking puffs of the cigarette, he weaves into more lanes, trying his best to move away from the police. At this time, Brian notices that several news helicopters are following him. He knows that he's now on television, and being broadcasted to millions of people in the area. Brian takes an unusual approach to this. He waves his hand up in the air at the helicopters following him, to tease everyone. Taking more puffs of his cigarette, Brian makes a sudden exit off the freeway, but quickly gets back on. He continues to tease the police officers, and the news helicopters which are following him. Brian takes another puff of his cigarette, laughing to himself.

Meanwhile, Jesse is now only a short distance away from "Home Base". Still shocked that the police officer allowed him and Russell through. Without causing any suspicion or attention to himself, Jesse remains on the highway at a moderate speed. He finally approaches his exit, and gets off leading towards the surface streets.

Jesse has noticed that for the past ten minutes, Russell has stopped screaming. Jesse has a feeling that Russell is dead because of this, and is scared that he didn't make it on time. He starts to pray and hope that everything will be alright. While on the surrounding roads in the area the unit is in, Jesse starts to speed up, wanting to get to his destination as quick as he can. He runs several red lights as he gets closer to the unit, scared to stop the car as it will stall in the street. This however might cause unwanted attention, by him speeding and not obeying traffic lights.

Jesse begins to cry, with tears falling down his face faster, the closer he approaches the unit. Feeling nervous because Russell is silent; as much as it made him feel upset that Russell was screaming and crying because of his pain, he at least knew that Russell was still alive. Now that the whole vehicle is silent, it doesn't seem as though things are going well.

Jesse reaches the corner the unit is located on, and makes a quick sharp turn. He then drives into the block where the "Home Base" unit is, heading slightly pass it. Jesse drives right outside Max's unit, and parks the car. This time, the vehicle remarkably does stall right on time, in the parking spot in front of Max's unit. Not even having the chance to calm himself down, Jesse immediately runs to the rear door, and opens it. He notices that Russell's face is even more pale than it was before, and Jesse panics, believing that Russell is gone.

He takes off Russell's sunglasses, and notices that his eyes are still dilated and not moving. Jesse removes the blanket, and the entire left side of Russell's shirt is covered in blood. Russell's chest and left arm are completely bloody. Jesse raises Russell's shirt, scanning over the bullet wounds, and how bad they look; they are still bleeding. Jesse then also sadly realizes that Russell is not breathing at all. Jesse then covers his mouth with his hand and starts to cry. He leans into Russell's forehead and kisses it. Jesse then not knowing what else to do, and upset at the current situation, runs to Max's unit, and unlocks the door. Max doesn't notice Jesse walk in. Max is in his wheelchair watching television with a sad look on his face. His vision is at the police chase Brian is in. Jesse looks at the screen, and for a couple seconds watches the police chase and understands it's Brian, but then Jesse quickly shouts out to Max.

"Max! Come here quick! It's Russell! I need your help! I'm scared! Come quick!"

Max looks at Jesse in a terrified way, and Jesse runs over to Max, pushing his wheelchair out to the Mercedes parked right outside his unit. Max then starts to cover his mouth, as he's looking at Russell. Max turns over to Jesse in shock, and then he turns his head back to Russell. Max then puts his fingers around Russell's neck, and cries out to Jesse.

"Fuck, he has a pulse, he's got a pulse. Um, go get me my spare wheelchair by the door."

Jesse nods his head, and runs into Max's unit to get his other wheelchair. Due to all the stress, Jesse didn't even check Russell's pulse at all. Russell is not blinking or breathing, but he still has a pulse, which for right now is a good sign. Max then tries to give Russell CPR, while he's still hunched in the rear seat. Jesse runs out the unit with Max's spare wheelchair, and watches as Max tries to revive Russell. Seconds later, Russell who's face is still pale from the blood loss he's experiencing, regains consciousness; he starts to cough and hack very heavily.

Russell then starts deep breath very heavily, and also moving his eyes rapidly, feeling disorientated. Jesse starts to cry, happy that Russell is alive. Max smiles at Russell, and Max starts to look at Russell's bullet wounds. Max then starts to assess Russell, while venting out his frustrations.

"Okay, he's breathing. These wounds though. Holy shit, this isn't good. These wounds are really bad. Damn it. This is not good. Damn it. What shall I do?"

Russell continues to feel disorientated, and sits back the seat. He is passed out to where he cannot hear or see anything, but he is conscious. Max continues to look at the bullet wounds on Russell's chest and arm. Jesse then feeling worried, responds to Max's concern.

"What's going on? Is he going to be alright? You can fix him right? Please?"

Max then starts to cry. While he's crying, he stares over at Jesse, struggling to speak.

"Well, I'm going to have to amputate his arm. Just by looking at it, I can already tell that's something I'm going to have to do. He has no more nerves in this arm, and time has passed too long, and he has lost so much blood, the nerves in this arm are infected."

Jesse then cries, and walks over and hugs Max. Max then starts to look at Russell's chest, and turns his view over to Jesse, and continues to explain more on Russell's condition.

"That's really not even half of it. The other bullet fragments are possibly near his heart. At least I'm hoping that they are just near, and not an impact wound. If they did hit his heart, then I'm afraid there isn't much I can do. If they only hit the area around his heart, it's still grim, but his chances of survival are better. I'm going to have to operate on him right now. I can't waste any more time."

Jesse nods his head, and with the help of Max, Jesse manages to sit Russell down on the other wheelchair. Jesse then pushes Russell into the unit, and Max directs him to a side door connecting the unit, which leads to a medium sized examination room.

Max being a licensed surgeon and retired criminal pathologist, has his own under the table operating room. He has only used this room on humans, counting Russell, three times. Max mainly uses this room to study medicine, and to perform experiments on cadavers that some of his connections send him. This room has a freezer containing medicine and other medical supplies, and also computers and other monitors. He has several tools and machinery in the room as well. All of this is more than likely illegal for him to have and own. However, Jesse is glad that Max has his own mobile hospital, opposed to taking

Russell to a legitimate hospital. Jesse with Max's assistance, manages to get Russell to lay down on the operating table. Max immediately starts to turn on all of his machines. Jesse watches Max get all of his tools together.

Max puts on his surgical gloves, and surgical mask. During this time, Jesse starts to fully undress Russell, so he only has his boxer shorts on. Once all the computers are powered up, Max tells Jesse to give him several different tools and items. Max then sticks an IV needle inside Russell's right arm, which he still has feelings and nerves connected to, and Max also gives him anesthetic medicine to temporarily knock him out. Jesse simply shakes his head at how skilled Max is. At this point, Max with his surgical mask on, grabs Jesse's hand and whispers to him.

"I can't allow you to stay in here, I'm sorry. Not only what I'm doing is highly illegal, and in some jurisdictions it's considered murder, but due to safety and health reasons, this is where you have to go. I have everything set, and he'll be fine. I'll let you know when I'm done."

Jesse nods his head, and walks over and kisses Russell who's under the anesthesia and knocked out, on the forehead. Jesse then kisses Max on the forehead, and closes the door to the room his operating station is in. Jesse has no reason to doubt Max's abilities. Jesse continues to walk out of Max's unit and locks his door. Jesse grabs the duffel bags located in the trunk of the Mercedes. They are all too heavy to carry at once, so he only grabs two, bringing them to "Home Base". Using the same set of keys he had to unlock Max's unit, he unlocks the front door. Jesse for a minute finds it weird that for the first time, he's the only one in this unit, and starts to find it odd and crazy.

He sets the duffel bags over by the sofa area, and runs back to the Mercedes to grab the other bags, shutting the trunk. Jesse walks back into the unit, and shuts and locks the door. He sets the remaining bags under the table, and sits at the sofa area. Jesse then starts to lay down on the sofa and closes his eyes, crying uncontrollably.

CHAPTER 23:

NOTHING WON, NOTHING LOST

The way things are currently standing, unfortunate tragedy is the main point of focus. In every perspective towards the previous events, the effects are that it seems that emotions are running in several different directions and ways. This particular day, is one which is causing much strain, tension and catastrophe. It seems as time progresses, more and more developments which are unprecedented, seem to sprout and reveal themselves. It is complex to explain why everything is being produced in this specific manner. Ordinarily, this was supposed to be a routine bank heist. Something that the men figured they planned enough to prepare for, and were assuming to finish the job without any hassle or issues. Approaching the robbery feeling confident, and leaving out of the situation as winners. That wasn't even centimeters close as to what actually happened.

Unfortunately, this day has gone to an ultimate level of disaster and terror. It doesn't make much sense, that the sorrow molded itself this way. Perhaps, it was the overconfidence which in turn, made an illusion of things appearing to be more simple than they actually are. If things are to happen for a reason indeed, despite the fact events turn out differently than hoped, it was meant to be somehow and someway. Even so, that still doesn't offer any type of reasonable explanation to why exactly scenarios are programmed in particular ways. Danger creeps itself in several methods, and it seems during situations where individuals are caught off guard.

It is also confusing to deal with all of the consequences and guilt. Knowing that it is bad enough that the event happened, but being forced to be involved with any type of upsetting and depressive repercussions which are formed from it. This is when emotions start to overpower your own control, and this turns into some type of trap that you need to get out of. Failure to remove yourself from said trap, will not allow you to heal and move forward. In any case, it's important to know that with every action, there of course is a reaction. With proper wisdom of obtaining the will to detect which traits and objectives are the ones which will bring positivity, and which will bring negativity.

Situations and adventures you encounter in life, can be rectified by proper usage of sorting out performances in a way that will bring you certain results. Results that can be pleasing for you to accept and live with, or results that are unpleasant and detestable. Having a clear approach to all of this, will make life meaningful; regardless of the outcome. In addition to that, things won't be as confusing or out of the ordinary to deal or settle with. Only acceptance will rise from it all.

Inside of the "Home Base" unit, Jesse remains on the sofa sobbing heavily. Not wanting to take in all the sad events, which this day has presented itself to him. The men all left this same unit a couple of hours ago, to simply rob a bank. They didn't intend to hurt or kill anyone. In this process, several people have been hurt and killed. Jesse shakes his head, while his eyes are closed; tears running down his face. Jesse punches the sofa with his fist, with much anger. All the depression pulsing through his body is causing him to act in such way.

Jesse is concerned over Russell's health, as Russell is currently being operated on by Max. Jesse feels slightly worried over that, but comfortable, as he trusts Max that he will take extra care of him. While Jesse is still crying on the sofa, he starts to relay the heist in his head. Jesse saw Russell and Victor shot in the heist, and also saw John; a past co-worker of his shot as well. All of those scenes running in his mind, causing stress and sadness. Jesse then starts to worry, and he feels much concern over Brian. For unclear reasons, Brian left Russell and

Jesse out in the street by themselves, and separated himself; with the intentions of later reuniting. Jesse doesn't understand why Brian didn't stay with them. He believes that Brian was possibly scared at how things were going, and feeling guilt from killing a police officer. Jesse then quickly remembers, that when he inside Max's unit to ask for his help with Russell, he saw that Max was watching a police chase on the television; presumably Brian being in the pursuit. Jesse then immediately sits up on the sofa, and turns the television set on. Every major network news station is showing the high speed chase that Brian is in. Jesse puts his hand over his mouth, in disbelief that Brian is trying to run away from the police. Jesse feels anxious, and his whole body starts to shiver. The anchorwoman explains updated information on the events which conspired.

"If you are just tuning in, you are now watching a high speed chase on the number 2 highway: The 'Angeles Crest' highway, of an armed robbery suspect. Police say this man, and others were a part of a deadly armed robbery earlier today. This man is one of the suspects."

Jesse continues to hold his hand to his mouth. He walks over to the kitchen area of the unit. Jesse opens the refrigerator, taking out a bottle of beer. He returns to the sofa area, to watch the police chase, while taking sips of the beer. The anchorwoman explains more on the event.

"They have been chasing the man for over an hour now. He is driving at an insanely high rate of speed, and not showing care for other drivers. Police believe he is heading up towards the 'Angeles National Forest', although it's not sure why he's travelling there."

As the anchorwoman continues to report on the high speed chase, Jesse is at an extreme loss of words and thoughts. He can't believe that he's safe and sound at "Home Base", yet Brian is running away from the police; in a chase miles away from where the safe house unit currently is. Jesse wonders if Brian intended to do this in some cosmic attempt to prove a point somehow. He sits back on the sofa drinking his beer, paying close attention to the chase. Jesse has been watching the live coverage for about half an hour now, still shocked that

Brian is managing to evade the police. Jesse is glued to television, feeling several different emotions from what he is viewing and witnessing on the television screen. As much as he doesn't want to watch, and feels captivated to turn away, Jesse continues to pay attention to the chase. He mostly finds it odd and thrilling, that he's watching Brian in a police chase. Jesse doesn't know how to react or feel; If he should be rooting for Brian speeding down the highway from the police, hoping that he runs away and escapes; or should he react some other type of way; concerned over Brian's safety.

Jesse then wonders if he's going to get in trouble as well, as he was also involved in the same robbery that Brian was in. Jesse didn't kill or shoot anybody like Brian did, but he was still there, and it's a guilt which is hard to explain and describe that Jesse is experiencing. It's also puzzling to Jesse, why Brian is running in a direction away from where their safe house is. Brian is heading nowhere near their unit, which is in San Pedro district of Los Angeles; south of where Brian is directing himself. Brian is chasing the police through the mountains, near the "Angeles National Forest", way further north. Jesse shakes his head and continues to watch the chase.

Brian is currently losing most of his self-control and conscious. He takes another cigarette, and puts it in his mouth, lighting it. Feeling an outrage of rushed emotions, Brian keeps driving, evading the police in this chase. Brian starts to wonder if Russell and Jesse made it back to the unit, as he's continuing to speed down the highway being chased by the police. Brian has a feeling that Russell and Jesse managed to escape, and were able to get lucky unlike him. He wanted to quickly separate from them because Brian, unlike Russell and Jesse, didn't kill a police officer, and they are innocent in that regard.

Brian believed if he separated himself, they could stand a better chance that way. Brian feels stupid that he wasn't smart enough to realize, that he didn't switch vehicles. He was so worried about multiple things, that he had gotten carless, and made the mistake of staying in the vehicle they escaped the bank in. Brian was hoping that it wouldn't have made a difference at all. Unfortunately, it turned out that it made a huge impact on how things evolved. Brian takes a puff of his cigarette, driving at high speed; over a hundred miles an hour. He amazingly is able to swift through cars, without hitting them or causing a collision or crash. Brian has a wide grin on his face, putting himself in this zone he's in. From this chase he's in, he's becoming a different version of himself, and turning into a more ruthless man. Brian before today, has never killed anyone, and still feels the guilt of shooting a police officer. He feels that the officer didn't deserve any of that at all.

Most of the pain Brian is feeling, is deep regret from the actions he has done today. It is now coming up on an hour into the police chase, and Brian remains on this same highway; getting closer to approaching the forest. His plan for now, still remains the same, and he's confident that it should work in his favor. Brian wants to run into the forest, finding a way to escape and hide, causing a distraction for the police to look for him. The police remain following him, preparing to adapt to whatever move that Brian makes next as the chase continues.

Detective Henderson has now caught up to Brian in the chase, and some of his colleagues, also follow Brian. While he's in the chase, Detective Henderson receives a call on his mobile phone, and he puts it on speakerphone. Some of the investigators at the police station are informing him that Victor has been properly identified by fingerprints, and that his name is Victor Romero. He did not have any prior criminal history or convictions, aside from issues in his youth, and parking violations. Detective Henderson then confirms this by saying the man mentioned his name was Romero. They also tell the detective that they are unable to come up with any possible leads as to who the other three men involved in the heist are. Detective Henderson is slightly frustrated over this, but he quickly gets himself together, dealing with the news. The detective is also told that the bank worker that was injured in the heist, which was John, is going to be fine. Detective Henderson then thanks the police agents on the phone, and disconnects the call. He remains right behind the rest of the officers, as they chase Brian, who's heading straight into the forest.

During this time, the police try to implement a "PIT" maneuver on Brian. If this is done correctly, this would make it so Brian would spin his vehicle out of control, immobilizing him; allowing the authorities to take him into custody that way. The officers are get into position, as Detective Henderson watches them attempt the move. As they are doing the formation to knock Brian right into their trick, Brian quickly is able to weave into the other lane, merely missing this. Detective Henderson slams his fist on the steering wheel with anger, aggravated that they missed the chance to correctly pin Brian together with that technique. The chase continues with the news helicopters being positioned right above Brian; recording all of the proceedings.

As the pursuit has now been ongoing for an hour and a half, the men then discuss performing a second "PIT" maneuver. If they are unsuccessful this time, they will leave this tactic alone. Detective Henderson laughs to himself and shakes his head, as he watches the patrol cars attempt to give the maneuver another chance. The patrol cars start the formation to once again try to knock Brian's vehicle out of control. Sadly, the men once again come up short, and Brian is able to quickly swerve away from their movements. Detective Henderson shakes his head again, upset at the incompetence of this police force, only solidifying his decision to retire.

Jesse remains watching the whole entire chase live on television. Still in much disbelief and shock at the way Brian is acting. Again feeling mixed reactions; being in fear of how the outcome of this chase is going to end. This is an interesting police chase, filled with many suspenseful moments. Not only because of the way Brian is driving, and how he's able to dodge all of the methods the police are using to disable his vehicle; also because Jesse personally knows Brian, so it's tough. It's an interesting way to put it, and Jesse keeps an open and clear mind to all of the events which are happening in the police chase.

While he's watching the chase, the news station reveals that it's going to take a quick commercial break. During this time, Jesse looks down at the duffel bags filled with cash under the coffee table. Jesse grabs two of the heavy bags, setting them on top of Brian's bed. Jesse then walks over by the table again, and grabs the remaining two bags. He also removes the industrial drill Russell used to hack into the vault, and sets the drill down on the floor. Jesse then dumps all of the cash out on the bed, looking at the large amount of money all scattered around. By looking at pile alone, he knows that compared to their previous two heists, this is the most they were ever able to get. Jesse then starts to count all of the money, separating it into several different groups of one thousand. Making sure that all of the piles are neatly put together in a row, due to the huge amount of cash there is. While he's continuing to count the cash, the news returns with the pursuit Brian is in. Jesse then decides to take a break from counting the money, and returns to the sofa area to watch.

With it now being two hours into the pursuit, the police are starting to become impatient with Brian. If he keeps this same rate of speed up and stays on this highway, before the hour is out, he will make it into the forest. This would be something the police rather not happen, but they are prepared and ready for regardless. At this time, as the "PIT" maneuvers proved to not be effective at all, the police are now willing to use spike strips to puncture Brian's tires. Unmarked patrol cars start to speed up away from Brian. When they get a set distance ahead of him, they lay out a big metal sheet of spikes on the road. By implementing this, it will make it so Brian's tires are punctured, and his vehicle will then stop; putting an end towards the pursuit.

Detective Henderson is not very confident that the spike strips will thwart this pursuit at all. The detective sits back in his seat; watching to see if he is going to be proven wrong, or if his original assertion is correct. As he suspected, Brian notices the spike strips, and makes a very clever move around them; making a quick side weave on the other side of the road. Detective Henderson shakes his head, and is not surprised.

Jesse who's watching the pursuit on the television, shakes his head, and can't believe how Brian is able to escape all of the tools the police are using to slow him down. Brian is feeling extremely indestructible at this point, and from the rage and adrenaline in his blood, it's going to take a lot more than that to stop him. The police remain right behind Brian, accepting that he is going to head straight into the forest very soon, despite all of their efforts to end the pursuit before then. Jesse takes a sip of his beer, and starts to frown and feel upset at how this chase is turning out. It now reaches the two-hour mark, and Brian is less than a mile away from entering the forest area. Once he's in that area, it will become much harder for the police to catch and apprehend Brian. Especially as the sun is starting to set; they are virtually heading onto nighttime hours. Nightfall and lack of sunlight in the forest, allows for an easy method to not be seen; which is good if you are trying to escape the police. This isn't good if you are the police, and trying to pursue a suspect. The pursuit carries on, with every move Brian decides to make, being unknown and unpredictable.

Brian reaches into his glove compartment, and starts to light his third cigarette. He takes puffs of the cigarette, and starts to tease the police once again. Brian begins to intentionally jerk and serve the car in a zig-zag fashion; laughing out loud while he's doing it. With him being very close from entering the forest, Brian starts to believe that his original plan is working out fine. His plan still remains the same, to continue the chase heading into the forest, then running and hiding away in the bush, until the time is right for him to eventually run out from hiding; escaping back into the city any way that he can.

Brian is now travelling inside of the forest. He stays on the highway, driving past the mountains, taking in the view. Brian has mixed emotions' feeling that if he has to be in a police pursuit, this is the perfect area. The sun proceeds to go down, as evening approaches.

Brian has now been driving in the forest for coming up on a half an hour now. Jesse is stuck watching the whole entire chase happen, still in awe from seeing Brian run away from the police. The news helicopters are having a slightly tough time, from the camera reception that the forest gives out from keeping up with him. As a result, the picture quality that the live stream gives out in the news program, starts to become buggy and lags. Brian decreases his speed while he's in the forest; the roads are quite winding, and one wrong turn could cause Brian to crash or dip his car off the road, leading to ugly results. The officers stay right behind Brian, even though continuing on with a pursuit in the forest is not safe by any means. They as well start to slow down, and distance themselves away from Brian; yet still making sure they don't lose track or him, or lose him out of their sight.

Detective Henderson follows them into the forest, not expecting at all for this pursuit to last this long. He knows that from this point, Brian is either going to hightail and run into the forest to hide, or his vehicle is going to eventually run out of gas. There is no other scenario or situation to happen. Brian cannot steal another car, as he's deep in the forest, and all the other roads have been blocked by the police as a result of this chase. Brian also can't turn back, as the police have also completely barricaded and closed the roads which are positioned behind him. The police are sure that it will not be long before Brian starts to tire, causing the chase to end. However, it seems that it's going to take a miracle to get Brian out of this beast he's morphed himself into.

Brian grins and laughs to himself, at the chaos he's caused in this chase. His hands continue to grasp the steering wheel, as he drives deeper and deeper into the forest. Brian is waiting for the appropriate time to stop the car, so he can run out and hide. He knows that his time to act upon that won't be long at all, and he needs to get ready. Brian while he's rushing down the highway in the forest, starts to scan for the perfect area to to dart into. Also minding that he needs to pick a spot that the helicopters will have a tough time capturing him from. Brian also needs to immediately act fast, as if he waits too long when pulling over, the police are more than likely going to fire a fuselage of shots at him. In turn, this will kill Brian. He needs to make sure whatever decision he makes, is logical.

Finally, nearly twenty minutes later, with it now being past 6 P.M., Brian starts to decrease his speed slower and slower. He believes he has now found an area he wishes to dash out to, and is most likely going to be running out in the next minute or so. Brian rolls down his window, so he can hear which direction the helicopter is circling around at. The helicopter is currently facing his right, so if Brian darts out from his driver's side at this moment, it will give him enough time to run into the bushes; without being seen or caught by the helicopter cameras above in the sky. Brian then decides to slow down his car, and he abruptly makes a complete stop. The ignition of the vehicle however, is still running. Brian starts to finish his cigarette, knowing that he's most likely going to run out of the car within the next few seconds. The patrol cars behind him stay put, as from their protocol rules since Brian did not open any car doors, at this point they must remain in their vehicles, just in case he decides to take off once again. The helicopter in the sky remains still, however the pilot now moves to the driver's side direction of Brian's vehicle. Jesse continues to watch Brian in this pursuit, in complete shock; scared to what Brian intends to actually do. The helicopter remains on the left side of Brian's vehicle now. Due to this fact, Brian changes his mind on running out at this point, and a few seconds later, he quickly speeds away.

The patrol cars waste no time by keeping up with him, as he heads even deeper into the forest. Brian now isn't feeling as wild and crazy as he was previously. For the first time in this pursuit, he's doubting himself, and has no idea what he's doing. If Brian keeps this attitude up, the unfortunate is mostly likely bound to sure happen. Detective Henderson follows the patrol cars, keeping in mind that is is possibly going to be his last police pursuit ever, as he plans to still retire and quit the police force.

The reception of the helicopters become worse, due to depths Brian is travelling, as he continues down the highway inside the forest. The sky continues to become dim. Brian starts to believe his only hope is that the darkness will allow him some type of redemption to escape the police. From all the technical errors the helicopter cameras are experiencing due to the bad reception, as Brian continues stays on the highway, getting to more distant areas of the forest; the news takes a break from broadcasting the chase.

At this time, Jesse decides to walk back over to Brian's bed; counting the rest of the money they were able to get from the heist. Jesse stacks all the cash neatly in separate groups, making sure that everything is properly counted, and he isn't missing anything. Jesse finishes the first duffel bag full of cash, and then moves onto the next one, with only three more to go. After counting all of the money in the second duffel bag, Jesse looks around the bed, and sees multiple amount of stacks neatly arranged in rows. Jesse then dumps the third duffel bag of cash on the bed, and starts to count the contents of it. This bag containing the most amount so far. He sets all of the stacks he counted from that bag on the bed, along with the others. When Jesse starts to reach for the final duffel bag, he hears the news station return from break. The news is now able to get a clear stream reception of the chase. Jesse runs back to the sofa, watching the action.

Brian now is driving at an interestingly slow speed through the forest. He is only driving at ten miles an hour. Jesse watches as Brian is travelling at this slow rate. The police officers stay right behind Brian, as he lowers his speed down to this level. Detective Henderson starts to shake his head, not knowing why Brian decided to drive this slow. Brian actually is trying to kill time by doing this. He wants to remain on the highway area, as the evening continues; giving him more time for darkness to seep into the area; also allowing more time for Brian to relax, before he has to prepare himself on running out of the vehicle.

He also knows that this is aggravating the police as well, so he can accomplish two things. These include teasing and playing with the police which he enjoys, and Brian is also buying himself some time. Detective Henderson then finally understands what Brian is up to, and informs the other officers. Upon finding out that Brian wishes to stay at this speed, so time can pass by without him leaving the area, a few patrol cars then intentionally speed up past Brian, to try to box him in.

Brian quickly figures out what they are doing, and increases his speed; directly passing the patrol cars. Now that Brian has returned to a faster speed, he starts to worry that the highway will extend out of the forest, and merge into highway 138, leading onto the main road.

Brian doesn't want for that to happen, and hopes that he will remain in the forest when nighttime falls. With Brian being now a third of the way out of the forest, and it now being 7 P.M., this pursuit which has been going on for several hours, continues. Brian keeps a moderate speed, as he's reaching the end of the forest highway. If he is going to run out and hide, he's going to have to make his choice rather quick.

What is on his side, is that he is still inside the forest. However, if Brian keeps the speed he's at now, he will be out of the forest in thirty minutes. So going by speed and distance, he still has time left, albeit a very little amount. As he remains on the road, Brian then notices that all of the patrol cars behind him have their lights on. Brian then follows this custom, and turns on his headlights as well. The sun has completely set, and it slowly and surely gets totally dark around the forest area. The helicopters up in the sky start to turn their spot lights on as well, as darkness is creeping up fast. Jesse stays locked to the television screen under immense shock and horror, being captivated by this pursuit. It's going in many different twists and turns, nobody, not even Brian himself, can really figure out what will happen next.

Detective Henderson while he's still following all the cars as nighttime starts to fall, then notices that Officer Livingston, who was the officer who originally pulled Brian over, bump into the back of Brian's vehicle. The detective doesn't understand why the officer did that, and is confused. Officer Livingston is starting to lose his patience with this pursuit, and wants for Brian to pull over. The officer feels he has wasted enough of their time, and there is already a barricade force waiting for Brian once he exists of the forest anyways.

Officer Livingston once again rams his police car into Brian, in an interesting attempt to get him to pull over. In actuality, this is only making Brian more frustrated. Brian gets angry over Officer Livingston continually ramming into his car. Brian then starts to swerve the steering wheel of his car, causing Brian's car to weave haphazardly; in an effort to throw the officer off. Officer Livingston also feels combative at Brian as well, and the both of them get into road rage by trying to knock into each other. The pursuit then takes an interesting twist, with the Officer Livingston and Brian swerving in and out from one another. When the officer bumps into Brian for the third time, Brian then has had enough. Right after that, Brian slows down and once again makes a complete stop for the second time in this pursuit.

As Brian has not opened any car doors, the officers must remain in their vehicles as apart of safety regulations and protocols. During this time while Brian is idle, he puts the car in neutral; he climbs to the back area of the vehicle, grabbing one of the rifles. Because the windows of the vehicle are tinted dark, they cannot see that Brian has climbed back, and everyone assumes he's still sitting in the driver's seat. After he has grabbed his rifle, Brian returns to the driver's seat, holding the gun. Brian has now lost it. He tells himself if that officer bumps into him one more time, he's going to shoot. Brian under immense psychopathic rage cannot control himself, and he then speeds and darts off again, continuing down the highway. Once the pursuit continues, all the officers speed up along with Brian. With the forest highway now being only ten percent length wise left, until Brian reaches the 138 highway back on the open road.

Officer Livingston a couple minutes later, rams his patrol car into Brian's vehicle once again. Detective Henderson smacks his hand across his face and shakes his head, not knowing why the officer once again did that. Brian keeping his promise, does the unfortunate. Brian does a quick abrupt stop yet again, and grabs his gun. Brian turns his body, aiming the gun out his back windshield, firing several rounds, breaking the glass. Brian watches as the bullets fly out to the police cruiser. He then sees a silhouette of a head drop, and the horn of the police cruiser sounds off. The rounds end up instantly killing Officer Livingston, as he's struck in his head multiple times. As soon as he was shot, the deceased officer immediately drops down to his steering wheel. Brian begins laughing to himself in a sinister manner, and he quickly speeds away. Congruently, patrol cars fire shots at Brian's vehicle, narrowly missing him. Other patrol cars continue the pursuit after him. Detective Henderson upon noticing the gunfire and what happened, pulls his car over to the highway, and slouches under his seat. He makes a call on his radio dispatch.

"This is Henderson; we have shots fired and an officer down. I repeat officer down. Suspect has fled. We are on the 2 'Angeles Crest Highway'. I have an officer down."

With the whole pursuit being broadcasted on television, all of the events were streamed to many people tuning in. The helicopter managed to capture the moment the officer was sadly killed by Brian.

Jesse gets up from the sofa, and walks to the other side of the unit. He falls down to the floor, being mortified that Brian did that. Jesse then returns to the sofa to watch the remainder of the police pursuit, shaking his head and crying. Detective Henderson gets out of his vehicle, and walks over to Officer Livingstons patrol car. He sees the unconscious body of the officer, and Detective Henderson lifts his head up away from the steering wheel. At this time, more officers arrive where Detective Henderson is, and the detective walks away from the scene, shaking his head. Detective Henderson walks back to to his patrol car, and starts to smoke a cigarette. He tells himself that he is truly done for the day, and has seen enough. He has no intentions of proceeding forward. He remains in his car, sitting back with his eyes closed, smoking his cigarette in peace.

Brian continues to move down the forest, with there being only a mile left before he reaches the end of the forest. Brian is no longer capable of making sound decisions, especially after killing Officer Livingston. Brian at this point has realistically given up, and he is a ticking time bomb. It now being shortly past 8 P.M., Brian finally gives in. For the final time, he stops the car; turning the ignition off. The shattered glass from the gunshots he fired, gives the police a clear picture inside his vehicle. When Brian reaches for another cigarette, the officers at this point think he's going to shoot at them again, and this time they have legal grounds to get out of their vehicles and subdue him. They instead perch themselves outside of their patrol cars. Brian puts the cigarette in his mouth, and lights it.

After he finishes the entirety of the cigarette, Brian sits to himself, and beings to cry. He then looks behind the shattered glass that he shot out, and feels an extreme overwhelm of guilt, and all the actions he caused during this pursuit. Brian then seconds later, opens the door of his car, and starts to sprint into the forest. Upon leaving the vehicle, Brian is struck an exorbitant amount of times all over his body by the officers. Mainly in his chest, and in his legs. Jesse immediately upon seeing this, starts to uncontrollably cry and gets up from the sofa; he curls up on the floor, appalled. Remarkably, Brian is able to crawl into the brush area, still alive. The officers chase after him, and Brian proceeds further and further into the forest. Brian is bleeding heavily from the bullet wounds, and has a complete lack of energy. He is feeling lethargic from being shot that many times from the officers. His mind isn't thinking clearly, and he stumbles into many areas of the forest, in total darkness. The officers at this point, have lost Brian, and they track all around the forest area in pursuit of him. The helicopter is unable to track Brian's exact whereabouts, but the last thing the helicopter camera captured, was Brian being struck as he ran into the forest. Brian walks through more areas of the forest, and he starts to climb up a cliff attached to a mountain.

As he's climbing the cliff, he can see the lights from the sirens on the highway. Astonishingly, Brian despite bleeding badly and having bullets all over his body, makes it to the top of the cliff. He looks around the horizon and notices that there is a possible side highway where he can escape and hide at. As Brian scurries down the mountain over to that area, a big police roadblock then emerges in his determined path, now making this plan impossible to take. Brian then becomes angry, and rolls down the rest of the mountain, accepting his defeat. After he rolls off the mountain, Brian starts to feel much pain and crawls all throughout the forest losing blood. He can hear the footsteps of the officers looking for him, and tries to crawl away from their direction.

The helicopter continues to swarm in the sky, using its spotlight to locate Brian. As he's still slithering through the forest and blending into the darkness, Brian finds a secluded area located right below a ridge; which makes for a good hiding spot. Brian lays face down, and looks up at the night sky. He pays close attention at the moon and stars, as he continues to bleed from the bullet wounds located in various parts of his body. Brian begins to cry and laugh, and he feels happy that this is possibly his final moments on earth. Brian can hear the officers come closer to his hiding spot, and he then starts to slowly struggle to sliver away from this location. Unfortunately, the helicopter pilot was finally able to spot Brian as he was crawling out, and shines the spotlight on him. Brian with every strength he has, gets on his legs and struggles to run, limping in the process. With the spotlight still shined on Brian, the officers instantly swarm around this area. They demand for Brian to get down on the ground and surrender, as they point their guns at him. Brian looks directly at the officers, and yells.

"FUCK YOU MOTHERFUCKERS! I'LL SEE YOU ALL IN HELL!"

Brian then runs away from them right after that, and several officers shoot Brian in the head, killing him instantly. The helicopter pilot did not jump out of the scene in time, and captured the whole incident live. Jesse watches as the pursuit has now come to sad end.

Jesse gets up from the sofa, and curls up on the floor again. It has dawned on him that Brian is now dead as well, and Jesse feels as if the world is no longer turning. Jesse continues to remain on the floor, sulking and feeling depressed at the situation which just happened. Jesse stands up, grabs the remote, and turns the television off. Jesse then finishes drinking his beer, and walks over to Brian's bed. He then empties the final duffel bag full of cash on the bed, counting the entire amount up whole. Jesse finishes counting and stacking the final amounts of cash, and arranges it all on the bed with the rest of the money. So he has the correct number, just to be sure, Jesse once again counts all the money for the second time; being that it is a large amount. Rearranging all the stacks together; lining them up accurately. Once he finishes counting the money up for the second time, he still cannot believe the grand total.

He gets up from Brian's bed and paces around the unit, with his arms crossed and staring down directly at the floor. The total amount of money the men took from the heist, ended up being two hundred and forty-seven thousand dollars. Jesse cannot react to that much money, and how great of a sum that actually is. Jesse using his great memory skills, then starts to add up all the money they have with all three heists combined. With the first heist, they managed to snag, ninety-two thousand dollars. The following heist, the guys took out, one hundred and thirty-seven thousand dollars. Adding all of that to this heist, the combined money from all three heists, is four hundred and seventy-six thousand dollars. Jesse is still shocked at all of that, and doesn't know what to do. It's only him in the unit, and all of that money starts to scare him, and he becomes tired after counting it. Jesse then shoves all the money off Brian's bed, and the cash is poured all across the floor of the unit. He then lays down, staring at the ceiling for a short while. Jesse beings to cry, and rests his eyes as he's laying down on the bed. He takes several moments to relax and calm himself, still trying to get his mind right; stretching himself on the bed and getting comfortable.

Jesse while he is lying in bed resting his eyes, daydreams to himself. He goes back to the "Sunset Credit Union" heist several weeks ago, to where this whole epic journey began. Before he left for work that day, he remembers his landlord threatening to kick him out of the building, and Jesse felt that his day at work was not going to be like any other. It turns out he was correct, as that day changed everything. Jesse had only been working at that bank for a short while, having no previous bank teller experience. Peter being the kind and gentle man he was, decided to give Jesse a chance and hire him. Jesse also had an interesting bond with Jennifer as well.

Jesse went into work that Friday, having a feeling something drastic was going to occur. Brian and his associate Scott went into the bank, and that changed everything. Scott ended up killing both Peter and Jennifer, which made Jesse wonder why he survived that ordeal? Jesse was also able to find an unexpected relationship with Russell. A man whom before that day, he only said less than ten words to. Following that, he met Kevin, who was Russell's estranged college buddy; Brian. who was the other man in the Sunset heist who ran away; and Victor, an interesting and ambiguous man who had plans to originally rob the bank right before Brian and Scott, but didn't and was too cowardly to do it, and watched the entire heist.

Jesse then continues to daydream about all the time he spent with the other four men. How Kevin being a funny pudgy man who liked to smoke weed and eat. Brian, being a handsome action movie star like man. Victor, being a scary and creepy looking man of complete and total mystery, and him being eccentric. Finally, Russell; a man whom before all of these ordeals, Jesse payed no mind to, and actually hated. Everyone at the "Sunset Credit Union" including Jesse himself, would always spread lies and rumors about Russell that were not true; saying that he was an evil man that you shouldn't talk to or mess with. Jesse now considers Russell a major part of his life, and someone he cares about.

Jesse then remembers all of the times he and the rest of the men spent together; both the ups and downs and sideways moments. He then remembers the heists, and the sadness. He remembers seeing Kevin die, he remembers seeing Victor die, he remembers only a few minutes ago seeing Brian die live on the television. Jesse laughs to mask and hide his pain, and opens his eyes. He stares at the ceiling, laughing at everything he and the other men have been through over the past several weeks, and trying to cover all the sadness and depression over with that. Jesse closes his eyes back on the bed, and now starts to fall asleep, from feeling tired and exhausted. He's only asleep for an hour, when he is awoken instantly. Jesse notices that Brian's cell phone is ringing over by his work station. Jesse jumps out of bed, and runs over looking at the phone screen to see who's calling. It's Max; Jesse answers the phone, and Max responds.

"Jesse is that you? I'm calling to let you know that I finished about five minutes ago. Everything went completely well. I'm sorry it took so long, but get over here now. Thank you."

Max hangs up the phone, and Jesse immediately leaves out the "Home Base" unit, locking the door. He then runs over to Max's unit. Jesse unlocks the door to Max's unit, and walks inside. Jesse continues heading towards Max's operating room, and walks inside. Upon entering, Jesse sees that Max and Russell are talking to each other, and they both stop when he walks in. Russell is laying down on the operating area, with nothing but his boxer shorts on. Jesse looks at Russell's left arm, and notices that there is only a small bloody stump directly under his shoulder, hanging off. Russell's left arm is completely gone. He then looks at Russell's chest area, and sees six horizontal scars near his heart. Jesse then immediately makes eye contact with Russell, and he starts to cry. Russell then smiles at him.

"Jesse don't cry, because if you cry, then I'm going to cry. You know that I hate crying."

Jesse laughs at Russell, and walks over to where he is. Jesse then kisses Russell on the cheek, and Russell uses his right hand and rubs Jesse's hair. Russell then responds to him.

"It's not so bad, I can still move my other arm just fine. It's going to be hard to get used to only having one arm. You have to look on the bright side of things. Isn't that right Max?"

Max who's starting to cry smiles at the both of them, and softly replies to Russell.

"That's true. Russell, if it were possible for me to save that arm, I would have. The truth is that I couldn't, and that's the way science and nature and the human body works. I think you should be more thankful that the bullet didn't strike your heart. If it hit you, I want to say maybe three inches away from where it struck, you would not be here talking to me. That's a fact."

Jesse then starts to rub Russell's hair, and Max then continues to speak to both of them.

"Some of the things I hate by working in medicine, would have to be seeing abused or hurt children. Seeing cancer kids, and shit like that. I hated having to remove limbs from people; even though I've done it a ton of times. I also hate the fact you can only do so much. There have been many times to where I've had my patients die because me and my other team members couldn't do anything, or beat nature and how the human body is. I couldn't take any of that."

Russell smiles at Max, and Russell then starts to sit himself up. Max then screams out to Russell.

"Hey, careful. I've only put those stiches in you a few minutes ago. I don't want them to pop out, and you'll have blood and guts gushing everywhere. Take it easy for now."

Russell then lays himself back down, and starts to laugh at Max. Max and Jesse both frown at him. Russell then quickly once again tries to sit himself up, this time he is able to successfully do it. While he's sitting up, Russell while he's looking at Max, talks to Jesse.

"Go back to the unit Jesse, and get me something to wear please. I'm ready to leave now."

Jesse nods his head at Russell. Max also nods his head at Russell, and Max proceeds over to the other side of the operating room. Max reaches inside a cupboard, and pulls out a brown paper bag. He then hands the bag to Jesse, while Jesse is on his way out to get Russell some clothes. Max then explains the contents of the bag.

"Now listen, he's going to be in a lot of pain shortly. He's all giddy because the medicine hasn't worked off yet, but believe me, he's going to feel uncomfortable. These are highly strong pain killers, and only give him one every six hours. This is important. Do you understand?"

Jesse nods his head at Max, and runs out of the unit, back to "Home Base", to get Russell an outfit to wear. He heads over to Brian's closet, trying to find something that could fit Russell. He manages to grab a blue polo shirt, and a pair of grey sweatpants. Jesse proceeds to back to Max's unit, and walks inside. He continues directly back to the operating room, and hands Russell the clothes. Jesse helps Russell dress himself, and he sets Russell down on Max's spare wheelchair.

Russell is still much too weak to walk. After setting Russell in the wheelchair, Jesse whispers to Max that Brian was killed during the police chase. Russell heard what Jesse said, despite him whispering, and Max starts to hug both Russell and Jesse. They both say goodbye to Max, and leave out of his unit. Jesse pushes Russell in the wheelchair over to "Home Base", and they both walk inside the building. After entering, Jesse pushes Russell over by the sofa area, and Jesse walks back to the front door of the unit, to lock it. Russell then while he's sitting in his wheelchair, starts to scream out in pain.

"Ugh, my chest fucking hurts. Give me one of the pills Max gave you. Ah, this hurts."

Jesse gets a bottle of water from the refrigerator, and opens up the pill bottle of painkillers. He hands Russell the bottle of water, and one of the pills. Russell swallows the pill, and he then shakes his head. Jesse then sits on the sofa right in front of Russell to speak with him.

"We got about a quarter million dollars in the heist. That's a lot of money. If I count everything up, we have over four hundred grand. Wow. I don't know what we're gonna do."

Russell stares down at the floor and rubs his head, he then under his breath responds.

"I want to give some of it to charity. I then want to split the rest of it up evenly, that includes us, with everyone we know. Including John. That's what we're doing, and that's final."

Jesse smiles at Russell, and walks over to hug him. Russell then while continuing to look down on the ground, puts his right hand under his chin, and talks to Jesse under his breath.

"I'm going miss not having an arm. Even though what I said to Max was true, at least I'm still living, I'm going to miss not having a left arm Jesse. I feel like half a fucking man."

Russell then starts to cry, which also causes Jesse to cry by seeing him upset. Jesse continues to hug Russell tightly and then softly responds to Russell.

"I know you're weak, but do you want to try to walk? I'll be here to help you. You only have to walk from that end of the coffee table to the other end. If you can't do it, don't feel bad. Do you at least want to try it out?"

Russell while looking down away from Jesse smiles, and nods his head. Jesse then goes around to the front of Russell, grabbing his right arm to help lift him up. Russell then very slowly manages to stand himself up off the wheelchair for a few seconds. Russell then with Jesse holding onto his back, is able to walk all around the sofa area for a while. Russell starts to cry out of joy, and walks several times around the coffee table, gaining more and more strength each time he does it.

While he's walking around the sofa area with Jesse grabbing him to make sure he doesn't fall, he starts to understand that life is going to be different from this point. Russell as morbid as it sounds, took for him to lose his left arm for him to finally stop being a selfish and terrible man. He then starts to realize that the past is the past, and what has already happened, has already happened.

There is nothing that he can do to turn back time and erase it. He has to accept that Peter is gone, Jennifer is gone, Kevin is gone, Victor is gone, and Brian is gone. From this point forward, Russell is going to have to become a better man, and be more appreciative of his new life. This wasn't Russell's time to go, even though from the way things were presented, he was defiantly meant to die during that heist. He was given another chance, and Russell doesn't want to take it for granted. The last thing he remembered was seeing John shot during the heist. Despite him being a man he truly hated, he doesn't look at John that way anymore, and is willing to let whatever issues they had faced in the past, be pushed aside.

Russell continues to walk around the coffee table, until he starts to feel tired. He tells Jesse that he is finished, and is too exhausted to continue. Jesse helps Russell back into the wheelchair. With the both of them now feeling hungry, Jesse opens up Brian's freezer; there is a frozen pizza inside. He sets the pizza in the oven. Jesse then grabs a beer, and walks over to Russell and hands it to him. Russell then asks Jesse to hand him the television remote, and he does. Jesse takes one of his magazines, and lays down on Brian's bed reading it.

After turning on the television, Russell watches the news report explaining that Brian was killed during the police chase. Russell shakes his head, and turns the television to another network, which is showing "Tom and Jerry" cartoons. He enjoys watching the cartoons, and Russell is feeling happier about himself. A few minutes later, the frozen pizza is now ready, and Jesse takes it out of the oven. Jesse cuts it up, and the both of them start to eat, sitting down over at Brian's kitchen area. As they are eating, they would occasionally look up and make eye contact with each other, but they remain silent. They are refusing to speak to one another, and it's an awkward silence. Eventually Jesse can't stay quiet anymore. He takes a bite of pizza, and begins to speak to Russell.

"So it's over now? It's just us. What happens now? What do we do now Russell?"

Russell looks down at the empty stump area on his left arm, and takes a bite of pizza. Under much heavy waves of emotions, Russell unintentionally starts to cry. He then angrily responds to Jesse.

"What do you mean it's over? It's just the beginning if you ask me. I don't have a fucking arm anymore. The fuck do you mean it's over? Nothing is over? I don't have a god damn arm."

Russell begins to flow many tears down his face, Jesse then gets up from his seat, and starts to wrap his arms behind Russell. Jesse cries as well, as he continues to wrap his arms around Russell. Russell takes a swallow of his beer, and starts to calm himself down.

"I guess this was to teach me some type of lesson. I'm now half the man I used to be, and I have a second chance to be nice now. I got us all of us into this shit. Kev is dead, Victor is dead, Brian is dead. All because of me. I had to lose an arm to be taught a lesson, right Jess?"

Jesse doesn't respond to him. Jesse simply wipes Russell's tears with his hand, off Russell's face. Russell then starts to stare into the distance, while grinning heavily. He then starts to have a little rant to himself, while Jesse caresses his face. Russell cries out several remarks.

"I may only have one arm, but I'm still Russell McCoy. Believe that shit. I may wake up tomorrow and be weirded out because I have one fucking arm, but I'm still Russell McCoy. There may be times to where I look to my left, and feel sad because I only have one arm, but guess what Jess; I'm still Russell McCoy. I'm not dead, and I'm still here Jess. I'm still here, and it's because of you. Take me over to the bed, because that pill made me sleepy."

Jesse laughs at Russell, and pushes him over to Brian's bed. He gets him out of the chair, and lays him down. Jesse then crawls on the bed and lays next to Russell. Jesse cuddles up close to Russell, resting his head on his chest, running his fingers over Russell's stiches.

"Max did a good job, and put you all back together again. Like Humpty Dumpty. Ha. Russell. I don't know, you should feel lucky that you're still here."

Russell while looking up at the ceiling, continues to cuddle Jesse and responds.

"Bullshit, I know exactly what happened Jesse. The last thing I remember was being in the bank, and seeing John get shot, and I was shot by the cop that came into the bank. But Max told me everything, that you told him. Brian kicked us out in the middle of nowhere, and I was this close from death. Brian managed to hotwire a random car that you drove off in, and a cop also pulled us over in roadblock that was put to look for us. The same roadblock Brian got caught up in. You had to drive me all the way back here, while I was on the verge of dying. I don't know how you managed to do all that shit, but if anybody is lucky, it's you."

Jesse then starts to close his eyes and while laying on Russell's chest, replies to him.

"I'm not lucky Russell, you are. You got shot a million times, and you're still here. If that isn't luck, then what the fuck is? Russell, you're a lucky man, and you got through it."

Russell then nods his head, and starts to close his eyes. He carries on talking to Jesse.

"Yeah, I'm a lucky son of a bitch aren't I? Max said that if it took you ten minutes longer to reach the unit, I would have been done, and gone. That is luck, and I was still meant to be here. But Jesse, I still feel like there is more I need to do, I'm not done."

Jesse brushes his head against Russell's chest and quietly snaps back at him.

"Russell, shut the fuck up, and go to sleep."

Russell smiles, as Jesse drifts off to sleep soon after that. Russell stares down at Jesse who's now deep asleep, and kisses him on his forehead. Russell then seconds later closes his eyes and drifts off to sleep as well.

CHAPTER 24:

NOTHING VENTURED, NOTHING GAINED

Throughout this whole entire adventure, there have been several different lessons learned. Many new experiences which came as a complete surprise, that many were faced with. Situations that you would never think of happening or taking place, which happened. It was due to all of these strange and unusual events, which transpired into this complexity of strange proportions. Analyzing all the details on how everything constructed itself, from beginning to end. Under much amazement and surprise, on how items were pieced together in a specific platform. Finding closure to know how to evolve yourself into acceptance, and dealing with scenarios that you do not comprehend. It should be known, that along the way several hints and tips were presented. Problem is, at the time you can't always have the knowledge to fully understand what exactly they are. Everything is indeed connected, and in order for certain things to appear and to come into light, other effects have to be in proper order as well. An agenda is made for a reason, so things are mapped and planned out accordingly.

Whether this agenda is mental or physical, agendas still have a main purpose. For now, it's important that values and conduct are appreciated moving forward; that's the only thing that should matter. Social studies and learning the structure of life, is necessary to achieve acceptance and comfortability with adapting yourself to the world.

Learning from examples and past history, is another way of properly obtaining safety. Perhaps also using a defense strategy to protect or hide yourself from any pain when faced with blissful ignorance. Having a second plan of attack, if you do not obtain victory with your first order of business.

Another thing to put into perspective, is that life is far too convoluted to understand all the core meanings behind it. Politics are a major part of most of it, and that can also merge the natural flow and order of things. Minds, moods and opinions can be forced and altered to support that groups narrative or company. Debating and arguing over several categories, which may or may not be trivial or dismissive.

It would have to be up to that particular person's prerogative, on what choices they wish to side themselves on, or what personal vices that they wish to stand behind. The way someone thinks and behaves, is completely on them; they have every right to feel that type of way. It is going to be impossible to explore all of these feelings more; hoping to gain some type of hidden message or plot, so it can make sense. When most of everything which happens in life, does not make a great deal of sense usually; it only falls together that way.

After realizing this, you can approach these agendas with the same open level headed view, and this will make whatever consequences involved with these agendas, easier to settle with. With all of that said, life is generally what you make of it, and how you perceive and observe it as well. The same person can approach the same exact agenda, and feel a completely different reaction from it, than another person did. It is all pertaining to the way you deal with these prospects, and the way you decide how much of it are you going to let dictate your life, and the way it's mapped out for you. The sooner you are able to fully understand this information, the better it would basically be for your entire life's goals and ambitions. The only thing that should matter is yourself; your own personal thoughts come before everything else. Being true to yourself, is important. If you keep yourself in top priority, the rest is simple to manage.

Russell and Jesse begin to wake up, still holding onto each other tightly. Jesse gets out of bed, and starts to help Russell out of the bed.

Russell stands himself up, yet starts to slip towards the ground from feeling weak, but Jesse manages to catch him. Russell, with Jesse supporting his back, limps over to the sofa area of the unit, and sits down. Jesse then proceeds over to the kitchen, to make himself and Russell something to eat. Russell shakes his head, and looks down towards the ground. Russell takes a quick glance at Jesse in the kitchen preparing some food, and he then returns to staring at the floor, thinking to himself.

During this same time, Russell looks over to his left, looking at the small empty stump next to his shoulder. He is finding it tough to get used to the fact doesn't he have a left arm anymore. Russell a few minutes later then starts to feel much pain, and cries and screams. Jesse feeling concerned, gives Russell one of the painkillers that Max gave him. While Jesse does that, Russell asks for a piece of paper and a pen. Jesse hands him those items, and Russell begins to write down several names. Figuring in all the money the men were able to take during the heist, came out to four hundred and seventy-six thousand dollars. Being that is a great amount of money, Russell wants to give it back, and share some of the wealth. It took him having to lose an arm, to feel generous.

The first thing Russell jots down, is donating fifty thousand dollars to each to children's hospitals, and cancer research hospitals. He then wants to donate fifty thousand dollars each to the "Wounded Warrior Project", which helps disabled veterans and armed servicemen, and the "Human Rights Campaign", which helps support LGBT issues and activism. With that, the men still have over two hundred thousand dollars left. The rest of the money, Russell wants to split it evenly between himself and Jesse, and everyone else who is close to them in their lives. They both will secretly disperse the money to these individuals, in a random act of kindness. As they both do not have that many friends, this shouldn't be that difficult for them deciding who to give the money to. Russell begins to write down names of these people, and why they are being included.

The first names that Russell writes, is giving a fraction of the money to Peter's family, and to his wife and children. He follows that by adding Jennifer's family as well. The third name that Russell includes is Yvette. Although he doesn't have the best relationship with her, he wants to include her in this list. Russell then adds the remaining individuals who worked at the "Sunset Credit Union", which include Sally, Tiffany and Abel. Russell then decides on whether or not he should write down John's name. It is no secret that Russell does not care that much about John, and decides to ignore adding John, and moves on jotting down names.

Following that, Russell adds Max's name to the list. If it weren't for Max, Russell would not be alive right now, so he wants to include him. While Russell is continuing to write down names, he adds Kevin's family back in Chicago to the list. Russell figures that they could make good use of the money as well. As Brian and Victor do not have any family that Russell knows of, he cannot split the money with any of their relatives at all sadly. Russell writes one final name down; which happens to be John. Jesse is making pancakes in the kitchen for himself and Russell to eat. Once he has finished writing down all the people that he wishes to share the money with, Russell calls Jesse over to read the list. He asks him if there is anyone he objects to, or if there is anyone he has forgotten or wishes to include. Jesse has no issues with the names Russell included. Altogether, Russell has included nine names to split the funds eventually with. With that, everyone, Russell and Jesse included, will take twenty-five thousand dollars each. Russell is satisfied with the list he made, and over the course of the following week, he plans to secretly give out the funds to everyone.

The men decide to stay in Brian's unit for the time being, still recuperating from the fiasco which happened on Friday. On Monday morning, Jesse is woken by Russell.

"Jesse, look, I'm walking! I can walk again! I'm back to my old self again! Yes!"

Russell now is able to walk without feeling weak or limping, and gallops around the unit without feeling tired or stumbling. Jesse gets out of bed, and walks over to Russell and hugs him. Russell then starts to do various stretches and exercises, to circulate himself.

"I got it all worked out now. I don't get tired anymore, I'm back to my regular self."

At this time, Max arrives at the unit, and begins to knock on the door. Max has the money they men had gotten during their first two heists, sitting on his lap. Jesse lets him in, and Max starts to move over to where Russell is doing his stretches, and speaks to both of them.

"Good morning the both of you. I'm glad to see that you've recovered rather quickly Russell. I'm proud of you, and you're a tough guy so I'm not surprised."

Russell smiles at Max, and Russell pats Max on the shoulder. Max continues to speak to them.

"I didn't mean to bother you guys, but in case you wanted these, I brought them over. It's your money, so you guys need to have it. I'll leave these here, and I'll be on my way now. Oh by the way Russell, if anyone asks on your arm, don't ask me how I did it, that's for me to know, and for you to never ever find out, but I managed to do some tricks on your medical history, and your amputation is legally listed from being caused by an automobile collision. So don't worry about that."

Russell nods his head Max. Russell then grabs the bags of money which are sitting on his Max's lap. Russell then sets both of the bags on the ground. Jesse then walks over to several different equal stacks of money laid of the coffee table, and hands of the stacks to Max. Max gives the both of them a puzzled look, and Russell then starts to explain everything to him.

"When I lost my arm, it made me a different man. Me and Jesse spending that much money doesn't make sense at all. That's so petty and disgusting. I decided to split it all between my friends, and the people who mean a lot in my life. Including you Max, I want you to enjoy."

Max smiles at Russell, and puts the stack of money in his pocket. Russell and Jesse then both hug Max, and say goodbye to him. Max on his way out the unit, says one final thing.

"Whenever you guys need me, or want to talk, you know where to find me. I may be a crazy old man, but I'm still your friend, and I'm always here. Take care boys."

Max leaves the unit, and Russell walks over to the door, to lock it. Following all of that, Russell crosses Max name off the list of people. They put all of the money they plan to share, in large legal sized envelopes, with that person's name labeled and attached to it. Russell and Jesse both decide that their goal for today, is to disperse all the money out to as many people as they can. They exit out of the unit, and get into Russell's car. Jesse gets into the driver's seat, with Russell sitting in the passenger seat, as he's not comfortable to drive yet.

They decide that as it's early into the morning, they can inconspicuously drop off the money without being seen by others. It will indeed be a random act of kindness. Jesse drives to Yvette's house first, and drops her money in the mailbox. They then drive to Peter and Jennifer's families' homes, and drop their money in their mailboxes as well. Russell struggles to remember where Abel lives, but finally remembers going to his residence at one time to attend a party. They give him his share of the money by dropping it in his mailbox.

As they cross more names off the list, they head over to more of their former coworkers at the "Sunset Credit Union", homes. Jesse vaguely remembers where Tiffany lives from visiting as a guest there once, and drops her envelope in the mailbox. Russell luckily also remembers where Sally lives, as he has been to her residence once before, and they drop her envelope in her mailbox. The men at this time decide to drive to the post office, and mail in the rest of the share of the money. Kevin's family are sent in their share of the money by mail anonymously. Russell and Jesse then mail in their donations to the charities they wish to send the money to. They put the money inside plastic bags, and put these bags inside big brown envelopes to mail out.

Jesse walks to the mailbox inside the post office, and mails in Kevin's families' money, and the donation charity money. Now the men only need to give John his money; then they would have then evenly spread the money out. Russell knows where John lives, but the men wait to send him his money. They both decide to take a break, and go to a diner for lunch. As they are sitting down in a booth, the waitress seems to react to Russell's missing arm, but she is respectable about it. Russell fibs that he lost his arm during a car accident, and the waitress carries on by serving the men. Once they finish their lunch, Russell and Jesse then walk back to the parking lot, to get back in their vehicle.

They head back to the unit, and Russell decides to take some of his pain medicine, as his shoulder stump and chest is starting to hurt him severely. Russell struggles to open the bottle with one hand, but he accomplishes this nevertheless. He sticks the pill in his mouth, and speaks to Jesse, while he's swallowing the pill.

"We're going back to my place tomorrow. I know you like hanging out here too, and so do I, but this is only a hideaway. None of my stuff is here, and you understand right?"

Jesse nods his head. While Jesse is laying down on the sofa, he responds to Russell.

"John is the only one left we didn't hand the money out to yet, right?"

Russell walks over to the sofa area, and sits right next to Jesse. Jesse lays across the sofa and rests his head on Russell's lap. Russell then responds to Jesse, while looking down.

"Yeah, we can drop his money off tomorrow. John lives right around the corner from me, go figure. He doesn't know where I stay, but I know where he stays."

The next morning, Russell and Jesse then head out of the "Home Base" unit, and direct themselves over to John's house. Jesse pulls up in front of the residence, and like he did with the others, walks up the door, and starts to drop the envelope in the mailbox. However, this time, John catches Jesse before he drops the envelope, and opens his front door. John is wearing a white buttoned up shirt, cargo shorts, and sandals. John is holding onto crutches under his arms, still weak from being shot during the heist, which has caused him permanent body damage. Jesse is stunned, as he and John make eye contact for several seconds; both of them shocked to see each other. John raises his eyebrows, and he scans the area.

He notices Russell sitting in the passenger seat, in a car on the curb. Both Russell and Jesse feel they are now in a tough predicament, as they were hoping they wouldn't be caught or seen dropping the money envelopes. John without acknowledging Jesse, snatches the envelope from Jesse's hand, and looks inside of it, noticing the large amount of money. John gives an angry expression towards Jesse, and Jesse remains silent. Using his crutches, John heads over to where Russell is. Russell then starts to panic, as John gets closer to the car door. John then stands outside the car door silent. Russell doesn't know what is going to happen, and why John is standing there staring at him. John stands outside the car door for a short while, and Russell reluctantly rolls down the window. John speaks to him.

"Russell, are you busy? If you aren't, can you come in for a little bit?"

Russell shakes his head, and walks out of the car. He and Jesse then walk inside John's house, and sit down in his living room. John is bisexual, but struggles with his sexual identity, as he feels that isn't anyone's business. He isn't a man that is involved with relationships, and lives a solitary life by himself. He isn't married, and has no children. John then puts the envelope down on the table in his living room, and speaks.

"Russell, I wanted to tell you that I'm sorry for everything I've done to you. I want to start over, and I want to be friends and not enemies. I want to start fresh again."

Russell looks down at the ground and is frozen with his emotions. John then walks into his kitchen, and brings out three beers, handing one to Russell and Jesse. John opens his beer, and takes several sips of it. He then starts to speak softly to Russell.

"I know we all have secrets Russell, and you know I could call the police on you and Jesse right now. The both of you will be in jail for a long time. I'm not going to though."

Russell opens his beer, and keeps his eye contact away from John looking at the floor. He takes sips from his beer, and John continues to shock both him and Jesse.

"You think I'm stupid? You think I wasn't going to notice you don't have a fucking arm? You could fool a fool and others, but Russell, I was in that robbery. I saw the tape. Nobody else is suspecting you guys but me. I know it was you Russell. Fucking confess."

Russell starts to feel scared, and he and Jesse sit in fear as to what John plans to do next. They are in complete shock, as they listen to John continue.

"I was shot in the fucking legs. I was there. I know you and Jesse were with that group that kept robbing those banks. You think just because gave money to everyone else, it makes up for it? That was really stupid of you guys to do that. You're lucky that I'm friends with you now Russell, and I have secrets myself. I'll make a deal with you Russell. You don't tell my secret, and I won't tell yours. Deal? Promise you won't tell anybody, or I will tell on you guys."

Russell looks over at Jesse, and responds to John.

"No John, you can tell me and Jesse. We're not gonna snitch. It's okay."

John takes a sip of his beer, and turns his head over to Russell, and starts to talk to him.

"I was involved with this inside robbery, when I was manager at the "California Savings Union" bank, around this time last year. It turned out ugly, and I was helping out some of these buddies I knew from college. Things didn't go as planned. All of my friends were killed in the robbery by the police, and I was never suspected because I was playing hostage, being manager of the bank. It's so terrible, and I still feel guilty on it. I've kept this secret until now. I'm just as guilty as the guys for planning an inside robbery. I fucked up, and I'm sorry. I feel bad. I don't want to work for banks anymore, those days are over."

Russell takes another sip of his beer, and responds to the story John gave.

"I knew not trust you at all John. I knew you were hiding something. I saw you taking money from cash terminals, and could have reported that shit to the authorities, but I didn't. You treated me like shit, and we could have been friends. It's because of you, I lost my damn arm John. I almost didn't rob 'First Federal'. But I did, because of you, and the way you always treated me. But you have your secret, I have mine. We're now even. It's a deal. Ha-ha."

Russell then looks at John, and they both stare at each other for a while. John then reaches out his hand for Russell to shake it, and Russell shakes John hand. John and Russell then start to cry, and John kisses Russell on the cheek. Jesse receives a notification on his phone, and he reads it. While he's staring at his phone, he talks to the other men.

"I don't mean to interrupt your conversation, but Yvette is getting married to her boyfriend Matt next month, and I was just now sent an invitation to attend. I know this is random for me to mention, but I thought that you guys would like to know this."

Russell then laughs and smiles at John, and softly asks him a question.

"Do you want to go to the wedding? I'll pick you up, and give you a ride there?"

John laughs at Russell, and nods his head. The both of them continue to chat and bond with each other; they are grateful on their newly found friendship. Over the course of the next few weeks, John kept Russell's and Jesse's secret to himself, and remained close friends with them in addition to that. John would invite them over to his place for dinner some nights. John didn't reveal any their behavior to the authorities, and didn't press Russell on any further information related to their heists. He simply allowed for them both to keep their secrets to each other. The individuals that received their money aside from John, had no idea where it came from, but they were appreciative to receive it. Detective Henderson retired from the police force, and now works at a hardware store. He decided to let the "Snowman Bandit" case rest.

Detective Henderson, along with the other investigators would sadly forever be unaware, that Russell and Jesse were the other men involved in the heists. Detective Henderson feels if the other two robbers were smart enough to escape capture, then he is willing to accept his defeat. Detective Henderson remains happy with his decision to retire, and goes on about his life.

With only a few days to go until Yvette's wedding, the men all try to get themselves situated before the big event arrives. Russell and Jesse wake up in his apartment, and quickly get dressed and ready. Russell wants to go out and buy a tuxedo for the occasion; also deciding to drive for the first time, since losing his left arm. Russell and Jesse head to the parking structure in Russell's residence. Russell sits in the driver's seat, and begins start the ignition. Jesse shows concern over him.

"Russell, I can drive if you want. If you don't feel ready, I can take care of it for you."

Russell ignores Jesse, and starts to drive as if he had two arms. Jesse is amazed at how quickly Russell was able to adapt to driving with only one arm. Russell continues down the road, without any struggle or issues at all. While he's driving, Russell responds to Jesse.

"So, because I have one arm, I'm not supposed to drive anymore? How is that fair? It's not fair, right? This is my life Jess, and I have to accept it. I have to accept that this is just how it's going to be, and I have to get used to it. That's how it is."

Jesse smiles and nods his head. Russell continues towards the tuxedo shop. Once he's there, Russell picks out a nice brand new black expensive tuxedo for himself, and is being fitted for it. The shop owner is very polite towards Russell only having one arm, and she still shows him excellent customer service, as she is measuring him. Jesse walks around the shop, seeking out an outfit to wear to Yvette's wedding.

During this time, John walks into the tuxedo shop with his crutches. Russell who's being fitted for the tuxedo, doesn't notice John walk in. John sits down on a chair waiting to be serviced, and Jesse notices John. John lifts up his finger to his mouth, alerting Jesse to hush and remain quiet, and Jesse smiles to himself. Jesse checks out more of the store. John continues to sit in silence, watching Russell get fitted for his tuxedo. Shortly after this, Russell eventually notices John, and they both laugh at each other. John gets up from the chair and walks over to hug Russell and speaks to him.

"John? What are you doing here man? You trying to pick something out?"

John looks around the tuxedo shop, as he's doing that he responds to Russell.

"Well, I was intending to window shop, but if there's something that catches my eye, I can't promise you that I won't check it out. I'm pretty tempted, there is some nice stuff here."

Russell nods his head, and the shop owner has Russell's tuxedo ready. Russell then walks into the fitting room to try it on. At this time, John then picks out a tuxedo for himself, and gets it fitted. Russell comes out of the fitting room with his tuxedo, and walks over to the mirror to get a better perspective over it. The tuxedo is a perfect fit. He's satisfied with it, and decides to purchase it. Russell walks back into the fitting room to change back into his regular clothes. Jesse then finds something that he likes which goes with his style, and decides to purchase that as well. He picks out a black vest, with a white dress shirt, a black bow tie, and dark black slacks. Jesse sits down in a chair by the entrance with the outfit he bought, as he waits for Russell to come out of the fitting room. John walks out of the fitting room with his tuxedo. He stands in front a mirror being comfortable with it. John then looks over at Jesse, and asks for his opinion.

"So, what do you think? Is it me? Would I look nice with this on?"

Jesse sincerely believes that John looks handsome in the tuxedo, and Jesse nods his head. John smiles at Jesse, and John has his mind made up to buy the tuxedo. John walks into the fitting room to change back, and Russell walks out during this same time. Russell purchases his tuxedo, and the outfit Jesse picked. Before he and Jesse walk out the store, he is stopped by John who is screaming out to him, to get his attention. Russell turns his head around towards John.

"Hey hey, Russ. Wait up. Let me take you and Jesse out to lunch on me. Say yes, you have nothing to lose. I have a surprise that I need to tell you as well."

Russell nods his head, and he John and Jesse all go out to lunch together. John takes them to a deli that he likes to go to, located nearby the tuxedo shop. The men all place their orders, and take a seat at a table. The men all sit quietly. Jesse is playing a game on Russell's phone. Russell is staring down, thinking to himself. John starts to wave his hand in front of Russell's face, to get his attention. John leans towards Russell, to mention something very important.

"I don't ever want to work in a bank ever again. I know you don't either Russell. There's a job fair at 'Northrop Grumman' tomorrow, they have open interviews for accountants. I figure me and you can go. I don't know, and don't give a fuck who stitched up your arm, but you can lie and say you had a car accident or something. Come on. I'll meet you there tomorrow."

Russell looks down at the table grinning at what John said, John then continues.

"Come on Russell, I know you don't work. I can tell by your face you're not working right now. We both can get hired, and start over this way. Please. You can come pick me up tomorrow, and we'll go together. It will be fun Russell. What have you go to lose?"

Jesse, although he has his attention to the game he's playing on Russell's phone, is eavesdropping on their conversation. Russell looks up at John, and nods his head. John smiles in support of him. Their food arrives at the table in minutes after that, and the men start eating.

Once they finish, John pays for meal, leaving the waitress a tip, and they all go about their separate ways, with Russell agreeing to pick up John tomorrow morning. The next day, Russell dresses for his job interview, and puts on a well-tailored dark blue suit with a red tie. This particular suit is one that Russell wears, when wants to feel lucky. Jesse is wearing a nice looking outfit as well. Which is a blue sweater vest, and black pants. Russell compliments Jesse on his attire, and Jesse then explains to Russell why he's dressed nicely.

"I figured that while you and John are that the job fair, I would try to get a job myself. On the way there, a 'Walgreens' is hiring for workers. I thought I give it a shot to see what happens."

Russell fastens his tie, and nods his head at Jesse, and responds to him.

"I'll drop you off, and once we're done I'll come back and pick you up."

Jesse is an agreement with Russell's plan, and both of the men then leave together. Russell drives over to John's house and picks him up. Jesse moves to the rear seat, and John hands Jesse his crutches, to which Jesse sets them down in the rear area. Russell continues to drive, dropping Jesse off at the drug store for his job interview. Before Jesse gets out the car, Jesse leans from the rear seat next to where Russell is sitting, and kisses Russell on the cheek.

"Good luck Russell, you're going to do fine. You're gonna get that job, I know it."

Jesse then leans across at John and kisses him on the cheek as well.

"Good luck to you too. Thank you for helping out Russell, that was real nice."

John smiles back at Jesse, and Jesse walks out of the vehicle. Russell drives away with John. Jesse is now heading towards the drug store, to inquire about their open positions which are available. Upon walking into the store, Jesse lets an employee know that he's here about the job opening. The employee he speaks to, happens to be the hiring manager. She gives Jesse an interview on the spot right there.

Jesse hands her his resume, and she's impressed at what she sees. Being that she enjoys Jesse's attitude and personality, she hires him to be an associate at the store as a cashier, and to stock items as well. She brings Jesse to the back of the store so he can fill out pertinent information regarding the job.

Russell and John have now arrived at their destination. "Northrop Grumman", is an aerospace defense company, which deals with engineering and science business as well. Russell and John notice an extremely long line of candidates standing outside the door. This causes Russell to feel frustrated, as he doesn't think his chances are high of being hired, from the amount of competition that is currently there. He decides to stay anyways. Russell hands John his crutches, and they both start to walk to the building. They fill out a great deal of paperwork while they are waiting to be called for their interview. Russell and John continue to sit in the waiting area for an extended amount of time, which makes Russell become stressed, as he's an impatient man. Finally, Russell is called first. John smacks him in the behind.

"Go get em' tiger. You're going to do great. Just relax, everything is going to be fine.

Russell smiles at John. Russell follows the interviewer, who is a very soft faced geeky and pudgy Caucasian man. He name is Chester Wright. He is the same age as Russell. Chester has puffy cheeks, and he also wears glasses. He has short styled black hair, and is wearing a striped brown suit. Once he's seated in the interview room, Russell introduces himself, and hands Chester his resume. Chester begins to chew on his pen, as he's reading Russell's resume. Chester then speaks to Russell, with his vision still directed at Russell's resume, and also while he's still gnawing on his pen.

"So you know, we don't discriminate against people who are disabled. We are an equal opportunity employer, so don't feel that we aren't accepting to handicapped people. We are."

Russell smiles and nods his head at Chester. Chester then sets Russell's resume down.

"Listen, I know you saw that big line out the door. It's okay though, don't fret. All of those are for different positions. I'm looking at your resume, and based on your experience, you're more than qualified to be an accountant. If you can deal with math, and numbers, and taxes, and figuring. You're hired. Be here on time, Monday through Friday, nine to seven with breaks, and the job is yours. Welcome to the team Russell."

Chester extends out his hand for Russell to shake it. Russell and Chester shake hands. Chester then hands Russell some forms to fill out, and once he's completed that, Russell walks back out to the waiting room. Russell doesn't see John, so he assumes he's currently being interviewed. As Russell is seated, he looks down and smiles; happy that he has a job again, and in a somewhat related field too. John finally emerges out of his interview, and he was hired by the company as well. Russell and John hug each other, and John kisses Russell on the cheek whispering to him.

"This is my way of making everything up to you man. We start over today."

Russell and John walk back to Russell's car, and Russell heads to the store to pick Jesse up. Jesse mentions that he was hired, and both Russell and John are proud of him. They then explain to Jesse that they got their jobs as well, and Jesse is overjoyed once he's notified of that.

Russell then decides to make an unexpected detour towards "Home Base". He wants to introduce John to Max, especially if they are going to be working together as friends now.

"John, there is this guy I want you to meet. He's the one that fixed my arm up, and saved my life. I also want to show you me and Jesse's secret hiding spot. You can't tell anyone this."

John rubs the back of his head, and laughs at Russell. He then responds to him.

"Who am I going to tell? I thought we were boys? Nobody will believe me anyways."

Russell looks over at John and laughs at him. Russell continues towards the "Home Base" area, and parks his car outside of the unit. He then walks over to Max's unit, and unlocks the door. All three of the men walk in, and Russell introduces Max to John. Max would occasionally wink at Russell, not revealing all of the information surrounding their history to John. After this, Russell walks John over to the "Home Base" unit, and gives John a tour of the place. Russell grabs several beers from the refrigerator, and gives one to John. As he's walking through the unit, John is in disbelief at what he sees.

"Holy shit, so this is where you guys did all the action at? You sly fuckers. Ha-ha."

Russell takes a sip of his beer, and smiles at John responding to him.

"I'm not saying shit. Those are your words, not mine. I never mentioned any of that."

John turns his head towards Russell and laughs at him. They end up staying in the unit for a while longer, with John complimenting the Oldsmobile convertible. Russell then says that he's going to take the car to Yvette's wedding, as he wants to show up in style. All the other cars Brian kept in the unit, Russell and Jesse donated to charity. Russell also plans to take the convertible to an auto show in Malibu; competing in a car competition at the event, next week. All of the men then proceed out of the unit. Russell shuts the door, and locks it right behind him.

They get back in Russell's car, and Russell drops John off back at his home. Russell and Jesse say goodbye to him. Jesse hands John his crutches, and John gets out of the car, waving to both of them. Russell continues on driving, heading back to his residence. Jesse climbs up to the passenger seat, and talks to Russell, facing him.

"John is a nice guy after all huh? See, he got you a job. Everything worked out didn't it? You have a new job working finances for aerospace, you have a new best friend..."

Russell then laughs very loudly at Jesse, interrupting him. Russell then corrects him.

"John is not my best friend. He's just a friend for now, and he's cool. We'll see."

Jesse smiles at Russell, and turns his head facing forward; Russell heads home. The day of Yvette's wedding arrives. Russell and Jesse wake up immediately, getting ready. Jesse who already has his outfit to the wedding on, notices Russell is struggling to put on his tuxedo. Jesse helps him. Russell starts to talk to Jesse, who's fixing Russell's bow tie.

"Even with one arm, I still look good don't I? I look good, smell good. I'm good."

Jesse and Russell then kiss passionately for nearly a minute. While they are kissing, they fall on Russell's bed laughing at each other. Russell then shoves Jesse away, snapping at him.

"Okay, that's enough of that shit. Go get the wedding gift. We don't have time to waste. We still have to go and get the car, and I have to pick John up."

Jesse quickly obeys Russell, and grabs Yvette's wedding gift. Russell and Jesse then quickly leave, and depart towards "Home Base". Russell parks his car outside the unit, and opens the garage gate. He looks over at the Oldsmobile convertible, not believing that he is finally having the chance to drive this car for the first time today. Russell opens the door, and starts the ignition. He lays down the top, and Jesse sits in the passenger side of the car. Russell drives the convertible out of the unit, and walks back to the garage door locking it. He gets back into the car, and gets on the highway.

The sunny weather and breeze, makes this a perfect day to drive a car like this. Many people are turning their heads at classic car, and Russell feels like a celebrity driving it. He drives the car towards John's house, and picks him up. John who has already seen the car, is impressed that Russell is driving it to the wedding. Russell is enjoying driving this car, and has always wanted to drive it, the minute he saw it. He continues to drive down the highway in style, on his way to Yvette's wedding. He finally reaches the venue, and he notices that many people are there. Being that Yvette is Hispanic, and her soon to be husband Matt is Caucasian, there are a mixture of different people attending the wedding.

Russell and John set their wedding gifts on the gift table, and they manage to take a seat in the back section of the wedding. It is a romantic outside venue, located in a private country club in Hollywood. There are many lovely peaceful conservation pieces, and natural flower arrangements being used as decorations. Russell, Jesse and John manage to see Tiffany, Sally, and Abel, but they do not go up and introduce themselves. They instead remain seated in the back area, waiting for the wedding to start.

Matt, Yvette's groom, soon walks to the altar of the wedding waiting for her to arrive. Yvette then walks down the aisle in her wedding gown, which the dress and veil are white as snow and very beautiful. Yvette walks up to the alter, and she and Matt are now married. Russell, Jesse, and John congratulate them, and watch them in joy.

During the reception that afternoon; Russell, Jesse, and John, sit with each other at a table in the back area of the reception area; situated near a bunch of trees and a pond. You can hear the water from the pond from where they are sitting, and it's a nice comfortable and relaxing section to be sitting in. It's a very quiet area, to where they can't be disturbed or seen by that many people. They are simply eating and drinking, trying not so much to blend in with the rest of the crowd, but to keep to themselves, and mind their business.

Russell gazes at several people in the crowd, some he recognizes, some that he doesn't. Russell then looks down at his plate, and the food they are serving at the wedding. It is cream of mushroom chicken and rice. It is actually not that bad tasting, and Russell seems to enjoy it. Jesse who's also looking around, speaks to Russell, and rests his head on his shoulder.

"This is a nice wedding. I don't know if I want to have my wedding like this. Possibly not. This is a little too fancy for me, but I don't know. I still want to get married someday."

Russell takes more bites of his food, and nods his head. John who's eating as well, being nosy, listens to Russell and Jesse's conversation; shaking his head at the both of them. John then takes out his phone, and starts to watch an MSNBC news finance stream. Russell takes a sip of some champagne, and with Jesse still laying on his shoulder, Russell responds.

"Well, in order to get married, you have to be in love with someone. Who are you in love with, and who are you in love with deep enough for them to want to marry you? Ha-ha."

Jesse then shakes his head while he's still laying down on Russell's shoulder. Jesse then closes his eyes, and continues to speak with Russell who's looking at the wedding venue.

"Yeah you're right. It's too bad I don't have anyone that loves me. Oh well."

Russell stares out into the distance of the wedding and shakes his head. He takes more bites of the food, and drinks some more champagne. The men remain sitting, watching the festivities at the wedding, and seeing the other patrons dance and play party games. The sun then starts to set in the outside venue, and the sky is now dark with the moon and stars out. From where Russell, Jesse, and John are sitting, it exhibits a lovely romantic setting. Jesse then starts to make out with Russell, as the the DJ is playing loud Hip Hop music from the dance floor, located far away on the other side of the wedding venue.

John watches in amusement, as they both kiss. He smiles at them, and goes back to watching the news stream on his phone. Russell feels that Jesse has had enough fun, and he is finished making out with him. Russell then pulls Jesse away and snaps back.

"It's all this wedding bullshit got you acting crazy. You have a cigarette?"

Jesse looks at him angrily, and rummages through his tote bag, grabbing a carton of cigarettes. Russell asks John if he wants to come smoke with them, and he refuses. Russell and Jesse then walk away from the table over by a secluded area near the pond, and start to smoke. They sit on a bench facing the pond, and Jesse lays his head on Russell's shoulder. Russell takes puffs of his cigarette, and begins to whisper to Jesse.

"Me and John start work in two days. You only work part time, but I'm going to be gone all day and all week. That's going to be alright for you?"

Jesse nods his head, and continues to lay down on Russell's shoulder. They both remain in this area for a short while, looking at the gorgeous and lovely view, then they walk back over to their table. At this time, John wishes to go home, and all three of them start to exit out of the wedding. Russell drops John off, and he and Jesse say goodbye to him. Immediately after that, Russell directs himself to "Home Base" to park the convertible. He gets back into his regular car, and proceeds to his apartment. He and Jesse go to sleep not long following that. On Monday morning, Russell gets himself ready for his first day of work at "Northrop Grumman". Jesse is already dressed for work in his Walgreens vest, in which Jesse picked up his uniform days before. Jesse doesn't have to be at work until noon; he is going to take the bus to get there. Jesse gets off work at seven like Russell does, so Russell offers to pick Jesse up when his shift is over. Russell stands in the mirror making sure his suit looks nice.

Russell is wearing a light gray suit, with a black tie, and black shoes. Jesse helps Russell look good for his first day. Russell reaches for his briefcase inside his closet and grabs it. He gives Jesse who's sitting on his bed, a kiss. Russell then looks in the closet mirror, speaking to Jesse.

"You be a good boy. I'll pick you up later. I gotta go to work."

Jesse tells Russell goodbye, and he lays down on Russell's bed, happy that Russell is going to work, but upset because he doesn't want him to leave. Russell walks out towards his car, and starts to drive. He notices how sunny the weather is for today, and hot humid it is, despite it being early on in the morning. Russell arrives at John's house, and picks him up. The two of them head to start their first day of work. Russell is shown where his cubicle is, and he and John both work in the same section.

Their computer monitors and work stations are positioned right next to each other. Despite this, Russell and John do not use this as an advantage to chit chat or fool around. They strictly get to work, and complete their work tasks. Russell despite only having one arm, is able to work quite well. He can file papers easily, type on his keyboard without any issue, and he can carry things just fine.

Russell is certain that he is going to like his new job as an accountant, and can see possible career growth. As John is doing his work, he looks over at Russell, proud of him, despite being handicapped without an arm. John starts to feel happy that he has this brand new life with Russell. They were former enemies, now they are turning into close friends, working in a different setting. John, like Russell, never wants to work in a bank ever again; this is a great way to deal with all of their insecurities. Russell himself is also appreciating his brand new lifestyle.

Even though he's not glad that he lost his arm from all the poor decisions and choices he made, he is happy that he was given a second chance, and can now live a life that makes him free to start over. Anything that happened before this point, Russell wants to wash away from his memory like it didn't exist. He concentrates on his work, filing all the appropriate documents and financial records in their proper order. This type of work comes simple for Russell, as it's something he's familiar with, working with finances and money.

As the day continues, he and John are doing rather well with it being their first day. Lunch time finally arrives, and he and John take their break. They head to the cafeteria to get themselves something to eat.

Jesse walks out of Russell's apartment, and locks the door; walking to the bus stop to start his new job. While he's standing at the bus stop, he starts to talk to an older African-American woman. They engage in small talk. Jesse gets on the bus, and rides the half hour ride to get to the Walgreen's he works at. He gets off the bus, and walks in the building to begin work. Jesse starts stocking several items on the shelf, entering them into the stocking database, using a small handheld scanner device to do so. Meanwhile, Jesse also checks customer's items out at the cash register as well.

Russell and John have now finished their lunch break, and they get back to work. The end of their shift arrives, and the men have completed their first day. Russell and John get into Russell's car, and Russell drives towards Walgreens to pick Jesse up from work. Jesse waits in the break room of the store, and Russell's texts him that he's outside. He walks out to Russell's car, and sits the rear seat. Instead of taking John home, Russell drives to get some Chinese food, and he invites John to his apartment. When they walk in, John is amazed at Russell's place. John takes a seat on the sofa, and Russell takes John's crutches and sets them on the side of the sofa. Russell grabs himself, Jesse and John a beer. John then starts to compliment Russell's apartment.

"I like how you have this. Never knew you were a man that was this styled. I like the sports motif, and all the jerseys you have up. It's interesting, and I like it."

Russell smiles at him, and takes a seat next to him on the sofa. All three of them then start to eat, and Russell turns on a muted NFL game on the television. He and John start to joke around with each other. Jesse is on the other side of the sofa, reading a magazine. John while he's staring at the football game on the television with Russell, starts to speak.

"Russell, I have your back man. Don't worry, if you need me I'm always here."

Russell while he's starting at the football game on the television, nods his head. Later on in the night, Russell takes John back home. Russell and John leave the building, with Jesse staying. Jesse walks into the bedroom, and starts to get into his sleepwear. Jesse then lays down on Russell's bed, reading a magazine with his headphones on. Russell soon returns from dropping John off, and joins Jesse on the bed; with with the suit he wore to work, still on. Russell then crawls across the bed to Jesse, and whispers to him.

"I had a long day at work, and I'm tired. You want to help me undress?"

Jesse looks up from his magazine, and laughs at Russell. He then helps take Russell's suit off, and Russell then lays down in the bed in his underwear. They both then fall asleep. Russell, Jesse and John continue on the rest of the week, adapting themselves to their brand new lifestyles; going about their second chance that they now have in their lives. One major thing on Russell's mind, is the car competition show on Saturday. Friday night after work, after Russell dropped John off at home, he and Jesse return to Russell's apartment; they slip into comfortable clothes. They also pick out a change of clothes; as they are going to sleep over and spend the weekend at the "Home Base" unit, so they can go straight to the competition the next day. Russell brings two large brown cardboard boxes that were shipped to his apartment with him. Jesse helps carry one of the boxes. Russell then drives over to the unit.

Once inside the unit, Russell opens up the cardboard boxes to Jesse's wonderment. Inside are several modified car parts, which belong to the Oldsmobile convertible that Russell plans to enter in the car competition. Russell then starts to open up Brian's tools, and starts to tinker with the convertible. Jesse hands Russell a beer, and Russell takes small sips of it, before he gets back to working on the car. Russell, remarkably with only one arm, is doing a good job of taking apart and detailing and modifying the vehicle. Jesse would occasionally help hand him tools, and to move things out of the way. Jesse would also take a rag, and wipe oil and sweat off Russell's face. While Russell is working, he grunts out to Jesse.

"Well, I'm not as good as Brian was. He would have been done already. I mean I only have one fucking arm, and I'm still getting the shit done right. If we don't get at least third place, I'm going to be pissed. This car is a classic, and I have to show it off."

Jesse wipes more oil and sweat from Russell's face as he's working on the car. Russell finally finishes his task, and the car is now ready for the competition. Jesse starts to add wax and polish to the car, and cleans the headlights and windows. Russell hops into the shower to clean up, and Jesse then gets into the shower after him. They both then lay down, and go to sleep.

The following day, Russell wakes up and notices that Jesse isn't in the bed. He gets his clothes on, gets ready regardless. He puts on a black polo shirt, some khaki shorts, and some flip flop sandals. While Jesse is still out, he walks over to where Brian's workstation is. Russell starts to go through several drawers looking for something, and inadvertently sees a portrait picture that Max took of himself, Jesse, Kevin, Brian and Victor, standing outside the unit together. Russell smiles to himself, and tapes the picture up on a board situated on top of the drawers. Russell also inadvertently finds Kevin's marijuana bag. He puts it in his pocket. Russell then finds what he was looking for, which is a small box; putting it in his pocket. A few minutes later Jesse who's wearing a striped and patterned white button up shirt, black shorts and sandals, walks into the "Home Base" unit. Russell can't believe what he sees, as Jesse walks towards Russell with a bulldog puppy.

"I named him Kevin. I wanted him to be a surprise before you woke up. So much for that. Ha-ha."

Russell picks up the dog as it licks his face. Russell finding this cute, responds to Jesse.

"Aww, this is nice. He's gotta come with us now, we can't leave him here when we're at the car show. Speaking of that, we're gonna be late for the contest, so come on. But before we go, I want to show you something."

Russell directs Jesse over to the photo he found, which he hung up on the wall. Jesse vaguely remembers the photo, yet is happy to see it. Russell also informs Jesse that he found Kevin's marijuana bag. Before they exit out the unit, Russell with one hand, remarkably begins to roll a marijuana joint successfully. He and Jesse then smoke it together. Russell then puts the marijuana bag, back in the drawer.

They then quickly prepare themselves for the car competition, and take the convertible out of the unit. Jesse walks back to the door and locks it. He grabs the bulldog in his hands, and Jesse sets the dog on his lap. With the top down, Russell then heads to the car show in Malibu. He makes a stop to get kibble at the pet shop, and then they proceed towards the classic car competition.

Once they arrive there, they see fifty other cars apart of the show roster. From classic Cadillac's, Fords, Chevrolets, and other models. However, there is only one other Oldsmobile in the roster, including Russell's car. Each of the cars are put into several different categories; from sports cars, to convertibles, to luxury cars, and trucks. Russell is competing in the convertible category. During the competition, so the judges aren't biased, the owners of the cars must wait in a separate area until scoring has finished. The judges look at all the cars, and they take a liking to Russell's Oldsmobile that he modified for the contest. It is now time for the scores to be revealed. Russell actually ends up taking second place in the competition. This is something he's happy with, despite the fact he wanted to win. As long as he got at the minimum third place, that was all that he cared about. After the scoring is finished, the car owners can hang by their cars, so visitors of the car show can ask them questions about the vehicle. Russell and Jesse stand by the car, with Jesse holding Kevin the bulldog, in his hands. An elderly Caucasian man walks by Russell and Jesse, and smiles at them both. The man takes a close inspection at the car and asks Russell a question.

"Out of all the cars here, I have to say this one stands out. It's my absolute favorite. If you don't mind me asking, where did you get such a beautiful car son?"

Russell adjusts his sunglasses, and smiles at the man, and then answers his question.

"I got her from a close friend of mine. He sadly passed away, but he was really into cars. I do agree, she is beautiful, and this is a one of a kind car. Yes, sir."

The man continues to look around the car, and carries on speaking with Russell.

"These Oldsmobile's are really rare, and really something. I'm surprised you only got second place, to me this car should have won for sure. This is a lovely car you got son."

Russell smiles at the old man, and he shakes Russell and Jesse's hand. Several more people come up to the car and ask Russell questions about it. As the day continues, attendees at the event, start to depart. At this time, Russell and Jesse, with Jesse still holding Kevin the bulldog in his hands, go and look at the other cars apart of the show. While they are walking through the car show, Russell still has an extreme bias to his Oldsmobile.

The other cars don't compare to his, and he is appreciative of the other vehicles, and the work put into them; he is adamant in believing that his car reigns supreme over the others. With it now being evening time, Russell and Jesse decide to take their second place trophy from the coordinators at the contest, and they then drive away from the car show. While he's driving, Russell speaks to Jesse.

"I'm hungry, so I'm going to go stop at In-and-Out Burger. Is that fine with you?"

Jesse turns his head over at Russell, and nods in agreement. Russell then heads straight there. He gets in the drive thru line, and places his order; which consists of four double double cheeseburgers, two orders of fries, and two cokes. The line as usual is quite long, so Russell turns on the stereo in the convertible. While he's in the drive thru line, Russell notices that many people are being captivated by the car, and look at in amusement.

Jesse is looking down at Kevin the bulldog, and petting his ears. Russell looks over at Jesse playing with the dog and smiles. Eventually, Russell makes it to the service window of the drive thru, and gets his order. After getting the food, he drives down a short distance to the beach; "Point Dume" beach in Malibu to be precise. Russell parks the convertible on a private section of the beach, and he closes the top of the convertible.

There is virtually no one else here at this beach, and it's a private intimate spot. He signals for Jesse to get out of the car. Russell locks all the doors, and opens the trunk grabbing a blanket; Russell is also carrying Kevin the bulldog. Jesse carries the food and the drinks. They get situated on a nice spot of the beach, having a perfect view of the evening Californian sun.

Russell lays the blanket down in the sand, and he and Jesse, sit down on the blanket. Russell sets the dog down on the blanket, and the dog starts to fall asleep. He and Jesse then begin to eat their food, looking at the ocean waves. The sky is blue, and the sun is giving out an orange streak into the sky. As they are eating their food, Russell starts to softly speak to Jesse.

"Jesse, I want to say that I'm really happy in my life right now. I'm blessed to have been given a second chance at life. This whole journey I've been with on you has been wild. I feel that there is only one thing left for me to do, and then I'll truly feel complete with my life."

Jesse looks out towards the sunset, and has an idea of what Russell is talking about, but doesn't want to rush into any conclusions; he remains quiet looking at the ocean. Russell then reaches into his pocket, taking out the small box. Without Jesse watching him, he opens the box and puts the contents inside of it, inside his hand. Russell then crawls over to where Jesse is and moves in front of him. Jesse laughs at him, and his full attention is now on Russell. Russell then kneels down on one knee, opens his palm, revealing a platinum ring band. Jesse immediately puts his hands across his mouth, and feels like he's living a dream. Russell then whispers to him.

"Jesse, will you marry me?"

Jesse with his mouth still covered, is still shocked. Russell remains kneeling in front of him, and Russell starts to put the ring on Jesse's finger. Jesse then gives his answer while crying.

"Yes Russell. I will."

Russell and Jesse hug and kiss each other for several minutes, while wrestling and cuddling each other as well. They then compose themselves and sit back up. Russell stares out into the beach, and observes the evening sky glow from the sun. He scans over the ocean, hearing the waves crash and roar towards the shore. Jesse then leans under Russell's chest, and Russell picks up Kevin the bulldog, petting the dog. Russell then whispers out.

"My life is complete."

Russell and Jesse watch the sunset. They then get back into the convertible, driving off into the distance. Russell continues to drive down PCH with the top down, blasting music. Jesse holds onto Kevin the bulldog tightly. They continue onto down the road, with the California night sky glowing. Russell carries on with his life, completely happy and feeling complete.

Los Angeles, a vibrant and loud city. A very populated city with an array of activity, and never that many dull moments apart of it. A city that has a lot of action and entertainment to offer, and for those to participate and take part in such agendas. A city that has many opportunities available. In this city, there are many who hold onto dreams of success in their life. Very driven on compassion and desire, with a very competitive edge for those to reign supreme above others in many aspects. This is a city which has many characters and personalities apart of it, all of which are finding their piece of the puzzle in the success and business ladder. It is also a city where crime and masterminding also come into play. In these difficult times to where those who have desires to achieve what they want, will do just about anything to obtain them, it becomes a very complex and complicated industry to understand. Everyone tries their best to fit into a loop or place to which they feel the most comfortable by, and willing to accept and understand their full potentials and abilities toward.

THE END

ABOUT THE AUTHOR

Brennen Tammons, was born in Los Angeles, California. He is an African American, gay writer. Having a unique imagination, allows him to explore diverse topics with his writing. He enjoys dancing, aerobic exercise, all types of music, (having a soft spot for jazz, soul, urban and electronic music), playing Nintendo games, and researching new topics and ideas.